Peter Loves<del>...</del> <del>...</del> <del>...</del> <del>...</del> <del>...</del>
to Death in <del>...</del>, <del>...</del> <del>...</del> <del>...</del> <del>...</del>,
Victorian detective, who went on to feature in seven
more books and two TV series. Lovesey's novels and
short stories have won him awards all over the world,
including both Gold and Silver Daggers of the Crime
Writers' Association, of which he was Chairman in
1991–2. In 2000 he joined the elite list of recipients
of the Cartier Diamond Dagger Award. He lives in
Chichester.

PETER LOVESEY OMNIBUS

The Last Detective
Diamond Solitaire

PETER LOVESEY

A *Time Warner* Paperback

This omnibus edition first published in Great Britain by
Time Warner Paperbacks in 2006

Copyright © Peter Lovesey 2005

First published separately:
The Last Detective first published in Great Britain by Scribners in 1991
First published in paperback by Warner Futura in 1992
Copyright © Peter Lovesey 1991

Diamond Solitaire first published in Great Britain by Little, Brown in 1992
First published in paperback by Warner Futura in 1993
Copyright © Peter Lovesey 1992

The moral right of the author has been asserted.

A CIP catalogue record for this book
is available from the British Library.

ISBN-13: 978-0-7515-3783-3
ISBN-10: 0-7515-3783-7

Printed and bound in Great Britain by
Mackays of Chatham plc

Time Warner Paperbacks
An imprint of
Time Warner Book Group UK
Brettenham House
Lancaster Place
London WC2E 7EN

www.twbg.co.uk

The Last Detective

PART ONE
The Lady in the Lake

Chapter One

A MAN STOOD THIGH-DEEP IN WATER, motionless, absorbed, unaware of what was drifting towards him. He was fishing on the north shore of Chew Valley Lake, a 1200-acre reservoir at the foot of the Mendip Hills south of Bristol. He had already taken three brown trout of respectable weight.

He watched keenly for a telltale swirl in the calm lake where he had cast. The conditions were promising. It was an evening late in September, the sky was overcast and the flies in their millions had just whirled above him in their spectacular sunset flight, soaring and swooping over the lake in a mass darker and more dense than the clouds, their droning as resonant as a train in the underground. The day's hatch, irresistible to hungry fish.

A light south-westerly fretted the surface around him, yet ahead there was this bar of water, known to fishermen as the scum, that showed a different pattern in the fading light. There, he knew by experience, the fish preferred to rise.

So preoccupied was the man that he failed altogether to notice a pale object at closer proximity. It drifted languidly in the current created by the wind, more than half submerged, with a slight rocking motion that fitfully produced a semblance of life.

Finally it touched him. A white hand slid against his thigh. A complete arm angled outwards as the body lodged against him, trapped at the armpit. It was a dead woman, face-up and naked.

The fisherman glanced down. From high in his throat came a childishly shrill, indrawn cry.

7

For a moment he stood as if petrified. Then he made an effort to gather himself mentally so as to disentangle himself from the undesired embrace. Unwilling to touch the corpse with his hands, he used the handle of the rod as a lever, lodging the end in the armpit and pushing the body away from him, turning it at the same time, then stepping aside to let it move on its way with the current. That accomplished, he grabbed his net from its anchorage in the mud and, without even stopping to reel in his line, splashed his way to the bank. There, he looked about him. No one was in sight.

This angler was not public-spirited. His response to the discovery was to bundle his tackle together and move off to his car as fast as possible.

He did have one judicious thought. Before leaving, he opened the bag containing his catch and threw the three trout back into the water.

Chapter Two

A LITTLE AFTER 10.30 THE same Saturday evening, Police Constable Harry Sedgemoor and his wife Shirley were watching a horror video in their terraced cottage in Bishop Sutton, on the eastern side of the lake. PC Sedgemoor had come off duty at six. His long body was stretched along the length of the sofa, his bare feet projecting over one end. On this hot night he had changed into a black singlet and shorts. A can of Malthouse Bitter was in his left hand, while his right was stroking Shirley's head, idly teasing out the black curls and feeling them spring back into shape. Shirley, after her shower dressed only in her white cotton nightie, reclined on the floor, propped against the sofa. She had her eyes closed. She had lost interest in the film, but she didn't object to Harry watching if it resulted afterwards in his snuggling up close to her in bed, as he usually did after watching a horror film. Secretly, she suspected he was more scared by them than she, but you didn't suggest that sort of thing to your husband, particularly if he happened to be a policeman. So she waited patiently for it to end. The tape hadn't much longer to run. Harry had several times pressed the fast-forward button to get through boring bits of conversation.

The violins on the video soundtrack were working up to a piercing crescendo when the Sedgemoors both heard the click of their own front gate. Shirley said bitterly, 'I don't believe it! What time is it?'

Her husband sighed, swung his legs off the sofa, got up and looked out of the window. 'Some woman.' He couldn't see much in the porch light.

He recognized the caller when he opened the door: Miss

9

Trenchard-Smith, who lived alone in one of the older houses at the far end of the village. An upright seventy-year-old never seen without her Tyrolean hat, which over the years had faded in colour from a severe brown to a shade that was starting to fit in with the deep pink of the local stone.

'I hesitate to disturb you so late, Officer,' she said as her eyes travelled over his shorts and singlet in a series of rapid jerks. 'However, I think you will agree that what I have found is sufficiently serious to justify this intrusion.' Her gratingly genteel accent articulated the words with self-importance. She may have lived in the village since the war, but she would never pass as local and probably didn't care to.

PC Sedgemoor said with indulgence, 'What might that be, Miss Trenchard-Smith?'

'A dead body.'

'A body?' He fingered the tip of his chin and tried to appear unperturbed, but his pulses throbbed. After six months in the force he had yet to be called to a corpse.

Miss Trenchard-Smith continued with her explanation. 'I was walking my cats by the lake. People don't believe that cats like to be taken for walks, but mine do. Every evening about this time. They insist on it. They won't let me sleep if I haven't taken them out.'

'A human body, you mean?'

'Well, of course. A woman. Not a stitch of clothing on her, poor creature.'

'You'd better show me. Is it … is she nearby?'

'In the lake, if she hasn't floated away already.'

Sedgemoor refrained from pointing out that the body would remain in the lake even if it had floated away. He needed Miss Trenchard-Smith's co-operation. He invited her into the cottage for a moment while he ran upstairs to collect a sweater and his personal radio.

Shirley, meanwhile, had stood up and wished a good evening to Miss Trenchard-Smith, whose tone in replying made it plain that in her view no respectable woman ought to be seen in her nightwear outside the bedroom.

'What a horrid experience for you!' Shirley remarked,

meaning what had happened beside the lake. 'Would you care for a nip of something to calm you down?'

Miss Trenchard-Smith curtly thanked her and declined. 'But you can look after my cats while I'm gone,' she said as if bestowing a favour on Shirley. 'You don't mind cats, do you?' Without pausing to get an answer she went to the door and called, 'Come on, come on, come on,' and two Siamese raced from the shadows straight into the cottage and leapt on to the warm spot Harry had vacated on the sofa as if it were prearranged.

When Harry came down again, Shirley glanced at what he was wearing and said, 'I thought you were going upstairs to put some trousers on.'

He said, 'I might have to wade in and fetch something out, mightn't I?'

She shuddered.

He picked his torch off the shelf by the door. Managing to sound quite well in control, he said, "Bye, love.' He kissed Shirley lightly and tried to provide more reassurance by whispering, 'I expect she imagined it.'

Not that tough old bird, Shirley thought. If she says she found a corpse, it's there.

Harry Sedgemoor was less certain. While driving Miss Trenchard-Smith the half-mile or so down to the lakeside he seriously speculated that she might be doing this out of a desire to enliven her placid routine with gratuitous excitement. Old women living alone had been known to waste police time with tall stories. If this were the case he would be incensed. He was damned sure Shirley wouldn't want to make love after this. Whatever there might or might not be in the lake, the mention of a corpse would colour her imagination so vividly that nothing he did or said would relax her.

With an effort to be the policeman, he asked Miss Trenchard-Smith to tell him where to stop the car.

'Anywhere you like,' she said with an ominously nonchalant air. 'I haven't the faintest idea where we are.'

He halted where the road came to an end. They got out and started across a patch of turf, his torch probing the space ahead. The reservoir was enclosed by a low boundary fence, beyond which clumps of reeds stirred in the breeze, appearing to flicker in the torchlight. At intervals were flat stretches of shoreline.

'How exactly did you get down to the water?' he asked.

'Through one of the gates.'

'Those are for fishermen only.'

'I don't disturb them.' She gave a laugh. 'I won't tell anyone you broke the law.'

He pushed open a gate and they picked their way down to the water's edge.

'Was this the place?'

She said, 'It all looks amazingly different now.'

Containing his annoyance, he drew the torch-beam slowly across a wide angle. 'You must have some idea. How did you notice the body?'

'There was still some daylight then.'

Fifty yards along the bank was a place where the reeds grew extra tall. 'Anywhere like that?'

'I suppose there's no harm in looking,' she said.

'That's why we're here, miss.'

He stepped in and felt his foot sink into soft mud. 'You'd better stay where you are,' he told Miss Trenchard-Smith. He worked his way through to the far side. Nothing was there except a family of ducks that put up a noisy protest.

He returned.

She said, 'Just look at the state of your gym shoes!'

'We're looking for a body, miss,' PC Sedgemoor reminded her. 'We've got to do the job properly.'

'If you're going to wade through every clump of reeds, we'll be out all night,' she said blithely.

Twenty minutes' searching resulted only in Miss Trenchard-Smith becoming more flippant and PC Sedgemoor less patient. They moved steadily along the shoreline. He shone the torch on his watch, thinking bitterly of Shirley alone in the cottage with those unlikeable cats while he danced attendance on this scatty old maid. Almost 11.30. What a Saturday night! In an impatient gesture he swung the beam rapidly across the whole width of the water as if to demonstrate the futility of the task. And perversely that was the moment when Miss Trenchard-Smith said, 'There!'

'Where?'

'Give me the torch,' she said.

He handed it to her and watched as she held it at arm's length. The beam picked out something white in the water.

PC Sedgemoor took a short, quick breath. 'What do you know?' he said in a whisper. 'You were right.'

The body had lodged among the reeds not more than ten feet from where they stood, in a place where waterweed, bright viridian in the torchlight, grew densely. Unquestionably a woman, face upwards, her long hair splayed in the water, a strand of it across her throat. The pale flesh was flecked with seedpods. No wounds were apparent. Sedgemoor was reminded of a painting he had once seen on a school trip to London: a woman lying dead among reeds, evidently drowned. It had impressed him because the teacher had said that the model had been forced to lie for hours in a bath in the artist's studio and one day the artist had forgotten to fill the lamps that were provided to keep the water warm. As a result the girl had contracted an illness that didn't immediately kill her, but certainly shortened her life.

The story had been given to the class as an example of obsessive fidelity to the subject. Sedgemoor had stood in front of the painting until the teacher had called his name sharply from the next room, for it had been the only painting of a dead person he had seen, and death is fascinating to children. Now, faced with an actual drowned corpse, he was made acutely aware how idealized the Pre-Raphaelite image had been. It wasn't merely that the girl in the painting had been clothed. Her hands and face had lain elegantly on the surface of the water. The face of the real drowned woman was submerged, drawn under by the weight of the head. The belly was uppermost, and it was swollen. The skin on the breasts had a puckered appearance. The hands hung too low to be visible at all.

'There's a wind blowing up,' said Miss Trenchard-Smith.

'Yes,' he responded in a preoccupied way.

'If you don't do something about it, she'll drift away again.'

The duty inspector at 'F' Division in Yeovil picked out the significant word from PC Sedgemoor's call. 'Naked' meant a full alert. You can generally rule out accident or suicide if you discover a naked corpse in a lake. 'And you say you handled it? Was that necessary? All right, lad. Stay where you are. I mean that literally. Stand on the spot. Don't trample the ground. Don't touch the corpse again. Don't smoke, comb your hair, scratch your balls, anything.'

Sedgemoor was compelled to ignore the instruction. He hadn't cared to admit that he was calling in from the car, where he had stupidly left his personal radio. He set off at a trot, back to the lakeside.

Miss Trenchard-Smith stood by the body in the darkness, sublimely unconcerned. 'I switched off the torch to save your battery.'

He told her that assistance was on the way and he would see that she was taken home shortly.

'I hope not,' she said. 'I'd like to help.'

'Decent of you to offer, miss,' said Sedgemoor. 'With respect, the CID won't need any help.'

'*You* were glad of it, young man.'

'Yes.'

She was unstoppable. Women of her mettle had climbed the Matterhorn in long skirts and chained themselves to railings. 'They'll want to identify her,' she said with relish. 'I'm no Sherlock Holmes, but I can tell them several things already. She was married, proud of her looks and her shoes pinched. And it appears to me as if she had red hair. It looked dark brown when you first brought her out, but I would say on closer examination that it was a rather fetching shade of chestnut red, wouldn't you?' She switched on the torch and bent over the face admiringly as if it had none of the disfigurement caused by prolonged submersion. 'No wonder she let it grow.'

'Don't touch!' Sedgemoor cautioned her.

But she already had a lock of hair between finger and thumb. 'Just feel how fine it is. Don't be squeamish.'

14

'It isn't that — it's procedure. You don't handle anything.'

She looked up, smiling. 'Come now, you just dragged her out of the water. Touching her hair won't make a jot of difference.'

'I've had orders,' he said stiffly. 'And I must request you to co-operate.'

'As you wish.' She straightened up and used the torch to justify her deductions. 'The mark of a wedding ring on the left hand. Traces of nail polish on the toes as well as the fingernails. Cramped toes and redness on the backs of the heels. Neither a farmgirl nor a feminist, my dear Watson. Where are they? They ought to be here by now.'

It was with distinct relief that Sedgemoor spotted across the landscape the flashing light of a police vehicle. He swung the torch in a wide arc above his head.

In a few bewildering minutes their sense of isolation was supplanted by activity on a scale the young constable had only ever seen in a training film. A panda car, two large vans and a minibus drove over the turf and halted and at least a dozen men got out. The area was cordoned off with white tapes and illuminated with arc-lamps. Two senior detectives approached the body and spent some time beside it. Then the scenes-of-crime officers moved in. The forensic team arrived. A photographer took pictures and a screen was erected. Miss Trenchard-Smith was led to the minibus and questioned about the finding of the body. The detectives took more interest in her green wellingtons than her deductions about the victim. The boots were borrowed, photographed and used to make casts. Then she was driven back to PC Sedgemoor's house.

Sedgemoor was not detained much longer. He made his statement, surrendered his muddy trainers to the forensic examiners, waited for them to be returned and then left the scene and drove home. Miss Trenchard-Smith and her cats were still there when he arrived a few minutes after midnight. She was still there at 1.30 a.m., drinking cocoa and reminiscing about her days in the ambulance service during the war. As she graphically expressed it, sudden death was meat and drink to her. This was not the case

15

with Harry Sedgemoor. He refused Shirley's offer of cocoa and went upstairs to look for indigestion tablets. He had to be on duty at eight next morning.

Chapter Three

IN THE BRISTOL CITY MORTUARY a body lay on a steel trolley. In profile the swell of the stomach suggested nothing less than a mountainous landscape. Or to an imaginative eye it might have been evocative of a dinosaur lurking in a primeval swamp, except that a brown trilby hat of the sort seen in 1940s films rested on the hump. The body was clothed in a double-breasted suit much creased at the points of stress, grey in colour, with a broad check design – well known in the Avon and Somerset Police as the working attire of Detective Superintendent Peter Diamond. His silver-fringed bald head was propped on a rubber sheet he had found folded on a shelf. He was breathing evenly.

Peter Diamond was entitled to put his feet up. Ever since the phone beside his bed at home in Bear Flat, near Bath, had buzzed shortly after 1 a.m., he had been continuously on duty. By the time he had got to the scene at Chew Valley Lake and viewed the body, the local CID lads had set the wheels in motion, but there had remained decisions only Diamond could make, strings that only the man in charge could pull. He'd pulled more strings than Segovia.

Clearly a naked body in a lake was a suspicious death, warranting the attendance of a Home Office pathologist. Resolved to get the top man rather than one of the local police surgeons who was simply empowered to certify that death had occurred, Diamond had personally called Dr Jack Merlin at his home seventy miles away in Reading and spelt out the facts. Fewer than thirty forensic pathologists were on the Home Office list for England and Wales, and several lived closer than Merlin to Chew Valley Lake.

Diamond had set his sights on Jack Merlin. Experience had taught him to shop around for the best. In practice two or three pathologists bore the brunt of the work for the whole of southern England, sometimes motoring vast distances to attend the scenes of crimes. Dr Merlin was grossly overworked, even without the emergency calls, obliged by the system to perform many routine autopsies a year to provide funds for his forensic science unit. Reasonably enough, if he was called out to a corpse, he liked to be assured by the detective in charge that his attendance was indispensable.

Without altogether succumbing to Diamond's early morning charm, Merlin had responded at once. He had got to the scene by 3.30 a.m. Now, ten hours later, he was performing the autopsy in the room next door.

The sight of that unoccupied stretcher had been irresistible to Peter Diamond. Ostensibly he was there to witness the post mortem. The emphasis on scientific and technical know how in the modern police increasingly made it the custom for senior detectives investigating suspicious deaths to watch the pathologist at work. Diamond didn't embrace the opportunity as readily as some of his colleagues; he was content to rely on the pathologist's report. Not for the first time on the way to a post mortem had he taken the slow route and meticulously observed the speed limits. On arrival he'd spent some time cruising along Backfields looking for a parking space. Upon finally checking in at the mortuary to learn that the pathologist had started without him and Inspector Wigfull, his reliable assistant, had already gone in, he'd grinned and said, 'Botheration. Bully for John Wigfull. Time out for me.'

For the now-dormant Detective Superintendent, those first hours had been as stressful as they always were when you had to impose order on a situation as disorderly as sudden death. But the CID machine was humming now, the procedures set in motion with the coroner, the scenes-of-crime officers, the missing persons register, the forensic science laboratory and the press office. He could justifiably take his nap while waiting for the news from Jack Merlin.

The door of the dissecting room opened suddenly and woke him. There was a whiff of something unpleasant in

18

the air: cheap floral perfume sprayed from an aerosol by a zealous technician. Diamond blinked, stretched, reached for his felt hat and raised it in a token greeting.

'You should have come in,' he heard Dr Merlin tell him.

'Too close to lunch.' Diamond hoisted himself ponderously on to an elbow. It was true that he wasn't used to missing lunch. He had stopped buying suits off the peg when he took up rugby and started thickening. The rugby had stopped eight years ago, when he was thirty-three. The thickening had not. It didn't trouble him. 'What's your snap verdict, then – subject to all the usual provisos?'

Merlin smiled tolerantly. Soft of speech, with a West Country accent redolent of blue skies and clotted cream, this slight, silver-haired man projected such optimism that it was a pity the people he attended were in no state to appreciate it. 'If I were you, Superintendent, I'd be rather excited.'

Diamond made a gesture in the direction of excitement by heaving himself into a sitting position, squirming around and dangling his legs over the side of the trolley.

Merlin went on to explain. 'It's the opportunity one of your sort dreams of – a real test of his sleuthing ability. An unidentified corpse. No clothes to identify her from a million other women. No marks of any significance. No murder weapon.'

'What do you mean – "*one of your sort*"?'

'You know very well what I mean, Peter. You're the end of an era. The last detective. A genuine gumshoe, not some lad out of police school with a degree in computer studies.'

Diamond was unamused. 'No murder weapon, you said. You're willing to confirm murder?'

'I didn't say that. I wouldn't, would I? I'm in the business of making incisions, not deductions.'

'I just want any help you can give me,' said Diamond, too weary to argue professional demarcations. 'Did she drown?'

Merlin vibrated his lips as if to buy time. 'Good question.'

'Well?'

'I'll say this. The body has the appearance you would expect after prolonged immersion.'

'Come on, Jack,' Diamond urged him. 'You must know if she drowned. Even I know the signs. Foam in the mouth and nostrils. Bulging of the lungs. Mud and silt in the internal organs.'

'Thanks,' said Merlin with irony.

'You tell me, then.'

'No foam. No over-distension. No silt. Is that what you needed to know, Superintendent?'

Diamond was accustomed to asking the questions, so he tended to ignore any addressed to him. He stared and said nothing.

Someone stepped out of the autopsy room carrying a white plastic bag. He spoke something in greeting and Diamond recognized him as one of the scenes-of-crime officers. The bag now on its way to the Home Office Forensic Science Laboratory at Chepstow was known in the trade as the guts kit.

'Drowning is one of the most difficult diagnoses in forensic pathology,' Merlin resumed. 'In this case, decomposition makes it even more of a lottery. I can't exclude drowning simply because none of the classical signs are present. The foam and the ballooning of the lungs and so on *may* be present when a body is retrieved from water soon after a drowning occurs. They may not. And if they are not, we can't exclude drowning. The majority of cases of drowning I've seen over the years have lacked any of these so-called classical signs. And after a period of immersion ...' He shrugged. 'Disappointed?'

'What else could have killed her, then?'

'Impossible to say at this stage. They'll test for drugs and alcohol.'

'You found no other signs?'

'Other signs, as you put it, were conspicuously absent. Chepstow may give us a pointer. This is rather a challenge for me, too.' Merlin didn't go so far as to rub his hands, but his blue eyes certainly gleamed in anticipation. 'A real puzzle. It might be more productive to determine what didn't kill her. She was definitely not shot, stabbed, battered or strangled.'

'And she wasn't mauled by a tiger. Come on, Jack, what have I got to go on?'

Merlin turned to a cupboard marked *poison*, unlocked it and took out a bottle of malt whiskey. He poured generous measures into two paper cups and handed one to the Superintendent. 'What have you got to go on? You've got a white female in her early thirties, natural reddish brown hair of shoulder length, five foot seven inches in height and about a hundred and ten pounds in weight, green eyes, pierced ears, a particularly fine set of teeth with a couple of expensive white enamel fillings, varnished fingernails and toenails, a vaccination mark just below the knee and no operation scars, the mark of a wedding ring on the appropriate finger, and, yes, she was sexually experienced. Aren't you going to make notes or something? This is the distillation of twenty years wearing a rubber apron, I'll have you know.'

'Not pregnant, then?'

'No. The swelling of the abdomen was due entirely to the putrefactive gases.'

'Can you say whether she has borne a child?'

'Unlikely is as much as I'm prepared to say.'

'How long had she been in the lake?'

'What sort of weather have we been having? I've been too busy to notice.'

'Pretty warm the last fortnight.'

'At least a week, then.' Merlin put up his hands defensively. 'And don't even ask which day she died.'

'Within the last two weeks?'

'Probably. I suppose you've checked your missing persons?'

Diamond gave a nod. 'Nobody fits.'

Merlin beamed. 'You wouldn't have wanted it so easy, would you? This is when your technology is put to the test. All those incredibly expensive computers I keep reading about in *Police Review*.'

Diamond allowed him to make his dig and get away with it. He felt he couldn't do otherwise, knowing, as he did, the conditions that Merlin and his colleagues were sometimes obliged to work in: public mortuaries with inadequate space, lighting, ventilation, plumbing and drainage. Mortuary building would never be high on the list of social priorities. Mind, there were points Diamond wouldn't mind making himself about pay and conditions of work in the police, but not to Jack Merlin. So he simply repeated in a tone of disparagement, 'Computers?'

Merlin grinned. 'You know what I mean. Major Inquiry Systems.'

'Major Inquiry Systems, my arse. Common sense and door-stepping. That's how we get results.'

'Apart from the odd tip-off,' said Merlin and added quickly, 'So what will you do about this woman? Issue an artist's impression? A photo wouldn't bear much resemblance to the way she was before she got into the water.'

'Probably. First I want to collect any evidence that's going.'

'What sort?'

'Obviously we're searching for the clothes.'

'At the scene?'

Diamond shook his head. 'In this case the scene is unimportant. The body floated there. I gather from what you said that it must originally have sunk to the bottom, and later risen, as they do, unless they're weighted.'

'Correct.'

'So it came to the surface and floated with the breeze across the lake. We have to search the perimeter.'

'How many miles is that?'

'Ten, near enough.'

'That represents a lot of cancelled leave, I should think.'

'It's a sod. But we may get lucky. The lake is popular with anglers and picnickers. I'll be putting out an appeal to the public on TV and radio. If we can pinpoint the place where the body was put into the water, that will give us a start.'

Merlin cleared his throat in a way that signalled dissent. 'There's a hefty assumption there.'

'A deduction,' said Diamond with a glare. 'Come on, what else am I to assume – that this young woman decided to go for a solitary swim when nobody was about, first removing her wedding ring and all her clothes, and then drowned? You'd have to be bloody naive to put this one down to natural causes.' He crushed the cup in his hand and dumped it into a bin.

Chapter Four

THE MURDER SQUAD WORKED FROM a mobile incident room from Sunday morning onwards. It was a large caravan parked on a stretch of turf as close as possible to the reeds where the body had been found. Each time Peter Diamond crossed the floor it sounded like beer-kegs being unloaded. The sound was heard until well into the evening as he directed the first crucial stages of the inquiry. Five telephones were steadily in use and a team of filing clerks transferred every message and every piece of information first on to action sheets and then on to cards. The standard four-tier carousel for up to 20,000 cards stood ominously in the centre of the room. Diamond felt comfortable with index cards, even if some of his younger staff muttered things about the superiority of computers. If there was no quick resolution to the inquiry, he'd be forced to install the despised VDUs, and God help the moaners when the things broke down.

The search for the dead woman's clothes was first concentrated on the sections of shoreline with easiest access from the three roads that enclosed the lake. A bizarre collection of mislaid garments began to be assembled, tokens of the variety of human activities around the lake. The items were painstakingly labelled, sealed in plastic bags, noted on the map and entered on the action sheets without much confidence that any were linked with the case.

Divers were brought in to search the stretch of water where the body had been found floating. It was not impossible that the clothes or other evidence had been dumped there. This was an exercise that had to be gone through, although most people, including Diamond, reckoned that the body had drifted there from further along the shore, or even across the lake.

At the same time, house-to-house inquiries were made in the villages and at each dwelling with a view of the lake, seeking witnesses to any unusual activity beside the water after dark in the previous month. A sheaf of statements soon confirmed what the squad already knew, that the area was popular around the hour of sunset with anglers, bird-watchers, dog-owners and courting couples. Nothing remotely resembling a naked body being dragged or carried into the water had been seen.

For Peter Diamond this dragnet process was a necessary, if largely unrewarding, preamble to what he thought of as real detective work: the identifying and questioning of suspects. For all the care that was being taken to refer to what had happened as an 'incident', this was a murder inquiry. He was as certain of that as the fact that one day follows another. Since his appointment to the Avon and Somerset murder squad three years previously, he had led five investigations, three domestic, two large-scale, all but one resulting in convictions. The odd one out was an extradition job, still to be resolved. It could drag on for another year. However, he was satisfied that he had nailed his man. An impressive record. And it might have been more impressive if his service in Avon had not been regularly interrupted by all the ballyhoo over the Missendale affair.

Four years earlier, a young black man called Hedley Missendale had been convicted of murder in the course of theft at a building society in Hammersmith, west London. A customer, an ex-sergeant-major, had tried to tackle the thief and had been shot in the head, dying almost immediately. The investigation had been headed by Detective Superintendent Jacob Blaize, of 'F' Division of the Metropolitan Police. Diamond, then with the rank of detective chief inspector, had been Blaize's second-in-command. Missendale, a known thief, had been pulled in quickly and had confessed under interrogation from Diamond. Then more than two years later, after Diamond

25

had won his promotion to superintendent with the Avon and Somerset force, a second man had confessed to the crime after undergoing a religious conversion. He had produced the gun used in the killing. A second investigation by a fresh team of officers had been ordered, and late in 1987, after serving twenty-seven months of a life sentence, Hedley Missendale had been pardoned on the recommendation of the Home Secretary.

The press, of course, had roasted the police. Blaize and Diamond had been openly accused in the tabloids of beating a confession out of an innocent black youth. An official inquiry had been inevitable. Jacob Blaize – broken by the strain – had accepted full responsibility for the errors and had taken early retirement. The press had switched the full force of their attack to Diamond. They had wanted his head on a platter, but he had stood up well to tough questioning at the inquiry. What had yet to be seen was whether his strong rebuttal of the criticism had influenced the board of inquiry. People said he was on a hiding to nothing, because the principal charge was that his forceful personality had secured the bogus confession, and he had fought his corner ruggedly at the hearings.

Eight months on from the hearings, the inquiry team had yet to publish its findings. Meanwhile, Peter Diamond was unrepentant, and willing to argue the rights of his conduct in the case with anyone rash enough to take him on. No one did; the mud-slinging went on from a safe distance. His response was to prove his worth as a detective, and this he was doing – between appearances in London – with fair success. The string of cases he had investigated in Avon had been properly handled without a suggestion of intimidation.

He was still finding the going tough in the new job. Although the men on the murder squad gave him professional support, they hadn't accepted him on a personal level. He had come in first as the streetwise detective from Scotland Yard, which understandably had created a certain amount of scepticism among detectives who had served all their careers in the West Country. Then, with ruinous timing, the Missendale story had broken.

The work somehow had to continue amid all the distractions. He had learned to live with stress. On any murder squad, the nerve of the man in charge was severely tested in those first hours at the start of a case. It was a kind of phoney war when nothing was happening. All these expensive resources were being deployed. Men were wanted for other policing duties. How long could you justify employing so many if results weren't apparent? Inevitably the CID were regarded as the top dogs, enjoying different conditions of service from the uniformed branch, working flexible hours, more mobile, more independent, and able to snap their fingers and call up reinforcements as soon as someone went missing, or a body was found. A certain amount of resentment was understandable. It was built into the system and it existed at all levels. Maybe it was more subtle nearer the top. It was there. So you lived with it.

Diamond had learned to hand off the opposition as if he was still playing rugby. He was proving a hard man to stop, a burly, abrasive character who spoke his mind. Computer technology was 'gadgetry', accepted with reluctance as an aid to the real detective work. Some of the career-minded people around him thought it a miracle or a travesty that a man so outspoken and with the Missendale Inquiry hanging over his head could have progressed to the rank of superintendent. They failed to appreciate that his bluntness was a precious asset among so many backbiters.

Whether he would ever earn respect in Avon and Somerset it was too soon to predict. His detractors said that his successes so far owed too much to help from paid informants. They couldn't fault him for using grasses; but they waited gloatingly to see him handle an inquiry when no help could be bought.

The Chew Valley case might be the one.

Sunday was disappointing. Nothing of significance was found.

On Monday Diamond recorded interviews for BBC Television and HTV West for their regional news broadcasts after the early evening news. An artist's impression of the dead woman was shown, followed by Diamond beside the lake appealing for help in identifying her. He asked for information from anyone who might have witnessed suspicious behaviour over the last three weeks. An invitation, he commented afterwards to the TV crew, to all the voyeurs in the valley to wipe the steam off their glasses and share their secondhand thrills, but he had to admit that it was worthwhile. A thirty-second spot on TV brought in more information than a hundred coppers on house-to-house duty all the week.

Late that night, while the calls were being processed, he called Jack Merlin and asked for the results of the laboratory tests.

'What exactly were you hoping for?' the pathologist asked in that benign, but irritating way he had of sounding as if he were from another, more intelligent form of life.

'The cause of death will do for now.'

'That, I'm afraid, is still an open question until all the results are in, and even then –'

'Jack, are you telling me those flaming tests are still going on? The autopsy was yesterday morning, thirty-six hours ago.'

For this petulant outburst, Diamond was given a lecture on the time-scale necessary for the processing of histological tissues, which required at least a week, and on the pressures the Home Office Forensic Laboratory was under. 'Currently they're so pressed that it could be weeks before they deliver.'

'*Weeks?* Have you told them it's a suspicious death? Don't they understand the urgency?' Diamond had picked up a pencil and put it between his teeth. He bit into the wood. 'You're still not willing to say if she drowned?'

'All I will say is that as yet the cause of death is not apparent.' Merlin was retreating behind the form of words he used in giving evidence.

'Jack, my old friend,' Diamond coaxed him. 'Can't you speak off the record to me? Can you help me with an estimate of the date of death?'

'Sorry.'

'Terrific!' The pencil snapped into two pieces.

There was a longish silence. Then: 'I am doing the best I can in the circumstances, Superintendent. I won't be steam-rollered. You must appreciate that the service is undermanned.'

'Jack, spare me the charity appeal, will you? Just call me the minute you reach an opinion.'

'I always intended to.'

Diamond dropped the phone and left it dangling below the worktop. The telephonist retrieved it without complaining and removed the pieces of pencil. Diamond ambled across the floor again to see what had come in as a result of his television appeal, knocking the carousel out of alignment as he went.

John Wigfull, his second-in-command, summed up. 'We've heard from seven callers convinced that the victim is Candice Milner.'

After a pause to decide whether the question should be taken seriously, Wigfull said, '*The Milners* – that soap on the BBC. Candice was written out of the story a couple of years ago, at least.'

'Give me strength! What else?'

'Two deserted husbands called in. In one case the wife left a note saying she was going away for a week to unwind. The home is in Chilcompton. That was six months ago.'

'Six months. She ought to be in missing persons.'

'She is. The photo doesn't bear much resemblance. We passed it over.'

'I'll take another look at it. You'd better send someone to talk to the bloke tomorrow. What else?'

'Slightly more promising, this. A farmer by the name of Troop from Chewton Mendip had a row with his wife three weeks ago and she hitched a lift with the lorry-driver who collects the milk-churns. Husband hasn't seen her since.'

'Didn't he report it?'

'He was giving her time to come to her senses. There's a history of fights and walk-outs.'

'And he reckons the picture looks like his wife?'

'He's not saying, sir. His sister-in-law thinks so. She was the one who phoned us.'

Diamond's eyes widened a fraction. 'Anything on file? Complaints of violence?'

Wigfull nodded. 'Just the one, on 27 December, 1988. Farmer Troop seems to have kicked his wife out of the house, literally, and refused to let her in again. The sister reported it. A PC from Bath was sent out and saw the bruises. The woman refused to proceed. She said it was Christmas.'

'Goodwill to all men.' Diamond took a deep, disapproving breath and let it out slowly. 'What can you do? You and I had better follow this one up ourselves, John. Chewton Mendip can't be more than five miles from the lake. I'll see the sister-in-law in the morning – and you'd better find out the name of the gallant knight of the churns.'

Wigfull grinned appreciatively. Any sign of good humour in the superintendent had to be encouraged. They weren't exactly bosom pals. Wigfull had been named as Diamond's assistant in the worst of circumstances, when the Missendale scandal had first made banner headlines. In the few preceding months, Diamond had made an impressive debut with Avon and Somerset and cleared up two murders, assisted by an inspector he had got along well with, called Billy Murray. But within hours of Diamond's involvement in the Missendale case becoming known, instructions had come from County Headquarters that Murray was to be transferred to Taunton, where a vacancy had arisen. John Wigfull, from CID (Administration), was his replacement. Rightly or not, Diamond was convinced that Wigfull was a plant, the Headquarters man under instructions to report any excesses. Unlike Billy Murray, Wigfull did everything by the book. He'd gone to a lot of trouble to ingratiate himself with the squad. He hadn't succeeded yet with his superior.

'Anything else?' asked Diamond.

'A fair number of sightings.'

'But of what?'

'Horizontal jogging, mostly.'

'No reports of violence?'

'Nothing yet.'

'Not much, is it? I may go on the box again towards the

30

end of the week. Let's see if Chewton Mendip amounts to anything. Is that where the sister lives as well?'

She was Mrs Muriel Pietri, and her husband Joe owned a motor repair business beside the A39 that had a sign that promised, 'Low Cost High Class Repairs. We Get You Back On The Road.' The police often visited the place to follow up hit and run accidents. Diamond himself called there early next morning. Someone lower in rank could have handled the interview, but the prospect of question and answer was so much more appealing than another morning in the caravan.

The sickly-sweet vapour of cellulose paint hung in the air as he manoeuvred his bulk unskilfully through a narrow passage between damaged vehicles, collecting rust on his grey check suit. He had brought a sergeant with him to take the statement.

Mrs Pietri stood at the open door in a floral print frock that she probably wore for visitors. She was made up for the occasion – the works: foundation, lipstick, mascara and some sort of cheap scent that made the paint quite fragrant in retrospect. A slim, dark-haired, slow-speaking woman, burning with the enormity of what she believed had happened. 'I do fear the worst this time,' she said in the broad accent of Somerset as she led them into her scrupulously tidy front room. 'Carl's behaviour is a proper disgrace. He do clout my sister summat wicked. Terrible. I can show you photographs my husband took with one of they Instamatics last time poor Elly came here. Black and blue, she were. I hope you'll be giving the bugger a dose of his own medicine when you visit him. He do deserve no blimmin mercy, none at all. Won't 'ee sit down?'

'You saw the artist's impression of the woman we found?' said Diamond.

'On *Points West* last night. That be Elly, without a blimmin doubt.'

'Sergeant Boon has a copy of the picture. Take another look at it, would you? It's only an artist's sketch, you understand.'

She handed it back almost at once. 'I swear to it.'

31

'What colour is your sister's hair, Mrs Pietri?'

'Red – a gorgeous, flaming red. It were her best feature, and it were natural, too. Women spend fortunes being tinted at the hairdressers for hair that colour and it never looks half so good as Elly's did.'

Her use of the past tense reinforced her conviction that the dead woman was her sister. Diamond made it just as clear that he was keeping an open mind. 'Flaming red, you say. Is that what you mean – pure red?'

'Natural, I did say, didn't I? Nobody's hair is pure red, except for they punks and pop stars.'

'I need to know.'

She pointed to a rosewood ornamental box that stood on the sideboard. 'That colour, near enough.'

'Her eyes – what colour are they?'

'Some folk called they hazel. They always looked green to I.'

'What height is she?'

'The same as I – five-seven.'

'Age?'

'Wait a mo – Elly were born two years after I. St George's Day. She must have been thirty-four.'

'You said that your husband took photographs of her.'

'Not of her face, my dear. The backs of her legs, where she were marked. It were in case she wanted evidence for a divorce. I don't believe I got a picture of her face, not since her and I were kids at school, anyways. We were never a family for taking pictures.'

'But you said your husband has a camera.'

'For his business. He do photograph the damage in case the insurance people get funny.'

'I see.'

'It were his idea to take they pictures of Elly's legs.'

'Photographing the damage.'

'I can find they if you want.'

'Not now. Tell me how you heard that your sister is missing.'

'Well, being that she lived so near, she used to call in here regular for a bit o' gossip Tuesday morning. She didn't come last Tuesday, or the Tuesday afore that, so I got on the blower and asked that bugger of a brother-in-law what happened to my sister.'

'And?'

'The blighter tells I this bit o' hogwash about Elly taking off with Mr Middleton who collects the milk. Your sister is a shameless woman, he did tell I, no better than the whores of Babylon. He called her other things, too, that you wouldn't find in the scriptures. Riled I proper, I can tell 'ee.'

'When is this supposed to have happened?'

'Last Monday fortnight, he did say. I didn't believe a word of it, and I were right. She must have been dead already, lying naked in Chew Valley Lake, poor lamb. Do you want I to come with 'ee to identify her proper?'

'That may not be necessary.'

'Will you be going over to arrest the bugger?'

'I want you to sign a statement, Mrs Pietri. The sergeant will assist you.' Diamond got up and walked out.

Over the radio he made contact with Inspector Wigfull. 'Any news?'

'Yes,' Wigfull answered. 'I just called at the milkman's cottage.'

'Middleton?'

'Yes.'

'And?'

'Elly Troop opened the door.'

Chapter Five

IN THE MODERN POLICE, AS any detective will tell you, a murder mystery is rarely, if ever, solved by scintillating deductions from clues that baffle inferior minds. Unless the killer's identity is so obvious that the case is cleared up in the first hours, the investigative process is likely to be laborious, involving hundreds of man-hours by police officers, forensic scientists and clerical staff. If any credit attaches ultimately to a conviction, it is diffused among numerous individuals, and has to be qualified by administrative delays, false assumptions and sometimes fatal errors. These days criminal investigation is not a sport for glory hunters.

After the unproductive interview with Mrs Pietri, Diamond returned to the mobile incident room and pounded the floor again. He demanded another look at the missing persons files for Avon and Somerset and the adjacent counties and vented his anger on a filing clerk when he found that the list hadn't been updated since he had last seen it. The atmosphere in the caravan was sulphurous as he reduced the girl to tears, blaming her for other shortcomings in the list that were apparently not her responsibility.

Inspector Wigfull's return should have defused the tension. Wigfull, the sunbeam of the squad, as Diamond unkindly dubbed him, always had a word of encouragement for everyone, including the civilian clerks, each of whom he knew by their first names. His was the shoulder to cry on. He smiled a lot, and when he wasn't smiling he still appeared to be, because of the tendency of his exuberant moustache to curl upwards at the ends. This time the mere sight of him coming up the steps – playing a catching game with his car keys – triggered Diamond into another tirade.

'You took your bloody time.'

'Sorry, sir. Mrs Troop was in a bit of a state. She needed advice.'

'John, if you want to join the bloody Marriage Guidance people and hold hands with weeping wives, why don't you go ahead? I happen to be working on a murder inquiry, and if that isn't your particular bent, I suggest you tell me right now so that I can ask for someone I can rely on.'

'She'd been assaulted by her husband, sir. I was telling her to lodge a complaint this time.'

'Social work,' said Diamond as if he were speaking of some disease brought on by lack of hygiene. 'You're supposed to be a detective. Meanwhile I'm stuck here like a lupin waiting for a bee.'

'Has there been a development?'

Diamond flung out his hand and knocked over a box of paper clips. 'Of course there bloody hasn't. How can there be when you're listening to sob stories over coffee in Chewton Mendip? Three days, and all I've got for it is a sunburnt scalp. We're literally up the creek until we can put a name to this corpse.'

'Should we have another look at missing persons?' the hapless inspector suggested.

There was a tensing of shoulders right around the room, unnecessarily as it turned out. Diamond, deciding that he had raised his blood pressure to dangerous levels, said in the mild register that he knew was more effective than a bellow, 'That is what I have been trying to do.'

'But in this area alone?'

'And Wiltshire.' He snatched up a sheaf of flimsy papers and flapped it. 'A bloody long list, growing by seventy-plus every week.'

Wigfull cleared his throat and said, 'Surely the PNC can help us.'

Diamond had to think a moment. His mind didn't work in abbreviations, and people who knew him better were more tactful than to press the cause of the Police National

Computer. 'Yes,' he said with contempt, '– by giving us twenty thousand names.'

'You limit it by keying in the data you have,' Wigfull tried to explain. 'In this case, females under thirty with red hair.'

In reality, Diamond had a reasonable grasp of the PNC's functions; otherwise he couldn't have survived in the CID. What he deplored was the general belief that it was the cure-all. 'For the present, we'll work with the county lists,' he said. 'I want updates on each of the names I've marked. Call the local stations. Get descriptions, real descriptions, not sodding data, as you insist on calling it. I want to know what they're like as people. By 3.30 this afternoon. I'm calling a conference.'

'Very good, Mr Diamond.'

'That remains to be seen. You may have sensed that I'm feeling somewhat frayed at the edges, Mr Wigfull. Somewhere out there is a murderer. We're making precious little progress towards arresting him. Jesus Christ, we don't even know how it was done.'

'Looks as if we'll need the PNC,' said Wigfull.

Diamond turned away, muttering, to check more responses to the local appeal for information. Copies of the artist's impression had appeared in Monday's *Bath Evening Chronicle* and the *Bristol Evening Post*. 'Two more for Candice Milner,' he presently called across to Wigfull. 'It says a lot about contemporary values when people can't discriminate between real life and a flaming television serial.' It would take a breakthrough of cosmic proportions to shake him out of this embittered mood.

Wanting to get away from the constant bleep of the phones, he chose to hold his case conference in the minibus parked beside the incident room. So at 3.30, the four senior officers in the squad sat with him in the rear of the vehicle in uncomfortable proximity and in turn reported their findings.

Wigfull's work on the phone had yielded results of a sort: he had fuller details of three missing women whose descriptions broadly tallied with the woman found in the lake. 'Janet Hepple is divorced, thirty-three, a part-time artists'

36

model in Coventry. Red hair, five foot seven. She left her flat seven weeks ago, leaving rent unpaid, and hasn't been seen since. Evidently this was out of character. Everyone spoke of her as honest and reliable.'

Diamond was unimpressed. 'And the second?'

'Sally Shepton-Howe, from Manchester, missing since 21 May, when she had a row with her husband and ran off. She sells cosmetics in a department store in the city. Hair described as auburn, green eyes, thirty-two, good-looking. A woman of her description was seen that night at Knutsford Services on the M6 trying to hitch a lift south.'

'Asking for it. Who else?'

'This is an odd one. An author, from west London, Hounslow. Writes romance. What are those books women buy everywhere?'

'Bodice-rippers?' someone suggested.

'No, the name of the publisher.'

'Don't ask me. I only read science fiction.'

'Anyway, she writes them. She's called Meg Zoomer.'

'Zoomer. Is that a pen name?'

'It's real, apparently, the name of her third husband.'

'*Third?*' said Diamond. 'What age is this woman?'

'Thirty-four. She appears to carry on as if she's one of the characters in her books. Hungry for romance. She wears a dark green cloak and grows her hair long. It's chestnut red. Anyway, she drives about in an MG sports car looking for experiences to use in her books.'

'Someone's having you on, John,' said Keith Halliwell, the inspector supervising the house-to-house inquiries.

'They'd better not be,' Diamond said gravely. 'This is a murder hunt, not a night out at the pub. Let's have the rest. When was Mrs Zoomer last seen?'

'The nineteenth of May, at a party in Richmond. She left soon after midnight with a man who seems to have been a gatecrasher. Everyone assumed he came with somebody else. Tall, dark-haired, aged about thirty, powerfully built, a trace of a French accent.'

'Straight out of one of the books,' commented Halliwell. 'What did he drive – a Porsche, or a four-in-hand?'

'Wrap up, will you?' Diamond snapped. He regarded

Halliwell as a pain, which was why he was on house-to-house. 'Who was the informant?'

'The woman who lives next door, sir. She took in the milk each day until there was no room left in her fridge.'

'Has anyone shown her the picture yet?'

'That's being done. And Scotland Yard are trying to locate Mrs Zoomer's dental records.'

'A model, a shopgirl and a writer,' Diamond summed it up, and sniffed. 'That's all?'

'Those are the missing redheads more or less fitting our description, sir.'

'I thought you would come up with more than that.'

Wigfull countered this by saying, 'With respect, sir, the PNC would have given us more.'

After an uneasy silence, Diamond said tamely, 'All right. See to it.'

Wigfull tilted an eyebrow in Halliwell's direction and it was his undoing.

'As we're going to cast the net more widely,' continued Diamond in a reasonable tone, 'maybe we should broaden our data-base.'

The jargon from the lips of the Last Detective ambushed everyone. 'In what way, exactly, Mr Diamond?' Wigfull innocently asked.

'Brunettes. People have different ideas about red hair. Our woman isn't what you'd call ginger. The hair is reddish brown.'

'More red than brown, sir.'

'Some people might call it brown. Check the brunettes on the PNC as well.'

That silenced Wigfull rather pleasingly. The conference continued for another twenty minutes, dispiritingly chronicling the failure of the door-to-door enquiries, the searches and the appeals in the media to throw up anything of real significance. At the end of it, when they had climbed out of the minibus and were flexing their limbs, Inspector Croxley, a quietly ambitious man – an ascending angel, by his own lights – who was co-ordinating the search around the lake, approached Diamond and said, 'I didn't raise this inside, sir, but it crossed my mind.

We're all assuming murder because she was found nude, but there isn't any evidence of violence.'

'Up to now. The pathologist's report isn't in.'

'If it does turn out to be the writer, I wonder what you think of suicide as a possibility, sir?'

'What?'

'Suicide. I saw a thing on television once about a famous writer. I mean a documentary, not a play. She was out of her mind, I admit, but she killed herself by walking into a river. Back in the 1940s, this was, in the war. She drowned. We know this Zoomer woman has fantasies about herself, the way she dresses and what have you. Suppose she got depressed and decided to do away with herself. Isn't this the way she might do it – a dramatic gesture?'

'Starkers? Did this woman on TV strip off before she drowned herself?'

'Well, no, sir.'

'That's gilding the lily, is it?'

'I beg your pardon.'

'The dramatic gesture. An extra touch?'

'Something like that. It's only an idea.'

'I'll say one thing for your theory, Inspector. I've heard of cases when people have left a heap of clothes on a shoreline. It's not uncommon. That Labour MP –'

'Stonehouse.'

'Right. The difference is that he faked his suicide. People were meant to find the clothes and assumed he'd drowned. What we have here, Inspector, isn't a pile of clothes and no corpse. It's a corpse and no clothes. You find me a pile of women's garments including a long, green cloak and I might buy your theory.' With a swagger, Diamond ambled off to the incident room.

Occasionally during the long summer, when his caseload had been lighter, he had bought sandwiches for lunch and found a seat among the tourists on one of the wooden benches in the Abbey Churchyard, the paved open area facing the West Front of the Abbey. There he'd regularly whiled away a pleasant twenty minutes reading *Fabian of the Yard*, which he'd acquired in the Oxfam shop for 10p.

Fabian of the Yard. Lovely title. No wonder so many big-name detectives from Fred Cherrill to Jack Slipper had used that ... *of the Yard* tag for their memoirs. *Diamond of Avon and Somerset* didn't have the same ring to it. Good thing he wasn't planning to go into print.

At intervals in those summer lunchbreaks he had looked up from his reading. The towers on each side of the great west window were decorated with sixteenth-century carvings representing angels on two ladders – to Diamond's eye more curious than decorative. These weatherbeaten figures were perched at mathematically precise intervals on the rungs of the two ladders reaching up to heaven. Many people assumed that it was a representation of Jacob's ladder. The official version, however, was that it was Oliver King's ladder, for the bishop of that name who rebuilt the church, starting in 1499, had stoutly insisted that the dream of a ladder to heaven was his own, and who can doubt the integrity of a bishop? Fixed in perpetuity in their positions, unaltered except by the eroding effects of wind, rain and contamination, those luckless angels seemed emblematic of hope deferred, rather than celestial promise. Peter Diamond knew the feeling. Staring up at the West Front one lunchtime, he had been charmed by a revelation of his own, picturing the senior CID of Avon and Somerset clinging to the rungs. The image often came back to him when he saw them together.

Midway through Wednesday morning came a call from Dr Merlin, the pathologist. For no obvious reason Diamond had started the day in a benign mood. He strolled across the room, thanked the girl who handed him the phone, put it to his ear and said, 'Glorious morning here, Jack. What's it doing in Reading?'

'Look here, I've been badgering the lab on your account,' Merlin announced, sounding quite piqued at the *bonhomie*. 'Off the record they've given me some early results.'

'And?'

'Nothing has been found to indicate conclusively how she died.'

'You call that a result?'

'It supports my preliminary opinion.'

'I never doubted you.'

The absence of doubt in Diamond's mind appeared not to settle the question for the pathologist. 'It's still quite conceivable that she drowned.'

Diamond sighed. 'We've been over this before. Aren't we any closer to a definite cause of death? Let's put it this way, Jack,' he added quickly, not wanting the phone slammed down. 'Is there anything I can rule out? Toxic substances?'

'Too early to say. Nothing very obvious, but you have to remember that if someone has drowned, especially in fresh water, there's a tremendous increase in blood volume – up to a hundred per cent within a couple of minutes – due to the osmotic absorption of fresh water through the lung membranes. This has the effect of diluting any concentration of drugs or alcohol in the blood by up to a hundred per cent. So any analysis result on a post-mortem sample may give only half the true value which was present just before death.'

'Jack, suppose she didn't drown. Suppose the body was dumped in the lake after death. Is there anything pointing to a cause of death?'

'Essentially she appears to have been a healthy young woman. We can rule out coronary artery disease or myocarditis, or diabetic coma, or epilepsy.'

'I sense that you do know something,' said Diamond. 'You're keeping me in suspense, you bugger.'

'I'm telling you these things, Superintendent, because without them my conclusion is tentative, at best. At the autopsy I found a number of pinhead haemorrhages in the eye membranes and there were some in the scalp and to a lesser extent in the brain and the lungs. The presence of petechial haemorrhages is open to different interpretations depending on other findings.'

'All right, mate, I get the point. You can't be a hundred per cent certain. But what would you put your money on?'

Down the line, Merlin's tone of voice revealed that he didn't much like his opinion equated with gambling. 'In the absence of external injuries, one is drawn along the road –'

'Oh, come on, man!'

'... of asphyxia as the cause of death.'

'Asphyxia?'

'So you appreciate the difficulty. Drowning is a form of asphyxia.'

Diamond groaned. 'But I just ruled out drowning.'

'I didn't.' After a pause, Merlin said, 'There's a phenomenon known as dry drowning.'

Diamond wondered briefly whether he was being sent up. 'Did you say *dry* drowning?'

'It happens in about one case in every five. The victim's larynx goes into spasm with the first intake of water and very little of it enters the lungs. They drown without actually gulping or inhaling water. Dry drowning, you see.'

'What about those haemorrhages you found?'

'Would be observed, as in any case of asphyxia.'

'Meaning she may have drowned after all? That doesn't help me much. It doesn't help at all.' Diamond was heating up again. 'This wasn't a swimming accident, Jack. People aren't allowed to swim in reservoirs. Anyway, she was nude. Her wedding ring was missing.'

'Are you listening to me?' said Merlin.

'Go on.'

'To answer your question, if you exclude drowning as a possibility, and if we can eliminate drugs and alcohol, the most likely explanation is that before she got into the water she was smothered with some soft object, say a cushion or a pillow.'

'We've got there,' said Diamond to his audience in the caravan.

'I didn't say that. I'm trying to balance the probabilities. Death by smothering is hard to detect at the best of times,' said the pathologist tartly.

'You said the same about drowning. I sometimes wonder, Jack, if you'd say the same about a dagger through the heart.' Diamond banged down the phone and looked around. 'Where the hell is Wigfull?'

'Outside, sir,' said a sergeant. 'The press has arrived.'

Diamond swore and left the room.

One of the filing clerks said to nobody in particular, 'I wish we were back in headquarters.'

42

'Why?' the sergeant asked her.

'He intimidates me, that's why. I don't like to be so near him. You can't get away from him in this poky caravan. There's more room in a proper incident room. And he breaks things. Have you watched him? He breaks things – paper cups, pencils, anything he gets his hands on. It gets on my nerves.'

The sergeant grinned. 'That's how he got where he is today, by breaking things.'

Outside, at a signal from Diamond, John Wigfull terminated the press interview and the two men took a walk along the edge of the lake, past fishermen spaced at intervals. Wigfull waited until Diamond had given him the gist of the news from Merlin, and then said with his habitual optimism, 'That's a big step forward.'

'It may be, when we eventually find out who she is,' Diamond said, and was moved to confide to his assistant, 'I can't even feel sorry for the woman without knowing anything about her – her name, her background. I need to care about what happened to the victim, but I don't. She's just a stiff. That isn't enough.'

'We know a certain amount,' Wigfull pointed out. 'She was married. She cared about her appearance. She wasn't a down-and-out.'

'I keep telling myself that. Someone ought to have noticed that this woman is missing by now. It's over two weeks. She must have had people she knew, friends, family or workmates. Where are they?'

'I'm following up those missing women we talked about yesterday and I've got a long list of brunettes who could be worth checking on.'

Diamond aimed a vicious kick at a fir cone.

They retraced their steps. Before they reached the encampment of blue and black vehicles inside the taped cordon, a police motorcyclist rode along the track and stopped by the incident room. He went inside, was evidently told where to deliver his message, came out and walked across to Diamond and handed him a brown envelope, sent from police headquarters at Bristol.

'My promotion, no doubt,' Diamond quipped as he

43

opened it. Inside was a faxed diagram. 'No,' he said. 'It's from the Yard. Mrs Zoomer's dental record. I regret to inform you, Mr Wigfull, that by the look of this your eccentric author has two superfluous wisdom teeth. Two more than our lady of the lake.'

Later that afternoon, the decision was taken to decamp. The house-to-house enquiries and the search of the lake perimeter had been completed. The scenes-of-crime officers had long since left. It made sense to transfer to Bristol.

The midges in their millions were casting their evening haze over the water when the last police car left the site and headed through Bishop Sutton towards the A37. In the back seat, Diamond remarked, 'You know what depressed me most about that spot?'

John Wigfull shook his head.

'Those goddam fishermen. They were showing us up.'

Just short of Whitchurch, a message came through on the car radio. It was the desk sergeant at Manvers Street Police Station in Bath.

'Don't know if this is relevant to your inquiry, sir. A man has come in and reported that his wife is missing. Her name is Geraldine Snoo, sir.'

'Snoozer?'

'Snoo. Geraldine Snoo.'

Beside him, Wigfull opened his mouth to speak, but Diamond put up a restraining hand.

The sergeant added, 'She's thirty-three and he describes her hair as auburn.'

'When did he see her last?'

'Almost three weeks ago.'

Diamond cast his eyes upwards in an expression of gratitude that was almost worshipful. 'Is he still with you?'

'Yes, sir.'

'Keep him there. For God's sake don't let him leave. What's his name?'

'Professor Jackman.'

'Professor? Hold on. You say his name is Jackman, and he's the husband, but you just gave me the woman's name as Snoo.'

'That's the name she's known by, sir. She's an actress. Well, that's an understatement. She's a star. Do you ever watch *The Milners* on TV? Geraldine Snoo played the part of Candice.'

Diamond had taken too strong a grip on the window handle. It jerked out of its socket.

Chapter Six

IF A SOAP-STAR HAD TO live anywhere, it might as well be Bath, that squeaky-clean city in the south-west. Ribbons of Georgian terraced houses undulate elegantly between seven green hills, diverting the eye from anything more unsightly. Stone-cleaning is second only to tourism as a local industry; the Yellow Pages list fifty-four firms. High-pressure water-jets have transformed old blackened buildings into gleaming backdrops for television plays of the sort the British are supposed to do best. With two thousand years of history, Bath chooses to ignore all but the Roman and the Georgian periods. Some people say that it's just a theme park, that if you want to see a real city you might as well drive the thirteen miles further west to Bristol. If you tried, as Peter Diamond did most mornings, you'd suffer the curse of a real city – its traffic. With the soap-star and the stone-cleaners, he was content to make his home in Bath.

His house on Wellsway was only twenty minutes' walk from here – south of the railway. Not the smartest end of town, but the best a senior detective could afford.

He almost waltzed across the car park and up the steps of Manvers Street Police Station. Already he had brushed aside the trifling embarrassment of his remarks about the people who had phoned in to say that the dead woman was a TV star. He didn't believe in fretting over past mistakes. Infinitely more was at stake than his own self-esteem. What mattered in a major inquiry was the ability of the man in charge to seize his opportunity when it came. Diamond was sure that the moment had arrived. His luck had changed now that he had turned his back on that pesky lake.

46

He was met by the desk sergeant, whom he knew well.

'Is he still here?'

The sergeant nodded and made a dumb-show of pointing towards a door.

Diamond scarcely lowered his voice. 'What line is he taking?'

'He's very concerned about his wife, sir.'

'He ought to be after three weeks.'

'He's been away from home a good deal, he says. He thought she was with friends.'

'And left it until now to go looking for her? What do you make of him?'

The sergeant vibrated his lips as if the question was all too much to cope with. 'He's not my idea of a professor, sir.'

'They don't all look like Einstein. Is he telling the truth about his wife? That's what I want to know.'

'I think he must be, else why would he come in here?'

Diamond answered with a look that said he could think of a dozen reasons. 'Does he know about the body in Chew Valley Lake?'

The sergeant nodded. 'Friends told him.'

'And what's a murdered wife between friends? Has he seen the picture we distributed?'

'He hasn't mentioned it.'

'Right. Don't stand there like a Christmas tree. There's plenty to do. I propose to set up the incident room here. We were on our way to Bristol, but this has changed everything. Get it organized, will you? And I need someone to take a statement.'

With the confident air of a man about to do the thing he enjoys best, he thrust open the door of the office where the professor who had lost his wife was waiting. 'My name is Diamond,' he announced, 'Detective Superintendent Diamond.'

It was immediately clear what the sergeant had meant. The man standing beside the window had the look not of a professor, but a sportsman. He might have just showered and changed after a five-setter at Wimbledon. Some padding in the shoulders of his black linen jacket clearly contributed to the effect, but he still didn't pass muster as an academic. He could not have been much over thirty. He wasn't wearing a tie, just a sky-blue cotton shirt sufficiently open to show a double gold chain across the chest. His thick, black hair was expensively cut and he had a Mexican style of moustache. Young men were running the money markets. Had they now taken over the universities? 'Gregory Jackman,' he introduced himself in a voice that was pure Yorkshire. 'Do you have any news of my wife?'

Diamond, in his customary fashion, declined to answer. 'You're a professor, I understand. Bath University?'

Jackman gave a nod.

'What's your subject?'

'English. Look, I'm here about my wife.'

A woman PC came in with a shorthand pad.

'You don't object if she takes notes?' Diamond enquired.

'No. Why should I?'

'Have a seat, then. Just for the record, I should tell you that you don't have to say anything unless you wish to do so, but what you say may be given in evidence. Now tell me about your wife.'

Jackman said, without moving towards a chair, 'I told them at the desk half an hour ago. They took the details.'

'Bear with me, professor,' Diamond said with painstaking courtesy. 'I'm in charge and I'd rather hear it from you than read it in the occurrence book. Her name, first.'

With a resigned air, Jackman planted himself on a chair and said, 'Geraldine Jackman, known to most people as Gerry Snoo. That's her stage name. She'll be thirty-four in a week or two if . . . God, I find this whole thing too appalling to contemplate.'

'Would you describe her, sir?'

'Do I have to? You must have seen her on television. *The Milners*. Right? If not, you must have seen the lager ad with the bulldog and the girl. That was Gerry. She did a few commercials after she left the BBC.'

There was a moment's hiatus. Diamond was studying his man's expression so keenly that he had to catch what he said by mentally playing it over again. 'Oh, I don't see much television. Let's assume I've never seen her. What colour hair does she have?'

'Reddish-brown. Chestnut red, if you like.'

'You said auburn to the sergeant.'

'Auburn, then.' On a rising note that showed the strain he was under, Jackman responded, 'What are you trying to do – catch me out? I wasn't dragged in here for questioning, you know. I'm here because my wife is missing. I'm told she may be dead.'

'Who told you that?'

'Some people who know Gerry extremely well saw that picture you showed on television. They said it was exactly like her. They told me they got in touch with you.'

'Not me personally. We had a massive response to our appeal for information,' Diamond smoothly explained. 'It takes time to check. But now that you have come forward –'

'Look, I want to know, one way or the other,' Jackman cut in. Concern was etched vividly in his features, but so it would be at this stage of the game, whether he was innocent or not. 'You found a woman. Where is she now?'

'At Bristol City Mortuary. Let's not leap to conclusions. It may not be neccessary for you to go there if it turns out that your wife's appearance is unlike the woman we found.' Patiently Diamond elicited a description, feature by feature, of Mrs Jackman, and it corresponded closely with the details of the corpse. Encouragingly closely.

He went on to ask, 'When did you last see her?'

'On a Monday, three weeks ago.'

'That would have been 11 September?'

'Er, yes. I left early for London. She was still in bed. I told her when I expected to be back, and then left to catch the 8.19 from Bath.'

'You had business in London?'

'I'm responsible for an exhibition about Jane Austen in Bath that opened that weekend. I had to see someone about a manuscript.'

Diamond had never read a book by Jane Austen. He found it difficult to identify with the detectives in TV whodunnits who quoted Shakespeare and wrote poetry in their spare time. Biography was his choice, preferably biography that included the words *of the Yard* in the title.

'And this exhibition kept you away for three weeks?'

'No, no. I was back on the Wednesday.'

Diamond straightened up in the chair and shut out all thoughts of Jane Austen. 'Home again?'

'Yes.'

'Then you knew your wife was missing as early as Wednesday, 13 September?'

'Missing, no.' The professor reinforced the denial with a sideways sweep of the hand. 'She wasn't home, but that wasn't any cause for alarm. She often stays over with friends.'

'And doesn't tell you?'

'I'm not Gerry's keeper.'

The answer jarred.

'But you are her husband. Presumably you like to know where she is.'

'I don't insist upon it.' There was a period of silence before Professor Jackman thought it appropriate to explain, 'We live fairly independent lives. We are two people who need space to be ourselves. We married on that understanding. So when Gerry isn't around for a day or two I don't immediately call the police.'

'We're not talking about a day or two, sir.'

'I thought we were.'

'You've had three weeks to notify us,' Diamond pointed out. He wasn't impressed by the slick explanations. The man was clever with words, as you would expect of a professor of English, but he couldn't gloss over the fact that he was suspiciously late in reporting his wife's disappearance.

'I wasn't at home all that time.' said Jackman. 'I've been buzzing about getting things organized for the new session. London, Oxford, Reading. I'm on too many committees. I was in Paris for a couple of days. I've given most of the summer to setting up this exhibition, so I'm way behind on my work in the English Department.'

'What did you think your wife was doing meanwhile?'

'Visiting friends. She knows plenty of people in London and Bristol.'

'She doesn't work, then?'

'Resting, as they say.'

'Do they?'

'Unemployed actors.'

'Ah.' Diamond knew the expression well enough. If he had appeared vague it was the way his mind worked. He had been thinking of the words so often seen on tombstones. *Only resting*.

Jackman may have sensed something, because he went on to say precisely what he had meant. 'Gerry has been off the box for eighteen months. She did a couple of commercials after she left the BBC, but otherwise the television work dried up.'

'Why is that? Because everyone still thinks of her as Candice Milner?'

Jackman nodded. 'That's part of it, certainly. There's also the fact that she's untrained as an actress. She was still in school when they offered her the role.' Given the chance to take refuge in a narrative of less immediacy, he grasped it. 'The way she was discovered was every schoolgirl's dream. The director picked her out of the crowd at Wimbledon. He went to watch tennis and found himself watching Gerry instead. In appearance she was exactly the young girl character he had visualized for *The Milners*. Extremely beautiful. You know the corny scene in all those Hollywood musicals when the Fred Astaire character says, "Lady, I don't care who you are, I *must* have you for my show." It really happened to Gerry, at eighteen. They tailored the part to her personality, so she played herself and became a household name. The other side of the coin was that she found it difficult to take on any other role.'

'Did that depress her?'

'Not at first. Being in a twice-weekly soap is very demanding, you know – a treadmill of learning lines, rehearsing and recording. Plus opening church fêtes on Saturdays and dodging the gossip writers. She wasn't altogether sorry when she was written out of the script.'

'And that was how long ago?'

'Getting on for two years now.'

'So how long had she been playing the part?'

51

'She started when she was eighteen and she must have been thirty-one when it came to an end. Poor Gerry. It came out of the blue. The first she heard of it was when they sent her a script in which the character of Candice stepped into a plane that was to crash over the Alps with no survivors. I can remember vividly how angry she was. She fought like a tigress to save her part, but ultimately the director got through to her that they couldn't any longer keep up the fiction that she was an *ingenue*. She turned her back on London.'

Jackman had related it with sympathy, yet there was a note of detachment in the account, as if he looked back with more regret than he presently felt. This didn't escape Peter Diamond, who had a sharp ear for evasion. The case might not be as complex as he had first supposed. He expected to crack it soon.

Rather than pussyfooting through more of the family history, Diamond took the drawing of the dead woman from his pocket, unfolded it and handed it across. 'This is the picture that went out on TV. What do you think?'

Jackman gave it a glance, took a deep breath as if to subdue his emotions and said, 'Looks awfully like Gerry to me.'

Within minutes they were sharing the back seat of a police car on the way to the City Mortuary.

'I ought to mention,' Diamond said, 'that the body we're going to look at has been under water for a couple of weeks. The artist's drawing was prettied up to go out on television.'

'Thanks for the warning.'

'If there's some means of identifying her by a mark or a scar . . .'

'I don't know of any,' Jackman said quickly, then added, as if in an afterthought, 'What happens if it turns out to be someone else?'

Diamond made a good show of remaining impassive. 'Now that you've reported your wife's disappearance, it's an inquiry anyway, and we'd take it from there. Someone else would handle it.'

'It's just possible that I was mistaken.'

Diamond didn't trust himself to comment.

They arrived soon after 9 p.m. and it took some time to make the necessary arrangements. Mortuary staff had a different set of priorities from the police. At length the attendant arrived on a pushbike and unlocked the door.

Diamond didn't say a word. He was too interested in watching Jackman.

The body was brought out and the face uncovered.

'It goes without saying that I can rely on your co-operation.'

Diamond's utterance was the first he had made since leaving the mortuary. He deliberately put it as a statement rather than a question.

Professor Jackman was sitting forward in the back seat of the police car, one hand covering his eyes. Vaguely, he said, 'What?'

Diamond repeated what he had said, word for word, like a schoolmaster being scrupulously fair.

Without looking up, Jackman answered, 'I'll do whatever I can to help.'

'Splendid.' Diamond waited while the car stopped at traffic lights and said nothing else until it moved off again. 'Tonight, I'll arrange for you to stay at the Beaufort, unless you prefer another hotel.'

This time the professor swung round to face him. 'A hotel isn't necessary. I don't mind going home. I'd prefer it, really I would.'

Diamond shook his head. 'Your house is off limits tonight, sir.'

'Why?'

'I want it examined first thing tomorrow – with your permission. Until then, it's sealed. I'm putting a man on guard tonight.'

'What do you mean – "examined"?'

'The forensic team. Scenes-of-crime officers. Finger-prints and all that jazz. You know?'

'*Scenes-of-crime*? You're not suggesting that Gerry was murdered under my own roof?'

'Professor, I'm not in the business of suggesting things,'

said Diamond. 'I deal in facts. Fact number one: your wife is dead. Fact two: the last place she was seen alive was in your house. Where else am I going to start?'

After mentally wrestling with that piece of policeman's logic, Jackman said, 'I don't see what difference it makes if I spend one more night in the place considering that I've been there on and off ever since Gerry went missing.'

Diamond let it stand as a protest that didn't merit a response. Instead, he asked, 'When you came to report your wife's disappearance this evening, how did you travel?'

'I took the car.'

'So where is it now?'

'Still in the National Car Park beside the police station, I hope.'

'Have you got the keys?'

'Yes.' Jackman was frowning now.

'May I borrow them?'

'What on earth for? You're not impounding my car?'

A reassuring smile spread across Diamond's face. 'Impounding, no. It's just the boring old business of checking facts. We make a print of the tyres, that sort of thing. Then if we can find another set of tyre-prints – say in front of your house – we can eliminate your own vehicle from our inquiries.' He was pleased with that answer. It sounded eminently reasonable, and he hadn't given an inkling of his real purpose, to examine the boot of the car for traces of the corpse. When he had been handed the keys he asked casually, 'Are you planning to be at the university tomorrow?'

'If my house is being searched, I'm going to be there to see what goes on,' Jackman stated firmly.

Chapter Seven

THE SEARCH OF PROFESSOR JACKMAN'S house was not, after all, begun 'first thing' the next day. The first thing, the first in Peter Diamond's day, was the bleep of the phone beside his bed at 6.30 a.m. A message from the Assistant Chief Constable, no less, relayed by the duty inspector at police headquarters. Diamond was instructed to report to headquarters at 8.30.

He was willing to bet it wasn't for a chief constable's commendation. This, he sensed, was trouble.

He flopped back on the pillow and groaned. Whatever the reason for this sudden summons, it couldn't have come on a more inconvenient morning. The complications! He had somehow to unscramble his arrangements of the previous evening. Vanloads of detectives, uniformed men and forensic scientists were due to converge on Jackman's house at 8.30 – precisely the time of the appointment in Bristol.

Sitting up again, he removed the phone-set from the bedside table and planted it on the duvet between his legs. His wife Stephanie, resigned to their bedroom taking on the function of a police station, wordlessly dragged on a dressing gown and went downstairs to put on the kettle. Diamond picked up the receiver and made the first of several calls, rescheduling the search for 11 a.m. He was unwilling to let anyone go into the house without him. In theory the responsibility could have been delegated to John Wigfull – a theory Diamond preferred to ignore. But he did ask Wigfull to visit Professor Jackman at the hotel and explain the change in arrangements.

On the drive to Bristol, he tried to fathom the thinking

at police headquarters. He concluded sourly that Jackman must have got busy on the phone in his hotel room the previous evening. When trouble loomed, people of Jackman's elevated status didn't go underground like petty crooks. They rose above it by rallying support from the old boy network.

This morning Mr Tott, the Assistant Chief Constable, was sitting behind his desk in white shirt and pink braces, a spectacle so unlikely as to cause any officer of lesser rank to hesitate in the doorway. But he greeted Diamond matily, using his Christian name, waving him towards the black leather settee under the window. As if utterly to remove all apprehension that a reprimand was in prospect, the Assistant Chief Constable got up, went to the door and asked for coffee and biscuits to be sent in. Then he perched himself on the arm at the far end of the settee with arms folded, looking – with his parted hair, flat to the scalp, and Guards' officer moustache – as if he were posing for an Edwardian photograph.

All this forced informality had a dispiriting effect on Diamond. The last time anyone had treated him with such a show of consideration was on a tragic occasion, when a doctor had given him the news that his wife had miscarried.

'Sorry to have messed up your arrangements,' Mr Tott said, managing to sound completely sincere, 'but it was necessary to see you at the earliest opportunity. How's the murder inquiry going, by the way?'

That 'by the way' was another jolt, for it implied that a matter quite different to the Jackman case was up for discussion. Diamond mouthed the next few responses while making a rapid mental adjustment. 'We identified the woman last night, sir. Perhaps you heard.'

'A television actress – is that right?'

'Yes, sir. She was married to the Professor of English up at Claverton.'

Mr Tott grinned amiably. 'So I heard. Better brush up on your Shakespeare, Peter.' He paused, unfolded his arms and said, 'And I'd better come to the point. Over there on the desk is an advance copy of the report on the Missendale Inquiry.'

Diamond had read the signal right.

'I see.' The bland response was the best he could manage after striving to suppress his troubled feelings for so long. More than eight months had passed since he had appeared before the board of inquiry – and more than two years since Hedley Missendale had been released on the orders of the Home Secretary and recommended for a pardon. A false confession, a wrongful imprisonment. Sections of the press had drummed the story up into a hate campaign against 'rogue policemen', with accusations of racism and brutality. A campaign targeted on Chief Superintendent Blaize and Diamond. Jacob Blaize had been hounded into ill-health and early retirement, which the press had maliciously and without justification written up as confirmation of their smears.

'I thought you should cast an eye over it as soon as possible,' Mr Tott said. 'You'll be relieved to know that none of the wilder accusations was shown to have any foundation.'

Diamond looked towards the desk. 'May I . . .?'

'Go ahead. That's why you're here.'

Numbly, he got up, crossed the room and picked up the report.

'The main findings are towards the end, of course,' said Mr Tott. 'You'll find the paragraphs from Page 87 onwards are of personal interest. Take your time.'

Diamond flicked through and found the summary of the findings. His name sprang out of the text. He scanned the page swiftly, getting the gist of the comments. *'We found no evidence of racial bias on the part of Detective Chief Inspector Diamond . . . This officer acquitted himself impressively under intensive questioning . . . As to Missendale's statement, there was nothing in it that conflicted with the evidence . . . It was reasonable for Chief Inspector Diamond to deduce, as the court did, that Missendale's statement was supported by the facts.'*

He turned the page, feeling curiously unmoved rather than vindicated after the months of abuse from the media. Then his eyes fixed on a sentence.

'Christ Almighty!'

Mr Tott had returned to his chair. 'What's wrong?'

' "*We are bound to state that Chief Inspector Diamond's physical presence and forceful demeanour must have appeared intimidating to Missendale,*" ' Diamond read out. 'That's out of order. I'm built that way. I can't help the way I'm made.'

'Yes, it's unfair,' Mr Tott agreed in a tone that attached no importance to the matter.

But Diamond wasn't willing to let it pass. 'Sir, there was no intimidation used to obtain the confession. The judge established at the trial that there was no oppression.'

'Of course, but the inquiry team was charged to re-examine everything.'

Diamond's eyes were already moving on. 'I just don't believe this! "*We view with concern the fact that hair samples from the woollen hat snatched from the assailant in the struggle were not compared with hairs from Mr Missendale.*" '

'What's the problem?' Mr Tott asked.

'We sent the hat to the lab.'

'But you didn't follow it up, if I understand this correctly. You didn't take hair samples from Missendale.'

'Sir, the man confessed.'

'It would still have been sensible to do so.'

Diamond stared at him in amazement. 'To what end, exactly?'

'As a comparison.'

'This was 1985, sir. Before genetic fingerprinting came in. Even if we had followed up, forensic couldn't have told us whether the hairs in the hat were Missendale's, or Sammy Davis Junior's. This report implies that if the samples had been compared, Missendale's innocence would have been established, but it simply isn't true.'

'The report doesn't go so far as to say that.'

' "*We view with concern*" . . .? It's suggesting somebody was at fault.'

Mr Tott said firmly, 'The point is that it should have been done routinely. Nobody is accusing you of withholding evidence.'

'They're accusing Jacob Blaize and me of fitting him up.'

'Oh, don't be so melodramatic, man! If that were the case, you'd be out of a job. Your integrity isn't in question.'

Diamond knew that he should have shut up at this point.

He still felt aggrieved. 'I told them at the inquiry what must have happened and they seem to have disregarded it. Missendale *was* fitted up, but not by me. He was a petty thief with a record, not much good at it. He had a low IQ. There were bigger operators in the background, too smart to be caught. It's obvious with hindsight that Missendale was their fall-guy. They wanted the other character, the guy who actually gunned down the sergeant-major, to keep pulling the jobs, so they made it clear to Missendale that if he didn't fake a confession, they'd wipe him out. He was safer in the nick. He had no future on the outside.'

Mr Tott nodded. 'I'll take your word for it. Organized crime is behind so much of our casework these days. But this sort of theorizing falls outside the scope of the inquiry. They were looking at the particular circumstances in which the miscarriage of justice was perpetrated.'

Diamond heard himself saying, 'I'm far from satisfied.'

'In a report that runs to over a hundred pages, it would be surprising if anyone was satisfied with all that it contains. I think you'll find that this lays the whole wretched business to rest. The media won't be interested in the points that seem to be exercising you.'

'But I don't believe it wipes the slate clean.'

'I think I hear the chink of cups,' said Mr Tott.

Diamond waited while the coffee was poured in genteel fashion from a chrome and glass container. When they were alone again, he said, 'I'd like to ask what effect this will have on my career with Avon and Somerset, sir.'

'None at all,' said Mr Tott, and the voice was metallic in its positiveness. 'What happened four years ago in London is history.'

'Plenty of mud has been slung my way since then.'

'Yes, and none of it has stuck.'

'But you won't deny that you clipped my wings?'

Mr Tott stirred his coffee and said nothing. It was transparently obvious that this was a reference to the replacement of Billy Murray by John Wigfull, the headquarters man.

'I'm not beefing about that. From your point of view it was a reasonable precaution after the Missendale thing blew up,' Diamond conceded. 'But I had a right to expect that this report would vindicate me, and I don't believe it has, not completely.'

'If it makes you just a little more punctilious about procedures, it won't be entirely wasted, Peter. You must admit that you can be rather resistant to technology. The scientific developments of the past few years are mind-boggling, I grant you, but it behoves us all to make an effort to work with them.'

'Up to a point, sir. There's still a lot that native intelligence can achieve. There's a danger in surrendering to technology.'

'Come now. I'm not suggesting any such thing. It's a question of balance, of proportion.'

Diamond closed the report and planted it on Mr Tott's desk. 'So what will happen next time some petty crook objects to the way I question him?'

'I would treat any complaint on its merits,' said Mr Tott, showing in his tone that indulgence can only go so far. 'And I would take exception to any suggestion that I might show prejudice. I see no mud sticking to you, and I hope I don't see a chip on your shoulder, either. Is there anything else you wanted to say to me?'

'In which regard, sir?'

'About your present investigation.'

'No, sir. Nothing else.' In the stress of the moment he had already said more than was politic.

'I appreciate that,' said Mr Tott. 'Wigfull's transfer to your squad was at my insistence. He is not – I stress this – he is not there as some kind of informer. I keep tabs on all my officers without assistance from the likes of John Wigfull. Is that understood?'

'Understood, sir.'

'And accepted?'

'Yes, sir.'

'Then I'll tell you about Wigfull.' Looking down at his cup, Mr Tott traced a finger slowly around its rim. 'Knowing as I did that this report was imminent, but not knowing its findings, I had to face the possibility – the worst conceivable scenario – that you might have to be

60

removed at short notice from the murder squad. I wanted a man capable of taking over, and without going into personalities, there was no one in your team I could confidently turn to. Wigfull was my choice. He hasn't, of course, been told the reason, but as a good detective, he may have worked it out for himself. I appreciate that his temperament and yours are not in tune. You, too, are a good detective. You are also a big man, as the report unjustly emphasizes. Be big in the best sense, big enough to get the best out of Wigfull.'

Shortly after 11 a.m., the convoy of cars and police vans streamed into the drive of Jackman's house some distance up one of the secluded roads off Bathwick Hill. The leading car was Diamond's BMW. Beside him sat Jackman. John Wigfull followed in his Toyota with two detective sergeants and a constable. The other vehicles brought a scenes-of-crime officer from headquarters, two forensic scientists and a team of uniformed officers in support.

Jackman's blue Volvo was at this moment undergoing forensic examination at Manvers Street. Diamond had commented when handing over the keys to the forensic lads, 'Don't disappoint me, will you? They always believe they've removed every trace.'

Brydon House looked suitable for a professor to inhabit, not quite within walking distance of the university, but convenient for it, as the estate agents had no doubt claimed when the Jackmans first took an interest in the property. It was an ivy-clad, four-square structure with a pillared porch and a first-floor balcony. Probably not much over a century old, it was set in spacious grounds behind a low drystone wall. Plots tended to be generous in size on the outskirts of the city and the houses were distinctive in design. The area was too far out from the centre of Bath for the planners to have insisted on uniformity, and quite modern buildings in garish reconstituted stone stood alongside mellowed Georgian and Victorian villas.

Diamond invited Jackman to open the door. Then he gripped the professor's arm, preventing him from entering. 'No, sir, you and I won't step inside just yet.'

61

Disbelief and bewilderment were combined in Jackman's look as two men in white overalls stepped forward, sat in the porch, removed their shoes and replaced them with socks made of polythene.

'If you don't mind,' Diamond said in his ear, 'we'll leave the spacemen to their work. How would you like to show me your garden?'

'This is a huge waste of everyone's time,' muttered the beleaguered Professor.

'I've got a brother-in-law in Doncaster,' Diamond volunteered as a way of easing the tension, 'and each time we visit him, I hardly set foot in the house before he draws me away from the ladies and says, "Come and see the back garden". Now I'm no gardener. I wouldn't pretend to know when to prune the roses, but I do know enough to see that Reggie's garden is a bloody wilderness. Some of the nettles are chest high. We poke about searching for the path while Reggie points to pathetic plants weighted down with blackfly and bindweed and tells me their names. After an hour of this, there's a shout from my sister that tea is ready, so we beat a route back to the house for a reviving cup. No sooner have I had a bite of cake than Reggie turns to me and says, "You haven't seen the front garden. Come out and see the front". I'm supposed to be a detective and I don't know why he does it. Is he afraid to go out there unaccompanied? Or is the house stuffed with stolen goods he doesn't want me to notice? I'm still trying to work it out.'

Jackman seemed unwilling to supply a theory, but he had, at least, consented to walk beside the superintendent. They made an incongruous pair, the broad-shouldered academic moving with sinewy step beside the fat policeman forced by sheer girth to throw out his feet in a ponderous strut. The setting for this spectacle consisted of stretches of lawn separated by clumps of shrubs and a number of well-established trees. There were enough apple trees at the far end to give it the status of an orchard.

Abruptly, Diamond moved from homely matters to the business of the day. 'Your wife. I need to know everything about her. Background, family, friends past and present –

and enemies, if any – daily routines, personal finances, state of health, drinking habits, hobbies, places she visited, shops she used.'

'We've only been married two years,' Jackman said in a tone that protested at the length and comprehensiveness of the list.

'Long enough to know all those things, surely?' Diamond pressed. 'We'll take it from the beginning. How did you meet?'

This approach yielded a dividend. Jackman made a sound that was halfway to being a laugh, shook his head wistfully as some memory surfaced and said, 'It was because of a pigeon, or so Gerry always claimed. The pigeon may or may not have existed, but it became part of our private mythology. She was motoring along Great Russell Street in her Renault 5 –'

'This was when?' Diamond cut in.

'Just over two years ago. As I was saying, she was driving along when this slow-witted or stubborn London pigeon allegedly stepped across the road and refused to take flight. Unable to bear the prospect of killing a living thing, Gerry swung the wheel and crumpled the nearside wing – of the car, not the pigeon – against a parked van. You must be hearing stories like this all the time.'

'I'm not in the traffic division.'

'Well, this was in the month of May, I think, and I was in my final term at Birkbeck College prior to taking up the professorship here. I'd been working in the British Library that particular morning and I came out for a lunchtime stroll. I didn't see the pigeon, but I heard the bump. I was the first to reach the car, open the door and enquire if she was hurt. I can see her now staring at me, pale with shock, and beautiful, surpassingly beautiful. She was suffering nothing worse than the shakes, so I helped her to move the car into a space, found her a seat in the nearest sandwich bar and ordered strong, sweet tea. Then, not missing a chance to play Galahad, I went to look for the van driver. He turned out to be a Buddhist monk.'

'A monk – in London?'

'Doing research, just as I was. I'd seen him once or twice

in the Reading Room. When I told him about the collision he was serenely unconcerned at one extra dent on his van. In fact, he went out of his way to praise Gerry's action in averting an accident to the pigeon. She was moving towards enlightenment, in his estimation. So I nipped back to the sandwich bar and set her mind at rest.'

'Advising her, no doubt, to go to the nearest police station and report the accident,' Diamond said sardonically.

Jackman stayed with his story. 'I found her perched on the high stool, dabbing the edges of her eyes with that amazing red hair. The bump was the first she'd ever had, she told me, and she felt stupid at having caused damage just to avoid a scruffy pigeon. I remember springing to the defence of the pigeon and upholding its rights to cross the street without being flattened. Made her smile again. She had a stunning smile. Then she announced that she was due at the Television Centre in twenty minutes, so I offered to drive her to White City. Embarrassing. It was transparently clear that I didn't know she was famous. I hardly ever watch the box.'

They stopped at the edge of the apple orchard, where the grass was too overgrown for comfortable walking. Diamond pulled off a long stalk and chewed it, pleased with himself for having the patience to listen to this boy-meets-girl stuff. There was time enough to get to the violence. 'You arranged to meet again, I take it?'

'Well, yes. We got on well. The attraction was mutual – though I suppose there was over-glamorizing on both sides. She had a few 'O' levels to her name, and that was all, so she was flattered to have a professor-designate in tow. And apart from finding her extremely attractive, as every red-blooded male in the country did, I rather basked in the envy of people who watched *The Milners* and couldn't fathom how some egghead professor had managed to hook television's top girl.'

'What about her conversation?'

'What do you mean?'

'Was she on your wavelength?'

'Oh, she was as bright as a button. If her schooling

hadn't been interrupted, she'd certainly have got to university.'

Diamond noticed something in the way Jackman made this remark. It was spoken with a measure of detachment rather than the pride you would have expected from a devoted husband. Yet everything else he had said — all the memories from two years ago — had been related with warmth. The story of their first meeting rang true. Undoubtedly the man had been charmed by her and it wasn't difficult to see why she had been attracted to him. He was handsome. He wasn't stuffy. He wasn't at all the stereotype of the lofty intellectual.

This was underlined when Jackman went on to say, 'We first made love under the stars in Richmond Park. Didn't realize the gates closed at sundown. Had to climb over the wall to get out, and our energies were somewhat depleted by then.' He smiled faintly. 'We came to a more comfortable arrangement after that. She moved into my semi in Teddington. We married in September, a registry office do followed by a trip up the Thames in a pleasure steamer for two hundred and fifty.'

Diamond took mental stock of the number, troubled by it. Tracing the victim's friends, if it came to that, was going to require a large task force.

'Surprising, really,' Jackman remarked. 'The worlds of academe and showbiz got on famously. They strutted their stuff to a jazz quartet until well into the next day.'

'This was September, 1987, you said? So when did you move to Bath?' Diamond asked.

'Directly. My term was about to start. Gerry was still with the BBC. We had no idea that her days with *The Milners* were numbered. She rented a flat in Ealing to use when she was filming. As I mentioned to you, we were each committed to our careers, so we tied the knot less strongly than is traditional. We kept separate bank accounts. The house here is in my name; I'd already found it and set the legal wheels in motion before I met Gerry.'

'Did she approve your choice?'

The professor put a hand to his face and passed it across his mouth and down to the point of his chin as he considered the question. 'I think she liked it, yes. It's a little far from the centre, but she had the car.'

'The Renault?'

'A Metro. She bought a new one. It's in the garage. Want to see it?'

'Later.' Now it was Diamond's turn to take stock. 'If her car is still in the garage, didn't that worry you when she went missing?'

'Not really. She often used taxis for getting about, particularly if she was likely to have a few drinks.'

'Was she a heavy drinker?'

'She could put it away, but I wouldn't say she drank to excess.'

Inside the house, John Wigfull, in the approved polythene oversocks, had been called upstairs by the scenes-of-crime officer to look at the main bedroom. They watched one of the forensic team, on his knees, collecting fibre samples on strips of adhesive tape.

Wigfull folded his arms and took in the essentials of the room. 'Twin beds, then.'

'Some people prefer them.'

'Would you – married to Gerry Snoo?'

A smile from the scenes-of-crime officer. 'I'm a simple scientist, John. No imagination at all.'

Both beds had been stripped to the mattress for forensic examination, enough to dispossess any bedroom of its character. It was a large, gracefully proportioned room decorated in a mushroom colour and pale green. There was a television set and video-recorder on a stand facing the beds. Two abstract paintings in the style of Mondrian enlivened the walls, yet to Wigfull's eye reinforced the feeling of hotel-like neutrality.

He got a strikingly different impression when he crossed the room and looked into one of the adjacent dressing rooms. It was a shrine to Gerry Snoo's television career. The walls were thick with silver-framed stills from *The Milners*, interspersed with press pictures of herself with celebrities at parties. Her dressing table had the mirror fringed with light bulbs that was supposed to be a feature of every star's dressing room, and the wall behind it was festooned with silver horseshoes, telemessages, greetings cards and sprigs of heather. Across the room was a folding screen entirely pasted over with press clippings. A system of shelving between the built-in wardrobe and the window was stacked with video-cassettes and paperbacks of *The Milners*.

'Missing the big time, would you say?' the scenes-of-crime officer called out.

'Looks remarkably like it.' Wigfull returned to the bedroom. 'Have you found much?'

'A few microscopic spots on the duvet that could be blood. May be significant, may be not. We'll see what the tests show. Plenty of prints on the surface of the dressing table, presumably her own. Hardly any elsewhere. I reckon the chest of drawers and the wardrobe have been wiped clean. Did he do it?'

'The husband, you mean?'

'Who else? Murder's generally in the family, isn't it?'

Wigfull gave a shrug.

The scenes-of-crime officer snapped shut the metal case containing his instruments. 'If he *is* guilty, I back your boss to nail him. I've seen the way Diamond works. It's cat and mouse with him. Playful for a bit. Then he pounces. If he doesn't bite their heads off he breaks their backbones.'

Wigfull said, 'Before it comes to that, I'd like to know the motive.'

'Obvious. They weren't sleeping in the same bed. She must have been getting it from someone else. Husband found out. Curtains for Candice.'

In the garden, Diamond was patiently unravelling the story of the marriage. 'You were telling me in the car about the blow it was when your wife was written out of the television serial. You seemed to imply that after the initial shock, she was quite positive in the way she faced up to it.'

'That's perfectly true,' Jackman answered. He was calmer now that the questions were more structured, more predictable. 'Of course she made her feelings plain to the director, but once she saw that it was a lost cause, she responded sensibly, I thought. She told me she meant to make up for the years she had missed.'

'What did she mean by that?'

'She had never been allowed the freedom girls in their teens are entitled to expect. At last she could break out – go on holidays, dance the night away, change her hair-style, put on weight if she wanted and never answer another fan letter. I suppose it was the teenage rebellion ten years delayed.'

'Not the ideal start to a marriage,' ventured Diamond.

The answer came on a sharper note, as if Jackman knew what was behind the comment. 'We didn't view it that way. As I told you, we had agreed to leave enough space to be ourselves and pursue our interests independently. We didn't want the kind of arrangement where one partner tags along forever making sacrifices.'

'But the basis of your contract – your understanding, or whatever you called it – had altered,' Diamond pointed out. 'She no longer had a career.'

'So what? Just because Gerry was unemployed I didn't expect her to stay at home and darn my socks. She put her energies into building a social life for herself. She gave up the flat in Ealing, of course.'

'Difficult for a woman used to London, coming down here and not knowing anyone,' Diamond remarked, resolute in his belief that the marriage must have been fatally flawed.

'Not for Gerry. Word soon got round that she'd moved down here. The invitations came in thick and fast.'

'Did you get invited, too?'

'Quite often. I couldn't usually join her. I had a brand new department to set up, and that took up most of my time. I gradually got to know the crowd she spent her time with. We had the occasional party here.'

'People from Bath?'

'Bristol. All around, I gather.'

'You gather? You didn't get to know them *that* well, then? Weren't they your sort?'

Jackman gave him a cold stare. 'People don't have to be my sort, as you put it. Anyway, I didn't make a point of asking them where they lived. If you want their names and addresses, I dare say I can find her address book.'

'You mean you don't even know the names of your wife's friends?'

'I didn't say that. There were some people called Maltby. They were from Clevedon, I believe. Paula and John Hare. Liza somebody. A tall fellow by the name of Mike – I'm not sure where he lived.'

'Don't bother,' said Diamond. 'I'll go through the address book, as you suggest. Did your wife ever mention falling out with any of the friends she made?'

'Not that I recall.'

'Shall we move on again?' Diamond started back in the direction of the house by way of stepping-stones across a lawn still damp with dew that would probably remain all day. 'I sense from what you've been telling me about your marriage that she might not have discussed her friends with you,' he commented as he picked his way gingerly across the path.

'Probably not,' the Professor answered from behind him. Nothing appeared to wrongfoot him.

Ahead, virtually in the centre of the garden, was a solidly paved area, darker at the centre. Diamond mistook this at first for a flower-bed, but as he got closer he saw that the blackness was the burnt-out foundation of a building, roughly octagonal in shape. 'Looks as if you had a fire some time,' he said conversationally.

'It was quite a feature of the garden,' Jackman responded with the urbanity of the practised host. 'A summerhouse. It burned down on the night Gerry tried to kill me.'

Diamond stopped with such suddenness that he practically lost balance. When he managed to find his voice again, it sounded quite different, shocked into a flat, breathless delivery. 'I don't know if I heard right, Professor, but I think we've jumped ahead a bit in the story.'

PART TWO
Gregory

Chapter One

IT WAS 5 AUGUST WHEN my wife Geraldine attempted to murder me.

The killing of a husband calls for a degree of disaffection, not to say loathing. Gerry was known to everyone as a warm, exuberant personality, a charmer. She was extremely good-looking, too. She had reached the stage of her life when 'beautiful' was beginning to give way to words that were no less appreciative, merely more dignified: words such as 'elegant' and 'soignée'. Her famous flame-coloured hair was gathered and fastened high on the nape of her long white neck. The fact that she favoured black skirts and blouses was in no way sinister; that was good dressing.

I'm bound to say that in the privacy of home it was a different story. In the last six months she had become increasingly difficult to live with. Her moods were unpredictable. She was subject to fits of temper, irrational outbursts when she would blame me for little things that thwarted her. I recall that she accused me of tampering with her car when it failed to start, of hiding her newspaper and of emptying the hot water tank when she had clearly left a tap running herself − silly, domestic things that she inflated into major incidents, claiming blatant evidence of malice on my part. Yet at other times she swung to moods of gaiety and amusement that could be almost as difficult to take, followed often by black, silent depression. All this worried me, naturally, but it stopped a long way short of personal violence, or so I believed.

With hindsight, I can see that the first intimation that Gerry was planning something came indirectly, from the

73

doctor. Towards the end of July I went for my annual check-up, a routine that my employers at the university insisted upon. After the nurse had weighed me, checked my blood pressure, water, reflexes and every function on her list, I was ushered into the consulting room for the verdict. My regular GP was not available, so for the first time I met the senior man in the practice. Dr Bookbinder is one of the old school, pitted and grizzled, with a bow-tie and cufflinks. He's the sort who refuses to go near a computer. Although he had an anti-smoking poster on his wall and kept the window open, his room reeked of cigars.

'How do you feel in yourself?'

'Fit as a butcher's dog,' I answered, and although I say it myself I looked it, clear-eyed, sturdy and cheerful.

'What are you – thirty-six, thirty-seven – indecently young for a professor. What's your subject? Nothing in the medical line, I hope?'

'English.'

'Fine.' Dr Bookbinder's brown eyes glittered as he looked at me over his glasses. 'You won't be telling me my job. I didn't know they bothered with the mother tongue up at Claverton.'

'I'm in the process of building up a department. The chair was created a couple of years ago.'

'Chair of English, eh? Sounds all right, but don't be tempted to sit in it too long. The sedentary life can lead to constipation and piles.'

'It's not all sitting. I stand up and stretch at intervals.'

'Splendid. Is it stressful?'

'The standing up?'

'The running,' said Dr Bookbinder. 'Of the department.'

'Not really. I don't have many students yet.'

The doctor glanced through the form containing the nurse's findings and stuffed it ham-fistedly into the buff folder that represented all of my life in medical terms. 'Haven't read anything so boring since that book about the hobbits – or was it the rabbits? In insurance terms, Professor, I would describe you as a ruddy good risk so long as you don't burn yourself out. You're married to that enchanting young woman who used to play Candice Milner on the television, aren't you? She's a patient of mine.'

I nodded.

'She was in here on Monday,' he went on. 'It's one of the perks of this job that I tend to see the ladies more often than the husbands. No insult intended.'

'None taken. I make a point of avoiding doctors unless it's inescapable,' I riposted, uncrossing my legs prior to making my exit. 'And since I'm not here to wangle a week off work, I shan't take up any more of your time.'

Dr Bookbinder made a downward movement of his hand to signal to me to remain seated. 'When Mrs Jackman makes an appointment they go bananas in reception.'

'The power of the box.'

'Want to know why she came to see me?'

Indiscretion was in the air. I didn't care for it. I remember saying guardedly, 'My wife and I respect each other's privacy.'

'Do you sleep together?'

My eyes widened. I pulled myself up in the chair in a formal attitude. 'Does that have some relevance?'

'I wouldn't ask it otherwise, would I?' said Dr Bookbinder.

After a moment's consideration, I said, 'If you mean in the same room, the answer is yes.'

'In that case I'm not being unprofessional. You must have noticed it.'

'Noticed what, Doctor?'

'Your wife's insomnia.'

'My . . . wife's . . . insomnia?'

'That's why I asked you about the stress. It crossed my mind that you could, quite unwittingly, be passing on your concerns about the job to her, but you tell me that isn't the case.'

Now, I don't care for half-baked psychiatry. I don't care much for psychiatry at all. So I told him, 'I don't often discuss my work with Geraldine.'

'Then we must look elsewhere for a possible cause of

anxiety. Could it be traced to some dissatisfaction with her present mode of life? She has to put up with rather less of the limelight now.'

'True. She does the occasional commercial, but otherwise the television work has dried up.'

'Why is that? Because everyone still thinks of her as Candice?'

'That's part of it, certainly.'

'You didn't notice she was losing sleep?'

'Frankly, no. We have twin beds and when my head touches the pillow, I'm off.'

'You don't enquire in the morning whether she slept well?'

'Not usually. My impression is that she's always sleeping soundly when I get up.' I paused. 'But I must say I feel very uneasy about this conversation, Doctor. If Geraldine is worried about losing sleep, she could have mentioned it to me. The fact is that she didn't. She came to you in confidence.'

'I made the not unreasonable assumption that you knew about the problem,' the doctor told me. He followed this up with an insinuation that I didn't like in the least: 'You are concerned, I take it?'

With difficulty I controlled myself. 'Naturally I'm concerned now that you've told me. I'll do whatever I can to help, if it's only making her cups of hot chocolate in the night.'

The doctor sniffed. 'You don't have to stay awake and keep her company. That's no way to tackle insomnia.'

'What do you suggest?'

Off-handedly he said, 'Don't bother – she'll get her sleep now. I've put her on phenobarbitone.'

I frowned. 'Is it as bad as that?'

'We've run through the milder hypnotics. She tells me they had little or no effect.'

'It's been going on for some time, then? I didn't know.'

'This is severe, intractable insomnia, Professor. We must break the cycle somehow, and in cases like this a good old-fashioned barbiturate will do the trick when some of the newer tranquillizers will not. When we have re-established the habit of sleep, the natural pattern should reassert itself in a few weeks.'

'You mean there's nothing I can do?'

'There's still the underlying problem. It *may* be physical, but of all the causes of sleep loss, anxiety is the most common. I can see that you're sympathetic, and that's helpful in itself, so if you can find out what is troubling her and do something constructive about it, you'll do more good than phenobarbitone in the long run. Please be discreet, however.'

'That's rich!' I said.

'Professor, as an intelligent man, I'm sure you won't need telling that a patient's confidence in her doctor is vitally important.'

'Point taken,' I told him, and this time I didn't hold back. 'And as an intelligent man, I ought to advise my wife to change her doctor. Good morning.'

I got up and walked out.

Before starting the car I sat for some time trying to understand why Geraldine should have been losing sleep and how it was that I had failed to notice. The possibility didn't cross my mind that the phenobarbitone was intended for me.

Chapter Two

LATER THE SAME MORNING AT the University of Bath, I found myself watching Miss Hunter – who is the personal assistant to the Dean of Letters – arrange six chocolate digestives on a plate. In the next room the University Steering Committee was in session and I had been summoned for item six on the agenda. I was due to go in with the coffee. After twenty minutes I was getting restless. I still hadn't got over that uncomfortable session with Dr Bookbinder. I remember helping myself to a biscuit and saying facetiously, straining to put myself in a better frame of mind, 'Peculiar name to give it – the Steering Committee. What do they do in there – ride around on pushbikes?'

Hilary Hunter likes a giggle. She seemed to enjoy the mental picture of five professors solemnly pedalling around the dean's office for the entire morning, but as a loyal PA she couldn't laugh at the dean's expense, so she turned and flicked the switch on the kettle. It had come to the boil twice already.

Another minute passed.

The buzzer on her desk sounded. She poured the coffee and picked up the tray.

I opened the door for her and murmured, 'Watch out for the race leader in the yellow jersey.'

It was like a nudge in the ribs for Miss Hunter. She made a snorting sound as she stepped through the door.

The dean said, 'Do you require a tissue, Miss Hunter?'

She shook her head.

'Leave the tray, then. We'll help ourselves. Jackman, do come and join us.' The dean gestured towards a vast chintz-covered settee. The comforts of life are important to him. He goes in for check-patterned woollen shirts and hand-woven ties. His flat cap and golf bag were hanging on the door. This year it was his turn to preside over the Steering Committee. The others were drawn from different faculties. I knew three of them slightly and sometimes propped up a bar with the fourth, Professor Oliver, the Art man.

'How is the fledgling School of English faring?' the dean asked in his ponderous way.

'Chirpy enough,' I answered.

'Ha – yes. Ready to take wing?'

'What's on offer, then – a trip to the States?'

The dean chuckled. 'You're an optimist.' He turned to his left. 'Isn't he an optimist? Professor Oliver, would you be so good as to explain?'

'Me?' Tom Oliver asked in a spray of biscuit crumbs. He needed something to chew. Smoke-free committee meetings are an ordeal for a man who habitually keeps a pipe alight. He took a gulp of coffee and swallowed hard. 'You probably know, Greg, that we're trying to buff up the university's image in the town.'

'The city,' said the dean.

'Correction. The city. There was some criticism a year or two back that we'd built the proverbial ivory tower up here at Claverton and were ignoring the burghers.'

'Now that's uncalled for,' said the dean.

'Burghers,' Oliver repeated. 'The good citizens. The suggestion was untrue, of course. With our strength in science and technology we've always been involved with local industry through sandwich courses. We provide a marvellous range of extramural courses. We have the Concert Society arranging musical events. At Christmas we let hundreds of shoppers use the car park for the park-and-ride scheme. And of course the students have their rag week and so on.'

'The sedan chair race,' contributed the Professor of Comparative Religions, a featherweight who annually agrees to be transported around the course.

'That, too. What I'm leading up to is that three years

ago, before you joined us, Greg, we held an exhibition in the Victoria Gallery.'

'The one over the public library,' chipped in the dean. 'Fine exhibition, it was, for a pioneering effort.'

A guarded look dropped like a visor over my features.

'It fell to me to organize it,' Oliver continued. 'My brief was to put on a show called *Art in Bath*, featuring painters who actually lived here at some point in their lives. A motley crew, I have to admit. Gainsborough, Sir Thomas Lawrence, Whistler, Lord Leighton and a few lesser lights.'

'Professor Oliver had one of his own on show,' said the dean. 'An abstract, mainly in pink, as I recall.'

Oliver said self-consciously. 'I needed to fill a space. I would have preferred to put on a complete show of modern work, but the Society of Bath Artists had its annual show in the gallery a month before, and I was told firmly that this must be different in character, a more traditional exhibition.'

Sensing, perhaps, that the positive aspects of the *Art in Bath* Exhibition needed to be stressed more, the dean came in again. 'There was a first-class response to our request for the loan of pictures – from private collections as well as the more obvious sources. That's partly the point of an exhibition such as this. It's a way of involving the local people, reminding them that we exist. It got into the papers and on local television and radio. Professor Oliver got to be quite a media man in the end.'

Tom Oliver's eyes rolled upwards at the memory.

By now I'd heard enough of this. I sat back and folded my arms. 'Let's have it, gentlemen. What am I lumbered with?'

The dean frowned. 'No one has *lumbered* you with anything, Jackman. I would have thought a professor of English might have employed a more felicitous word than that.'

'Clobbered?'

'We seem to be at cross-purposes,' said the dean. 'I know you don't mince words, Jackman, but there's no cause to be obstructive before we have even outlined the proposition. I see this as a shining opportunity for the English Department to make a name for itself. You know, as the newest department in the university you have a lot of ground to make up on those of us who were here at the beginning. And with only two years' intake of students to administer I wouldn't have said you were overburdened. You won't be awarding degrees for another year.'

'Fair cop,' I said. 'You want me to bang the drum this year. Do I have a free hand?'

'Within limits.'

I shrugged. 'I don't have a free hand.'

'We have a proposal — rather an engaging one — originating from the city council itself. It has this committee's strong support, naturally.'

'What is it?'

'*Jane Austen in Bath.*'

There was a silence.

'Jane Austen, the writer,' added the dean, whose sarcasm wasn't complicated by subtlety. 'In case you weren't aware of it, she lived in the city for several years.'

'You learn something every day,' I said. 'Is that the deal — just Jane?'

'And Bath. The theme, the rationale, of the exhibition is a celebration of Jane Austen's years in Bath.'

'A celebration?'

'Exactly.'

I drew a deep breath and let it out slowly. 'Pity she isn't still around to enjoy the irony of this.'

The dean bristled. 'You had better explain that remark.'

'Jane Austen's years in Bath were no cause for celebration. She was pretty pissed off with the place.'

'Professor Jackman!'

'All right — it was the least happy phase of her life.'

'That's rather sweeping, isn't it?'

The professor of comparative religions reached for the last chocolate biscuit and said, 'What is happiness? What did happiness amount to for Jane Austen? We are dealing in abstractions here.'

'As I recall it,' I said, 'when the Reverend George Austen informed his family that they were to move here from

81

Steventon, where Jane was born and brought up, she passed out. Fainted. They had five years in Bath. It failed lamentably to come up to Steventon in her estimation. She had a series of unhappy experiences about that time – a broken engagement, the deaths of friends. Her father died here. They had to move into more humble lodgings, and after they finally left she described it as a happy escape. Happiness amounted to escaping from Bath.'

After another uncomfortable pause the dean said doggedly, 'The fact remains that she was a resident. And one of the world's great novelists.'

'Not one of the great novels was written in Bath.'

The dean glared over his glasses. 'Correct me if I'm mistaken, Professor. Bath does, as I recall, feature prominently in the novels.'

I looked around the room at the other members of the committee. 'There's no ducking this, is there?'

'It isn't something to be *ducked*. It's an opportunity, Jackman. Everyone who has heard of it so far is extremely excited about the prospect. The city librarian and his staff have promised every assistance.'

My heart sank. 'People have been told already?'

'One or two crucial individuals.'

'I wish you'd brought me in earlier.'

Oliver said, 'Greg, we only heard about it ourselves this morning.'

I sighed heavily, got up and walked to the window. 'And I'm supposed to find enough exhibits to fill the Victoria Gallery?'

'The Assembly Rooms,' said the Dean with an air of triumph. 'We have been offered the Assembly Rooms.'

'God – that's even bigger.'

'It couldn't be a more appropriate venue. Do you appreciate the significance? Jane Austen must have danced there many times.'

Tom Oliver said, 'Actually, Dean, it was gutted by bombs in the last war.'

'And perfectly restored.'

'Right,' I said, turning to face them. 'It's a bloody great ballroom. How am I supposed to fill it? So far as I can

82

remember there's one postcard-size portrait of Jane by her sister, and that's in the National Portrait Gallery because no other picture of her exists. If I get a loan of that, which is unlikely, it's not going to fill a hundred-foot ballroom.'

The dean shuffled his papers. 'I'm confident that if you embrace the opportunity as Professor Oliver did three years ago, we shall have an admirable show.'

I turned to the professor of comparative religions. '"Embrace the opportunity" – how's that for an abstraction?'

Tom Oliver, wanting to be helpful, said, 'You might make use of the novels in some way.'

'Open at certain pages and displayed in glass cabinets?' I said. 'Not exactly riveting, is it? It isn't going to pull in the crowds when they can pick up the same books in any shop in the town.'

'City,' murmured Oliver.

'You could photograph the houses she lived in,' said the dean.

'And blow them up to actual size?' At this stage, I was in no mood to take any suggestion seriously. 'True, if I back them with hardboard and stand them upright like theatre scenery, that might help to fill the bloody Assembly Rooms. I could dress my students in period costume and have them disport themselves around the scenery, commenting, "Upon my word, the gentlemen of the Steering Committee are deserving of our plaudits, for a happier conjunction of town and gown than this was never conceived." '

'Come off it, Greg,' said Oliver before the dean could erupt. 'When you've had time to think it over, you'll have some bright ideas.'

'It's window-dressing, isn't it? Jane Austen is a name to pull in the tourists. Nobody stopped to consider what Jane herself really thought of the place. I suppose it's too late to point out this slight ethical objection to the genius who suggested it.'

'But that is the very reverse of all we're trying to achieve,' the dean pointed out to me. 'We want to make a gesture of support to the city, not humiliate them by scoring academic points. And, yes, it is too late. Far too late.'

I asked fatalistically, 'How long have I got?'

Oliver said, 'It's essentially a summer exhibition.'

'. . . opening on 9 September for three weeks,' said the dean as if he were passing sentence.

'That takes care of *my* vacation,' I said.

'I'd like a progress report this time next week, if that isn't too much to ask.'

I happen to be blessed or cursed with acute hearing. As I was leaving the outer office, I overheard the dean saying, 'What an obstreperous fellow. I don't recall this side of him emerging when he was interviewed for the chair.'

Oliver said, 'You weren't here, Dean. It was during your sabbatical.'

'Ah.'

'He's very well regarded by his students.'

'I can believe it.'

'He won't let us down.'

'He had better not.'

Chapter Three

PLENTY OF PEOPLE CROSS PULTENEY bridge without even realizing that they're passing over the Avon. The reason, of course, is that it's lined on either side with buildings, like the Ponte Vecchio in Florence. You can't see the river without going into one of the shops and looking out of a window. I heard that when Robert Adam designed the thing in 1769 he had the Ponte Vecchio in mind, but if there's any resemblance, it's superficial only. Adam's bridge is charming and original, a Palladian structure built over the three arches, with a central Venetian window and domed tollhouses at either end.

The tollhouse on the west side, opposite the library, functions as a coffee shop called David's. I had come here after my meeting with the Steering Committee. My presence had nothing to do with the new assignment; I had come to David's to unwind. After the sessions with Dr Bookbinder and the Steering Committee, I thought I was entitled to a break. I couldn't stomach the Senior Common Room. My nature rebels against the attitudes and assumptions of most provincial academics. As the professor of a newly formed department I feel obliged most days to sit and listen to regurgitated points of view from the *Guardian* and *Independent*, or the failings of the cricket selectors, or the union, or the photocopier. Not that day.

David's is a haven for me. On the day nearly three years ago that I arrived in Bath to be interviewed for the chair of English, it seemed a happy omen when I chanced upon this *bijou* establishment no wider than a railway carriage, with its aroma of cappuccino, its narrow back-to-back seats and linen tablecloths and the quiet clientele lingering over newspapers provided by the owner. At one end is a framed picture of Michelangelo's *David*. At the other the modern David dispenses tea and coffee from a serving area designed to utilize the limited space to the maximum. David is slim and supple, an essential requirement; one needs almost to be a limbo-dancer to get behind the counter.

The most favoured seats enjoy a view of the river. The broad sweep of water below the bridge is dominated by the weir, a white, U-shaped structure in three tiers. However, its elegant lines mask a deathtrap. Thousands of gallons converge and drop on a confined area that forms a whirlpool where, year after year, foolhardy swimmers and canoeists come to grief.

I took a seat by the window, easing my weight downwards in a practised way to avoid rocking the person at the next table. I ordered a coffee, and thought about the interview in the surgery. The hell with Bookbinder. Later I would tell Geraldine exactly what had been said. Honesty in our marriage was more important than medical ethics that had already been muddied by the doctor.

I glanced at the front page of *The Times* and pushed it aside, and took from my pocket a paperback of *Northanger Abbey* that I had picked off my bookshelf in the office before walking down Bathwick Hill. I searched for and found a remark Jane Austen had put into the mouth of Isabella Thorpe: '*I get so immoderately sick of Bath; your brother and I were agreeing this morning that though it is vastly well to be here for a few weeks, we would not live here for millions.*' It was like a balm. I felt restored by the words, which were much as I had remembered them. Of course it's erroneous to impute the views of fictitious characters to their author, and in justice the book does also contain some complimentary remarks about the city, but in my mood at that stage it pleased me to picture the councillors touring their exhibition and finding gracious pictures of Georgian Bath captioned with caustic quotes from Jane.

I sipped the coffee, telling myself to put subversive thoughts out of my mind. The exhibition had been dumped in my lap. It was my baby now, so I had better start to love it. A celebration of Jane Austen in Bath. In principle, I was more than willing to celebrate the six completed novels. If not, I was in the wrong job. The celebrating of their creator was more of a problem for me. I have never had any desire to join the legion of devotees who call themselves Janeites. Not that I find much to object to in Jane's character. In fact, the occasional waspish comments in her letters make her seem more worldly, more approachable, than the 'gentle Jane' of the novels. My difficulty is more fundamental. I am out of sympathy with those who venerate writers and study their lives minutely. Any piece of literature has a life of its own, complete and independent of its author. So I baulk at the trend of modern criticism to bury creative work in biographical data.

My thoughts were diverted momentarily by something I saw from the window. Below, three young boys had ventured out to the end of the weir and found a footing where driftwood collected. The current was not as strong there as in the centre, where it raced over the edge, the result of several days of steady rain. The lads were picking up bits of wood and hurling them into the middle for the sheer joy of disturbing the shimmering uniformity of the flow.

The scene illustrated my difficulty rather aptly. There must be visual stimulation in this exhibition. Pages of text, however elegant, were not suited to public display unless they were supported by strong images. Yet the novels provided few striking pictorial possibilities. I always find illustrated editions of the Austen novels depressing to look at. They are little more than fashion plates. The dynamism is all in the text. Thinking it over, I could photograph the locations Jane Austen had used in *Northanger Abbey* and *Persuasion*, the two novels set in Bath, but to what effect? Who wanted to look at photos of Milsom Street and the Pump Room when they could see the places for themselves? No, I was going to be compelled to set aside my objections and use the biographical approach, providing pictures of Jane's family, the houses she had lived in and the people she had met. The illustrations would be static, but at least they would not seem insipid.

Then how about moving pictures? It might be worth setting up a video and screening extracts from a television dramatisation that had actually been filmed in Bath. I recalled a production of *Persuasion* not long ago. Presumably the BBC had obtained permission from the Bath City Council to film on location, so it wouldn't be unreasonable to ask for their co-operation in return.

I visualized several rows of chairs in front of a large screen at one end of the ballroom, and felt more optimistic. My gaze returned to the weir.

One of the boys was stepping along the edge towards the centre. A stick, presumably one he had thrown, had lodged almost at the cusp of the curve. The other two watched as he moved quite confidently towards it. He looked about twelve or thirteen, and sturdy in physique. It was still a foolhardy thing to try. Notices on each bank of the river warned of the danger of swimming and canoeing here.

I remember telling myself with one voice that the boy was a little idiot and with the other that kids of that age needed physical challenges. If they weren't walking along the weir they would probably be skate-boarding down the ramps in one of the city car parks. The boy reached the centre and drew the stick out of the water. He held it aloft like Excalibur.

Feeling, perhaps, that this was excessive, one of the others picked up a chunk of wood and slung it towards the show-off. It didn't hit him. He saw it coming and swayed aside. But he must have underestimated the strength of the current, because he was forced to take a step sideways to keep his footing. It took him closer to the edge. He seemed to sense the danger and teetered there for a moment with arms swaying. Then he was forced to step down to the next level.

The move was sensible. The concrete tiers were quite wide at that point and the difference in levels was no more than a few inches in depth. The force of the water seemed not to be a problem for him. He might easily have stepped up to safety.

He was unlucky, however. His foot slipped, he lost balance and fell on his back. The water carried him down to the next level.

I got up fast, concerned that the boy would be swept into the maelstrom of converging water. I believe I called out to David, 'Someone in trouble', and ran out of the shop and across the bridge. Others may have seen the incident from Grand Parade, which overlooked the weir, but I was closer to the side with access to it. At the far end, I turned right, grabbed the iron handrail and hurried down the enclosed flight of steps to the stone pier that supported the bridge. I ran to the railing. I had a clear view. The boy was not in sight. The other two stood as if petrified, staring at the place where the water poured off the weir and formed a bubbling vortex.

On this side of the river a sluice forms part of the weir construction, a huge floodgate on a pivot surmounted by a platform. To reach the weir on foot I would need to dash about a hundred yards to the steps on the far side and cross the platform. The lifebuoy was almost as far away, attached to the railing beside the sluice. There wasn't time.

I wrenched off my jacket and shoes, climbed over the railing and jumped. The drop to the river was about fifteen feet. I went under, surfaced, coughed out some filthy-tasting water, and started swimming. My actions up to this moment had been automatic. Now, as I struck out for the weir, the doubts came. Had there really been three boys down there, or only two? What a pointless and embarrassing exhibition this would be if the kid in trouble had picked himself up already.

My right hand touched a solid structure under the water. I grasped the stone surround of the weir and with difficulty hauled myself upwards, getting my leg up first and scrambling up sideways. I managed to stand upright, close to the point where the boy had gone for the piece of wood. The current dragged at my legs.

The boys at the end of the weir were waving and shouting.

I shouted back to them, 'Can you see him?'

'He keeps going under,' one called out in an accent

redolent of Latin primers and striped schoolcaps.

'Where? Where did you see him?'

The boy pointed. 'There, sir! Over there!'

I glanced left and saw an arm exposed in the foam, a hand with fingers extended. Almost at once it sank from view.

I yelled, 'Get the lifebelt! Get some help!'

I didn't give much for my chances in the torrent but you can't watch a child drown. I stepped down two tiers and felt my foot slip, so I dropped to my knees and crawled around the ledge to the point nearest to where the arm had appeared. I could see graphically how the inundation of water produced a churning effect that would prevent the boy from climbing back or being carried downstream. He would be submerged repeatedly until he drowned.

Desperately I scanned the seething surface for another glimpse of the boy and suddenly saw him thrust upwards again a mere two or three yards ahead. This time it was the torso that appeared, turning in the water like a log, apparently lifeless.

I launched myself after it, arms outstretched to make a grab. The cold water struck me like a charging rhino and forced me down. I went under, swallowing copiously. My ears roared. I was turned over, buffeted and disoriented. My head glanced against something solid. But I succeeded in getting a hold on the boy. I had him by the thigh.

I drew the limb to me and clung to it with both hands. The conflicting currents tossed us about as if we were cork. We were dragged down, hauled along the bottom, thrust upwards, spun around and slapped in the face. But I continued to hold the boy. And by degrees I was conscious of a lessening in the force of the buffeting. Now, when we came to the surface, there was time to inhale. I glimpsed foliage overhead, which meant that we were being carried to the outer extremity of the weir where the current was less strong.

My shoulder scraped against the stone embankment. I found a foothold. I took a gulp of air and adjusted my hold on the boy, drawing a hand under his back, lifting the face clear of the water. It was lily-white and lifeless. The head lolled back.

With this limp burden in my arms, I battled against the flow until I stumbled on to the lowest level of the weir at the outermost edge, just below the point where the boys had stood. I might as well say it, even if it sounds like something out of the *Boy's Own Paper*: the urge to do whatever I could to save this young life was giving me more strength than I knew I possessed. First I was kneeling. Then I managed to draw my right leg into a position where I could force myself fully upright. I staggered across the structure and climbed upwards to a place where the end of the weir had been built up to form the wall of the sluice. It was wide enough to have been planted with trees.

Crouching, I rested the small body on the ground, and the daunting realization came to me that if the boy was to have any chance of survival, some life-saving technique was crucial. I had only the vaguest notion of what was necessary. As if prompted by my thoughts, a child's voice beside me said, 'Kiss of life. Try the kiss of life, sir.'

It was one of the boys from the weir.

I struggled to remember what one has to do. Resting a hand on the forehead of the unconscious boy, I tilted back his head. A trickle of water seeped from the edge of the mouth, so I turned the head, but no more was emitted. The mouth and nostrils appeared to be clear of weed or other obstructions.

The kid at my side said, 'You have to pinch his nose and blow into his mouth.'

I tried it. His lips felt clammy and gave no promise of life. I expelled several breaths, and saw the chest rise as the air penetrated the lungs. Nothing else happened. I seemed to be making no progress, so I tried pressure on the chest, pressing repeatedly on the lower half of the breastbone.

Without taking my eyes off the pale face, I asked the boy, 'Did you go for help?'

'Nelson went. The boy that threw the wood.'

The significance of the identity of the wood thrower was

wasted on me. I was fast losing confidence in my ability to restore consciousness.

I stopped kneading the chest and put my fingers to the pulse beside the boy's Adam's apple. If there was any life there, it was too faint to detect. I lifted the left eyelid. No movement. I pinched the nostrils closed again and clamped my mouth over the boy's.

It was difficult to tell at such close proximity, but it seemed to me that as I blew the second breath into the boy's lungs, the eye that I had examined gave a twitch. It remained shut, but the muscles around it appeared to flex. I could not be certain that it had happened. And I was not sure whether I had caused the effect myself with the pressure of my hand against the nose.

I stopped the blowing and drew back to get a better look. As I was putting my hand towards the eye, it opened and the iris moved. Both eyes opened fully.

The moment was profoundly moving. It was a deliverance. An acquittal. A life had been given back.

I murmured, 'Thank God!' I am not religious, but no other words could encapsulate my feelings.

The boy coughed and spluttered.

'I'm going to turn you on your side,' I told him, and the joy of communicating was never so exquisite.

The boy took several short breaths and then vomited some water. I massaged his back.

'He's all right! You saved his life!' The other boy knelt close to his friend. 'Are you all right, Mat?'

'Is that his name – Mat?' I asked.

'Matthew. And I'm Piers.'

'All right, Piers, let's have the shirt. We'll put it around his shoulders.' And as the boy on the ground started to turn his head, I told him, 'We'll get you home soon, Matthew.'

Piers announced, 'Here comes Nelson with the Old Bill.'

I turned to look. Not merely Nelson with the Old Bill, but up to twenty people were strung out along the river bank, running towards the weir. First they would have to climb a flight of steps and cross over the sluicegate. I took the opportunity to put in a word on Nelson's behalf. 'Piers, if I were you, I wouldn't say any more about the piece of wood that was thrown. Matthew walked along the weir and fell in. That's all you need to tell anyone.'

'I suppose it is.'

'I'm certain of it.'

'Right you are, sir.'

Matthew himself managed to speak in a croaking voice. 'It wasn't deliberate.'

I glanced down at the pale face, the red-lidded eyes and the dark hair flat to the forehead. He looked a bright kid. 'That's right, son,' I told him. 'Some time in our lives we've all done daft things we'd like to be overlooked.' The 'son' came naturally to my lips although I had neither son nor daughter. At the marvellous moment when Matthew had opened his eyes, I had experienced something not unlike the joy and relief a father must feel at the miracle of childbirth.

Piers said, 'The gentleman saved your life, Mat.'

I said, 'I think Mat needs to rest.'

It wasn't a policeman Nelson had found, but a traffic warden. He led the rescue party up the steps and over the platform. They had to climb over a railing and let themselves down.

Someone had thoughtfully picked up my jacket and shoes. While I was putting them on, the boys gave their version of what had happened. The siren of an approaching ambulance cut the explanation short. A blanket was handed down. Matthew protested that he would rather go home, but he was wrapped in it and hoisted up.

It was my opportunity to slip away. The role of gallant rescuer didn't appeal to me. I'd rather be known as the obstreperous fellow who winds up the dean.

Chapter Four

LATE THE SAME AFTERNOON, I was drinking coffee in the kitchen of my house on Bathwick Hill, when the drum-roll sound of the rollers on the garage doors signalled Geraldine's return from her pub lunch. In quick succession came the thump of the Metro door, the clatter of heels across the concrete floor and the rasp of the door handle. She flung open the door. All those years in television and she still couldn't resist making an entrance.

This one was perfectly set up for her. 'Christ,' she said when she saw the white bathrobe I was wearing. 'What's going on – infidelity?'

I smiled. If she was being humorous – and I couldn't be sure these days – it was worth encouraging. 'Want a coffee?'

She nodded. She was pink from the Pimm's she'd been putting away. Her skin was drawn tight from cheek to jaw. For almost a decade the BBC make-up department preserved the peachy softness of her youth. Now it was gone. She had been written out of the series for two years, yet the image of Candice was impossible to forget when you looked at her. She was still a strikingly attractive woman, but the changes were striking, too – a poignant illustration of why the framed wedding photo in most homes gets consigned to a drawer after a few years.

She told me, 'For a moment just now I thought you were dead.'

'Dead?'

'I saw the suit hanging up in the garage. At first glance I thought you were in it. What on earth is it doing there?'

'It got wet, or at least the trousers did. I had a ducking

today. My things smell of river water so I hung them out there.'

'*River* water? Are you serious?'

I spooned instant coffee into a cup, poured on the boiling water and told her about the boy in the weir. When I had finished, she said, 'You could have drowned doing that. You could *really* have been dead.'

There wasn't the depth of concern in her voice that the statement warranted. On the contrary, there seemed to be a note of wistfulness.

I let it pass. As a literary man I know the mind's limitless facility for flights of imagination. 'Unlikely,' I said cheerfully. 'I have a charmed life, like the pigeon in Great Russell Street.'

'*That.*'

'You haven't entirely forgotten, then?'

'I'm not likely to.'

These days, the Great Russell Street pigeon seemed to have become a bird of ill omen. Our marriage might have broken up already, were it not for the way we had chosen to conduct it. Although Geraldine no longer had professional commitments, we had kept to our pact to conserve a strong measure of independence. I would go abroad on courses without expecting Geraldine to tag along; and she took her own skiing holidays. We each had our own cars, beds, newspapers, books and records. She went to church; I didn't. We sometimes went separately to dinner parties. The theory was that when we did spend time together, the experience was more precious because it was by choice, not circumstance. And for the first few months it had worked, sexually and emotionally.

Given the free-ranging style of our marriage. Gerry's altered life after she lost her part in *The Milners* didn't threaten to spoil things too much. She had a pile of money from television and she spent it liberally. She soon linked up with a lively crowd from Bristol who were only too happy to hoist her on to the social merry-go-round she had missed before.

Now, two years on, our independence was about all we could agree on. Her erratic moods, the rages and the accusations, had turned the space we had created into a gulf. The sex had become perfunctory, and we both needed to be half plastered to perform it. Our conversations were strained even when Geraldine switched to her exultant, highly animated states, because our worlds hardly overlapped. She had friends I had never met. 'They would bore you,' she'd say, 'and, God, would you bore them!' There was an assumption in the way we treated each other that it would have to end in a separation.

However, I hadn't yet grasped that Geraldine's notion of separation was more absolute than mine.

And I still felt some responsibility towards her. I said casually as we sat drinking the coffee, 'I went for my medical this morning. I saw Bookbinder, your doctor.'

Geraldine gave me a sharp look. 'I didn't tell you Bookbinder was my doctor.'

'You didn't tell me you were being treated for insomnia, either.'

'Bloody hell!' The jar of coffee tipped over as she swept her arm outwards. 'That's private and confidential. You had no right to ask.'

'Hold on, Gerry,' I told her. 'Before you hit the ceiling, Bookbinder volunteered the information. He expected me to know all about it. I told him I didn't. It's news to me. I must say, I haven't noticed you lying awake.'

She didn't answer. She glared at me with her green eyes, threatening any minute to prove the truth of the axiom about redheads and their temper.

I said in conciliation, 'Gerry, I don't want to make an issue out of this. If you haven't been getting your sleep, I'm sorry. On the few occasions I've had a wakeful night myself lately, I've heard you breathing evenly and assumed you were out to the world. But I suppose the tablets have solved the problem.'

Her eyes widened and narrowed almost as quickly. 'You heard about those, too? What else did you bloody find out? Did you read my notes at the same time?'

After my attempt to take the heat out of the exchange, I found her response abusive. I rapped back, 'You'd better complain to your doctor, not me.'

She vented her fury in a piercing attack. 'Snake in the grass! You've been trying to find out things, haven't you? Prying into my treatment. What are you plotting? Going to my own doctor behind my back – it's disgusting!'

The usual tack. I said, 'Will you listen to me? I'm getting heartily sick of this persecution mania of yours. I was sent in to Bookbinder because my doctor – Marshall – is away. I went in to get the result of my medical.'

'You fixed a date when you knew Marshall was away.' She stabbed the space between us with her finger. 'You trumped up this medical just to get in to my doctor and find out what my medication is.'

'Give it a rest, will you?'

'It sticks out a mile! What are you up to, that's what troubles me. Are you trying to get something up with him behind my back? That's it, isn't it? You're in league with my doctor now, you bastard.'

'If this was behind your back, why do you think I told you about it?' I pointed out.

'Because you're bloody devious, that's why,' she shouted. 'You're covering your tracks, pretending it's all out in the open when it isn't. Why did you mention it at all if you knew it would upset me? You're up to something, there's no question of that.'

'Have you finished? You want to know why I mentioned this. I'll tell you. It's the reverse of what you're suggesting. The reason I spoke out is that I've always believed in being straight with you. And there's another reason: I'm damned sure you shouldn't be drinking or using the car if you're on phenobarbitone. A taxi might be sensible next time.'

'Go to hell.' She snatched up her bag and walked to the door.

I said, 'I mean it. You're going to kill someone if you carry on like this.'

She started to laugh.

I gave up trying to reason with her.

Chapter Five

THURSDAY AFTERNOON OF THAT WEEK found me standing in front of a television camera beside one of the seven marble fireplaces in the main Assembly Room in Bath, the location so recklessly nominated for the forthcoming Jane Austen exhibition. As it happened, this wasn't directly concerned with the exhibition. I had been invited there in another connection, to contribute to a BBC *Points West* item about the history of the building. Even so, my thoughts kept darting ahead to September. The place was even more vast than I remembered. My gaze travelled up a Corinthian column and across the ornate ceiling to the orchestra gallery.

'Professor, would you mind coming in closer to Sadie?'

'If Sadie can stand the excitement,' I answered.

'Enough. Hold it there.' The highly-strung New Zealander who was directing this interview asked the lighting man if he was happier and got a thumbs-up. 'Fine. Are we okay for sound?'

While they continued to set up the shot, I spoke confidentially to Sadie, who was to interview me. 'Before we start, I'd like to get one thing straight. Just now you mentioned the *Jane Austen in Bath* Exhibition. At this stage dear Jane is just a twinkle in my eye, and a faint one at that. I only heard about it myself a couple of days ago. You'd better not ask me what my plans are.'

'No problem,' she said. 'Didn't Dougie make this clear? I won't ask you anything about it. After we screen the interview we'll mention that you're planning to hold the exhibition in September. That's all — a little advance publicity. We can drop it if you like.'

'No, it ought to go in.'

'Today's item is just about the uses the Assembly Rooms have been put to over the centuries. All we want from you, Professor, is something about what went on here in Jane's time.'

'You mean behind the pillars?'

A look of disquiet crept over Sadie's features. She said, 'We were rather expecting that you would stress the more formal aspects, the dress balls and so on. I'm recording two more interviews to bring out the slightly more disreputable uses it was put to in more recent times. Apparently it was used as a cinema between the wars.'

'A cinema?' Still with a straight face I said, 'I can't imagine *anything* more disreputable than that.'

Every television interviewer dreads a wisecracker. Sadie eyed me without amusement and said firmly, 'Everything will be edited, by the way. It doesn't have to go out until Friday. Dougie wants at least two takes in case of a problem, so if you cough or anything, you needn't worry. It won't be transmitted.'

'My dear, I never worry.'

Sadie wetted her lips, turned away and said, on a lower note that I think was directed at the crew, 'You worry me, ducky.' She nodded to Dougie, the director.

'Quiet please,' he said. 'We're going for a take. Take one – and action.'

We didn't get past Sadie's first question before Dougie said, 'Cut'. Something was amiss with the sound. While they checked it, I awarded myself a short break. I left the fireplace, strolled across to a row of Chippendale chairs that the crew used between takes and picked up a newspaper someone had left there, the *Bath Evening Chronicle*. The headline ran: SHY HERO IN WEIR RESCUE.

I sat down and read on:

An unknown man plunged to the rescue of a drowning schoolboy at Pulteney Weir yesterday afternoon and hauled him to safety. The boy, Matthew Didrikson, twelve, of Lyncombe Rise, a day pupil at the Abbey Choir School, was unconscious when brought to the bank, but his rescuer revived him with the 'kiss of life' method of resuscitation. He was taken to the Royal United Hospital suffering from shock and water inhalation, but was not detained. Matthew's rescuer, a well-dressed man of about thirty-five, left the scene without identifying himself.

Mr David Broadbent, a retired optician, saw the entire incident from Grand Parade. He said, 'The boy was playing with two others beside the weir and he started to walk out to the centre. The current was strong after all the rain we've had lately. The lad appeared to wobble and slip and the next thing he was in the water below the weir. The man must have seen it from Pulteney Bridge or thereabouts because he came running down the steps by the bridge and jumped straight in. He didn't hesitate. He swam to the weir and went in after the lad. It was heroic because people have drowned there in the past. Somehow he got a grip on the boy and they were washed to one side, and he climbed out and dragged the boy on to the bank and gave him the kiss of life. I think the Royal Humane Society should be informed, because that man deserves a medal.'

Dr Rajinder Murtah, who attended Matthew at the hospital, said, 'The boy undoubtedly owes his life to the prompt and sensible action of this unknown man.' Matthew's mother, Mrs Dana Didrikson, who is employed by Realbrew Ales Ltd as a driver, said, 'I would dearly like an opportunity to thank the brave man who saved the life of my son.' Matthew, apparently none the worse for his adventure except for superficial grazing, will return to school tomorrow.

A police spokesman said, 'At least three people have drowned at Pulteney Weir in the last ten years and there have been any number of incidents involving swimmers or canoeists. People don't realize that it's so deep below the weir that you could sink a double-decker bus there. For anyone caught in the undertow, it's a deathtrap.'

A voice at my shoulder said suddenly, 'There's no escape. I've tracked you down.'

'What?' I slapped the paper face down.

Sadie said, 'We're going for another take.'

On the evening the interview was screened I was caught up in a Board of Studies meeting, so I missed it. Gerry saw it and thoughtfully switched on the video-recorder, which she failed to notice was tuned to Channel 4, so when I got in I sat through ten minutes of a gardening programme before I realized what had happened. But it was meant as an olive branch after the shindy we'd had about my visit to Dr Bookbinder, and I thanked her for making the attempt.

'It's funny,' she remarked. 'You always look different when I see you on the box – almost dishy, in fact.'

'*Dishy*?' I said, pretending to take umbrage. 'We were discussing the social *mores* of Bath in Jane Austen's era. That was my donnish look.'

'I wasn't taken in by that,' she said. 'It's just an act, isn't it? Greg Jackman putting it across that he's the professor, just like some actor hamming it up as Julius Caesar.'

There was more than a germ of truth in her comment, but I didn't much care for the analogy.

Some time after ten that evening, when I was sipping a cognac prior to checking that the doors and windows were locked, the phone rang. Gerry was taking a shower, so I picked it up, expecting to find myself talking to one of her many friends who called at all hours with titbits of gossip.

'Is it possible to speak to Professor Jackman?' a woman's voice asked.

'Speaking.'

'I thought I recognized your voice. I'm sorry to be calling so late. Is it terribly inconvenient?'

'Well, you found me at home,' I said cautiously, trying to work out whether this was one of my students wanting to contest a grading. 'Do I know you, then?'

'No. My name is Abershaw – Molly Abershaw.' She paused as if I might have heard of her, then resumed, 'From the *Bath Evening Telegraph*.'

I said, with more tact than I usually employ, 'Now that you mention it, I believe I have seen your name in the paper.'

'And I saw you on television earlier this evening.'

That was why she had recognized my voice. I felt more comfortable with the call now that I had some idea of its provenance. 'You picked up the reference to the Jane Austen exhibition, I suppose?'

'Yes, indeed. That's in September, I gather?'

'Correct,' I told her, refraining from adding that it scarcely merited a ten o'clock call this evening.

'You'll be wanting to publicise it, I'm sure,' she went on. 'We'd like to run a feature nearer the time.'

'Fine,' I said, not wanting to prolong the conversation now that the necessary goodwill had been exchanged. 'It's early days yet, but I'll be happy to co-operate. And as you obviously have my home number as well as the university's, there should be no difficulty getting in touch.'

'I'd like to ask you something else,' she put in quickly. 'I don't know if you know my paper. It probably gets pushed through your door twice a week. It's free, but we have a very good name for our news reporting. Earlier this evening I was speaking to the young schoolboy who was almost drowned at Pulteney Weir on Monday. He saw you on *Points West* tonight and thinks he recognized you. He believes you were the man who saved his life. Are you able to confirm it, Professor?'

I hedged. 'Why exactly are you asking me this, Miss Abershaw?'

'I thought that was obvious. It's a matter of public interest. It was a very brave act and it deserves to be written up.'

'But it *was* written up, on the day after it happened.'

'Yes, in the *Evening Chronicle*. They weren't able to reveal the name –'

'. . . of the shy hero.'

'Exactly.'

'And you're hoping to get an exclusive?'

'Was it you, Professor?'

Stupidly I admitted that it was, and from the elation that came down the line she might have turned a cartwheel. 'Listen, I don't want any fuss,' I added, too late, of course. 'Anyone would have done what I did, seeing the boy in difficulties.'

She laughed. 'That's a load of balls.'

'What did you say?'

'Give me a break. This story has been written a million times before without a single line being altered. Man saves child, or old lady, or kitten – and then walks away without identifying himself. And when he is finally traced, he says, "Anyone would have done the same thing". Would they – hell! These days, nine out of ten would look the other way.'

I took refuge in the same well-worn formula she was attacking. 'I don't know what you want from me, Miss Abershaw, but the incident is over, as far as I'm concerned.'

She said, 'My paper will print your name. I thought you might like to be credited with a few intelligent remarks. Would you mind if we sent a photographer round in the morning to get a picture of you?'

'Yes.'

'That's very good of you. Would about nine be convenient?'

'I said yes, I *would* mind. I'm not posing for pictures.'

With steel in her voice, she said, 'We are a major local newspaper, Professor. We work closely with the university, publicising events.'

'Agreed, but this isn't an event requiring publicity.'

'With respect, I believe it is.'

'We'll have to differ, then.'

Then she played her trump. 'Don't you want to know how young Matthew is getting on?'

There was a threat of adverse publicity here. I said without much show of concern, 'Right. Tell me. How is he?'

'He's fine, but he'd like to meet you and thank you personally.'

'Oh, no,' I said. 'I'm glad he's all right and that's the end of it, as far as I'm concerned. Thank you for calling, Miss Abershaw.' I put down the phone.

Out of curiosity mingled with apprehension, I picked up a copy of Molly Abershaw's paper the next day. It was even more embarrassing than I expected. The main story, in banner headlines, was:

The mystery man who leapt to the rescue of a schoolboy at Pulteney Weir last Monday and used the kiss of life to revive him was today revealed as a Bath University professor. He is Professor Gregory Jackman, thirty-seven, of Bathwick, who was appointed to the newly-created Chair of English in 1987. The *Evening Telegraph* this week appealed for help in tracing the hero of the rescue, who walked away from the scene without identifying himself. A number of our readers phoned with detailed descriptions of the man, but appropriately he was spotted by the boy he rescued, twelve-year-old Matthew Didrikson, from the Abbey Choir School. Matthew recognized the professor when he appeared on the *Points West* programme on television last night, in a filmed report about the Assembly Rooms.

Said Matthew when the *Telegraph* phoned him last night, 'I'm positive that the professor is the man who saved my life. I switched to the programme by chance and there he was. It was really amazing.'

The *Telegraph* contacted Professor Jackman late last night and he confirmed that he carried out the rescue. After making sure that Matthew was fully conscious and the ambulance was coming, he had walked away because, in his own words, 'The incident was over as far as I was concerned'. He said he was pleased to be told that Matthew has now made a complete recovery.

It made me squirm, of course, but I suppose it could have been more of an embarrassment. I had to be thankful that I'd given my last lecture that term, for the article would have been a perfect excuse for some kind of stunt from my students.

As it was, I planned a low-profile weekend. The only social occasion was a party that Waterstone's bookshop was throwing at lunchtime on Sunday to publicize a new book of poems by Ted Hughes, the Poet Laureate, who was coming to sign copies. I had never met Hughes, but I liked his work and the issues that he espoused, and I wanted to be there. If I could get away reasonably early I hoped to drive down to Hampshire later the same afternoon to look at the house where Jane Austen had once lived in the village of Chawton. It was set up as a museum, so I was duty-bound to make a visit there soon, on the cadge for exhibits.

The weekend was one of those precious, if uncanny, intervals in an English summer when the weathermen were prepared to hold out the prospect of sweltering heat. Across the nation last year's shorts were tried on for size and straw hats were dusted off. Tables and chairs appeared outside pubs and cafés. Sales of suntan lotions, insect creams, lager and lettuce increased phenomenally. And, unbeknown to me, my wife prepared to murder me.

On the Sunday morning, I needed to catch up on some office work, so I put in a few hours at the university before the sun made further work impossible. Then I drove down to Bath for the signing party, which was marred for me by an unexpected incident. When I arrived soon after twelve, the crush around the table on the first floor where Ted Hughes was already signing was a fine testimony to the literary taste of Bathonians, even if some had lowered the tone by climbing on to stools to get their sight of the great man. I looked for someone I knew and spotted a group of kindred spirits from the university. We were soon deep in discussion about trends in modern poetry.

The large woman who practically elbowed one of my companions aside and addressed me by name was unknown to me, although the voice was familiar. She introduced herself as Molly Abershaw, the reporter who had phoned me late on Thursday. I was peeved, to put it mildly. I reminded her that I had nothing else to say to the press.

Miss Abershaw had obviously had time to work out her battle-plan, whereas I was reacting predictably. On reflection, I may have over-reacted. She said with a smile that she wasn't there to get a statement, she simply wanted to introduce someone to me. Then she reached behind her and thrust a schoolboy in front of me – Matthew, the child I had pulled out of the weir. The poor kid looked thoroughly uncomfortable. Miss Abershaw tried to prompt him into some kind of statement of gratitude, but before he opened his mouth I said it was unnecessary.

You can imagine the mystification of the people I was with. They knew nothing of my adventure in the weir. But Molly Abershaw hadn't finished yet. She said that the boy's mother had come to meet me. By this time, I was in no frame of mind to be civil with anybody, and when a camera flashed and I realized that I had been well and truly set up, I acted fast. I grabbed the photographer, who was obviously from the newspaper, and insisted that he expose the film and hand it over. The wretched man was rigid with fear, and that's not a response I'm used to getting from people I meet. I demanded that roll of film and got it.

Not the sort of incident one expects at a literary party.

Chapter Six

AS SOON AS POSSIBLE AFTER the incident at Waterstone's I left the party. The drive to Chawton compelled me to think of other things. The cottage where Jane Austen spent the last eight years of her life is located this side of Alton, just off the A31, and is furnished as a museum by the Jane Austen Society, not a place I would normally have sought out, but the Steering Committee had concentrated my mind wonderfully. I took note of a number of items – manuscripts, family portraits and other memorabilia – that I decided were worth making enquiries about for a possible loan. My list didn't include the lock of Jane's hair recently dyed bright auburn, or the microphotographs of pieces of her skin still attached to the roots. I had ditched most of my donnish scruples, but there were limits, even with a hundred-foot Assembly Room to fill. Before leaving, I explained my interest to the curator and sounded him out about the possibility of borrowing items. It seemed I would have to approach the Society. There were the usual complications over insurance.

The worst of the day's heat had passed when I started for home, yet it was still an uncomfortable drive with the sun steadily penetrating the windscreen at a low angle. I stopped for a pint and a salad in Marlborough and got back to Bath shortly before nine – to an extra infliction. The mindless beat of disco music carried to me from my own garden even before I saw the line-up of large cars in the drive. I recognized a red Porsche and a grey vintage Bentley: Geraldine's Bristol crowd. The whiff of charcoal fumes and kebabs was in the air. A far cry from Jane Austen.

107

The front door stood open and a bearded man I had not met sat across the doorstep, tapping the disco rhythm with his fingertips on a 1935 Silver Jubilee biscuit tin belonging to me that was quite a collector's piece, and usually displayed on the Welsh dresser. 'Hi,' the man greeted me without looking up. 'What have you brought?'

'Nothing. I live here.'

Now the man raised his face to squint at me. 'With Gerry, you mean? Nice work, man. Want to come in?'

I stepped over his legs and walked through the house, and found Geraldine dancing on the patio opposite an estate agent called Roger, in striped shirt and red braces, who never missed these shindigs. Gerry gave me a wave. The music was deafening, so I turned down the volume.

Continuing to wriggle her hips, she called out, 'You're too early for the food. It needs another half-hour to get up some heat. You've got time to get into something more relaxing.' She was relaxing in an emerald green jumpsuit. Her feet were bare.

To say that I wasn't in the party mood would be an understatement. I said, 'For Christ's sake, Gerry – you might have told me you were planning this.'

'Didn't get the chance, dear heart. You were up and away too early this morning. Never mind, I've fixed you up with a date.'

'What?'

'A date. Skirt, or whatever charming expression you fellows use these days.' The cassette ran out and she stopped dancing and came over to me and tried to loosen my tie. Her manner was elated in a way that it rarely was when I was alone with her. I guessed she was on vodka, because I couldn't smell drink on her breath. 'So get yourself into something sexy,' she told me. 'She'll be here any minute.'

I said, 'Jump in the pool, Gerry.'

'I'm not shooting a line,' she persisted. 'This woman with a name like a man's called on the phone an hour ago and asked for you. Wait, it's coming to me. Some nineteen-forties film star with dreamy eyes and a trilby. Dana Andrews. That was it. Her name is Dana.'

'I don't know anyone called Dana.'

'You will shortly. She was so desperate to speak to you that I invited her to my barbecue. She's the mother of that schoolkid you rescued from the river.'

'Mrs Didrikson.' It had been that sort of day. 'You birdbrain. Those people are a menace. They turned up at the Ted Hughes signing.'

'What's come over you, shyboots?' said Geraldine. 'I thought publicity was meat and drink to you.'

'Not this local hero stuff. I've had a bellyful. Look, I'm not having the press invading my house – least of all while this is going on.'

'She's coming alone, she told me,' said Geraldine.

'Yes, and pigs might fly.'

I went up to the bedroom, picked some fresh clothes off the hangers, looked into the *en suite*, discovered a woman already using the shower, and had to wash in the bathroom instead. And would you believe it, someone had removed the mirror from the wall.

My first idea had been to tell Geraldine to give the Didrikson woman her marching orders the moment she arrived. But Gerry couldn't be relied on, even when sober. I would do it myself. I dressed, returned downstairs, stepped over the man in the doorway and looked in the drive to see if another car had arrived yet. I walked out to the road. It was completely dark by now and blessedly cool.

In my days as a smoker this would have been a fine time to light up. I had no desire to join Geraldine's barbecue. I had nothing in common with her friends, although I was resigned to joining them ultimately. Trying to sleep would be futile.

I heard the approach of a car from the direction of Bath. Before it came into view, the headlights on full beam glowed high above the walls and hedges. Its progress was slow, as if the driver was looking for a particular house. Then the car itself appeared and the lights dipped. A Mercedes. It halted just across the road from where I was standing, but no one got out.

The driver was a dark-haired woman. She wound down

the window and said, 'Would I be better off parking in the road?'

'Are you here for the barbecue?'

'Not exactly,' she said, hesitating. 'You *are* Professor Jackman?'

'That's right, but my wife is giving the party. You can park there if you like. Not much comes along at this time of night.'

She said, 'I think we're at cross-purposes. I just wanted a few minutes with you, Professor.'

'You're Mrs Didrikson?' I hadn't expected the woman to arrive in a Mercedes.

'That's right. Didn't you get the message that I was coming?'

'If you want to talk, this isn't the place,' I said, seized with a pleasing thought. I could outflank Molly Abershaw, who had no doubt set up this meeting, and escape the party for a while by getting a lift to the nearest pub. 'It would be easier in my local – the Viaduct. Do you have any objections?'

She hesitated. 'Well, no – if that's what you'd like,' she said.

I got in, chatted about the weather and the tourists for a mile and admired the way she took the Mercedes round the tight bends on Brassknocker Hill. She handled it as if she enjoyed her driving. I was curious why she hadn't chosen to drive something more like a sports car, for she was really too short for the Mercedes. She was propped up on two thick cushions.

The pub was busy. As she wanted something non-alcoholic, I suggested a St Clement's and ordered a large cognac for myself.

'I was so upset by what happened in Waterstone's today that I had to get in touch with you,' she plunged in as soon as we had our drinks. 'Believe me, it came as a total shock to Matthew and me when that photographer appeared. We were there in the belief that it was a chance to meet you informally and thank you for what you did. It seemed a good idea when Molly Abershaw suggested it. Now I'm kicking myself for being so dumb. Can you forgive me?'

I had given her no more than a glance in Waterstone's. The incident had been so unexpected that I had barely registered who the boy was before the camera flashed and triggered my angry reaction. Dana Didrikson's deep-set brown eyes now studied me with apprehension as she awaited my response. She didn't look as if she was out for more publicity. The shape of her face, the high forehead and neat mouth and chin, suggested intelligence without guile. Her small hands were clasped tightly.

I said, 'Forget it, Mrs Didrikson. I blew my top, and I'm not too proud about that. Your son has fully recovered from the ducking, I hope.'

'Completely,' she said. 'I can't dismiss it just like that. Not without thanking you for saving his life — and words seem totally inadequate.'

'All right,' I said, smiling. 'In a moment you can buy me a drink and we'll both feel easier.'

'And the cleaning bill for your clothes?'

'They were due for cleaning anyway.'

'I should think the suit must have been ruined.'

I shook my head. 'You don't know my dry-cleaner. He's a genius, an artist. He should be restoring Leonardo's frescoes. Instead he has my trousers to clean.'

She was one of those women whose beauty is in their smile. 'And now I've taken you away from your party.'

'My wife's party,' I told her. 'Isn't it truer to say that I've taken *you* away from it? Gerry invited you, didn't she?'

'Oh, I didn't intend to stay.' She blushed. 'Sorry — that sounds rude. I'm rather tired. It's been a heavy week.'

'What's your job?'

'I'm a company driver, for a brewery.'

'You sound like someone worth getting to know.'

Another quick, self-conscious smile. 'I don't get samples. And the car belongs to the firm.'

'Is it hard work?' I asked.

'I have to earn a living.'

'Are you, er . . .?'

'Divorced.' She said it evenly, without emotion. 'Mat's father went back to Norway. We married too young.'

'Is it difficult to raise a son? I don't have children.'

She looked down at her drink, considering the answer. I particularly noticed that – the fact that she didn't trot out some superficial statement. 'It's a matter of being alert to the way he develops. Mat's twelve now, coming up to Common Entrance. He's coming to terms with manhood. He's neither small boy nor man. I keep reminding myself not to be too surprised by his behaviour. My worry is that he'll lose his respect for me. How am I going to be a support to him if he disregards me? I see signs of it and I'm torn between checking him and clutching him to my bosom.'

'Difficult. Does he have any contact with his father?'

'No. We don't hear from Sverre. Mat is fiercely proud of his dad's reputation – he's a chess international – and he has a collection of press-cuttings and some photos I gave him, but it's like worshipping a wooden idol. There's no response.' She drew back from the table and flicked her dark hair behind her shoulders. 'How did I start on this? Are you ready for that second drink?'

I watched her carry the glasses to the bar, exchanging some banter with a couple of men she recognized at another table. She was small, yet she conducted herself with confidence. Work must have toughened her. I felt privileged that she had been willing to tell me about her conflict in being both mother and father to Matthew. When she returned with the drinks, though, she made clear her wish to turn to other matters.

'Did I catch it right on television the other night – are you putting on an exhibition about Jane Austen?'

'Under protest, yes. I drew the short straw. In my spare moments I drive around southern England looking for exhibits. There's a worrying shortage. If you hear of a firescreen she embroidered or a bonnet she wore going cheap, I'm the man to contact.'

'*Anything* to do with her?'

'Absolutely. Strictly speaking, it's the *Jane Austen in Bath* Exhibition, but I won't turn any offer down – lace handkerchiefs, teapots, old shoes, tennis rackets.'

'Tennis – in Jane Austen's time?'

'Joke – I've got to fill the Assembly Rooms with something.'

'She lived in Gay Street, didn't she?'

'She did, indeed. Forgive me being tactless, but how did you know that?'

'It's part of a project Matthew is doing at school.'

'Obviously I should enlist Matthew's help. Yes, apart from Gay Street there were three other houses in the city where the Austen family resided: in Sydney Place, Green Park Buildings and Trim Street. She also stayed at Queen Square before the family moved here, and at 1, The Paragon, where her scandalous old aunt lived.'

'Jane Austen had a scandalous aunt?'

Now that I had vilified Aunt Jane and made Mrs Didrikson curious, I felt duty-bound to tell the story. 'It's been rather glossed over in the biographies. The aunt may have had The Paragon for her address, but she wasn't such a paragon herself. She was put on trial for shoplifting, which was a capital offence. She was supposed to have stolen some lace from a milliner's. Do you know the dress shop on the corner of Bath Street and Stall Street, just opposite the entrance to the Baths?'

'You mean Principles.'

I smiled at the name. 'There's irony. Yes, that would be on the site of the shop. Well, one August afternoon in 1799, Aunt Jane bought a card of black lace there and walked out with a card of white that she hadn't paid for. Shortly afterwards, the manageress stopped her in the street and challenged her. Aunt Jane claimed that they must have made a mistake in the shop, but they pressed charges and she spent seven months in custody waiting for her case to come up.'

'That must have been an ordeal in those days.'

'It could have been worse. Because she moved in elevated circles, she was allowed to lodge in the warden's house instead of a prison cell and her husband moved in with her. Jane Austen almost went too. Her mother offered the services of Jane and her sister Cassandra as additional company, but the accommodation wouldn't stretch to it.'

'Good material for a writer.'

'Whether Jane would have thought so is another

question. The warden's wife had a habit of licking her knife clean after cooking fried onions and then using it to butter the bread.'

Mrs Didrikson grimaced. 'But I suppose it was preferable to bread and water. What happened at the trial?'

'Aunt Jane was acquitted eventually, and it used to be accepted that the poor old biddy was the victim of a trumped-up charge and perjured evidence, but modern writers who have analysed the quality of the evidence are more sceptical. She seems to have got off mainly on the strength of her reputation as an upright citizen. Witnesses galore were called to defend her character – members of parliament, a peer of the realm, clergymen and shop-keepers. All this was stressed by the judge in his address to the jury, coupled with the suggestion that a rich, respectable woman had no need to go shoplifting.'

'Which is not necessarily the case,' she remarked. 'Rich women do steal. There can be motives other than personal hardship.'

I nodded. 'Lucky for Aunt Jane that post-Freudian psychology hadn't been heard of in 1800.'

'Still, it *is* fascinating. I hope you can use the story in your exhibition.'

'I dare say I will. You see, it's not so peripheral as it first appears if you think what might have happened if the jury had convicted Aunt Jane.'

'Hanging?'

'Realistically, transportation. She would have ended up in Botany Bay. And then the Austen family almost certainly wouldn't have come to live in Bath the year after the acquittal. They lodged with her while they looked for a house of their own. *Northanger Abbey* and *Persuasion* might never have been written.'

'Ah, but who knows what else might have come from Jane's pen? Was she a blood relative?'

'No, Aunt Jane was a Cholmeley. She married Uncle James and became Mrs Leigh Perrot.'

'Mrs what?'

'Two words: Leigh and Perrot. She lived to a great age – over ninety.'

'Innocence rewarded?'

I shook my head. ' "The good die early, and the bad die late." '

The softening of her features each time she smiled challenged me to amuse her more. Before I tried again, however, she hoisted her bag on her shoulder and said, 'I don't want to seem rude, but would you like me to drive you back?'

'Already?'

'I shouldn't keep you from your guests.'

'I'm not too anxious to get back to the barbecue. Ah, but you said you were tired,' I recalled. 'I shouldn't have started on my Aunt Jane story.' I drank up. 'Let's go.'

Chapter Seven

AS THE MERCEDES CRUISED UP the winding incline of Brassknocker Hill, I said, 'I've been thinking about your son. This may sound stupid after what happened, but does he like swimming?'

'I think so,' Mrs Didrikson answered. 'He can manage a length or so. It isn't his strongest sport, by any means. They don't do enough at the school. Too much of their time goes on singing, in my opinion. I shouldn't complain, should I, as I was daft enough in the first place to send him to a choir school?'

'What I'm leading up to is that we have a pool at the university. Oddly enough, it isn't much used at this time of year when most other pools are crowded. Nearly all the students have gone down. Do you think he would enjoy a swim?'

'Professor, you've done more than enough for Mat already.'

'I'd like to meet him again. After all, he and I did meet first in the water.'

She smiled faintly. 'He wouldn't remember much about that.'

'He'll remember the rebuff he got from me in the bookshop this morning. An incident like that can be wounding to a kid his age. I'd like to show him that it was nothing personal. How about one evening after school?'

The road ahead levelled out. After thinking about it for a moment she answered, 'I'm sure he would enjoy it.'

'Tuesday?'

'All right. I'll bring him in the car.'

'Say about seven? Why don't you join us?'

She answered tersely, as if she had seen the invitation coming, 'No, thank you.'

I had meant only to be civil and I underlined this by saying neutrally, 'Just as you wish. Do you know where the pool is at Claverton?'

She laughed. 'You're talking to a former taxi driver.'

A Rolling Stones number boomed across Bathwick Hill when we stopped in the road opposite the house. Near-hysterical shrieks issued from the back garden.

'Good thing your neighbours don't live too close,' Mrs Didrikson commented. 'When we have a barbecue we have to watch the decibels.'

'And I'm willing to bet that the moment you strike the first match there's always someone who pointedly marches out to take her washing off the line.'

'Always.'

'Will you come in for a drink? A bite to eat? A quick kebab?'

'Thank you, but I'd like to get back and tell Mat how this turned out. He was rather anxious.'

I understood. I knew from the way that she spoke that it wasn't just an excuse. I got out, wished her goodnight and watched her reverse the Mercedes in a neat arc and drive back at speed in the direction of Bath. A capable woman. Beneath that armour-suit of independence was a person of wit and integrity, qualities I rate highly.

The night was clammy, with barely a breeze. The temperature had not dropped much since sundown. The smell of fried bacon mingled not unpleasantly with the heavy scent of honeysuckle. I strolled around the side of the house in the direction of all the noise.

The floodlights around the swimming pool had been switched on and most of the party were standing around it, being entertained by three women and two men who had stripped off all their clothes and were chasing each other around the perimeter, with the object of pushing someone else into the water before they themselves took a ducking. Geraldine's friends like to think of themselves as feisty – the feistiest people around – and the strain showed at times. I automatically assumed that Gerry was one of the three until I spotted her still in her jumpsuit, merely in the role of observer, her hand hooked over the shoulder of Roger the estate agent. The chase around the pool reminded me of a series of cartoons by James Thurber called *The Race of Life*, the naked figures pale, paunchy and intense, more quaint than erotic. It was impossible to say how long this had been going on, but the screams and laughter were forced at this stage, as if bestowed out of charity. At last one man was caught from two directions and he leapt off the side, tugging two women in with him. A mighty splash, hoots of laughter, and then the others plunged in as well. It would not be long before they were singing, 'Come and join us', and grasping for the ankles of anyone rash enough to stand close to the edge.

I remember looking at my watch and recalling Mr Woodhouse's dictum in *Emma* that the sooner every party breaks up, the better. Mr Woodhouse, a standard-bearer for the modern obsession with health, would undoubtedly have had something pertinent to say on the perils of skinny-dipping.

Turning my back on the pool, I wandered across to the patio, where the barbecue wanted some attention if I was to cook myself a steak. With a hand-shovel I drew some ash off the charcoal to reveal glowing embers and fanned them into more activity. The meat was set out on a tray covered with wire mesh. Plenty was left. I lifted the cover, picked up a steak and some bacon, tomato pieces and mushrooms and spread them on the grid above the fire.

Presently I was conscious of somebody at my side. Geraldine looped her arm around mine and said, 'Where have you been hiding all evening?'

'I went out for a bit. Enjoying your party?'

'Immensely., Didn't your lady friend turn up after all?'

'She came. She couldn't stay.'

'Pity.' She looked at the steak. 'I saved enough for both of you. You must be famished by now. Want me to take over?'

'There's no need. You go back to your friends.'

'They don't need me. They'll only drag me in the pool and ruin my clothes. Listen to them.' She picked up a fork and turned over a slice of the bacon. 'Besides, I can't neglect my nearest and dearest.'

'Your snake in the grass, you mean.'

'What?'

'You called me a snake in the grass the other day. I'm suppose to be plotting God knows what with your doctor.'

She squeezed my arm. 'Darling, you know me by now. I'm a Leo. I can't help my personality. I roared a bit, as Leos do, that's all. Could you blow on the charcoal, or the steak will never get done? I saved some of my home-made sauce for you. They were on it like vultures. It's in the house.'

'Where?' I asked. 'I'll get it.'

'It's all right. You keep an eye on this. I know where I tucked it out of sight.'

I moved the tomatoes to the side of the grill to stop them from burning, my mind on other things. Almost enough material was now promised for the exhibition. The next challenge was how to present it interestingly. My earlier reluctance to get involved had been supplanted by a strong desire to make a success of the show. I still refused to make it a paean to life in Bath. I was resolved that Jane's feelings about the city should be scrupulously represented.

Then Gerry was back with a jug of sauce. 'You're going to enjoy this. Got a plate?'

I picked one up from where they were stacked. 'Hey, don't drown it.'

Too late; she had liberally coated everything. She said, 'Why don't you come down to the pool with it? You know most of them.'

'Thanks. I'll eat it here, while it's hot.'

'You don't really hit it off with my wacky friends, do you, Prof?'

'I'm not complaining.'

'I'll make some coffee in a mo and move the whole thing indoors. They'll be glad of a warm drink after their dip.' She cleared some plates from a table and handed me a knife and fork, and a paper napkin. 'Listen, I knew you'd be wanting some sleep after being out all day, so I made up the camp-bed in the summerhouse. You can slip away whenever you wish. They won't disturb you there. I left half a bottle of Courvoisier and a pack of cigars beside the bed.'

Such wifely consideration was so rare from Gerry that I at once suspected an ulterior motive. I found it difficult to believe – even of Gerry – that she would have the gall to invite her admiring estate agent up to the bedroom while her own husband spent a night in the garden, but what other construction was there to put on it?

I said, 'I'm not tired.'

'That's all right, then,' said Gerry with such implacable charm that I was reassured. 'Just remember it's there if you want to escape before the party finally breaks up.'

She went off towards the house, leaving me alone on the patio eating my supper. The food was good, the sauce a trifle too peppery for my taste. I scraped some off the steak. Presently I was aware of someone standing nearby, holding a beer glass. It was Roger, the estate agent, his moon face glowing greenly in the artificial light.

'Hello there, brother Gregory. What's this – second helpings?'

I gave him a look without much fraternity in it. 'I only just got here. I've been out.'

'Business or pleasure? The latter, I hope. Six days shalt thou labour.'

'. . . and have a barbecue on the seventh?'

Roger laughed. 'Speaking of labour, I have to be at my charming best in the office tomorrow morning.'

'Gerry's making coffee,' I informed him.

'I think we'll have to skip it. Have you seen anything of Val?'

'Val?'

'My wife.'

'Er, no.' I refrained from adding that I'd always assumed Roger was a bachelor from the way he carried on with Gerry.

'She was one of the first in the pool,' said Roger.

'Perhaps she's gone indoors to get dry.'

'No, there she is!' said Roger, and called out, 'Val, darling, we're about to leave. Come and say goodbye to your host.'

Val came over. By this time, she had got back into her clothes. When dressed, and with her damp hair flat to her head, she looked even more like one of James Thurber's creations. Her stare was withering. 'So you're the husband.'

I felt like the owner of an unruly dog.

Roger smiled feebly and said, 'She means thank you for having us. Come on, my water nymph. Party's over for you and me. Nighty-night, Greg.'

They moved off around the side of the house. Presently I heard their car start up and move away. I wondered if Gerry knew they had left.

When I had finished eating I strolled across to the house for a coffee. There, I couldn't avoid getting into conversation with some people who were vaguely connected with the Bristol Old Vic and wanted to impress me with their theatrical gossip. The vagueness was more of my making than theirs because unusually my concentration had started slipping. Black coffee didn't help. I was getting more weary by the minute.

Unable to listen any longer, I muttered some excuse and wandered out through the patio door. All that I could think about was that camp-bed in the summerhouse. I moved as if wearing one of those early diving suits with weighted boots. It wasn't the drink that had done this; I'd had nothing since the cognacs in the pub and they never make me sleepy. Then I was conscious of pointed heels clattering on the patio behind me, and Gerry was at my side.

'Greg, are you all right?'

'Just tired,' I answered, and I heard myself slurring the words. 'Going to bed now.'

'Can you make it that far?'

'Yes.'

My thigh came painfully into contact with a table. I turned my head, but Gerry had already gone back to her party. The impact sharpened my wits momentarily. I thought, I've been given something. I'm drugged. I groped across the table and found the mustard-dish, pulled it towards me, scooped up a generous amount on

121

my finger and pushed it into the back of my throat. Instantly I retched, staggered to a tub of geraniums and heaved up as much as I could of the barbecue supper. My head spun when I raised it. I still felt profoundly tired. I thrust my finger down my throat a second time, with a result almost as copious. The sweat on my forehead turned icy. Down the patio steps I tottered, then perilously around the edge of the pool, across the lawn and as far as the summerhouse, an octagonal wooden structure open to the elements on two sides.

True to her promise, Gerry had made up the camp-bed there. I dropped on to it like a felled tree, too exhausted to remove even my shoes.

It felt as if I were levitating. Not a pleasant sensation.

Home-made sauce, I thought, as I pushed my finger down my throat again.

The next thing I knew was when I stirred, opened my eyes, and tried to remember where I was. It was still dark and quiet, yet something had disturbed me. My limbs felt heavy and my thinking was slow. I closed my eyes again.

Another sound, a movement close to me.

I remembered that I was in the summerhouse and that it was open on two sides. Possibly a breeze had got up and disturbed something. But the sound had been heavy, as if some living thing were in there with me. A fox? They sometimes crossed the garden.

Without otherwise moving, I opened my eyes. A faint light from the moon enabled me to make out a human figure – Geraldine, wearing a dark tracksuit. I wondered vaguely why she had come, but I was too weary to supply an explanation. I was too weary even to ask her.

I closed my eyes again.

A faint bubbling sound broke through my muzzy perceptions, as if liquid were being poured from a narrow-necked bottle. I looked, and that was exactly what was happening. Gerry was emptying the Courvoisier bottle, holding it upside down so that the contents tipped on to the floor. I registered that she must be drunk to do such a crazy thing. Too dazed to intervene, I observed her passively, as if watching a surrealist film too bizarre to interpret.

When the bottle was empty, Gerry turned, bent down and picked up another that she must have brought in. She unscrewed it and began liberally dowsing everything, including the bed. I murmured a protest that came out as a Neanderthal-sounding series of grunts.

Geraldine ignored me. Next she picked a cigar from the box she had left by the bed, put a match to it and started smoking! Extraordinary — she never touched cigars. I watched her put it to her mouth and draw on it so that the tip smouldered and glowed. Then she crouched down and it was difficult to see her.

My eyelids drooped. It had been an effort to keep them open so long.

Sightless I may have been, but my sense of smell continued to function. I sniffed and caught the acrid whiff of smoke. It crept into my nostrils and made me open my mouth and cough. I heard a hissing sound. I opened my eyes and saw that the bed was on fire. Not merely the bed, but the entire floor was alight with trails of fizzing blue flame.

If I continue to lie here, I thought, I'm going to be incinerated with the summerhouse.

PART THREE
The Men in White Coats

Chapter One

THE INCIDENT ROOM IN MANVERS Street Police Station was not as crowded as the caravan had been. Paperclips no longer danced in their boxes each time Peter Diamond walked across the floor. Nor could the filing clerks feel his breath on the backs of their necks. Loose papers and file cards were not so likely to be brushed off the edges of desks. The carousel of cards, instead of dominating the room, had been relegated to a corner. Four Trojan horses – as Diamond dubbed them – in the form of computer terminals, stood on a table near the door. The Police Committee had decreed that no major inquiry should be without its computer back-up, irrespective of the prejudices of one cantankerous detective.

'We'll soon have them up and running, sir,' Inspector Dalton, who came with the computers and four civilian operators, had rashly promised.

To this, Diamond had responded, 'Up where? Up yours, as far as I'm concerned.'

Apart from that, the air of desperation beside the lake had been supplanted by confidence. They were working to a purpose now. In the hackneyed, but comforting phrase, a man was assisting the police with their inquiries. He had been in the interview room for an hour and a half.

Diamond and John Wigfull came out for a sandwich. Neither was wearing a jacket. The Last Detective was in his element. He had loosened his tie and unfastened the top button of his shirt. His confidence was high and he wanted everyone to know. He didn't so much as glance at the computer screens. He expected all fresh developments in the case to come from the interviewing of Professor

Jackman. With his weight securely deposited on a desk, he snapped open a can of beer and remarked to Wigfull, 'You know what this amounts to – this story about the fire?'

Wigfull waited. He was no reader of minds.

'He's laying the foundations for his defence,' Diamond said. 'Mentally he's already in court, pleading mitigation. She tried to kill him on this previous occasion, so when it happened a second time he defended himself. Didn't know his own strength. Panicked. Tried to get rid of the body by dumping it in the lake. See if I'm not right, John.'

Wigfull's eyebrows were raised. 'That isn't the way he told it yesterday.'

Diamond was unmoved. 'They always start by giving you the clean-as-driven-snow gambit. Left her sleeping peacefully and never saw her again. He's had plenty of time to concoct his story. That's only his first line of defence. He doesn't really expect to hold it long and he won't.'

'You think he's ready to admit he killed her?'

'Not yet. Jackman's got a good head on his shoulders, remember. First, he wants to win us over and show himself in the best possible light. But this stuff about the summer-house, this shows how his mind is working.'

'You don't believe it, sir?'

Diamond said nothing, letting his silence make the point.

'The summerhouse *was* burned down,' Wigfull pointed out.

'Agreed. Did he report it at the time? No. He can give it any slant he wants.'

'Should we ask forensic to take a look at the site, see if the evidence bears out his story?'

'It's already in hand.' Diamond couldn't help sounding smug. He enjoyed keeping mentally ahead of Wigfull, who was no idiot. With the air of an achiever, he tugged at the packet containing the egg and cress sandwich he had ordered. 'Mind you, the lab will take weeks to come up with anything helpful. You and I can crack this today.' Unable to find a way into the packet, he squeezed it. The result was a pulverized sandwich. Furious, he flung the whole thing at the nearest waste-bin and missed.

'Want one of mine, sir – lettuce and tomato?' offered

Wigfull.

'Rabbit food. Let's have another go at him. I need an early supper tonight.'

'Are you going to caution him?'

A guarded look closed over Diamond's blunt features. 'Is that advice, or what?'

Wigfull reddened. 'I thought if we have reasonable grounds, we ought to issue the caution.'

Diamond jabbed a finger against his assistant's shirt-front. 'Don't ever tell me my job, Inspector. What I told you just now – about his guilt – was a gut feeling. If you and I are going to work as a team you'd better get one thing straight: if I speak my thoughts aloud, that's my privilege. If I want yours, I'll bloody ask for them. Understood?'

'Understood, sir.'

'I cautioned him last night, before he said a bloody word to me. Remind him when we go in.'

Professor Jackman glanced down at his watch as they returned. He seemed so well in control that he might have been about to put the questions to them. On the desk in front of him was an empty mug and one biscuit, the last of a packet of three. Diamond reached for it and scooped it into his mouth in one rapid movement.

The constable taking shorthand slipped in unobtrusively behind them and took her place to the rear of Jackman, just as Wigfull was reinforcing the caution.

Diamond didn't waste time over small-talk. 'Getting back to the fire in the summerhouse, Professor, I take it that you got out without serious injury.'

Jackman's response was even more to the point. 'Yes.'

'You managed to rouse yourself when you sensed the danger?'

'Not without difficulty. It took an exceptional effort.'

'You're certain that you were drugged?'

'I'm convinced of it. She must have used the phenobarbitone she had from the doctor. God knows how many tablets she'd crushed and mixed in the sauce she gave me. If I hadn't made myself sick, as I told you, I wouldn't have recovered consciousness at all.'

'You were lucky.'

'You can say that again. In a matter of seconds I would have been incinerated. My shoes and trousers were smouldering when I got out.'

'I suppose it's too much to hope that you kept them?'

'The shoes and trousers? I threw them away. They were no use any more.' His eyes narrowed. 'You *do* believe what I'm telling you?'

Diamond answered equivocally, 'I saw the burnt-out summerhouse.' He leaned back in his chair and clasped his hands behind his neck. 'What interests me, Professor, is what happened next. Your wife had tried to kill you. What did you do about it?'

'I was in no state to do anything. I flopped down on the lawn at a safe distance from the flames and watched the fire burn itself out. I still had some of the drug in my system and I must have fallen asleep, because the next thing I knew it was daylight and I was aching in every bone. Everything seemed like a dream except that I had in front of me the heap of ashes that had been the summerhouse. I went into the house to look for my wife. She'd behaved like a madwoman but she was no fool. She'd quit the place.'

'How did you know?'

'Her car wasn't in the garage.'

'So what did you do?'

'Slept a few hours more. I was still too muzzy to go looking for her. And when I came to, I started slowly clearing up after the party. I needed to occupy myself in a practical way.'

Rebuking him mildly, as if remarking on a social gaffe, Diamond said, 'You didn't notify us.'

'You?'

'The police.'

'I wanted Gerry's explanation.'

'But you didn't know where she was. She could have killed herself. People frequently do after murdering a spouse.'

Jackman said dryly, 'People clever enough to dress up a murder as an accident don't spoil it by committing suicide. I knew she would come back.'

130

Diamond exchanged a glance with John Wigfull. 'You're telling us you just started clearing the dishes?'

Jackman rested his elbows on the table and leaned forward to make a point. 'Look, I'm here of my own free will. I'm telling you what happened. I don't expect to have my behaviour called into question.'

With the air of a man whose behaviour had been questioned too many times to matter any more, Diamond commented, 'We're simply trying to understand why things turned out as they did. Let's move on, shall we? When *did* you see your wife again?'

'The same day, early that evening.'

'She came back to the house?'

'Yes.' Jackman related the events with a directness that was vivid and convincing. 'She didn't come into the house immediately. I watched her leave the car on the drive and walk around the side to the garden. She was wearing the black tracksuit that I remembered seeing her in. She stood for a moment staring at the gutted summerhouse. She didn't go too close to it, just stood about thirty yards away, fingering her hair. Then she turned and approached the house. She came in by the patio windows, which were still open.' He smiled slightly. 'Of course, she was shocked out of her skin when she saw me sitting in front of the TV with my feet up. She damned near passed out. I had to pour her a drink. I didn't accuse her right out. I wanted to see what she would make of it, so I asked where she'd been all day. She said she'd gone out early and spent the day on a deckchair in Parade Gardens catching up on her sleep. She said she couldn't face being in the house. Quite possibly she was telling the truth.'

'And what happened when you *did* broach the little matter of the fire?'

'She denied it, naturally. Said I must have dreamed the bit about her coming into the summerhouse. She insisted that I must have dropped a lighted cigar and set light to the place myself – which you can bet is the story she would have put about if she'd succeeded in killing me. There's no chance that it was true,' Jackman said quickly, as if sensing that he'd given them an opening. 'In the first place, she definitely drugged me.'

'Let's say that someone drugged you,' said Diamond.

Jackman was quick to scotch that amendment. 'Listen, Geraldine had the drug in her possession. She had the sauce put aside for me. She insisted on collecting it herself. She poured it all over the food. Within a short time of eating it, I was three parts slewed. She'd put the cigars and the spirits ready beside the camp-bed in the summerhouse. It was all set up. And I'm certain it wasn't a dream when I saw her there because I noticed what she was wearing. She was still wearing that black tracksuit when she came back the next day.'

'You mentioned that already. You've been over this many times in your mind, haven't you?'

Jackman nodded. 'And the conclusion is irresistible.'

'All right, Professor,' said Diamond cheerfully, as if he accepted every word of the story. 'Why do you think it happened?'

'Why did she try to kill me?'

'Yes.'

Jackman lodged his face ruminatively against his hand. 'I put it down to her mental state. As I explained, some time before that evening she was showing symptoms of paranoia. She imagined I was plotting her downfall, or something. It was illusory, a fantasy, but plainly very real to her. I didn't appreciate how serious her mental state had become – until that night.'

'Did she have any history of disturbance?'

'Only what I've described. I'm no psychiatrist.'

'Paranoia,' Diamond repeated, and with a gleam of mischief looked across at the constable taking notes. 'Do you want the professor to spell that?'

The PC shook her head.

Diamond swung back to Jackman. 'And how about you? Did you feel persecuted?'

Jackman tensed and drew back from the desk. 'What?'

'Persecuted or threatened, at least. I should think you were entitled to feel like that after what happened.'

'I wouldn't describe it in those terms.'

'Would you care to describe it in your own terms then?'

The professor hesitated, and when he spoke it was with reluctance, as if he were being drawn into alien territory. 'Naturally there was a loss of trust on my part. I had to be on my guard in future.'

'You thought you could look after yourself?'

'She wasn't going to rush at me with an axe, or something. At least, that's the way I saw it. A lot of planning had gone into the summerhouse incident, mainly to ensure that the killing would be passed off as an accident. She didn't want to be caught. If she plotted another attempt on my life, I thought I was capable of picking up the signals before it got really dangerous.'

'Brave man,' commented Diamond, without actually meaning it.

Jackman leaned forward to solicit more understanding. 'When you've lived with a person, married them, shared their joys and disappointments, you've got to believe you have some influence, some hope of making sense to them. Okay, the magic had gone from our marriage, but we didn't have to destroy each other.'

There was a silence. Neither Diamond nor Wigfull would say one word to deflect him from what sounded like the beginning of a confession.

Jackman appeared to see the expectation in their eyes, because he said, 'I'll put that another way. I was willing to take my share of responsibility for what had happened. We'd made mistakes in our marriage. I'd alienated Gerry by failing to reach out to her mentally. The best thing I could do was try and remove the suspicions she harboured.'

'Give her the benefit of the doubt?'

'There *was* no doubt,' said Jackman flatly. 'She tried to kill me and failed. The fact that I knew for certain was my safeguard.'

Someone tapped on the door and opened it. Diamond wheeled around in his chair, ready to raise hell. He couldn't abide interruptions when he was interviewing a witness. But the intruder was the police doctor, accompanied by a constable carrying a kidney-shaped steel bowl containing a syringe and other items. 'Ah,' said

Diamond, reconciled. He turned back to address Jackman, whose face was a study in disbelief and alarm, 'I asked the doctor to step in. We'd like to take a sample of your blood for the forensic lab. It's a routine procedure. I take it we can rely on your co-operation?'

'Just a blood sample?'

Diamond grinned unkindly. 'What did you expect – a truth drug?'

Chapter Two

WHILE THE TWO DETECTIVES STOOD outside, Wigfull took the opportunity to ask, 'What's next?' His superior wasn't much of a communicator.

'This.' Diamond picked up a book and held it at the level of his shoulder as if he were about to swear an oath in court, except that the book had a laminated cover of pink elephants. 'Geraldine's address book.'

'You want to go through the names?'

Diamond confirmed it with a grin. 'With the help of our friend in there, of course. Let's give him some rope, John.'

'And see if he hangs himself?'

'You're out of date, chum.'

Wigfull nodded. Diamond's views on the death penalty were well known. He firmly believed Britain's decline as a world power could be traced back to 1964, the year of abolition. This wasn't the moment to get him on that old hobbyhorse. 'How will he give himself away?'

'By pointing the finger at someone else.'

'To sidetrack us, do you mean?'

'*Assist* us,' Diamond said, affecting a pained look. 'We don't want to make any premature assumptions about our professor, do we? He is co-operating to the best of his ability. You're a devious bastard.'

'You're a sarcastic one,' said Wigfull.

Diamond beamed.

When they returned to the interview room, they found Jackman buttoning his cuff, looking less self-assured than he had previously appeared. 'Why did you want my blood?' he asked at once.

'You make me sound like a vampire,' said Diamond. 'I

135

told you. It's standard procedure these days. Have you heard of genetic fingerprinting?'

'Yes, but what does it have to do with me?'

'There were traces of blood on the quilt of your wife's bed.'

'I didn't notice any.'

'They weren't very obvious.'

After a pause that was open to several interpretations, Jackman asked, 'Was she attacked in bed, then?'

'That's impossible to say yet. We don't even know if the blood was her own. There may be a perfectly innocent explanation if she scratched herself accidentally, as we all do from time to time. Or it may be significant. Either way, we won't know this side of next week. The forensic science lab isn't noted for quick results. And if your sample happens to match the bloodstains, I'm sure there's an innocent explanation. We can talk about it now if you want.'

Jackman shook his head. 'We'd be wasting our time.'

'As you wish.' Diamond dropped the address book on the table and they began the process of going through names. Whether anyone's address book is an indication of character is debatable, but Geraldine Jackman's was chaotic. For the few full names and addresses that appeared under each letter, many more were entered under forenames alone, often with no address listed, only a phone number. Some were circled or heavily underlined and many were scored through. Additional jottings had been added on most pages, times of trains, appointments, bank balances and densely-patterned doodles strung across the entries like an illustrated guide to cobwebs. A detective of the school of Sherlock Holmes would surely have deduced enough from those elaborate pages to convict the murderer and state exactly how the crime had been committed and when. Diamond's more workaday method was to observe Jackman's demeanour and listen to his comments as together the three men attempted to compile a list of Geraldine's friends.

Painstakingly, in the course of the next hour and a half, the task was completed – or as nearly completed as it was ever likely to be. By concentrating on local addresses and phone numbers, Jackman identified more than thirty of his wife's friends of the past two years. A scattering of names remained mysteries, but his willingness to assist was not in doubt. He went meticulously through the book interpreting the jottings. He could be faulted only in one respect. Inconveniently, he omitted to suggest that any of the names was a potential suspect.

Far from satisfied with the exercise, Diamond started probing with less subtlety. 'When you were telling us about the barbecue, you mentioned an estate agent by the name of Roger, the character who was dancing with your wife.'

'Yes. He's in here somewhere. Roger Plato.' Jackman leafed through the pages. 'Under "R". Two phone numbers, work and home.'

Diamond reached for the book and peered at the entry as if he hadn't noticed it previously. 'His wife isn't mentioned.'

'As far as I know, she didn't go about with the Bristol crowd.'

'She came to the barbecue, you said.'

'Yes. I didn't know of her existence until that evening.'

'But your wife knew, presumably.'

Jackman gave a shrug.

Diamond snapped the book shut and said on a sudden aggressive note, 'Was Plato sleeping with your wife?'

The attempt at a shock-effect was too obviously stage-managed. Jackman showed that he was unimpressed and unruffled. 'Isn't that a matter you should discuss with Roger, rather than me?'

Diamond reverted smoothly to his more civil approach. 'Let me phrase it differently, then. Did you suspect that he was sleeping with her?'

Paradoxically, this caused a flicker of annoyance. 'No, I didn't. She wouldn't have been so obvious about it. She flaunted Roger like a new hat.'

'Was there some other man?'

'I can't say. I simply do not know.'

'Did you care?'

Jackman hesitated. 'Yes.'

'So the openness you talked about in your relationship didn't extend to taking lovers?'

At this stage in the interview the professor made a bid to seize the initiative by demanding, 'Why are these questions necessary, Superintendent?'

Diamond answered candidly, 'Because jealousy may be the motive I'm looking for.'

'Jealousy on whose part?'

Unaccustomed to finding himself on the end of a sharp question, Diamond cast his eyes up to the ceiling and answered, 'A wife who is being cheated, possibly.'

'Or a husband?' said Jackman angrily. 'You've made it plain enough that I'm your principal suspect, so why don't you say it?'

'Principal witness,' Diamond insisted. 'You're my principal witness up to now. I need your help. I'm not going to throw accusations at you when you're helping us.' He reached for the address book again. 'There are several names here that we passed over quickly. Andy. No surname. Bristol phone number. Did you meet a friend of your wife's called Andy?'

'No.'

'Was anyone of that name at the barbecue?'

'I've no idea. I doubt whether I saw everyone who came.'

'You mentioned stepping over someone in the doorway who was using your Coronation biscuit tin as a drum.'

'Silver Jubilee biscuit tin. I didn't discover his name.'

Diamond tried another. 'Chrissie — does that mean anything?'

'No.'

'Fiona?'

'Look, if I'd recognized the names, I would have told you when we were going through the book. I thought I had made it abundantly clear already that we didn't live in each other's pockets. Gerry had a life of her own and I shared a part of it, just a part.'

Diamond gave a tolerant nod and eased back in the chair. 'Let's concentrate on *your* life, then. Take us through the weeks leading up to your wife's disappearance. How long was it after the barbecue that she went missing?'

'The barbecue was on 5 August. The last time I saw Gerry was Monday, 11 September.'

Diamond glanced at Wigfull, who made a mental calculation and said, 'Just over five weeks.'

'So how did you fill the time?'

Jackman gave an exasperated sigh. 'For Christ's sake! I was working my butt off organizing a bloody exhibition.'

The Jane Austen exhibition didn't interest Diamond. 'What about your personal life? What was going on at home?'

'Nothing much. We were pretty suspicious of each other after what had happened. I think Gerry deliberately kept out of my way as much as possible – to let me get over it, I suppose. And I was getting in late.'

'Did you continue to sleep together?'

'If you mean in the same bedroom, yes.'

Wigfull put in, almost out of curiosity, 'How could you relax, knowing she'd tried to kill you?'

'I felt safer knowing she was in the same room than if she were somewhere else in the house, where God alone knows what she might have got up to.' He made it sound reasonable.

Diamond, too, was making strenuous efforts to sound reasonable. 'So this was the pattern of your life for the five weeks up to her disappearance: long days preparing the exhibition?'

'Correct.'

'It can't have been very relaxing.'

'Sometimes at the end of the day I went for a swim.'

Diamond raised his finger. 'Ah – I was going to ask about the swimming. You spoke earlier about the boy you rescued. What was his name?'

'Matthew.'

'Yes. You invited him to the university pool.'

'I mentioned it in passing,' Jackman said. 'I don't see why it should interest the police.'

Diamond leaned forward on his elbows, covering his face in an attitude of fatigue or discouragement and ran both hands over his forehead and the bald curve of his head. 'Professor,' he finally said, 'everything interests the police in an inquiry as serious as this. Everything.'

With a slight upward movement of the shoulders, Jackman said, 'Fair enough. Matthew came for his swim. He came a number of times. I would generally meet him outside the sports centre about seven.'

'With his mother?'

'She drove him up to Claverton, but she didn't join us. He and I had the pool to ourselves most evenings. I helped him lose some faults in his overarm style. He'll develop into a useful swimmer if he keeps it up.'

Notwithstanding his recent declaration, Diamond didn't want to know any more about Matthew's progress as a swimmer. What really intrigued him was the pretext that the swimming lessons must have given Jackman for regular contact with Matthew's divorced mother. He had noted how approvingly Jackman had spoken earlier of Mrs Didrikson, even commenting on the beauty in her smile. 'And when the swim was over . . .?' he ventured.

'Mat went home.'

'In his mother's car?'

'Most times.'

'The exception being . . .?'

'When I drove him home on a couple of occasions.'

'Did you go into the house – for a coffee, or something?' Diamond added as if it scarcely mattered what the answer might be.

His casual air failed to woo Jackman, whose equanimity snapped. 'For pity's sake! What are you driving at now? Do you want me to say the swimming was just a front for secret meetings with Mrs Didrikson? Give me strength! This isn't 1900. If I really wanted to spend time with the woman I wouldn't have to find some fatuous excuse.'

'Perhaps you'll answer my question, Professor.'

'Perhaps you'll tell me what it can possibly have to do with my wife's death.'

'That remains to be seen. Are you tired? Would you care for a break?'

Jackman sighed impatiently and said, 'On two or three occasions I was invited in for a coffee. Is that what you wanted to know? And since you seem bent on pursuing this line of questioning, I took Mat to a cricket match at Trowbridge one afternoon and to a balloon festival at Bristol. I like the boy. I have no son of my own and it pleased me to spend some time with him. His mother was working on both occasions. Are you willing to believe that people sometimes act on innocent motives?'

'My beliefs don't come into it,' said Diamond. 'What about your wife? Did she mind you taking the boy to cricket and so on?'

'Why should she?'

'Perhaps with her suspicious mind she took it that you were making inroads with the boy's mother.'

'Her suspicious mind, or yours?' demanded Jackman. 'Look, Gerry was capable of twisting anything into a conspiracy, but don't forget that she invited Mrs Didrikson to her barbecue in the first place, so she could hardly object if I exchanged a few civil words with the woman next time I happened to meet her. That's all it was. I haven't been to bed with her.'

'How *was* your wife in those last five weeks of her life?'

'Her behaviour, you mean? I didn't see a great deal of her. She spent the mornings lying in bed talking on the phone to her friends.'

'Anyone in particular?'

'The entire galaxy, so far as I could tell. When we did meet she was pretty insufferable, either too moody to speak or spoiling for a fight – which I didn't give her.'

'Was she like that with everybody?'

'No, she turned on the charm when the phone rang and it was one of her friends. She could be in a towering rage with me and then pick up the phone and say a sexy "Hello, Gerry speaking", before she knew who was on the other end. That's the mark of a good actress, I suppose.'

'What sort of things were you fighting over?'

Jackman clenched his fists and thumped them on the table. 'How do I get this across to you fellows? *I* didn't fight. The aggro was all on her side. The issues were trivial. Example. The hand-mirror from her dressing table went missing and she accused me of taking it. What would I want with an ebony-handled mirror from a woman's vanity set? I told her one of the women at the barbecue must have taken a fancy to it, but Gerry wouldn't accept that any of her friends was light-fingered. That's the sort of piddling thing she was getting agitated about. In the end, to shut her up, I offered her a shaving-mirror I'd once used. She didn't need it. She had three adjustable mirrors fixed to her dressing table, another in the bathroom and any number of wall-mirrors around the house. But she told me she'd already been to the bathroom cabinet and helped herself to the shaving-mirror. I didn't inquire what made a hand-mirror so indispensable. In the mood she was in she wasn't amenable to logic.'

'You're suggesting this was another symptom of the paranoia you mentioned?'

'I'm not suggesting anything. I'm stating what happened. I have neither the expertise nor the energy to go into her mental problems. How much longer do you propose to keep me here?'

Sidestepping the question, Diamond said, 'I want to go over the last couple of days of your wife's life in detail. This is a useful time to take a break while you think about it. I dare say you could do with something to eat by now. I'll send someone out for sandwiches if you tell them what you'd like. Would you care for a warm drink or a beer?'

'I thought you served bread and water to people like me.'

Chapter Three

PETER DIAMOND REMOVED HIS JACKET and draped it over a filing cabinet, slipped his hands under his braces and fingered the sweat on his shirt front. The questioning had not developed as promisingly as it should have done. This professor was turning out to be a stronger adversary than he had first appeared. There was progress of a kind – some of the replies were less guarded now – but Jackman was still mentally well-defended. By declining to incriminate anyone else, he had resisted the lure that most guilty men would have accepted gratefully. Anyone in his position should have seized the opportunity to unload suspicion on to one of those names in the address book.

Far from discouraged, Diamond relished the challenge. At this stage, a tactical shift was indicated, a shift that might test the mettle of somebody else, as well as the professor. Without looking up from a copy of the evening paper that was on his desk, he told John Wigfull, 'I think we should make this more of a two-hander from now on. You take him through the events and I'll catch him off balance when I see a good opening.'

How satisfying it was to see the jolt this gave to Wigfull, who had been quite resigned to a passive role. Diamond had always run his own show up to now, regardless of the fact that Wigfull had led at least two murder inquiries of his own before being assigned to this dubious role as understudy. It wasn't because he had a low opinion of the inspector's ability, rather the reverse. According to Wigfull's personal record, he had joined the police at twenty-four, transferred to the CID in his second year and worked his way swiftly through the ranks. He was the bright lad everyone had tipped for high office, the possessor of a degree from the Open University. He had swanned through the promotion exams and made the rank of inspector at a disgustingly early age. Then had the temerity to clear up a couple of domestic murders in Bristol. Bad luck for him that the Missendale Report had exonerated Diamond, or he would certainly have been heading this inquiry by now.

'How are you holding up?' Diamond asked the professor solicitously when they returned to the interview room – and then spoilt it by showing that he had no interest in the answer. 'The hours leading up to your wife's death: are you ready? Inspector Wigfull will be putting the questions.' He rested an elbow on the table and sat chin in hand, like Nero in the Colosseum, prepared to be entertained by the contest.

Wigfull had taken the chair opposite Jackman. His curly moustache and widely-set brown eyes made him appear less formidable than Diamond. He started in a tone that was mild to the point of diffidence, nodding briefly before saying, 'If I have it right, sir, you said that you last saw your wife alive on Monday, 11 September.'

'Yes.'

'Have you been able to recall anything at all of that weekend?'

'I'm unlikely to forget it,' Jackman answered, but without irritation. 'The *Jane Austen in Bath* Exhibition was officially opened by the Mayor on that Saturday. I was racing around like the proverbial blue-arsed fly.'

'Last minute panics?'

'One, anyway. I'll come to that. In fact, everything was in place by Thursday evening. I don't suppose either of you managed to see it, but I think it was a reasonable show. I won't say we filled the Assembly Rooms, but by some artful use of display stands and video equipment we managed to do interesting things with the space. There was some gratifying comment in the national press, and we made the local TV news programmes. But you don't want to hear about the exhibition.'

144

'If it had any conceivable bearing on what happened . . .' said Wigfull.

There was a harsh intake of breath from Diamond and some ostentatious squirming on his chair. He could see the interview being sidetracked.

'I can't imagine how it could have played a part,' Jackman admitted, keeping his eyes on Wigfull, 'but Gerry's death is inexplicable to me, anyway. Shall I go through the weekend, as you asked? On that Friday, I spent most of the day at Heathrow meeting a weekend guest.'

Wigfull's eyes widened. 'You had a house guest that weekend?'

Jackman answered casually. 'He was Dr Louis Junker, an American academic from the University of Pittsburgh. He's a specialist on Jane Austen, which is more than I can say about myself. Junker has published a number of papers on the novels and he's doing the research for a major biographical study. He got to hear about the exhibition and arranged his vacation around it. We corresponded through the summer and I invited him to spend the weekend of the opening with us. Unfortunately his plane was delayed six hours. Instead of arriving about 10 a.m. on Friday, it came in at 4 p.m. Good thing the exhibition was all set up the night before.'

'Had you met Dr Junker before this?'

'No, we'd merely corresponded. It's not uncommon for academics to offer to put colleagues up. I've enjoyed hospitality myself on my visits to America.'

'Was he with you for the entire weekend?'

'Until Sunday. He attended the opening and stayed all afternoon. Said a lot of generous things. I was run off my feet that day doing interviews and showing VIPs around, so I had to leave him to his own devices. Well, not quite. Gerry escorted him. She volunteered, much to my surprise, because she doesn't usually show much interest in what goes on at the university. She seemed to hit it off with Junker. I don't know what they found to talk about — she never opened a serious novel in her life.'

'Was she acting normally?'

'Depends what you mean by normally. She could turn on the charm with other people. Her crazy outbursts, when they came, were mostly directed at me.' A sigh escaped from Jackman's lips, as if to chide himself for the bitterness he had just revealed. 'Anyway, by Saturday evening, we were all exhausted. The exhibition closed at six and the three of us had a pub meal and came home. Sunday morning we spent quietly with the papers and then went to the local for a pint and a sandwich.'

'You and Dr Junker?'

'Yes. Gerry lingered in bed as usual. She was up in time to see our guest leave. I drove him to the station about 3.45.'

'You said something just now about a panic.'

He nodded. 'That happened later the same evening.'

'On the Sunday?'

'Right. I can't say whether this has any connection with Gerry's death. As a result of all the publicity in the run-up to the exhibition, I'd been offered a number of items with Austen connections – a model of a ship once captained by Jane's brother Frank, some silhouette pictures of characters from novels, early editions with special bindings and so on. Most of it was unsuitable for my purposes, but on the eve of the exhibition I was made a present of two letters dating from the year 1800 that, if genuine, could cause a sensation in literary circles. They were apparently written by Jane Austen to her Aunt Jane, who lived for some years in Bath.'

'Some present!' Wigfull commented.

As if concerned that he might have overstated the importance of the letters, Jackman said, 'They were quite short and they said nothing very startling, but their interest to scholars would be considerable. Obviously I couldn't put them on display without authentication. However, I was mightily excited about them, as you may imagine, and keen to add them to the exhibits if they proved to be genuine. Naturally I showed them to Dr Junker. He knows Jane's handwriting better than I, and his opinion was that she had written them.'

'Really? And how did you say you came by them?'

'They were handed to me by somebody who had seen me plugging the exhibition on TV. The donor didn't want any publicity, and I promised to respect that wish. I believe they were part of a batch of old letters sold by a philatelist for the postmarks. This was before postage stamps came in. Before envelopes were used. Letters would be written on one side of a sheet of paper, addressed on the other, then folded and sealed. The Post Office would frank them. People collect them for the postmarks, but they're not so sought after as are letters bearing Penny Blacks and other early Victorian stamps, and you can sometimes pick them up for peanuts.'

'Unless they happen to have been written by a world-famous novelist.'

Jackman permitted himself a fleeting smile. 'You mean unless the seller is smart enough to know what he is selling. These were signed *Your affectionate niece, Jane*. Janes were pretty thick on the ground in 1800. You'd need to know that Mrs Leigh Perrot was Jane Austen's maternal aunt.'

'What sort of price would a Jane Austen letter fetch?'

'Hard to say. There are about a hundred and fifty letters extant, and they rarely come up for sale. I think one could be sure of a five-figure bid in a London auction.'

'I wonder if the donor had any idea of the value,' Wigfull mused.

Jackman shook his head. 'Highly unlikely. I intended to offer them back if they proved to be genuine.'

His use of the past tense prompted Wigfull to say, 'Something went wrong?'

Jackman looked sheepish as he admitted, 'They went missing from my desk drawer. I should have had them under lock and key. Foolishly, I didn't. That Sunday evening, when I happened to go to the drawer, they weren't there. Of course I took everything out and went through all the papers. I pulled out the drawer to see if they had fallen behind it. I asked Gerry if she'd taken them out for any reason. She said she hadn't.'

'She knew of the letters' existence?'

'Oh, yes. She was present when Junker examined them. Gentlemen, I felt sick to the stomach. I was damned sure somebody had been to that drawer and taken them. Of course I went through the house searching – I was at it until well after midnight – but there was no reason why those letters should have been anywhere but in the desk. Finally, I had a blazing row with Gerry and accused her of stealing them. It was bloody ironic – I must have sounded just as paranoid as she had when she'd accused me of tampering with her car and things like that. Quite a head case.'

Diamond had contained himself admirably. Now he couldn't resist coming in with, 'A blazing row? What do you mean by that? Did you knock her around?'

'No. I don't go in for violence.' Jackman glared at him, affronted at the suggestion.

'When was this – Sunday night or Monday morning?'

'Monday, I suppose.'

'You *suppose*?'

'I mean it must have been in the small hours. I told you I spent the whole evening looking for the letters.'

'Where did this row take place – in the bedroom?'

Jackman's expression began to take on a hunted look. 'Yes, as a matter of fact. She was already in bed.'

'Asleep? You woke her up and accused her of stealing them?'

'Hold on,' said Jackman. 'She was still awake.'

'You didn't take hold of her and shake her?'

'Absolutely not.'

'A blazing row, you said.'

'There was shouting. I said she must have taken them to spite me. I demanded to know where they were.'

'Tell me precisely where you were standing when this exchange took place,' demanded Diamond.

Jackman hesitated, frowning. 'I don't know. I moved. I wasn't in the same position.'

'Moved towards the bed?'

'Possibly. I didn't touch her, if that's what you're still on about. I didn't lay a finger on her.'

'Not at that point?'

'Nor later.'

'The next morning?'

'No.'

'Sometimes, Professor, people have blazing rows and don't remember very much of what they said and did.' Diamond had switched to a more measured tempo. Interrogation ceases to be productive after a few minutes at the rhythm he had struck.

'That isn't the case,' Jackman insisted. 'I remember precisely what happened. We shouted some abuse at each other and she laughed at me, which only made me more angry. She said I deserved to lose the letters for not having locked them away. She was right, of course, but I didn't enjoy the way she rubbed it in when I suspected her all the time of having hidden them somewhere out of mischief or malice. After a while we just stopped talking to each other.'

'Would you describe yourself as a man with a short fuse?' Diamond asked, reluctant to step down as the interrogator.

'What do you mean – a quick temper? No, I don't often lose control.'

'But you did on this occasion.'

'Only in the sense that I spoke my angry thoughts spontaneously. If I'd attacked her physically – which is what you seem to want me to say – do you think I'd be telling you this?'

Diamond gave a benign smile and commented, 'Sometimes it's a relief to talk about it.'

The response to that suggestion was that Jackman's mouth clamped shut, whereupon Diamond withdrew from the skirmish and gestured to his assistant with a lordly extended hand.

There was a pause. Then: 'Did you consider the possibility,' John Wigfull ventured, 'that Dr Junker had taken the letters?' It was as neat a way as any of restoring communication.

After sustaining his silence a moment longer, the professor consented to answer. 'Of course it occurred to me later. Gerry was the obvious suspect, but I couldn't discount Junker. It's an unpleasant fact that academics aren't above stealing. They become so engrossed in a field of study that they consider it their right to acquire original documents and first editions, dishonestly if necessary.

149

Every university librarian has horror stories of light-fingered researchers. To answer your question, yes, I began to believe that Junker couldn't be ruled out.'

'But he'd left your house by then?'

'Hours before. As I told you, I'd driven him to the station in time to catch the 4.12 to Paddington. He was planning to visit Professor Dalrymple at University College on the Monday, and then he was going on to Paris to begin his vacation. The more I thought about it, the more I convinced myself that I should go after him. So after not much sleep Sunday night, I got up early on Monday and caught a train to London.'

'The 8.19, you told us when you first reported her disappearance.'

This small feat of memory by the inspector clearly impressed Jackman, if not Diamond.

'Yes.'

'And that was the last time you saw your wife. Was she awake?'

Jackman tilted his head. 'I told you that, too.'

'What exactly was said?'

'I told her I was going after Junker, to ask about the letters.'

Across the table, Diamond shifted in his chair and said, 'That wasn't the way you put it to us. You said you had to see various people about the loan of manuscripts.' A comment calculated to show that he, too, retained a memory of what had been said before.

Without turning to look at Diamond, Jackman said, 'When I first spoke to you, I didn't think it would be necessary to bring up the business of the missing letters.'

'You wanted to keep it to yourself?'

'If possible, yes.'

Diamond commented to Wigfull, 'Worth picking up these discrepancies. Carry on.'

'What happened?' Wigfull asked the professor. 'Did you catch up with Dr Junker?'

'He didn't, after all, visit University College. He missed his appointment with Dalrymple, which made me suspicious. He'd phoned Dalrymple from Heathrow with some excuse about a late change in his flight arrangements to Paris, so I beetled off down to Heathrow with all speed and took the first flight I could to Paris.'

'Did you know where he was staying?'

'No, and I knew he hadn't made a reservation, because he wasn't expecting to leave London before Tuesday, so when I arrived at Charles de Gaulle, I went straight to the Tourist Information Office at the airport and asked for their help. I said I needed urgently to find a colleague. He *had* called there and they'd sent him to a small hotel near the Sorbonne.'

'Was he there?'

'Not when I arrived, but he had taken a room. I booked in at the same place and settled down to wait for as long as necessary. Finally, about eleven, he came in. He was surprised to see me, but not obviously alarmed. I explained my reason for being there, putting it as delicately as I could that maybe the Jane Austen letters had got among his papers in error – an invitation, in effect, to return them to me, and no recriminations. I'd thought it through. I didn't want to bring charges. I just wanted those letters back.'

'Did he have them?'

Jackman shook his head. 'I'm satisfied that he didn't. If he *was* deceiving me, he did it brilliantly. He was troubled for me and yet sufficiently shocked that I could have suspected him of taking them. He invited me up to his room and we went through his luggage together. He turned out his pockets, his wallet, everything. I had to admit in the end that Geraldine must have taken them. I flew back the next day, meaning to get the truth from her – and of course she wasn't there.'

'You didn't regard it as a police matter?'

'The theft of the letters? Who else could have taken them but Gerry? I believed I could get the truth from her without making it public. And I didn't want the donor of the letters to know that they were missing.'

'You haven't given us the name of this generous benefactor.'

'I told you. It's confidential.'

Diamond said, 'Come off it, Professor. This is murder we're investigating, not kiss and run.'

Adamantly, Jackman said, 'I gave my word. That's it.'

'There's such a thing as obstructing the police in the course of their inquiries, you know.'

'I am not being obstructive. It has no direct relevance to Gerry's death.'

'That's for us to decide.'

'No,' insisted Jackman. 'The decision is mine.'

Chapter Four

'ANY QUESTIONS?'

Diamond eyed the CID officers assembled in the briefing room at Milsom Street. He expected no questions. His instructions had been plain enough. He wanted the interviews with the murdered woman's friends to establish when they had last seen her alive; when they had last spoken to her on the telephone; what had been said; and, finally – an invitation to the purveyors of gossip always encountered in such an exercise – whether they knew of any reason why she might have been murdered.

'Go to it, then.'

Alone in the briefing room, Diamond turned to Wigfull. 'You, too, John. The boyfriend, Roger Plato. And his wife. What was her name?'

'Val.'

He hadn't expected so immediate and confident a response. In a burst of *bonhomie*, he remarked, 'Instant retrieval, eh? Why do we clutter the place with computers when we've got you? Take an hour off from the custody suite, John, and see what you can get out of the Platos. They're too important to leave to boys straight out of training school.'

As a good detective, Wigfull was bound to respect the reasoning behind the command, but he was plainly unhappy at being shunted to other duties. 'What about the professor? We haven't finished with him, have we?'

'He can stew for a bit,' Diamond said airily.

The prospect of the professor stewing for any appreciable time failed to satisfy Wigfull. 'He was getting stroppy in there. He's free to leave unless we formally arrest him.'

'He's torn, isn't he?' said Diamond. 'He doesn't want to be unco-operative. That could go against him later.'

'We've had twenty-four hours of his co-operation.'

'And barely scratched the surface. There's more to come, depend upon it.'

'Will you arrest him, then?'

'Would *you?*'

In the minds of both men were the time limitations set out in the Police and Criminal Evidence Act. An officer of Diamond's rank was entitled to detain a suspect for up to thirty-six hours without charging him, after which a magistrate's warrant would have to be obtained.

'I'd want to see the lab report first,' said Wigfull.

'We won't get that tonight.'

Wigfull said flatly, 'He won't spend another night with us.'

'And if we let him walk out of here,' said Diamond, 'he could do a runner.'

After a moment's further thought, Wigfull said, 'We can check whether he was on that flight to Paris on 11 September.'

'That's already in hand.'

'And the University College professor – Dalrymple?'

'Boon is dealing with it.'

'So what's the plan, sir?'

Diamond avoided a direct answer. 'The case is stacking up nicely. Opportunity: plainly – he was in the house with her. Motive: the marriage was on the rocks and she was bloody dangerous by his own account.'

'It doesn't justify killing her.'

'I'm not postulating a cold-blooded killing,' Diamond's irritation sounded in his voice. 'It's most likely to have happened during a violent argument. Those letters went missing, and – rightly or wrongly – he accused her of stealing them. A woman with fire in her belly isn't going to take that sort of abuse. She lashes out. If it *was* a violent row that Sunday night and he stuffed a pillow over her face and killed her, he'd know that it was curtains for his

154

career – unless he disposed of the body. He put it in the car and drove to the lake and dumped it there after removing the clothes and the wedding ring. Next day, to establish some kind of alibi, he behaved as if his wife was still alive and he suspected the American of stealing the letters.'

The explanation, compelling as it was, appeared not to have swept up Wigfull in its wake. 'If the letters were the cause of the argument that resulted in her death, why did he mention them to us?'

'Because he's a clever bugger, John. The way he tells it, they're his alibi. I've no doubt he was telling the truth when he said he flew to Paris and saw Dr Junker. I'll bet you a double whiskey if we can trace Junker he'll testify that the conversations took place exactly as Jackman described them. And has it occurred to you –' Diamond said, smoothly disguising the fact that it had only just dawned on him '– that the missing letters could be one enormous red herring? He could have killed her for some totally different reason.'

'That is a possibility,' Wigfull generously admitted.

Diamond nodded, drew closer and thrust a fat finger in front of the inspector's face. 'I've given you motive. And now . . .' A third finger. '. . . his conduct. He behaved like a guilty man, waiting over two weeks – until after the corpse was discovered – before reporting that she was missing. Why? Because he hoped she would sink to the bottom of the lake and stay there. Once she was found and we put her picture on the telly, he had no option but to come forward. People were certain to recognize the actress who played Candice Milner.'

'Even the murder squad, eventually,' murmured Wigfull.

The irony didn't deflect Peter Diamond. 'He'd had plenty of time to concoct a story. It's not bad, but it's far from perfect. He's scared out of his shoes by the prospect of what the lab will come up with. Did you see his face when the doctor came in to take the blood sample? That could nail him well and truly.'

'The men in white coats have their uses,' Wigfull remarked.

Diamond gave a half-smile. 'As a last resort, yes. They

may even prove that his car was used to transport the body. So, being an intelligent man, Jackman lays the foundations for a fallback position – impresses upon us what a nutter Geraldine was, and how dangerous she had become. If the forensic evidence proves beyond doubt that he smothered her and dumped her in the lake, he's all ready to pleed that he was provoked past endurance. He'll get a nominal sentence.' The way Diamond spoke the last words left no doubt of his view on lenient sentencing.

It was an intriguing test of Wigfull's true role in the investigation. Was he really only there in reserve, as the Chief Constable had asserted, or was he supposed to prevent an outbreak of intimidation? If so, Diamond had set him a problem. In the time it would take Wigfull to get to Bristol and obtain a statement from the Plato couple, Diamond was capable of tyrannizing the professor into a confession. More by accident than design, the language he had just been using was spiked with aggression: so many of the terms he had used to analyse Jackman's situation were physical. '*He's torn . . . scared out of his shoes . . . Did you see his face?*'

'If you're planning another session with him, I'd like to be present,' Wigfull stated resolutely.

'No problem,' Diamond airily said. 'I'll wait for you.'

'But will *he*? I could interview the Platos later.'

A grunt of dissent from Diamond. 'The whole point of the exercise is that everyone is interviewed at the same time. We don't want one set of friends phoning another to warn them that the rozzers are on their way and tell them the questions they have to answer. Roger Plato is a big cheese, John. He's yours, right?' He pushed a piece of paper at Wigfull. Upon it the addresses of all of Geraldine Jackman's friends had been listed.

With undisguised reluctance, Wigfull took the paper and looked for the address of the Platos.

Diamond yawned, stretched and said, 'I might go out for a breath of fresh air.'

He walked with Wigfull through the reception area. Immediately a group of people who had been sitting in a huddle got up and surrounded them. The press.

'Any developments, Mr Diamond?'

'None at all. Why don't you get off home? I intend to, quite soon.'

'You're interviewing a man? Are you holding him?'

'Will you be charging him?'

'We're interviewing anyone able to help.'

The detectives made their way out to the forecourt where the cars were parked. Wigfull got into his Toyota, started up and drove out.

Diamond watched him go. Then he turned and marched briskly back up the station steps.

Chapter Five

DIAMOND MARCHED THROUGH THE INCIDENT room without a word to anyone. Information was flowing in at a rate that kept six civilian clerks and the computer operators fully occupied. A heap of action sheets and computer print-outs awaited inspection, but there was a higher priority for the man in charge. He was confident that he could extract a confession before John Wigfull returned from Bristol.

He pushed open the door of the interview room.

Jackman, on his feet in a stance that was assertive, if not actually combative, his face taut, obviously primed for the third degree, said, 'Look, I'd like to have something clear from you. Am I under arrest, or what?'

'*Arrest*?' Diamond repeated, as if the word were unknown in the modern police.

'I came here of my own free will, to help you. I could walk out.'

Diamond conceded the truth of this with a nod. 'But I'd rather you didn't. We haven't cleared everything up yet, have we?' He felt profoundly encouraged that his man had become so tense. The laid-back academic had been a difficult adversary.

Jackman's expression had darkened. 'What else is there? I've told you everything I know.'

Diamond smiled benignly and said, 'You've been extremely helpful, sir.' A deferential touch that heralded a significant change of tactics. 'Did I say earlier that my name is Peter, by the way? I wouldn't mind making this more informal now that we're alone.'

The offer drew a hollow laugh from Jackman.

'Informal?' His eyes travelled scornfully over the acoustic wall-linings.

'We haven't been taping the conversations,' Diamond was able to say truthfully. 'Wouldn't do it without telling you. That's why the girl was taking notes.' He paused briefly to make certain that the shorthand-writer's absence was fully appreciated. 'If you want to move somewhere else, it can be arranged. I would have suggested an evening stroll outside, but we'd have the press for company. You know how they are, Gregory.'

Jackman, already unsettled by this outbreak of *bonhomie*, winced at the mention of his name. 'Greg, if you must.'

'Sorry . . . Greg.'

Diamond might have been talking to his oldest friend. Contrary to the rumours that had circulated after his transfer to Avon and Somerset, he didn't actually bully suspects into submission. He was more subtle. He liked to win their confidence. When he judged that the moment was right, his normally abrasive manner gave way to a charm that was difficult to resist after hours of interrogation. By that stage, a smile from Peter Diamond was more productive than a clenched fist. He had believed at the time that this was how Hedley Missendale had been coaxed into confessing; the lad had appeared so bemused that he'd poured out the story as if he were proud to join the company of Bonnie and Clyde and hold-up murderers in general. In Diamond's book, that isolated mistake hadn't destroyed the effectiveness of the technique.

'You'll have to forgive me for some of the things I said earlier,' he went on in the same companionable vein. 'In my job you get so obsessed with the facts of a case that human considerations get pushed aside. I mean, it's easy for me to overlook the fact that you came here as a volunteer, to render assistance.'

'Which I have rendered to the point of exhaustion,' said Jackman acidly. He seemed to find the charm resistible.

Diamond nodded. 'Too true. You could probably do with another coffee, Greg.'

Perplexed by the change, but correctly spotting it as a

cynical manoeuvre, Jackman leapt from there to a wrong conclusion. 'Is this where you soften me up before your oppo comes back and puts the boot in?'

This brought a smile of genuine amusement from Diamond as he savoured the notion of John Wigfull, Mr Clean from headquarters, laying into a suspect. 'He's gone to Bristol to talk to a witness.'

'It was meant as a joke,' said Jackman unconvincingly.

Diamond grinned again. 'I'm beginning to understand your sense of humour.'

'I think I would like that coffee.'

'Fine. Let's go down to the canteen. I don't know about you, but I'm famished.' He looked at his watch and picked up the phone. 'Do you mind?' he asked Jackman. 'I ought to have phoned before this. She's used to this, but she likes to be told.' He pressed out a number. 'Me,' he said presently into the mouthpiece. 'How's it going? . . . I'm not quite sure, my love, but soon as I can. What are you up to yourself? . . . I'd forgotten it was on . . . Well, yes, of course, but don't wait for me.' He replaced the phone and said to Jackman, 'She's watching the football. When I'm at home and want to look at it, she complains. I'll never understand women.'

He deliberately pursued this theme at some length downstairs over toasted sandwiches and coffee, to a background of old Beatles' songs and a noisy card game in one corner led by a former sergeant, now employed as a civilian computer operator. Once or twice Diamond's reminiscences of quirky women he had met succeeded in relaxing the muscles at the side of Jackman's face, the next thing to raising a smile. Encouraged, he went on to talk disarmingly of his difficulties courting Stephanie, his wife who, when they had met, had been Brown Owl to the local troop of Brownies. He had visited them in Hammersmith as community involvement officer, to instruct them in road safety, and had been enchanted by their winsome leader. A fuse had been lit that evening, and almost every spark and splutter in the consequent relationship had been witnessed by little girls in brown uniforms.

'I must have been bloody dedicated to put up with it,' he

recalled. 'Steph had to take me seriously when I turned up at the summer camp with a couple of donkeys. The desk sergeant at Hammersmith had opened a sanctuary for old mokes after he retired. He was a good mate. I think those donkeys swung it for me. Steph and I got engaged soon after. I was slimmer in those days.' He grinned. 'Relatively. Well, I could sit astride a donkey without someone complaining to the RSPCA.'

He paused, crammed the last of the sandwich into his mouth, and asked, 'Do you believe in love, Greg?'

'In *love*?'

Diamond nodded. 'Is there such a thing, or are we all deluding ourselves? Is it just a con trick by songwriters and authors? Desire I can understand. Admiration and respect. But love is something else. I mean, did you love Geraldine when you married her?'

Jackman gave him a long look. 'Is this what you've been leading up to? You want to know more about my relationship with my wife? Why didn't you come straight out with it?'

'Skip it, if you feel like that,' Diamond responded, piqued. 'I'm only trying to find some common ground.'

'Peter, my old chum,' Jackman said sarcastically, 'if it's going to get you off my back, I'll tell you anything.' He cleared his throat and said, 'I'd better rephrase that. If there are things you want to ask, let's get them over with. I want to get home tonight. Yes, I believe I loved her. Later we ran into problems, but I retained some tender feelings towards her. Does that cover it?'

'Apart from her good looks, what was her appeal?'

'I thought we'd been over this. I was flattered that she seemed to prefer me to the glamorous TV people she worked with.'

'That isn't love.'

'Look, what are you trying to prove now – that I'm devoid of human feelings – some sort of psychopath? Do you have some theory about murder that you want to slot me into? I loved Gerry because she was like no one else I'd ever met. She was witty, observant, brave and optimistic. In a unique and mysterious way, her mind was in touch with mine. The same things amused and delighted us. Will that do?'

The tribute was brief, but convincing.

'And then it went wrong,' Jackman continued. 'Catastrophically wrong. That precious contact between our minds was lost. I don't know why. Up to a point I can understand – her career falling apart – but why she turned on me as if I was the enemy, I'll never know. With her friends she was still the same Gerry, bubbling over with vitality. Not any more with me.'

'She made your life intolerable,' Diamond prompted. 'You made that clear.'

'No,' Jackman was quick to correct him. 'Not intolerable. I didn't use that word. The point is that I *did* tolerate her.'

'That'll teach me to feed words to a professor of English,' said Diamond wryly, not wanting to stem the flow. 'Let's just say that she was being difficult. Why didn't you divorce her, Greg? Wasn't that the obvious way to deal with the problem?'

Jackman let out a sharp breath as if to mark a protest that he was being prodded into the bull-ring again. 'You're still implying that I solved the problem by killing her.'

'I didn't say that.'

'You didn't have to.' He pushed away the plate with his half-eaten sandwich. 'If you want to know, I wasn't opposed to divorce, and nor was Gerry. I think we both knew that we were travelling rapidly down that path, but we hadn't discussed it.'

'Why not?'

'First you've got to remember that we'd only been married two years. Okay, I'd seen astonishing changes in Gerry's personality in that time, but I could understand why. She'd been through a traumatic time, having to leave the BBC, pull up her roots and come and live in the country with me. It wasn't the way we'd planned to run our lives. Maybe I was being naive, but I was convinced that the woman she had become wasn't the real Gerry. She needed more time to adjust to being an ordinary human being instead of a media figure.' His eyes darted left and right, signalling a disclosure more profound. No one else in the canteen could have heard anything over 'She Loves You'. 'This is going to sound quite loopy, but I sometimes felt as if some demon had taken possession of her. If I could have exorcised it, we might have saved our marriage. To come back to your question, I didn't talk to her about divorce because I didn't want to abandon her. The love we had felt for each other ought to have got us through the crisis.'

'You still had blazing rows.'

'Of course – she was bugging me at every opportunity.'

'Did you kill her, Greg?'

'No.'

Question and answer, straight out.

'Without premeditation, I mean.'

'Ah.' Jackman opened his eyes a fraction wider. 'That's the bait, is it? Manslaughter, rather than murder.'

'You've studied the terminology, then.'

'I do read other things, besides Milton and Shakespeare. No, Mr Diamond, I won't settle for manslaughter. I'm not settling for anything you suggest. If you want to stitch me up, that's going to be your mistake entirely. Don't expect me to conspire in it.'

Diamond ground his teeth. For a moment he didn't trust himself to go on.

'Speaking of writers,' Jackman added, 'I think it was a character in a Joe Orton play who said that policemen, like red squirrels, must be protected. Your bushy tail could be at risk if you make a mistake over me.'

How it happened so swiftly, Diamond was uncertain, but there was no denying that the interview had been turned around and he was on the defensive now. An unpleasant suspicion crept into his mind that this smart-mouthed professor knew about the Missendale case. Maybe the thought was timely; the temptation to pound the truth out of him had to be suppressed at all costs.

Instead he swallowed his pride and turned for support to the men in white coats. 'You can't buck the lab reports. If you killed her, the forensic evidence will stitch you up, as you put it, not me. Your blood, fingerprints, the samples from your car. I'm willing to wait a few more hours.'

'What does my car have to do with it?'

'The body must have been transported to the lake by some means.' He thought as he heard himself saying these things, I'm losing my grip. I was supposed to be charming the truth from him, not scaring him rigid.

'I'm allowed to have fingerprints on my own car,' Jackman said, frowning.

'Yes, but if, for example, some human hair was found in the boot and proved beyond doubt to have been your wife's, you would have some questions to answer.'

Jackman looked dubious. 'Can they identify hair like that?'

'It isn't the hair itself,' Diamond backtracked. 'It's the microscopic particles of skin attached to the roots.'

'*Did* they find any hairs?'

'They're very assiduous. They find all sorts of dust and debris.'

'You *are* going to stitch me up.'

'You should stick with Milton and Shakespeare, Greg. You're way off beam.'

Jackman said defiantly, 'You have a hunch that I killed her, and you won't let go.'

The whole tone of the conversation had changed irreversibly. Diamond shook his head slowly for a measured interval, conveying the message that he had more than a hunch, infinitely more.

Jackman said, 'How do I convince you that you're wrong?'

'You begin by explaining why you waited almost three weeks before notifying us that your wife was missing.'

'I should have thought that was obvious.'

'Not to me.'

'I wasn't surprised to find she'd gone. She'd stolen the Jane Austen letters and was unwilling to face me with the truth.'

'Where did you think she was?'

'With some friend or other. She wasn't short of bolt-holes.'

'Did you phone around?'

'I tried the obvious people and got nowhere. It was quite

164

possible that she'd asked them not to tell me anything.'

'But you didn't report to us that she was missing. You didn't even report that the letters were missing.'

'Because I wanted to deal with it myself,' Jackman insisted. 'I was certain that she'd taken them. If I ran straight to the police and branded her as a thief, what was that going to achieve? I didn't want the story getting to the newspapers.' His answers were sounding plausible, disturbingly plausible.

'How *did* you deal with it – apart from phoning her friends?'

'I thought she might try to get the letters valued, so I made inquiries at auctioneers and dealers in the West Country as well as London. Again, I drew a blank.'

'Let's get this clear,' said Diamond. 'You're telling me now that you expected her to sell the letters? You told us earlier that you thought she must have taken them out of malice.'

Jackman nodded. 'That was my first assumption. I didn't think their cash value was of any importance to Gerry. She wasn't short of funds, as far as I was aware. Then a few days after she'd gone, her bank statement arrived. I opened it in hopes of getting some clue to her whereabouts. She was overdrawn almost three thousand pounds.'

'*Overdrawn?*'

'I found her credit card statement and she was carrying a fifteen hundred pound debt there. She'd run right through her money.'

'How?'

'Most of it was signed out to cash amounts. She was borrowing money on the credit card, which is plain stupid at the rates they charge.'

'Yes, but what would she have spent so much money on?'

Jackman lifted his shoulders in a gesture of uncertainty. 'Living it up with her so-called friends.'

'Running through a fortune?'

'I don't know if you could call it a fortune. I had the impression she was very well off when we met. The television money was good, and there were plenty of extras.'

Footsteps clattered on the tiled floor. One of the constables from the incident room crossed the canteen and put an end to the conversation by telling Diamond that he was wanted urgently on the phone.

'Who is it?'

'Inspector Wigfull, sir.'

'From Bristol?'

'Yes.'

'Bloody better be urgent. Wait here with the professor. I'll be back shortly.'

Cursing Wigfull under his breath for having the gall – he was damned certain – to check up on him, he snatched up the phone when he got to the interview room. 'Yes?'

'Mr Diamond?' John Wigfull's voice was tense.

'Who else?'

'I just spoke to the Plato couple. They told me something I think you ought to know right away, sir. On the day Professor Jackman last saw his wife – the Monday – she phoned the Platos some time between ten and ten-thirty.'

'In the morning?'

'You see the point, sir? If Jackman caught the 8.19 to London, as he claimed, and then went on to Paris, he couldn't have killed her. She was alive after he left. Mr Diamond – are you there?'

Diamond dropped the phone without answering. He shouted across the room, 'Sergeant Boon!'

'Sir?'

'Did you check the professor's movements as I asked?'

'Yes, sir.'

'With what result? Come on, man!'

'It all checks out, sir. He saw Professor Dalrymple at University College, London, some time before eleven on 11 September and he was on the 1410 Air France flight from Heathrow to Paris.'

For a moment Diamond had the look of a deflating balloon. Then he managed to say in a small voice, 'Have a car at the back door directly. The professor is going home.'

Chapter Six

THE FIRST FROST. PEOPLE HAD talked all summer of the damaged ozone layer and the greenhouse effect, unable to accept that weeks of steady sunshine were possible in the English climate. Now normality was restored. On this chilly morning the geraniums in the window-boxes of Bath had a wan, defeated look that Peter Diamond noted with a cynical eye as he waited in a traffic queue on his way up Manvers Street towards the police station. This year the Parks and Gardens Department had spared no effort in trying to wrest the title of top floral city from Bath's main rival, Exeter. Every sill, ledge and surface had been stacked with pots, even the roofs of the bus shelters. Not a lamp-post had been without its hanging basket. Such enthusiasm! Such commitment! To no avail; Exeter had retained the title. Bath's abundant flowers were losers.

Diamond, too much the policeman to take a few wilting geraniums as his text for the day, still wished someone would cart them away.

The bus ahead slowed as it approached a stop. Diamond moved out to overtake, only to discover that the entire line of traffic in front had stopped. Not a promising start to the day, stuck out there, obstructing the opposite lane. Fortunately someone behind flashed his headlights and backed a few yards. Decent of him. Diamond shunted back into line and looked in the rearview mirror to see who the Good Samaritan was. A fellow in a Toyota. Big moustache, wide grin. John Wigfull, of all people. Probably thinking what a dumbo his superior was for failing to notice that the bus was one of the bright yellow open-top double deckers for tourists. Every kid in Bath knew that the city tour buses didn't use the regular stops.

He switched on the radio, and after the crackle as the automatic aerial went up (he hadn't wiped it clean for weeks), he heard the newsreader saying on Radio Bristol, 'Detectives are today expected to step up the hunt for the murderer of Geraldine Snoo, the former star of the long-running BBC television serial *The Milners*, whose unclothed body was recovered from Chew Valley Lake at the weekend. She was identified by her husband, Professor Gregory Jackman, of Bath University, who is understood to have given the police —'

'. . . a pain in the bum,' Diamond muttered as he switched off.

The bus ahead started moving again, giving the full view of its back end. To underline its commitment to tourism, the company had given names to each of the buses, chosen from the city's illustrious past. Diamond had just noticed what this one was called. It was the *Jane Austen*. Much more of this and he would feel that the gods were mocking him.

Almost too late, he spotted the entrance to the police station and spun the wheel violently without giving a signal. A good thing it was only Wigfull who was following.

Neither man referred to the incident when, soon after, they were joined in Diamond's office by Halliwell, Croxley and Dalton. A crime conference, so-called; let no one suggest that the murder squad was up a gum-tree. Up a ladder was more like it — that stone ladder on the front of the Abbey, clinging rigidly to their positions. And now four rising detectives had better chip in some ideas, and fast.

Diamond decided on a low-key opening. 'More forensic reports — for what they're worth,' he told them first. 'The men in white coats are still hedging over the date of death, but 11 September looks the strongest bet. She was certainly dead before she got into the lake — as if we didn't know. And asphyxia remains the most likely cause of death. Damn all there.' He snatched up a second sheet. 'This is the report on the cars, Jackman's and the victim's. No indication that either was used to transport the body. No significant traces or fibres. Either the murderer was useful with a vacuum cleaner or we're looking for another vehicle.' Muttering, he turned to a third lab report. 'Blood groups. The victim was Rhesus Positive O and so was her husband. You'll recall that someone found traces of blood on the quilt. They proved to be too minute to analyse in preliminary tests.'

'The heat's off the prof, then,' Keith Halliwell observed, and must have wished he hadn't after the glare he got from his superior. He doubled his rate of chewing. Everyone on Diamond's murder squad needed some recipe for survival; young Halliwell's was to fantasize that he was a case-hardened New York cop. He was never seen in anything but leather and denim.

Diamond returned his eyes to the sheet of paper in his hand. 'It says here that the blood sample on the quilt has been sent for DNA analysis – genetic fingerprinting – which ought to please the press boys, if no one else.'

This prompted Croxley, usually the most reticent of the DIs, to speak up in the name of science. 'It is an infallible identity test.'

'And bugger all use to us unless we find a suspect with a matching profile,' said Diamond.

Croxley turned pink.

Halliwell rashly tossed in a suggestion in support of Croxley, 'Okay, so if they get a profile from the blood on the quilt, we keep sending in blood samples until we get a match, like they did for that rape and murder case in the Midlands.'

Mercifully, Wigfull beat Diamond to the draw. 'Come off it, Keith. If you're talking about that case in Leicester, there isn't a chance in hell of us mounting a similar exercise. The police up there were working within quite narrow parameters – looking for a male, between seventeen and thirty-four, in three small villages, about four and a half thousand men – and that took months to complete. We don't even know the sex of our killer.'

Dalton said, 'The reason they finally caught the bloke was that somebody talked. He fiddled the test. Persuaded some other berk to take it for him.'

'If you've quite finished,' Diamond said morosely, 'I wouldn't mind talking about the case in hand. I may be an incurable optimist, but what I propose for this morning is a brain-storming session.'

That silenced them all.

He took his time measuring the effect of the announcement before resuming. 'First, let's have an update. Yesterday evening's interviews. Mr Dalton, would you report?'

Dalton, who was responsible for the computer back-up, stared in horror. 'We haven't processed them yet, sir.'

'Why is that?'

'It's too soon.'

'I thought this all went on computer.' Diamond glanced about him as if in need of advice, really just taunting the hapless inspector, who was so desperate to impress that he made an easy target. 'We have umpteen thousand quids' worth of hardware in there. Why don't we have a print-out in front of us?'

'The data has to be keyed in first, sir.'

'You don't have to hammer us with jargon. I thought the main advantage of using the blasted things was to speed up the investigation.'

'It is, Mr Diamond – but the input is a manual function.'

'Skip it, then. I've already cast an eye over the reports myself. I found nothing remarkable' – he paused – 'with one notable exception.'

For a moment it seemed as if no one was willing to provide Diamond with the cue he wanted. Then Inspector Croxley found the silence too stressful. 'What was that?'

Diamond announced in a throwaway tone, 'As a result of one of the interviews, we have learned that Geraldine Jackman was still alive on the morning of Monday, 11 September. She made a phone call. John, be so good as to repeat what you learned from Mr and Mrs Plato.'

'Well, it appears that –'

'No,' Diamond interrupted him. 'Facts, if you don't mind, not appearances.'

A ripple of tension showed in Wigfull's jaw as he made another start. 'Mrs Valerie Plato told me that she took a call some time between ten and ten-thirty. The caller claimed to be Geraldine Jackman.'

'Is there any doubt?' Diamond pounced on the possibility.

'Not so far as I'm aware, sir,' Wigfull said tightly. 'But I don't know for a *fact* that the voice on the phone was Geraldine's. I have to take the Platos' word for it.'

'Go on.'

'She asked to speak to Roger, the husband. He was at home that morning. Roger Plato came to the phone, and his wife remained in the room. At this point, with your permission, sir, I should like to refer to my notes.'

Diamond couldn't be certain whether this was deliberate sarcasm. Nobody was so foolhardy as to smile.

Notebook open, Wigfull continued, 'Mrs Jackman stated that she was sorry to be a nuisance, but she needed some help. She said there had been a spot of bother with Greg – Professor Jackman – and she needed to get away from the house for a few days, to clear the air, as she put it. She wanted to know if she could come and stay with the Platos. Well, Valerie Plato was at her husband's side and she made it very clear that she wasn't having that woman under her roof.'

'Why not?' Halliwell asked. His ignorance was excusable. As the least experienced officer, viewed with suspicion for his quasi-American style, he had been delegated a series of doorstepping jobs that had kept him out of the incident room all week.

'Plato had been knocking around with her,' Wigfull answered.

'Is knocking the operative word?'

'Valerie Plato thought so. Roger strongly denies it.'

'With a name like his?'

'Actually I believe him,' said Wigfull. 'I questioned him separately. He said it wasn't that serious, just a pairing-off because their respective spouses didn't usually go to the parties. He said Gerry Jackman wasn't looking for a lover.'

'Maybe Valerie Plato sized it up differently.'

Diamond said irritably, 'We could spend the rest of the morning saying maybe. Get back to the phone call.'

'That was it, really,' said Wigfull. 'Plato told Gerry Jackman it wasn't convenient for her to come and stay, and she rang off.'

'In an angry frame of mind?'

'Apparently not. She must have guessed she was on a loser when Valerie picked up the phone first.'

'And that was all she said about the row with Jackman, that she'd had a spot of bother and wanted to get away from him to clear the air?'

'Yes. She didn't sound unduly distressed, according to the Platos.'

'Did she phone anyone else after that? What did we get from the other interviews last night?' Croxley asked in his west of Ireland accent.

'Sweet Fanny Adams,' said Diamond in the less lilting sound of South London.

'So the call to the Platos was the last evidence that she was alive?'

'The last we have.' Diamond spread his hands, inviting contributions.

An uneasy silence. If brains were storming, the lightning was slow to strike.

He scanned the faces. 'In that case, gentlemen, in the absence of anything more brilliant, it looks as if we're forced to fall back on the Diamond method of investigation — good, old-fashioned doorstepping. Get your lads out to Widcombe, Halliwell. I want reports on everything and everybody seen in the vicinity of John Brydon House on Monday, 11 September. Check the neighbours, the milkman, the newspaper boy, the postman. Got it?'

'Sir.'

'Well, what are you waiting for?'

Halliwell left the meeting fast, no doubt with a sense of relief.

'And now what else?' Diamond demanded of the rest of his team.

'I could be out of order here, sir,' Dalton guardedly prefaced what he was about to suggest, 'but I think it's worth finding out how Valerie Plato spent the rest of that day. Rightly or wrongly, she seems to have been suspicious of Gerry Snoo's intentions, this famous television star

172

making a pitch for her husband. The call could have made her pretty desperate when she heard Gerry openly asking to move in with them.'

Diamond turned to Wigfull. 'He thinks the Plato woman is a suspect. What do you say to that?'

The theory earned a grudging nod. 'It's not impossible. She's the quiet type, reasonable-looking, but not what you'd call glamorous. She *may* have panicked in a fit of jealousy, I suppose.'

'Does she have an alibi?' Dalton asked.

'Does she have a car?' said Diamond.

'A car, yes. A Volvo. Being in the property business, they're quite well off. He drives a Rover. As for the alibi, they were both at home until about one, and then Roger left to do a valuation. Valerie went shopping in the afternoon.'

'No alibi,' said Dalton.

'Hold on,' said Wigfull. 'If she went shopping, presumably people in the shops will have noticed her.'

'And if she went to a supermarket?'

'She may have kept the till receipt.'

Dalton shrugged and withdrew from the discussion.

'How was she when you spoke to her?' Diamond asked Wigfull. 'Did she appear nervous?'

'Not particularly. Reserved.'

'And the husband?'

'He was more jumpy, but then he would be, with his wife at his side, thinking he was lying about the relationship.'

'Did you get the impression that they'd had a row about it?'

'I'd put money on it.'

'And yet you seem to be playing them down as possible suspects.'

'Yes, sir. But you might want to talk to them yourself.'

'Thank you for that advice, John,' Diamond said with sarcasm. He leaned back in the chair and rested his palms on his stomach, as if to measure the span. 'Gentlemen, I don't mind telling you I am not exactly blown away by your – um – input.'

Doggedly, Wigfull defended his corner. 'I believe the

Platos told me the truth, sir. It's worth pointing out that their statement fits in with Professor Jackman's.'

'Go on.'

'It supports what Jackman told us about the Jane Austen letters that went missing. If Geraldine did take them, as he suggests, she wouldn't have wanted to face him on his return from Paris. So it's not surprising that she started phoning around for some place to lay up for a while.'

'A bolt-hole.'

'Well, yes.'

'Jackman's term, not mine,' Diamond explained. 'He told me last night that she wasn't short of bolt-holes. That's the reason he gives for taking so long to report her disappearance. He assumed she was still alive until he heard about the body in the lake.'

Dalton remarked, 'The sixty-four thousand dollar question is what happened after the Platos gave Mrs Jackman the brush-off. None of the other friends appears to have heard from her.'

'Unless one of them is lying,' said Croxley.

Diamond screwed his face into a look that overlaid curiosity with a glare. 'What is that supposed to mean?'

'Well, sir, that the next person she called on the phone was her murderer. Someone who offered her sanctuary and then killed her.'

'What for?'

Croxley seemed unable to supply a plausible motive, so the irrepressible Halliwell suggested, 'For the Jane Austen letters. She must have taken them with her.'

'Killed her for a couple of letters?'

'They were worth a bit.'

'Over ten thousand, by Jackman's estimate,' Diamond admitted. 'But these people Geraldine was keeping company with weren't complete idiots. They would know the dangers involved in trying to sell letters as rare as these. I don't buy it.'

'Even so,' Wigfull quietly put in, 'it might be sensible to alert the dealers in antique letters. There can't be so many.'

He was rewarded with a glacial stare from Diamond and the terse instruction, 'Action it, then.'

'If it were me, I'd take them to America,' said Dalton. 'Get a better price.'

Diamond was shaking his head. 'I'm not convinced that the letters provide a credible motive. I'm not even totally convinced of their existence.'

'You think the professor is lying about them?'

'He was evasive.'

'About where they came from?'

'Yes.'

Dalton shrugged. 'So let's put the heat on him.'

Diamond flapped his hand dismissively. 'Too late for that.'

'There is another way of checking whether these letters exist at all,' Croxley was emboldened to say, 'and that's by getting a statement from the American, Dr Junker. Isn't he supposed to have examined them?'

'Junker.' Diamond snapped his fingers. 'Yes – I'd written him off, thinking he was still touring in Europe. He should be back in America by now. We'll try and raise him. Which university does he teach in?'

'Pittsburgh,' answered Wigfull.

'We'll call him at once.'

'I wouldn't, sir,' said Wigfull.

'Now what's the problem?'

He'd taken out a pocket calculator. 'The problem is that now is 5.10 a.m. over there.'

Chapter Seven

DIAMOND'S CALL TO DR LOUIS Junker was connected shortly after 3 p.m. He was using an amplifying phone so that Wigfull and Dalton, who had joined him in the office, could hear the responses.

'Who is this?' the voice from Pittsburgh asked.

'Detective Superintendent Peter Diamond, from Bath, in England. You won't know my name, sir.'

'That is correct.'

'I'm enquiring into the death of Mrs Geraldine Jackman, of Brydon House in Bath.'

There was an understandable pause. The three detectives waited.

'Mrs Jackman – she's *dead*?'

'Sadly, yes.'

'Greg Jackman's wife? Dead?'

'Her body was recovered from a reservoir. It appears that she was murdered.'

'*Murdered*?' The voice climbed an octave. 'You can't possibly mean this.'

'She was last seen alive on Monday, 11 September. I understand that you were a guest of Professor Jackman at Brydon House at about that time.'

'September 11? Let me collect my thoughts a moment, will you? No, I left for Paris on the previous day . . . Now listen, Mr, em . . .'

'Diamond.'

'Mr Diamond. I know nothing about this, nothing. It's a total shock to me.'

Diamond boomed reassurance down the transatlantic cable. 'Dr Junker, there's no suggestion that you are implicated in Mrs Jackman's death. I am simply hoping that you can help me to piece together the events of that weekend. Do you mind?'

There was a silence sufficient for Dalton to murmur flippantly to Wigfull, 'He's calling his lawyer on the other phone.'

Junker's voice started up again. 'If you really think I can help, I'll do what I can. I'm still trying to comprehend this. Is Greg okay?'

'Professor Jackman is fine.'

'The last time I saw him was in Paris. He flew out to talk to me. Which day did you say she was killed?'

'I said she went missing on Monday, 11 September.'

'That Monday? Oh my God . . . that was the day he met with me in the hotel − late. It must have been around eleven in the evening. He told me he flew out in the afternoon. Look, if you're putting the heat on Greg Jackman, I think you should tell me. He was very good to me. They both were.'

Junker was a fast talker, and disembodied words in an unfamiliar accent can be difficult to take in. Diamond had a tape-recorder running and he could analyse the responses later. He still needed to conduct the interview effectively, to a structured pattern of question and answer.

'Dr Junker, nobody has been charged with this murder, if that's what you're suggesting. I'm simply asking for your help to establish some facts about the weekend prior to Mrs Jackman's disappearance.'

'Whatever you want.'

'Thank you. Let's take it from when you first got in touch with Professor Jackman.'

'That was back in July. We hadn't met before this summer. I wrote him when I heard about the Jane Austen exhibition he was putting on in the city of Bath. The nineteenth-century novel is my principal field of study. It so happens that I'm currently writing what I hope will become the definitive biography of Jane Austen. Do you need to know my background?'

'Not at this stage, sir. So you decided to come over?'

'In point of fact, I was coming to Europe on vacation. I

adjusted my schedule to take in Bath to visit the exhibition, and Greg Jackman was kind enough to invite me to his home for the weekend.'

'I believe he was at Heathrow to meet you.'

'That's correct. This was on that Friday. Unfortunately there was some technical trouble with the airplane and the flight was delayed for hours. It was heroic of Greg to wait so long. I recall that we landed at 4.10 in the afternoon, almost seven hours late, and I didn't expect to see him, but he was there to shake my hand as if it was still only nine in the morning. Then we drove along the freeway to Bath. We stopped someplace for a sandwich. I couldn't tell you where.'

'Doesn't matter.'

'The trip took about two, two and a half, hours and we talked about his work and mine, as I recall. My memory of that evening is a little disordered. I was bushed, to be frank with you. I guess it was around 7.30 when we finally reached Brydon House, and I had been travelling a long time. Gerry – Mrs Jackman – came out to meet me. She was a dream; beautiful, just beautiful. There's no other word. Did you know she was a television actress? She was all ready to cook for me and I had to tell her that I was too tired to wait for a full meal, or to appreciate it, so she fixed me a sandwich and coffee. Greg went off to another room. He had some late calls to make about the exhibition. The poor guy hadn't figured on spending most of that day at the airport. Well, after I had eaten, Gerry showed me to my room and I took a shower.'

Now that he had got over his reservations about talking to the police, Junker was proving to be a witness with copious recall, almost too copious.

Diamond said, 'Dr Junker, if nothing else of importance happened that evening . . .'

'But I haven't told you about the caller.'

'The what?'

'The caller. Someone who came to the house – right?'

Diamond gripped the arms of the chair and sat forward. 'I understand. Please go on.'

'This was how I got to hear about the Jane Austen

letters. The shower revived me a little and I put on a change of clothes and went downstairs, figuring that if I could stay on my feet a couple of hours more, I would adjust to your English time and beat the jet-lag. When I got down, I heard Greg's voice from a room at the front of the house, so I looked in there. He had somebody with him and it wasn't Gerry. A short woman with brown hair. They were standing over a table examining a document. I apologized for interrupting, but Greg called me in. It was obvious that he was fired up about something because he forgot to introduce me to the lady. He said, "Louis, you came at just the right moment. Feast your eyes on these!" Right off, I saw the reason for his excitement. Believe me, my heartbeat tripled. We were looking at two original letters in Jane Austen's hand. No question.'

Diamond listened impassively, avoiding Wigfull's eye. Having repeatedly questioned the existence of the Jane Austen letters, he could expect some gloating looks from that quarter. Not that he cared much. A good detective took nothing for granted.

Junker plunged into a description of the letters so detailed that it was unrealistic to harbour doubts any longer. Both had been penned in September, 1799, to Mrs James Leigh Perrot, Jane's aunt, at the Warden's House, Ilchester Gaol, where the accused lady was awaiting trial on a charge of shoplifting. They were written from Steventon, and signed *Yr affectionate niece, Jane*. The first had apparently been written in support of an offer from Jane's mother to send her two daughters to reside with the Leigh Perrots (Uncle James had joined his wife in captivity) in the Warden's House until their ordeal was over. Jane's *'chief wish'* was that her aunt and uncle *'might be persuaded to ease the desolation of this undeserved confinement'* by sharing the experience with their loving nieces. The second, written after the offer had been welcomed, but declined, nicely complemented the first. Jane had not been able to suppress her sense of relief. It was lighter in tone and more spontaneous, short, but gossipy, and altogether more typical of her letter-writing style.

'Of course you have to guard against forgeries,' Junker

went on. 'But I'd bet my last dollar that these letters were genuine. The style, the handwriting, all of it was so right. Even the spelling. Jane had an endearing blind-spot about the word 'believe', quite often reversing the 'i' and the 'e', and it cropped up in the second letter.'

By now the three detectives, agog to discover the identity of the donor of the letters, had heard more than they cared to know about Jane Austen's style and orthography.

To nudge the conversation in the right direction, Diamond said, 'A generous gift, then?'

'Amazing. Did I give you a physical description of the letters?'

'Thanks – but I can get that from Professor Jackman. What interests me more is the woman who was in the room that day. Had she found the letters herself?'

'So I was told.'

'You said you weren't introduced.'

'Not when I first came in. Greg was just too excited to notice. He did the honours later. Her name – I think I have this right – was Mrs Didrikson.'

Dana Didrikson.

One mystery solved. This time Diamond's eyes locked with Wigfull's.

Intriguing possibilities opened up. Gregory Jackman's refusal to reveal the name – allegedly because his benefactor wished to remain anonymous – was open to new interpretations now.

'Did you catch the name?' the voice from Pittsburgh asked.

'Yes. I've heard it before, in another connection. Tell me, did the gift of these letters come as a total surprise to Professor Jackman?'

'I'm sure of it. He was jubilant. Who wouldn't have been?'

'Mrs Didrikson must have been excited, too.'

'I wouldn't say so.'

'No?'

'I don't know the lady, but I'd say she was pretty cool about the whole thing. She didn't say much at all.'

'She must have told him where they came from.'

'She already had, before I stepped into the room. I heard

180

the story later, how she had tracked down the letters through some dealer in postage stamps.'

'Do you think she knew their value?'

'Sure. She knew they were worth a bundle. I said in her presence that I was certain they would fetch a high price at auction. The weird thing is, it had no appreciable impact on her. I got the impression that she just wanted to hand them over and get the hell out of the place. Greg talked about giving them back to her when the exhibition was over, but she insisted they were a gift – a gift to him personally. Apparently this was her way of thanking him for some action of his in rescuing her son from drowning. Does that make any sense to you?'

'It fits the story we have.'

'Right. Well, by now I was beginning to sense that I shouldn't be there. Greg needed to talk this thing through with her. I mean, I have no idea what the lady's personal circumstances were, but she was parting with an extremely valuable item. I edged diplomatically toward the door, meaning to leave them to work things out. Just then the door opened and Mrs Jackman walked in. No, that's an understatement. She made an entrance like she was the star guest on a talk-show. She was reeking of expensive perfume and dressed in a skin-tight black gown that reached to the floor. This was the lady who only a half-hour before had been wearing a check shirt and faded blue jeans and had fixed me a sandwich. Okay, I thought, maybe they're planning to go out for dinner, even if Greg is still dressed in the casual clothes he wore to the airport. Anyway, he greeted her warmly and told her about the letters. She and Mrs Didrikson obviously knew each other, but there was a chill between them from the beginning and it didn't warm up much when Gerry Jackman gave the letters one quick glance and commented that she would never understand why people bothered to collect musty old things like that when they had no literary merit whatsoever.'

'Was she trying for a reaction?'

'That was the way I read it. Actually, she didn't get one. Mrs Didrikson didn't say a word. Greg tactfully attempted

181

some kind of counterstatement, and I backed him up as well as I could, whereupon Gerry stepped really close to me – practically toe to toe – gave me a sexy look and asked me what was big on Broadway just now. She was blatantly upstaging Mrs Didrikson. I felt extremely uncomfortable. I answered her truthfully that I didn't live in New York and didn't keep up with the theatre. She persisted in engaging me in conversation to the exclusion of the others until Mrs Didrikson made it clear that she wanted to leave. Then Gerry broke off what she was saying and suggested to Greg that he take Mrs Didrikson out to dinner.'

'That evening?'

'Yes, to thank her for all the trouble she'd taken to find the letters. I didn't know what game Gerry was playing and I still don't. Greg said that he couldn't abandon me, his house-guest, on my first evening, to which Gerry said she'd enjoy entertaining me. Dressed like that – she and I alone in the house – can you imagine?'

'Did he take up the suggestion?'

'No. Mrs Didrikson scotched it by saying she was busy that evening. He saw her to the door. In fact, he went out to the driveway with her, I imagine to have some private words. I was left with Gerry long enough for her to run a finger down my backbone and say that she couldn't be blamed for trying.' Dr Junker coughed nervously as if he were still undergoing the experience. 'Jesus, I'm an academic, Mr Diamond. I wear thick glasses and I'm forty-six years old. I have a receding hairline and a larger-than-average nose. I'm not accustomed to attractive women making passes at me. No one makes passes at me. In my position, what would you have done?'

Interesting as it might have been to have heard Diamond's answer, he refused to supply it. Instead, he asked, 'Are you telling me that something happened between you and Mrs Jackman? Is that what you're saying?'

'No, sir! I'm saying that I didn't take up the offer.' After the strong denial, Junker's voice changed to a discernible note of regret.

'I imagine it wouldn't have been easy, with Professor Jackman around.'

'You think she didn't mean it? That she was putting me on?'

'How can I say?' answered Diamond, his patience running out. 'I'm a policeman, not an agony aunt. What happened next?'

'She poured me a drink. Then I heard Mrs Didrikson's car move off and Greg came back. We spent some more time studying the letters. Quite properly, Greg decided they needed authenticating before he put them into the exhibition. The earliest he could arrange it was Monday. God, I wish I'd had the good sense to photograph them. You haven't found them, I suppose?'

'No.'

'That's too bad.'

'And after you'd finished your drink, Dr Junker?'

'I went to bed. I slept. Boy, did I sleep! I came to my senses around eleven next day. When I went downstairs, Greg had already left for the exhibition.'

'You and Mrs Jackman were alone, then?'

An uneasy laugh came down the line. 'True, only she wasn't acting up like she had the night before. She was curiously different toward me. Kind of friendly, but in no way suggestive. She drove me to the Assembly Rooms for the opening ceremonies and stayed with me the whole of the afternoon – which must have been insufferably boring for her. The exhibition, I mean. I photographed almost every item. To give Greg his due – it was a terrific show.'

'Did you have much conversation?'

'Sure.'

'Did you learn anything of interest about Mrs Jackman, her problems, her plans?'

'Sorry,' said Junker. 'We kept off personal matters. After my experience the previous night, I figured it was safer to stick with the nineteenth-century novel.'

'Did you meet anyone? Any of her friends, for instance?'

'A couple of guys from the English Department who wanted to talk to me about a piece I wrote for *The Times Literary Supplement* a while back, that was all.'

'Nobody who knew Mrs Jackman?'

'Plenty who recognized her. She must have signed her

autograph a dozen times. I don't think she met anyone she already knew. She told me her friends weren't the book-reading sort.'

'That was probably true.' Diamond continued to fish for unconsidered suspects. 'Did you mention the letters to anyone?'

'No way. Greg and I had agreed to say nothing about them to a living soul. In the academic world, you keep a hot property like that under wraps until you're one hundred per cent certain.'

Diamond continued to probe as Junker continued his account of the day, but the story that emerged was substantially the same as he had got from Jackman: the pub meal after the exhibition had closed for the day. The decision to retire early. Next day, a quiet morning with the Sunday papers in another pub.

'Just you and Professor Jackman?'

'Yes. The lady was still in bed, or so I understood.'

'Then this was the first opportunity Jackman had of speaking to you alone since the episode on Friday evening?'

'Correct.'

'Did he refer to it?'

'Briefly. He tried to make some kind of apology and I said it wasn't necessary. He said Gerry had these unpredictable phases. I shrugged it off with some chauvinistic remark about women in general. That was all. We returned to the house after lunch, and pretty soon after, it was time to leave. Gerry was downstairs to wish me goodbye. She acted normally, we shook hands chastely and that was the last I saw of her. Greg drove me to the station in time to catch the London train. Next morning I was due to visit with a professor at University College.'

'Dalrymple.'

'You're well informed. Actually, I had to cancel. When I booked my flight to Paris I didn't realize how far out of town Heathrow is. There was no way I could fit in Edgar Dalrymple and catch my flight.' Junker paused. 'You want to know about my meeting in Paris with Greg?'

'If you please.'

'It won't take long. I went out for a meal Monday and when I got back I was amazed to see him standing in the lobby of my hotel. He told me the Jane Austen letters were missing and asked if it was possible that I'd taken them by mistake. You can imagine how I felt. It was obvious what he was thinking. I hadn't disguised my envy when those letters had dropped into his lap. Now it looked like I'd abused his hospitality by stealing them. Mr Diamond, I assure you that I hadn't – and there's no way I could have taken them in error. We searched my things together. My luggage, my room, everything. I believe I convinced him finally that I didn't have them. He said Gerry must have taken them out of spite. No one else knew about them. I had to agree with him. I said maybe she resented the fact that another woman had given him this unique present. It could help to explain why she'd behaved so oddly at the time.'

'What did he think of your theory?'

'Not much. He said these histrionic scenes were pretty common. I guess he was more concerned about recovering those letters than trying to analyse his wife's behaviour. We parted in a civilized fashion. He promised to call me if the letters turned up. I said I might see him at breakfast, but in the morning he checked out early. I heard no more from him.'

By means of sign language, Diamond invited Wigfull and Dalton to pass him any questions they might want to put, but they shook their heads. He wound up the conversation and ended the call.

Nobody moved.

'Why the mystery?' said Wigfull after an interval.

'Explain.'

'Mrs Didrikson. Why didn't Jackman tell us it was Dana Didrikson who supplied him with the letters?'

'Are you looking for an answer,' said Diamond, 'or do I sense that you have it ready?'

Wigfull spread his hands to show how obvious his conclusion was. 'He's shielding her. He knows she killed his wife and he's shielding her.'

'Not too successfully,' commented Diamond.

'He expected it to come out, but he didn't wish to point the finger.'

'Why not?'

'Because he doesn't really blame her. He thinks she deserves to get away with it. It's not impossible that he loves the woman.'

Diamond's surprise at this confident analysis was surpassed only by his disbelief that it should have come from Wigfull, the plant from headquarters. He didn't object to anyone on the squad going for broke with some blinding theory . . . but *Wigfull*. He could only assume it was a rush to the head, a momentary loss of concentration, and he actually warmed to the man for showing that he was human. 'John, I'd like to hear more. What could her motive be?'

'Infatuation.'

Diamond glanced towards Dalton, who was preserving a statuesque neutrality.

'It's the classic set-up,' Wigfull said in support of his theory. 'She's a single parent, not too well-off, working her butt off to keep her kid in a private school. Jackman is the white knight, the fearless, good-looking fellow who rescued the boy from the jaws of death. She finds out he's a professor, loaded, with a big house and a wife who is not only making his life a misery, but actually tried to kill him. Dana sees him as the solution to all her problems if he'll ditch the wife. Inconveniently, he won't. He's so chivalrous, so loyal a husband, that he hasn't any plans for a divorce. So . . .' He climaxed his argument by drawing an extended finger across his throat, not a mime that fitted the facts, but sufficient to make the point.

'We'd better talk to her,' said Diamond, reserving judgement.

'Would you like to leave it to me?' Wigfull asked.

Diamond grinned. It wasn't a generous grin.

Chapter Eight

HARSH WORDS WERE SPOKEN IN Diamond's BMW when he missed a vital turning because Wigfull, navigating, was too late in pointing it out. Wigfull said in mitigation that Mrs Didrikson's address (which they had got from the phone book) happened to be situated between Widcombe and Lyncombe in the section of the map that lay along the centrefold and was not quite aligned after a repair with adhesive tape. In spite of the difficulties, he was confident of finding another way through. Diamond, sensitive to the charge that he was a cack-handed map-restorer, shifted the attack by commenting that the road Wigfull had got them into had not been built for the modern automobile. He'd never liked these hills south of the city, their pitted roads lined by uncompromising stone walls ten or fifteen feet high, overhung with dreary evergreens.

Wigfull stayed silent until the next problem arose. Unable to make a U-turn, they were obliged to take a route up a steeply inclined lane with a passage so narrow that it ought to have been designated one-way. As proof that it was not, they met a Post Office van making its way down, and were forced to reverse. At the second try, they got three-quarters of the way up before another vehicle appeared at the top, a red Mini, small, yet sufficient to obstruct the way. In common courtesy, the driver should have given way and backed up. He continued to advance, however, with his headlights on full beam.

'You know what they say in traffic division,' said Diamond. 'Always watch out for the ones wearing hats and driving red cars. This looks a prize specimen.' He stopped the car.

'I'll handle it,' Wigfull volunteered, unfastening his safety belt. The atmosphere was improving in the BMW now that they were united in the face of a common nuisance.

Diamond took a second look at the driver, who had also come to a halt. 'No. Leave him. He's ninety, if he's a day, poor old codger. Probably forgotten how to get into reverse.'

'In that case he shouldn't be on the road.'

Wigfull plainly felt that the sympathy was misdirected. He'd taken plenty of stick; why should some inconsiderate old man get away with it?

'Something tells me to let this one alone, John,' Diamond told him, turning in his seat and starting to back down the hill.

'Bet you wouldn't have done this in London,' Wigfull commented.

'You're right. I've gone soft as a cider apple since I came down here.'

'I hadn't noticed.'

At the foot of the hill, the old man in the Mini revved powerfully and passed them, recklessly removing his hand from the wheel to raise his hat.

'You see?' said Diamond. 'Politeness breeds politeness.'

Their third attempt was successful. They turned right at the top, negotiated two tight turns and found the name of the street chiselled into the wall. High above the street level was a terrace of six small Georgian houses set back from the road, each with its own iron gate. The Didrikson house was the second. Like the others, it was in need of cleaning, stained most heavily below the cornice and sills. They drew up outside and toiled up three sets of stone steps to a front door painted royal blue.

'Someone's in,' Wigfull said.

'Good – I wouldn't want to make this trip too often.'

Their knock was answered by a boy in the grey trousers, white shirt and striped tie of one of the more exclusive schools in the area – presumably the lad Professor Jackman had pulled out of Pulteney Weir.

'Hello, son,' Diamond hailed him. 'Is your mother in?'

This amiable greeting was answered with, 'We don't buy anything at the door.' The boy could have been any age from twelve to fourteen, at that stage of life when the features grow out of proportion and the look on the face expresses resentment at the process – or at the world in general.

'We're from the police,' said Diamond.

'Where's your warrant?'

'What's your name, son?'

'Matthew.'

'Matthew what?'

'Didrikson.'

'Well, Matthew Didrikson, do you ever watch *The Bill*?'

'Sometimes.'

'You want to pay more attention, then. We don't have warrants unless we're searching a place. We just want to see your mum. I'm asking you again. Is she in?'

'She goes out to work,' said the boy.

'We'll come in and wait.' Diamond stepped forward.

Momentarily the boy blocked the doorway in defiance, then took a step back as Diamond put a huge foot over the doorstep.

Wigfull, behind him, had spotted a movement along the hall. 'Someone's going out the back!' he said.

'Grab them.'

In the first stride of the pursuit, Diamond was stopped by a vicious kick in the groin. As any ex-rugby-player would, he reacted to the swing of the foot by attempting to swerve, with a simultaneous jack-knifing action. The movement would have saved him if he had not acquired so much extra poundage since giving up the game. His agility was unequal to the intention. True, the impact might have been more damaging had Matthew Didrikson been wearing leather rather than rubber. It still felt like being impaled on a heat-seeking missile and savaged by a Rottweiler at the same time. And the boy followed it up by making a diving grab for Diamond's thigh.

Acting on instinct now, Diamond handed him off and pitched forward on to his hands and knees, bellowing in agony. Somewhere behind him, the boy thudded against the wall.

The pain was extreme. Numbness would take over eventually, Diamond promised himself. Could he wait that long?

His eyes were shut tight. Through his groaning he heard Wigfull's, 'Leave it to me.' A superfluous offer.

By degrees, the pain spread and became less intense. Diamond opened his eyes. They watered copiously. Just as well, he told himself grimly, because he doubted whether the organ intended for watering would ever function again. He looked round for the juvenile delinquent who had maimed him. Prudently for his survival, Matthew Didrikson had fled through the front door.

With the help of a table-leg, Diamond succeeded in hauling himself off the floor. In a fair imitation of a Sumo wrestler charging his opponent, he lurched a few steps and found a chair. There he sat, conscious of nothing but the fire below. How long he was there, he neither knew, nor cared.

'You all right, sir?'

He looked up.

The fatuous question came from Wigfull.

'Do I look all right?' Even the vibrations of his own voice gave him pain.

'It was obviously Mrs Didrikson I saw,' Wigfull informed him. 'I didn't catch her, unfortunately. The house backs on to another street. She ran through the yard and drove off in a black Mercedes. I got the number.'

'So what do you want – a pat on the back?'

'I suppose you don't happen to have a personal radio on you?' Wigfull ventured.

'What would I want with a bloody bat-phone?'

'We could put out a message.'

'There's a phone on the table beside you,' said Diamond. 'Come on, man!' With that, he began to feel marginally better.

Wigfull got through and ensured that the motor patrols would be alerted. 'In that fast car she's probably heading for the motorway,' he said when he had finished. 'They'll pick her up in the next hour with any luck.' He continued to fuel his optimism. 'Well, we're quite a bit further on, funnily enough. The lady does a bunk and confirms herself as the number one suspect, in my book, anyway. She's going to regret this. Look, would you like me to see if I can find some sort of painkiller?'

'The first sensible thing you've said,' Diamond told him.

A short time later, he lowered himself gingerly into the passenger seat of his car. The codeine Wigfull had found in the bathroom was beginning to work. Wigfull closed the door gently on him and walked round to the driver's seat and got in.

Then he gave an embarrassed cough.

What's the matter with him now? Diamond thought.

'The keys.'

'Why didn't you think of it before? Why didn't I, come to that?' Nothing is so awkward as fishing in your pocket when you're seated in a car, or as perilous, when you're sore down there.

It was an effort and a pain, but Diamond prised them out and handed them over and they drove off. He didn't offer to map-read. It was up to Wigfull to remember. They took the two sharp turns and then steered left to the top of the narrow hill that had caused such problems on the way up. Wigfull stopped the car.

'Not again.'

The way down was obstructed.

Diamond started to laugh. It was ridiculous to do so, because every movement gave him a spasm of pain, but he couldn't prevent it. He shook with laughter.

The car halfway down the hill was a stationary black Mercedes — stationary because it had met another vehicle coming up. They were bonnet to bonnet, quite literally. The vehicle the Mercedes had hit was a red Mini with the headlights full on. The driver, familiar in his trilby, had got out and was standing beside the cars examining the damage. There was a figure still seated in the Mercedes.

'Can't be too serious if his lights are still working,' said Wigfull. 'I'll trot down and see.'

Diamond got out and hobbled after him. This was going to be worth the discomfort.

Chapter Nine

THE DAMAGE TO THE VEHICLES was slight, no more than a flaking of paint from the Mercedes and a small dent in the nearside wing of the Mini. But it was enough to provide a pretext. Having established that neither driver was injured, Wigfull solemnly took particulars from the old man – a retired doctor – who owned the Mini, while Diamond opened the door of the Mercedes, introduced himself and asked the woman inside to hand him the key.

'Thank you. Now would you move across to the other seat?'

She obeyed, her hands trembling as she put them out to support herself.

'Sure you're all right?'

'Yes.'

He lowered himself towards the driver's seat, then realized just in time that he wouldn't fit. The level of the seat had been raised by two squares of foam rubber, leaving so little space below the steering wheel that it would have courted disaster to squeeze the already suffering portion of his anatomy under there. 'I'll have to move these.'

She shrugged her consent and he managed the manoeuvre at the second try.

'You're Mrs Dana Didrikson?'

'Yes.' Her face had turned the colour of skimmed milk, accentuated by the brown hair that framed it. A neat, finely-shaped mouth and dark, intelligent eyes that now had a hunted look. Without it, Diamond might have guessed that she was a teacher or a social worker.

Capable of murder? he asked himself as he said aloud,

'Would you care to tell me how this happened?'

'I was driving too fast. It wasn't his fault. I thought I'd stopped in time.'

'Why the hurry?'

She let out a sigh that said this was playing games because they both knew the reason. 'I was trying to escape.'

Simple cause and effect. Naturally she'd hurried because she was trying to escape. From her deadpan manner, she might have been talking about the weather.

Diamond couldn't match her composure. He quivered. The adrenalin coursed through him. The breakthrough was happening. All those miserable hours by the lake, in the caravan, on the phone to Merlin, at case conferences, watching the pesky computer screens, teasing out information from the professor — were about to be rewarded.

His throat had gone dry. He dredged up the one word that mattered. 'Escape?'

'Out of the back of the house. Didn't you see me?'

'We saw you.'

'Well, then.' More words, apparently, were superfluous. Not wishing to say one syllable that might discourage her candour, he kept to practicalities. 'Your car was parked at the back, I take it?'

She nodded. 'I got in and drove too fast. What's going to happen to me?'

'We're going to require a statement. Would you wait here, please?' He hauled himself out of the seat and approached Wigfull, who was still going through the motions of questioning the elderly Mini driver. 'Reverse the Mercedes, John. She's willing to cough the lot, I think.'

The old man said at once, 'If she's admitting responsibility, I'd like it noted.'

'Thank you for drawing it to our attention, sir,' said Diamond. 'An officer will come and see you in due course.' He returned to the Mercedes and got into the back seat, behind Dana Didrikson. 'Back to the house,' he told Wigfull when he got in.

At the top of the hill, he transferred to his own car and drove the short distance, and somehow his soreness was

193

less disabling now. Wigfull followed in the Mercedes and they parked both cars in front of the Didrikson house.

The door stood open as they had left it. Sensing that a second escape bid was unlikely, Diamond allowed Mrs Didrikson to go in first. She called out a name.

'If that's your son you're calling,' said Diamond, 'he went out through the front as we came in.'

She said, 'He had no reason to run off.' More loudly, she called, 'Mat, are you there?'

Wigfull explained, 'He attempted to stop us from entering, ma'am. We could do him for obstruction and assault. He caught Mr Diamond well and truly.'

She said with contempt, 'He's just a schoolboy.'

Diamond signalled to Wigfull not to pursue the matter, a fine instance of altruism in the line of duty. 'We'll be wanting to interview you at some length, Mrs Didrikson.'

'Here?'

'Down at Manvers Street. It's late already. You might wish to put a few things in an overnight bag.'

'You want me to come to the police station? Can't you talk to me here?'

'That won't be possible.'

'What about Mat? I can't leave him alone all night. He's only twelve, you know.'

Diamond assured her that the boy would be taken care of in her absence. The Abbey Choir School had a house for boarders in Lansdown Road. While Mrs Didrikson, accompanied by Diamond, went upstairs to pack her bag, Wigfull spent some time on the phone arranging for a patrol to find the boy and drive him to the school to spend the night there.

Dana Didrikson's bedroom revealed little about the character of its owner, unless it was that she was tidy-minded and self-effacing. Emulsioned walls in the magnolia shade so popular with decorators. Fitted shelves, wardrobes and a double bed. Free-standing dressing table. A wall-to-wall carpet in a neutral stone colour. And matching curtains. No pictures, photos, books, stuffed animals or discarded clothes. Perhaps the reason why it so resembled a hotel room was that Mrs Didrikson's work as a chauffeur allowed her little time for anything but sleeping there.

She took a bag from the top shelf of the wardrobe and put in a few things. 'Now may I pack a bag for Matthew?'

Diamond gave his consent. He could hear Wigfull still on the phone downstairs.

They had to go up another flight to the boy's room, which had a more lived-in look. Cardboard birds and bats, made from modelling kits, were strung from the ceiling. Pop posters adorned the walls and socks and record-sleeves were scattered about the floor. An unfinished chess game stood on the top of a desk. Decidedly more lived-in, not least because its occupant was lying on the bed behind the door.

'Mat – I thought you were out,' his mother said. 'I called out and you didn't answer.'

He was on his stomach leafing through a comic, only his dark hair visible. He didn't look up.

'Mat – do you hear me?'

Still without turning to look at her, the boy said, 'They're the fuzz. They knocked me over and forced their way in. I asked them for a warrant, but they took no notice.'

'*Knocked you over?*'

Diamond explained, 'I pushed him aside when he aimed a kick at me.'

'Against the wall,' Matthew stated vehemently. 'You bashed my head against the wall and knocked me over. What do you want, anyway?'

'Your mother is going to give us some help with a matter we're investigating,' Diamond said, expressing it more sensitively than he thought the kid's attitude deserved. This looked a prime example of a boy in want of a father's authority and playing hell with his hapless mother. He went out to the landing and called downstairs, 'John, the kid's up here. He was here all the time.'

Back in the boy's bedroom, Mrs Didrikson was explaining to her son why it would be necessary for him to spend a night at school. Matthew made an unsuccessful appeal to be allowed to remain alone in the house, then turned his back on everyone and went back to his comic. His mother packed a bag for him, watched indulgently by Diamond, who felt a stirring of pity for the kid, in spite of everything. One night as a boarder was likely to be an underestimate.

PART FOUR
Dana

Chapter One

THIS IS ABOUT WHAT HAPPENED to Geraldine Jackman, isn't it? You want to know how I got involved with the Jackmans. I'm willing to talk about it now, if you'll let me tell it in my own way, but this is going to be quite an effort for me. I'm not one of those twittering women who broadcast their life stories to everyone in the supermarket queue. By nature I'm a private person, which sounds like a way of keeping people at a distance and often is, but I wouldn't describe myself as shy, which always makes me think of a five-year-old covering her face at a birthday party. It's more true to say that it doesn't come naturally to me to confide in anyone else. As a result, I'm sometimes accused of being unfriendly, or stand-offish. I constantly struggle to break out of it because, believe me, when you're a single parent, you have to speak up for yourself and your child.

After Sverre, my former husband, left me three years ago, I drove taxis, and you might think that was a peculiar way for a social misfit to earn a living. Actually it was my salvation. I learned to put up a front and shelter behind it. I could hear myself playing the part of the taxi driver and saying these mundane things about the traffic and the tourists and what I'd just heard on the radio, knowing all the time that the real me was a million miles back from the action. None of it touched me personally. But this situation is another thing altogether. Blood from a stone.

All right, let's plunge in. At the time I met the Jackmans I'd given up the taxi-driving. I had a job as chauffeur with Mr Stanley Buckle, the managing director of Realbrew

Ales. That's how I got to drive the Mercedes. It doesn't belong to me.

I was offered the job by Mr Buckle himself one evening when he used my cab for a trip from Bath to his home in Bristol. On a few previous occasions he had been my passenger and I'd got into conversation and found him pleasant enough, with just a suggestion of the mild flirting a woman cabbie gets from middle-aged males. Nothing I could take exception to. At that time I didn't know he was the Realbrew boss. I had a vague idea he had stakes in several businesses in Bath and Bristol, and of course I'd seen his beautiful house overlooking Clifton College, so I was pretty certain he wasn't stringing me along when he offered me the job. At the end of the run home, he simply asked me how much I took in fares in a good week and offered to match it with a regular salary in return for a six-day week and no nights. I would be allowed to use the company car whenever I wished, as long as I kept an accurate log of mileage.

I didn't hesitate. The taxi-driving had been a living, but it was a treadmill. Until that evening I'd seen no possibility of escape.

Of course you know about my son's fortunate rescue from drowning last July. You'll have heard about it from Greg – Professor Jackman. That was one of the most horrible days in my life, and not just because of what happened to Mat. I was in trouble with the police before I even heard about Mat. Not here in Bath, or you'd have known about it, wouldn't you?

I'm sorry. This doesn't sound very coherent, does it? I'd better tell you exactly how that day turned out, because it all links up with what happened later on.

Early in the morning, Mr Buckle rang me. He needed the car, so would I drive over to his house at Clifton by 9 a.m.?

This usually meant that he was making a business trip to London, and wanted to be ferried to Bristol Parkway in time to catch the train; the InterCity service was a full hour quicker than a belt along the motorway. But when I arrived at the Buckle residence that morning I had to revise my ideas. It was building up to be a really hot day, by the way. Not a cloud in the sky. The Filipino maid escorted me to the rear of the house, where my boss, flaunting a straw hat, powder-blue shorts and mirror sunglasses, was stretched out on a lounger beside the swimming pool. The only concession to business was a cellphone within arm's reach on the paving. He waved me towards a metal chair.

Mr Buckle was in a mood to match the weather. He apologized for bringing me out so early and offered me a fresh grapefruit juice. Then he asked me if my son had got his Common Entrance result yet.

I told him Mat wasn't taking the exam until next year when he'd be thirteen.

He said, 'In that case, take a tip from me, Dana. Give him a rest from books now. Let him get out and enjoy the summer.'

I nodded. Men are always giving me advice I don't ask for, as if male solidarity requires that Mat doesn't end up as that reviled creature, a mother's boy.

With that off his chest, Mr Buckle pitched his voice lower. 'The reason I asked you to come is confidential.' To reinforce the point he tapped the side of his nose. 'Family jewels, right?'

I shaped my mouth into an 'O' that was meant to imply that I understood without agreeing to anything.

'Far be it from me to lead young ladies off the straight and narrow,' he confided to me with a wolfish grin. The irony was that he was right. Charmian, the tigress he lived with, would claw out his vitals at the swerve of a roving eye. She'd made that very clear to me the first time we had met. 'What I'm proposing is rather naughty,' Mr Buckle went on. 'You're a Realbrew driver, and the Merc is a Realbrew car, but I have other stakes in business, as I'm sure you know. I want to borrow you for the day, so to speak. There's a small consignment of goods awaiting collection in Southampton. All my regular drivers are spoken for. Would you be an angel on this occasion and help me out?' His eyes uplifted in appeal reminded me of one of those plaster dogs used as collection-boxes for animal charities. 'It is extremely urgent.'

I hesitated. If he had given me my orders straightforwardly, I wouldn't have thought twice about them. The
way he'd asked made me suspicious. In view of his lifestyle
I'd sometimes wondered if all his activities were strictly
within the law. The last thing I wanted was to get drawn
into some racket. 'What exactly is it?' I asked.

'Teddy bears.'

After an interval to be certain that I'd heard correctly, I
said, '*Teddies*?'

'Eight hundred teddies made in Taiwan. Very small.
About this size.' He made a space between the thumb and
forefinger of one hand. 'They don't weigh much at all.
They're in four cartons that will easily fit into the car.'

An alert was sounding in my head. My brain hammered
out possibilities like a teleprinter. Southampton docks . . .
import licence . . . dangerous toys . . . hidden drugs . . .

'The paperwork is all in order, if that's what you're
thinking about,' he said to reassure me. 'You just show the
pass I'll give you, Dana, collect them from the warehouse
and bring them back here. Well, not here. There's a
lock-up garage in Whiteladies Road. I'll give you the key.'

'May I ask what the urgency is, if it's just a load of
teddies?' I enquired, trying to sound merely curious.

He spread his hands as if it were obvious. 'Come on, you
must have heard of the big charity day at Longleat House.
The Teddy Bears' Picnic, this Saturday. Every bear of any
distinction is there. Hundreds of teddies. And children, of
course. I've been asked to supply these mini-bears for
souvenirs, and I can't let the kiddies down.'

'Oh.' I could almost hear that song about the teddy
bears' picnic. Suddenly I felt extremely foolish.

And Stanley Buckle was grinning.

I agreed to make the delivery, of course.

I was on the A36 approaching Warminster when I was
stopped. The trip had gone smoothly enough until then. I
had found the warehouse in Southampton docks without
difficulty, signed for the teddies and loaded the four
cartons into the back of the Mercedes. I'd travelled some
forty miles on the return and was through Heytesbury

when I noticed a red car following me. At one stage I moved over, but they made no attempt to overtake, so I put my foot down a little because I didn't like being tailgated. A mile or so further on, I looked in the mirror again and saw a blue flashing light on the roof of the pursuing car. It hadn't been there before. The two men inside weren't wearing police uniforms as far as I could make out, but they were flashing their headlights like crazy, so I stopped at the next lay-by, and so did they.

I wound down the window.

The man at the car door told me he was from the police. He held up an identity card that looked official. He told me to turn off the engine and remove the key.

I obeyed, and the conversation went something like this.

'Did you know you were exceeding seventy miles an hour just now?'

'I wasn't aware of it.'

'Do you know the limit, miss?'

'Sixty on this stretch.'

'Where are you travelling?'

'Bristol. I've come from Southampton.'

'Business?'

'Yes.' As I spoke I thought of the packages in the boot.

He asked for my name and some form of identification. Then he asked the nature of my business. I described myself as a driver. There was a horrid sense of inevitability about the whole thing. I was asked to step out of the car and somehow I knew it wasn't to be breathalysed.

The second man had got out of the red car and walked over to join us. He showed me his identification. He was a detective inspector.

'Is the boot locked, miss?'

'I believe so.'

'Would you unlock it, please?'

I obeyed and pulled up the lid.

The four cartons lay there. I thought of my boss at leisure beside his pool while I went through this ordeal. If they found something and charged me, I would bloody well see that Mr Buckle took the rap. There might be honour among thieves, but I was no thief. Nor did I knowingly have possession of whatever items of contraband might be in those boxes. I would lose my job, but that would be less of a disaster than acquiring a criminal record.

One of the policeman asked, 'What's in those, miss?'

'Teddy bears,' I said, trying to sound convincing. If I was going to plead not guilty it was vital to stick to the story I'd been fed.

Glances were exchanged. The first said, 'What did you say the name of your firm is?'

'You didn't ask me. It's Realbrew Ales Limited, but I was asked to collect the teddies as a personal favour to my boss.'

'Personal. He likes bears, does he?'

I explained about the picnic at Longleat.

'I think we'd better have a look at these teddies. Would you mind opening one of the cartons?'

Squirming on the hook, I said, 'They don't belong to me. I require some authority.'

The inspector nodded. 'You can tell the owner we identified ourselves as policemen and asked for your co-operation. I take it you're willing to co-operate?'

I was handed a penknife. The pulse was still thumping in my head. I cut a line along the vinyl tape that sealed the lid.

'Remove the packing, miss.'

I lifted aside a layer of foam rubber – and a tremor of relief ran through me as I saw twenty-five small yellow teddy bears in five ranks lying on a bed of polystyrene.

The police insisted that I lift out each layer of bears until they had seen the entire contents of the box. Two hundred bears. Then they asked me to unfasten the other cartons. There was nothing to be gained by protesting; clearly they expected to find something. I felt the same flutter of nerves at each layer, but rank after rank of teddy bears gazed innocently up at me until the entire consignment had been checked.

The inspector picked up one of the bears and turned it over, examining it minutely. He and the other policeman withdrew a few yards and conferred. I watched them twist the teddy's head and limbs. The inspector gave it a shake and held it to his ear. He put it to his nose and sniffed it. The whole thing would have been laughable if I hadn't felt so intimidated by their suspicion.

Whatever they'd decided, it required some authority, because the inspector went to their car and used the two-way radio.

I tried to contain my anxiety by busying myself repacking the cartons until the policemen approached me again. The inspector handed me the teddy bear.

'In view of the way you have co-operated, I won't be reporting you for exceeding the speed limit on this occasion, miss, but take this as a serious warning. The limit is for your own protection as well as that of other road users.' He said nothing about the bears.

I murmured something suitably contrite.

The pair of them returned to their car and drove away.

Mr Buckle was still beside the pool when I returned to his house. He had turned the lounger the other way to stay facing the sun and his skin looked as if it might be sore later. He wasn't alone. There were two other middle-aged fellows in shorts playing cards under a sunshade beside the pool. They didn't look up. A third man was swimming lengths with a slow breast-stroke, and I had to look twice at his long hair, fanned on the water, before deciding that it wasn't white, but pale blond. He glanced across and assessed me in the way that men do. Apparently I wasn't worth even a passing nod.

My boss was asleep. I had to say his name twice. Then he stirred and asked me what time it was.

I told him and asked if we could speak privately, to which he said there was nothing he couldn't discuss in front of his friends.

So I told him what had happened on the road.

He paid close attention and didn't interrupt or comment.

'I think I'm entitled to know what it was all about,' I said in conclusion, and it was more of a demand than a request.

He rubbed the back of his neck. 'All this is a puzzle to me, Dana. Did they mention my name at all?'

'No.'

'That's the way they work, of course. You commit some minor traffic offence and they throw the book at you. Did they test your tyres and brakes?'

I shook my head. 'Didn't I make that clear? They weren't interested in the state of the car.'

'Well, it's nearly new. They could see that,' he said, 'so they tried to get you on something else. You did well to keep your cool, my dear.'

Still sure that I had been duped in some way, I went so far as to say, 'I think they were acting on a tip-off. They seemed so sure of themselves.'

He didn't seem impressed. 'I doubt it,' he told me firmly. 'It's their mentality. They see a big shiny Mercedes and they think it must be part of some scam. You'd better get used to this sort of thing happening, or drive more slowly.'

'You sound like one of them.'

He grinned and asked if I would care for a swim. He could find me a two-piece if I wished. 'Or just the one piece, if you feel inclined,' he added.

He was playing the philanderer again. Presumably Charmian was out for the afternoon.

I made some excuse and was about to leave when he remembered that there was a phone message for me. Would I call the switchboard at the office urgently? He handed me his cellphone.

And that was how I learned that my son had been taken to hospital.

Chapter Two

YOU CAN IMAGINE THE TURMOIL I was in. Anita, the switchboard operator at Realbrew, broke it to me as gently as she could, saying that apparently Mat had been taken to the Royal United only as a precaution after falling into the river, but when you get news like that about your own son you immediately put the worst construction on it. You think everyone is glossing over the seriousness of what has happened so as not to panic you.

Horrific possibilities filled my head while I was driving at high speed to the hospital, putting my licence and my livelihood in jeopardy. Things are never as straightforward as people would have you believe. Matthew was my only child, my entire family. I parked the car in the bay outside Casualty Reception, ran up to the entrance, took a deep breath to control myself, walked in and announced who I was.

I recognized the receptionist, but she gave me one of those plastic smiles that are supposed to ease the strain in Casualty, and told me that Matthew was being examined by Dr Murtah. I asked if he was injured in any way, and she wouldn't tell me a blessed thing, except to take a seat. Oh, and I remember that she half turned away and then took a second look and asked if she had seen me before.

I simply hadn't the mental energy left to remind her that I worked for Realbrew and had brought in a man whose arm had been fractured on the production line the previous week.

I went to a seat in the front row and rubbed the backs of my arms. The gooseflesh wasn't because the place was cold. This was July, remember. I'm often accused of taking life too seriously. No use protesting that I like a good laugh; as I told you, I'm guarded in my reactions to all but the closest friends. That's no bad thing. Anyone who drives for a living has good reason to treat the rest of humanity as wolves and vampires.

Presently, a white-coated man came over to me. He introduced himself as Dr Murtah and invited me to follow him. As we went through a swing door, he announced in the rather formal speech that Asians use that the young fellow – meaning Mat – should be none the worse for his misadventure. There was superficial grazing. And he'd had a jab in his backside. Dr Murtah had thought it wise to give him a precautionary shot of penicillin in case of infection.

He asked me whether Mat often played by the river, and I answered truthfully that I'd had no idea he was there. I could only assume he must have been playing truant from school.

'He is a scholar at the Abbey Choir School, he tells me.'

'Yes. A day boy.'

'Far be it from me to interfere, Mrs Didrikson, but when all is said and done he seems a good lad. We don't want a repeat of this misadventure. If I were you, I would ask your husband to read him the Riot Act. I wouldn't chastise him this time. He had a pretty unpleasant physical shock. However, I would leave the young tearaway in no doubt.'

'I understand.' I didn't say I was divorced. 'Thank you for attending to him, Doctor.'

He waved me into a cubicle and left me with Matthew, a distinctly chastened young tearaway sitting up on an examination couch.

'Mum.' Mat's eyes glistened.

I went to him and held him a moment, not saying a word. I didn't trust my tangled emotions.

He said, 'I'm –'

I put a hand over his lips. 'Later. We'll talk about it later. Not here.'

He said, 'They lent me this dressing gown. My clothes are still wet.'

'Doesn't matter,' I told him.

A nurse came in and asked if we had any transport, and I confirmed that we had. She told me Mat had better wear the dressing gown and sandals home, and I promised to return them later.

I tried to let the practical arrangements fill my mind. I stooped to help Matthew get his feet into the sandals, but he put his hand to them first. He didn't want to be mothered, you see. When he stood upright I was reminded that he was an inch or so taller than I – at twelve years old. It's curious how the relationship has altered since he gained that extra height. It's so easy to fall back into the old ways and treat them as babes in arms.

As we passed through the swing doors again, the receptionist stepped forward with a form in her hand and asked me to fill in a few details. She said it had to be done, and it wouldn't take a minute.

It was just a matter of my name and address and Matthew's date of birth and the name of our GP. While I was filling it in, I was surprised to overhear Matthew in conversation with someone. I looked up and saw him by the tea trolley with an overweight girl with cropped blonde hair and large earrings. She was wearing a blue linen coat, unbuttoned, over a red teeshirt and white jeans and at first it appeared that she was in charge of the trolley. Then she and Matthew came away from it carrying cups and I realized that the coat wasn't a uniform. It was part of her ensemble.

I went over to them. 'I thought you'd appreciate a cuppa,' the girl explained with a dimpled smile. 'Shall we sit down for a minute? How about the back row, Matthew?'

It crossed my mind that she was possibly something to do with the almoner service. I was handed a paper cup. 'Thank you, but I don't think I know you.'

'You may have heard of the name,' she told me. 'Molly Abershaw.'

I hadn't. I didn't know it and I hadn't seen her before. The remark smacked a little of self-importance, I thought.

'You want to get home, I know,' she told us both, 'and I shan't keep you longer than it takes to drink the tea. Did you want a biscuit, by the way, Matthew? I always forget to ask. I have to watch the calories myself.'

I'm repeating what she said, more or less, because it gives you an insight into the sort of person Molly Abershaw is, and she had a big influence on what happened. You must have come across her sort, with the cheek of old nick, brazenly going up to people as if they were the oldest of friends.

Matthew had the good sense to refuse the biscuit.

'This is such an exciting story,' Molly Abershaw insisted on telling us. 'I was out at Bathford when I got the call. I really put my foot down on the A4. I was thinking if I don't watch out I'll be in the news myself. It's so important to be first on the scene. My photographer is on his way. We'd like a shot of you, Matthew.'

'You're a reporter?' I said, hearing the disfavour in my own voice.

'Didn't I say? The *Evening Telegraph*. You don't mind, do you? A rescue story is such a joy to write when we so often deal in tragedy and disaster.'

I told her curtly that we'd rather not have anything in the newspapers.

'Mrs Didrikson,' she protested, 'it's unavoidable. If we don't run the story, the other papers will. It was a major incident by local standards. We won't print distortions, I promise you. That's why I'm talking to you, just to verify the facts. *Do* say you'll answer my questions.'

'What's the point?' I said, looking for somewhere to get rid of the tea. 'I wasn't even there. I know less about what happened than you do.'

Matthew added in support, 'And I don't remember much.'

She was very persistent. 'Listen, I'm not trying to harass you,' she said. 'I just need to check the essential facts. I don't even know yet whether there's a 'c' in your name.'

'There isn't,' I told her.

'It's unusual.'

'I'd rather not prolong this.'

Instead of taking this as a rebuff, she dipped into her handbag and produced a notebook. 'All right. Just the essential facts. How old are you, Matthew?'

Matthew glanced towards me to see if he should answer and I gave a nod, foolishly telling myself that we might get rid of her after she'd taken a couple of notes. 'Twelve.'

'And you were playing by Pulteney Weir. With friends?'

'Yes.'

'How many?'

'Two.'

'Who were they?'

'I don't want to get them into trouble.'

'Why – did they push you in?'

'No, I fell. I walked along the edge and tipped over.'

'And nearly drowned, I gather.'

'I don't know much about it.'

I stood up. 'There – that's all the help we can give you. Now, if you'll kindly allow us to pass, I want to get my son home.'

'But we haven't covered the rescue yet.'

'You heard what he said. He doesn't remember.'

'You *must* remember the man who saved you, Matthew. You saw him when you opened your eyes.'

'Yes.'

'Did you find out his name?'

'No. He was dark and he had a moustache.'

'What sort of moustache?'

Matthew put both hands to his face and traced his fingers from under his nose to the edges of his mouth. 'Like this.'

'Mexican style?'

He nodded. 'He was wearing a striped shirt and tie.'

'Smartly dressed, then. A young man?'

'Not very.'

'Middle-aged, would you say? Over forty?'

'Not as old as that.'

'Did he say anything to you?'

'He was talking to Piers mostly.'

'Your schoolfriend?'

Matthew let out a short, troubled breath. 'Please don't put his name in the paper. We were supposed to be in school.'

'You were playing truant, then?'

211

I just had to assert myself. 'I don't think this is a matter for the papers,' I told her. 'It's up to the school to deal with it, and I'm sure they will. Come on, Mat.' I made a move towards the door.

'I wish our photographer had got here,' said Miss Abershaw. 'I can't ask you to wait.'

'No, and we wouldn't.'

She walked with us out of Casualty and offered to drive us home.

I told her we had transport.

I looked along several lines of cars gleaming in the sun, trying to remember where I'd left the firm's black Mercedes. I had been in such a distracted state when I arrived.

'It's over there,' said Matthew, pointing.

Miss Abershaw was still standing beside us. 'You drive a Mercedes?'

Matthew came out with, 'My mother is a chauffeur.'

I said bitterly, 'Yes, put it in your notebook. Do you want the mileage as well?'

'I was only thinking that we all have to work for a living,' she commented, almost as an apology.

I hesitated as she felt for her keys. Do you know, the remark got through my defences? The girl's persistence had annoyed me, but a voice inside told me that she was doing a difficult job. She'd been sent by her editor to cover this story. It was not far removed from my own line of work — my boss, Stanley Buckle, sending me off to meet important clients at Bath or Bristol railway stations. Some of those VIPs turn out to be pretty unfriendly. I said, 'I'm sorry. It's been a hell of a day.'

'Do you think if Maxim, our photographer, called at your house in an hour or so, he could get a picture?'

I got into the car, picked up a card and scribbled our address on the back.

She said, 'Thanks. I really appreciate it. Will your husband be at home?'

'I'm divorced.'

Matthew spoke up and announced, 'My Dad played chess for Norway.'

I closed the door and started the engine. When we had driven out of the hospital gates I told him, 'You didn't have to say that, about your father.'

'It's true. I'm proud of him.'

I didn't say any more.

Chapter Three

MATTHEW STAYED AWAY FROM SCHOOL the next day, but
not because of illness. I decided he should have a day's
grace before he was called to his headmaster's study. It was
almost the end of term, anyway. You know the Abbey
Choir School, of course. There's the prep school which
Mat attends, and the main school for boys of thirteen and
upwards. He won't start there for another year. They take
Common Entrance in the year of their thirteenth birthday,
and his will be in February. The high flyers go on to some
of the best public schools in the country, but the majority
just move up to the senior school. The prospectus makes a
big thing about traditional values. Parents have to sign a
form allowing their boys to be 'chastised' for misbe-
haviour. It's supposed to be the right way of encouraging
respect and loyalty and most parents seem to accept it.
Truancy leads inevitably to a slippering.

I was educated at a comprehensive, a large one, and I
must confess that I find the public school methods quite
alien. I've agonized over whether I'm right to keep
Matthew at the school. Yet three years ago, when he was
nine, I pleaded with the head to admit him. It was at the
time when my husband Sverre had just deserted me. At
that low point in my life the prospect of bringing up a son
unaided terrified me. I'd failed completely in all my
relationships with men — my beer-swilling father whom I
grew to despise, the brothers I treated as rivals and still do,
and the husband who gave me up not for other women,
but for *chess* — so what right had I to raise a son to
manhood?

Well, I tell myself that the school is a male institution

and Matthew is learning to live among men, supported in the complexities of growing up. That's the justification, and now he's in the choir and everything, I doubt if I'll move him. I've worked damned hard to scrape together enough to pay the fees, first as a taxi driver, and now a company chauffeur.

I'd be happier if I really believed in the system. I accept that scripture and church music must play a prominent part in the curriculum of a choir school, and that Latin has to be obligatory, but why does everything else have to be treated in an old-fashioned way? In English they spend hours on clause analysis. The reading list ends at Dickens. The maths master bans calculators from the classroom. Games seem to consist of learning to hold a cricket bat correctly. There's no joy in it. You don't have to be an educationalist to see that there is too much cramming. And the use of corporal punishment is repellent. That's my opinion, anyway.

Surprisingly, Matthew has never asked to change schools. The only thing that he takes strong objection to is singing at the occasional Saturday wedding in the Abbey, obliging him to give up part of his one free day in the week. Otherwise he hardly ever complains. This truancy (at my school it was known more uncouthly as bunking off and I did it often) was a new development, unless he had been remarkably clever in covering it up.

When I asked him about it, he dismissed it lightly. Without looking away from the television, he said, 'Mr Fortescue was away on jury service, so our form was sent to the library. Three of us decided to go for a dip. That was all.'

'You picked a dangerous place for a swim, Mat.'

'We didn't swim. We were messing about in the water.'

'Whatever it was, it was dangerous. Why did it have to be you who went along the weir? Why not one of the others?'

'They dared me.'

'Oh, Mat!'

He turned his face towards me, ran his fingers through his hair and said on a note that signalled something of significance, 'Ma.'

'Yes?' I had ceased to be 'Mum' recently. I took it as a sign of Mat's wish to appear more mature. At the hospital he'd forgotten about this, but now he was the young man again.

'I'm sorry I caused all this trouble. It won't happen again.'

I hadn't been looking for an apology. I just wanted to reach out to him. I said, 'You're not alone in doing stupid things. I've done them. Everyone has, at some stage.'

He stared at me in surprise. 'He said that.'

'Who?'

'The man who got me out. He said almost the same thing as you just said. He used the word 'daft' – 'daft things'. He said some time in our lives we all do daft things. Something like that.'

I commented that he sounded a nice man, adding that I wished we knew who he was, so that we could thank him. Apart from anything else, his clothes must have been ruined.

Matthew said, 'It's funny that you should say the same thing.'

'I suppose it is.'

'We ought to find out who he is. I think I'd like to meet him again.'

'Well, I can't think where he would have gone in a set of wet clothes,' I told him. 'Maybe he went to the taxi rank by the Abbey. Tomorrow I'll ask the fellows I used to work with.'

I turned up the sound on the television. The strain of talking about the incident was difficult for both of us.

I was greeted warmly at the Abbey rank next morning, and there was the inevitable mickey-taking from the drivers about the Mercedes and my supposedly up-market status. At the first opportunity I asked about yesterday's incident. Nobody remembered a fare in wet clothes, but several of the fellows had early copies of the evening papers. I was handed the *Telegraph*. Prominent on the front page was the picture of Matthew under the headline *SHY HERO IN WEIR RESCUE*.

I read Molly Abershaw's report and had to admit that the story was broadly correct. I didn't remember a rather pious-sounding quote attributed to me, but the gist of it was true. Mat and I *did* want to trace the man who had gone to the rescue, and thank him personally.

I handed back the paper and asked the drivers to let me know if they heard anything.

My visit to the taxi rank made me nearly forty minutes late for work. When I got there, I slammed on the brakes at the sight of another black Mercedes parked in the space reserved for the chairman. The company owned two such cars, one for me to drive, the other for Mr Buckle's exclusive use. Wouldn't you know it! My boss's appearances at the Bathford site were pretty few and far between, and he was never usually in so early. In my fatalistic mood, I knew before talking to Simon, the office supervisor, that Mr Buckle had left word that he wanted to see me as soon as I reported for work.

Stanley Buckle bought a controlling interest in Realbrew in 1988, when it was on the point of collapse after years of ineffective management. He invested heavily in new plant and brought in a new team to run it, and already it looks as if the firm's decline has been halted.

Upon joining Realbrew Ales, I learned that Mr Stanley Buckle isn't everyone's idea of Santa Claus. He sacked half the existing staff when he took over, and several others have gone since for various shortcomings. Being summoned to his office isn't reckoned to be a promising way to start the day.

I tapped on the door and went in, prepared to be penitent – if necessary, to plead for mercy, offer sackcloth and ashes, anything . . . I needed this job. I couldn't afford to go back to taxi-driving. I'd sold my cab and the money had gone on a dozen essential things.

So it was immensely reassuring that Mr Buckle smiled as he looked at me over his half-glasses. Dressed as usual in a dark pinstripe that must have been Italian and outrageously expensive, and with the customary red rosebud in his buttonhole, he was giving out a distinctly roguish message for the time and place. He stepped around the desk and approached as if to embrace me.

The thought raced through my brain that if this was the price he wished to exact for my late arrival, I'd better settle for it. Physically, he was bald and beginning to be paunchy under the skilful tailoring, not exactly my fantasy lover, but this need not amount to any more than a token smooch. He reached out and grasped my upper arm, pulling me firmly towards him. Then, against all expectation, he pressed his hot hand against mine and shook it.

'Congratulations, my dear!'

My confusion must have been starkly obvious.

'. . . upon your boy's fortunate escape!' he explained. 'I read it in the paper. Miraculous! I spotted the name. Unusual name, yours. But I couldn't be certain until I saw the reference to Realbrew.'

That was what had pleased him: free publicity in the local papers. Saved by the power of the press!

He said, 'How about some coffee? What this must have done to your nerves! Is the boy really none the worse?'

'He's fine,' I assured him. 'The reason I'm late —'

'Late!' Mr Buckle cut in. 'We didn't expect to see you at all after a ghastly experience like that. Are you sure you wouldn't like the day off?'

'That's very generous,' I succeeded in saying, 'but it happened the day before yesterday.'

'Never mind. If there's anything we can do, just mention it.'

That evening I got home after Matthew. He was watching the TV and eating baked beans on toast. I didn't enquire what had happened when he'd reappeared at school; he must have had enough humiliation.

'There was a phone call,' he told me. 'That jumbo-sized reporter, Miss Abershaw.'

I sighed, partly in annoyance at Molly Abershaw and partly in her defence — against masculine insensitivity. 'Mat, she can't help her size. What did she want this time?'

'She asked if I could remember anything else about the man. She said she would call back when you got in. She *could* help her size if she dieted.'

'What exactly did you say to her?'

'There was nothing much I could say. I mean it isn't as if he had a safety pin through his nose. He was just an ordinary bloke with a moustache. I told her that.'

I asked him tentatively if he had any homework.

He switched off the TV. 'Plenty actually. The usual Latin vocab. And old Fortescue has given us a pig of a history project. We've each been given a street in Bath and we've got to write its history.'

'What's yours?'

'He really planned this. He said as I was given the kiss of life I should have Gay Street. It got a cheap laugh, of course.'

'Some of those masters are no better than the boys they teach. What are you supposed to do tonight?'

'Draw a large plan of it. We've got to show every building. Then tomorrow we start trying to find out when everything was built and who lived there and all that stuff.'

'It sounds more interesting than Latin verbs,' I said by way of encouragement.

The phone rang.

Molly Abershaw. She asked if I had seen the paper.

'Yes, I did,' I admitted in a tone that surrendered nothing.

'And did you like it?'

'Like it?' I said. 'I wouldn't put it as strongly as that. We're not accustomed to being in the newspaper, as I'm sure you must appreciate. But we can't complain. You kept to the facts of what happened. My boss was pleased you mentioned his company by name.'

On the other end of the line, Molly Abershaw was matching me in poise. 'Just out of interest, I was wondering whether you found out any more about the man who saved Matthew's life.'

'No,' I told her. 'Nothing else. I've been asking around, but with no result. That quote you attributed to me in your report – the one about wanting to thank him personally – I really meant it.'

Now the voice became more animated. 'That's why I wanted to talk to you, Mrs Didrikson. I've got this idea for a follow-up. I thought we might run a "Find the Hero" piece, appealing to our readers to help.'

'I see.'

'You don't sound too overjoyed.'

'To tell you the truth,' I said, 'I thought there wouldn't be any more in the papers.'

'But you said you'd like to find him.'

'Well, yes.'

'This is as good a way as any. What I would like from you is another quote to say how keen you are to find this man.'

'Obviously I am. He put his own life at risk and saved my son. We'd dearly like the opportunity to say how grateful we are, but –'

'Great. And Maxim would like to take a picture of you and Matthew together. He can do it first thing tomorrow if you like, before Matthew leaves for school.'

'That would be early. He leaves at 8.30.'

'No problem. Maxim will be with you soon after 8.00. And Mrs Didrikson . . .?'

'Yes.'

'Would you mind asking Matthew the names of his two friends? I'm hoping that they might remember some detail that would help us find the man.'

I was wary. 'I'm not sure about that. Couldn't we keep the boys out of it?'

'I just want a word with them. I'm wondering if between us we can get a description good enough to publish an artist's impression of the man.'

'The police do that to identify criminals,' I pointed out.

There was a moment's silence, then: 'I hadn't seen it that way, and I doubt if our readers would. Anyway, I would like to hear from those boys. They can talk to me on the phone tomorrow. Do you have our number? It's on the back page of the paper.'

I said that without making any promises, I would speak to Mat about it.

'Fair enough. And of course if Mat should remember anything else, I'll be delighted to hear from him.'

'I'll tell him.' I put down the phone. It was a strain being subject to so much interest. I had some sympathy with Matthew's rescuer if he wanted to remain unknown.

Chapter Four

ON FRIDAY, MATTHEW CAME INTO the kitchen and opened the fridge. I asked him what he was hoping to find.

'Some of that custard,' was his answer.

'You're an optimist,' I told him. 'You had the last of it yesterday. There's ice cream in the freezer if you're really desperate. What have they given you for homework this weekend?' Time always seems to be so short that my conversations with my son are reduced to this sort of exchange. I don't like playing the over-anxious mum, but that was how it must have seemed to him, and it certainly seemed so to me. At this age, he doesn't often want to share his thoughts, so we keep to the practicalities, and homework is inescapable.

He told me he'd been given a Latin translation to complete, a scripture reading for a test on Monday and – I quote – 'that sodding history project'.

'*Matthew*.' I'd heard much worse language when I was driving taxis, but from my own child it was wounding. 'What exactly are you objecting to?'

'We're supposed to find out the famous people who lived in the street and write something about their lives. It's easy for Piers. He was given the Circus, and there are plaques with the names up. I'm stuck with Gay Street, worse luck.'

'Well you must do some research. That's the point of the exercise, I expect.'

'Research?'

'Don't be so dumb, Mat. There must be books you can look up.'

'Where?'

'The library, for a start.'

'You've got to be joking.'

'Not the school library. The public library. We'll go tomorrow. I'll show you where to look.'

'What time tomorrow? You work Saturdays.'

'I can't say just now, love. I'll try and make time.'

He gave me a look that said he didn't have much faith. Then he turned his back on me and slouched into the back room. I heard him switch on the TV. I felt the tension in my neck and shoulders. If I couldn't spare the child enough time to help him with his homework, what was the point of it all? And my sense of despair wasn't helped by Mat's ungraciousness. I have to remind myself repeatedly that his behaviour is normal in an adolescent. He hasn't acquired the maturity to cope with his hormones – if they ever do. His father's example is no encouragement.

There was a sudden shout from the back room of, 'Ma, come here.'

It riled me. 'You don't speak to me like that, Matthew.'

'Quick.'

The urgency in his voice galvanized me. I found Matthew on his knees in front of the television set with his finger against the screen.

'That's him!'

'Who?'

'*Him* – the man who saved my life.'

On the screen I glimpsed a dark-haired man with a moustache, and then the camera moved on to other things, the interior of some lofty room with pillars and chandeliers. Then a young woman in a blue shirt was shown asking a question.

Matthew said, 'They'll show him again.'

'Who is it?'

'I don't know. I just switched over.'

The woman on the screen was asking some question that involved Jane Austen.

The man's face appeared again, responding confidently, spacing his words in a way that suggested he was used to being interviewed. There was an amused glint in his eyes as if he found the whole subject faintly ridiculous.

'That's him – with the moustache,' my son insisted.

'Thousands of men have moustaches like that.'

'I know.'

'It can't be the same man, dear.'

'Why not? It is.'

'Out of all the faces you see on television? This programme could be coming from Scotland, for all I know. Anywhere.'

'Ma, this is Channel 1. *Points West*. If you shut up and listen we might find out his name.'

The man on the screen was saying, '. . . in *Persuasion*, she wrote of the public rooms having to take second place to what she described as "the elegant stupidity of private parties". A touch of sour grapes there, I suspect. She didn't get the invitations she would have liked. These parties, or "routs", as they were called, were pretty wild affairs for their time, free from the rules and conventions that operated in the Assembly Rooms. So the numbers attending the balls were thin. In one of her letters, Jane writes of being cheered up when scores more people arrived at the Rooms after the private parties broke up. Can you picture her sitting here drumming her fingers on the chair-arms while she waits for the action?'

I said, 'He's talking about Bath.'

'So the pattern of social life was changing?' said the interviewer. 'Poor Jane missed the best years here.'

'Yes, by the time her family got here, Bath was socially on the skids. Brighton had taken over as the fashionable place. The Prince of Wales preferred the seaside air, so everyone of note started going down to Brighton instead.'

The interviewer turned towards the camera. 'And the Assembly Rooms began to be put to different uses. Professor Jackman, thank you. An exhibition about Jane Austen in Bath is being organized by Professor Jackman here in September. To take up the story of the Rooms in more recent years –'

Matthew turned down the volume. 'See? That's who it was,' he said elatedly. 'His name is Jackman.'

'But that man was a professor.'

'So what? He still got me out of the water. Ma, we've got to thank him properly.'

'We'd look awfully silly if you were wrong.'

'I'm not.'

'Mat, it's easy to make a mistake. People look different on television.'

'He didn't.' He pressed his lips defiantly together. 'Don't you want to find him?'

I hesitated. This threatened to become an issue between us. It could easily be settled. 'Of course I'd like to find him, if this is the right man, but I'd like you to see him properly before we approach him, not just on television. I wonder if he's in the phone book.'

Matthew went to fetch it.

Any lingering suspicions in my mind about the consignment of teddy bears had to be shed on Saturday morning. Mr Buckle asked me to deliver them to the Women's Institute tent in the grounds of Longleat House in time for the Teddy Bears' Picnic. The wild theories I had concocted in the small hours that some of the bears were stuffed with heroin or diamonds looked pretty silly now. And my boss was looking smug.

He hadn't finished with me, either.

'Little lady, I keep reading about you in the papers. Did you see the *Telegraph* last night?' He handed me a copy. 'Page Four.'

I turned to the page and saw a picture of myself with my arm around Matthew below a headline, '*HELP US FIND OUR HERO*'. I just said, 'God!' and didn't read on.

'I hope this fellow will turn up soon,' Mr Buckle remarked.

'Thanks.'

'If by the start of next week, say, he's still not found, I propose to offer a reward of £100 for anyone who can name him.'

I swallowed hard, not liking the idea one bit. Probably it was my boss's way of compensating me for the hassle I'd had from the police over the teddy bears. 'That's generous,' I said in a way that was meant to show appreciation without much enthusiasm.

He missed the subtlety entirely. 'Not at all,' he said. 'A gesture like this will do no harm to the firm's reputation.'

'What I was going to say is that I'm not sure if a reward is appropriate. Rewards get offered for information about bank raids and burglaries.'

'And lost pets,' he said. 'I see no difficulty.'

I didn't question his logic. Instead, I said, 'Don't think I'm ungrateful, Mr Buckle. I just don't want this man to feel hounded. He may prefer to remain unknown. He's entitled to his privacy, if that's what he wishes.'

'Fair point,' he conceded. 'Who knows, he might have a reason not to have been in Bath that day.'

'True.'

'We all like to slip the leash occasionally, wouldn't you agree, Dana?'

I answered evenly, 'In my case, it doesn't apply. But I'm not ungrateful for your offer — I mean the offer of a reward.' I left on my errand.

I made sure when I collected the four cartons from the lock-up that no one had disturbed them since I had deposited them there. To be completely certain, I checked that all eight hundred bears were present. Then I drove down to Longleat and handed them over to the WI for distribution to the children. It was all done by 10.30 a.m.

Having made such good time, I felt justified in slipping the leash – although not quite as Stanley Buckle had meant – to keep my promise to Matthew. I picked him up at home and we drove up Bathwick Hill in search of an address called John Brydon House. The owner, according to the phone book, was the only G. Jackman resident in Bath. I faintly remembered having driven past a house of that name on some occasion, but I wasn't going to make demands on my memory now.

I told Matthew, 'I'm making no promises. We'll just find the house and park the car somewhere near and see if he's about.'

'Suppose he doesn't come out?'

'Then we'll have to think of something else.'

'You mean knock at the door?'

'Don't keep on so, Mat. I told you I'm making no

promises.'

Really, he was right. The proper course of action was to call at the house. Trying to sneak a sight of the man without his knowledge was underhand, but I know how unreliable my son can be. He fantasizes. From the days when he first strung words together he peopled the streets of Bath with goblins, aliens from outer space, pop stars and characters from soaps. Although he has lately been more restrained with his sightings, I still thought it would save blushes all round to let him get a look at Professor Jackman from a safe distance before we attempted to introduce ourselves. I was pretty sure in my own mind that Mat would be forced to admit to a mistake.

We turned left and drove slowly for some minutes looking at the names of houses. Presently the street took on a more countrified look as the spaces between the plots increased. John Brydon House came up on the right. Matthew spotted the name on a gatepost a moment before I did.

I drove the Mercedes fifty yards or so further and stopped out of sight of the house, which was set back from the road in its own grounds. More grey than the local limestone, and extensively covered in ivy, it was neither Georgian nor modern; Victorian or Edwardian was my guess. A maroon Volvo stood on a wide, semicircular drive.

'AOK, chief,' said Matthew, slipping into one of his cops-and-robbers roles. 'Shall we stake out the joint?'

I wasn't equal to that kind of wit. 'Someone is at home, apparently. We'll walk slowly past.'

We got out and followed the line of the drystone wall that fronted the drive, trying not to stare at the house too obviously. Where the wall came to an end we paused beside an overhanging pyracantha bush that formed a useful screen, with a narrow view of the house and drive.

Matthew asked, 'Want to walk past again?'

'I think we'll stand here a while.'

'There's a path down there. If we cut through to the field we could see the back of the house. He might be gardening.'

'Don't agitate,' I told him.

Matthew gave a shrug and hoisted himself on to the wall

227

and sat bouncing his heels off the stones. Somewhere above us a blackbird warbled. It was good to hear. Bird-song is rare in my life.

Matthew said casually, as if to fill in the time, 'Mighty Molly gave us a bell last night.'

This time I didn't pull him up for insulting one of my own sex. 'You didn't tell me. What time was this?'

'Quite late. When you were running your bath. I told her you couldn't come to the phone.'

'What did she want this time?'

'Same as before. Did we have any news? She said quite a lot of people phoned the paper after she printed some stuff about wanting to find the hero. Some of them were watching when I was rescued. She said they described the man for her, but not one of them recognized him. I told her I could. I told her he was on the television.'

'Oh, Mat!'

He folded his arms and stared at the sky. 'What's bugging you now?'

I felt like wringing his neck. 'You told her that? Did you give her Professor Jackman's name?'

'Course I did.'

'You great ninny! Suppose you made a mistake.'

'I didn't. I keep telling you.'

'Mat, would you look at me when I'm talking to you? You don't say things like that to the papers unless you're one hundred per cent sure, and even then it isn't always wise to talk to them.'

'Why? We're not ashamed of anything. She was bound to ask me if I had anything else to tell her. Did you want me to tell a lie?'

'You could have told her . . . oh, what does it matter now? What are we doing skulking behind this bush if the whole thing is public knowledge?'

'It was *your* idea to come here,' Matthew pointed out ungratefully. He jumped down from the wall. 'Shall we call at the house, then?'

'I think we must. She will have phoned him by now, I'm sure of that. And Matthew . . .'

'Yes?'

'Leave the talking to me.'

'Be my guest.'

Mat's condescension stung me. I sensed an assumption of male superiority in the remark. It had got through to me in almost everything Mat had said this morning. It came from the school, I was convinced. I couldn't allow it to take hold. I was mother and father to him and I needed his respect. So I grasped him by the sleeve of his blazer and told him firmly, 'If you give me that kind of lip, young man, you'd better find someone else to dig you out of messes like this, because you're going to lose my sympathy here and now.'

His eyes widened and suddenly he looked very childish. 'Sorry, Ma.'

Saying, 'Come on. Let's get it over with,' I stepped out towards the house.

We had not even reached the entrance when Matthew said, 'Someone's coming out.'

I glanced over the wall and saw a man on the porch.

'That's not him!' Matthew said in a stage whisper. 'Ma, that's not him.'

I saw for myself that the man now moving briskly and with a bit of a swagger towards the Volvo in the drive was nothing like the professor we'd both seen on TV. This was a hunk of muscle and sinew not much over twenty, with swept-back straw-coloured hair and no moustache. He was in a cornflower-blue short-sleeved shirt, white jeans and white trainers. Some flicker of memory led me to think I'd seen him before in different surroundings. Generally when I recognize people they turn out to have been fares in my taxi, but you know how it is when your brain can't place someone. Mine was telling me this handsome young buck had never been in my taxi. I'd seen him in some other setting. I placed my hand over Matthew's wrist. 'We'd better leave it a few minutes. We'll walk past.'

We had not taken a couple of steps when a scene of pure melodrama unfolded. From the still-open door of the house came a voice in shrill protest: 'You can't walk out on me, for Christ's sake! Come back!' Then a woman with long, loose red hair appeared in the porch and dashed after the man, catching up with him as he opened the car door. She must have been some years older than he, with a face that was still pretty, yet with a strained, stretched look to the skin.

All this happened as Matthew and I passed the front of John Brydon House. I didn't like to take too obvious an interest, particularly as the woman was barefoot and wearing a pink silk dressing gown open to the thighs. I need not have troubled. The actors were too caught up in the drama to care about who was watching. The woman reached out and got a grip on the gold chain at the man's throat. She was trying to stop him from getting into the car. She cried out, 'Don't go, Andy, you can't do this to me! Come back in, please, please! What do you want me to do, get on my knees and beg?'

The man called Andy didn't answer. He was prising her fingers one by one from the chain as if he didn't want to risk snapping it by thrusting her away from him. Meanwhile she clutched a mass of his blond hair with the other hand, but that didn't appear to trouble him. Having succeeded in saving the necklace, he gripped her wrists, forced her to her knees and then toppled her off balance with a light, contemptuous push. She cried, 'Bastard!' as her shoulder made contact with the gravel, but a stronger shove could have made it a lot more painful.

By the time the woman was on her feet again, Andy had got into the car and slammed the door. He started up the engine. She drummed her fists on the window and cried, 'Andy, I didn't mean that!' The Volvo crunched on the gravel, swung into the road and headed towards Bath. The woman ran as far as the entrance and watched it go. She was sobbing.

Matthew and I had raised our walking pace from a stupefied shuffle to a quick march towards our own car, which fortunately was parked in the opposite direction from the route the Volvo had taken. We got in and closed the doors.

'Who do you think they are?' Matthew asked.

I told him I hadn't the faintest idea.

'It's the right house.'

230

'I know. Phone books aren't always up to date. Maybe your professor sold it to these people and moved somewhere else. Anyway, I don't propose to knock on *that* door.'

'What was she shouting about?'

'It's none of our business. Something private.'

'Like sex, do you mean?'

'Matthew, that's enough.'

'She wasn't wearing anything under that dressing gown. Was she a prostitute, Ma?'

'Don't be ridiculous.' I started the car.

'I was only asking. You hardly ever talk to me about sex.'

Liberated youth! At his age, I almost died of shame when my mother told me what to expect – without once mentioning the reproductive organs by name.

I reversed the car and drove past the house. The woman had gone and the front door was shut. We drove down into Bath and parked in one of the spaces opposite the Orange Grove. I was glad to have the distraction of the other promise I'd given to Mat – the visit to the local history section in the central library. I took him downstairs and we passed a quiet half-hour taking books off the shelves and looking for references to Gay Street. We discovered it was named after someone called Robert Gay, who had owned the land on which it was built. 'Big deal!' said Mat. But we managed to compile a list of former residents and visitors that included John Wood, Tobias Smollett, Josiah Wedgwood, Jane Austen and William Friese-Green. Matthew wrote down the names and said he hadn't heard of any of them.

'You've got to find out. That's the purpose of the exercise,' I told him, trying to generate some enthusiasm. 'We'll walk to the reference library now and I'll show you where to look.'

I left him making notes from the *Dictionary of National Biography* and went to buy a fresh parking card. When I got back to the car a large, familiar and not too welcome figure was waiting beside it.

Molly Abershaw greeted me by saying that the fellows on the taxi rank had spotted my car and suggested that I wouldn't be long in returning to it. Today she was in a multi-coloured poncho that she had probably bought from the Latin-American craft shop. 'I thought you'd like an early copy.' She handed me an *Evening Telegraph*.

The main story was headed PROFESSOR'S RESCUE PLUNGE. I read it rapidly. Clearly Mat and I could have saved ourselves some trouble if we'd picked up a telephone instead of peering over the wall of John Brydon House. Professor Jackman was confirmed as the hero of Pulteney Weir.

Molly Abershaw beamed and said, 'I must admit I'm quite chuffed with it. This has been my story from the beginning. It's really satisfying when you can follow it up like this.'

'So you spoke to the professor yourself?'

'After Mat put me on to him, yes. He's a bright lad.'

'Do you mean Mat?'

Molly Abershaw quivered with amusement. 'Both, I assume, but I did mean Mat, yes.' It was clear from the way she continued to smile that she had something else to raise. 'You didn't mind me speaking to Mat?'

'How could I object?' I said reasonably. I refused to be lured into saying anything controversial. 'He answers the phone if I'm out.'

'Very capably, too. Most kids his age speak in monosyllables. I'm sure the school makes a difference.'

'Possibly.' I was wary. I didn't want the school mentioned in the paper again and nor did Mat.

'May I ask, will you be going to see Professor Jackman to thank him personally?'

This was where Mat would have blurted out a graphic account of the incident at John Brydon House. Thanks to Mr Fortescue and his history assignment, however, the press was denied a salacious story. I answered with well-chosen words, 'We'll find some way of expressing our thanks, certainly.'

'I knew you would, and I can arrange it for you.'

'Oh, that won't be necessary,' I said quickly.

'You do want to meet him?'

'Yes, but –' My poise was gone.

232

'Shake his hand and all that?'

'Well, I expect so.'

'He's going to be at Waterstone's bookshop tomorrow. There's a signing by Ted Hughes and all the local literati are invited.'

'I couldn't possibly go.'

'Why not? It's open to the public. That's the point of these parties. It's all about selling books. You and Matthew can sidle up to the professor and have a quiet word with him over a drink. Much easier than calling at his house or going up to the university.'

I wavered. It did sound painless.

Molly Abershaw added, 'And Mat won't have to take any time off school.'

'He's quite busy with services on Sunday.'

'In the afternoon?'

I conceded that on balance no better opportunity was likely to present itself for expressing thanks to Professor Jackman. Fickle creature that I am, I found myself wondering what to wear.

'I'll probably see you there, then,' said Molly Abershaw.

Chapter Five

THAT SUNDAY LUNCHTIME, WATERSTONE'S BOOKSHOP in Milsom Street was teeming with people wanting a glimpse of the Poet Laureate, or his autograph. Just out of the scrum, Mat and I were at a temporary standstill between the fantasy and crime sections. We were keeping watch for another distinguished man.

Mat, under heavy protest, was in his red and white striped school blazer, grey trousers, white shirt and tie. I'd told him he couldn't turn up to an occasion like this in his usual Sunday choice of teeshirt and jeans, which the choir wore under their cassocks at the Abbey services. He'd grumbled to me that if any of his form-mates spotted him walking up Milsom Street in school uniform, his life would be hell next time he saw them. I'd pointed out that I could expect some flak myself from the taxi drivers if they saw me in a skirt.

'That's him!' Matthew said suddenly.

'Where?'

'In that group on the far side, close to the books.'

'There are books all around us.'

'Against the wall, under the *fiction* notice, just in front of the woman with the green hat. He's with the tall black man and that bald man with a bow tie.'

'Is that him?' I said. 'I imagined he was taller when I saw him on the television.'

'That's him all right,' Matthew insisted. 'He *is* quite tall.'

'Well, yes. It does look like him. You're right.'

Professor Jackman was talking animatedly to the people with him. With the black moustache and darting eyes and the hands vigorously reinforcing what he was saying, he looked more like a gondolier haggling over a fare than an academic. A communicator, obviously. No doubt his lectures were worth attending. I found myself wanting to get closer to hear what he was saying. Yet I was petrified by the prospect of interrupting him to introduce my son and myself. His reaction was impossible to predict.

Matthew, too, shrank from seizing the opportunity now that it had come. 'His hair is standing up more than when I saw him,' he said to me, blatantly marking time. 'Of course, it was wet. And he wasn't wearing a jacket.'

'That one is tailor-made, by the look of it,' I murmured. 'He must be hot.'

'So am I,' said Mat.

'There's a woman serving orange juice over there,' I said. 'Shall we see if it's for everyone?'

We'd not moved a couple of steps when I felt my arm touched and held. The air was warmer and there was a clank of metal jewellery. Molly Abershaw had found us.

'You're heading in the wrong direction, my loves. He's over there. My, you're looking smart, Mat. Come on, I'll introduce you.'

She cleared a route across the room, with Mat and me following like foot soldiers after a tank. The group around the professor was still listening keenly to his conversation.

'Professor Jackman?'

'Yes?' He turned, eyebrows raised at being interrupted in mid-flow.

'My name is Molly Abershaw. We spoke on the phone yesterday morning. I'm from the *Evening Telegraph*.'

The muscles at the edge of his mouth tightened. 'I thought it was agreed, Miss Abershaw, that I don't have any more to say to the press.'

The tank might have stopped advancing in one sense, but in another it trundled on. 'Relax, Professor. I'm not asking for a statement. I just want to introduce somebody to you – well, it's more of a reunion than an introduction, in point of fact. Remember young Matthew?' She placed her hand on Mat's shoulder as if there might be some uncertainty in identifying him. 'You can say your piece, Mat.'

Before Matthew opened his mouth, Professor Jackman said tersely, 'There's no need.'

'This is his mother, Mrs Didrikson,' said Molly Abershaw. 'They've come here specially to meet you.'

The bald man with the bow tie said, 'What's this, Greg – your past catching up with you?'

Molly Abershaw took a tighter grip on Matthew's shoulder and pushed him closer to the professor, saying at the same time, 'Stand back, Mrs Didrikson.'

Then a fresh voice said, 'Professor, would you look this way please?'

A camera flashed.

It was unexpected by everyone except the photographer and Molly Abershaw. In the mass of people I hadn't seen a camera until that moment. I was furious. The whole thing had been set up like an ambush and Mat and I appeared to be parties to it.

Professor Jackman said, 'What the hell is going on?'

'Hold it like that. One more,' said the photographer, a tall and bearded youth in a pink shirt.

The professor moved fast. He stepped forward, reached across the bookcase that the photographer was standing behind, grabbed him by the wrist and told him to open the camera and expose the film.

'I can't do that.'

'If you can't, I will.' He forced the hand and camera upwards.

'You'll damage it!' the photographer said.

'Do it, then.'

Molly Abershaw said, 'Hey, you've no right –'

'Correction,' the professor said without relaxing his grip. '*You* had no right. Bloody nerve you people have got. This is a party for Mr Hughes, not a football match.'

Heads were turning and conversation had ceased around us.

'All right, let go of my arm,' said the photographer.

Professor Jackman released his grip.

The photographer pulled the release to open the camera.

'Take out the film and give it to me,' the professor

ordered. 'Yes, I want the film.' He pocketed it and turned away, looked at some people, said, 'Incident closed', and returned to the group with whom he had been in conversation.

He had his back to us. I couldn't possibly speak to him now and nor could Matthew. I was mortified and angry, more for Mat's sake than my own. It was a horrid outcome to Mat's decent wish to express his thanks, and Molly Abershaw was to blame. Not the professor. His angry reaction was understandable. We had been cynically used, all of us.

I glared across to where Molly Abershaw was conferring with the photographer.

'Leave it, Ma,' said Mat.

He was right. There wasn't any point in another scene. We left it.

PART FIVE
A Pain in the Head

Chapter One

IN MANVERS STREET POLICE STATION, Diamond handed Dana Didrikson a mug of coffee and told her that a message had just come through about her son. Young Matthew had been delivered to his school boarding-house by a police patrol and they had left him watching the Benny Hill Show with some of his friends. 'So now you can relax,' he told her with a slight smile that conceded the absurdity of the suggestion, even if it was kindly meant.

She didn't respond, except to pass a slow glance around the interview room, its acoustic walls stained with coffee, cigarette-burns, hair-grease and undetermined substances. Over the past hour she had given a fair impression of a co-operative witness, recalling her first encounters with the Jackmans in a frank, dignified manner, as if the escape bid earlier in the evening had never happened, and it had always been her prime intention to talk to the police. Looking at her childishly small left hand as it rested quite flat on the wood table, apparently free of tension, Diamond was encouraged to think that Dana Didrikson was at peace with herself. Was it too much to hope, he wondered, that she had now resolved to confess to the murder and would presently explain in her unruffled style exactly how and why she had done it?

'Shall we go on?' he said, impatient to bring the interview to its climax.

Another tape was switched on, and John Wigfull, observing the letter of the law as usual, went through the ritual of assigning it with its number and stating the time and date.

'Let's take it from the party at Waterstone's, then,'

Diamond cued her. 'You were obviously embarrassed by what had happened there.'

'Mortified.' She shook her head, remembering, and then explained how later that same day she had plucked up the courage to phone Jackman at home. He had been out, and Geraldine had answered, been perfectly charming and invited her over the same evening to a barbecue. It had seemed a good opportunity of speaking to the professor, without any obligation to stay for long. Better still, when she had got there she had been met outside by Jackman himself. He had suggested driving to a pub and over a couple of drinks they had ironed out all the misunderstandings.

Wigfull, chose to comment, 'So you two got on well when you were one-to-one?'

She declined to answer, and no wonder, Wigull's interruption, in Diamond's estimation, was about as well-judged as three cheers at a funeral. This wasn't the time to probe her relationship with Jackman – not when she was just getting into her narrative stride again.

Leaving a distinct pause as the remark sank away, Mrs Didrikson continued, 'He told me about the exhibition he was organizing in honour of Jane Austen, and the problems he was having collecting exhibits. Somehow the talk led on to Jane Austen's aunt, who was had up for shoplifting in Bath. Greg told me the story and funnily enough that rang a bell in my head, although I said nothing at the time. Oh, and he generously said he'd like to meet Mat again. He offered to take him swimming in the university pool.'

This time Diamond himself interrupted her, flagrantly doing the very thing that had caused him to glare at Wigfull. 'Tell us about Jane Austen's aunt.'

'The shoplifting episode?'

'No. The reason it rang a bell.'

She took a sip of coffee first, and still the hand was remarkably steady. 'Well, you have to know that her name was Mrs Leigh Perrot. I think I told you about Mat and his history homework, and how I took him to the library to look up the famous residents of Gay Street.'

'The aunt lived there?'

She shook her head and betrayed some slight irritation.

'I'm trying to tell you, if you'll give me a chance. We started in the local history section in the basement at the main library, as I mentioned. The shelves were stuffed with books about Bath and Bristol and the towns round about, as you would expect, and while we were looking along the titles my eyes lighted on one that looked as if it had strayed from the zoology section. At a quick glance, I thought the title was *In Search of the Parrots*. When I picked it up, I realized my mistake. The word was *Perretts*, and it was by a George Perrett, a local man who had written this book about his family history. It didn't help our Gay Street researches, so I returned it to the shelf, but later, when Greg told me the story of Mrs Leigh Perrot, I privately decided to go back to the library and have a closer look at the book. It was just possible that I might discover something of interest to him ... and I thought how marvellous it would be if I could find out something he didn't know, something that might be of use in the exhibition, just as a mark of thanks for rescuing Mat.'

'You didn't say anything to Professor Jackman at the time?'

'No, there was no certainty that the book would mention Mrs Leigh Perrot.' And then Dana Didrikson pressed her hands together, locking her fingers tightly, slipping the reins of her composure as she recalled the moment. 'But it did,' she said with satisfaction. 'Tucked away in the middle was a paragraph pointing out that many of the Perrett family weren't considered worthy of mention in the various archives and what a pity it was that they had been so law-abiding, or they might have rated a mention somewhere, *like a certain Mrs Leigh Perrot*, who had been tried at Taunton in 1800 for shoplifting.' Her eyes dilated like a baby's. 'The name leapt out at me. It had to be Aunt Jane! And – even more exciting – the author added that there was a bundle of papers in the Wiltshire County Record Office containing an account of the trial and a letter signed by one of the Leigh Perrot family.'

'The Wiltshire CRO. That would be Trowbridge,' Wigfull put in stolidly, just to air his erudition, so far as Diamond could judge, but it sounded like a real dampener.

Thankfully Mrs Didrikson was too hyped up by the memory of these events even to pause. She went on to describe how she had gone to Trowbridge at the first opportunity and put in her application for the papers. 'To be honest, it was quite an anticlimax when they were put in front of me. The letter had been written by someone called John Leigh Perrot, and when I eventually deciphered the handwriting I found nothing of interest. And the account of the trial was very dull. I had a word with the assistant there, just in case they happened to have anything on file about Aunt Jane. He looked through a card index and consulted a computer, and found nothing. I was about to give up when one of the more senior people, an archivist, I think, came over and asked which name I was researching. I told her and she looked up the details of the acquisition of the papers I'd seen. She said one of her colleagues had been involved. Well, to cut it short, she made a call and this person on the end of the line was able to confirm that quite a stack of Leigh Perrot family letters had been offered for sale to the Record Office back in the 1960s, or whenever, and they had taken only a representative sample. Whoever had dealt with it had been unaware of the connection with Jane Austen. But they had the name of the man who had offered the letters, a Captain Crandley-Jones, from Devizes.'

'And you traced him?'

'Eventually. It took longer than I hoped. He wasn't in the phone book.'

'Meanwhile Professor Jackman had no idea you were on the trail of these letters?'

She shook her head. 'I didn't say a thing about it. It might so easily have come to nothing.'

'Then you contacted this man in Devizes?'

'His son-in-law. The captain had died, but I was given the address of his executor, the son-in-law, who lived on the Isle of Wight. I wrote to him and heard nothing for over two weeks. I thought the trail had gone cold, and of course there were only a few days left before the exhibition opened. Then one evening in the first week in September he phoned me. He said he'd been going through the captain's papers, and he'd found a receipt for the sale of a collection of sixty-three Perrot family letters. Sixty-three! The purchaser had been a stamp dealer in Crewkerne, named Middlemiss. He'd bought the lot in 1979 for £150. Naturally I drove down there the next day, and this time I was in luck . . . more luck than I could have dared to hope for. Mr Middlemiss still lived at the same address, and he still had the bulk of the Perrot letters. He'd bought the collection because some of the letters bore early postage stamps, which he'd sold at a good profit, I gathered. Then he'd put the rest into a box file and hadn't touched them since. He brought out the box and let me examine the contents.' Mrs Didrikson squeezed her eyes shut for a second. 'I can't begin to convey the excitement I felt going through those dusty old letters. They were in various hands and I suppose they covered a period of about eighty years. Some of them had squares cut out, where postage stamps had been. Fortunately the ones that interested me would have been written before stamps came into use, whenever that was.'

Like the bright boy in school, Wigfull supplied the date: 1840.

But Dana Didrikson was too gripped by her story to notice. 'Imagine how I felt when I found two short letters dated as early as 1800, addressed to Mrs James Leigh Perrot, at The Warden's House, Ilchester Gaol, and signed *Yr affectionate niece, Jane*. I'd struck gold.'

'Did Middlemiss realize their significance?' Diamond asked.

'I'm afraid I didn't tell him.'

'Naughty.'

She took it as a serious rebuke. 'I could never have afforded the price he'd ask. As it was, he wanted thirty pounds for them, and he thought I was just researching my family history. I paid cash and left. Was that dishonest?'

'No, it's fair game,' Diamond commented. 'The first rule of the open market: an object is worth no more and no less than your buyer is willing to pay for it. He was pitting his knowledge against yours. You were smart enough to know it was worth a bit and he didn't. You'd have been a fool to enlighten him. You needn't lose any sleep over it, except that you could probably have knocked him down to twenty-five pounds. They expect you to haggle.'

'I know – but I couldn't have stood the suspense.'

'So you got out fast.'

'And drove home picturing the moment when I would hand them over to Greg.'

'You were still in touch with him at this time?'

Mrs Didrikson hesitated, gripped the edge of the table with both hands and eased back, as if she sensed a trap in the question. 'I'd seen him on several occasions when he took my son swimming.'

'And to the cricket and the balloon festival,' Wigfull prompted her with sledgehammer subtlety.

That did it: frigidly, she remarked, 'You seem to know everything already.'

After an uncomfortable interval, Wigfull attempted to repair the damage. 'What I meant was that Professor Jackman went out of his way to be kind to your son.'

'Well, yes,' she conceded.

'Which gave you even more reason to make him a present of the Jane Austen letters.'

Diamond asked, 'When did you hand them over – the same evening?'

Again she paused before answering. Her fluency had gone and Diamond knew who to blame. 'Not that evening,' she answered eventually. 'A couple of days later.'

'On the eve of the exhibition, I heard,' said Diamond. 'What made you leave it so late?'

More unease showed in the way she grasped at her hair and flicked it off her shoulders. 'I, em . . . When I got back from Crewkerne, there was, em . . . an ugly scene with Geraldine Jackman. To my utter amazement, she was in my house, sitting in my living room drinking coffee.'

'Alone?'

'No. What happened was that while Mat was swimming with Greg up at Claverton, somebody phoned the Jackman house from Chawton – that's the cottage in

Hampshire set up as a kind of Jane Austen museum – to say that permission had been given for Greg to borrow several extra pieces for his exhibition. Understandably, he was keen to go down to Chawton straight away, so he asked his wife to run Matthew home in her car, which she did. Out of politeness Mat thought he'd better invite Geraldine in for a coffee, and she accepted like a shot, which explains what I walked into. What I cannot explain is the vicious and quite unprovoked attack that woman made on me almost the moment I stepped into my own living room.'

Diamond briefly locked eyes with Wigfull in case he was moved to interrupt again. 'A physical attack?'

'No, I don't mean she hit me, but the force of it was almost physical. This was the first time we'd actually met, you understand. We'd spoken on the phone some weeks before, when she invited me to her party, and she'd sounded quite charming. I couldn't believe this was the same woman. In fact, I didn't know who she was for a moment. She just bombarded me with abuse.'

'What sort of abuse?'

'Do I have to repeat it?'

'Everything you can remember, please.'

Dana Didrikson fingered her hair again and looked down into the coffee mug, speaking in a low voice. 'She began by asking me who I thought I was kidding by driving around in a Mercedes when I was really the town bicycle.'

Wigfull asked, 'The what?'

'For Christ's sake, John,' Diamond rounded on him. 'Carry on, Mrs Didrikson.'

'I was more surprised than offended. I asked who she was and she said she happened to be married to the man I was currently humping. This was in front of my son, a twelve-year-old.' She looked up, her face creased in distress at the memory. 'Can you imagine? I asked him to leave the room. Poor child, he looked blitzed. And before he was through the door she launched into an accusation so twisted in its logic that I couldn't believe she meant it. She said I'd used Matthew as bait, to catch her husband.

Having discovered that Greg was childless, I'd dangled Mat in front of him – those were the actual words she used – knowing how much he wanted a son of his own.'

'What did you say to that?'

'The truth – that she was talking bloody nonsense and I'd never slept with her husband. Then of course she did her best to justify her crazy notions by bringing up the times I'd invited Greg in for coffee after he'd brought Mat home from the pool. I mean, a coffee and a biscuit in my kitchen isn't grounds for divorce, and I told her so. But in Geraldine's eyes everything was part of this web I'd spun – the swimming, the days out, the drink I'd bought Greg in the Viaduct . . . someone had seen us, of course. There was no shaking her. In the end I just stopped protesting and let her carry on in the hope she'd get it all out and go. That's what happened. She hadn't come to listen to my point of view. She just wanted to let off steam, and by God, she did. Finally she stormed out.'

'She didn't actually threaten you, or give you some kind of ultimatum?'

'No, it was just a torrent of abuse.'

'How did you feel at the end? Bloody angry, I imagine.'

'Dazed is more like it. Reeling. The first thing I did was talk to Mat and tell him that the woman was obviously unhinged. He apologized for letting her into the house, but she had been perfectly agreeable until I showed my face. That's how it is with that kind of madness. Ninety-nine per cent of the time they seem perfectly sane.'

Diamond nodded.

'Just in case Matthew was tempted to believe any of her crazy claims, I gave him a solemn promise that they were all untrue. We agreed that Greg had a terrible problem with a woman like that on his hands. I told Mat that after what had been said I didn't think he should go swimming with Greg again.'

To Diamond's ear, this struck a note of bathos, but he treated it solemnly. 'How did he take it?'

'Manfully, for a kid of his age. Oh, he couldn't see the sense in it at first. After all, Greg had been like a second father to him through the months of July and August. So it was a wrench. I had to point out that Greg himself would be bound to put a stop to the swimming in view of what Geraldine was saying.'

'Did he see the point then?'

'Yes.'

All of this had given Diamond some vital insights. The incident may not have provided a direct motive for murder, but it had clearly struck deep into Dana Didrikson's psyche. Not only had her moral conduct been under attack; so had her integrity as a mother – and that was enough to goad any woman dangerously. Even this long after the incident, a feral outrage had shown in her eyes and voice as she spoke of Geraldine Jackman.

He steered her back to the main line of inquiry. 'And you had another problem on your hands – the Jane Austen letters.'

'Now do you understand why I didn't hand them over the same evening?'

'But you did eventually.'

'Yes. After a couple of sleepless nights. I thought why should I let that pathetically jealous woman deprive Greg of the satisfaction of owning those precious letters? They were of no use to me, but in his hands they were sure to make a stir in the literary world. They would guarantee the success of his exhibition. After the tremendous risk he'd taken to save my son, I'd have to be an absolute wimp not to face another roasting from Geraldine. So on the Friday evening, the night before the opening, I steeled myself to call at the house.'

'You could have posted the letters, surely, and avoided seeing Mrs Jackman?' said Wigfull.

'They were too precious to put in the post. Besides, there wasn't time.'

Diamond commented with more understanding, 'And I daresay you wanted to see his reaction when you produced them.'

The corners of her mouth curved, confirming that he was right. 'If I'm honest, yes. I phoned first, to make sure he was going to be there, merely telling him I had something I wanted to give him, and would it be convenient if I came over right away. And I took the opportunity over the phone to thank him again for his kindness to Mat and me, and to make clear that I'd decided that the swimming sessions must come to an end.'

'Did you say why?'

'I think he knew. No doubt Geraldine had told him her suspicions. She wasn't noted for being reticent. Anyway, he didn't press me. And when I got to the house it was Greg who opened the door, much to my relief, of course. And when I showed him the letters in the front room, oh, it was a terrific moment! I was *so* pleased I'd come. He was over the moon. He made me tell him exactly how I'd tracked them down, every detail. And then a man I didn't know came in, an American.'

'Dr Junker.'

'That was the name. He seemed to be an authority on Jane Austen, and when he saw the letters he was agog with excitement. He was confident that they were in Jane's hand. So when Geraldine Jackman made an entrance a few minutes later, she didn't get the attention she felt was hers by right. She played up like a spoilt child.'

Fascinating as it was to listen to a fresh point of view on an episode that was becoming familiar, Diamond fixed his mind on the facts as he continued to listen, rather than looking for insights into character. Dana Didrikson's account corresponded impressively closely with what Jackman and Junker had said. She had noticed Geraldine's blatant passes at Junker and she repeated that lady's mischievous suggestion that Jackman should show his gratitude by taking her — Dana Didrikson — out for a meal.

'Just for the record, you made no arrangement to visit the house again?'

'Didn't I make that clear?' she said. 'I was ending our association with the Jackmans.'

'And did you?'

'Yes.' She leaned back, fatigue showing in her brown eyes. 'That's it. I've nothing else to tell you.'

Diamond stared at her, uncertain for a moment whether she had spoken out of mischief or defiance. Suddenly he

250

was fazed, mentally unprepared for the show to stop in mid-performance.

'You mean you need a break now?'

'No,' she said. 'That isn't what I mean.'

'Come now, Mrs Didrikson,' he said gently. 'There must be more to come. We know there's more.'

Her eyes may have given a clue that he was right, but she wasn't willing to admit to it. 'Am I under arrest, then?'

'Not up to now.'

'In that case I'd like to leave.'

'In that case,' said Diamond, 'I shall be forced to arrest you.'

'For what?'

'Driving without due care and attention will do.'

'That's absurd.'

'Sorry. You're nicked, Mrs Didrikson.'

'What does that mean?'

'It means we can detain you for twenty-four hours, or thirty-six, if I so decide.'

Her lip quivered. 'But I'm expected at work tomorrow. My boss relies on me to drive him about.'

'He'll have to use a taxi, won't he?' He looked at Wigfull. 'Stop the tape there. We'll need a fresh one shortly.'

Chapter Two

'BEFORE WE GO BACK, JOHN . . .'

'Yes?'

'A word.'

Wigfull, eyebrows arching above that comic-opera moustache, appeared to have no idea what was on Peter Diamond's mind. Leaving Dana Didrikson in the interview room to mull over what she had so far failed to disclose, the two detectives had busied themselves independently for twenty minutes or so, Diamond at his desk, Wigfull at a phone in the incident room. They now faced each other at the top of the stairs.

Diamond came to the point. 'We're at cross-purposes in there. I get her going and you keep chucking spanners in the works.'

'Such as . . .?'

'You know damned well what I mean.'

'If you have a complaint about me, I'd rather you specified exactly what it is, Mr Diamond.'

How typical of his whole nitpicking approach, Diamond thought in a spasm of anger which he had difficulty in containing. 'It's more fundamental, John. You and I are not on the same wavelength. You're basically hostile to the woman and it shows.'

This was received with a cold stare. '*I'm* hostile? *She* did a runner.'

'That doesn't mean we have to come down hard.'

'Great,' muttered Wigfull, plainly implying that this kind of talk from the man who had put Hedley Missendale away didn't cut much ice.

Diamond would not allow himself to be deflected. 'Look,

the object is to get at the truth.'

'Yes, and the truth is that she was besotted with Jackman and murdered his wife.'

To Wigfull, it was all so obvious.

'You could be right, but there's still another dimension to this,' Diamond told him.

'The sob story, you mean?'

'I can't say. There's definitely more to come, if we give her a chance to tell us.'

'In other words, you want me to button my hairy lip.'

The note of self-mockery was a concession, a step back from cold-eyed hostility, and Diamond acknowledged it with a grin. 'The chance of that has gone. She's dug a bloody trench for herself. We've got to move in, but to a purpose. In my judgement, she won't respond to threats.'

'Okay, I said I'll shut up.'

'No, I want you to chip in. I need your command of the details. That's how we'll tackle her, with the truth, testing her story with the facts we know to be true, you and me, John, working as a team.'

This earned a grudging nod from Wigfull, and a sharp enquiry as to what line the questioning was to take.

Diamond was equal to it. They would begin by suggesting to Dana Didrikson that she had been at the Jackman house on the day of the murder. Whatever her response, they would commit her to an account of her movements on that Monday. Only when they had got a full picture of her day would they probe her motives or point out inconsistencies. It was the structured interview so beloved of training school instructors, and Wigfull couldn't fault it. Diamond added, to bring a human dimension to the exchange, that all this would be at great personal cost, because his wife Stephanie was using the late nights as ammunition in her campaign to have her kitchen modernized. She was serving him burnt offerings nightly.

'You should get her a microwave oven,' Wigfull advised him.

'I don't trust them.'

'They're part of the new technology. I wouldn't be without ours.'

'That figures,' said Diamond, prepared to believe that Wigfull's home was indistinguishable from an electricity showroom.

'Maybe you saw me on the phone just now,' Wigfull went on. 'I wasn't calling my wife. I don't, now that we have a microwave.' While Diamond was pondering the cause and effect behind that, Wigfull added casually, but with a note of archness. 'As a matter of fact, I was phoning Mrs Didrikson's employer, Buckle.'

'What for?'

'I told him she wouldn't be in to work tomorrow.'

'Wasn't it a bit late for that?'

'I got him at home.'

'I see.' Slightly put out, but wary, Diamond started walking towards the interview room. 'She'll be grateful, I'm sure.'

Behind him, he heard Wigfull raise his voice to say, 'I didn't do it out of the goodness of my heart, Mr Diamond. I asked him if she reported for duty on Monday, 11 September.'

He wheeled around.

Wigfull was looking as smug as a cat in the best chair. 'And she didn't. Buckle checked his diary. She took the day off. She wasn't at work on the day of the murder.' He spaced the words like an actor in a radio serial rounding off an episode. It demanded a burst of music.

Diamond wasn't moved to supply any. He merely nodded his head.

'You knew already?' Wigfull piped in disbelief.

Diamond answered in throwaway style, 'The statements are in from the door-to-door lads. I've just been through them. A woman in a black Mercedes was seen turning into the drive of John Brydon House shortly after 11.15.'

It was a much better pay-off.

She had her back to the door when they returned, and the tension was evident in her stance. A slight figure staring out of the window at the lights of Bath, arms crossed in front of her. Diamond was moved to think how little he'd learned of this woman's character in the two or three hours of question and answer. Part of the difficulty was that she'd obviously rehearsed her story in her mind, knowing that sooner or later the police would catch up with her. The smoothness of the performance had given few insights, save for those bursts of waspishness at Wigfull's interruptions towards the end. Admittedly she had projected a strong sense of moral obligation, whether towards her disagreeable son, her dodgy boss or the knight in shining armour, Professor Jackman, but how much of that was window-dressing remained to be discovered. One other pointer Diamond had noted: the still-potent sense of triumph in her account of the quest for the Jane Austen letters – the letters that looked increasingly like the spur to murder.

'Shall we resume?' he said.

'I've nothing else to tell you.' She need not have spoken. He could read the defiance in the set of her shoulders.

He nodded to Wigfull to run another tape and speak the preliminaries. When it was done, he reminded her of the formal caution before saying, 'We've just had some information about you, Mrs Didrikson.'

All this had no appreciable effect.

'We know you visited Geraldine Jackman on the day she was murdered. You were seen.'

This time a tremor of shock went through her, which she tried to convert into the action of rubbing her arms.

Diamond concluded his statement. 'So there must be something else to tell.'

Wigfull said, in his new, non-aggressive guise. 'Why don't you sit down?'

She half-turned and looked over her shoulder, in two minds, and then walked to the table and took her place opposite Diamond, her eyes glazed, as if too much was going on in her brain for it to interpret what she was seeing.

'You do admit going to the house?' Diamond put to her.

She dipped her head in what may have been meant as a positive response.

'Why?' Diamond asked, already departing from the structured interview he had proposed. 'Why did you go there?'

She spoke in a whisper too low to register on the recording equipment, 'To ask her to hand over the letters.'

'Geraldine?'

She nodded, and said in a slightly louder voice, 'I was sure she had them hidden in the house.' Her eyes began to function intelligently again. 'It was obvious that she must have taken them.'

Wigfull asked, 'How did you know they were missing?'

'Greg phoned me early that morning, about half past seven. He believed Dr Junker had taken them. He was going after him, on the train to London.'

'But why should he have told you about it?'

'He was sure Geraldine would call me out of spite, just to gloat. He didn't want me to hear it from her.'

On rapid reflection Diamond decided that this explanation was plausible. It was reasonably consistent with Jackman's suspicions of his wife.

'And did Geraldine call you?'

'No.' Mrs Didrikson leaned forward, her dark eyes suddenly in strong focus again. 'Which makes it even more certain that she had the letters herself. Greg was mistaken. I was positive she had them.' She used the word 'she' with unconcealed contempt, with a passionate dislike that had not been expunged by the killing. The animus between the two women must have amounted to more, far more, than the events so far described had justified.

Diamond knew he was in danger of being sidetracked, and this time he kept to the record of what had happened on the fatal Monday. 'So what did you decide to do about it?'

'I didn't do anything at first. I waited some hours. It really got to me, that she could be so bloody-minded. I was in such a state that I phoned my boss and made some excuse to get off work. About eight-thirty I drove Matthew to school and did some shopping in Bath. Had a coffee in one of those places by the bus station and did some thinking. While I was sitting there, a phrase came back to me, something Geraldine had said when I handed the letters over to Greg. She tried to rubbish them. She called them musty old things with no literary merit.'

A detail, Diamond noted, that they had heard almost verbatim from Dr Junker. Dana Didrikson hadn't previously mentioned it herself.

'You *must* understand the appalling thought that came to me,' she said, scanning their faces for a sympathetic response. 'She wouldn't think twice about destroying those precious letters. She would put a match to them rather than admit to Greg that she'd hidden them out of spite. It was up to me to stop her. It mattered more that she was stopped than any misgivings I had about crossing swords with her again.'

'So you drove out to Brydon House?'

'Yes.'

'What time?'

'When I got there? I suppose about half past eleven. Maybe slightly earlier. I rang the doorbell. Got no answer. Assumed she was out. Walked around the side of the house to see if by any chance a door was open. And the back door was.' She paused and stared at the back of her right hand, as if the memory was too taxing on her nerves to continue.

'So you let yourself in?' Diamond prompted.

'Yes.'

'And?'

'I called out. Called her name several times. Got no reply. Decided to make a search.'

'Go on.'

'Starting with the bedroom. If I'd been in her position, that's where I would have hidden them. So I went upstairs and called her name once more in case she hadn't heard before. I located their bedroom and looked inside. She was there.'

'What?'

'In bed. She was in the bed.'

Diamond kept his eyes on her.

It seemed that Dana Didrikson couldn't bring herself to say that Geraldine had been lying dead, but it was implicit in the way she had spoken. That was what she had intended to convey.

Diamond's first response was to treat it as another attempt to cut short the questioning. He didn't believe her.

Nor plainly did Wigfull. 'Are you serious?'

She answered, 'I'm telling you what I saw.' She had removed her hands from the table, but beneath it she was pressing them together with such force that her head and shoulders trembled.

'Mrs Didrikson,' said Diamond, 'for the record, I must ask you to state your meaning clearly. You said she was in the bed.'

'Yes.'

'And . . .?'

She whispered, 'Dead.'

'You're certain?'

'I didn't imagine it.'

'You'd better describe what you saw.'

She took a long breath. 'She was lying face upwards. Her eyes were open and seemed to be staring at the ceiling until . . . until I saw that they didn't move. Her face was a dreadful colour, as if she'd put on a facepack. Her lips were blue.'

Lividity, notably of the lips and ears, is a sign of asphyxiation. 'Did you touch her, feel her pulse or anything?'

'No. She'd gone. It was obvious.'

Painstakingly, as if they accepted every word of her story, they got her to describe the scene. Diamond had laid the ground rules: they would test the facts she gave them, and this was the method, inducing her to talk, suppressing their scepticism until the right opportunity came.

The body, she told them, had been lying diagonally in the bed, the congested and livid face at one edge, the auburn hair tousled, some of it below the pillow that lay beside her head in the normal position. Both arms were under the pale green quilt. Mrs Didrikson had not disturbed the bedding, nor touched the body, but enough of the shoulders were visible for her to see that it was clothed in a white sleeveless nightdress. She had noticed no scratches on the flesh.

The bedroom itself had revealed no obvious signs of a struggle except an empty glass tumbler lying on its side on the bedside table nearest to the corpse. The second bed had a matching quilt folded back on itself, and she thought she remembered a man's pyjama trousers lying across the pillow. She had not looked into either of the dressing rooms. The door to the bedroom had been open and the sash window partly raised. The curtains had been drawn back, giving abundant light.

'What did you do?'

'I thought I was going to faint. I went to the window and took some gulps of fresh air. Then I fled the room without looking at her again. I think I drew some water from the tap in the kitchen. I was functioning like a robot, as if it wasn't me.'

Diamond couldn't allow this to pass. 'Explain.'

'I suppose what I mean is that I was on autopilot.'

Wigfull said eagerly, too eagerly, 'Not responsible for your actions?'

She glared at him. 'You're trying to trap me, aren't you?'

It was left to Diamond to provide reassurance. 'We're trying to understand you, Mrs Didrikson.'

'Haven't you ever been shocked rigid?' she said. 'Don't you see that I'm trying to explain what it means to be in shock? I knew what I was doing throughout, if that's what you're asking. I felt stunned by what I'd seen.'

'And after you drank the water?'

'I left.'

'The way you'd entered – by the back door?'

'Yes. I made my way back to the car and drove home.'

'And then?'

'Had some brandy, I think.'

'What time was this?'

'I can't remember exactly – some time between twelve and one.'

'Would your son remember?'

'No. He has school dinners.'

'So what did you do next?'

'Sat and thought for a bit. Then put on the television to try and shut out the image I had in my brain.'

'You didn't report what you'd found?'

'No.'

'Not that afternoon, nor the evening, nor the next day,

nor ever. Why not? Why didn't you notify us?'

She was silent.

'Did you discuss it with anyone at all?'

She shook her head.

Diamond rested his hands on the table and drew himself up in the chair. 'You'll appreciate that it doesn't reflect too favourably.'

Still she made no comment.

'See it from our point of view,' he suggested to her. 'When we called on you this afternoon, you ran out of the back door. When we caught up with you and asked you to help us, you told us a certain amount and tried to have us believe that it was all you knew. You only admitted going to the house on the last day Mrs Jackman was seen alive because we told you your car had been seen there. And now you ask us to believe that you found her dead and for some undisclosed reason decided to do nothing about it. It isn't good, Mrs Didrikson. In fact, it stinks.'

Ripples of shock or tension disturbed her cheeks. Her lips remained tightly compressed.

He tried repeating the case against her point by point, demanding explanations, but she refused to speak at all. At his side, he could sense Wigfull's impatience with the procedure. The man was agitating to try the theory he'd been nursing all day.

It couldn't be less productive than the last ten minutes, so Diamond gave him a nod.

Wigfull said without preamble. 'Let's face it, Mrs Didrikson. You and Jackman are lovers, aren't you?'

It rocked her. 'No!'

'What's wrong? He was unhappily married. You're divorced. You met by chance, found each other attractive, and did what millions of people do.'

'That isn't true,' she said vehemently. 'There was nothing like that.'

'No sex?'

'No.'

'Come on, Dana, we're grown-ups.'

'You're wrong,' she insisted. 'We never did anything like that. Never. Not even a kiss.'

260

The way she spoke the last four words revealed more than she meant to. Wigfull paused a moment and suggested with a knowing smile, 'But you wouldn't have minded a kiss.'

She reddened and said, 'This is intolerable.'

'But true?'

'I've given my answer.'

'Fair enough, you say you didn't sleep with him.'

'And it's the truth.'

'I hope everything you tell us is the truth. Let me suggest something else to you. You thought the Jane Austen letters would please him.'

'What's wrong with that?'

'You went to no end of trouble to acquire them. In your heart of hearts, didn't you hope to rise in his estimation?'

'I may have done,' she conceded.

'The letters weren't just a way of thanking him for saving Matthew's life. They were a bid for his affection.'

'That wasn't why I did it.'

'But that afternoon when you drove home from Crewkerne with the letters in your car, you must have fancied your chances a little bit, Dana. Am I right?'

Again the colour rose in her cheeks.

'You're entitled to your private fantasies,' Wigfull pressed on. 'No one can blame you for that.'

With an intake of breath that sounded very like a hiss, she answered, 'Even if I did, it's not what you were saying a moment ago.'

'But it's broadly true?'

'I wouldn't say broadly.'

'Marginally, then?'

'I suppose so.'

Wigfull had scored a useful point, and he wanted more. 'And you came home to Geraldine and a right old rollicking. She accused you of — what was the word? — humping her husband, which wasn't true, and she brought your son into it, which infuriated you. More to the point, she scotched those romantic thoughts of yours, however marginal they may have been, and made it impossible for you or Matthew to go on seeing Professor Jackman. You were in two minds about what to do with the letters.'

The more Wigfull steamed on, the more Diamond felt that he was fitting the theory around insufficient facts. From the way Dana Didrikson had conducted herself so far, she wasn't about to break down and confess. She would stonewall all night if necessary. They needed stronger evidence. With commendable restraint, he let the monologue run its length and listened to Dana Didrikson's firm denial. Then, while Wigfull recovered his breath, Diamond asked her if she wouldn't mind having her fingerprints taken and submitting to a blood test in the morning.

She agreed, whereupon Diamond called an end to the interrogation for that day.

Outside, Wigfull was generous enough to admit that he had been over-eager, and the forensic back-up was necessary. 'We must also have her car checked for traces.'

'Yes. I intend to ask her for the keys in the morning.'

'No need.' Wigfull felt in his pocket and dangled a key-ring a foot from Diamond's nose. 'I drove it last, remember?'

Smart-arse, Diamond thought.

Chapter Three

HE AWARDED HIMSELF A LIE-IN until eight the next morning, followed by a decent breakfast — and why not? His presence wouldn't be required first thing in Bath. The fingerprinting and the blood test were laid on for eight-thirty and the car was due to be taken away for forensic examination at about the same time. Meanwhile Wigfull could play at being chief of the murder squad for an hour.

So a fortified Peter Diamond drove into the city at an hour when the sun was high enough to pick out all of the tiered ranks of Georgian housing in the familiar, yet still spectacular view from the slope of Wells Road, the gleaming limestone terraces topped with slate roofs as blue-grey as the backcloth of Lansdown. In the foreground, the castellated railway viaduct with its Gothic arches contrived to blend into the scene, dominated from this view by the pinnacled tower of the Abbey beyond it, and softened by patches of gold and copper foliage. A day when Diamond was almost willing to forget that the backs of most of the elegant streets and crescents were eyesores of blackened masonry, abandoned for two centuries to the ravages of the weather, builders and plumbers. Almost, but not quite. The policeman in him couldn't overlook the hidden side, just as he never took the citizens of Bath entirely at face value.

He hoped that cynicism hadn't taken permanent root in his character. He preferred to think of it more positively, as professional discernment. Experience had taught him that you cannot discount anyone as a possible murderer. Faced with a model of innocence, a bishop or a flower-arranger, you needed to be that much more alert, to guard against slack thinking. The Jackman case demonstrated the principle neatly. Who but a case-hardened policeman would be willing to believe that a professor from the university could be drugged and almost incinerated by his paranoid wife; and that a respectable working mother would suffocate the obnoxious woman and dump the body in a lake? Actually, if pressed to charge Mrs Didrikson on the evidence so far, he would jib. Certainly she had been evasive and obstructive, but he remained less sure than Wigfull of her guilt. She had discredited herself with her evasions, and now some evidence was needed. By the end of the day he expected to have it from the forensic lab. And at the end of the day he would be sorry; he had a sneaking regard for the woman. Perhaps in the last analysis there *was* a dash of the romantic in him.

Then his spirits took their usual downward lurch at the sight of the four-square institutional-looking building wedged between the Baptist church and the National Car Park. The best you could say for Manvers Street Police Station was that it was one of the few buildings in Bath that looked no worse from the rear. Inside, it was typical of pennypinching post-war architecture, drably functional and fitted with cheap wood and striplighting, a workplace where you needed to make a conscious effort to start the day cheerfully. His 'Grand day out there, isn't it?' drew no response from the men on duty, which was understandable, yet worrying. He wasn't used to being ignored and there sprang into his brain a suspicion that everyone else in the place knew something to his discredit and didn't wish to give him the bad news. The sergeant at the reception desk suddenly started leafing through the phone book and the computer operators in the incident room appeared mesmerized by their screens. All this was threatening to become a chapter out of Kafka until he caught the eye of Croxley and asked what had happened to Wigfull and was stutteringly informed that he was with the Assistant Chief Constable. Mr Tott had appeared without warning at 9 a.m. and asked to see Diamond. Soon after, Wigfull had been called upstairs. It was now 9.48.

The obvious assumption, Diamond reassured himself, was that the official copies of the Missendale Report had arrived, and Mr Tott was obliged to hand him one in person. If that were so, there should be no sweat. His own belated appearance need not be an embarrassment; he could supply a hundred reasons for being elsewhere in the course of duty. But he still didn't fathom how Wigfull came into it. And it did seem odd that the Assistant Chief Constable was acting as a delivery-boy.

He went up to the carpeted meeting-room on the top floor where Mr Tott installed himself on his rare visits. The girl posted as sentinel in the outer office asked him to wait. If John Wigfull was making some excuse on his behalf, it was a protracted one. A further ten minutes passed before the door opened and Wigfull emerged. On seeing Diamond, he gestured with open hands and a lift of the shoulders that he was powerless to influence whatever was going on. Diamond was making a dumb-show of asking what it was about when the Assistant Chief Constable appeared in the doorway and crooked his finger.

'Shut the door behind you.'

Ominously there was no invitation to be seated. Mr Tott, in uniform today, all braid and silver buttons, positioned himself at the far end of the oval table. On its surface were a cup and saucer, two biscuits on a plate, Mr Tott's peaked cap and his white gloves, but no copy of the Missendale Report. He seemed unwilling to speak. In fact, he looked immobile, a wax figure in a costume museum, assistant chief constable *circa* 1910. Diamond wondered fleetingly whether it was a sign of incipient paranoia if you believed you were being persecuted by men with ridiculous moustaches.

He decided he had better apologize for being unavailable earlier.

The substance of what he said was ignored, but it did induce an utterance from Mr Tott. 'I gather from Inspector Wigfull that you expect to charge the Didrikson woman with the Jackman murder.'

'It's possible, sir.'

'*Possible*? You put it no higher?'

'Not until I have the lab reports.'

'But you held her overnight?'

'Yes, sir.'

'And she is still downstairs?'

'I believe so.'

This encounter was markedly less friendly than their previous one. Mr Tott let out a troubled gust of breath and started pacing the section of floor at the far end of the room. 'You'd better tell me precisely what happened when you arrested her. I've already had Wigfull's account, you understand.'

'Is something up, sir?' Diamond asked in the hope of finding out what this was about before he committed himself. Clearly something *was* up.

'I am waiting, Superintendent.'

A lapse in procedure? he asked himself as he outlined what had happened. Some pettifogging breach of the Police and Criminal Evidence Act?

When he had finished, Mr Tott said, 'The boy.'

'Matthew?'

'Yes. He tried to stop you from entering the house?'

'We wanted to speak to his mother, as I explained.'

'And he challenged your right to go in?'

'He did more than that. He put in the boot, sir.'

'A twelve-year-old?'

'He caught me where it hurts most.'

'So you retaliated?'

With petrifying certainty, Diamond saw the drift of this cross-examination. 'That isn't what happened, sir. He was clinging to me and I pushed him away, as I described to you.'

'What you neglected to say is that he hit a wall.'

'It was a very narrow hallway, sir.'

'Do you deny that he was thrown against the wall, and hit it head-first?'

While his mind leapt ahead, picturing dire possibilities, Diamond tried to cling to the facts. 'He couldn't have been badly hurt because he got up and ran off.'

Mr Tott uncharitably allowed the remark to stand as long as it took Diamond to modify it.

'He wasn't hurt – was he?'

In a voice as dry as antique tapestry, Mr Tott said, 'He was admitted to hospital last night, as an emergency.'

'*Hospital*? Whatever for?'

'He blacked out. The school quite properly called the emergency number. It seems that concussion has been diagnosed.' Mr Tott gave out the information routinely, as if he were a hospital spokesman. Routinely and unsparingly.

'He was all right when I saw him last,' Diamond said, conscious how feeble this sounded. 'Conversing normally, quite relaxed.'

'The effects aren't always immediate,' commented Mr Tott, and then continued with the bulletin. 'They are taking X-rays, in case the skull is fractured. It's too early to tell if there is permanent damage.'

The whole thing was so incredible that Diamond wanted to ask if anyone had considered whether the boy was play-acting, but he checked himself. Such a suggestion was most unlikely to ease his predicament. Mr Tott was taking it seriously, and Mr Tott wouldn't take kindly to being duped.

Instead, he confined himself to a defence of his own actions. 'If the kid did crack his head on the wall, it was accidental. He kicked me in the privates first and then made a dive for my leg. All I did was push him away. John Wigfull saw it. He was right behind me, sir.'

Mr Tott shook his head. 'That's where you're mistaken. Inspector Wigfull didn't see it. His attention was directed to Mrs Didrikson. He had just caught sight of her making her getaway through the back of the house. He wasn't looking at you or the boy.'

Thanks a bunch, John, Diamond thought bitterly. Any brother officer with an ounce of loyalty would have given me some backing. Wigfull *knew* there was nothing deliberate in the hand-off.

'Whatever the rights and wrongs of it,' Mr Tott said in a cold, judicial tone, 'I have to consider the way it could be interpreted by others, outside the police. I mean the school and the parent. This morning I took a pretty irate call from the boy's headmaster.'

'Oh, no!'

'The school had not been informed that the boy had received a blow to the head.'

'It wasn't a blow, sir. Nobody struck him.'

'I'm not here to argue terminologies, Diamond. This is too serious for that. The headmaster registered a complaint and he assumes – not without reason – that Mrs Didrikson will wish to do the same.' He tilted his head back a fraction, signalling a significant statement. 'In the circumstances, I have asked Wigfull to take over the investigation into Geraldine Jackman's death. With the acting rank of chief inspector.'

'What?' Diamond's skin prickled and a pulse started thumping in his head.

'I'm relieving you of your command, pending a possible inquiry into your conduct. I have no option. What has happened may already have undermined our case against this woman.'

Even the semblance of respect cracked now. 'This must be Toytown. It's bloody Toytown. I don't believe it.'

'Have a care what you say, Superintendent.'

But Peter Diamond was in no frame of mind to care any more. 'Too late for that, Mr Tott. I've got your number now. I know what this is – your golden opportunity. You're terrified of my record. All that horseshit about no blame attaching to me from the Missendale inquiry and you hit the panic button at the first whisper against me. It suits your book beautifully. Your stooge was sitting in, waiting for me to screw up, and now he takes over. Well, I just hope he delivers. You bloody deserve each other. As for me, I'll save you the trouble of an inquiry. I'm quitting. You have my resignation.'

After which, he had nothing else to do but walk out and down the stairs.

Chapter Four

TOO ANGRY TO SPEAK TO anyone, he left the building and crossed the street, only to realize that even the timing of his exit was ill-judged, for the pubs wouldn't be open for another hour. He started walking, past the bus station towards Stall Street, telling himself that by degrees the anger would recede. He didn't regret what he had said. Every word had been justified, and if he had expressed it more diplomatically, he would still have been there trying to find an exit-line. All right, he could be called impetuous, wrong-headed and insubordinate, but he still had balls. To have capitulated to Tott, allowing himself to be sidelined, excluded from the murder squad, condemned to see out the rest of his career from behind a desk, would have been emasculation.

Regrets? None that would cause him to reconsider. He hadn't been long enough with Avon and Somerset to make strong friendships. And – it was no less true because he beefed about it so often – his job satisfaction had been in steep decline in recent years. The scientists were taking over CID work. The great detectives of the past – the idols of his early years in the force, like Bob Fabian, Jack du Rose and 'Nipper' Read – now seemed as remote as dinosaurs. They were honest-to-God detectives. They'd have been hamstrung by the paraphernalia of modern technology – computers, cellphones, photofits, police programmes on television, ultrasonic surveillance and genetic fingerprinting. Maybe he was rationalizing what had just taken place upstairs, but he didn't see how he could have lasted much longer in the modern police. He'd chalked up some modest successes over the years. Pity he was denied the satisfaction of clearing up the Jackman murder. Yes, that was a genuine regret.

His biggest concern was the shock this would be for Stephanie. Poor Steph was going to hear it cold. If *he* was stunned by the suddenness of his going, how much worse would it be for her? At least he'd been there at the time and brought it on himself. Steph hadn't been given the slightest warning that this would happen. Her world was about to cave in and she was likely to cave in with it. Even after the shock subsided, she would sink into a deep despair about the mortgage and the bills and the cost of staying alive. He would deal with those things as they happened, but Steph was a born worrier.

On his right as he made his way up Stall Street was an electricity showroom, and the sight of all those appliances in the window gave him a thought. As impulsively as he had quit his job, he marched in and asked to see the microwave ovens. Big enough to cast aside his principles in an act of mercy, he decided to go for broke, selected the one with the biggest display of controls and paid for it by cheque. They promised to deliver it to Mrs Peter Diamond the same afternoon. That, he told the salesman, would be the good news.

Coming out, he continued past the colonnaded entrance to the Baths and came to the Abbey Churchyard, his lunchtime haunt in summer. At this end of the year there were fewer tourists, so he had a wooden seat to himself. Only the pigeons remained in any numbers, and they converged on him at once, too single-minded even to coo as they searched the flagstones by his feet for crumbs. Then a loose dog, a black retriever, came running from the direction of Abbey Green, and the pigeons took flight. Diamond watched their whirring ascent. They formed into a tight flock within a moment of taking to the air and when they had wheeled out of sight behind him, he was left gazing up at the Abbey front, those stone angels perpetually trapped on the ladders. The consoling thought came to him that he could stop identifying with them now. Just as he started to look away, something strange made an impression on his vision, demanding a longer inspection. He squinted up at the stonework. He had spotted a feature of the carving he had never previously noticed. It was not a trick of the light, nor a failing of vision. One of the angels – the third from the top – wasn't sculpted in the attitude of climbing, but was upside down. No question. That angel was coming down head-first.

He couldn't summon a grin, but he nodded and said, 'You and me both, mate.'

He didn't, after all, make straight for the nearest pub. Apart from the bitterness he felt towards Tott, something else rankled – his strong suspicion that the whole thing had been founded on a deception. He didn't believe Matthew Didrikson had blacked out. It couldn't have been more than twenty minutes after the alleged incident in the hall that he'd seen the boy lounging on his bed, not in the least distressed, doing his best to convince his mother that what had happened amounted to deliberate assault by the police. In his rugby-playing days, Diamond had seen a number of genuine cases of concussion and not only had the effects been immediate, but the victims hadn't been able to recall the events immediately before they were hit. If the kid *was* shown to be faking, Diamond still couldn't turn back the clock and get his job back: he accepted that. But a disturbing possibility was beginning to dawn on him. His sudden resignation might be interpreted as an admission that the boy *had* been treated violently. Taking the worst possible scenario, he might find himself being sued for assault, facing ruinous damages. And it was too late now to turn to the police for support.

In this sombre cast of mind, he resolved for his own protection to find out the truth about the Didrikson boy's condition. Back to Manvers Street, then, to collect the car and drive along the Upper Bristol Road.

He had no qualms about showing his police identity to the woman in reception at the Royal United Hospital. Matthew, she told him, had been moved out of Casualty into a general ward. There, the ward sister confirmed that the boy had been X-rayed and they were waiting for the results. He had not suffered any further symptoms of concussion since being admitted and, yes, he was well enough to receive a visitor. In fact, some people from his school had been in earlier.

She pointed out the room where Matthew was supposed to be, but Diamond didn't find him there. He tracked the boy to the day room, where he found him watching television, a cigarette drooping from his mouth, supplied, presumably, by the only other occupant of the room, an old man who had fallen asleep in his chair with an ashtray in his lap.

It wasn't Diamond's job to issue a health warning, so he asked without a hint of disfavour, 'How are you doing?'

'I might be going home this afternoon.' Matthew had the trick of speaking without removing the cigarette. His gaze didn't shift from the television screen. He was in a grey hospital dressing gown, slumped in a low, steelframed armchair, his slippered feet supported on a coffee table, hands clasped behind his head.

'You're obviously feeling better, then.'

'Mustn't grumble.'

'No more blackouts?'

Matthew swivelled his head enough to take in Diamond without otherwise altering his position. 'It's you. Did they send you to check up?'

'They can phone the sister if they want,' Diamond pointed out by way of denial. 'You must like this place.'

A wary look passed across the brown eyes. 'Come again?'

'It's the second visit this year, isn't it? You nearly drowned.'

'That was yonks ago,' the boy said scornfully. 'They didn't keep me in.'

'How's the swimming coming on?'

Matthew's eyes slid back to the television. 'I had to jack it in, didn't I? Mrs Jackman kicked up a stink about it. She's dead now, serves her bloody right.'

'Do you remember the day it happened?' As he spoke the question, he thought, this is crazy. Hardly two hours have passed since I chucked in the job, and here I am refusing to let go, hanging on to some chance remark by

272

this bumptious kid in the hope of a new slant on the Jackman murder. Technically finished as a policeman, I can't let go. I'm continuing to function, like a headless chicken running around a yard.

'That was the day I went back to school,' answered Matthew.

'Monday, 11 September?' The question and answer routine – so much easier than small talk.

'Mm.'

'And your mother drove you there?'

'Yes.'

'Before you left, do you remember the phone ringing?'

'Yes. It was Greg, for my mother. You probably call him Professor Jackman,' he added with condescension.

'You don't recall what time he phoned?'

'Quite early. Well before eight. Ma was still in her nightie. She was hopping mad.'

'What about?'

'The phone call. She'd only just given Greg some really valuable letters some famous author wrote hundreds of years ago and they were missing. Greg thought some American guy had swiped them and he was going after him.'

'And your mother – what was her opinion?' Diamond asked.

'She was certain Mrs Jackman had them.'

'How do you know?'

'She told me when she was driving me to school.'

'What time was that?'

'Half-eight. We have to be there by quarter to.' He reached for the remote control and switched channels.

'Don't you like school?'

'It's full of little kids. I have to wait till next year to take Common Entrance. Then I'll just move up to the main school.'

'If you pass.'

'No problem. I'm in the choir.'

Diamond had transferred to a grammar school at eleven and to his mind there was something wrong with a system that held back boys of Matthew's size and maturity. 'Do

273

you mind being driven to school by your mother – a big lad like you?'

'It's better than walking.'

'You could take a bus.'

'I'd rather take a Mercedes.'

The remark confirmed how much emblems of status still mattered in school, any school. The boy's manner grated with Diamond, but he remembered his own adolescence well enough to understand the insecurity that lay behind it. Just as well, because the impulse to box the kid's ears – if only metaphorically – was strong, and a set-to would be disastrous. So with restraint – and curiosity unslaked – he concentrated on Matthew's memories of the day Geraldine Jackman had been killed. The choristers, he learned, had passed a dull morning in and around the Abbey vestry being issued with a clean set of robes; and in the afternoon the timetables and textbooks had been given out for the eight Common Entrance subjects.

'And was your mother there to meet you at the end of the day?'

'She never is. I get a lift with my friend's father as far as Lyncombe Hill. It's only an old Peugeot, but he's a school-teacher, so what can you expect?'

'You're interested in cars, Matthew?'

'If you mean decent cars, yes.'

'Ever tried driving one?'

'Give me a break – even if I had, I wouldn't tell one of the fuzz.' The last word held more disdain for being spoken in the well-honed accent of a private education.

Diamond followed up the possibility he'd raised. The assumption behind it – that the boy had contrived to murder Geraldine Jackman himself, then transported her body to Chew Valley Lake and dumped her there – bordered on the absurd, but now that he had started, he might as well go on. 'Some kids of your age manage to learn without going on public roads. It isn't illegal. I've heard of schools that give driving lessons on the premises.'

'All we get is piano lessons,' Matthew said, making plain his discontent.

'Maybe your mother –'

'You're joking, of course.'

'She could take you somewhere quiet, like an empty beach or a deserted airfield.'

'She won't even let me ride the dodgems.'

It wasn't deception. It was the authentic protest of a frustrated child and the end of Diamond's short-lived speculation. He had to dismiss the notion of Matthew at the wheel of the Mercedes or any other vehicle.

'Anyway, as soon as I'm old enough I want to get a Honda MT5,' said Matthew.

'So you do fancy yourself as a driver?'

'It's a bike, you dingbat.'

'Watch it lad.' The reproof sprang unbidden, and Diamond added more jocularly, 'I might just mention cigarettes to sister on the way out.' Doggedly, he reverted to the original line of questioning. 'That evening we were talking about . . . you didn't actually say if your mother was at home when you got back from school.'

Matthew took a last drag on the cigarette and stubbed it out. 'She was there.'

'How did she appear?'

'What do you mean?'

'Her manner. Was it different from other days?'

Matthew turned to look at Diamond again. 'You think she did the murder, don't you?'

'Did she go out in the car that evening?'

'No.'

'You're telling the truth, I hope.'

'Of course.'

Diamond said, 'Let me put something to you, Mat. You might think that what you're doing is the best way to help your mother out of a tight spot, but it might not work like that.'

Matthew flicked the televison to the testcard and looked up. 'What do you mean?'

'For a start, creating this diversion. The reason you're here in hospital. I don't believe you cracked your head that hard. I don't believe you blacked out. My first thought was that you were making a protest about having to spend the night at school.'

'That's not true!' Matthew said vehemently.

'But now I think it wasn't selfishness. I reckon you did it for your mother's sake. You thought we'd stop questioning her if you were taken ill. We'd have to bring her to see you.'

The boy was frowning. 'Well, you will, won't you?' Once again, it was the child speaking.

'It isn't up to me, son.'

The significance of what Diamond had just admitted went over Matthew's head. 'My ma wouldn't kill anyone.'

'If that's what you really believe, acting up as you did last night isn't going to help her.'

'You *did* shove me against the wall. That was the truth.'

'Yes,' said Diamond, 'and you kicked me in the goolies, but I didn't make a production number out of it.'

Matthew grinned.

Given time, Diamond reckoned he could achieve an understanding here, if nothing more. The bravado was paper-thin. Behind it was a kid pining for his father.

But they were interrupted by the ward sister. 'Your X-rays are through, Matthew, and we can't find anything amiss. I think we can safely send you back to school.'

'Right away?'

She winked at Diamond. 'After four, I think.'

Steph took the news infinitely better than he'd expected.

'When the microwave oven arrived, I knew something ghastly must have happened. I'm glad you thought of me. Of course, it's barmy getting me a present.'

'Stupid.'

'Not stupid. No, I won't have that. Daffy, if you like, but I always knew you were daffy – well, ever since that day you brought the donkeys to the brownies' camp.' She smiled. 'Not everyone appreciates you.'

'Too true. I wasn't right for the job. I was an ogre.'

'You're not a violent man.'

'Tell that to Mr Tott. Steph, let's face it, man-management wasn't my strongest suit. I got by because I drove people hard. No one was given any favours.'

'That isn't bad management. After all, you weren't running a playgroup.'

He was forced to smile.

She said, 'In your job it was no good trying to be popular.'

'No, but I had to command respect, and I'm not sure it was there any more. I should have kept up with technology. I was the only one on the squad without a pocket calculator. I still do mental arithmetic.'

'I don't think you ever settled down in this place.'

'It's not the place. It's the frustration. The top dogs provide you with all these aids and expect you to be super-efficient, but when all's said and done you're investigating people; dodgy people, dangerous people, frightened people. And the villains are more sophisticated than they would have been twenty years ago. You've got to talk to them, get inside their minds and tease out the truth. That's what I joined the CID to do. These days it's slide-rule policing. You have to justify the bloody hardware. Supposedly there's this infallible forensic back-up, but they're understaffed, and the results take weeks, months to come back. Meanwhile what do you do with your suspect? The law won't let us hold him indefinitely. Is it any wonder that we try for confessions? All these cases of statements taken under duress that you hear about – it's the result of pressure – pressure in a system that isn't functioning properly.' He sighed and shrugged. 'Sorry, love. I didn't mean to unload it all on you.'

'Better out than in,' Stephanie commented. 'But if you can face it, I'd like some help with my new piece of hardware. Let's see if we can work the microwave.'

Together they cooked a passable meal of steamed plaice and vegetables in a miraculously short time. They cracked open a bottle of Chablis and agreed that it wouldn't be wise for him to rush off to the Job Centre in the morning. He would take a week off, do up the kitchen (which now looked too scruffy to house the microwave) and think about his future.

In the morning he wrote his formal letter of resignation.

Chapter Five

ON THE FOLLOWING MONDAY THE *Bath Evening Chronicle's* main headline was *GERRY SNOO KILLING – BATH WOMAN HELD*. The essential facts were few. Dana Didrikson, a thirty-four-year-old company driver, had been brought before the magistrates on a charge of murdering television actress Geraldine Jackman on or about 11 September last, and had been remanded in custody. The proceedings had lasted only a few minutes.

With new priorities pressing, Peter Diamond turned to the Situations Vacant. He had to let go, he kept telling himself. The letting go was briefly delayed by a mental picture of John Wigfull cock-a-hoop in the charge room at Manvers Station, but the hell with it, he thought – I've moved on.

Traditionally, ex-policemen looked for work with private security firms. All morning, he had worked through the Yellow Pages, trying his luck with what he had always thought of as Mickey Mouse organizations. Some of the names made him squirm as he spoke them. 'Is that Secure and Sleepeasy?' 'Somerset Sentry-Go?' The only result of this phoning – apart from all the metered units he'd used – was the discovery that his seniority didn't have the pull that he'd counted on. If anything, it was a handicap; the people he spoke to didn't see an ex-superintendent riding the vans or on foot patrol in the big stores, and they were unwilling to take him on as an executive. His experience with murder squads wasn't a recommendation for dealing with business clients.

The Yellow Pages also listed a number of detective agencies offering vast ranges of services. On enquiry they turned out to be one-man outfits run by retired police sergeants uninterested in taking on an ex-superintendent as a sidekick.

In the next two weeks, he broadened the search, trying for office work of any description, and still got a series of rejections. Too many middle-aged men were touting for white-collar jobs, he was unkindly told, and had he thought of labouring? As this generally involved climbing ladders or wheeling barrows over planks, activities ill-suited to a fat man, he didn't warm to the suggestion.

His luck changed in the last week in November. 'I've been offered *two* jobs,' he was able to tell Stephanie one Friday evening. 'Two jobs that I am singularly qualified to perform.'

'Two – that's marvellous,' she told him. 'Are they safe?'

'Safe? I should say so! You know the new shops in the Colonnades, just off Stall Street? Well, they want a Santa Claus to rove around the precinct chatting to the kids and so on. Ho, ho, ho! All under cover. Three of us were interviewed and I got it on the size of my waist. I start tomorrow, for a limited season.'

'Oh, Peter.' Stephanie's face creased in dismay.

'What do you mean – "Oh, Peter"?'

'I know jobs are thin on the ground, but . . .'

'But what?'

'A detective superintendent dressing up as Father Christmas?'

'A DS no longer,' he reminded her.

'It's such a comedown.'

'Not at all. Santa is a VIP to twenty per cent of the population. The rest won't know me from Adam.'

She sighed. 'What's the other job?'

'Barman-cum-bouncer at the Old Sedan Chair, evenings only.'

'Where's that, for pity's sake?'

'The new pub in that road behind the theatre.'

'Don't they get a lot of rowdies from the disco club?'

'That's why they need a bouncer, my love.'

One evening he saw in the paper that Dana Didrikson had

gone through the committal proceedings at the magistrates' court and had been sent for trial at Bristol Crown Court on the charge of murder. He turned to the sports pages and tried to interest himself instead in a fitness report on Bath's crop of rugby international players.

He proved to be a popular Santa, in spite of the fact that he had nothing to give away except balloons stamped with the Colonnades logo. The role appealed to him and he filled it with a gusto and panache that had never characterized his police career. The awestruck faces of small children, eyes shining with anticipation, enchanted him. As a childless parent, he had never had much difficulty convincing himself that kids, like dogs, were in the main a nuisance. Now, behind the white nylon whiskers, he shamelessly played Dad.

One afternoon on the top floor of the Colonnades he saw Matthew Didrikson and a couple of friends playing some game that involved the glass-sided lift that served the three levels of the precinct. The shop-owner who had interviewed the would-be Santas had been sufficiently impressed by Diamond's police background to speak of the nuisance sometimes caused by boys of school age running about the concourse, but as Diamond had pointed out, a man in a Father Christmas outfit wasn't best-placed to control tearaway kids. As it happened, Matthew and his friends weren't kicking cola cans about or bumping into old ladies. The worst that could be said about them was that they were monopolizing the lift. It was a slack time, early in the afternoon, and he decided to leave them to it.

Shortly after, they must have tired of the game, because they came over to poke fun at Father Christmas. No small children were about, no danger of illusions being shattered, so he submitted to the send-up, which was as bawdy as he expected from schoolboys their age – did he have a fetish for black wellies? . . . or were stockings his hang-up? . . . and (pointing to the balloons) didn't he know what you were supposed to do with condoms?

They found their own wit so hilarious that there was a delay before Diamond's riposte got through: 'If you want to know, I get my kicks from shopping choirboys to their headmaster.'

The glee changed abruptly to near-panic. 'He knows us!' Two ran off. Only Matthew remained, staring him out with his dark eyes, and commenting, 'I know that voice, and that's a naff disguise.' It was serious criticism this time.

He was straight with the boy. He explained that he was no longer working with the police, and this was his job.

Matthew matched him in candour by admitting that he and his friends had slipped out of school for an hour. They were supposed to be rehearsing carols in the Abbey at four, and no one would bother about their whereabouts before then.

Diamond took the opportunity to ask something that had been on his mind since he'd read that Dana Didrikson was in police custody, charged with murder. 'Where are you going to be over Christmas?'

'With Nelson – one of my friends. And his parents. I'm spending all the hols there.'

'Kind of them.'

'Nelson owed me one.'

Diamond recalled what he had heard of the accident at Pulteney Weir. The boy who had flung the stick that had caused Matthew to slip had been called Nelson. A three-week stay wasn't bad compensation for one wild act of mischief.

Until hearing of this invitation, Diamond had assumed that the school would board Matthew somewhere during the holidays, perhaps at the house of one of the teachers. Quite an ordeal for any kid. Since their conversation in the hospital, Diamond's dislike of Matthew had lessened. He understood some of the reasons behind the brashness. If the truth were told, he had a strong streak of alienation in his own personality. In fact, his sympathies had shifted so far as to consider asking the boy over to their place for a day. He'd discussed it with Stephanie, and she had given her consent. She'd always liked kids. Now, after all, the offer wouldn't be necessary. Matthew would be better off with company his own age.

Matthew may have sensed the thaw. Revealing strains he

would not have owned to in front of the other boys, he asked, 'How long will she have to wait for the trial?'

'Your mother? Quite a few months, I'm afraid.'

'Will she get off?'

Diamond hesitated, torn between honest opinion and comforting lies. 'It depends on the evidence. Look, I think you'd better find your friends and get to that choir practice. Your mother has worries enough, without hearing that you're playing truant. Have a good Christmas, son.'

The bar work each evening was gruelling after a day on his feet parading the precinct. Thankfully there were intervals when he could shift his weight to a stool. The clientele were mostly under twenty – taking breaks from the disco across the street – generally amenable, but out to impress and not always exhibiting youth in its most appealing form, thus providing a counterbalance to Santa's small clients during the day. Even the most winsome kids grew up into teenagers.

The weeks passed, and so did his stint as Santa Claus. He and Steph spent Christmas quietly. A card arrived from the CID lads, a sombre scene of a decrepit old man dragging a yule-log along a snowy lane. Maybe that was how they pictured him in his new life. They had all signed it, including Wigfull. And when he looked at the names – Keith Halliwell, Paddy Croxley and Mick Dalton – they appeared remote, an indication, surely, that he *had* let go.

So much so, that one evening in mid-January he had to think hard before putting a name to the man in a black padded jacket who strolled into the Old Sedan Chair and said, 'How are you? I was told I might find you here.' A voice that was more Yorkshire than West Country. The penetrating eyes, broad face and black moustache of Professor Gregory Jackman.

Diamond gave his barman's nod. 'What can I get you, Professor?'

'A cognac. Have one with me.'

He turned down the offer with good grace, making clear that no other drink would tempt him. Whether the visit was out of curiosity, or had some ulterior purpose, a dignified aloofness recommended itself.

'I was told that you left the police,' Jackman ventured after he'd taken a sip of the cognac. He'd picked an evening when the disco was closed, and a mere handful of drinkers were in, at tables some distance from the bar.

Diamond busied himself washing glasses, so Jackman provided his own comment on what had happened since they'd last met. 'It's a bastard.'

Without looking up, Diamond said, 'I'm coping.'

'I meant the fact that you jacked it in. That really sunk Dana.'

'Leave it out, will you?' said Diamond. 'That's a closed book for me.'

'It isn't for Dana. She's accused of a crime she didn't commit. If nothing is done, she'll be sent down for life.'

'You expect me to do something about it?'

'She needs help.'

Diamond turned his back and reached for more empties. 'That's the job of her defence lawyers.'

'I've talked to her solicitor. She has no answer to the prosecution case.'

Diamond plunged the glasses in the water. 'She did it, then.' If his indifference to Mrs Didrikson's plight came across as callous, he was under no obligation to spare Jackman's feelings.

Some new people – a party of five Americans – entered the bar and stood by it settling the question of who should stand the round and what they would choose to drink. Jackman went silent until they had been served their drinks and taken them to a table.

'You don't really believe she's a murderer,' he said.

'What I believe or don't believe is of no more importance now than how I feel about the Channel tunnel or women priests,' said Diamond. 'I'd rather not prolong this, Professor.'

'Greg. You called me Greg when you were interviewing me.'

Diamond sighed, unwilling to believe that a man of intelligence had been taken in by an interrogator's ploy.

'How *do* I get through to you?' Jackman asked.

'That isn't the question,' Diamond said. 'The question is what do you want from me? And the answer is that I have nothing to offer except a drink.'

'You lived with the case for weeks. You did the groundwork. You must have come up with alternative theories, even if they were later set aside. That's how you can help – by suggesting avenues we haven't considered.'

'We?'

'Her defence. I told you I'm in touch with her solicitor.'

'Is that wise?' Diamond asked, intrigued, in spite of his determination to remain uninvolved. 'Surely the prosecution will be out to establish a relationship between you and Dana Didrikson. By actively taking up her case, you hand them a trump card.'

Jackman ran his hand through his hair and down the back of his neck, where it remained. 'I know. It's a dilemma. But I *do* care. I care passionately. Can I be frank with you? There's no relationship between Dana and me, not in the way it's generally understood. We haven't been to bed. We've never even talked in intimate terms. But over these difficult weeks I've come to regard her as someone . . . Oh, let's face it – I care about what happens to her. I want to get her out of this mess. And you're perfectly right. My involvement can only damage her now. God, I sound like something out of a third-rate Victorian novel.'

Diamond felt the creeping unease that any man feels when another bares his soul. Up to now he'd thought of Jackman as the flinty academic, urbane and self-possessed.

Nor had the soul-baring finished. 'And Dana has shown quite touching faith in me.'

'In what way?'

'Ask yourself why she didn't call the police on the day she found Gerry's body. She came to the house and found her lying dead in bed. Anyone would have assumed that I'd murdered my wife, wouldn't they?'

Diamond answered with a neutral twitch of the lips.

Speaking in the partisan tone of a smitten man, Jackman went on, 'She's incredibly good to me. Even after the body was found in the lake, she didn't come forward. When you went to interview her, she made a run for it. All very suspicious in the eyes of the law. But I'm certain she did it to protect me. She didn't want to be instrumental in getting me charged with murder.'

'How did you know she made a run for it?'

'From her solicitor. He's got the police file with all the statements.'

'In that case,' said Diamond, 'you're more up to date than I am. How much has she admitted?'

'Only that she went to the house and found the body.'

'She's sticking to that?'

'Of course.'

There was an assumption in that 'of course'. Diamond was expected to concur in Dana Didrikson's innocence. However, he remained unconvinced. Once or twice before he'd heard such rationalizing from men in love. Or guilty men.

'Has the solicitor discussed the forensic evidence with you?'

Jackman sighed and spread his hands in a gesture of helplessness. 'It couldn't be worse. They've established that her car was used to transport the body. Particles of skin tissue and some body hairs were found in the boot. The scientists proved by DNA analysis that they came from my wife.'

To say that it couldn't be worse was no exaggeration. The case was buttoned up now.

Out of charity for the man's state of mind, Diamond softened his conclusion. 'I understand your concern, Professor. These days you can't buck the scientists. There was a time when forensic evidence gave rise to different interpretations. Each side had its own set of experts. But with genetic fingerprinting, it's cut and dried. Faced with evidence like that, I'd have charged Mrs Didrikson with murder myself.' Bloody ironic, he thought as he said it. Peter Diamond conceding infallibility to the men in white coats.

'Surely there's room for doubt,' said Jackman. 'What if someone else used the car?'

'You mean she lent it to the murderer? You'd have to ask her. She said nothing about it when I interviewed her.'

'But would she? At that stage you didn't know the car had been used to move Gerry's body.'

'Her lawyers will have to ask her, then. I wouldn't place too much hope on it.'

Silence dropped between them as divisively as if the grille over the bar had been lowered.

Jackman hesitated, locked in thoughts of his own, staring down into the brandy glass and rotating the dregs of his drink. Finally, he said, 'That inspector who took over from you.'

'John Wigfull? Chief Inspector now.'

'Yes. Don't get me wrong, Mr Diamond, but one hears a lot in the press about wrongful convictions. From my observations of the man, he's highly ambitious. He seemed almost fanatically –'

Diamond cut in sharply, 'Don't say it, Professor. I'm not stabbing former colleagues in the back.'

'I'm trying to account for the inexplicable.'

'Obviously. Drink up, will you? I have some tables to clear.'

An hour after getting to bed dog-tired, he was still actively engrossed with what he had heard from Jackman. Stupid. He had no desire to get involved again. Any assistance he gave the defence would be taken as sour grapes, an embittered attempt to get back at John Wigfull.

From all he had heard, the case against Dana Didrikson was unassailable now that the forensic team had linked her car to the crime. Jackman's doting support would only strengthen the prosecution's hand. The motive couldn't be spelt out more clearly if Jackman had chartered a plane and flown over the city trailing a banner with the words 'Dana loves Greg'.

Yet he'd always felt that there was another dimension to the murder. Loose ends dangled tantalizingly. That strange business of the fire, and the question whether Geraldine Jackman had really meant to kill her husband. Was she paranoid, as Jackman had asserted more than once?

Then there was the extraordinary scene Dana Didrikson and Matthew had witnessed in the drive of John Brydon House, when Geraldine had fought with the man she called Andy, apparently to stop him from leaving. Was Andy her lover, wanting out?

And why hadn't the Jane Austen letters turned up?

He must have fallen into a shallow sleep for a time, because when he woke, it was still only 1.55 by the clock, and he was repeating question and response in the kind of maddening litany that troubled sleep induces: 'Who have I overlooked? Louis Junker, Stanley Buckle, Roger Plato, Andy somebody, Molly Abershaw . . .'

He sat up and thought, why am I bothering?

Nobody else does, except Jackman.

Wigfull is sleeping the contented sleep of a man who has wrapped up a case.

Maybe I'll sit up a little longer and think.

Chapter Six

HE PHONED JACKMAN AT THE university the next morning
– disregarding his own judgement that it was unwise to get
involved. The slender possibility that Dana Didrikson was
innocent of murder impelled him to pass on an idea that
had come to him in the small hours. 'Look, I've
remembered something that could possibly have a bearing
on the case. I'm passing it on to you because I believe it
might bring out the truth, but I don't want you
mentioning my name to the lawyers, or anyone else, do
you understand?'

'What is it?'

Jackman was too eager for Diamond's peace of mind.

'You guarantee to keep me out of it?'

'Absolutely.'

'It concerns Mrs Didrikson's car.'

'Go on.'

'You said the forensic tests established that your wife's
body had been placed in the boot of the Mercedes, right?
The assumption is that Mrs Didrikson drove with it to the
lake. When I interviewed her some days ago, she told me
she had to keep a log of every journey.'

'A log?' Jackman picked out the word and repeated it
without yet understanding its significance.

'It was a company car. The mileage showing on the
gauge had to be written in the book each time, even for
private trips. Get hold of that log, and you can find out
what use she made of the car on Monday, 11 September
and the days immediately after. If someone else used the
car to transport the body from Widcombe to Chew Valley

Lake, that's a round trip of thirty miles. It must show up in the figures.'

'Jesus Christ, you're right!' Jackman paused and then, sensing a catch, said with less buoyancy, 'But what if it doesn't show?'

'It has to. The only way a journey of that length could be wiped from the record is by falsifying the log . . . either inventing a trip to some other place, or making it appear part of a longer run. The point is, she would have noticed if there was a bogus entry.'

'True.'

'And if she falsified the log herself, it should be simple to check. One way or the other, you'll know.'

'Yes.' The enthusiasm was ebbing from his voice.

'Do you follow me, Professor?'

'Thank you, yes. I'll be in touch.'

'There's really no need.' Some people are afraid of the truth, Diamond thought. He put down the phone and looked for something else to do. It was a problem having so much time to fill.

Almost a week passed before Jackman phoned the bar one evening at a moment when it was under siege from the disco clientele.

'Who is this?'

'Greg Jackman. I've blown it.'

'What? I can't hear you.'

'The mileage log. I've really screwed things up for Dana.'

'Listen, this isn't a good time. People are lining up in front of me here.'

'Shall I come over?' Jackman asked, his agitated state obvious in his tone.

'No, it's too damned busy.' Diamond put his hand over the mouthpiece and promised two tattooed customers with punk haircuts that he would serve them directly. Then he told Jackman, 'I'll be on the go until closing.'

'Come to the house, then.'

'When do you mean – *tonight*?'

'Thanks. I'll be waiting.'

He'd meant to protest, not acquiesce. With so many people crowding the bar, he hadn't time to make himself better understood.

After the last customers had been persuaded to leave, and the doors were bolted, he thought of phoning Jackman again, then dismissed the thought. It wouldn't put the man off. The desperation behind the voice wasn't going to recognize that people were entitled to their sleep.

It was after midnight when he drove up to John Brydon House. Jackman came to the steps and put a hand on his upper arm like a despairing relative receiving the doctor on a visit.

'I really appreciate this.'

Diamond's heavy evening had left him bereft of cordialities. He said grouchily, 'I don't know why I came. I've damn all to tell you.'

They went inside. The interior was cold. Presumably the heating had gone off and Jackman had been too distracted to notice.

'You'll have to forgive the state of the place,' Jackman explained. 'You people . . . Sorry, let me start again. The police left it in a hell of a mess and I haven't straightened it out yet.'

'They must have been looking for the Jane Austen letters.'

'They needn't have troubled. I already searched the house from top to bottom. My files are going to take months to sort out again.'

The piles of books on the living room floor and the pictures removed from the walls didn't trouble Diamond; he'd seen searches before. Authorized them. He picked up a replica T'ang horse from an armchair, deposited it on the floor and sat down heavily, still in his raincoat. 'I'm not staying long.'

'Coffee?'

'Let's get to the point. It's the car log, is it?'

Jackman nodded. 'It's missing.'

'It should have been in the car.'

'Well, it wasn't. The police files contain no reference to it. I checked with Dana's solicitor. He said if it had been there, a copy would have been included in the file that was sent to the Crown Prosecution Service and made available to the defence.'

'True.'

'There's nothing – no reference to a log. Mr Siddons – the solicitor – has spoken to Dana. She insists that she always kept the log in the glove compartment of the car.'

'It was there the last time she drove the car?'

'The day you took her in for questioning.' No imputation of malpractice was discernible in Jackman's words. His own conduct preoccupied him. 'I was so concerned when I heard it was missing that I did the dumbest thing. At the time I didn't appreciate how damaging it could be. I went down to the police station and demanded to see Chief Inspector Wigfull. Did it off my own bat, without telling Siddons. I asked Wigfull if the police were holding the log.'

Diamond winced. 'That *was* unwise.'

'I mean, I didn't accuse him of perverting the course of justice, or anything like that. It was all very civilized. I told him Dana insisted the log had been in the car. He said it hadn't been found.'

'John Wigfull wouldn't tell you that if it wasn't true,' said Diamond in all sincerity. His former assistant was too much the police college man to sully his career with misleading statements.

Gregory Jackman drew no comfort from the assurance. He emitted a long, tremulous sigh that signalled more alarming depths in his confession. He was standing stiffly in front of a white, denuded bookcase like a convicted man lined up for mugshots.

'I made a blinding error by drawing it to their attention – handed a trump card to the prosecution. Siddons is incensed. He says they might have missed the significance of the bloody log. Now they'll seek to suggest that Dana destroyed it.'

The gravity of what had happened came home to Peter Diamond. Almost certainly the disappearance of the log would now be used against Dana Didrikson.

He asked precisely what she had told her solicitor.

'She's adamant that she never took the log out of the car except on the last day of each month when it went in for checking at the Realbrew office. She always got it back the next day. She's telling the truth. I know it.'

'Does she remember any discrepancies?'

Jackman shook his head slowly. 'She doesn't. She says it was up to date. The last entry would have been the day you arrested her.'

'Invited her for questioning,' Diamond corrected him. 'Was it all written in her own hand?'

'Yes.'

'She's positive?'

'Utterly.'

'So we must expect her to say so in court.' He took a grip on the chair-arms. 'I'm not surprised your Mr Siddons is busting a gut.'

Jackman looked about him as if he wanted to pace the floor, a feat rendered unlikely by the chaos of books and ornaments.

Diamond, meanwhile, was searching his own soul. 'I take a share of the responsibility,' he admitted. 'I started this hare.'

And should have seen where it was leading, he went on to tell himself. Dana Didrikson would have been better off if the log had never been mentioned. The prosecution were sure to question her about it now, and the more she insisted that it had been properly kept, the stronger would be the implication that she had destroyed it.

A sense of guilt oppressed him, adding to his burden of self-reproach.

'I could do with a coffee after all, if you don't mind.'

While Jackman was busy in the kitchen, Diamond brooded in the armchair. The probability was strong that Dana Didrikson was the killer, but to treat her guilt as a certainty was a cop-out. His interference had stacked the odds more heavily against her. If he could think of something to redress the balance, he had a moral duty to mention it.

Yet when Jackman returned with the coffee, nothing of comfort was said by either man.

*

At Realbrew Ales next morning, he started to expiate his error. 'No,' he told the receptionist, 'I don't have an appointment. On a visit like this it isn't the practice to announce that we are coming. Kindly inform the Managing Director – Mr Buckle, if that is he – that he has a visitor.'

'I'll see if he's free. Your name, sir?'

'Diamond.'

'And what shall I say you have come about, Mr Diamond?'

'Taxation.'

It worked. She mouthed an 'Oh', pressed a button on the intercom and spoke into it with her hand cupped over her mouth and her eyes on Diamond as if he were pointing a gun at her.

While waiting to be shown upstairs, he pictured the panic in the manager's office. From all he had heard of Stanley Buckle, his relationship with the tax authorities was likely to be precarious.

'You'll have to bear with me, old chum,' were Buckle's first words when the confrontation came. 'I'm supposed to be in Bristol for a meeting in twenty minutes, and you know what the bloody traffic is like.'

He got up from behind his desk and shook Diamond's hand, clearly resolved to disarm the threat if at all possible. The hand was warm and damp. Shorter than Diamond had pictured him, neat-featured, with slicked-back, receding black hair, Buckle beamed benignly and gold gleamed at the edge of his mouth. His choice of clothes was about right for a wheeler-dealer with a spread of business interests . . . fawn-coloured suit with brown shirt and a pale yellow silk tie that was probably called champagne-coloured by the fashion house it came from. A rosebud was in his lapel.

'I won't detain you long,' Diamond promised.

'Tax matter, is it?'

'It's not unconnected.'

'Nothing personal, I hope?' A smile.

Diamond shook his head. He could be amiable, too. 'Strictly business. I believe you have extensive business interests in the West Country, Mr Buckle.'

'That's putting it strongly,' said Buckle. 'I do a bit of importing in addition to my work here.'

'Importing what?'

'Novelty goods, cheap toys – that sort of thing. I supply quite a number of toyshops and stationers with items from the Far East.'

'Japan?'

'Hong Kong and Taiwan principally.'

'You ship the goods over and distribute them?'

'Yes. It's concentrated in Bristol and Bath. I charge the Value Added Tax. It all goes through the books.'

'Is it a good living?'

'I get by.'

'I heard that you have a large house in Clifton.'

'So what? There's no law against it.'

With what he intended to appear as the air of an inspector, Diamond whipped a buff folder from the brief-case he was carrying. From it he produced the Guide to Value Added Tax that he had picked up that morning from the VAT office in Ham Gardens House. 'You've studied this, Mr Buckle?'

A wide, defiant grin. 'Next to Charles Dickens, it's my favourite reading. Have a seat.'

The seats – apart from Buckle's vast executive chair – were fashioned out of beer-kegs. Diamond lowered himself on to one, and found it inadequate. 'So you do your own returns?'

'Actually no, squire. I have an accountant. Want me to give him a call?'

'Not just now. I presume you keep tabs on the figures anyway.'

'Figures in which sense?' Buckle punctuated this with a wink.

'The input tax. Mileage of all the vehicles in use by the company.'

Buckle became more serious, adjusting the knot of his tie and trying to make it seem a confident gesture.

'I think you'll find that our returns are accurate.'

'Do you keep a record, sir?'

'Naturally.' He opened the bottom drawer of his desk and took out a red ledger book. 'It's all in here. Every Realbrew vehicle is listed.'

Diamond held out his hand for the book. His hopes were dashed the moment he opened it. The mileage was in monthly totals. As evidence, it was no help at all. He went through the formality of asking how the figures were supplied and heard about the mileage logs kept by each driver.

'And when the logs come in, do you photocopy them?'

'No. I don't believe in paperwork for its own sake.' Buckle made a pistol of his fingers and pressed them to his head in a mime of suicide. 'Now tell me it's obligatory.'

Diamond opened a page of the ledger fully in front of him. 'The Mercedes-Benz 190E 2.6 Automatic Saloon.'

'Which one? The company owns two. One is for my personal use and the other is driven by the company chauffeur.'

'Two cars of the same model?'

'Bought at the same time. It all went through the books quite properly and I keep my own log religiously. You're welcome to examine it if you wish.'

'Yes, please. And the other . . .?'

'. . . should be with the other vehicle which – unfortunately – is not on the premises at the present time. If you'll excuse me a moment . . .' He called someone on the intercom and asked them to fetch the log from his car.

'The other vehicle, the one the chauffeur drives,' Diamond said. 'Is that the one being held by the police?'

Buckle's eyes snapped into sharper focus. 'You're bloody well informed.'

'It's public knowledge, sir. I can examine the log for that car at the police station – is that what you're telling me?'

'Not really,' answered Buckle. 'I gather it's gone missing. The Old Bill were on to me about it. They wanted to know if the log was on the premises here. There was no reason why it should have been. The system is that the books are kept in the cars and checked at the end of each month. The job never takes more than a day.'

'Your chauffeur's in trouble, I understand,' Diamond ventured.

'To borrow a phrase of yours, it's public knowledge,' Buckle said smoothly.

Equally smoothly, Diamond asked, 'Is she guilty?'

'I should think so. She was in pretty deep with the dead woman's husband. Mind, I'm not faulting her as an employee. She was a good driver. Reliable.'

Diamond felt a gut contempt for this man. He was finding it hard to subdue. 'She drove the one car, did she?'

'Just the one. She never used mine, if that's what you're asking.'

'It wouldn't have mattered if she did,' Diamond pointed out, 'seeing that they're both company cars.'

'True. But mine is exclusively for my own use.'

'And did you ever have reason to drive the chauffeur's car, sir?'

'Never. I had my own. Look here, if there's any suspicion that I'm on the fiddle in some way, you'd better come out with it.'

'I'm more interested in Mrs Didrikson,' Diamond candidly answered. 'You said she was reliable. Was she at work on the day of the murder?'

'She took the day off, but I don't see what this has to do –'

Diamond overrode the protest. 'And the next day? Was she at work the next day?'

'She was late. When she got in about half past ten she looked to me as if she'd been up all night. I didn't go to town on her. With a chauffeur as dependable as Dana, you know there had to be a damned good reason. I've told all this to the police.'

And Diamond could imagine what John Wigfull had made of it. Stanley Buckle was going to be a formidable witness for the prosecution, apparently believing the best of his chauffeur, while disclosing facts that were open to the worst interpretation.

'Who exactly are you?'

Diamond was saved from replying by a secretary who

brought in a small black book. 'The log?' he said, holding out his hand. 'Thank you, my dear.'

All the entries were in one hand, presumably Buckle's. The book was fully up to date and appeared to have been kept as meticulously as Buckle had claimed. The monthly totals tallied with the office ledger. On the critical day of 11 September two short journeys of nine miles were entered, and the same on 12 September.

Diamond thanked Buckle, said he would delay him no longer and left. On the way out, he looked for Buckle's Mercedes in the car park. It was parked in the space reserved for the managing director. The mileage on the clock matched the latest figure in the book.

His morning's work had come to nothing. The case against Dana Didrikson looked stronger still.

Chapter Seven

THERE FOLLOWED A HIATUS OF three months during which Peter Diamond tried to persuade himself that he could do nothing more for Dana Didrikson, that it would be better for all concerned if he let the law take its course. His thinking came down to this: he expected her to be found guilty, and his knowledge of the case suggested that the verdict would be right. He didn't expect the trial to last long. It wouldn't surprise him if she changed her plea to guilty.

She would serve probably a dozen years of the life sentence and be released on licence. She was no danger to society. Most of the murderers he'd known had been like her – a group apart from other criminals . . . people driven by family pressures or their own obsession to commit one crime in their lives.

And yet . . .

A vestige of unease lingered in his mind. Certain things about the case still challenged an explanation. The Jane Austen letters had not been found. No doubt the prosecution would suggest that Geraldine had destroyed them in an act of jealousy, and Dana Didrikson had killed her in a fit of outrage fired up by her infatuation with Jackman. Yet Geraldine had known that those letters were valuable. According to Jackman, she had been overdrawn three thousand pounds. Mightn't she have seen the letters as a way out of her financial mess?

Maybe it was mistaken to assume that Geraldine would make that kind of calculation. According to Jackman she had been mentally unstable, if not actually unhinged.

According to Jackman . . . So many of the assumptions

in the case depended on Jackman's statements. He had interpreted the fire in the summerhouse as an attempt on his life, a manifestation of Geraldine's paranoia. It was worth remembering that Jackman's field of expertise was English literature, not psychiatry.

What other evidence had he provided of her mental illness? There were the persecution fantasies such as her belief that he was conspiring with her doctor. There was the time she had accused him of stealing the hand-mirror from her vanity set.

The incident had appeared trivial when Jackman had described it, and still did. Other mirrors were in the house, and Geraldine had already taken possession of Jackman's shaving-mirror, yet she had got into a state because hers was missing.

Hardly worth repeating. People – perfectly sane people – were forever getting into huffs with each other over things they foolishly mislaid.

Diamond plumbed his memory for more significant evidence of Geraldine's instability, and recalled that some had been provided by Dana Didrikson herself. Dana had witnessed that curious scene in front of John Brydon House when Geraldine had wrestled with the blond man called Andy to try and prevent him leaving. And on another occasion, Dana had arrived home and been deluged with what she had termed a torrent of abuse from Geraldine, apparently unjustified.

One night in April, six months since he'd quit the police, he was going over the incidents in his mind when the realization came to him that changed his understanding of the case. Ironically, something he had disregarded galvanized his thinking – the mirror Geraldine had lost.

The next morning he phoned Jackman and asked to meet him at John Brydon House. There was no reluctance on Jackman's part. The voice, bleak in its greeting, abruptly changed when Diamond spoke. 'It's you – I thought you'd lost interest.' The words gushed from him with hope on tap again. 'I tried reaching you several times.'

Diamond knew. He'd avoided the calls.

'This could take some time,' he said when he got to the house. 'I want to make a search.'

Disappointment spread across Jackman's face. 'They already did. They pulled the place apart.'

'I know. I'll start in the bedroom. Okay?'

'If you're looking for those letters, forget it.'

'I'll start in the bedroom.'

Jackman's back was stiff with dissension as he led the way upstairs. Apparently he had built himself up to expect some blazing insight that would transform the case, not just one more search of his home.

Diamond went straight to Geraldine's dressing room and found the switch for the frame of lights around the dressing table. The publicity photos on the walls gleamed. While Jackman watched him from the doorway, he opened the centre drawer and began examining the contents, sifting through the jars and tubes of face-creams, opening them, sniffing them, and, in the case of a box that turned out to contain talcum powder, dipping his finger in and tasting it. He took the drawer right out of its housing, placed it on the floor and explored the space. He repeated the exercise with the other drawers.

Jackman asked, 'What are you hoping to find?'

'Do you remember telling me about the fuss she made when her hand-mirror was missing?'

'Yes – but it turned up later in the garden, of all places. Is that what you're looking for?'

'In the garden, was it? Maybe someone else used it.' He didn't enlarge on this. He replaced the drawers and turned to the wardrobe, running his hand along the shelf. He scooped out some silk scarves and a black straw hat. Then he knelt and began rummaging among the boots and shoes. 'Mirrors have many uses. It's just an idea I have.'

But there was nothing in Geraldine's dressing room to support the idea, so he said, 'Do you mind if I make a search in yours?'

Jackman shrugged.

His room was as austere as a sauna after Geraldine's, the walls devoid of decoration, the chest-of-drawers functional, all the surfaces bare except for a newspaper and a couple of books of poetry. 'Do you want to open the drawers yourself?' Diamond asked.

'Be my guest.'

They contained nothing remarkable. Nor did the bathroom and the other rooms upstairs, for all the painstaking search. After two unprofitable hours, Diamond accepted the coffee Jackman offered. They sat in the kitchen and Jackman started angling again. 'I'm still not sure what you hope to find.'

'Do you cook for yourself?' Diamond asked.

'I wouldn't describe it as cooking. Without Marks and Spencer and the microwave I wouldn't survive.'

This wasn't the time to embark on a debate about microwave cookery. Diamond feared that Stephanie hadn't yet mastered their new oven. Some of the meals that came up sizzling were cold by the time you got them into your mouth. There had been government warnings about food insufficiently cooked. In any other circumstances – across the bar of the Old Sedan Chair, for instance – he would have got into a helpful discussion now. However, his sleuthing took priority.

'Was she much of a cook?'

'Gerry? That's a laugh.'

'Except for barbecue sauce, I take it?'

Jackman looked unamused.

'So what do you keep in those jars marked tarragon and oregano?'

'Tarragon and oregano. Just to impress her friends.'

Diamond worked his way through the spice-rack, unscrewing the lids. The jars still had their seals. He tore each of them aside and sniffed the contents. 'When the police made their searches, they didn't bother with your kitchen, then?'

'You bet they bothered. They stripped the cupboards bare.'

'But they didn't look in these.'

'You couldn't hide an antique letter in a jar that size.'

'True.' He moved along the fitted units, opening the cupboard doors.

'What do you want – sugar?'

'No, thanks.' A large box of drinking-straws had taken his attention. 'Are you lemonade drinkers?'

'What?'

'The straws. A box of 500. Plenty have gone. I suppose you had them for the party.'

'I didn't notice.'

He replaced the box and took out a half-used packet of flour and set it on the kitchen table.

'Going to bake me a cake?' Jackman morosely jested.

Diamond was sniffing again. 'Do you have a spoon – a large one? Thanks.' He dipped deep into the flour, scooped up a spoonful and tipped it back, repeating the process several times. Then he returned the bag to the cupboard and took out an unopened one. It was folded at the top and fastened with a small piece of Sellotape.

This time he felt some resistance when he dug the spoon into the flour. Encouraged, he said, 'I'll have that plastic bowl from the sink.'

Jackman handed it to him without a word.

He tipped the contents of the flour-bag into the bowl and immediately found what he had come for: three small polythene bags about the size of table-tennis balls containing a substance as white as the flour.

He picked at the wire fastening around one and opened it. 'Do you mind turning on the light?'

The powder inside glistened. It was definitely not flour, but crystalline in form.

'Drugs?' whispered Jackman.

Diamond wetted his finger, dipped it into the bag and tasted the substance. Bitter. He washed out his mouth at the sink. 'Cocaine – the champagne drug. Didn't you know your wife used it?'

Jackman's expression switched rapidly from disbelief to shocked acceptance. It was the reaction Diamond would have expected. 'I see – the straws.'

'Not only the straws,' Diamond told him. 'I don't know how familiar you are with cocaine use. The stuff has to be chopped into fine powder first. They use a razor blade and a mirror. Glass is an ideal surface. They form the powdered coke into a line and sniff it through a straw or a

302

rolled banknote. Your wife didn't have many banknotes left.'

'You mean she spent all her money on this?'

'It isn't cheap.'

Jackman was tugging abstractedly at the side of his face. 'Jesus Christ. How could I have failed to see it?'

'Too engrossed in your job. From what you told me about your marriage – your worlds hardly overlapped, I think you said – you weren't best placed to make sense of what was happening. It's taken me a hell of a time to work it out, and I'm supposed to be a detective, or was.'

'Her odd behaviour – was that totally due to cocaine?'

'I don't know about totally. I think it's safe to say she wasn't mad. My understanding of the drug is that after the well-being wears off, the user – I'm speaking of heavy users – can be prey to all kinds of fears and anxieties. They think people are against them. Paranoid delusions leading to violent behaviour are well-known symptoms.'

'I'm surprised her bloody doctor didn't get on to this. So when she tried to kill me she must have been high with cocaine.'

'She'd probably been snorting it at the party.'

'Is this what they call crack?'

'No, crack is cocaine dissolved in warm water and heated with an alkali, like baking powder. It comes in the form of flakes or crystals. Try that and you have an immediate compulsive addiction. A physical addiction. This isn't crack.'

'But it is addictive?'

'Psychologically, yes. It can take some time. I would guess from the size of your wife's overdraft that she was hooked.'

Jackman was silent for a moment, piecing together the logic of what had seemed incomprehensible at the time. 'I'd like to find the bastard who supplied her.'

'So would I,' said Diamond. 'And fast.'

'You think it has some bearing on her death? You do, don't you?' He smacked his hand on the table. 'My God, it could change everything!'

Diamond was way ahead of him. 'There was an incident

that took place on the drive in front of this house last summer, witnessed by Mrs Didrikson and her son. It was a Saturday morning. I think you were out at the time. You were very busy with that exhibition. The two of them – Dana and Matthew – were in the road hoping to catch a glimpse of you. Mat had seen you on television and recognized you as the guy who rescued him from the weir. Instead, they saw a man come out of the house – clean-shaven, strongly built, with straw-coloured hair. Blue shirt, white jeans and trainers. Oh, and he had a gold chain around his neck. Know anyone like that?'

'Nobody springs to mind.'

'He had a maroon-coloured Volvo. His name was Andy.'

'Andy? The only Andy I know is fat and sixty. What happened?'

'He walked out towards the car and your wife came running after him, wearing a dressing gown. Her feet were bare, but she was in too much of a state to bother. She didn't want him to leave. She was asking him to come back in. She called him Andy and said something like, "Do you expect me to go on my knees and beg?" She had quite a wrestling match with him before he shoved her away and drove off.'

'Dana saw all this?'

'Yes, and reasonably enough she took it to be a lovers' tiff. She steered Mat away in some embarrassment. Now that we know about the cocaine, I'm tempted to see the incident in a different light.'

'This Andy was her supplier?'

Diamond gave a nod. 'That's my assumption. Probably he was holding out for a higher price. More than your wife was willing to pay at that time.'

'We've got to find him.'

'That isn't easy. If I were still in the police, I'd bring in the drugs squad. They're better placed to find him. We ought to report this, anyway.'

Some reluctance may have escaped in Diamond's voice, because Jackman immediately said, 'We're in a different ball-game here. This isn't just about our civic duty. Dana faces a life sentence, and that Inspector Wigfull's reputation is on the line. He's handed the prosecution a neat case of murder with an eternal triangle motive and evidence to back it. He doesn't want it complicated with a drugs connection.'

'He couldn't stop it.'

'Yes, but he can soft-pedal. I think we should follow this up ourselves. It's the first scrap of hope for the defence. Let's not chuck it to the opposition right away.'

Diamond was uneasy. As a senior policeman, he would have come down hard on anyone who failed to report a drugs find, however small. Yet he'd also known as a senior policeman how murder inquiries worked. New evidence wasn't greeted as good news when the file had already been passed to the Crown Prosecution Service. Jackman's remark about soft-pedalling was persuasive. And the earlier cock-up over the car-log still troubled him. By drawing attention to its disappearance they had undoubtedly handed the prosecution a trump card. Why not hold this one back to play when the time was right?

Following it up for themselves, as Jackman had suggested, would be fraught with difficulties, but thanks to a well-trained memory, Diamond had one possible lead. 'Cast your mind back a few months. Do you recall going through your wife's address book with me? I'm pretty sure one of the names we didn't pin down was Andy.'

'You're right! It didn't mean anything to me.'

'There was no address, just a phone number. If we could get that number . . .'

'Right on!' Then Jackman's expression altered. 'But the address book must be still in the hands of the police.'

'The defence solicitor could ask to examine it. They can't refuse. It's a reasonable request, and he doesn't have to say what he's looking for.'

'I'll call Siddons right away.'

It was easy — too easy for Diamond's cynical mind, which warned him that nothing you really want comes without hassle. Siddons the solicitor went straight to Bath Central and saw John Wigfull. The address book was produced for him. Within an hour of asking for it, Jackman had Andy's phone number.

The snag came when they tried it. An Asian voice answered. The Bristol number was an Indian restaurant in the St Paul's district of the city. They didn't know anyone called Andy. It gradually emerged that the restaurant had opened in January, having taken over empty premises that had been boarded up for a couple of months. Before that, it had been a gents' hairdressers.

Diamond succeeded in contacting the estate agent who had handled the transfer of the property. The man wasn't too pleased to be asked about Andy. He'd had to deal with a number of inquiries from a variety of callers. The barber's name had not been Andy. He had been Mario, and he had died in the flu epidemic just before Christmas. The estate agent gathered that Mario the barber had made a secondary income by taking messages for scores of dubious people who called into the shop from time to time.

Diamond put down the phone and told Jackman, 'It's a dead end.'

Chapter Eight

MATTHEW DIDRIKSON SAT EATING HIS second slice of chocolate fudge cake in Charlotte's Patisserie in the Colonnades. Facing him were Jackman and Diamond. They had sought out a table under an arch at the rear of the shop; even so, they looked conspicuous among the shoppers and business people refreshing themselves for the journey home. Diamond, in the crumpled check suit he habitually wore, was shoehorned into the space between the table edge and the upholstered seat that went halfway around; and Jackman, elegant in brown corduroy and a black shirt, could have been straight out of a colour magazine fashion feature. Matthew was wearing a white shirt, striped tie and navy pullover, having peeled off his school blazer at the first opportunity. Diamond had predicted that at this hour of the day they would find the boy somewhere in the Colonnades making a nuisance of himself on the escalators or in the lift, and he'd been right. It remained to be discovered what they would get in return for their bribe of unlimited cake.

'How's your head these days?' Diamond asked. 'No more blackouts, I hope?'

Clearly sensing that he had the high ground here, Matthew was in no hurry to respond. He glanced towards some schoolgirls at a table nearby, ran his fingers through his dark hair, and finally admitted, 'It's all right.'

'It's some time since we spoke. It was here, wasn't it? I was in disguise, if you remember.' When that got no reaction, Diamond added, 'I don't think Professor Jackman knows I played Santa, unless you mentioned it.'

Jackman said quickly, 'It's Greg. He calls me Greg.'

This earned a smirk from Matthew, a more positive response than Diamond had achieved so far, so Jackman took up the conversation. 'Mat and I haven't seen much of each other for a while, come to that. His mother wanted it that way after a misunderstanding and of course I respected her decision, but we had some good days out, didn't we, Mat?'

Matthew nodded.

The set-up was fast becoming ridiculous, two grown men trying to coax information from a schoolboy over afternoon tea. Diamond tried to sound less avuncular. 'Have you been to see your mother in the remand centre?'

A nod.

'This week?'

'Sunday.'

'How's she bearing up?'

'All right.'

It was difficult to tell whether the brevity of the responses demonstrated unwillingness to answer or a wish to consume the cake without interruption.

'Mat, we're trying to help her,' Jackman said.

Diamond added, 'And it's up to you to help us.'

Matthew made no comment at all.

'I don't know if you understand how serious this is,' Diamond said gravely. 'Do they teach you anything about law at that school of yours? Your mother is being put on trial for murder, but she has a barrister to defend her and he must try to show that there is reasonable doubt. Follow me, Mat?'

The boy pushed aside the empty plate and wiped his lips. 'Yep.' He looked away from the table, over his shoulder.

'Another piece?' Jackman suggested.

'If I can have a Coke to wash it down.'

'Bring me some change, then.' He handed over a five-pound note.

While Matthew was at the self-service counter, Diamond said, 'Talk about sweeteners. Does this come out of Mrs Didrikson's defence fund?'

'Couldn't justify it on what we've heard so far,' said Jackman.

When the boy returned and put the plate of cake on the table, Diamond reached out and moved it deftly out of range. 'Now I want you to cast your mind back. Your mother told me about an incident she witnessed in front of Professor Jackman's house one day last summer. You were with her.'

Matthew was silent. His eyes were on the cake.

'There was some kind of dust-up between Mrs Jackman and a man.'

'Andy.'

'What did you say, son?'

'Andy. The man's name was Andy.'

'You've got a good memory, obviously. We'd like to find this Andy. You see, if he and Mrs Jackman were seen grappling with each other – as I understand they were – he has to be regarded as a possible suspect. Let's test that memory of yours and see exactly how much you can tell us about him.'

'What's the point?'

Diamond reined in his irritation. 'Son, we explained. Reasonable doubt.'

'I mean why ask me, when you can see him for yourself?'

'If we knew where to find him, we would. That's the point.'

'I know where.'

'What?'

'I know where you can see Andy. I've seen him heaps of times.'

The entire seat creaked as Diamond braced. 'Where?'

'In the Baths.'

'The Roman Baths, do you mean?'

'Mm.'

He slid the cake back towards the boy. 'Tell me more.'

'I told you,' said Matthew. 'If you want to talk to Andy, that's where to look.'

'He works there?'

'Don't know.' Matthew stuffed some cake in his mouth. 'Listen, all I know is that I've seen him down there quite a few times.'

'What were you doing down there?'

'Nothing much.' The dismissive answer appeared to be all they would get. Then the boy's bravado triggered a statement that was the longest Diamond had ever heard from him. 'I go down after school. It's a spooky place. I like it. The kids in my form started this dare. You have to go right through the Baths without being caught by the security men. You walk into the souvenir shop in Stall Street, and when no one is looking you whizz down the stairs marked *staff only* – which is really the exit – and you're inside. You have to watch out for the security men, of course, but if you're smart you can walk right through the whole of the Baths and come out in the Pump Room. No one stops you there because it's the restaurant. I've done it zillions of times. It's a doddle.'

'And that's where you see Andy?'

Matthew nodded.

'Doing what?'

'Pointing at stuff and talking mostly.'

'He's a guide, then?'

'Sort of. He has these students with him.'

'*Students*?' said Jackman, reddening suddenly.

'Not every time. Sometimes he's alone.'

Diamond was far ahead, assessing the implications, but the process of question and answer had to be completed. 'So he may be a lecturer of some sort?'

'Don't know.'

Matthew added nothing else of significance. And little was said at that stage between the two men. If Andy, the presumed supplier of Geraldine's cocaine, had connections with the university, Jackman was going to face some questions himself.

When they got up to leave, Diamond invited Matthew to visit the Roman Baths with him after school on Monday, the next opportunity. 'Meet me here,' he suggested, adding craftily, 'and if you're early, there may be time for another slice of fudge cake. Then you can help me do some detective work. But I want one thing clear: we enter the Baths the regular way, through the front. I'm too visible to creep down the back stairs.'

Matthew grinned and went off to look for his friends.

Out in Stall Street, Jackman was burning to say something. 'Before you ask, there's no school of archaeology at the university.'

'History?'

Jackman was actually shaking his head when he clapped his hand to his forehead and said, 'Wait a minute. I'm wrong. A section started up this year. Just a handful of lecturers and first-years. I can't say I know any of them. That's the truth.' He paused. 'I suppose you want me to make inquiries.'

'If you can manage it without alerting anyone,' Diamond said. 'I want to surprise Andy.'

'Want some support?'

'There's no need. I'll let you know what happens, naturally.'

'Actually I'd quite like to be there,' Jackman offered with a self-conscious clearing of the throat. 'I haven't seen much of Mat in recent weeks. I like the kid.'

'That isn't the point of the exercise,' Diamond told him in the tone he'd once used to keep the murder squad in line. 'I'll be in touch.'

If the truth were told, he liked the kid, too, for all his rough edges.

Jackman phoned on Monday with news of a part-time lecturer attached to the University history section. He was called Anton Coventry, and was known as Andy. His specialism was the history of Roman architecture, and he was presently leading a study of the Roman Baths with a first-year group from the School of Architecture and Building Engineering. They met on Mondays and Thursdays at 4.30. By special arrangement they had the use of the Baths those days for an extra hour after the public had left, until 6.00. Jackman's inquiries had confirmed that Coventry had blond hair and dressed in a macho style. Moreover, he was a triathlon specialist.

'A what?'

'Triathlon. It's a sport, the ultimate in endurance, a kind of triple marathon, involving running, swimming and cycling.'

'Sounds to me like the ultimate in folly. Triathlon. When you mentioned it first, I thought maybe someone had invented the ideal sport for people like me, giving you credit for trying, and the hell with achievement.'

'Trying, yes. I get it,' said Jackman without amusement. 'Coming back to Andy, I find it hard to square a passion for fitness with pushing drugs.'

'Nothing strange in that,' said Diamond, the pure-born cynic. 'Drugs are commonplace in sport.'

'I'd like to make it clear that I've never met the guy, so far as I'm aware,' Jackman stressed.

'Point taken.' Diamond grinned unkindly as he put down the phone.

On Monday afternoon, Matthew must have raced out of school or skipped a lesson, because he was waiting in the Colonnades by the entrance to the patisserie. Consequently there was ample time for the cake. Diamond, under instructions from his doctor to limit the calories, confined himself to a frugal black coffee, averting his eyes from the boy's plate as he issued instructions. 'Get this clear, Mat. Your purpose in being there is to satisfy yourself that the man in the Baths is the same one you saw having a set-to with Mrs Jackman in the drive of John Brydon House. If you made a mistake, or can't be sure, then you must have the guts to say so, right? But whatever happens, I want you to stay quiet while we get a look at him, and remain hidden after that.'

If proof of Mat's commitment were required, it came when he put down the cake half-eaten and suggested they started. Diamond told him there was plenty of time to clear his plate.

'I can't. I'm too excited,' Matthew admitted.

Diamond's self-control wavered. 'Pass it across, then.'

At 4.20 pm, they left the Colonnades, crossed Stall Street and entered the Baths. To reach the ticket office, it was necessary to pass through the Pump Room, the meeting-place of Georgian society that now serves as a restaurant. The tea-time ritual was fully in session, every chair occupied, the waitresses in their black waistcoats,

312

white blouses and aprons trying zealously to keep up, and the trio at the near end lustily performing the Toreador music from *Carmen*. It was a relief to penetrate to the more serene atmosphere beyond.

Not many visitors were entering the Baths at this stage of the day. The woman in the ticket office warned them that the exhibition closed to the public at 5.00. Attendants would ask everyone to leave. Diamond gave a nod of understanding. As soon as they were out of earshot, Matthew, the veteran interloper, confided to Diamond that he knew hundreds of places to hide.

Diamond didn't care to admit that he'd never previously made the official tour of the Baths. Two terms of Latin in his youth had killed any interest in the Romans. Once he had attended a civic dinner in the Pump Room, preceded by cocktails beside the Great Bath; looking up to admire the lighting supplied by flaming torches attached to the columns, he had tripped on the uneven paving and spilt most of his drink down the dinner jacket he'd hired for the evening.

They came first to the remains of the temple of Sulis Minerva, picked out by discreetly sited lighting, so that the weathered limestone effigies of the gods glowed red-gold on the altar. The tourists down there were lingering to gaze, if not to read the guide-notes, but Matthew, striding through as if it were his home, said, 'You don't want to waste time here. Andy covered this bit a month ago. He's doing the Great Bath this week.'

They moved along a walkway and down several flights of stairs, taking a series of turns that confused Diamond's sense of direction until they passed a window that looked down on to an open-air bath. The surface of the water was bubbling. 'That's only the sacred spring,' Matthew mentioned dismissively, seeing Diamond hesitate. At a still lower level, they heard a steady rush of water and saw the arch where the overflow from the spring tipped out as a miniature waterfall.

Ahead was daylight and the Great Bath, its blue-green rectangle overhung with steam. After the spotlights in the tunnelled approaches, the sense of space and light could not fail to impress. The Bath itself was some seventy feet by thirty, with steps down to the water. Rows of columns on stone piers surrounded it, supporting a canopy for the flagstoned aisles where Romans once promenaded, watching the bathers. The stretch of water was open to the sky. Visitors stood in ones and twos along the aisles, staring up at the columns and the sculptured figures mounted above them. 'Most of it's Victorian,' Matthew informed Diamond. 'The Roman stuff barely comes up to your knees.' His education had profited from his trespassing in the Baths.

Diamond wasn't there for the architecture. A group of young people had gathered at the far end. Their style of dress and their absorption in conversation, rather than the surroundings, confirmed them as students. The lecturer had not appeared yet.

For the moment, Diamond had no need to get close to the students. Around the sides of the Bath, under the canopy, were a series of recesses where miscellaneous bits of masonry were displayed on stone plinths. Most were too low or too narrow to be useful to someone of Diamond's size, but at the centre of the south side was a larger bay that housed an assortment of broken pilasters and columns. It looked possible to get behind it without attracting attention.

He and Matthew strolled casually around the pool until they were level with the bay. After glancing around, he touched Matthew's arm and steered him behind the plinth. They didn't even need to crouch.

Visitors continued to drift by for the next ten minutes, and then two of the security staff came through, evidently to warn any lingerers that the exhibition was about to close. Mercifully, although they passed quite close to the plinth, they didn't look behind it.

By degrees the surrounds of the Bath emptied except for the history class and its hidden observers. The daylight was starting to fade. High above the Great Bath, the figures of the Roman emperors appeared more dramatic against the sky.

'You okay, son?' Diamond enquired.

Matthew nodded.

A moment later, footsteps clattered on the flagstones

quite close to them, steps too brisk for a sightseer, even a belated one trying to get round. And it wasn't one of the attendants.

'It's him,' Matthew whispered. 'Definitely.'

Andy Coventry passed within a few feet of them on his way around the perimeter to his students – his head and torso visible from their vantage-point, the shoulders so broad and well-muscled that the black teeshirt he was wearing seemed like a second skin. The striking feature was the bleached mass of hair swept back from the forehead over the skull in the style of some sports idol of the 1950s.

Diamond said, when it was safe to speak, 'Let's watch for a bit.'

There was some lively barracking from the students when Coventry approached them. He was probably ten minutes late. He opened a sports-bag and took out what presently proved to be a number of steel measuring-rules and handed them round. His voice was audible only in snatches across the water, but it was clear that he was issuing instructions, setting the class some kind of project. He knelt beside one of the original Roman piers supporting a column and measured its length and height. There was some discussion about the additonal masonry used to reinforce the structure that had once supported a timber roof. The students had produced clipboards and were recording the information. Coventry started assigning them in pairs to the six main piers along the north side of the bath.

In a few minutes, all of the students were busy, measuring and taking notes. Satisfied, apparently, that they were usefully occupied, Coventry picked up his bag and strolled away from the class towards one of the exits at the west end.

Diamond put a restraining hand on Matthew's shoulder. This was going to require the stealth of a professional. He left the boy, stepped back into the shadows and crept off in the direction Andy had taken. Conscious of his size, he moved with a lightness of step more appropriate to a much slimmer man.

A suspicion had dawned in Diamond's brain even before Andy had appeared with the sports-bag. The next few minutes, he sensed, would be crucial to the investigation he had started all those weeks ago and was pursuing to its climax.

The need to remain unnoticed was essential, and so was the need to see what Andy Coventry was up to. It meant venturing into a complex of warm and cold baths at the west end of the Great Bath – with a high risk of discovery now that no visitors were left. He passed through the open door. Making use of every feature of the building that offered the possibility of cover, he approached the circular cold plunge bath known as the frigidarium and stared around its perimeter for a sighting of his man. The subdued lighting was a mixed blessing.

He seemed to have lost the trail already. The walkway system lined with plexiglass sides began again in this section. All he could see as he peered over the handrail opposite was the site of another bath, practically empty of water. Obliged to move on into a section still more in shadow, he found himself looking down on a sunken area where columns of copper-coloured bricks stood in ranks like the Terracotta Army discovered in China. He knew what it was from postcards he had seen: an early form of central heating. The columns had once supported a floor, enabling hot air from a charcoal-burning flue to circulate in the cavity. Above, in their Turkish bath, Romans had once sat and sweated and been oiled, scraped and massaged. The hypocaust, as it was labelled, was one of the most notable features of the Baths, mainly because of its function, and also for the strange, unforgettable spectacle of more than a hundred of these knee-high columns, filling the floor space in symmetrical formation, no less impressive for being worn and damaged, a chromatic mix of copper and ochres that time had rendered into what could easily have passed for a masterpiece of modern art.

If Diamond's thoughts had really taken on aesthetic overtones (which is doubtful), they must have been galvanized by the sight of Andy Coventry crouching down on the floor among the columns at the far end.

Diamond froze, undecided whether to go down there. Coventry hadn't looked up; he was absorbed in whatever he was doing.

The right course, Diamond decided, was to watch and wait. He backed away, out of Coventry's sight, up a flight of stairs that led to the toilets.

There was an interval of two or three minutes when nothing happened; then the scrunch of shoes on the gritty under-floor of the hypocaust, followed by the sound of Coventry hoisting himself back on to the walkway; and brisk steps as he returned to the Great Bath.

Peter Diamond was down the steps and over the barrier before the drumming of the footsteps had ceased. With agility born of urgency, he sidestepped between the columns until he came to the place where he had seen Coventry. As he had anticipated, there was a cavity near one of the vents to the flue. He knelt, put his hand inside and touched something most unlike a Roman relic. It was soft, smooth and light in weight.

He lifted it out – a plastic bag containing a white, glittering substance.

In appearance it was identical to the cocaine he had found in the bag of flour in Jackman's kitchen. He felt inside the cavity again and located similar bags, stacks of them, too many to remove now.

As a hiding place for drugs, the hypocaust had advantages. Unlike much of the site, it was dry. The cavity was masked by one of the brick columns, and nobody had reason to look there, because this section of the Baths had been comprehensively excavated. The public were kept well back behind the plexiglass. Yet it was neutral ground that Andy Coventry could visit twice-weekly without fear of being seen. Whether collecting or depositing, he could carry the stuff in and out of the building in his sports-bag. And who in his right mind in the Avon and Somerset Drugs Squad would suggest the Roman Baths for a bust?

Diamond stood up. The immediate problem was what to do about it. He was entitled to make a citizen's arrest. But was that the wisest course of action? Ideally he wanted to question the man about the murder. Drug-dealing was dangerous and despicable and Coventry would take the rap for it, but not immediately.

Then the lights went out.

This part of the building had no windows. It was pitch-black. Diamond reached out to steady himself. He didn't want to blunder into those columns of bricks and lose his balance. His first thought was that the lights had been routinely switched off now that the place was officially closed.

His second thought was more alarming, prompted by a sound somewhere ahead like the scuffing of a shoe on limestone grit. Of course it might simply have been a fragment of stone dislodged by some natural means. He doubted that. Suppose Coventry had returned and spotted him at the hiding place. Suppose he had deliberately cut the lights.

It wasn't wise to remain where he was.

There was no question of finding a way through the hypocaust. He would have to edge along the back wall like a spider trapped in a sink. Tentatively he slid his hand along the surface, put out a foot and shifted his weight sideways. He paused, listened, heard nothing, and repeated the move, this time finding one of the columns in his way. Still with his palms flat to the wall, he edged around the obstruction, intent on putting as much distance as possible between himself and the cavity where the drugs were hidden.

By this means he negotiated three more columns. He was feeling his way around a fourth when he heard a scrunch from the far side. No doubt about it: someone had climbed down from the walkway and let himself on to the gritty surface of the underfloor.

A voice, definitely Coventry's, called out, 'I know you're there, fatso.'

Diamond made no response. Remaining still and silent was the best way to limit the damage.

Coventry was on the move. The steps were quick and even. Either he was willing to risk skinning his knees on the columns of the hypocaust, or he knew the layout perfectly.

It was a test of nerve. Diamond waited, tense and poised to defend himself.

Coventry was heading for the place where the drugs were hidden. He must have moved right along one of the aisles between the columns, because he didn't falter. Only when he reached the wall did he stop.

There was a short silence. Then Coventry spoke up again. 'All right, you bastard, let's see where you are.' With that, a cigarette-lighter flamed.

He held it at arm's length and moved it in a wide arc, casting long shadows across the floor of the hypocaust. Inevitably, the flame picked out Diamond.

The triathlon was Coventry's sport, but he could certainly have made a success of all-in wrestling. He came at Diamond as if he'd just rebounded off the ropes. The lighter went out – too late to be of help to Diamond, who stepped back to avert the force of the charge, and fell. A brick column that had endured for two thousand years was flattened under his bulk. On a reflex learned in rugby scrums, he brought his knees and arms to his chest and swung his body hard to the right. He felt a searing pain in his side as he was crushed against the debris. One of his ribs had snapped. Using the leverage of his thighs, he succeeded in forcing the man aside and followed it up with a jab with the elbow that made contact with yielding flesh.

The pain in his side was severe. In a hand-to-hand fight, he wasn't going to last long. He groped in the darkness and made contact with another of the columns. Blessedly, it took the strain. He hauled himself on to his haunches. Then something hard hit his head.

Coventry must have picked up a brick and swung it wildly. The full force would have brained Peter Diamond. Instead, it scraped down the side of his skull, raking the skin just behind his right ear, and sank into the muscle tissue of his shoulder. He staggered, held on to the column, and lurched forward. His shoulder went numb.

Andy Coventry meant to kill him.

He was upright and moving between the columns with no idea which direction he was taking, except that it had to be away from his assailant. The darkness was absolute.

Heightened by the deprivation, his other senses gave him a vivid animal awareness. The dank, dead smell of the stones filled his nostrils. The chill ripped through his flesh. The crunch of his steps resounded from the roof and walls. This was the blind rush of the hunted. He didn't care if he transformed the hypocaust into a heap of rubble, so long as he survived. Taking huge, audible gasps, he stumbled through the black void, hands outstretched.

And stopped.

His hands were flat against a smooth surface which had to be the plexiglass side of the walkway. Reaching up, he found it impossible to make contact with the rail, so he worked his way to the left until a stone obstruction stopped him. The wall again. Behind him, he could hear the crunch of Coventry's steps.

He reached up with his right hand to see if there was any chance of scaling the wall, and got an agonizing reminder of the injury to his rib. Using the left hand instead, he discovered a ledge about three feet above the ground. He got his knees up to the level and hauled himself higher. A second step now presented itself. Laboriously, he scrambled up, made contact with the plexiglass again and then — mercifully — the rail of the walkway. He got his legs over and felt the flat rubber surface under his feet. Now he could discern a faint gray light. Daylight. He staggered towards it, conscious that Coventry must reach the walkway at any moment.

The Great Bath was ahead. There, common sense argued, he would be safe from further attack. Coventry could hardly carry on the fight in front of his students.

Diamond assessed his injuries as he moved. The rib was the most disabling, and there was also blood trickling down his scalp from the head-wound. He could feel its warmth on the side of his neck. The blood was conspicuous. When he reached the Great Bath, he didn't want the students crowding around him asking questions. Somehow he must hold himself together and convince anyone who was watching that he was walking normally. That the blood, if they noticed it, was some sort of blemish, a strawberry mark on the skin. Then he needed only to get to one of the doors leading to an exit.

He would have to leave Matthew to find his own way out. Thank God the boy was familiar with the place. He was smart enough to escape.

But Diamond was not. Within a few yards of the entrance to the Great Bath, he was surprised by a sudden movement to his right. He turned. Enough daylight had penetrated the place to show him Andy Coventry coming at him with a spade, a heavy-duty, long-handled spade of the sort used by builders. There was no escape this time. Wielded like a sledgehammer, it was about to cleave Peter Diamond's skull.

PART SIX
Trial

Chapter One

A BLACK BAR ACROSS WHITE. A thin black bar, dividing the field of vision like a cable across the sky.

Too uniformly white for sky. It had to be something else.

A ceiling.

A cable across the ceiling? No. Something more rigid. A black bar. A rod. Or rail.

Maybe a rail. There was something right about a rail. A connection, but with what?

With a sound. The rustle and scrape of something metallic. Curtain rings. So why not a curtain rail?

What would a curtain rail be doing across a ceiling? Curtains were for windows. No window here.

Unless this was a bed, a hospital bed with curtains for privacy. That would explain the scrape of the rings. It ought to be easy to check, because the rail would go at least three sides around the bed.

Unfortunately it wasn't so easy when one couldn't move one's head to left or right. When one felt muzzy and tired, too tired really to care . . .

'He opened his eyes again, sir,' the voice of a woman announced, a woman difficult to place.

'Didn't move his lips, I suppose?' A man's voice.

'No.'

'Poor sod. Keep your ears open, just in case. I know it's bloody tedious, but it has to be done. You want to try talking to him when you're here by the hour. Anything that comes in to your head. Tell him the secrets of your love life. That's what the nurses do. Anything to stir up the brain cells.'

'Do you mind? My private life isn't for Mr Diamond's ears, sir.'

'Relax, Constable. Even if he heard you, which is doubtful, he wouldn't remember a thing. Well, I'm off. See you tomorrow.'

'Gutso.'

'Mm?'

'You see?' The voice was triumphant. 'It is a response. He heard. Peter Diamond, you fat slob. What do we have to do to bring you round? What's your taste in music? The Hippopotamus Song, I reckon.'

'He's moving his lips, sir.'

'Jesus Christ, he is. Peter? Can you hear me?'

'Mm.'

'Again.'

'Mm.'

'Terrific. Mr Diamond, do you understand? This is Keith Halliwell. Remember me? Avon and Somerset Police. Your old sidekick, DI Halliwell.'

'Halliwell?'

'He spoke! Did you hear that, Constable?'

'Yes, sir.'

'Brilliant. Put a call through to Mr Wigfull. We're in business at last.'

His eyes were open, and instead of the curtain rail in front of them, there was a face, a dark face dominated by a moustache. A face he didn't particularly care for.

'Mr Diamond?'

'John Wigfull.'

'How are you feeling?'

'I can't move.'

'Don't try. Your head's clamped. You're lucky to be alive.'

The trite remark irked Diamond, even at this level of consciousness. 'Where am I?'

'In the RUH. You've been in a coma. They said if you did come round, there was no obvious physical damage to the brain, but no one can stay in a coma too long. Do you follow me?'

326

'Perfectly,' said Diamond.

'You were found in a pool of blood in the Roman Baths. The Didrikson boy alerted us.'

'Good lad.'

'Your skull was cracked and impacted. The only reason your head isn't in two pieces is that the spade was curved at the edge. Do you remember being struck?'

'Not really.'

'It may come back to you slowly. We'll be needing a statement.'

'You pulled Coventry in?'

'You remember a certain amount then?'

Diamond summarized what he remembered, up to the moment when Andy Coventry had set off in pursuit of him.

Wigfull informed him that the drugs squad were holding Coventry on a charge of possession. 'We'll do him for dealing, as well. He had two kilos of cocaine stashed away in the Baths.'

The brain was functioning, sluggishly, but reliably. 'He was supplying Mrs Jackman, the woman who was murdered.'

Wigfull frowned. 'What's your evidence for that?'

'The boy and his mother witnessed Andy coming out of the house.'

'The Jackman house? When was this?'

'Months ago. Last summer. You remember. Mrs Didrikson told us in her statement. Geraldine Jackman was begging Coventry not to leave.'

'That was Coventry?' Wigfull's tone was sceptical.

'The boy is certain of it.'

'What exactly are you suggesting, Mr Diamond — a drugs angle on the Jackman case? Is that the best the defence can think up?'

'I'm talking facts, John. Geraldine Jackman was snorting coke. Go to the house. You'll find packets of cocaine hidden in bags of flour in the kitchen.'

Wigfull moved away from the bed, out of Diamond's limited range of vision. 'The post-mortem samples were negative for drugs. If you cast your mind back, Dr Merlin ordered a full screening test for drugs and alcohol. Chepstow found nothing.'

'This is something you should check with Merlin,' Diamond advised. 'It doesn't mean she hadn't used cocaine. Unlike cannabis, it doesn't hang about in the body for long. A few days at the most. If she hadn't snorted the stuff in the few days prior to her death, it's unlikely that traces would have shown up in the samples.'

'Even if what you're saying is true, it's a side issue,' Wigfull insisted. 'Nobody's suggesting Gerry Jackman was nice to know. That's no part of the prosecution case. All right, you tell me she was a junkie. I'll see that it's investigated, but the fact remains that Dana Didrikson killed her. The evidence is unassailable.'

'When is the trial?'

'In just over a week.'

'A *week*?'

'You've been here ten days. Take it easy. They bring the papers round. You won't miss a thing.'

Later that morning, he met the surgeon who had pieced together his splintered skull. The operation, he learned, had been a five-hour job, and no one had been able to predict with confidence that he would come out of the coma, let alone come out of it with his brain unimpaired. The contraption clamped around his head was essential to his recovery. In twenty-four hours it would be replaced by something that permitted more movement. As for other injuries, two of his ribs had cracked, and there were superficial abrasions, but there was no reason why he shouldn't be on his feet in a week.

'On my feet and out of here?' Diamond asked.

'On your feet and as far as the toilet, Mr Diamond. As a ward sister once remarked to me, bedpans are nobody's cup of tea.'

At least he had an opportunity to think. The matter that exercised him most was Andy Coventry's behaviour. He would dearly have liked to question the man, only it wasn't possible, now or later. John Wigfull must have taken a statement already, but John Wigfull was blinkered.

The ferocity of the attack had been out of all proportion. Coventry could easily have killed him. Was a crack over the head with a spade a reasonable response to being caught with a couple of kilos of cocaine? People can panic, certainly. The chances were that Coventry wasn't a big wheel in the drugs trade, not an importer or a trafficker, just a pusher, probably with no form at all. Those are the people who are liable to strike back when threatened. The real professionals weigh the consequences.

However, there was a more persuasive scenario. Andy Coventry had clearly been Geraldine Jackman's supplier. He'd kept her in cocaine and systematically emptied her bank account. Fine, until her funds ran out. She had been heavily overdrawn at the bank. He must have watched her become increasingly desperate, knowing that ultimately there would be no point in offering the stuff to someone who couldn't pay. Maybe he'd told her the arrangement was at an end. Then – the scenario ran – Geraldine had got in touch again. She'd offered something of value in exchange for drugs. Coventry had gone to the house, and she had shown him the Jane Austen letters she had pilfered from her husband.

Coventry must have been unimpressed. He would have foreseen the problems in turning the letters into cash. The discussion had turned ugly. Gerry, in one of her towering rages, had threatened to expose him as a pusher, and the hell with the consequences for herself, because without cocaine her life was closing down anyway. Andy Coventry, driven desperate, had silenced her for ever.

Through the months since then, the man must have lived in dread of the truth emerging. When he became aware in the Baths that someone had been watching him stow away drugs, he had panicked. He had killed once to stop someone blowing the whistle on his dealing, so why not a second time?

Towards the end of the week Gregory Jackman came to the hospital on a visit. Hollow-eyed and drooping at the shoulders, he looked ten years older than when Diamond had seen him last. 'The drug story has broken,' he explained. 'They came to the house – Chief Inspector Wigfull and some people from the drugs squad – and I showed them the bags of flour. Today it's all over the tabloids. *Drugs Find in Prof's House*. *Dead Woman's Cocaine Habit*. The top brass in the university don't like it one bit. I've been told to take a year's sabbatical directly the trial is over.'

'Told? Do they have the right?'

'Asked, then. They're being as decent as they can. I'll get a year's salary, but the understanding is that I'll go to America on a research fellowship, and while I'm there I'll apply for other posts.'

'Welcome to the club,' said Diamond.

'What?'

'It's the old heave-ho. Will you go?'

'Try and stop me.'

'Can it really be as quick as you say?'

'Thanks to the wonders of fax, yes. The only thing to be settled is the day I fly out. I've been called as a witness, naturally.'

'Presumably a prosecution witness.'

'Yes. It's a warrant. I've talked to Dana's lawyers. I don't seem to have a choice in the matter. It's the way they want to play it, apparently.'

Diamond explained the strategy. 'These days the forensic evidence is often so cut and dried that you don't call defence experts to challenge it. If the defence calls no witnesses except Dana, they'll have the right to make the final speech to the jury before the judge sums up.'

Jackman said bleakly, 'I just hope they've talked to Dana about this. God knows what she's going to make of me appearing for the prosecution.'

'She still intends to plead not guilty, does she?'

Jackman tilted his head, surprised by the question. 'Certainly. Is there any reason why she shouldn't?'

'I don't know. Wigfull was here a day or two ago, looking as smug as a winning jockey. He's sure they'll convict.'

'So I gathered.'

'Nothing has altered, then?'

Jackman said gloomily, 'It looks as hopeless as ever. I thought perhaps what happened to you would help the defence by pointing to Andy Coventry as an alternative suspect.'

'Well, doesn't it?'

He shook his head. 'Her lawyers don't want to go down that road.'

'Why not, for God's sake?'

'They say it doesn't address the crucial points that the prosecution will raise – the fact that Dana admits she was at the house on the morning of the murder, and the evidence that her car was used to transport the body to Chew Valley Lake. That forensic report is dynamite. She has no answer to it. And that leaves out all the circumstantial stuff about motive. A good prosecutor will have her on toast.'

Privately, Diamond had to admit that the lawyers were right.

By Friday he felt sufficiently recovered to phone Siddons the solicitor and ask whether the defence team were fully aware of Andy Coventry's involvement in the case.

'Absolutely,' Siddons assured him. 'The drugs bring another dimension to it. Mrs Jackman's outbursts obviously had their origin in her cocaine habit.'

'Yes, but have you considered the possibility that Coventry killed her?' He outlined his theory.

From the tone of Siddons' responses – the polite, yet qualified murmurs that came down the phone each time Diamond paused – it was clear that the solicitor wasn't exactly turning cartwheels of joy at the other end. He thanked Diamond mildly for his interest and said, 'Unfortunately for us, your theory isn't tenable. Coventry was questioned by the police about his movements at the time of the murder, and he was three hundred miles away, in Newcastle. For the entire week. They checked it. He was lecturing to an Open University course at Hadrian's Wall. It's a cast-iron alibi. Infuriating, isn't it?'

Chapter Two

DEPRESSING AS IT WAS, THE doctors were right. Peter
Diamond was still in hospital when Dana Didrikson's trial
for murder opened at Bristol Crown Court. True, he'd
reached a stage of convalescence when he was no longer
considered enough of an emergency to justify occupying a
room of his own near the sister's office; instead, he'd been
moved into a six-bedded ward near the stairs that was, in
effect, a poker school. The inmates were all concussion
cases restored to sufficient consciousness to tell a sequence
from a flush. Their slick play was a testimony to the
nursing. Diamond had never been much of a card-player,
so after a few hands to demonstrate goodwill he had
escaped to the day room and the morning papers.

There was not much call in the RUH for the quality
newspapers, according to the newsagent who supplied the
wards. Diamond's information about the first day of the
trial had to be drawn from the tabloids. Among the glam-
our shots of Gerry Snoo and banner headlines of the
ANGRY GERRY'S LAST HOURS variety were meagre
accounts of the court proceedings. Diamond managed to
glean that Dana had pleaded not guilty and a jury of eight
men and four women had been empanelled. Prosecuting
counsel, Sir Job Mogg, QC – known in and out of the courts
as 'Claws' – had opened the prosecution's case with his
outline of the events leading up to the charge of murder.
Reference was made to the accident at Pulteney Weir that
had brought Dana Didrikson into the ambit of the Jackmans. She was portrayed as a single parent – *DESPERATE
DANA*, in one paper – struggling to bring up a son and
stretched to pay his school fees. Jackman's fatherly acts of
kindness to the boy in the summer months were seen as

the seed of a motive – *LONE MUM'S LOVE PLOT* – nurtured by Dana's discovery that the Jackman marriage was in crisis. The lengths to which she had gone to obtain the Jane Austen letters as a gift for Jackman were stressed as significant, and so was the acrimonious visit of Mrs Jackman to her home – *GERRY'S MAN-STEALER FURY*. It was pointed out that Dana had admitted visiting the Jackman house on the morning of the murder when she'd heard that the letters were missing. Motive and opportunity were thus spelt out to the readers at least as vividly as they had been to the jury.

The papers all insisted that recent developments in forensic science would dominate the case. The Crown would be calling experts in DNA analysis – genetic fingerprinting – to prove that the body had been placed in the boot of Dana's car prior to its being recovered from Chew Valley Lake. She had sworn a statement that the car had never been driven by anyone but herself. And she had been unable to explain the disappearance of the mileage log.

Thus outlined, the prosecution case appeared formidable. So, also, did the hostility of the tabloids towards Dana. Diamond had long ago ceased to believe in unbiased reporting. But he did feel embittered by two feature articles eulogizing genetic fingerprinting as the infallible method of detection. No direct reference to the Jackman case was made, but when an editor chose to publish such a piece on the day a major trial opened, the inference was clear. One paper had a centrespread of forty mugshots of murderers and rapists trapped by the DNA test in the past two years.

The old antagonism stirred again. He'd thought he had got it out of his system when he'd quit the police. Yet here he was bridling at the assumption that science had taken over completely from the detectives.

He heard a sound behind him and saw a staff nurse and probationer approaching with a trolley.

'How is my Mr Diamond this morning?'

'Just about coming to his senses,' he answered. He'd given up trying to speak normally to this Nightingale who reduced every exchange to the level of the children's ward.

'Ready to have his dressing changed?'

'Indeed. And if staff could arrange to make it a little flatter to the head — a little less obtrusive, shall we say? — Mr Diamond would be mightily obliged.'

'Why? Going to the pictures, are we? Or a football match?'

There was a supportive giggle from the probationer.

Diamond said, 'A murder trial, actually.'

'What are you saying?'

'That your Mr Diamond will shortly be leaving you. Discharging himself.'

A shocked silence was followed by, 'We'll see what Sister has to say about that.'

'Fair enough. And when she's said it, Mr Diamond will thank Sister sincerely for her tender, loving care and bid her good day.'

By 11.30 he was sitting in the public gallery in Bristol Crown Court listening to Dr Jack Merlin giving evidence. The pathologist was being as cautious as ever, declining to name a cause of death. Pressed by the prosecution to comment on asphyxiation as a likely cause, he would say only that it was not inconsistent with the findings. The main thrust of the forensic screening that had followed the autopsy had been towards toxicology to determine whether drugs or alcohol had been present. The screening tests carried out by the Home Office forensic laboratory had proved negative. Under cross-examination, Merlin admitted that there was a threshold point for analytical suitability, and that samples from a corpse submerged in water for more than a week might not yield significant traces. However, he believed it was unlikely that death had been caused by a toxic substance.

Merlin was followed in the witness box by another forensic scientist, called Partington, who spoke somewhat long-windedly about fibres found in the bedroom at John Brydon House. Peter Diamond's attention moved elsewhere.

Dana Didrikson, dressed in a dark green suit, listened from the dock, her hands clasped in her lap. She had her brown hair pinned back severely, perhaps to discourage the suggestion that she was a husband-stealer. She wore no make-up. Image was an important consideration, and her solicitor would have advised her to dress demurely. It appeared to Diamond that the months in the remand centre had marked her. She'd put on weight – not much, but enough to give her face a decidedly mumpish look that combined with her sagging posture to suggest that she was already resigned to a long prison sentence.

'The colour was distinctive?' Sir Job Mogg was saying to his witness.

'Certainly,' the scientist responded. 'A shade of dark red or maroon achieved by dyeing the garment with some home dye. We matched it with samples taken from a lambswool jumper found in the defendant's home.'

The judge – a world-weary Welshman – intervened. 'Sir Job, unquenchable as my interest is in the findings of the forensic science laboratory, I should like to know where this line of questioning is taking us.'

'My lord, the Crown is seeking to establish that the defendant was present and wearing the garment in the bedroom where the murder took place. Taken together with the hair samples and the skin tissues also found in the bedroom, and subjected to DNA analysis, the evidence is fundamental to the prosecution case.'

'The evidence of what?' persisted the judge. 'My understanding is that several weeks passed before the house was searched. We cannot safely conclude that these fibres and tissues were deposited on the day Mrs Jackman was murdered. Suppose the defendant visited the house some day after 11 September?'

'In that case, my lord, with the greatest respect, it would be highly relevant to inquire what the defendant was doing in Professor Jackman's bedroom some day after 11 September, or – one might conjecture – some night.'

There was some subdued amusement at this and defence counsel was on her feet. 'My lord, I must object.'

'Sit down,' said the judge. 'That remark was unworthy of you, Sir Job.'

'I withdraw it unreservedly, m'lord, and apologize to the court.' Smoothly, Sir Job added, 'We now pass on to the matter of the Mercedes car driven by the defendant. Did you examine the car, Mr Partington?'

'I did. On 11 October. I removed samples of skin and hair

from the boot of the vehicle and subjected them to DNA analysis.'

'For the benefit of the court, would you now explain the signficance of such a test? This is what is commonly known as genetic fingerprinting, is it not?'

'Yes. It is a way of producing genetic profiles of individuals which are unique in each case except for identical twins. The genetic material known as DNA can be extracted from samples of blood, skin, semen or hair-roots and separated into strands. Chemicals known as restriction enzymes are used to chop the strands into unequal pieces which are sorted on a piece of gelatine by a process known as electrophoresis. We then tag the bits with radioactive probes and expose them to X-ray film to produce a series of black bands not unlike the bar codes used in supermarket checkouts.'

'Every one unique to the individual?'

'Exactly. So that comparisons can be made with certainty.'

'And you produced genetic profiles of the traces of hair and skin found in the boot of the Mercedes car driven by the defendant?'

'Yes.'

'With what result?'

'They matched the samples taken from the victim.'

'Matched them absolutely?'

'In every respect.'

There was a pause in the proceedings while comparative photographs of the results were passed around the jury.

'Is there anything else you can tell the court about the skin and hair found in the car?'

'We found four hairs altogether, all matching the victim's DNA profile. Three were from the pubic region, suggesting that at some stage the body in the boot was unclothed.'

'And the skin particles. How many did you find?'

'Twenty-three.'

'So many. Is that indicative of anything?'

'It suggests to me that the body was dragged across the lining of the boot, causing some scaling. There may also have been some movement when the car was driven.'

'Summing up, then, Dr Partington, you are quite certain in your mind that the body of Mrs Jackman was conveyed somewhere in the boot of the defendant's car?'

'Entirely certain.'

'Thank you.'

Dana's defence counsel rose to cross-examine the witness. She was Lilian Bargainer, QC, a doughty, silver-haired advocate, ample in voice and girth. Diamond had been cross-examined by her on one occasion. The defence was in capable hands.

'Dr Partington, there is just one thing I would like to have clear. Is it possible, is it conceivable, that the skin and hair samples you took from the boot of the car could have been introduced there?'

'What exactly do you mean?' Partington knew very well what she meant. It was a defence red herring, dangled in front of the jury in case they were influenced by stories of police corruption.

'If some person of malicious intent wished to convey the impression that the car had been used to transport the body somewhere, might he or she have misled you by planting some skin and hair samples in the boot?'

Dr Partington was categorical. 'No. The appearance and positioning of the skin samples was entirely consistent with a body having lain there and been lifted in and out. They adhered to and mingled with the fibres of the inner lining entirely as one would expect. In my opinion, it would not be possible to reproduce this effect artificially.'

'Thank you.'

The court adjourned for lunch.

In the corridor outside, Diamond spotted Jackman briefly, but he was in conversation with a lawyer, possibly the solicitor, and it seemed inopportune to approach them. So it was a solitary lunch in the pub across the road, where the head-bandage attracted wary looks from other customers.

He next saw Jackman in the witness box. The people in front, in the first row of the public gallery, craned for a better view. In the dock, Dana Didrikson lowered her eyes as if taking an interest in the state of her fingernails. Her expression remained placid, but she couldn't do anything about a nervous twitch in a muscle close to her jawbone.

After Jackman had taken the oath, he was steered gently by Sir Job into the account of his marriage that he had given in his statement to Diamond many weeks ago. To his credit, he adhered closely to the original, admitting the imperfections in his relationship to Geraldine, the steady increase in arguments and accusations. Some of it was going to make juicy reading in tomorrow's papers, in particular the night Geraldine had set fire to the summerhouse.

'You were convinced that your wife intended to kill you?'

'Yes.'

'Yet you chose not to report the incident to the police.'

'That is correct. She was mentally unstable, or so it appeared at the time. As I now know, she –'

Sir Job cut in sharply, 'We're dealing with matters as you understood them at the time, Professor. Would you tell the court whether you had met the defendant, Mrs Didrikson, prior to the fire in the summerhouse.'

'I saw her that evening, yes.'

'Where precisely? At your house?'

'She came to the house. I met her outside, in the road.'

'Why was that? Didn't you want her at the party for some reason?'

'It wasn't appropriate. She hadn't come for a social evening. She came to clear up a misunderstanding.'

'So you cleared it up in the road?'

'We went to a pub.'

'In her car?'

'Yes.'

'At your suggestion?'

'It was a place to have a conversation.'

'And a couple of drinks, I presume. It didn't cross your mind that your connection – I employ the word in a platonic sense – your connection with Mrs Didrikson might have come to the notice of your wife?'

'She knew of it. She took the phone call.'

'Ah.'

Jackman had been lured into deep water and now he was floundering. 'But it didn't amount to anything at that stage.'

'*At that stage?*'

'I mean a connection in the sense you hinted at. Then, or

later.'

'Come, come, Professor,' said Sir Job, smiling indulgent-ly. 'I scrupulously avoided suggesting anything that may have happened later, but since you have raised the matter, would it be true to say that the platonic connection blossomed into a friendship?'

Jackman blushed deeply. He was making a terrible hash of this if he wanted to help Dana. 'A platonic friendship.'

'A friendship that lasted through the summer?'

'We met a few times, but it was for the boy's sake. I took him swimming a number of times.'

'And to other places?'

'A cricket match, on one occasion, and a balloon festival.'

'And at the end of these outings, you returned young Matthew to his mother?'

'Naturally.'

'She must have felt some obligation to you?'

'No.'

'No?'

'I mean that wasn't the intention at all. I had no ulterior motive.'

'But your wife thought otherwise.'

At this, defence counsel rose to object that Sir Job appeared to be cross-examining his own witness. For some minutes both counsel and the judge were embroiled in an argument over the legal niceties.

Diamond listened unhappily. He'd come here to follow the trial at first hand instead of reading the garbled newspaper accounts, and it wasn't at all as he had hoped. Power-less to influence what was going on down there, he sensed that Dana's attitude of resignation was pre-empting the verdict. The prosecution were riding high.

The examination-in-chief was resumed. 'Professor, we were discussing your late wife's reactions to your occasional meetings with the defendant. Would you tell us what she had to say on the subject?'

'She twisted everything.'

Sir Job glanced towards the judge, who said wearily, 'Tell the court what your wife said, Professor.'

'She hinted that I was having an affair with Mrs

Didrikson.'

'Only hinted?'

'Well, towards the end she was more specific.'

Diamond ached inwardly. This was disastrous for the defence. Far better if Jackman had come out with the worst Geraldine had said. By his reluctance to tell, he appeared to be confirming that he and Dana had been lovers.

'What did she say precisely?'

'You want the exact words?' Jackman hesitated. 'She said we were shagging like rabbits. It was a complete and utter lie.'

Sir Job said, 'Did you say lie, or lay?' The quip was well-timed. General laughter covered the embarrassment and the cheap point was scored. The defence would gain nothing by protesting.

Jackman's misery continued for another hour. Sir Job went on to secure the important admission that Geraldine had visited Dana and accused her of using Matthew as bait. He took Jackman through the events of the weekend before the murder and made much of Dana's gift of the Jane Austen letters.

'She wanted you to have them as a gift – these letters of potentially great value?'

'Yes.'

'A farewell gift?'

'That was my understanding. After what had taken place between my wife and Mrs Didrikson, it would be impossible for me to go on seeing the boy.'

'And you accepted the letters?'

'Yes – but if they proved to be genuine, I always intended to return them to her after the Jane Austen exhibition was over.'

'So this farewell was more of an *au revoir* than a final parting. When were you next in contact with Mrs Didrikson?'

'On the Monday morning. I phoned.'

'The day your wife was to be murdered? What did you have to say to Mrs Didrikson that Monday morning?'

Scarcely a statement of Jackman's had passed without being given a damaging twist by Sir Job. It was cross-examination masquerading as evidence-in-chief, and so skilfully had it been done that the defence would only have damaged its own case by repeatedly objecting. By the time Sir Job had done, the jury must have been convinced that Dana was a woman in the grip of an infatuation, and that Jackman had encouraged her.

The cross-examination proper was cut to the minimum. Lilian Bargainer looked over her half-glasses at Jackman and asked, 'Professor, can you account for your wife's erratic behaviour in the months prior to her death?'

'I believe I can. She was using drugs.'

'There is evidence of this?'

'Yes. On 25 April, the police found packets of cocaine hidden in the house. I understand that a person addicted to cocaine may exhibit symptoms of paranoia.'

The judge interrupted. *'Drugs?* I heard no mention of drugs before this. Sir Job, is the prosecution aware of this? You made no reference to it in your outline of the case.'

Prosecuting counsel coughed and wrapped his gown protectively around him. 'We are aware of it, m'lord. A man has been charged with supplying the deceased with cocaine. The matter has no connection with the case for the Crown.'

'That may be so. I am surprised we have not heard of it already.'

'I intend to call a police witness at a later stage, m'lord. Undoubtedly the matter will be touched upon. I do not wish to over-state its importance.'

The judge turned to Mrs Bargainer. 'I take it that you attach some significance to it. Did you wish to pursue this matter with this witness?'

She said, 'I think the point is made, my lord. I shall, of course, wish to cross-examine the police witness in due course.'

The rest was routine questioning, attempting to mend some of the fences broken by the prosecution. Jackman did what he could.

When the court adjourned for the day, Diamond didn't stop to speak to anyone. There seemed no point any more. Anyway, his head ached. He went home to take some painkillers.

341

Chapter Three

HE WAS IN THE SAME seat in the public gallery next morning. By the time Dana was brought in, every place was taken. She looked small, too small to be the focus of this elaborate ritual.

The court rose for the judge.

Prosecuting counsel remained standing when everyone else sat down. 'My lord, with your permission, before we commence the proceedings, I beg to advise the court of some new evidence which has come to light.'

'Sir Job, you know the position regarding new evidence,' said the judge. 'The prosecution is not at liberty to spring surprises on the court.'

'Then I must request an adjournment. I assure you that the matter is crucial to the proper administration of justice.'

The judge fingered his wig, thought for a long interval, and then announced testily. 'The court is adjourned for thirty minutes. Both counsel will attend in my retiring room.'

Diamond filed out with the others, sensing that there would be a longer delay than the estimated half-hour. Something sensational must have occurred.

The recall came after almost two hours.

'After hearing submissions from both counsel, I have decided to allow the prosecution to present its new evidence,' said the judge. 'We shall then adjourn until tomorrow to allow the defence to consider the implications.'

With the tact of a lawyer who knew he had stepped close to the limit, Sir Job pitched his voice on a low, unassertive note. 'Call Chief Inspector Wigfull.'

In the public gallery, Diamond's toes curled.

Wigfull stepped up and took the oath in a voice redolent with self-congratulation. To Diamond's prejudiced eye, the moustache seemed to have been brushed upwards, into an exultant curve.

'Chief Inspector, would you tell the court what you informed me this morning,' said Sir Job in little more than a whisper.

Wigfull had no reason to be humble. A stiffening of the shoulders, a tilt of the head, and he plunged into his story. 'Early this morning, I conducted a further search of the defendant's house in Bath. It has not been occupied since she was taken into custody. In the course of the search, one of my officers, Detective Inspector Halliwell, removed the drawers from the dressing table in the bedroom, the defendant's bedroom, and discovered something fixed with Sellotape to the underside of the section that housed the drawers. It was in a position where it would not have been visible by simply removing the drawers. Inspector Halliwell felt underneath and detected a transparent folder. He immediately drew it to my attention.'

'Describe it, please.'

'The folder contained two antique letters with the signature "Jane". They were dated in the year 1800. From descriptions given to us previously by Professor Jackman, I believe them to be the letters written by Jane Austen that had allegedly been stolen from his house.' Sir Job addressed the judge. 'M'lord, the Crown submits these letters as Exhibit Six.' He handed a folder to one of the court officials, who passed it up.

After a cursory examination, the judge asked whether the defence wished to put any questions to Wigfull at this stage, and Mrs Bargainer said she reserved her cross-examination. The judge gave his customary warning to the jury not to discuss the case, and called the adjournment.

Diamond had watched Dana Didrikson while this scene was enacted. Her composure had shattered. A look of extreme shock had registered on her features. Her counsel approached her and an earnest exchange took place.

The corridor outside was abuzz with Wigfull's announcement. Every phone was occupied by the press. In the crush, Diamond managed to catch Jackman's eye. He was in animated conversation with a grey-suited, silver-haired man who had to be Siddons, the solicitor, but their words were lost in the turmoil. They both gestured to Diamond to join them. He had some difficulty. Someone – a reporter – recognized him and asked for a comment. He refused point-blank and forced a passage through the jostling, shouting crowd.

'What do you make of it?' Jackman demanded, and then answered his own question with, 'It's devastating. Couldn't be worse. I thought my showing yesterday was damaging enough, but this on top . . . a disaster.'

'It looks bad,' Diamond agreed.

'They wouldn't have fitted her up, would they?'

Siddons, shocked, said, 'Come now!'

Diamond said, 'No chance. John Wigfull isn't the sort. He plays the rules. And I can vouch for Keith Halliwell. No, they found the letters for sure.'

'Why didn't they find them before? They searched the place weeks ago.'

'Two possibilities,' said Diamond. 'Either someone overlooked them, or they weren't there at the time.'

'*Weren't there?*'

'Feel like a drive to Bath?'

On the dual carriageway near Keynsham, Jackman unburdened himself of some guilt. 'You know, I felt a bloody hypocrite when I was giving evidence yesterday. I had to make it appear as if all my dealings with Dana were altruistic . . . that I acted out of sympathy for young Mat. I like the boy, it's true, and I enjoyed taking him swimming, but I looked forward to every meeting with Dana. You know. I've tried to explain.'

'Say so, then,' said Diamond, ever a man for frank speaking. 'You love her.'

'All right,' Jackman muttered. 'I do. I was hoping against all the odds that the jury wouldn't convict. Then I was going to ask her to come to America with me. And the boy. A clean break for all of us.' He sighed. 'No chance of that now.'

'You believe she did it?'

'I can't believe that, feeling as I do about her, but I can't see that she'll get off now.'

Diamond didn't comment.

They drove up to Lyncombe and the terraced block where Dana had lived. A uniformed constable was stationed by the front door. They could see him from the end of the street.

'Drive on. There's a way into the back garden from the street behind,' Diamond said, recalling the day Dana had escaped to her car when he and Wigfull had called at the house.

He picked his trilby off the back seat and covered his bandaged head. Without obvious subterfuge, but in silence, they entered the back garden and approached the back of the house. Diamond bent to examine the door-frame, and in particular the lock. It was an old-fashioned mortice that had probably been in use for forty years. By aligning his eye with the edge of the door, he spotted the shapes of finger-bolts at top and bottom. No one had forced an entry that way.

He examined the kitchen windows and found no signs, but when he came to the sash window to the sitting room and traced his finger along the lower edge, he located a distinct indentation in the painted surface of the ledge.

He invited Jackman to feel it.

'The window's fastened securely inside,' Jackman said. 'I wouldn't say it's been forced.'

'We'll find out presently.' Diamond returned down the garden path and got into the car. 'Would you drive us round to the front?'

This gave the impression that they were just arriving. The young constable at the door recognized him as he opened the gate. 'Mr Diamond?'

'We'd like to see inside, if you don't mind.'

'Sir, I'm under instructions from Mr Wigfull.'

'You'd better come in with us then, and see we don't steal

345

the silver.'

Whether or not the news of Diamond's departure from the force had percolated to this level of the uniformed branch, the voice of authority prevailed. With the constable in tow, they went straight to the back sitting room and examined the window-fastening. The frame had a substantial brass fitting of the kind that rotated on a pin and slotted snugly into a catch to secure both sections of the window in the closed position.

'Nothing wrong with that,' Jackman observed.

Diamond turned to the constable. 'See if you can find me a screwdriver, lad.'

A few minutes later he unfastened the four screws that held the main fitting in place, and lifted it clear of the wood. Then he stood back. 'See what you make of that.'

If Diamond's tone of voice wasn't quite so self-admiring as Wigfull's had been in court, it was a near-run thing. It was undeniable that the wood below the fastening had recently been splintered. You could see where the screws had been forced. Tiny splinters of clean, white wood had been jammed into the holes to give the screws something to bite into when they were replaced.

'The intruder got in this way and tidied up afterwards,' he said. 'I spotted a chip of fresh wood on the floor between the boards. Years ago, in the days when real detectives worked out of Scotland Yard, we had a saying: "Give your eyes a chance".'

Ideally, the dictum merited a moment's contemplation. It got none at all from Jackman. 'When was the break-in? Last night?'

'Could have been any time in the past two weeks. The letters were hidden upstairs ready to be discovered if and when they were needed.'

Diamond grinned from ear to ear. After so many months in the doghouse he was entitled to be satisfied. The discovery was detective work at its finest, worthy to secure his place in the pantheon with Fabian of the Yard and the other trilby-hatted heroes of yesteryear.

346

Chapter Four

LILIAN BARGAINER, QC, DISPOSED OF John Wigfull next morning with appropriate irony.

'Chief Inspector, the entire literary establishment salutes you today for recovering the missing letters of Miss Jane Austen. The newspapers are bracketing your name with Sherlock Holmes and Miss Marple. Pray, how did you make this happy discovery? Was it, to paraphrase Miss Austen herself, the result of previous study, or the impulse of the moment? Was it sense, or sensibility, that guided you to the hiding place?'

Wigfull frowned and said, 'I'm afraid I don't follow the question.'

'I'm surprised it causes any difficulty to a man of your acuteness. Let me put it another way. Who tipped you off?'

He swayed back like a boxer. 'I'm unable to answer that.'

'Somebody did, presumably. Surely you didn't order the search of the house yesterday morning on a whim?'

'Well, no.'

'So . . .?'

Wigfull passed the tip of his tongue slowly around his lips.

After an appreciable pause, Mrs Bargainer said, 'Do you understand what I am asking this time?'

'Yes.'

'Then you really must give an answer.'

He said softly, 'There was a phone call –'

'Speak up, Chief Inspector.'

'There was a phone call to the main police station in Bath late the previous evening. The caller rang off before we could get his name.'

'So you were tipped off. You didn't tell us this in your statement yesterday.'

'I didn't consider that it was needed at that stage.'

'I'm pleased to hear it. I really didn't have you down as a glory-hunter. Now we know. An anonymous caller. Do I have it correctly now?'

'Yes.'

Mrs Bargainer drew her gown aside and rested her hands on her hips. 'Let us consider another point. When you gave us this startling information yesterday, we were supposed to deduce, were we not, that the defendant, Mrs Didrikson, had obtained the letters and hidden them in her dressing table herself?'

'I simply reported what I found,' Wigfull said guardedly.

'And – you can tell us now – were you surprised to have made such a discovery? After all, you had searched the house from top to bottom on a previous occasion.'

'We must have overlooked it the first time. As I explained –'

'Oh, don't sell yourself short, Chief Inspector. Have you considered the possibility that someone entered the house some time in recent days and planted those letters there?'

Wigfull looked across to the table where the prosecution team were seated, but no help was forthcoming. 'I don't think that's likely. The place has been kept locked.'

'So would it surprise you to be informed that the sash window in the sitting room at the back has recently been forced, and the fitting repaired and screwed back into place?'

'Is that true?' said the hapless Wigfull.

'That is my information. You are the detective, Mr Wigfull. I suggest you investigate. Your findings will interest us all, as will your deductions afterwards. We accept that your statement yesterday was made in good faith. However, craving the court's indulgence, I venture to describe the testimony as somewhat coloured by pride and prejudice. No further questions, my lord.'

The judge looked faintly amused. He leaned forward, his chin propped on his right hand. 'Sir Job?'

Some hurried shuffling of papers at the prosecution table underlined their confusion. 'At this point, m'lord, we propose to move on to the chief inspector's evidence-in-chief.'

'Then I suggest you do.'

The next hour and fifty minutes was an exercise in damage limitation, a painstaking recapitulation of the police investigation. By switching back to the discovery of the body in Chew Valley Lake and plodding systematically through the process that had led to Dana's indictment, Sir Job contrived point by point to rehabilitate Wigfull as a credible witness.

To Wigfull's credit, his testimony was equal to the challenge. He spoke with restored assurance, making a point of facing the jury as he gave his responses, and his language was simple and direct. He didn't hesitate again. He must have been aware that Diamond was watching from the public gallery, yet he described the first phases of the inquiry, when Diamond had been in charge, with impeccable recall – the search of the lakeside and the delay in identifying the body; the television and press appeals for information; and how Professor Jackman had eventually come forward and identified the body. Sir Job took him through the search of John Brydon House, the interviews with Jackman and the transatlantic phone conversation with the American academic, Dr Junker (an affidavit from Junker had been filed by the prosecution). Wigfull explained how checks had been made at University College and with Air France that established an alibi for Jackman, and how the focus of the investigation had then switched to Dana.

'What happened when you went to interview her?'

'She ran out of the back of the house. I gave chase, but she got into the Mercedes and drove away. It happened that she met another car in a narrow road near the house – met it head-on. There was a slight collision.'

'She was unhurt?'

'Yes, sir.'

'And did she admit to running away from the police?'

'Her words were, "I was trying to escape." '

So it went on through the morning, this process of assembling a case that would allow no reasonable doubt. Sir Job omitted nothing. He took Wigfull through the interview of Dana and established that she had insisted she had no more to tell when in reality there had been much more to come. He plotted the stages of her disclosures, showing how she'd eventually admitted to having visited the Jackman's house on the morning of the murder and had seen Geraldine lying dead in bed. Finally, he testified that when the reports had come back from the forensic lab confirming that the body had been placed in Dana's car boot, he had formally charged her with murder in the presence of her solicitor.

It was 12.50 when Sir Job concluded the examination-in-chief. The court adjourned for lunch. Dana, ashen after the morning's ordeal, was led down to the cells.

Siddons, her solicitor, was waiting for Diamond at the foot of the stairs from the public gallery. 'Do you have a few minutes? Mrs Bargainer would *so* like to meet you.'

'Her memory can't be too hot,' Diamond commented. 'She cross-examined me in this court six months ago.'

They invited him to join them for lunch across the road. Out of her wig and gown, Lilian Bargainer passed for one of the mainstays of the lounge bar, drinking dry sherry from a schooner and dragging at a cigarette that she held between thumb and forefinger. 'God, what a production old Claws is making of it,' she said. 'He's working on the principle that if Wigfull talks for long enough the jury will forget the balls-up of the missing letters. Never fear – I'll remind 'em.' She gripped Diamond's sleeve. 'Peter, old sport, I owe you one for that. What are you drinking?'

'Orange juice,' said Diamond, tapping his head-bandage.

She pushed a ten-pound note at Siddons. 'Be an angel. Get one for yourself. I mean a beer or something. And see what food there is.' Alone at the table with Diamond, she said, 'I want to tap your brain.'

'Gently, if you must.'

'I cross-examine Johnny Wigfull this afternoon. I intend to keep it short and devastating, but I mustn't miss anything. What are the weak points in the evidence?'

'I wouldn't trouble with the weak points if I were you,' Diamond told her. 'Go for the strong one.'

'The body in the boot?'

'Right. If you hadn't suggested this meeting, I was going to whisper in Siddons' ear.'

'Ah – so you know something?'

'I wouldn't put it so strongly as that – particularly after brain surgery. I don't know how reliable the little grey cells are, but they've been working overtime to catch up.'

He wasn't really underselling the importance of what he was about to tell her. He quietly relished this moment as much as he relished the sensation to come in court. For all her hail-fellow manner, Lilian Bargainer had a shrewd brain. She would appreciate this. She would understand its significance, a triumph of canny detection over the men in white coats.

'Get to the point, my love. Time's at a premium.'

'If I'm right about this, there's a detail – an important detail – you can check with your client. She won't appreciate the significance, by the way.'

'She's in no shape of mind to appreciate anything, sport, but I'm willing to try.'

'Ask her to cast her mind back to that morning she took Matthew up to John Brydon House and saw the blond man walking out on Geraldine.'

'The pusher – Andy Coventry?'

'Yes. In her statement, she told me he appeared familiar at the time, but she couldn't place him. I think we may be able to refresh her memory. Ask her if she could have seen him swimming.'

'Swimming? You'd better explain, you cryptic old bugger.'

Wigfull looked apprehensive as he entered the witness box again. With good reason. His rehabilitation had owed everything to Sir Job Mogg. Lilian Bargainer wouldn't be wearing velvet gloves for the cross-examination. Up in the public gallery, however, Peter Diamond was in a forgiving mood. The last words he had spoken to Mrs Bargainer were, 'Wigfull's not a bad detective. He's wrong, but he's not bad. You don't have to wipe the floor with him.'

She was on her feet. 'Chief Inspector, I shan't detain you long. You've given the court a copious account of your investigation, but you neglected to mention that the late Mrs Geraldine Jackman was a user of cocaine. Did you not consider this of relevance?'

'It came to our notice only recently,' Wigfull stated with a smoothness suggesting he had anticipated the question.

'But it doesn't affect the present case?'

'That is correct.'

'That is your judgement.' She turned towards the jury and rolled her eyes upwards as if in despair of the police. Then she swung back to Wigfull. 'There is one other matter I should like to clarify, and that concerns the interrogation of the accused, Mrs Didrikson. She was taken by ex-Superintendent Diamond and yourself to Bath Central Police Station for questioning on Tuesday, 10 October. Am I right? You may refer to your notes. I want to get this clear.'

Wigfull produced his notebook and thumbed through it. '10 October. Yes.'

'She was detained overnight? Is that correct?'

'Yes.'

'And on 11 October her car was collected for forensic examination?'

'Yes – but with her permission.'

'Granted. Your personal conduct towards Mrs Didrikson cannot be faulted. I believe you went so far as to notify her employer, Mr Buckle, that she would not be able to drive him in the morning.'

Wigfull agreed modestly, 'That's true. I did.'

'A very considerate thing to have done, if I may say so,' Mrs Bargainer complimented him.

Plainly, Wigful saw an opportunity here. 'Yes, but there was another reason for doing it. I wanted to check with the employer, Mr Buckle, whether the accused had reported for work on the day of the murder. And she hadn't.' He glanced towards Sir Job and was rewarded with a nod of acknowledgement for scoring a point under cross-examination.

'So when did you speak to Mr Buckle?' Mrs Bargainer asked.

'Some time between eight and nine in the evening.'

'The evening of 10 October?'

'Yes.'

'Thank you, Chief Inspector.'

There was a moment's hiatus before the court fully grasped that Mrs Bargainer had finished the cross-examination. The whole exchange had taken less than two minutes.

Wigfull looked as bemused as anyone.

The judge asked whether the prosecution were proposing to re-examine. They were not. Wigfull was told to step down. Sir Job and his team had been thrown again. The disarray at their table was all too apparent.

'Are you calling another witness?' the judge enquired.

'Directly, m'lord,' said Sir Job, scattering paper across the floor.

The witness was Stanley Buckle, dressed for his appearance in a three-piece dove-grey suit and an Institute of Directors tie. The usual rosebud was missing from his buttonhole, possibly in recognition of the solemn occasion. Once in the box, he reinforced the punctilious image by making a performance of putting on half-glasses to read the oath. He exuded importance; it was in the tilt of his chin and the set of his shoulders.

Sir Job's junior, by comparison a man with a poor posture and an unfortunate high-pitched voice that would probably ensure that he remained a junior for ever, was assigned with the undemanding task of establishing how the Mercedes car came to be in the prisoner's possession.

'She was the driver for my company, Realbrew Ales,' Stanley explained.

'She kept the car overnight?'

'Yes. There was an understanding that she could use it privately outside office hours provided that journeys were entered into the log.'

'All journeys were entered into a log?'

'That's what I said.'

'To your knowledge, Mr Buckle, did any person other

353

than Mrs Didrikson ever drive that car?'

'Not a soul. It was new when we supplied her with it.'

'The log – is it kept in the car?'

'That's the drill. We check it at the end of the month and enter the mileage in our ledger.'

'Did you know that the log was not in the car when it was taken for forensic examination?'

'I heard about that. We made a search at Realbrew just in case, but I didn't expect to find it. Dana got it back from the office on 1 October. It should have been in the car, as I believe she told the police.' Buckle glanced across at Dana for confirmation and she actually gave a nod. He added gratuitously, 'I'd like to have it put on record that she was a respected member of my staff.'

'We are obliged to you.'

When Lilian Bargainer rose to cross-examine, nothing in her manner suggested that this would be anything but a formality.

'Mr Buckle, you described yourself as the Managing Director of Realbrew Ales, but you have a number of other business interests, don't you?'

'I didn't think you needed to know. I'm a supplier of novelty goods to stationery shops and other outlets. I'm also on the boards of several companies in the entertainment business.'

'Novelty goods?'

'Toys, Christmas crackers, metal puzzles – you name it . . .'

'You import these items, presumably?'

'Well, yes.' Buckle answered in a way that showed he was more interested in talking about other matters.

'From the Far East?'

'In the main.'

The judge, too, was uneasy and signalled it by resting his hands on the bench and leaning back stiffly against his padded chair.

Lilian Bargainer made no concessions. 'The toys. Would they include such items as miniature teddy bears from Taiwan?'

'Certainly.'

'Last summer you asked Mrs Didrikson to collect a consignment from Southampton Docks.'

'That's right.'

'She told you, I believe, that she was stopped on the way back by two policemen in plain clothes who searched the cartons containing the bears. Is that so?'

'That's what she told me.'

The judge leaned forward to interrupt. 'Mrs Bargainer, I am trying to see the pertinence of these questions.'

'The matter has direct relevance to the case, my lord, as I shall presently demonstrate. Mr Buckle, you're obviously – literally, in fact – a man of the world. You must have divined the reason why the police were interested in this consignment. Toys from the Far East, collected by a company driver from the docks.'

'They were clean,' said Buckle, affronted. 'Teddy bears – for charity. They were handed out to kids at Longleat.'

'So it emerged,' Mrs Bargainer conceded. 'But clearly in the view of those policemen there were grounds for suspicion that you were importing drugs.'

Sir Job bounded up to interrupt. 'M'lord, I can't believe my ears. This is outrageous. It's a blatant attack on the reputation of the witness. Nothing in Mr Buckle's testimony can warrant such character assassination.'

'Both counsel will approach the bench,' the judge instructed them.

From the gallery, Diamond strained to overhear the earnest argument that ensued. If the judge ruled in favour of the prosecution now, Mrs Bargainer's task would be next to impossible. In the dock, Dana nervously repinned a strand of hair. Whether she fully understood the significance of this moment was unclear, but she could not have failed to sense the tension in the court.

After almost ten minutes of wrangling, counsel returned to their positions. Sir Job was crimson, Lilian Bargainer still serene.

'My apologies, Mr Buckle – for the delay,' she resumed. 'I have been asked to come quickly to the point, and I shall. Is it a fact that Anton Coventry, known as Andy, is an associate of yours?'

Buckle's hands gripped the ledge of the witness box. 'I've met a man of that name, if that's what you mean.'

'I mean a little more than that. Have you entertained him at your house?'

'Well, yes.'

'He swam in your pool on at least one occasion?'

'Yes.'

'Doubtless you've heard that he is at present in custody on several charges, including offences relating to the supply of cocaine?'

'I read something about it in the paper.' Buckle was unconvincing. It was too late now to distance himself from his odious friend.

'Did you know that Andy Coventry is alleged to have supplied cocaine to the late Mrs Jackman?'

Buckle was silent.

'Come now. It is public knowledge, is it not?' Lilian Bargainer probed.

'Why ask me, then?' said Buckle.

'Why not admit it, then?' she rapped back. 'We're getting closer to the truth, aren't we? The whole truth that you promised to tell, Mr Buckle. I put it to you that you came under police suspicion as an importer of illegal substances. My client's trip to Southampton at your behest to collect the teddy bears was just a charade, a diversionary tactic to spike their guns, was it not? How interesting that when she returned to your house at the end of the day you were entertaining, among others, Andy Coventry.'

Sir Job rose to protest that the charges against Coventry were *sub judice* and the imputation was misleading, and Mrs Bargainer withdrew her last comment.

'But you agree with my account of the facts?' she pressed Buckle.

'The whole thing is irrelevant,' he said without conviction. 'I'm here to talk about the car.'

Mrs Bargainer smiled. 'Very well, let's talk about the car. The Mercedes 190E 2.6 Automatic that you bought when Mrs Didrikson joined Realbrew Ales. You bought two cars of that model for the company at that time, didn't you?'

'Yes.'

'One for your personal use and the other for Mrs Didrikson's?'

'Yes.'

'Good.' She beamed at Buckle; he didn't smile back. 'I'm going to ask about the use you made of the cars, notably on Monday, 11 September and Tuesday, 10 October last year. Am I making myself clear, Mr Buckle? The first date was that of Mrs Jackman's murder. We have already heard from you that Mrs Didrikson did not report for work that day, so presumably you had to drive yourself about?'

'Yes.'

'And ever since Tuesday, 10 October, you have been without a chauffeur, because that's the day Mrs Didrikson was taken in for questioning by the police. When were you informed?'

'I can't recall.'

'Chief Inspector Wigfull testified that he phoned you between eight and nine that evening, 10 October.'

Buckle shrugged. 'Fair enough.'

'I must insist on a better answer than that. Do you recall being telephoned?'

'All right. It was some time that evening. I didn't check my watch.'

'It's important, you see, because there was a delay of some twelve hours before the Mercedes Mrs Didrikson drove was collected for forensic examination. The car stood outside her house for twelve hours. When it was collected, we now know, the impossible was shown to have happened. The scientists proved with their genetic fingerprinting that the body of Geraldine Jackman had been in the boot of that car. I say it was impossible because Mrs Didrikson has told me so, and I believe her.'

Buckle stared rigidly ahead like a guardsman being bawled at by a drill sergeant. Actually Lilian Bargainer had not raised her voice one decibel.

The skill of this cross-examination was profoundly satisfying to Peter Diamond. Compelled to hear his own deductions voiced by proxy, he was locked in to every word the barrister uttered.

'I put it to you that the impossible can only be explained

this way. When you got the call from Chief Inspector Wigfull, you decided on a plan to confuse the police and divert suspicion from yourself. For it was you, wasn't it, Mr Buckle, who deposited the body of Geraldine Jackman in Chew Valley Lake?'

Nobody protested and Buckle made no pretence of a response. A paralysing curiosity gripped the court as Mrs Bargainer talked on. 'On the night of 11 September you drove there with the dead woman in the boot of your Mercedes. And when, a month later, you heard that Dana Didrikson was being held overnight, you thought of a way of confirming the police in their suspicion that she was the murderer. The spare keys for her Mercedes were held by your company. You drove up to Lyncombe where the vehicle was parked. You opened the boot and unclipped the fabric lining.'

Buckle's eyes flicked towards the jury, as if in search of a doubter. The looks that met his were not encouraging.

'Are you listening, Mr Buckle? You unclipped the lining. Then you removed the lining from the boot of your own car, the lining the body had lain on, and fitted it into the other car. Do you deny it?'

Peter Diamond so completely identified with the question that he started to say aloud, 'Speak up'. He clapped a hand to his mouth.

Buckle was saying, 'You've got me totally wrong. I didn't kill Gerry Jackman. Before God I didn't.'

'You put her in the lake.'

He hesitated.

'You put her in the lake,' Mrs Bargainer insisted. This had become a contest of wills.

Buckle stared around the court. In the dock, Dana had put her fingers to her throat.

'Do you deny it?' Lilian Bargainer demanded.

He capitulated. 'All right, I did. I put her in the lake.' As a murmur from all sides of the court broke the tension, he added more loudly, 'But I didn't kill her.'

Mrs Bargainer frowned, put her hand to her face and let the fingers slide down to the point of her chin in an attitude of incomprehension. 'You're going to have to help me, Mr Buckle. What you are claiming now is curious, if not incredible. Let's have this clear. On the night of 11 September you drove to Chew Valley Lake with the body of Mrs Jackman and deposited it in the water, and yet you didn't kill her. You insist on that?'

'Yes.'

'Why? Why behave in such an extraordinary fashion?'

He was silent.

'You must explain, Mr Buckle, you really must if we are to believe you.'

His mouth remained closed.

Mrs Bargainer said, 'Let's approach this another way. You didn't kill her. Did you know she had been murdered?'

'No,' said Buckle, freed from his constraint. 'That's the point.'

'Good. I'm beginning to understand. You found her dead, is that right?'

'Yes.'

'You didn't know she'd been murdered, is that right?'

'Yes.'

'You thought she'd overdosed.'

'Yes – I mean no.' Buckle stared about him. He'd been snared, and he knew it.

Lilian Bargainer said without even a hint of irony, 'You said yes and you meant no. Which is it? I put it to you that your associate Andy Coventry was supplying Mrs Jackman with cocaine that he got from you. You're the importer and he was the pusher. Am I right?'

Sir Job sprang up, but the judge gestured to him to be seated.

'You had better consider your position, Mr Buckle,' said Lilian Bargainer. 'It's too late now to deny your involvement in drugs. If you do, you lay yourself open to suspicion of murder. Which is it to be?'

Buckle swayed slightly in the witness box, sighed heavily, and then the words tumbled from him. 'What happened was this. Come September, Andy bunked off to Scotland on some course. He was her supplier, like you said. I got word from my contacts that she was shouting for the stuff. She was making trouble about Andy being unavailable. Big trouble. She was threatening to blow the whistle on us. So I went to see her on the Monday.'

'Monday, 11 September?'

'Yes.'

'What time?'

'About lunchtime. When I got no answer at the front I went round the back. The kitchen door was open. People with the habit aren't too clever about things like that. I called out and still got no anwer, so I tried upstairs. She was dead on the bed. It got to me, I can tell you, finding her like that. She's overdosed, I thought. They say cocaine can kill you, just the same as heroin. I could see real trouble ahead if the doctors opened her up. So I decided to move her. That's what I did. Carried her downstairs and put her in the car. That night I dropped her in the lake.' He closed his eyes and added, 'I was hoping that would be the end of it.'

'And the Jane Austen letters?'

'They were stuffed down the front of her nightdress, like she was hiding them. I thought it must be something she meant to trade for the coke, so I took it. I didn't even look at them till later.'

'And what happened when the body was found in the lake?'

'I was really scared – but not a word was said about drugs. She'd been smothered, the papers said. I realized what I must have done – I'd moved a murdered corpse. The next thing, they arrested Dana – my driver – and it was all too close to home for my liking. I could be done as an accessory. So when the chance came, I switched the linings, just like you said. I only did it to cover myself. Dana had been stupid enough to kill her, I thought, so I wasn't causing her any more aggravation than she deserved.'

'What happened to the log?'

'I burnt it, obviously.'

'Obviously?'

'Well, every trip was accounted for. If the police had seen it, they'd have found out that her car wasn't used to move the body, wouldn't they?'

'And presumably you falsified the log in your car?'

360

He nodded. 'It's a simple matter when you're behind with the entries, as I was.' Then Stanley Buckle drooped like a bull pierced with bandilleras.

But Mrs Bargainer had another ready. 'Let's turn to something else that was brought to the court's attention. I put it to you that when you heard Coventry had been arrested, you broke into Mrs Didrikson's empty house and taped the letters into her dressing table as another diversion.'

Buckle hesitated.

'Why did you do that?' said Mrs Bargainer gently, as if he had made the admission already.

He dipped his eyes. 'As a kind of insurance. I was dead worried the drugs would come up at the trial, and they did – on the first day. So I needed to switch the interest back to the letters. I phoned the police and told them to look in the house. Until today I believed Dana was guilty. I wouldn't have done it otherwise. Have I said enough?'

'More than enough for me,' the judge acidly commented. 'Does the prosecution propose to re-examine?'

Sir Job declined. 'And in view of the testimony we have just heard, we shall not be calling any further witnesses, m'lord.'

'The prosecution case is closed?'

'Yes, m'lord.'

Up in the public gallery, Peter Diamond sat back in his chair, mentally spent.

Lillian Bargainer rose again. 'I submit, my lord, that the case we have heard from the prosecution is not strong enough to lay before the jury.'

The judge agreed and directed the jury to acquit Dana Didrikson.

Dana covered her face and sobbed.

Chapter Five

'YOU LOOK LIKE A PIECE of chewed twine,' Stephanie told him that evening after they'd eaten. 'And no wonder. Why don't you get an early night?'

'Presently.'

'If it's the news you're waiting for, I saw it all at 6.30. She appeared at the press conference and scarcely said more than a couple of words. She didn't even smile. The papers are offering terrific money for her story, but she's told them what to do with it. You've got to admire her.'

'Yes.'

'That QC of hers was a woman, I noticed. She must have been brilliant to fathom what really happened. You can't put that down to feminine intuition.'

'I don't,' said Diamond.

'What a brain!'

'Lilian Bargainer?'

'Well, yes. That Inspector Wigfull was way off beam and so were you.'

The injustice wounded him less than being coupled with Wigfull. 'Off beam? What about?'

'The cocaine. You should have been on to that from the beginning.'

'We got diverted. The forensic tests were negative. They didn't show Geraldine Jackman was using the stuff. Yes, I know,' he added sheepishly. 'I'm the one who says never rely on bloody scientists.'

'What went wrong with the tests?'

'She hadn't taken any of the stuff before she was killed. Not for some days. She was desperate to get some, which was how Buckle was drawn into it. The irony is that she had several packets in the house, the ones I found. They must have been left over from one of the parties she gave, and she forgot they were there. She focused totally on her supplier.'

'And he killed her.'

'Oh, no,' said Diamond.

'I mean Buckle. He's been arrested.'

'Yes, but on a drugs charge.'

She frowned. 'Isn't he the killer, then?'

'No.'

After he declined to add any more, she said, 'I suppose you know who it was, cleverclogs. You ought to be back in the police.' As if instantly regretting the remark, she reached out and squeezed his hand. 'But I'm glad you aren't. I see more of you.'

'Hm.'

'Let's have a pub lunch tomorrow, just the two of us.'

He shook his head. 'Sorry, I'm already booked for lunch.'

'Oh? Who with?'

'The murderer.' He reached for the TV remote control.

Conceding no hint of surprise, curiosity or concern, she said, 'All right, Saturday.'

He got to bed soon after. Stephanie's insouciance and his cussedness kept them both awake for a few hours more. Some time after midnight, he told her everything.

Chapter Six

HE SAT HUDDLED UNDER A big black umbrella on a bench in front of the Abbey, his raincoat buttoned to the neck and the collar up around his ears, touching his hat brim, indistinguishable from the plainclothes men seen in grainy black and white films of forty years ago. He had bought two portions of fish and chips from the shop at the end of Abbey Gate Street. They waited, wrapped, in his lap. A fine drizzle had blown in from the Bristol Channel and settled over the city. It was so misty that half the Abbey front was invisible. Even the pigeons had abandoned the place, but he was content to be there. This was what it was all about.

He was keeping a close watch on everyone who crossed the paved churchyard. Most were shoppers or tourists. A line of schoolchildren chattering in French approached the West Door and went in. From Stall Street came the opening bars of the Bruch Violin Concerto; the busker played regularly, backed by a taped orchestra. He had done well to find a dry pitch this morning. But he would have done better to have waited a few minutes longer, because the Abbey bells started chiming midday.

'Do we really have to talk here?'

The voice came from behind Diamond. He turned and saw Matthew Didrikson at his shoulder. 'Come and sit down. It's dry under the umbrella, and the fish and chips won't stay warm for ever.'

The boy came around the bench and accepted the packet Diamond handed him. He remained standing.

'At least we can talk in private here,' Diamond said. 'Have you seen your mother?'

'Yesterday evening. Greg took us out for a meal. It's impossible at home with the press and all that.'

'A celebration feast?'

'Not really.' Matthew stared down at the pavement, frowning. 'Greg's going to America.'

'Yes, I heard.'

'He wants my ma to go with him and bring me, too.'

Diamond asked straightforwardly, 'Did you tell them you killed Mrs Jackman?'

Matthew caught his breath and shivered. He continued to look downwards. Today the child in him was more obvious than the man.

'You should.'

'I can't.'

'Why not?'

'It's too much.'

'You mean after everything she's been through?'

Matthew gave a nod.

'I believe she knows,' said Diamond. 'That's why the acquittal left her unmoved. In her heart of hearts she has a sense of what really happened, Mat. And she's staying silent because she's your own mother and she loves you. But she knows the truth has to come out, and she'd rather hear it from you than someone like me.'

The boy was scanning Diamond's face to satisfy himself that the words were totally sincere. 'Are you going to tell?' A playground phrase.

'I will if necessary.'

His frankness measured up to the scrutiny, because Mat said, 'I'll speak to her.' He looked away, at a child crossing the yard on a BMX bike. 'Will I go to prison?'

'Not prison. You're under age.'

'Will there be a trial, like my mother had?'

'Probably.' This wasn't the time to speculate on the problems the judicial system faced in dealing with a twelve-year-old accused of murder. Nor was it useful to explain what detention during Her Majesty's Pleasure would really amount to. 'Want to sit down?'

This time Matthew accepted. He had to sit close to Diamond to get under his umbrella. There was moisture at the edges of his eyes. 'I didn't mean to kill her. When I went to the house, I only meant to find those letters. I knew she must have taken them just to spoil everything.'

'Why don't you tell me about it from the beginning? That Monday morning your mother had a call from Professor Jackman to say the letters were missing.'

'She was really upset. I could tell how angry she was, and I was angry, too. Mrs Jackman was a wicked woman. I hated her. She called my ma some horrible things and it was only because of her that I couldn't go swimming with Greg any more. *He* didn't want it to stop. He'd been really kind to me. He saved my life when I fell in the weir. Greg wasn't using me as some kind of worm on a hook, like she said, just because he fancied my ma, or something. He was . . .'

'Like a father?'

'Yes.' Then Matthew rapidly added, 'I still love my real father.'

The 'real' father who preferred playing chess, who hadn't bothered to come to England for the trial. The reality was that the father had rejected his son. Matthew's blind loyalty suppressed a terrible, deadly despair.

'What happened on that Monday morning?'

'When Ma was driving me to school I could see she was all screwed up about those letters. I decided to try and get them back from Mrs Jackman. On the first day of term, we always have to hang around the vestry for hours while they issue us with clean robes. They're too busy with the little kids to bother with us older boys. You can go off round the shops and nobody gives a monkey's. I went up to Bathwick Hill on a minibus. I knew the house, of course. I thought I might find a window open somewhere, but it was easier than that, because the back door was open. I just turned the handle and walked in. Nobody was about. I crept upstairs and found her bedroom. She was in there, still asleep. I wanted to look for the letters, but I was afraid she might wake up and catch me.'

'Did she wake?'

'Not until I lifted the duvet over her face. She was lying on her back and I pulled it up to cover her eyes. I don't think I would have killed her if she'd stayed asleep. She moved, and I pressed the duvet down. She struggled, but it was no good because her arms were trapped under the quilt. The more she struggled, the harder I pressed. I was kneeling on her. I was angry and frightened at the same time. I didn't panic, exactly, only I didn't want her to wake up and find me there, so I kept on pressing and pressing down on her face until she went still. I was even more scared then, when I knew what I'd done. I pulled the quilt down again and uncovered her face. I knew she was dead. I didn't stop to look for the letters, or anything. I just ran out.'

'Caught the bus back to Bath?'

'Yes.'

'Later on, when you heard that the body had been found in the lake, you must have been amazed.'

'Yes.'

'What did you think had happened?'

'First, I thought Greg must have found her in the bedroom and moved her, to make it look as if she killed herself. Later, I believed my mother put her in the lake. They said her own car was used. I didn't know what to do. If I owned up, I could get my ma into trouble. That day you came to our house and she tried to run away, and you caught her, I didn't really have concussion. I thought you might have to release her if I was taken to hospital.'

Diamond gave a nod and said nothing.

'I'm sorry you lost your job because of me,' said Matthew.

'Forget it,' Diamond told him. 'You probably saved my life by getting help as quickly as you did after Andy Coventry brained me in the Baths. That could have been permanent. Eat up your fish and chips.'

In the silence, Diamond weighed the significance of what Matthew had told him. The Crown Prosecution Service would have a real problem deciding the sensible way to deal with this. In reality, it would save everyone a headache if Jackman and Dana flew off to America and took the boy with them. There was no extradition of minors.

367

As if he read the thought, Matthew said, 'I want to own up properly. If I go to the police, would you come with me?'

'Sure.'

'First I want to tell Ma.'

'Okay.'

'What do you think she'll do?'

'I don't think she'll be in any hurry to go to America.'

'And Greg?'

'It wouldn't surprise me if he changes his plans when he hears what you have to say.'

They finished their lunch and got up to leave. Diamond rested a hand lightly on the boy's shoulder. Ahead, the mist was starting to lift, and he could make out one of those stone angels on the lowest rung of the ladder, caught in the attitude of moving upwards.

Diamond Solitaire

Chapter One

AN ALERT SHATTERED THE SILENCE in Harrods, a piercing, continuous note. The guard on duty in the security control room, Lionel Kenton, drew himself up in his chair. His hands went to his neck and tightened the knot in his tie. On the control panel in front of him, one of the light-emitting diodes, a red one, was blinking. If the system was functioning properly, someone — or something — had triggered a sensor on the seventh floor. He pressed a control that triggered the video-surveillance for that floor. Nothing moved on the monitors.

Kenton was the senior security guard that night. He was so senior that he had a shelf above the radiator for his exclusive use. On it were framed photos of his wife, two daughters, the Pope and Catherine Deneuve; an ebony elephant; and a cassette rack of opera tapes. Puccini kept him alert through the night, he told anyone so philistine as to question opera in the control room. *None shall sleep.* Listening to music was more responsible than reading a paper or a paperback. His eyes were alert to anything on the panel and his ears to any sound that clashed with the music.

He silenced Pavarotti and touched the button that gave him a direct line to Knightsbridge Police Station. They must already have received the alert electronically. He identified himself and said, 'Intruder alert. I'm getting a signal from the seventh floor. Furniture. Section nine. Nothing on screen.'

'Message received 2247 hours.'

1

'Someone is coming?'

'It's automatic.'

Of course it was. He was betraying some nervousness. He tried another survey of the seventh floor. Nothing untoward was visible, but then he hadn't much faith in video surveillance. Every terrorist knows to keep out of range of a camera.

And he had to assume this was a terrorist.

Twenty-two night security officers were posted in various parts of the store. He put out a general alert and asked for a second check that all the elevators were switched off. The security doors between sections were already in position and had been since the cleaners left. In the business of counter-terrorism nothing can be taken for granted, but really it wasn't feasible to break into Harrods. The intruder – if one was up there – must have hidden when the store closed and remained out of sight. If so, someone's job was on the line. Someone who should have checked section nine. You weren't allowed one mistake in this line of work.

His second-in-command that night, George Bullen, burst in. He'd been patrolling when the alert sounded.

'Where's it from?'

'Seventh.'

'It bloody would be.'

The furniture department was high risk: a brute to patrol. Wardrobes, cupboards, chests of drawers and units of every description. The nightly check for devices was a wearisome chore. It was conceivable – but in no way excusable – that the guard on duty had been so bogged down opening cupboards and peering into drawers that he'd missed someone lurking out of sight behind the damned things.

Another light flashed on the console and one of the monitors showed headlights entering the delivery bay. The police response couldn't be faulted. Kenton told Bullen to take over and went down to meet them.

Three patrol cars and two vans already. Marksmen and dog-handlers climbing out. More cars arriving, their flashing alarms giving an eerie, blue luminosity to the

2

delivery bay. Kenton felt a flutter in his bowels. The police weren't going to vote him security man of the year if this emergency had been triggered by a blip in the system.

A plain-clothes officer stepped out of a car and ran across to him. 'You're?'

'Kenton.'

'Senior man?'

He nodded.

'You put out the call?'

He admitted it, and his stomach lurched.

'Seventh floor?'

'Furniture department.'

'Points of access?'

'Two sets of stairs.'

'Only two?'

'The section is sealed off by security doors.'

'No lifts?'

'Switched off.'

'Any of your lads on the stairs?'

'Yes. That's routine. They'll be guarding the stairways above and below level seven.'

'Lead the way, then.'

Thirty or more uniformed officers, dog-handlers and men in plain clothes, several carrying guns, came with him as he set off at a run through the ground floor to the first stairway. A squad of a dozen or so peeled off and raced up that staircase while he led the remainder to the next.

Mounting seven floors was a fitness test for Lionel Kenton. He was relieved to be told to stop after six and a half, and even more relieved to find four of his own security staff in position as he'd claimed they would be. Now he had a chance to recover normal breathing while radio contact was made with the party on the other stairs.

'What's the layout here?'

Essentially the police marksmen wanted to know how much cover they could rely on. One of Kenton's team, a burly ex-CID officer called Diamond, gave a rapid rundown of the furniture display positioned nearest to the stairs. Peter Diamond was the man responsible tonight for

3

this section. You poor bugger, thought Kenton. You look more sick than I feel.

A team of three marksmen went up the final flight. Others took up positions on the stairs. The rest moved down to the landing below.

This was the worst – waiting for the unknown, while others went up to deal with it.

Someone offered Kenton some chewing-gum and he took it gratefully.

Perhaps six nerve-racking minutes went by before there was a crackle on the senior policeman's radio and a voice reported, 'Negative so far.'

Two dogs and their handlers were sent up to help.

Another long interval of silence.

Security Officer Diamond was just to the left of Kenton. He had his hands clasped, the fingers interlaced as if in prayer, except that the fingernails were white with pressure.

The last dregs of Kenton's confidence were draining away when someone announced over the scratchy intercom, 'We've got your intruder.'

'Got him under restraint?' said the man in charge.

'Come and see.'

'You're sure he's the only one?'

'Positive.'

The tone was reassuring. Strangely so, as if the tension had lifted altogether. Police and security staff dashed up the stairs.

The seventh floor lights were fully on. The marksmen had converged on a section where armchairs and settees were displayed. But they weren't in the attitude of gunmen. They were lounging about as if at a wine and cheese party. Two were seated on the arms of chairs. There was no sign of anyone under arrest.

Suddenly cold with his own sweat, Kenton went over with the others. 'But you said you found someone?'

One of them flicked his eyes downwards, towards a sofa.

It was the kind of vast, black corduroy thing that an advertising executive would have in his outer office. At one end was a heap of scatter cushions, brilliant in colour.

4

The face looking out from under the cushions was that of a small girl, her hair black and fringed, her eyes oriental in shape. Nothing else of her was visible.

Kenton stared in bewilderment.

'Ah, so,' said the senior policeman.

Chapter Two

'YOU'RE SACKING ME.' PETER DIAMOND, the guard
responsible for section nine on the night the child was
found, spoke without rancour. 'I know the score.'

The score was heavily against him. He wasn't young.
Forty-eight, according to his file. Married. Living in West
Ken. No kids. An ex-policeman. He'd got to the rank of
detective superintendent and then resigned from Avon
and Somerset over some dispute with the Assistant Chief
Constable. A misunderstanding, someone said, someone
who knew someone. Diamond had been too proud to ask
for his job back. After quitting the police, he'd taken a
series of part-time jobs and finally moved to London and
joined the Harrods team.

'I shouldn't say this, Peter,' the security director told
him, 'but you're bloody unlucky. Your record here has
been exemplary apart from this. You could have looked
forward to a more senior post.'

'Rules are rules.'

'Unfortunately, yes. We'll do the best we can in the way
of a reference, but, er . . .'

'. . . security jobs are out, right?' said Diamond. He was
inscrutable. Fat men – and he was fat – often have faces
that seem on the point of turning angry or amused. The
trick is to guess which.

The director didn't mind exhibiting his own unease. He
shook his head and spread his hands in an attitude of
helplessness. 'Believe me, Peter, I feel sick to the stomach
about this.'

'Spare me that.'

'I mean it. I'm not confident I would have spotted the

kid myself. She was practically invisible under the cushions.'

'I lifted the cushions,' Diamond admitted.

'Oh?'

'She wasn't on that sofa when I did my round. I definitely checked. I always do. It's an obvious place to plant a device. The kid must have been somewhere else and got under them later.'

'How could you have missed her?'

'I reckon I took her for one of the cleaners' kids. They bring them in sometimes. Some of them are Vietnamese.'

'She's Japanese, I think.'

Diamond snapped out of his defeated mood. 'You *think*? Hasn't she been claimed?'

'Not yet.'

'Doesn't she know her name?'

'Hasn't spoken a word since she was found. Over at the nick, they spent the whole of today with a string of interpreters trying to coax her to say something. Not a syllable.'

'She isn't dumb, is she?'

'Apparently not, but she says nothing intelligible. There's almost no reaction from the child.'

'Deaf?'

'No. She reacts to sound. It's a mystery.'

'They'll have to go on TV with her. Someone will know her. A kid found in Harrods at night – it's just the sort of story the media pick up on.'

'No doubt.'

'You don't sound convinced.'

'I'm convinced, Peter, all too easily convinced. But there are other considerations, not least our reputation. I don't particularly want it broadcast that a little girl penetrated our security. If the press get on to you, I'd appreciate your not making any statements.'

'About security? I wouldn't.'

'Thank you.'

'But you can't muzzle the police. They have no interest in keeping the story confidential. It's going to break somewhere, and soon.'

A sigh from the director, followed by an uncomfortable silence.

'So when do I clear my locker?' Diamond asked. 'Right away?'

Chapter Three

THE PRIEST LOOKED INTO THE widow's trusting eyes and rashly told her, 'It's not as if it's the end of the world.'

The words of comfort were spoken on a fine summer evening in the sitting-room of a country villa in Lombardy, between Milan and Cremona. Pastoral care, Father Faustini termed it. Ministering to the bereaved, the sacred obligation of a priest. True, the ministering in this instance had continued longer than was customary, actually into a second year. But Claudia Coppi, cruelly widowed at twenty-eight, was an exceptional case.

Giovanni, the husband, had been killed freakishly, struck by lightning on a football field. 'Why did it have to be my husband when twenty-one other players, the referee and two linesmen were out there?' Claudia demanded of the priest each time he came on a visit. 'Is that the Lord's will? My Giovanni, of all those men?'

Father Faustini always reminded Claudia that the Lord works in mysterious ways. She always gazed at him trustingly with her large, dark, expressive eyes (she had worked as a fashion model) and he always told her that it was a mistake to dwell on the past.

The priest and the young widow were seated on a padded cushion that extended around the perimeter of the sunken floor. As usual, Claudia had hospitably uncorked a Barolo, a plummy vintage from Mascarello, and there were cheese biscuits to nibble. The sun had just about sunk out of sight, but to have switched on electric lights on such an evening would have been churlish. The scent of stocks, heavy on the cooler air, reached them through the open patio doors. The villa had a fine garden,

9

watered by a sprinkler system. Giovanni, not short of money – he'd made it to the top as a fashion photographer – had called in a landscape architect when the place was built. For Father Faustini, the remote location of the villa meant a three-mile trip on his moped, but he never complained. He was forty and in good health. A rugged man with tight, black curls and a thick moustache.

'You're doing so much better, now,' he remarked to the widow Coppi.

'It's window dressing, Father. Inside, I'm still very tense.'

'Really?' He frowned, and only partly out of concern for the tension she was under. It was a good thing the room had become so shadowy that his disquietude wouldn't be obvious to her.

'My usual problem,' she explained. 'Stress. It shows up in the muscles. I feel it in my shoulders, right across the top.'

'As before?'

'As before.'

There was a silence. Father Faustini was experiencing some tension, also.

Claudia said, 'Last week you really succeeded in loosening the muscles.'

'Really?' he said abstractedly.

'It was miraculous.'

He cleared his throat, unhappy with the choice of word.

She amended it to, 'Marvellous, then. Oh, the relief! I can't tell you how much better I felt.'

'Did it last?'

'For days, Father.' While he was absorbing that, she added plaintively, 'There's no one else I can ask.'

She made it sound like a plea for charity. Father Faustini sometimes fetched shopping for elderly members of his flock. He often collected medicine for their ailments. He'd been known to chop wood and cook soup for poor souls in trouble, so what was the difference in massaging Claudia Coppi's aching shoulders? Only that it set up conflicts within himself. Was it right to deny her Christian help because of his moral and spiritual frailty?

On the last two Friday evenings he had performed this service for her. Willingly he would have chopped wood instead, but the villa's central heating was oil-fired. He would have fetched shopping with alacrity, but she had a twice-weekly delivery from the best supermarket in Cremona. She had a gardener, a cook and a cleaner. What it came down to in practice was that the only assistance Father Faustini could render to Claudia Coppi was what she was suggesting. The poor young woman couldn't massage her own shoulders. Not well enough to remove muscular tension.

There was another factor that made him hesitate. Once a week in church he heard Claudia Coppi's confession, and lately – he wasn't certain how many times this had occurred, and didn't intend to make a calculation – she had admitted to impure thoughts, or carnal desires, or some such form of words. It wasn't his custom to ask for more details in the confessional once the commission of a sin was established, so he couldn't know for sure that there was a connection with his visits to the villa.

'I found something you could rub in, if you would,' she said.

He coughed nervously and crossed his legs. This was new in the routine. 'Embrocation?' he queried, striving to limit his thoughts to muscular treatment, remembering the overpowering reek of a certain brand favoured by footballers. The stuff brought tears to the eyes.

'More of a moisturizer really. It's better for my skin. Really smooth. Try.' She reached out and smeared some on the back of his hand.

He wiped it off immediately. 'It's scented.'

'There's a hint of musk,' she admitted. 'If you'd like to hold the pot, I'll just slip my blouse off.'

'That won't be necessary,' he quickly said.

'Father, it's silk. I don't want it marked.'

'No, no, *signora*, cover yourself up.'

'But I haven't unbuttoned yet.' She laughed and added, 'Is it as dark as all that?'

'I wasn't looking,' he said.

'That's all right. I've got my back to you anyway.'

11

As she was speaking he heard the blouse being slipped off her shoulders. Now he was in a real dilemma. She sounded so matter-of-fact, so nonchalant. By protesting, he was liable to inflate this into a moral crisis. It could appear as if he were letting himself be influenced by things she had said in the confessional.

'Not too much at once,' she cautioned. 'It goes a long way.'

He suppressed his misgivings, dipped in a finger and spread some over his palm.

Claudia's back was towards him, as she had claimed. He reached out and applied some of the moisturizer to the back of her neck.

She said, 'Oh dear, the straps are going to get in your way.'

'Not at all,' protested Father Faustini, but the brassière straps were tugged aside, regardless.

On the previous visits, he'd been persuaded to massage Claudia without using a liniment, through her T-shirt. This was a new experience. The contact with her flesh unsettled him more than he cared to admit. He traced the slope of her shoulders, feeling the warmth under his fingers. The smoothness was a revelation. When his hands cupped the round extremities of her shoulders he was compelled to pause.

She sighed and said, 'Bliss.'

In a moment he felt sufficiently in control to resume, spreading the moisturizer liberally across the shoulder-blades and up the spine to her neck. She had her head bowed so that her long, dark brown hair hung in front of her. He gave some attention to the deltoid muscles, gently isolating them, probing their form. In spite of what Claudia had said about tension, everything felt reasonably flexible to him, but he was the first to admit that he was no physiotherapist.

'Let me know if I'm causing any discomfort,' he told her.

'Quite the reverse,' she murmured. 'You have the most incredible hands.'

He continued to apply light pressure to the base of her neck until quite suddenly she raised her head and drew the hair back behind her shoulders.

12

'Enough?' he enquired. He hoped so. The movement of her hair across the backs of his hands had given him a physical sensation not to be encouraged in the priesthood.

But Claudia Coppi remained unsatisfied. She told him that there was still some tension at the tops of her arms.

'Here?'

'Yes. Oh, yes, just there. Do you mind if I lean back against you, Father? It's more comfortable.' She didn't wait for his answer.

The back of her head was on his chest, her hair against his cheek. In the same movement she placed her hands over his own and gripped them firmly. Then she pushed them downwards.

He hadn't discovered until now that she had altogether uncovered her breasts. She guided his hands over them. Exquisitely beautiful, utterly prohibited breasts offered for him to experience. For a few never-to-be-forgotten seconds of sin, Father Faustini accepted the offer. He held Claudia Coppi's forbidden fruits, passing his hands over and under and around them, thrilling to their fullness and their unmistakable state of arousal.

A monster of depravity.

With a supreme effort to banish fleshly thoughts, he blurted out the words, 'Lead us not into temptation,' and drew his hands away as if they were burned.

Tormented with shame, he stood up immediately and strode resolutely through the patio doors and around the side of the house without looking back. He didn't respond to Claudia Coppi's, 'Shall I see you next Saturday?' He knew he had to be out of that place and away.

He thought he heard her coming after him, probably still in her topless state. As swiftly as he could manage, he wheeled his moped out to the road, started it up and zoomed away.

'Fornicating fool,' he howled to himself above the engine's putt-putt. 'Weak-willed, degenerate, wanton, wicked, wretched, sex-crazed fellow. Miserable sinner.'

The little wheels bore him steadily along, his headlight picking out the road, but he was barely conscious of the journey. His thoughts were all on the depravity of his conduct. A man of God, a priest behaving like some beast of the field, only worse, because he was blessed with a mind that was supposed to be capable of overcoming the baser instincts.

How will I answer for this on the Day of Judgment? he asked himself.

God be merciful unto me, a sinner.

Precisely at which stage of the journey he became aware of what was ahead of him is impossible to say. Certainly he must have travelled some distance before he was ready to submit to anything except the writhings of his tormented conscience. It had to be spectacular, and it was. Father Faustini stared ahead and saw a pillar of fire.

The night sky was alight above the Plain of Lombardy, fizzing with hundreds of brilliant fiery points. Their origin was a fiery column, perhaps three thousand metres away, and towering over the land. Emphatically this was not a natural fire, for it was more green than orange, bright emerald green, with flares of violet, blue and yellow leaping outwards. Father Faustini was seized with the conviction that the Day of Judgment was at hand. Otherwise he might have suspected that something had been added to the Barolo he had swallowed, because what he was seeing was psychedelic in its extraordinary combination of colours. He'd seen large fires before, and mammoth firework displays, but nothing remotely resembling this.

What else could a wretched sinner do in the hour of reckoning, but brake, dismount, go down on his knees and pray for forgiveness? He felt simultaneously panic-stricken and rocked with remorse, that this should happen on the very night he had transgressed, after a lifetime of blameless (or virtually blameless) service in the Church. He knelt on the turf at the roadside, his hands clasped in front of his anguished face, and cried, 'Forgive me, Father, for I have sinned.'

He couldn't discount the possibility that his lapse with Claudia Coppi was directly responsible for what was happening. By speculating that his few seconds' fondling of a pair of pretty breasts had hastened the end of the world, he may have been presumptuous, but he felt an ominous sense of cause and effect.

He sneaked another look around his clasped hands. The state of the sky remained just as awesome. Streaks of fire were leaping up like sky-rockets, leaving trails of sparks.

As yet there were no avenging angels to be seen, nor other apocalyptic phenomena. He heard no trumpets, but nothing would surprise him now.

Instead he saw two brilliant lights, so dazzling that they made his eyes ache. And immediately there came a low droning, becoming stronger. The source wasn't supernatural. A car, its headlights on full beam, was moving at high speed towards him along the road, from the direction of the pillar of fire. Father Faustini could understand people fleeing from the wrath to come, but he knew that they were deluding themselves. There could be no escape.

And so it proved.

The engine-note grew in volume and the lights intensified in brilliance. Ordinarily, Father Faustini would have waved to let the driver know that he was dazzled. But of course he wasn't mounted on his moped. He was on his knees at the side of the road. He'd abandoned the bike when he'd first seen the pillar of fire. Abandoned it where he had stopped, in the middle of the narrow road.

The car was racing towards it.

He clapped his hands to his head.

There simply wasn't time to drag the moped out of the way. He could only hope that the driver would spot the obstruction in time and steer to the side. It might be academic at this late stage in the history of the world whether an accident – even a fatal accident – mattered to anyone, but Father Faustini had always been safety-conscious and he couldn't bear the thought of being responsible for anyone's death.

In truth, the driver of the car would share some blame, for his speed was excessive.

What happened next was swift and devastating, yet Father Faustini saw it in the curious freeze-frame way that the brain has for coping with danger at high speed. The car bore down on the moped without any let-up in speed

15

until the last split-second, when the driver must have seen what was in front of him. The rasp of tyre-rubber on the surface of the road as the brakes were applied made a sound like a siren's blare. The car veered left to avoid the moped, and succeeeded. But it hit the curb, went out of control and ricocheted to the opposite side. Father Faustini registered that it was a large, powerful saloon. The white light from the headlamps swept out of his vision and was replaced by intense red as the car skidded past with its brake lights fully on. It mounted the curb and started up a bank of turf that bordered a field. The band of rear lights lifted and spun in an arc. The whole thing was turning over. It was thrown on its back not once, but three times, tons of metal bouncing like a toy, smashing through a fence and finally sliding on the roof across the ploughed earth.

One of the rear lights was still on. It went out in a spray of sparks. Smoke was rising from the wreck.

Father Faustini's legs felt about as capable of holding him up as freshly cooked pasta, but he stumbled across to see if he could get anyone out before the entire thing caught fire.

The weight of the chassis had crushed the superstructure. The priest got on his knees beside the compressed slot that had once been the driver's window. There was a figure inside, the head skewed into an impossible angle. Too late for the last rites.

Round the other side was the passenger, another man, half on the turf. Literally. The other half, from the waist down, was still trapped inside. The halves were separated at the waist.

The priest crossed himself. A wave of nausea threatened, but it was vital to stay in control because the air reeked of raw petrol and the whole wreck was likely to turn into a fireball any second. Still troubled that someone might be alive and trapped inside, he lay on his stomach to try and get a sight of what had been the back seat. He needn't have troubled. There wasn't a centimetre of space between the torn upholstery and the impacted roof.

As he braced to get up, a sound like the rushing mighty

16

wind of the Pentecost started somewhere to his right. The petrol had caught fire.

He sprang up and sprinted away. Behind him, there was a series of cracking sounds followed by an almighty bang that must have been the petrol tank exploding. By then, he was twenty metres away and flat to the earth.

He didn't move for a while. His nerves couldn't take any more. He actually sobbed a little. It was some time before he thought of saying a prayer. In his embattled mind, the car-crash had overtrumped the Day of Judgment.

Finally, he sat up. The wreckage was still on fire, but the worst of it was over. Filthy black smoke was taking over and the stench of burning rubber stung his throat and nostrils. He stared into the flames. The charred, mangled metal that remained barely resembled a vehicle.

Every muscle he possessed was trembling. With difficulty, he got to his feet and walked past the burning wreckage towards the moped, which still stood untouched in the centre of the road, a testimony to his stupidity and his responsibility for this tragedy.

Beyond, the night sky was still rent by the vast pillar of fire that had so distracted him. The colours were still unearthly in their brilliance and variety. Even so, Father Faustini was forced to reconsider whether it could really be Judgment Day. The shock of the car-crash had altered his perception. He couldn't explain the phenomenon. There had to be a reason for it, but he hadn't the energy left to supply one.

He got astride the moped, started up and rode off to report what had happened.

Chapter Four

A SATURDAY EVENING PERFORMANCE IN the Metropolitan Opera House, New York. Domingo and Freni in full voice, before a packed, enthralled house. The entombment scene was drawing to its climax. United in Verdi's tear-jerking *O terra addio*, the tragic lovers, Radames and Aida, embraced in the crypt, while the massive stone slabs that would bury them alive were lowered inch by agonizing inch. Off-stage, the priests and priestesses chanted their relentless chorus, and the unhappy Amneris prayed for Radames' eternal soul. There are moments in an opera when no one minds too much if people wriggle and sway in their seats, straining for a better view, or trying to bring relief to aching buttocks. But when *Aida* reaches its poignant finale, when the slave-girl is expiring in the arms of Radames, and the lights are slowly dimmed to signify the sealing of the tomb, the stillness in the auditorium is palpable, from the orchestra stalls right up to the sixth tier.

Or should be.

This evening in the Center Parterre, the most expensive seats in the Met, there was a disturbance. Of all things at this heart-rending moment, a series of electronic beeps shrilled above the singing, a call-signal considerably louder than the wristwatch alarms that are always going off in cinemas and theatres. Some philistine had brought his pager to the opera.

The most absorbed of the audience ignored the source of the sound, refusing to have their evening blighted. Not everyone was so forbearing.

'Jesus Christ – I don't believe this!' a man spoke up in

18

the row immediately behind, regardless that he was adding to the disturbance. Others took up the protest with, 'Knock it off, will you?' and stronger advice.

In the third row, the source of the bleeps, a silver-haired man in black-framed bifocals, tugged aside his tuxedo, unhitched the pager from his belt and pressed a button that silenced it. The entire incident had lasted no more than six seconds, but it could not have been more unfortunately timed.

And now the curtain was down and the performers were taking applause, and in the Center Parterre as many eyes were on the man in the third row as on Domingo. Dagger thrusts of obloquy struck at the offender. Try as he did to ignore them by energetically applauding and focusing his eyes fixedly on the stage, he could expect no mercy from the offended patrons around him. New Yorkers are not noted for reticence.

'I know who I'd bury alive.'

'How do jerks like that get admitted?'

'I bought a ticket for a fucking opera, not a business conference.'

The jerk in question continued vigorously clapping through six or seven curtain calls, until the house lights were turned on. Then he turned to his companion, a stunning-looking, dark-haired woman at least twenty years younger than he, and attempted to engage her in such earnest conversation that the rest of New York was shut out.

She wasn't all that impressed. It was some consolation to those around as they got up and started to file out that the lady was unwilling to gloss over the lapse. In a short time, her voice was raised above his and snatches of the tongue-lashing she was giving him threatened to shake the chandeliers. ' . . . never been so humiliated and if you think after this I'm going to tag along for dinner and a screw, forget it.'

Someone called out, 'Attagirl! Dump him!'

And that is what she did, flouncing off between the rows of seats, leaving her escort staring after her and shaking his head. He didn't attempt to follow. He remained seated, judiciously letting the people he'd upset get clear. And when everyone had filed out of his section of the auditorium, he took out the pager again and keyed in a set of numbers.

Having got something on the display, he delved into his breast pocket and, impervious to the surroundings, took out a cell-phone and pulled out a length of aerial.

'Sammy, were you trying to reach me, because if you were, you could have timed it better, my friend.' While listening, he settled deep in the seat and propped his feet over the row in front. 'The hell with that. I sure hope for your sake this item of news measures nine point nine on the Richter Scale.'

What he then heard was enough to cause visible disturbance in Manfred Flexner. He withdrew his feet from their perch. He crouched forward as if it might enable him to hear better. His free hand raked through his hair.

Six minutes later, shaking his head and trying to stay calm, he reeled out of the opera house into the plaza of the Lincoln Center and took some gulps of fresh air. At this time of night the esplanade was thick with sables and minks, the audiences from the ballet and the Philharmonic jostling the opera-goers in the scramble for taxis. Flexner had his chauffeur waiting across the street with the limousine, so he had no reason to rush, but he wasn't going home yet.

He stared into the floodlit fountain for a while. Inside the last half-hour he'd interrupted an opera, lost his companion and slipped forty points on the international stock markets. He needed a drink.

The world was not a happier place next morning. He watched the Alka-Seltzers fizzing in the glass on his desk and brooded on what might have been. Pharmaceuticals were Manny Flexner's business.

Pharmaceuticals.

And here he was relying on the product of a rival company. He'd worked all his life in the expectation one day of finding a market leader like Alka-Seltzer that would become a steady seller for the foreseeable future. His was the traditional story of a Lower East side boy with a head for business who'd made some bucks driving taxis, lived frugally for a time and invested his earnings. Realizing, as all entrepreneurs do early in life, that you get nowhere using self-help and savings, he'd borrowed from the bank to buy a share in a small business supplying labels to pharmacies. When self-stick labels came in, he'd just about cornered the market, and made enough to borrow more cash and move into the supply side of pharmaceuticals. The 1960s and 70s had been a prosperous time in the drugs industry. Manny Flexner had taken over a number of companies in the USA and expanded internationally, buying shrewdly into Europe and South America. One of the Manflex products, Kaprofix, a treatment for angina, had become a strong source of income, a steady seller throughout America and Europe.

The story had a downturn. The pharmaceuticals industry relies heavily on the development of new drugs; companies cannot survive without massive research programmes. In the early eighties, scientists working for Manflex had identified a new histamine antagonist with potential as a treatment for peptic ulcers. It was patented and given the proprietary name of Fidoxin. The potential market for anti-ulcer drugs is enormous. At that time, Smith Kline's Tagamet dominated the field with sales estimated at over a billion dollars. Glaxo were developing a rival product called Zantac that would eventually outsell every drug in the world. But Manny Flexner was in there and pitching.

The early research on Fidoxin was encouraging. Manflex invested hugely in studies and field trials designed to satisfy the federal panel that advised the Food and Drug Administration, for no drug can be marketed without the FDA seal of approval. By 1981, Manflex was set to beat its rivals in the race to a billion-dollar market. Then, at a late stage, long-term side-effects were discovered in patients taking Fidoxin. Almost every drug has unwanted effects, but the possibility of serious renal impairment is unacceptable. Reluctantly, Manny Flexner had cut his losses and abandoned the project.

Too much had been gambled on that one drug. Through the 1980s Manny had been unwilling to sink so much into any research project. The recession in 1991 had hit Manflex harder than its rivals. Thanks mainly to the old standby, Kaprofix, the company still rated in the top ten in America, but had slipped from fourth to seventh. Or worse. Manny didn't care to check any more.

Today was the worst yet. He had the *Wall Street Journal* in front of him. Overnight, his stock had plummeted again in Tokyo and London. The reason?

'The biggest firework display in history is what they're calling it,' he told his Vice Chairman, Michael Leapman, throwing the paper to him. 'A twenty billion *lire* burn-up. The flames could be seen thirty kilometres south of Milan. How much is that, Michael?'

'About twenty miles.'

'The *lire*, for God's sake.'

'Not so bad as it sounds. Say seventeen million bucks.'

'Not so bad,' Manny repeated with irony. 'An entire plant goes up in smoke, a quarter of our Italian holding, and it's not so bad.'

'Insurance,' murmured Michael Leapman.

'Insurance takes care of plant and materials. There were research labs in that place. They were testing a drug for depression. Depression. I hope to God some of the stuff is left because I need some. Research is irreplaceable, and the market knows it. Do we have any news from Italy? Is it a total write-off?'

Leapman nodded. 'I spoke to Rico Villa an hour ago. The scene is a heap of white ash now.' He crossed the room to the drinks cabinet and took out the scotch. 'Can I pour you one?'

Manny shook his head and indicated the Alka-Seltzer.

'Then you don't mind if I do?' Thirty-seven, six-foot two, and blond, Michael Leapman was less volatile than his boss. He was half Swedish. Supposedly the Swedish half kept him from throwing tantrums. He'd joined Manflex five years ago through no action of his own, when Flexner had bought the small company he managed in Detroit;

Leapman had proved to be the only valuable acquisition from that takeover, a creative thinker with fine organizational skills. He'd developed a good rapport with his tough little boss. Within a year he'd been invited to join the board.

'Anyone died yet?' Manny enquired in a voice that expected nothing but bad news that day.

'Apparently not. Seven people were hospitalized, two of them firemen. They inhaled fumes. That's the size of it.'

'Environmental damage?'

Leapman raised an eyebrow. His boss wasn't known for his green sympathies.

'That could really put us in trouble,' Manny explained. 'Remember Seveso? The dioxin fumes? Wasn't that Italy? How many millions did the owners have to shell out in compensation?'

Leapman helped himself to a generous measure of Scotch. 'No poison fumes reported yet.'

The tension in Manny's face eased a little. He took off his glasses and wiped them with a tissue that he took from a Manflex dispenser.

'We can ride this,' Leapman said confidently. Providing reassurance was one of his most useful talents. 'Sure, it's going to bruise us. The markets will mark us down for a week or two, but we're big enough to absorb it. The Milan plant wasn't a huge moneymaker. Rico kept reminding us it was in need of modernization.'

'I know, I know. We were going to inject some capital later in the year.'

'Now we can give priority to the two plants near Rome.'

Manny replaced his glasses and studied Leapman. 'You don't think we should rebuild in Milan?'

'In the present economic climate?' His tone said it all. Rebuilding was out.

'You're right. We should consolidate with what we have out there. We can sell the Milan site.' Having weighed the options, Manny seemed satisfied. 'What I want now is for someone to go to Italy and tidy up, sort out the staffing problems, salvage anything we can from this mess.' He hesitated, as if casting about for a name. 'Who do you think? Would you say David can handle it?'

'David?' The name wrongfooted Leapman. He was fully expecting this assignment for himself.

'My boy.'

'No question.' He knew better than to try and talk the boss out of handing the assignment to his son, whatever he privately thought. Young David Flexner – young, but by no stretch of imagination still a boy – conspicuously lacked his father's enthusiasm for the business world, yet Manny cherished the unlikely hope that he would make a contribution eventually. After four years in business school and three on the board of Manflex, David should have been ready for responsibility. In reality, all his energies went into amateur film-making.

Towards the end of the morning, the screens in the large office adjacent to Manny Flexner's were registering some improvement in the group's ratings. Taking its cue from Tokyo and London, Wall Street had over-reacted to the first news of the fire. Now the market was taking a more measured view. The Manflex group was showing a sharp fall, but it wasn't, after all, in dire trouble.

Manny exhibited his positiveness by treating his son to lunch in the four-star-listed Quilted Giraffe, in the arcade of the Sony Building on Madison and 55th Street. Freshness was a watchword there. Even the wine list came on a computer print-out to underline that it was updated each day. 'You know this place, Dave?'

'No.'

Manny was twice-divorced and lived alone. Technically alone, that is to say. In reality he had a string of women friends who took turns to join him for dinner in New York's top restaurants and afterwards passed the night in his house on the Upper East Side. So he knew where to eat well. And the diet had to be good to keep up his stamina. He was sixty-three.

But lunches were strictly for business.

'I recommend the salmon with sweet-hot mustard. Or the duck salad with sour cherries. No, try the salmon. It really is something. You heard about the burn-up in Milan?'

Clearly his son hadn't looked at the business section of whichever newspaper he read. David had gone past the stage of youthful rebellion. He was a grown-up rebel, with dyed blond hair that reached his shoulders. Blond hair looked wrong on a Jewish boy, in Manny's opinion. The dark green cord jacket David had put on was a concession to restaurant rules. He often attended Board meetings in a T-shirt.

Manny filled him in with the painful essentials and told him his plan for dealing with the Italian end of the problem.

'You want *me* to go there? That could be difficult, Pop,' David said at once. 'How soon?'

'Anything wrong with tonight?'

David smiled. His engaging smile was both an asset and a liability. 'You're not serious?'

'Totally serious. I have up to two hundred people without a job, unions to deal with—'

'Yes, but—'

'An insurance claim to file and for all I know, lawsuits pending. Things like this don't get sorted if you ignore them, David.'

'How about Rico Villa? He's there, and he speaks the language.'

Manny pulled a face and shrugged. 'Rico couldn't close a junior softball game.'

'You want me to fly out to Milan and wield the hatchet?'

'Just point out the facts to these people, that's all. Their workplace is a pile of ash now. There's no future in rebuilding it. If anyone is willing to transfer to Rome, fix it. Talk to the accountants about redundancy terms. We'll give the best deal we can. We're not ogres.'

David sighed. 'Pop, I can't just drop everything.'

Although Manny had expected this, he affected surprise. 'What are you saying, son?'

'I have commitments. I made promises to people. They depend on me.'

Manny gave him a penetrating stare. 'Do these commitments have anything remotely to do with Manflex?'

His son reddened. 'No, it's a film project. We have a schedule.'

25

'Uh huh.'

'I'm due on location in the Bronx Zoo.'

'Filming animals, huh? I thought you said you made promises to people.'

'I was talking about the crew.'

The waiter arrived a split-second before Manny was due to erupt. Father and son declared a truce while the gastronomic decisions were taken. David diplomatically elected to have the salmon his father had recommended. It would be no hardship. When they were alone again, Manny started on a different tack. 'Some of the best films I ever saw were made in Italy.'

'Sure. The Italian cinema is up there among the best. Always was. *The Bicycle Thief. Death in Venice. The Garden of the Fitzi-Continis.*'

'*A Fistful of Dollars.*'

David gave a fair imitation of the sphinx. 'Ah — you mean spaghetti westerns.'

Manny nodded and said with largesse, 'You could get among those guys. Take a couple of weeks over this. Tidy up in Milan, my boy, and you have a free hand. Go to Venice. Is that a reasonable offer?'

Such altruism from a workaholic was worthy of a moment's breathless tribute, and got it.

Finally David confessed, 'I know you want me to step into your shoes some day, Pop, but I think I should tell you that the drugs industry bores the pants off me.'

'You're telling me nothing.'

'But you won't accept it.'

'Because you won't give the business a chance. Listen, Dave. It's the most challenging industry there is. You stay ahead of the game, or you die. It's all about new drugs and winning a major share of the market.'

'That much I understand,' David said flatly.

'One breakthrough, one new drug, can change your whole life. That's the buzz for me.'

'You mean it can change a sick person's life.'

'Naturally,' Manny said without hesitation. 'Only what's good for sick people is good for my balance sheet, too.'

He winked, and his son was forced to grin. The ethics

26

may have been clouded, but the candour was irresistible.

'Research teams are like horses. You want to own as many as you can afford. Once in a while one of them comes in first. But you can never be complacent. When you *have* the drug, you still need government approval to market it.' Manny's eyes glittered at the challenge. He didn't smile much these days, but occasionally a look passed across his tired features, the look of a man who once picked winners, but seemed to have lost the knack. 'And in no time at all the patent runs out, so you have to find something new. I have teams working around the globe. Any moment they could find the cure for some life-threatening disease.'

David nodded. 'There was a strong R & D section in the Milan plant.'

Manny said with approval, 'You know more than you let on.'

'I guess you really believe I can handle this.'

'That's why I asked you, son.' He gestured to the wine waiter. When he'd chosen a good Bordeaux, he told his son, 'This trouble in Italy has gotten to me. I always believed that someone up there was on my side. You know what I mean? Maybe I should think of stepping down.'

'Pop, that's nuts, and you know it. Who else could run the show?' Then David's eyes locked with his father's penetrating gaze. 'Oh, no. It's not my scene at all. I keep telling you I'm not even sure that I believe in it. If it was just a matter of making drugs to help sick people, okay. But you and I know that it isn't. It's about public relations, keeping on the good side of politicians and bankers. Thinking of the bottom line.'

'Tell me a business that doesn't. This is the world we live in, David.'

'Yes, but the profits aren't in drugs that cure people. Take arthritis. If we found something to stop it, we'd lose a prime market, so we keep developing drugs to deaden the pain instead. They're not much different from aspirin, only fifty times more expensive. How many millions are being spent right now on me-too arthritis treatments?'

Manny didn't answer. However, he noted with approval

his son's use of the trade jargon. A 'me-too' drug was an imitation, slightly reconstituted to get around the patent legislation. There were more than thirty me-toos for the treatment of arthritis.

David was becoming angry. 'Yet how much is invested in research into sickle-cell anaemia? It happens to be concentrated in Third World countries, so it won't yield much of a profit.'

'I was idealistic when I was your age,' said Manny.

'And now you're going to tell me you live in the real world, but you don't, Pop. Until something like AIDS forces itself on your attention, you don't want to know about the real world. I don't mean you personally. I'm talking about the industry.'

'Come on, the industry was quick enough in responding to AIDS. Wellcome had Retrovir licensed for use in record time.'

'Yes, and hyped their share price by 250 per cent.'

Manny shrugged. 'Market forces. Wellcome came up first with the wonderdrug.'

David spread his hands to show that his point was proved.

The waiter approached and poured some wine for Manny to sample. After he'd given it the nod, Manny said slyly to his son, 'You know more than you sometimes let on. When you become chairman, you'll be God. You can try injecting some ethics into the drugs industry if you want.'

David smiled. All these years on, his father still had the *chutzpah* of a taxi-driver.

'So we'll get you a seat on tonight's Milan flight,' said Manny, taking out his portable phone.

Chapter Five

KENSINGTON LIBRARY WAS BUILT IN 1960, yet the reference room upstairs has an ambience emphatically Victorian. The carpet is a dispiriting olive green and the chairs are upholstered in dark leather. Notices everywhere urge the readers to beware of pickpockets and to tell the staff immediately if they see anyone mutilating or taking newspapers. True, certain of the papers are heavily in demand. The *Evening Standard*, which arrives early in the afternoon, can be seen only on request – not because of anything unseemly in the contents, but because it would go from the open shelves and not be found again. The assistants at the desk get to recognize the beady-eyed men who hover from two p.m. onwards, each hopeful of being the first to spot a secondhand car bargain, a tip for the greyhound racing, or a job.

Peter Diamond – formerly of Harrods security staff – had become one of the job-seekers.

He got his turn with the *Standard* and ran his thumb down the columns. If he could imagine himself filling any of the posts on offer, he would hurry to the nearest phone. Most of the ads were couched in a friendly style – *Call Mandy* or *Ring Trish* – and you were encouraged to picture a sweet-natured personnel officer on the end of the line eager to talk you into a thirty-grand job with bonus and pension. Today, as usual, no Mandy or Trish in London seemed to have an opening for a forty-eight-year-old ex-detective who couldn't be relied upon to patrol a floor of Harrods.

He gave up. The *Standard* reported another rise in unemployment with the headline DESPAIR OF

LONDON'S JOBLESS. The despair wasn't much in evidence in High Street Kensington, apart from the droop of Diamond's shoulders. Young women with laminated carrier bags stuffed with goodies from the department stores stood by the curb waving for taxis. Middle-aged men in designer tracksuits jogged in the direction of Holland Park. The lunch crowd were still installed in Al Gallo D'Oro, the Italian restaurant across the street.

For the past seven months, Diamond and his wife Stephanie had subsisted in a basement in Addison Road, a one-way street where the traffic noise is almost unendurable without double-glazing and ear-plugs. The house was a stuccoed three-storey building with rotting window frames that never stopped shaking. Across the road was St Barnabas, a great smog-stained block with a turret at each corner, not by any stretch of imagination an attractive church, but one that might have been improved by exterior cleaning. Someone had tried to distract attention from the grime by painting the doors in bold Oxford blue, only it wasn't visible from the Diamonds' fox-hole. Apart from the towers of St Barnabas, all that they could see as they peered up were the topmost levels of multi-storey flats. It was a far cry from the view across Georgian Bath that they'd enjoyed until a year ago.

Not wishing to be idle, Diamond had refreshed the walls and ceilings of the flat with a coat of emulsion called primrose on the colour-chart. Turned out every drawer and cupboard, oiled every hinge, brushed the chimney, checked the electric plugs, changed the washers on the taps and fitted draught-excluders to all the doors. The drawback to this admirable zeal was that he was no handyman, so oil and paint got on the soles of his shoes and was transported everywhere; the taps dripped worse than ever; the doors stuck halfway; soot fell into the living-room whenever the wind blew; and the cat had moved into the airing-cupboard for sanctuary.

Stephanie Diamond would have joined the cat if she could. She worked two mornings in the Save the Children shop and had lately upped this to four, just to be out of the house. To discourage the DIY, she'd started bringing home jigsaws people had donated, getting Peter to occupy himself assembling them to see if pieces were missing before they were sold in the shop. It was not the good idea it had first seemed. She woke up one night at four a.m. with something digging into her back.

'What on earth . . .?' She switched on the bedside lamp.

Diamond turned over to see. 'Well, what do you know! It's that corner piece I was missing.'

'For crying out loud, Peter.'

'Fancy a cuppa?'

She remembered the taste of the tea since he'd descaled the kettle. 'No, go back to sleep.'

'God knows how it turned up here, of all places.'

'Oh, forget it.'

After an interval he said, 'Are you awake, Steph?'

She sighed. 'I am now.'

'I was thinking about the kid.'

'Which kid?'

'The Japanese girl I got sacked over. Why would anyone abandon a kid like that? She was nicely dressed. Clean. In no way neglected.'

'Perhaps she ran away from home.'

'And turned up on the seventh floor of Harrods? I can't believe that.'

'Fretting over it won't help,' said Stephanie. 'She's not your responsibility.'

'True.'

He was silent for a while.

She was almost asleep when he said, 'There must be a way of keeping all the pieces in one place.'

'Mm?'

'The jigsaws. I was thinking if I were to help in the shop—'

She sat upright. 'Don't you dare!'

'I was going to say I could do the jigsaws there, and if pieces went missing at least we'd know they were on the premises.'

'If you so much as set foot in that shop, you'll leave it on a stretcher when I've finished with you, Peter Diamond.' A bold claim – considering she was about seven stone and he

31

eighteen, but she knew what havoc he would wreak —
innocently, let it be said — in all that clutter. She'd known
when she married him that he was accident-prone. He was
badly co-ordinated. Some fat people are graceful movers.
Her husband was not. He knocked things over. In the
street he failed to notice curbstones. Hazards like
dog-mess seemed almost to seek him out.

'This getting old — I don't care for it,' he said at breakfast
next morning.

'Fishing?' Stephanie said.

He gave a shrug.

'All right, I'll say it. You're not *that* old.'

'Too old for work, apparently.'

'Snap out of it, Pete.'

'You want to see them lining up for unemployment
benefit. Younger men than me. Much younger, some of
them. Kids, straight out of school.'

She heaped streaky bacon on his plate. 'Things could be
worse.'

'You mean one of those unemployed kids could be ours.'

She looked away, and he cursed himself for being so
boorish. In her first marriage, to a shop manager, Steph
had miscarried three times. She'd lost another baby when
she married Diamond. That time she'd suffered complications that were finally resolved by a hysterectomy.
Surgery had been the cure-all in the early seventies. She'd
lost her womb, but not the maternal urge. Before he met
her she'd taken on the role of Brown Owl to a pack of
brownies. Did it for years, and did much more than Baden
Powell had ever intended. Always willing to be a second
mum to small girls whose parents neglected them. They
were all young adults now and she still wrote to some of
them.

He put his hand over hers and said, 'Sorry about last
night, love.'

Her face creased into a bewildered look. 'Last night?'

'In bed.'

She stared at him with wide eyes.

'The jigsaw piece.'

'Oh!' She laughed. 'I'd forgotten *that*. I thought you

were on about something entirely different. It didn't make sense at all.'

The day was fine after more than a week of overcast skies and rain, so instead of joining the queue in the library again, he called in at the newsagent's, treated himself to his own copy of the *Evening Standard* and took it into Holland Park to read. Finding that nothing in the jobs columns grabbed him, he put the paper aside and basked in the sun for a while on one of the wooden benches facing the pond beside the Orangery, watching people walk their dogs and push their prams along the length of the arched cloister. Everyone but he had some accessory, some visible reason for being in the park. A model aeroplane, a tennis racket, a camera, a spiked stick for picking up waste paper.

He got up decisively. Hell, he had no cause to be idle. He'd remembered an urgent job of work. Overnight a couple of air bubbles had appeared on the freshly emulsioned kitchen ceiling. Stephanie hadn't said anything, but he was sure she'd noticed them. He'd see if he could rub them out with sandpaper.

At home, trying to be tidy, he spread the sheets of the *Standard* across the kitchen floor below the bit of ceiling he was about to sand. Then he stood on a kitchen chair and examined the job. There were two bubbles the size of marshmallows. No question – they had to be removed. He picked at one with his fingernail. The paint was dry, so he gave it a tentative pull. It was pliant and springy, like plastic. He pulled harder and suddenly a sizeable piece of the coat of paint detached itself from the ceiling and flopped over his head and shoulders like a bridal veil.

He swore, stepped down from the chair, extricated himself, and examined the damage. This was no longer a simple sanding job. The entire ceiling would have to be stripped and repainted. Worse, it needed washing before he applied the paint. It was obvious even to an incompetent that the grease and grime from years of cooking should have been removed before the first coat was applied. The emulsion hadn't adhered. By seeking quick results, he'd wasted an entire can of paint. In a couple of hours, Stephanie was going to come back from

33

the shop to find her kitchen under occupation again.

Resigned to the major redecoration, he tugged off the rest of the coat of emulsion. It came away in large pieces and spread like dust-sheets over the units, table and chairs. That done, he put on the kettle. He deserved a break before he washed that ceiling.

But it never did get washed, or repainted. Something more urgent came up.

When Stephanie got home, she found the kitchen a disaster area, the sheets of dried emulsion festooned over everything, the ceiling as gruesome as it had looked the day they moved in, newspapers and sandpaper scattered around the floor and a half-filled mug of cold tea on the table. Diamond wasn't there. He finally came home about seven, apologizing profusely.

'But I've had an interesting afternoon, Steph.'

'So it appears.'

He related the episode with the paint. 'So when it was all off the ceiling I made myself some tea, feeling gutted after what had happened, and while I was drinking it, I happened to pick up a section of the *Standard* that I'd spread on the floor to protect it, you see?'

'You could have fooled me.'

'I just wanted something for distraction, something to read and—'

'You found a job in the paper? Oh, Pete!' She turned to him, arms spread wide.

'A job? No.'

Her arms flopped down. 'What, then?'

'I was telling you. I picked up the paper and saw this.' He handed her a scrap of newspaper.

She read:

MYSTERY GIRL STILL UNCLAIMED

The small girl who was the cause of a bomb scare when she was found in Harrods five weeks ago has still not been claimed or identified. The girl, believed to be about seven, and Japanese, is unable or unwilling to speak. A publicity campaign to find her parents has so far been unsuccessful despite extensive enquiries among the Japanese community. Meanwhile she is in the care of Kensington & Chelsea social services department. A spokesperson said, 'We're at a loss to understand why no one has come forward yet.'

'Poor mite,' said Stephanie, ever ready to brush aside her own concerns to take pity on a child. 'She must be terrified. First the police, and now the social workers. I'm not surprised she's silent.'

'Then you don't mind if I try and help?' said Diamond.

She gave him a wary look. 'If I did, would it make a jot of difference?'

'I found out where she's being kept.'

Stephanie frowned, stared and then allowed her face to soften. 'That's why you dropped everything and went out? To see this little girl? Peter, you're a softie at heart.'

'Softie?' he said. 'You're calling an ex-cop a softie?'

'You always had time for kids,' she insisted. 'Who got a job as Father Christmas last year?'

'That was work. This abandoned kid is a challenge, Steph. A chance to do what I'm trained for instead of standing on a chair washing a ceiling – which I will do, I give you my word. Face it, I've got experience. I was a bloody good sleuth.'

'With a heart of gold.'

He rolled his eyes upwards in dissent – and found himself staring at the grease-marks. 'Anyway, I tried the town hall, and they weren't willing to release information. I don't blame them. I could have been a weirdo, or something. They were perfectly entitled to show me the door. I went round to the police, told them I was ex-CID, and got an address. Some kind of assessment centre. Of course, when I got there, the kid had been moved on. I needed to be a bloody Sherlock Holmes to track her down. They put me onto some child psychiatrist, and he was no help, but his secretary took pity and handed me the address of a special school in Earls Court.'

'Special?' Stephanie said dubiously. 'You mean for kids with mental problems?'

He nodded.

'Is she retarded?' said Stephanie.

'No one actually said so, but that's where they've sent her.'

'They must think she is. What kind of place is it?'

'It's residential. I didn't get there this afternoon, but I'm going to try tomorrow. Apparently they haven't given up entirely. A Japanese teacher visits the school and tries to get her to speak. Up to now she's had no success.'

She was frowning. 'If everyone else has failed, what can you do about it? You don't speak Japanese.'

'I don't propose to try. It's just possible that everyone is too preoccupied with the speech problem. I'd like to try other lines of inquiry.'

'Such as?'

He wouldn't commit himself. 'I'd need to win the kid's confidence first. I've got the time to do it, Steph. For once in my life, I haven't got someone breathing down my neck.'

'Well . . .' said Stephanie, letting her eyes slide upwards.

'Don't say it. I'll scrub the damned ceiling tonight.'

Chapter Six

ONE USEFUL THING DIAMOND HAD learned in the police is that anyone with an air of authority can get admitted anywhere, with the possible exception of 10 Downing Street. The children's home was a detached Victorian house just behind the Earls Court exhibition building. The woodwork around the windows needed replacing and brickwork was visible here and there where weathering had invaded the layer of stucco. The local authority had more urgent priorities.

He rang the bell and a woman in an apron came to the door. Raising the 1940s trilby he still wore in private homage to the great detectives of past years, he said, 'Morning, madam. You must be Mrs . . .?'

'Straw.'

'Mrs Straw, Mrs Straw . . . ' he said thoughtfully as if deciding whether she qualified for the holiday of a lifetime in the Caribbean.

She waited, intrigued.

He said, 'You're not the head of this school?'

'No,' she said, fingering her apron. 'I'm the general help.'

'A general! General Help.' He made a gesture towards a salute.

She didn't smile. 'You want Miss Musgrave.'

'Miss Musgrave. Of course!' He stepped forward, compelling her to stand aside. 'Peter Diamond, General Help, here to speak to Miss Musgrave.'

She succeeded in saying, 'You have an appointment.' If she meant it to sound like a question, as she probably did, the attempt was foiled by a huge, disarming grin from

Diamond. The upshot was that Mrs Straw's utterance ended on a descending note and became a statement. She added, 'Miss Musgrave is very busy.'

'Don't I know it!' Diamond said.

'You know Miss Musgrave?' she said with relief.

He shrugged like a Frenchman in a way that could mean everything or nothing. 'She'll see me, I think.' He was in the hall now and Mrs Straw was closing the door. From the depths of the house came the cries of children. 'She's not in class, is she?'

'If you'd only wait, I'll tell her you're here.'

At that moment a face appeared around a door halfway up the hall. Diamond called out, 'There you are, Miss Musgrave.'

It wasn't a stab in the dark. The face was weighing him up with the look of a person in authority.

'Peter Diamond,' he told her, advancing with his hand extended. A man of his size in motion isn't easy to stop. 'Mrs Straw here was telling me how busy you are, but perhaps you can spare me a minute. I'm not selling anything.'

Miss Musgrave must have been in her thirties, tall and slim, with blonde hair drawn back to a small ponytail and tied with a black ribbon. She didn't immediately accept the handshake. She asked, 'What is this about, then?'

He beamed. 'It's about one of the children, the Japanese girl. I may be able to help.'

'You'd better come in.'

Her office evidently doubled as a classroom. There were three infants' chairs and tables. Her own desk had a line-up of painted masks made from egg-boxes. The floor was spotted with paint. A menagerie of stuffed animals sat on the filing cabinet. Children's paintings ranging from competent to inept were taped to the walls. Diamond found it congenial. In the absence of a spare adult-sized chair, he perched himself on a wooden chest with a flat lid that he reckoned would take his weight.

Miss Musgrave asked if he wanted a coffee. She had a full cup on her desk.

'No thanks. I really don't mean to be a nuisance.' At this

stage he judged it wise to throw himself on her mercy. 'I used to be in the police as a detective superintendent. Used to be. I must make it plain that I'm here in a private capacity.' He explained about losing the Harrods job. 'I saw the little girl that night, and I'm appalled that after — what is it? Six weeks? — her people haven't been found.'

'I'm sure the police are doing their best,' Miss Musgrave said.

'No question of that.'

'Meanwhile we're making her as comfortable as we can. She does need specialized care. That's *my* province, Mr Diamond.' She sounded defensive, yet well in control. From the guarded looks she was still giving Diamond, she hadn't much cared for his steamroller tactics in gaining admittance.

'It's not easy, I imagine, when a child doesn't speak at all,' he ventured.

'We deal with a variety of problems here.'

'With limited resources, no doubt.'

'If you're hinting that Naomi isn't being given the attention her predicament deserves, Mr Diamond, you're mistaken. She's been the subject of the most intensive tests and inquiries.'

'Naomi — you know her name?'

Miss Musgrave shook her head. 'We have to call her something. One of the staff from the Japanese Embassy suggested it as a name that their people and ours have in common.'

'Naomi. That's Japanese? I thought it was Old Testament.'

Hosanna! His early days as a choirboy paid off. Miss Musgrave's expression softened. A man who knew his Bible couldn't be wholly disreputable. 'What exactly are you here for, Mr Diamond?'

'To help the kid find her people.'

'Oh — and how will you succeed when everyone up to now has failed?'

'By being the Sherlock Holmes round here — except that I come free.'

'That's fine as far as it goes, but I don't know what the

police would say about it.'

'The police are up shit creek without a paddle, as Sherlock used to remark to Dr Watson.'

She put her fingers to her mouth, possibly, Diamond suspected, to hide a faint smile.

He pointed to the cup and saucer on her desk. 'Your coffee's getting cold.'

She lowered her hand and she was definitely smiling. 'It's Bovril. Is that an example of your detective skills?'

He made a pistol shape with his fingers and held them to the side of his head.

Miss Musgrave, serious again, said, 'Naomi can't answer questions, so I don't see what good you can do.'

'I can observe.'

'And make deductions?' She mocked him with her eyes.

'You've got to admit the kid needs help.'

This was a telling point with Miss Musgrave. She took a long sip of the Bovril. 'If you're serious, come back at two this afternoon. I'll be taking the autistic class. In this room. You can come in and see what happens. Then perhaps you'll understand the difficulty.'

An adult-sized chair had been installed just inside the door for Diamond. It wasn't possible for a man of his bulk to be unobtrusive in an office so small, but Miss Musgrave didn't mind and the children scarcely gave him a passing glance. They were shepherded in by Mrs Straw and another woman who looked mightily relieved to be handing them over.

One of them, a boy, was screaming, as if in rage rather than pain. On entering the room he broke away from Mrs Straw, ran to a bookcase, swept the bottom shelf clear of books and squeezed into the narrow space underneath, where he continued to scream.

'That's Clive,' Miss Musgrave told Diamond above the racket. She made no move to restore the books to their places or to calm Clive. 'And this is Rajinder.'

Rajinder moved erratically, with a springy step, both arms flexed and his wrists limp. He went to one of the infant chairs and sat there, rocking, it seemed, in time to

Clive's screaming.

'Come on, you two,' the second teacher urged the rest of the class, who seemed reluctant, not without cause, to enter. 'Tabitha, Naomi, we can't wait all day for you.' She cupped her hand around the back of one child's head and drew her in, a pale, worried-looking girl of about seven with fine blonde hair, presumably Tabitha. She had thick plastic glasses fastened with a band around the back of her head like a tennis player's. She had scarcely taken a step into the room when Miss Musgrave remarked to the other teacher. 'She needs changing. Do you mind?'

Tabitha was recalled and Naomi was ushered forward in her place. Diamond had seen the child briefly that night in Harrods, and remembered how impassive she had looked, surrounded by security guards. This morning she had the same preoccupied expression, as if her eyes saw nobody. There was clearly a level at which her mind was functioning efficiently, because she moved normally, straight to a chair and sat down, composed, indifferent to Clive's screaming and Rajinder's rocking, or to the presence of the adults. Someone had fastened a white ribbon in her hair and she was in a red corduroy dress, black tights and trainers.

'She'll stay like that for as long as I let her,' said Miss Musgrave. 'I can get through to the others. Outwardly they appear more disturbed than Naomi, but she's inaccessible, and it isn't just the problem of language. It must be some form of autism.'

Diamond had seen television programmes about autistic children who appeared physically normal, but tantalizingly locked in their inner worlds. They exhibited a range of behaviour that could include tantrums, grimacing, avoidance of all human contact, inappropriate emotional reactions such as laughing when someone else was hurt and, in rare cases, strange feats of memory enabling them to play music they had heard only once before, or doing complex drawings of scenes and buildings only briefly visited. From what he remembered, there was controversy about how autism should be treated. He'd watched a disturbing film of mothers forcibly embracing their

41

struggling children until they stopped resisting, which could take hours. In some cases, the results had been encouraging.

Miss Musgrave closed the door and took a pencil and worksheet to the howling Clive. To Diamond's surprise the boy took it, went silent and started to write or draw, still in his cramped position under the bookshelves. Rajinder, also, was persuaded to take a worksheet and give it his attention, though he needed a patient explanation of what was required.

'Now see what happens with Naomi.' Miss Musgrave held out a pencil. Naomi stared ahead and didn't move. Gently, Miss Musgrave took the child's right hand and positioned the small fingers around the pencil.

Diamond said, 'It's not for me to interfere, but do the Japanese hold pencils like that?' He took a pen from his pocket and demonstrated. 'I thought they held them upright, like this.'

Miss Musgrave's first reaction was a cool stare. Then she accepted the validity of the information.

The child allowed her fingers to be repositioned. A clean sheet of paper was placed on the table in front of her. Miss Musgrave stood behind Naomi and guided the pencil, making a mark on the paper. 'Now prove me totally wrong, Naomi, and draw a picture.' But Naomi's eyes weren't on the paper, and as soon as Miss Musgrave stepped back, the hand was still.

'I've had mutes before,' Miss Musgrave said, 'and they can usually be persuaded to use a pencil.'

'She's mute?'

'Silent, anyway. Not dumb. She makes little sounds if she's surprised in any way.'

'That's something.'

'Some autistics never learn to speak.'

Rajinder seemed to take this as a challenge and started repeatedly saying, 'Miss,' until Miss Musgrave examined his drawing, praised it and provided him with more paper. From the bookshelves came a new sound. Clive, tiring of paperwork, had taken a toy car from his pocket and was spinning the wheels with his finger, watching them intently.

'He'll do that for the rest of the lesson if he's left. It becomes obsessive,' Miss Musgrave said. 'He fits the stereotype of the autistic child.'

'Meaning what?'

'He shuns the company of others. Doesn't use eye contact. Refuses to be cuddled. Throws these tantrums if he feels his privacy is being invaded.'

'And is Naomi like that?'

'She's the aloof type. The muteness is a symptom.'

'Have you tried cuddling her?'

'She's indifferent to it. Passive. That's another kind of abnormality in these kids.'

'The others, Rajinder and Tabitha – are they autistic?'

'Yes.'

'Does Clive speak?'

She nodded. 'But he tends to repeat things parrot-fashion.'

'Does he progress at all?'

'A little. Listen,' she said, 'if you want to try and get through to Naomi, please feel free.'

The invitation was tempting, but he knew better than to accept. On first acquaintance a man his size terrified any kid if he went close. 'At this stage,' he told Miss Musgrave candidly, 'I'd rather get through to you. That's my game-plan for today.'

She tensed. 'What exactly do you mean?'

'I want to convince you that I won't be a nuisance. I want to come here again. And again. I can sit here and observe, or I can make myself useful, but I want to be here. I don't kid myself that I can work a miracle for Naomi. I sense that if she's going to give me any clues at all, it's going to be slow progress. How would you feel about having me here on a regular basis?'

She didn't answer at once. She went over to attend to Clive, who started screaming again at her approach. For a moment she wrestled with him for the toy car. In the struggle he bit her hand and she cried out in pain. 'If I don't do this,' she told Diamond, 'the entire lesson is wasted. Now *will* you let go?' She snatched the toy from Clive and he set up a piercing wail. 'You'll have it back presently. Now do me a drawing of the car. A drawing.' The child subsided by stages and picked up the pencil.

Massaging her hand, Miss Musgrave returned to Diamond. 'Before I say anything about this suggestion of yours, would you tell me something about yourself?'

'Whatever you want to know.'

'All right, then. Why did you leave the police?'

He hesitated. 'I resigned. I blew my top in front of the Assistant Chief Constable.'

'What about?'

'A kid. A boy of twelve. I was accused of hitting his head against a wall.'

She stared. After an interval, she said, 'At least you're honest.'

'Okay,' he added, 'I'm hardly a suitable person to invite again. Forget it.' He picked up his hat.

'Sit down, Mr Diamond,' she told him firmly. 'Did you do it?'

'Do what?'

'Hit the boy?'

'No, but it's academic now. He came at me and I pushed him aside. He knocked his head on the wall. I wasn't believed, so I said some things I lived to regret.'

'Have you got kids of your own?'

He shook his head.

'You're married?'

'Yes.'

'But you like them?'

'Kids?' He nodded.

She held out a hand. 'My name is Julia.'

Chapter Seven

'ANY IDEA HOW THIS HAPPENED?'

David Flexner gazed at two blackened pillars rising some ten feet above the rubble that had once been Manflex Italia's Milan plant. Immense heat had melted those pillars into stark, Dali-esque images in the ashen landscape. All this, and a perfect, cloudless sky. What a location for a film, he found himself thinking.

He had been driven there by Rico Villa, the plant manager, whose Zegna suit and D'Anzini shoes weren't the best choice for stepping through ashes. Rico always dressed the part of the business executive, but David, casual as usual in white denims, black T-shirt and faded red running shoes, regarded him as a kindred spirit, one of the few in his father's employ that he might actually have chosen to drink with.

'Some electrical fault, I guess,' Rico answered. 'Isn't that what usually starts a fire?'

'Or a lighted cigarette.'

'I don't allow smoking here.'

In that gutted ruin, Rico's use of the present tense amused David. He had to turn his face away in case Rico noticed. 'Smokers will always find somewhere.'

'That's true, but the Saturday shift had finished when the fire started. The plant was empty except for the two security guards.'

'A fire can take some time to get going,' David pointed out, adding with more tact, 'but I guess the fire service are making a report.'

'The fire team and the insurance investigators, too,' said Rico. 'The boys from Prima Roma Assurance came out

45

here the next day to see what they could find.'

'Any theories yet?'

'Nothing anyone will say.'

'How about arson? Someone with a grudge against the company.'

'Arson?'

'Was anyone dismissed in the last six months?'

Rico was shocked. He pressed his hand to his mouth as if unwilling to admit the possibility. 'I guess five or six for absenteeism and petty theft. The personnel records went up in smoke with the rest. We won't have their addresses any more.'

'Then the computer wasn't linked to our offices in Rome?'

'Some files were. Not personnel. That's against the data protection legislation.'

'We'll have to rely on memory, then. How's yours, Rico?'

Rico made a negative gesture.

'Let's check with some of the people who worked in personnel. Draw up a list of everyone they can remember who was fired and anyone else with reason to dislike the company.'

'I'll see to it.'

'Fine.' David stared around at the devastation. 'Must have been one hell of a fire. Where was your office in this heap?'

'To your right, approximately sixty metres,' Rico answered bleakly. 'Nobody would know.'

'Lose anything personal?'

He shrugged. 'My certificates. I had them framed on the wall. Membership of the Institute of Pharmacists and so forth. They can be replaced. And some photos of my family. They can't.'

'What will you do? Do you want to move to Rome?'

'Not really. I'm fifty-three. My home is here. My father is in a retirement home. I have kids in school. I guess I'll look carefully at the redundancy terms.'

'Jesus, Rico, we can't afford to lose you,' David heard himself say, and it was a perfectly obvious thing to say, except that he surprised himself by so readily taking on the role of spokesman for Manflex. Until now, he'd never truly identified with the company. He only attended Board meetings out of loyalty to his father. 'We'll find some way of keeping the family together. For the present, you're wanted here in Milan, so no problem. We need a temporary office. Can you find one?'

'Michael, I'm dying.'

Michael Leapman jerked around to look at Manny Flexner. There was no hint of amusement in his features, but that wasn't necessarily significant. Manny was capable of the straightest face when stringing hapless people along. He was a shameless liar in the cause of fun. And Manny's style of humour frequently eluded Leapman.

At Manny's suggestion, they were walking through the Essex Street Covered Market in the Lower East Side after lunching on blintzes and beer in Ratner's. This place throbbing with life, filled with pungent aromas of breads and cheeses, hardly seemed right for such a morbid announcement, but you could never be sure what Manny was up to.

'Did I hear you correctly?'

'How would I know?'

'I thought you said you were dying.'

'Correct.'

'You really mean that?'

Manny nodded solemnly. 'I saw my physician this morning. He sent me for tests a while back. Now he has the results. It's inoperable. I have maybe six months, maybe nine.'

Leapman stared at him. There was still no indication that some kind of black humour was intended. 'But that's not possible.'

'Precisely what I said to the doc. I have my faculties. I can read the paper still, eat a good meal, take a woman to bed when I want, and I don't disappoint. I'm not the biggest in that department, but what I got is in working order. He said fine, some people aren't so lucky. They languish and droop. At least I was going out in style. I said I didn't believe him. He asked if I wanted a bet. I said

47

okay, Doc, fifty bucks I'm still alive for Thanksgiving. I thought I was on a sure thing, but he suggested we put the money in a brown envelope and leave it with his receptionist because he didn't want to trouble my executors. That really brought it home to me, Michael. My executors. He meant it.' Manny exhaled, vibrating his lips. 'I called off the bet.'

'You should get a second opinion,' said Leapman, trying sincerely to be helpful while he assessed what this grim news would mean for his own prospects. He believed the story.

'More tests, more bad news.' Manny groaned at the prospect. 'No thanks. I'd rather spend my last days on earth profitably, robbing banks while I have my strength left.' He turned to a woman behind a fruit and vegetable stall. She must have overheard the last statement, because she was goggle-eyed. 'Ignore me. I'm in shock. How much are your pineapples, ma'am?' He chose one and felt it for firmness. 'Do you buy many pineapples, Michael? They can look fine outside, like me, and when you put in the knife, they're rotten. No offence,' he told the woman. 'I'll take this one.'

They reached the end of the market and made their way back down Delancey Street. 'Still, this isn't all bad for Manflex,' Manny remarked altruistically. 'We can do with a change at the top.'

Leapman's flesh prickled.

Manny went on smoothly. 'My shares will pass to Davey. He'll have a controlling stake, and he'll be fine.'

'For Chairman, you mean? David?' Leapman tried to sound casual, but the shock couldn't be stifled.

'I can't put it better than Shakespeare: some guys are born managers, some achieve management and some, like my son, have it thrust upon them.'

'The market won't like it,' said Leapman, impervious to Shakespeare.

'Davey taking over, you mean?'

'Your going.' An answer more tactful than honest.

'What choice do I have?'

A pause. 'Fair point.'

'He'll need your support,' Manny said.

'He can depend on it.'

'And the know-how. You have a grasp of the business. He doesn't.'

'Of course I'll help any way I can.' Michael Leapman was functioning on autopilot. The news of Manny's illness was bad enough. The prospect of his son taking over the Chairmanship was beyond everything.

Manny shifted the pineapple to his left hand and rested his right on Leapman's shoulder. 'Thanks, Mike. You don't have to tell me the sharks will be circling, but I have confidence in the boy. I like the way he's shaping up. As a matter of fact, I called Rico last night. Davey's doing a great job in Milan, and that isn't easy, closing down a plant.'

It was a skill that might soon be required nearer home, Leapman thought cynically. 'Have you told him?'

'Told him what?'

'This terrible news your doctor gave you.'

'Not yet. It's not easy over the phone.'

'You'll wait, then?'

'Davey doesn't need to be told at this stage. Maybe not at all.'

Frowning, Leapman said, 'But you just told *me*. Surely you owe it to him. He needs time to adjust.'

'Weren't you listening just now?' said Manny. 'About management being thrust upon him? It's better he doesn't have time to think about it. Knowing Davey, he'd look for an out.'

Leapman didn't pursue the point. Maybe Manny was right from the company's point of view, given the staggering premise that David Flexner had to be installed as the next Chairman. What was the point in getting steamed up about David's sensibilities when his own had been ruthlessly trampled over?

And now the misguided old jerk was weighing the group's prospects without mentioning the obvious fact that Manflex might be vulnerable to a takeover. 'We're lower down the league than I'd like to be, but we're not in bad shape right now. We still have a good cash-flow.'

'Mainly from Kaprofix.'

'What's wrong with Kaprofix? It's helped millions of people with angina.'

'Nothing – except that it's a declining asset.'

'Since I put the lid on development costs, we boosted the operating margin by 2.6 points. You talk about Kaprofix as if it's all we've got. We have a wide base of steady-selling products. The surplus from the pension fund was over ten million last year. Sure, we could do with a big-selling new drug—'

'Soon,' said Leapman.

'What?'

'Soon – we could do with it soon.'

'I wouldn't argue with that.'

Leapman wasn't letting it pass so lightly. 'We missed out on beta-blockers, salbutamol for asthma, L-dopa for Parkinsonism, H2-antagonists—'

'Okay, okay,' said Manny irritably. 'I get the point. We staked too much on Fidoxin. That was the biggest fuckup of my career. On the other hand, we've got a clean record. No one ever sued us. I can meet my Maker knowing I never damaged anyone through negligence.'

'Leaving aside environmental damage,' Leapman couldn't stop himself saying.

'What do you mean?'

'We did get fined for polluting French and Italian rivers.'

'Piss off, Michael.'

They walked on in silence for a bit, each feeling the strain of the changed situation.

'Will you say anything to the Board while Davey's away?' Leapman eventually asked.

'About my condition? There's no need. I'll step down and then they'll find out.'

'So you want me to regard it as confidential?'

'For the time being. How did I come to confide in an obstinate schmuck like you? What a mess.' He turned and looked at Leapman. There was just a glimmer of amusement in the look, yet the rest of the face was sad, undeniably sad. This time, Manny Flexner wasn't kidding.

Chapter Eight

THREE BLACK LIMOUSINES CRUISED ALONG the stretch of
Eighth Avenue opposite the lake in Central Park and
presently halted and disgorged a number of large men in a
motley collection of tracksuits. Enough for a football team,
except that footballers would never have looked so ill at
ease. They were peeking over their shoulders as if
someone they knew might be spying on this freak show.
The last to climb out of the front car was Massimo Gatti, a
man of influence in the Italian-American community – or
at least that section of it that requires round-the-clock
bodyguards. Unlike his minders, Gatti was short and
overweight, with high blood pressure, which was why he
had taken up jogging.

As a preliminary, he went through a token exercise to
limber up, flinging his arms outwards like a cheerleader
and simultaneously running on the spot. Some of the
others in the party attempted sheepishly to do the same.
Then Gatti moved off at a sedate jog, and with his
henchmen in tow he could easily have been taken for a
shorter, fatter embodiment of a recent President of the
United States. The limousines inched forward, staying
parallel with the joggers.

As usual in the park, New York's fitness freaks were out
in force. This morning Michael Leapman was among
them. He'd asked for an urgent audience with Gatti, and
this was the arrangement, a refreshing variation on the
working breakfast. Having spotted the group, he raised
his pace and strode across to meet them. He was one of
those envied beings who rarely take exercise, but succeed
in keeping in shape.

'Hi, Mr Gatti.'

They had met before, through a chain of intermediaries too tedious to list. Leapman's inside knowledge of the drugs industry – the legitimate drugs industry – had appealed to Gatti. In the depressed world of finance, pharmaceuticals were one of the few commodities that promised good returns. Medical supplies were necessities, and as nearly recession-proof as anything could be. A stake in the industry was what Leapman had offered, and Gatti had found it irresistible.

Gatti may have nodded in response to the greeting, or the dip of the head may have been part of his running action. It wasn't in his nature to greet people, even in less demanding circumstances. After just a few minutes of slow jogging, he was moving with a spastic jerkiness and taking noisy gulps of air.

A long exchange was clearly out of the question, so Leapman drew alongside and came quickly to the point. 'There's a hitch in our arrangement, I'm sorry to say.'

Gatti stopped jogging and turned away from Leapman, flapping his hands at his entourage to step back and give him some privacy. They reversed several paces. The procession set off again with a decent gap in the ranks.

'What are you trying to tell me?'

Leapman resumed, 'Manny Flexner saw his doctor for a check-up and found that he has only a few months to live.'

'So?'

'So that's the problem.'

'His problem, not mine,' Gatti wheezed.

'With respect, it isn't so simple as that. He says he's going to step down.'

'Resign?'

'Yes.'

'What's wrong with that?'

'He wants to nominate his son to replace him.'

'He has a son?'

'Yes.'

'You didn't tell me.'

'I'm sorry, Mr Gatti. I know I should have mentioned it before now. I didn't rate David Flexner at all. He takes no

52

interest in the business.'

'Is he on the Board?'

'Yes, but—'

'You didn't rate him, huh?'

'Well, no.'

'Flexner's own son? You didn't rate him?'

The questions appeared to indict Leapman and he was becoming alarmed. 'He sits through the board meetings and says nothing,' he said in his own defence.

Massimo Gatti stopped running again. The pursuers stopped, too far off to overhear anything. Across the band of grass separating the park from the roadway, the three limousines also came to a halt. Leapman stood tamely, waiting for Gatti to recover his breath. 'We made an agreement, Mr Leapman,' the little man eventually succeeded in saying. 'You needed funds. You came to me with a proposition. Fine. My people were impressed with your scheme. So we backed you. We did as you suggested. We took out the factory in Milano. And two good men were killed.'

Horrified, Leapman was quick to say, 'That wasn't my suggestion, Mr Gatti. You wanted to buy in at the lowest price. I wouldn't have recommended arson.'

'Good men killed,' Gatti reiterated. 'For nothing.'

'Not for nothing. Let's be frank — the fire achieved what you wanted. Manflex shares plunged on the news. The price recovered a little after you started buying. It *was* you, wasn't it? You and your associates, buying at rockbottom prices?'

There was no response.

'The shareholders are losing confidence,' Leapman insisted. 'Manny Flexner's position as Chairman is untenable. I'm certain I could have achieved a board-room coup. Manny has no rescue plan. The cupboard is bare.'

'So what's different?'

'He's dying, and it's altered the equation. People who would have supported me are going to back his son out of sympathy or loyalty. Manny's dying wish and all that crap. There's no way I can pull this off right now.'

Gatti stared at him. 'Mr Leapman, I don't give a shit who is Chairman. You enter a billion dollar agreement with me, you deliver. You know what happens when an agreement breaks down.'

Just three days after his arrival in Italy, David Flexner was installed in a temporary office suite in Milan with telephone system, fax machine, photocopier, word-processor, computer and PA – whose name, fittingly, was Pia. She had short, Titian-red hair and garnet-coloured eyes. Pia was so watchable that David had instantly decided she would get the female lead if he ever actually got to make a film in Italy, never mind whether she could act. The fact that she also spoke English like a BBC newscaster and could use all the hardware seemed of trifling importance when she first walked in. She was not, he hazarded from the swing of her hips, a diehard feminist. Nor, for that matter, was he.

Diverting as the gorgeous Pia was, in the crisis resulting from the fire there wasn't time to observe her. Rico Villa had set up appointments with the insurers, the union representatives, the employment office and the main city newspapers, who would be the chief means of getting information to the staff. A meeting of all the Manflex Italia employees had been set for the following Saturday morning. They were to gather in a cinema south-west of the city. By then David would have something positive to offer in the way of redundancy terms. He'd spent yesterday with the accountants. Reluctant as he was to devote his life to the pharmaceuticals industry, what had happened in Italy was a problem he could handle with energy and sensitivity. Hundreds of people had lost their livelihood, and he would do his damnedest to treat them decently and fairly.

Towards the end of Thursday afternoon, Pia swanned in with two men who were definitely not on the roll. They were far too brash to be employees. They studied David with long, level looks as if mentally measuring him for his coffin. Unwilling to be intimidated, he made it obvious that he was assessing them, their off-the-peg suits and their uninteresting striped ties. One, in his forties, had his hair trimmed to about half an inch. 'These gentlemen are from the police,' Pia said superfluously. She turned to check on their names. They spoke no English, apparently. The short-haired one was a Commissioner, which sounded pretty senior. His name was Dordoni. The other must have been too low in rank to merit an introduction.

'Do you have any information about the fire yet?' David asked, getting in first.

Pia translated, listened and then gave the response, which was not an answer. 'The Commissioner is asking for a list of all the staff employed at the plant.'

'No problem. We can provide that.'

'He wants a check on everybody.'

'A check?'

'To know if they are still alive.'

'That isn't so simple. Would you explain to him that we're not in contact with everyone. We're having this meeting Saturday and we'll take names there. What is this about? My understanding is that no one was killed in the fire.'

The translation process began again. Commissioner Dordoni spoke rapidly, as if irritated by the delays, looking directly at David with moist, black eyes that reminded him of fresh sheep-droppings.

'He says a car . . . ' Pia stopped and checked something with Dordoni. ' . . . an Alfa Romeo Veloce saloon, crashed on a country road three thousand metres – that's about two miles – from Manflex Italia on the evening of the fire. The petrol tank ruptured and the wreck was badly burned.' She turned back to Dordoni for more of the story in Italian, and presently added, 'The remains of two men were found. Badly burned. Very badly. They have not been identified.'

'And he's trying to connect this with the fire at the plant?'

'He says the Alfa Romeo was coming from the direction of the Manflex plant. They can tell by the skid-marks that the car was travelling at high speed when it left the road. Apparently it turned over a couple of times. Inside the trunk they found five empty gasoline containers.'

David hesitated, frowning.

Pia said helpfully, 'I think he's implying that these men

may have started the fire at the plant, but he hasn't exactly said so yet.'

'What does he want from me?'

She had another brief exchange with Dordoni before turning back to David. 'He says the fire service investigators haven't ruled out the possibility of arson. He's asking if you know of anyone who might have wished to destroy the plant.'

'The answer is no.'

Commissioner Dordoni didn't require a translation. He countered with a frenetic outpouring of Italian.

Pia, caught in the middle and handling her role with admirable cool, lifted her eyebrows a fraction and explained, 'He wants me to tell you it's unwise to refuse to co-operate with the police.'

'If that's a threat, Pia, you can tell this arrogant jerk that I resent it. I spoke the truth. I've no reason to suspect anyone we employ, or have employed.' Having let rip, David had second thoughts. 'No. Hold it. Tell him this. The possibility is very disturbing indeed, and he'll have our full co-operation.'

This undertaking lowered the temperature a little. Dordoni and his assistant got down to facts – the names of the two security men, the times of shifts, the number of employees and so on, all of which David supplied. They also demanded a list of the staff, with addresses, but he couldn't supply one, not before Saturday's meeting.

'If he'd describe these two men, we can make some enquiries and find out if anyone recognizes them,' he told Pia.

Dordoni gave a sinister laugh when this was translated, and made a rubbing motion with his finger and thumb while speaking his reply.

Pia impassively translated, 'The men were incinerated beyond recognition. It's possible that the forensic pathologists will give some information, but that is likely to take weeks or months.'

'What about the car?'

Dordoni revealed that the registration plates had been removed from the Alfa Romeo. Very little that would be useful was left.

David turned to Pia. 'Would you ask him a question from me? If these men haven't been identified, is there any evidence at all that connects them with our company?'

She conferred with Dordoni. 'He says no.'

'It's circumstantial, then.'

'Is that a question?'

'Don't trouble,' he told her. He wasn't scoring points. 'Ask him how this crash happened.'

Pia sounded reluctant to put the question. 'He already told us. The car was going too fast. It turned over.'

'Yes, but why? Was it being chased?'

She turned back to Dordoni and succeeded in getting the unhelpful answer, 'Nobody knows.'

Dordoni nodded to his assistant, preparing to leave. He wasn't waiting for any more idiot questions.

'Was another vehicle involved?' David pressed him.

Pia translated quickly.

Dordoni shrugged. At the door, he appeared to decide, after all, that he would volunteer something else. He turned and delivered a couple of sentences.

Now Pia gave a shrug. 'The car was travelling on a perfectly straight stretch of road. It went out of control, but they don't understand why. They can see from the tyre-marks that it didn't have a blow-out. It's an extraordinary thing to happen. They are calling it – I think you have the expression in England – an act of God.'

Later in the afternoon there was an opportunity to get Rico Villa's views on the mysterious car crash. He was dismissive, scornful of the suggestion that arsonists had started the fire. 'Why won't they admit that coincidences happen? Typical of the police, always looking for the first solution that suggests itself. Two serious incidents on one evening and they have to connect them.'

'Only a couple of miles from each other,' commented David, slipping into Dordoni's role.

'A couple of drunks turn their car over. What's so sinister about that?'

'How do you know they were drunk?'

'You're in Lombardy now, my friend. Have you tried

the *Oltrepo Pavese*?'

'They did have those empty petrol cans in their trunk.'

'They were probably farmers. If you have farm vehicles to keep on the move, you collect extra petrol to take back with you.'

'But he said the registration plates were missing.'

'Kids. Souvenir-hunters. They'll help themselves to anything.'

David wasn't overly impressed, and said so.

'Okay,' Rico lobbed one back, 'in a couple of days we can take a roll-call. Then we'll know if anyone from Manflex Italia is missing. Want a bet?'

'The guys in the car don't have to be Manflex employees,' David said. 'Like Dordoni said, they could have been sacked. Or they could simply be troublemakers from outside.'

'Let it go, Dave,' Rico advised, putting a hand on his shoulder. 'We have more important things to do right now. The police are going to take months over this. Years, probably. And then it's quite likely they'll file it as unsolved.'

For the first time in their friendship, David Flexner had a stirring of unease about Rico.

Chapter Nine

'WHAT EXACTLY DO YOU *DO* in that school?' Stephanie asked one evening as they waited to eat. A chicken casserole in the oven was sending out a rich aroma, but the vegetables still required their seven minutes in the microwave.

'A lot of sitting around.'

'Can't you make yourself useful in some way?'

'Occasionally. Today I was doing the job I do best – putting a jigsaw together. An eight-piece jigsaw.' Diamond offered the statement blandly, knowing Stephanie would pounce on it. Sometimes he took a wry pleasure in being the prey to his wife's sharp remarks.

'How many pieces went missing?'

'Unkind! Not a single one. They're the size of your hand.'

'This is for the children's benefit, I take it?'

'Naturally.'

'So you work with them, fitting the pieces together?'

He smiled. 'Some hope! I fit them together and they pull them apart.'

'Does Naomi join in?'

His voice altered, the by-play over. 'Naomi? No.'

'Why not? Jigsaws are pretty basic, when all's said and done. Language isn't involved.'

'She doesn't join in anything. She's completely passive.'

'Maybe she's terrified of the others.'

'She was like this before she was brought to the school.'

'Terrified?'

Diamond nodded. She was almost certainly right.

'But they insist she's autistic?' Stephanie asked.

'The diagnosis isn't carved in stone,' he said. 'Anyway, as far as I can tell it's a convenient label for a pretty broad spectrum of maladjusted kids. Clive, for instance, has these tantrums and has to find some corner of the room he considers the safest from invasion. Naomi's not like that. She'll sit where she's told. She's silent. Totally switched off. Her behaviour is nothing like Clive's, but they're both thought to be autistic. Is that ready?'

He'd been interrupted by five electronic bleeps. The microwave oven was a symbol of more affluent times. He'd bought it on the day he resigned from the police, but it looked older than that, copiously speckled during the redecoration of the kitchen. Some of the marks had been impossible to remove.

'Standing time,' Stephanie reminded him. 'The veggies need their standing time. I don't know if you remember Maxine Beckington, one of the brownies. She didn't last very long with us, but she was a bright little thing.'

'That was probably why,' said Diamond.

'Why what?'

'Why she didn't last. If she was as bright as you say, she probably objected to dancing around the toadstool on the grounds that it was a phallic symbol.'

She gave him a glare. The brownie movement wasn't a topic for levity. 'I was about to tell you that Maxine's mother had another child, a boy, and he was the envy of all the other mothers because he was such a contented baby, willing to lie in his pram for as long as they left him. I saw him myself – a beautiful child with gorgeous big blue eyes. He never cried. They never missed a night's sleep. But after a time, this angelic baby started to make them uneasy. They realized he didn't cry even when he was hungry. If they hadn't fed him as a matter of routine, he would have starved, still without complaining. It was uncanny. What started out as a blessing turned out to be deeply worrying, and with good reason. He was eventually found to be autistic. Your Naomi sounds similar.'

Diamond pondered the suggestion. 'Yes, I can imagine her as a baby acting like that, but we shouldn't make these comparisons.'

'Why not?'

'It's unscientific, that's why. One thing I've learned from Julia Musgrave is that autism has to be diagnosed by an expert. You can't pick out a single symptom as typical. Any characteristic you name – the aloofness, the odd movements some of them make, the difficulties with speech – could be the result of some other condition. You recognize autism by a whole range of things. And they vary. Not all autistic babies behave like the kid you just described. Some of them fight and scream from Day One and refuse to be comforted.'

'Dreadful for the mothers,' Stephanie concurred. 'And they look like normal children.'

'Prettier, sometimes. You used a word to describe that baby: angelic. Autistic kids tend to have large eyes and remarkably symmetrical features. They really seem to be other-worldly.'

'Is Naomi like that?'

'Well, yes.'

'Does she scream and fight?'

'Never.'

'What if she's provoked?'

Diamond frowned at the idea. 'No one wants to give the kid a hard time. She's had enough shocks already.'

'Don't the other children sometimes bother her?'

'They don't fight each other. They're too enclosed in their own worlds.'

Stephanie picked up the oven gloves and took out the casserole. Together they served up the meal. When they had savoured a few mouthfuls, Diamond said, 'I'd like to know how the geniuses at the Police Training College would cope with young Naomi. She'd test their information-gathering techniques all right.'

'It sounds to me as if you're warming to the challenge.'

'Me?' He raised his eyebrows in mock surprise.

Stephanie said, 'You and this kid remind me of something my science teacher told us at school, about when an irresistible force meets an immovable object. How do you resolve it, then?'

＊

Julia Musgrave was more amenable to his proposal than he felt entitled to expect. The ten days he'd spent observing the class and occasionally assisting had disposed of any fears she may have had that he was a potential nuisance. After classes and in the staffroom he'd shown by his questions that he was quick to appreciate the difficulties of teaching handicapped children.

The staff, as one would hope in a special school, were strongly committed. They amounted to four full-time and three part-time helpers, plus the redoubtable Mrs Straw, who besides guarding the front door had a list of duties that included playtime supervision, first aid, general filing and heating up the lunches supplied by the meals-on-wheels service.

Diamond had persuaded Julia Musgrave to release Naomi from class for the last hour of Friday afternoon. In a one-to-one situation, he would try patiently to dismantle the child's wall of indifference. They would have the staffroom to themselves. This small room at the back of the house doubled as a work and rest area. Desks were ranged along the walls and there was a table with coffee-making facilities under the window at one end. Three armchairs were grouped around a low table on which were scattered magazines and newspapers. Diamond had brought in one of the small chairs and spent some time deciding where to place it. Eventually he settled for a position facing one of the armchairs. He poured hot water onto instant coffee and sat in the armchair.

Mrs Straw appeared in the doorway. 'Miss Musgrave asked me to bring Naomi here.' She made it obvious from her tone that she thought the headmistress must have flipped. She still harboured some resentment at the way Diamond had bluffed his way into the school. However, she produced Naomi from behind her skirt and ushered the child to the chair.

Composed as usual, Naomi sat facing Diamond. She was wearing the red corduroy dress and black tights.

'She'll be all right with me,' he assured Mrs Straw. 'You

don't have to stay.' When she continued to linger he added, 'Would you mind closing the door as you go?'

Left alone with Naomi, he tried what he thought was a reassuring smile. The small girl didn't alter her expression or her gaze, which seemed to be focused on the far end of the room, regardless that Diamond's substantial form blocked the view.

A number of times in his police career he'd interviewed shy or disaffected children. None had succeeded so successfully as Naomi in making him feel not merely small, but imperceptible. She sat demurely, hands together on her lap, feet crossed at the ankles, showing no interest whatsoever in the unfamiliar surroundings.

Diamond reached for his coffee and was taking a sip when it occurred to him that Naomi might appreciate a drink. Orangeade and other soft drinks were banned in the school for the effect certain additives were supposed to have on children, but milk was permitted. He got up and half-filled a paper cup from the carton beside the kettle. He handed it to Naomi and she took it with both hands and put it to her mouth.

It wasn't a breakthrough, he knew. She must have been eating and drinking these past weeks to have stayed alive. But at least it was a positive action. He watched her drain the cup.

'More?' he enquired, pointing to the carton. 'Naomi.'

No response.

He held out his hand for the cup. She ignored it.

'All right,' he said evenly. 'Hang on to it if you want.' He topped up his own cup with coffee and returned to the armchair. Faced with such indifference from one so small, he felt more than usually gross. Partly to restore some self-esteem, he privately declared time out while he finished drinking.

Under the fringe of black hair, Naomi's almond eyes gazed steadily ahead, rarely blinking. If she saw anything of Diamond, it was the area where his tie met the lapel of his jacket, but in fact her eyes weren't focused there. Even if he contrived to slide down in the armchair to get on a level with the child, he still wouldn't achieve genuine eye contact.

The absence of eye contact was, he knew, a characteristic of the autistic behaviour pattern. Taken together with Naomi's refusal to speak and her indifference to what was happening around her, it made a diagnosis of autism more likely than any other. Diamond knew from conversations with Julia Musgrave and from his reading that parents, and sometimes teachers, had the greatest difficulty in accepting the reality of the condition, still less its inflexibility. Tantalized by evidence that these children were unimpaired in many respects and normal in appearance, the people who cared about them tried unavailingly to unlock the personalities imprisoned by the illness. Quite possibly he was engaged in the same futile exercise.

The coffee finished, he sat forward in the armchair and extended his right hand towards the child until his forefinger lightly touched her chest.

'Naomi.'

She didn't react in any way.

He brought the hand back and reversed the finger to indicate his own chest. 'Diamond.'

This establishing of identities was the first step in understanding. A baby learned to say 'Mama', 'Dada' and 'Baba' before anything else. Once the concept of meaning was grasped, the world of language opened up.

Still no response.

He repeated the actions and the words several times without result.

If she wouldn't respond verbally, perhaps he could coax her to make a significant gesture. He reached out and removed the empty paper cup from her hand. Then he took her fingers in his hand, feeling their warmth. Leaning towards her, he pressed her hand against his chest and spoke his name.

Not a flicker of comprehension. He let go of her hand. It dropped limply in her lap.

Without much confidence that she would get the idea and point to his chest, he said, 'Diamond.'

Nothing.

If only he could elicit some response, it would be a

platform to build on. He squirmed to the edge of the armchair and leaned so close that all she had to do was lift her hand to touch him. He repeated, 'Diamond?'

Naomi dipped forward and for a moment he thought she had twigged what to do. Her eyes were on him. Then she sank her teeth into his nose. She bit hard.

'Jesus Christ!'

The pain was severe. Diamond yelled and pulled away. He clapped his hand to his nose. She'd drawn blood. It started dripping steadily.

He got up and looked around for something to staunch the flow. Finding nothing, he went to the door, leaving Naomi self-possessed again, still on the chair, her hands resting in her lap.

Mrs Straw, in the kitchen, didn't disguise her amusement. 'What's she done – bashed you on the nose – a scrap like her?'

He ran the cold tap and dipped his face under it.

Presently Mrs Straw produced cotton wool and liquid antiseptic from the first-aid cabinet. Diamond asked her to take Naomi back to Miss Musgrave. The one-to-one was over for today. First blood to Naomi.

What was it about noses, that nobody took them seriously? If the point of his chin had been covered with Elastoplast, people wouldn't have grinned at the sight of him. He knew he looked ridiculous, but the plaster was necessary. The bleeding had persisted, in spite of the smallness of the cut. Naomi's sharp front teeth had opened a flap of skin at the tip and it was most reluctant to dry up.

At least Julia Musgrave's smile was accompanied by sympathy. 'It's one of the hazards of the job, I'm afraid. I've been bitten in most places, but my nose has escaped up to now. How did she do it?'

When he'd explained, she said, 'You invaded her space. They have a pathological fear of anyone getting too close. You've seen how Clive runs to the bookcase the minute he comes into my office.'

'When you say "they", you mean autistic kids?'

'Well, yes.'

65

'Naomi isn't like that,' Diamond insisted. 'She sits where she's told. She doesn't run off.'

'Didn't I warn you that their behaviour isn't all the same? It's a mental condition, Peter, not a physical thing like mumps which always produces the same symptoms. With some of them it takes an aggressive form, while others are passive.'

'You explained this to me the other day.'

'Well, then.'

'So why did she bite me? Hasn't anyone invaded her space before?'

Julia Musgrave nodded. 'I see what you mean. This is the first time she's bitten anyone, or shown any tendency to fight.'

'Is it possible she learned it from Clive?'

'The biting? I suppose it is, but they don't imitate each other much. They're too independent.'

'You keep saying "they",' Diamond objected testily. The bite, and the amusement it had created, had made him irritable. Some of his old colleagues in the police would have said his true character was beginning to emerge. 'Let's suppose Naomi isn't autistic. Suppose she has some other problem that stops her from speaking. Mightn't she be influenced by what the other kids do?'

Julia Musgrave sighed. 'I can't help thinking you're heading straight up a cul-de-sac. People find it so hard to accept that their kid is autistic.'

'Naomi isn't mine.'

She gave him a long look, not without sympathy, but accompanied by the slight smile that hadn't left her lips since she'd seen the injury. 'Let's say that you're taking a special interest. That's the agony with these children. They look bright. They can show glimmers of intelligence, even of brilliance in some cases. The textbooks call such children idiot savants.'

'Cruel,' Diamond commented.

'It's a cruel condition.'

'For the parents, I mean.'

'Oh, yes. It's harder to accept than having a child who is moronic. Some autistic children can sing quite intricate

66

tunes before they're a year old. I've known a four-year-old who remembers every bar of a Beethoven symphony. They can do incredible things with numbers. They can hide some favourite toy and then weeks, months later, go straight to it. People marvel at such things and persuade themselves that there's a genius trying to get free, that it's simply a matter of finding the miracle cure. It isn't so, Peter. These kids are impaired for life. The memory may be functioning with super-efficiency, but the rest of the brain isn't. They can't reason as you or I can. They can't interpret the facts they know to any purpose. It's incredibly frustrating, but you have to accept it if you work with them.'

'Of course.'

'You're not discouraged?'

'I'm not a quitter, Julia. I'm ready for the next round.'

She regarded him with a kind of pity. 'It isn't a boxing match, in spite of the evidence to the contrary.'

He peeled off the Elastoplast on the way home in the tube, not wishing Stephanie to see it. The small cut had dried, but the area still felt sore. It was too much to hope that Steph wouldn't notice the minute he stepped through the door.

She said, 'Lunchtime drinks today?'

'Naomi.'

'I thought you told me she was only this high.'

'Yes, but I was sitting in an armchair.'

'With the child on your lap?' She paused. 'Have you *got* a lap these days, my love?'

'Not on my lap, for God's sake. I don't want child-molesting added to my record. No, I was leaning forward in the chair, trying to get her to touch me.'

'Pete, that sounds even more deplorable.'

'To identify me. To show that she understood my name.'

'She's Japanese, my love.'

He switched on the TV.

Later she said, 'Maybe you ought to try a different approach.'

67

'Such as?' He spoke sharply. He was still feeling frayed.

'You seem to be trying to get through to her on the basis that she isn't autistic. Have you thought of doing the other thing? In other words, testing whether she *is*?'

'How do I do that?'

'Better ask.'

After two more arid sessions in the staffroom with Naomi (keeping his distance) he was close to being persuaded that no progress was possible, and he admitted as much to Julia Musgrave. They were in the school garden during what was wishfully described in the timetable as playtime. Rajinder and Naomi were seated on swings of the kind that had side supports and safety-bars, being kept in motion by Mrs Straw. Not one of the trio seemed to be taking any pleasure in the exercise. Tabitha, sucking her thumb, was watching dolefully and Clive was hiding behind a sack of grass-seed in the gardener's shed.

'I've got to admire your persistence, Peter,' Julia Musgrave told him, 'but I have to say that I think you're right. You're up against a brick wall. Have you talked to the police? They took away the clothes Naomi was found in. I wonder if they found any clues.'

'You can stop wondering,' he told her. 'I know one of the inspectors there. The kid's things were sent off to the lab, and after a couple of weeks a five-page report came back, saying – in a nutshell – that they appeared to have been worn by a dark-haired female child. Oh, and they had the Marks and Spencer label. That cuts it down to five million, I should guess.' He picked a sprig of lavender and rolled it between his finger and thumb, watching the bits drop on the path. The scent was a favourite of Steph's. 'My wife thinks I'm going at this the wrong way round.'

'How do you mean?'

'She says instead of looking for signs that Naomi isn't autistic, I ought to be examining all the evidence that she *is*. Normality is impossible to prove.'

'It's a questionable concept anyway. She sounds like a bright lady, your wife.'

'Brighter than me, for sure.'

'Why don't you talk to Dr Ettlinger? He's coming in to look at Naomi this afternoon.'

Ettlinger was a child psychiatrist attached in some unspecified way to the school, a short, troll-like man with a prodigious crop of wiry black hair. It wasn't clear whether he'd been appointed by the local health authority or was a freelance who had persuaded Julia Musgrave that there might be something in it for the children. As Peter Diamond was only there himself by courtesy of Julia, he was in no position to object, but his private assessment was that Ettlinger ought not to have been let within a mile of young kids. The man was abrasive, opinionated and humourless. In spite of that, he seemed to have convinced everyone at the school that he was an international authority on autism, and presumably it was true.

'You'd better not waste my time,' he told Diamond waspishly when approached in the staffroom. 'I'm Teutonic. I have no interest whatsoever in the weather, or cricket, or cars.' From anyone else, the remark might have been meant to amuse. Not from Ettlinger.

'It's a professional matter, Doctor,' Diamond assured him, uncomfortably kowtowing. The days when he could pull rank on smart-mouthed forensic experts were just a memory now. 'I'm interested in Naomi, the Japanese girl. She's here because they believe she's autistic.'

'Correct.'

'So you agree that she is?'

'I didn't say that. I was merely confirming your statement.'

'But have you formed an opinion yet?'

'No.'

'Is that because you have doubts?'

'Certainly not,' Ettlinger snapped. 'Dubiety is unscientific. I am open-minded. Do you understand the difference? *You* may harbour doubts. I am open-minded.'

Diamond was tempted to remark that the state of Ettlinger's mind interested him less than Naomi's, but he checked himself.

Ettlinger added, 'I would need to study the child in a more systematic way than I can on occasional visits. She is not my patient.'

'I understand she shows some of the classical symptoms of autism.'

'*Classical*?' Ettlinger almost choked on the word, he was so indignant. '*Classical*? The condition wasn't given a name until 1943, and it wasn't studied in a serious way until the 1960s. How can you speak of symptoms as classical?'

'Typical, then.'

'I could object to that as well.'

Diamond didn't give him the opportunity. 'She doesn't speak. She avoids eye contact. Is that the profile of an autistic child? Because if it is, Naomi fits it perfectly.'

'What you have just described, Mr Diamond, may be indicative of autism; it is also the appropriate behaviour of well-brought-up young women throughout much of Asia. Have you thought of that? One cannot discount the possibility that her behaviour is governed, to some degree at least, by her culture.'

A persuasive point that Diamond accepted. He supposed he had borne it in mind up to now without articulating it. 'But not to speak at all, not even to the woman from the Japanese Embassy?'

'That, I grant you, is exceptional.'

'How do you recognize autism, then?'

Ettlinger sighed and glanced up at the staffroom clock.

'All right, how does anyone recognize it? Are there tests?'

'What do you mean?'

'X-rays, blood-tests, scans. I'm no expert.'

'There are no objective tests of that kind,' said Ettlinger with disdain. 'One looks at the behaviour. What I will say is that every child who fits this syndrome suffers from some degree of speech impairment, ranging from mutism to aphasia – which is confusion over the proper sequence of letters and words. Every child, Mr Diamond.'

Diamond placed a mental tick against Naomi's mutism.

'It is also true by definition that the autistic child is manifestly indifferent to other people, especially other children. Autism comes from the Greek, as you probably know. *Autos*. Self. Right?'

Another tick.

'However, one would expect to observe other impairments, such as problems of motor control.'

'Odd ways of walking, you mean, like Rajinder?'

'Yes.'

'Naomi isn't like that. She seems well co-ordinated.'

Ettlinger nodded. 'Some of them are. Curiously, they sometimes have the ability to keep their balance better than other children. They climb on furniture and leap around in a sure-footed manner. They could probably perform prodigious feats on a tightrope.'

Which wouldn't be easy to test, Diamond thought.

'And they won't get dizzy if they spin around.'

'That's something I didn't know.'

'It's commonly observed.'

'Anything else?'

Ettlinger spread his hands. 'Much else, Mr Diamond. Repetitive behaviour, such as head-banging, or rocking, or staring into a mirror, or spinning things. The wheels of a toy, for instance. You must have watched Clive do that.'

'Of course. I don't think Naomi does it.'

Ettlinger was already onto other symptoms of autism. 'Abnormal reactions to sensory experiences, such as pain, or cold or heat. Hostility to being touched lightly.' There was the hint of a smile.

'You heard what happened to me?'

'I can see.'

'Was that to be expected of an autistic child?'

'They bite, yes.'

'I mean does it make the diagnosis more likely?'

'It's a small indication. Next time you should try being more boisterous, and see if she responds to it. They often enjoy a good romp.' The moral objection to a strange man 'romping' with a small girl seemed not to have occurred to Dr Ettlinger.

'Is anything known about the cause of the condition?'

A laugh came from deep in Ettlinger's throat. 'The cause, you say? Nobody knows. No known cause and no cure. There are theories. More theories than I have time to list, my friend. Personally, I am inclined to believe that the problem is organic, rather than emotional. It has nothing to do with the way the children are reared, as was once suspected. It goes back, in my opinion, to pre-, peri- or post-natal injury or illness affecting the brain. And don't ask me what can be done. Every week, practically, I read of some Svengali claiming spectacular success. Cures, even. You can hug these children, reward them, punish them, isolate them, put them on diets. They can be trained to some extent. I don't deny it. But so can chimpanzees. Personally I would rather train a chimpanzee. They're capable of affection, you know. Autistic children give none. They are tyrants.'

Diamond had heard all this with mounting distaste. 'That's hardly a scientific word, is it? Tyrants?'

The little doctor glared. 'Think of a better one. Spend as long as you like observing Naomi and think of a better one – if you can.' He turned his back on Diamond and went over to talk to someone else.

Chapter Ten

THIS MORNING DIAMOND WAS EQUIPPED with a pad of drawing paper and a marker. If this intractable little girl wouldn't respond to sounds, he'd decided, maybe it *was* a problem of language. He was going to see whether symbols would do the trick. He moved his chair next to hers and placed the pad on a low table in front of them. Then he drew a large circle and added a smaller one on top. A body and a head, evoking childish memories of beetle drives on wet afternoons in English holiday camps. Except that this was meant to represent his body and his head. He added stick legs and arms, followed by the facial features, with a scribble of hair above each ear to establish the margins of his bald dome. He held it up for Naomi, beamed encouragingly and said, 'Diamond.' He pointed to his chest.

Possibly, he persuaded himself, her eyes gave his artwork the credit of a glance. They certainly didn't linger on it. And she remained silent.

He touched the drawing and then tapped himself on the head.

'See? Diamond.'

Not a muscle twitched.

Refusing to be discouraged, he folded the picture over and drew a smaller figure on the next sheet, with the suggestion of a skirt and a passable attempt at fringed hair.

'Naomi.'

He pointed to her. Indicated her hair. Then added a flourish to the drawing, a small bow poised on top of the head. 'Like it?' He chuckled a little, and was conscious how forced it sounded. 'It's you.'

Not only was she unamused, she hadn't even looked.

Determined not to be thwarted, he turned back to the first drawing, tore it from the pad and set it on the table beside the second one, to make clear the contrast in size. 'Big Diamond. And little Naomi. Diamond. Naomi. Me and you.'

She seemed frozen.

Several more attempts to establish the significance of the drawings came to nothing.

'Would *you* like to draw?' He slid the pad across the table in front of her. Once on television he'd seen a boy suffering from autism who could do remarkable drawings of buildings from memory, precise in detail and perfect in perspective. After a visit to London the boy had made sketches of St Paul's and other buildings equally ornate. Two books of his drawings had been published.

Diamond wasn't expecting fine art from Naomi. He was willing to settle for a mark on the paper, of any sort. He took hold of her left hand and carefully inserted the marker between her fingers. He'd noticed that she used the left when she held a paper cup. Plenty of thought was going into this.

Naomi declined to grip the marker and let it flop out of her hand.

'I think you could do this,' he said, more for his own morale than the child's. 'I really think you could.' He replaced her fingers around the marker and guided her hand to produce a shaky circle on the drawing pad. 'There!'

The accomplishment was lost on Naomi.

'Suit yourself, miss.' More disappointed than he cared to show, he turned his back on the child and stepped over to the table where the coffee things were. He might as well switch the kettle on now so that the teachers didn't have to wait when they came in at lunchtime. That would be the sum of his achievements for this lesson. He checked the water level, pressed the switch and stared out of the window, listening to the kettle begin the moaning note that was sometimes mistaken for a child crying.

Then he was conscious of a light touch on his right hand. Unbidden, Naomi had got up from her chair and reached up to place her palm against his.

He stared down, amazed. Elated. Did he dare feel

elated? She didn't return his glance, but what she had done was enough. It was the first positive gesture she had made towards him, or towards anyone in the school, so far as he knew. He let his fingers gently enclose the small hand. He and Naomi stood together in front of the window in silence, in some sort of harmony, the irresistible force and the immovable object.

The kettle was coming to the boil and it had some fault in the mechanism that stopped it from switching off. He let it steam for a time and then leaned forward and with his left hand switched off the wall-socket. Naomi took it as the signal to remove her hand from his and go back to her chair. He turned, smiling to let her see that it wasn't meant as a rejection. She didn't respond.

His eyes were misting. For pity's sake, he thought, I'm not going soft, am I? Peter Diamond, ex-CID?

At lunchtime, he told Julia Musgrave about the drawing session. They sat together on a bench under a sycamore tree in the school garden eating sandwiches. By then he was able to be more objective, admitting that it might be a mistake to place too much significance on the incident.

'No, we need all the encouragement that's going in this work,' she said. 'Some kids never make a spontaneous gesture of friendship like that to another person. Never. It's terrific news, Peter. Let's face it, no one else has made any progress with her. I think the woman from the embassy has despaired of ever getting through. She didn't come at all this week. She phoned instead. They're talking about sending Naomi to a school in Boston that specialises in autism. It's run by Japanese teachers.'

'Boston?' Diamond said, aghast. 'Send her to America? That's going to confuse the kid even more.'

'They're getting remarkable results. Several children from this country have been taken there. It may be the best solution for her. We're making no progress here — well, not until this morning.' She paused, looking at him earnestly. 'They call it the Boston Hagashi School. Apparently *hagashi* means hope in Japanese. Don't you think that's a beautiful idea?'

If it was, he wasn't receptive to it. 'Look, I know you

mean to do right by Naomi, but suppose she isn't autistic?'

'It's not really my decision, Peter. She's in the care of the local authority.'

'Who'd be very relieved to have her taken off their hands, no doubt.'

'Now you're being cynical.'

'Tell me something, then. What precisely is being done to find her parents?'

She sighed. 'The police are making enquiries. No one has given any worthwhile information, so far as I can gather. No one has reported her missing. Where are the parents? Somebody definitely looked after her up to the time she was found. She was clean and decently dressed. She's been abandoned, Peter, and I don't think the parents are going to change their minds. Young mothers sometimes come forward to reclaim newborn babies left on doorsteps, but this is something else.'

'Agreed.'

'I often meet parents who feel they can't cope any longer with disturbed children – only they don't just leave them in Harrods and walk away.'

'What is it, six weeks now?' Diamond asked, making a point rather than seeking the answer, which he knew.

'Almost.'

'In the first week, her picture was in the papers.'

'And on television. Nothing came of it.'

He said thoughtfully, 'The picture was only a still, and it was only on the regional news. I'd like to get her on to a national TV programme, like *Crimewatch*.'

Julia Musgrave frowned. 'We don't know that a crime is involved.'

'Abandoning a child her age?'

She shook her head. 'It's not the best way to reach her parents. Somewhere out there is a very distressed mother.'

'All right, let's see if we can get Naomi on a chat show.'

'A *chat* show?'

'You'd do the chatting, but she'd be seen by millions.'

'Peter, I'm not sure that it's right to put a disturbed little girl in front of television cameras.'

He understood her reluctance without supporting it.

76

'I'd agree with you if she was a gibbering idiot, or scared of people, like Clive. But you and I know how she'll conduct herself on television. She'll stay as calm as ever. Self-possessed. She's in control. You can't deny that. And if she appears live, it's going to make a far bigger impact than a still picture. There's a very good chance that someone will recognize her.'

'I'm not at all happy about this.'

'And I'm far from happy about the kid being whisked off to America when her parents may still be here in England. Let me make some enquiries. This is just the kind of story they like to take up on TV. She's a very appealing child.'

'Exactly,' she said with passion. 'I don't want her used. We don't have the moral right to turn her into an object for people to goggle at. If she's on television, you can bet the papers will take it up. We'll have all sorts of well-meaning folk offering to adopt her, sending her toys—'

'Does she have any toys?'

'She isn't interested, Peter. We have a whole menagerie of stuffed animals.'

'How about toys with wheels?' he asked suddenly, recalling Dr Ettlinger's observation.

'She isn't a spinner, rest assured. Look, television is an entertainment medium. Naomi isn't entertainment, she's a vulnerable child with a serious impairment.'

'Julia, people aren't going to laugh at her, for God's sake.'

She regarded him steadily. 'If this had been Clive or Rajinder whose people we couldn't find, would you take them on television?'

'Probably not in a talk show,' he conceded.

'And why not?'

'Their behaviour wouldn't do them credit — but they're different. You and I know that Naomi would acquit herself impeccably.'

'Oh, yes?' A glint came to her eye. 'How do you know she wouldn't bite the cameraman?'

He had to smile at the prospect.

Julia's attention switched abruptly to Mrs Straw, who was bearing down on them from the direction of the house. From the manner of her approach, the carriage of her shoulders and the swing of her thighs, she had something awesome to announce, and she was going to make sure that it received its proper attention.

'What is it, Mrs Straw?' Julia asked.

'I think you should look in the staffroom, Miss Musgrave. Somebody stupidly left a marker pen lying about. The Japanese girl found it, and she's scribbled all over the walls, and they were only papered three months ago. You never saw anything like it!'

The vandalism in the staffroom provided Diamond with his first opportunity of detective work since leaving Bath. The perpetrator of the graffiti had done an effective job, for the walls were copiously covered in aimless scribble. Nor had the furniture escaped. The thick, black lines had turned the lower half of the room into what one of the teachers described as a Jackson Pollock. The reference went over Diamond's head, although it sounded apt.

Nobody, he learned by questioning Mrs Straw, had actually seen Naomi at work with the marker. The child had been found with it later in the dining room. She had refused to give it up. 'I had to prise her fingers off one by one,' Mrs Straw asserted. 'She was all set to do it all over the school.'

This, it turned out, was a false accusation. Doubtful that Naomi was the culprit, Diamond was able to demonstrate her innocence. When he examined the staffroom walls, he found that the scribbles ran higher than she was capable of reaching. Thus it was that the real culprit was apprehended in his usual hiding place behind the grass-seed in the garden shed. Not only was Clive's reach four inches higher than that of any other child in the school, his hands and clothes were stained with black marks. It transpired that he'd wandered into the staff-room at a time when nobody was about and had done the deed, afterwards throwing the marker away in the garden. Later, Naomi had picked it up.

'I'm afraid Mrs Straw is a vengeful woman,' Julia Musgrave confided to Diamond. 'She does work hard for the school, though. I don't think we'd manage without her.'

'She was right about one thing,' he admitted. 'I was daft

to leave the marker out.' In this confessional vein, he went on rashly to promise to redecorate the staffroom – a severe penance indeed. This little crisis had sidetracked them from the more vital issue of whether it was right to put Naomi on television; not for long, he was resolved.

As he was leaving, calculating how many cans of emulsion he'd need, Julia called his name and came after him into the corridor.

He stopped, uncertain what to expect.

'You can have your marker back,' she told him. 'Believe it or not, the ink isn't all used up yet.'

He pocketed it, slightly puzzled. The marker belonged to the school anyway. She must have known.

She said, 'You don't really have to go to all that trouble – over the staffroom, I mean.'

'It's no sweat for me,' he lied.

'I appreciate the offer, only I wouldn't want you to think it will change anything.'

'Except the colour of the staffroom,' he said, grinning.

When he turned, he almost fell over Naomi. She must have been standing extremely close behind him, apparently waiting, because she stretched up her hand towards him. Twice in a day, he thought. This is too amazing to be true.

He extended his hand towards hers, but immediately she pulled it away. She didn't, after all, wish to renew the contact.

'Have it your way,' he said, wryly reflecting that even at that tender age, women played fast and loose with decent men's affections.

Sure enough, she proffered the hand a second time, only now her palm was outstretched as if she were asking for money.

'What is it, Naomi?' he asked, bending lower. 'What are you trying to say?'

Her eyes had lost that habitual glazed look. She was focusing on him intently, her forehead creased in concern. She began jabbing her hand at him repeatedly like a beggar in a Cairo bazaar.

He asked, 'Are you hungry?'

Whatever the problem was, she was really trying to communicate – a huge advance after six passive weeks – and the least he could do in return was discover what she wanted.

'It can't be money.'

As he bent even closer to her upturned face, she reached for his jacket, pulled it open and dipped her free hand into the inner pocket.

'Young lady,' he said, 'you're sharper than anyone suspected.'

Only it wasn't his wallet she was after. It was the marker that he'd stowed away in there after seeing Julia. Naomi whipped it out and clutched it to her chest with both hands, as if she wanted nothing so much in the world.

'God help us!' he said to her. 'What do I do now?'

It was quite a dilemma. If he let her keep the thing, someone – Mrs Straw, knowing his luck – was certain to see it and inform the rest of the school that they had a fifth columnist in their midst. Julia Musgrave would feel betrayed. If, on the other hand, he insisted on taking the marker back, the first shoots of affection he'd cultivated would be trampled upon, destroyed for ever. He remembered Mrs Straw's saying how she'd needed to prise Naomi's fingers away one by one. Clearly, that pen was a treasure to the child.

He decided to let her keep it, and run the risk that Clive might snatch it away and go on a graffiti-spree again. He was pretty confident Naomi wouldn't lightly give up her prize.

Gently, he put a hand on her shoulder and steered her in the direction of the staffroom. She was as compliant as ever now that he'd made it plain that he wasn't going to take back the marker. Coming into the staffroom without thinking about Clive's handiwork, he was freshly shocked at the extent of the scribbling. No one was sitting in there, and he could understand why. He escorted Naomi to the wall where the scrawl was thickest.

'You see what happened?' he said, hoping she would share his outrage, even if the words meant nothing to her. 'Clive did it. You wouldn't, would you?' He swept the air with his hands to reinforce the message.

She stood solemnly facing the vandalized wall. Troubled that he might have been too heavy-handed, he reached out impulsively to stroke her hair, then decided he shouldn't.

An action like that could be misinterpreted, by others, if not the child. But his hand was already on her head, so he ruffled the dark hair instead – and still felt it was a liberty he shouldn't have taken.

The drawing pad he'd used earlier remained on the table, open at the picture he'd done of Naomi. He folded the pad and handed it to her. 'This is for drawing. You can have it. It's yours. Yours. All right?'

She appeared to understand. Her eyes briefly met his and she tucked the pad under her arm.

'Now let's find where you should be at this hour of the day.'

He found the class in a lesson that was down on the timetable as music, and consisted of indiscriminate tambourine-banging while the teacher, a cool young girl wearing a black fedora, strummed something on the guitar. Naomi settled cross-legged on the floor away from the others, continuing to hold the drawing pad and marker. She declined to take the tambourine Diamond found for her. He nodded to the teacher and left.

Now Julia Musgrave had to be told of his decision to entrust the marker to Naomi. He didn't want the news to be passed on by Mrs Straw, or anyone else for that matter. He believed he could make a persuasive case.

Julia wasn't alone in her office, but she called him in. Her visitor was a bearded, balding man in a brown corduroy jacket with patched elbows. An envelope file rested across his thighs and from his neck a thick pencil hung on a cord, all of which suggested to Diamond that this was a social worker. He was mistaken.

'Dr Dickinson is a child psychiatrist,' Julia explained. 'He's here to make an assessment of Naomi.'

'Another assessment?' said Diamond, mildly enough considering the warning bells that were sounding in his head.

'On behalf of the Japanese Embassy,' Dr Dickinson put in, using the kind of we-all-understand-how-the-world-goes-round tone that expects no disagreement. 'They want my opinion as to whether the child is autistic. The general idea is that she'll be sent to the Hagashi School in Boston if it appears that she'd benefit. She's a fortunate child.'

'Why is that?'

Dickinson frowned. 'The fees are out of most people's reach — about thirty thousand pounds a year.'

'I'm not impressed by money.'

Dickinson said cuttingly, 'Well, I'm extremely impressed by everything I've read about the school. As Naomi, I gather, is Japanese, this must be a happy arrangement.'

'You think so?'

'Mr Diamond has some reservations,' Julia Musgrave quickly added.

'Oh, and what's your specialism?' Dickinson asked witheringly.

'Testing the truth,' said Diamond. 'I'm a detective, or was until recently.'

Dickinson caught his breath and turned to Julia Musgrave. 'Really, I can't begin to understand why a detective . . .'

Julia Musgrave briefly explained the reason for Diamond's presence in the school and finished by remarking that only that morning his perseverance had paid a wonderful dividend.

'Oh, and what was that?'

'Naomi got up from her chair and held my hand,' Diamond informed him. 'It may not sound much, but it's a real advance.'

'Let us hope so,' the psychiatrist commented in a tone that suggested the reverse. 'Unfortunately the condition of autism is full of false dawns — not that I question the accuracy of what you experienced. It's so tempting with these children to draw unscientific assumptions from their behaviour. You assumed when she took your hand that she wished to express some trust, or affection. On the contrary—'

'But I didn't say that,' Diamond interrupted him. 'All I said was that she got up from the chair and held my hand. And speaking of unscientific assumptions, I'm surprised to hear you talking about autism in relation to Naomi before you've actually seen her.'

'I specialize in autism,' Dickinson said icily. 'I wouldn't have been invited here unless the child had exhibited autistic tendencies.'

Julia Musgrave judged it right to interrupt the exchange.

'Peter, what was it you came in about? Something urgent?'

'Something I'd like you to hear from me before you get it from anyone else,' he answered, and went on to tell her how it was that Naomi was back in possession of the marker. 'You don't mind?' he said finally, encouraged that she'd nodded more than once as he was relating the episode.

'It's a risk I'm willing to take,' Julia answered. 'Anything is preferable to that passive state she's been in for so long. Yes, I'm really heartened. She's being positive at last.'

Without much tact, Dr Dickinson offered his interpretation. 'This is very characteristic. Autistic children frequently become possessive about objects, to an exceptional degree, I mean. Mirrors, wheels, bits of crumpled paper. They refuse to be parted from them. It's compulsive.' He took a writing-pad from his folder and made a note.

'Oh, is that a pencil?' Diamond remarked. 'I thought it was a necklace.' Afterwards he regretted saying such a bitchy thing, not because he cared a sparrow's fart about Dickinson, but because it wasn't clever to fuel the man's evident dislike of him, which could easily prejudice his assessment of Naomi. Talking first and thinking after was a failing that had got Diamond into trouble in the past, and would again. He had the sense to leave Julia's office after that.

He slumped into an armchair in the staffroom, bemoaning his lowly status in the school. In his days in the police, he would have overruled Dickinson or any other headshrinker if a child's interests were under threat. He wouldn't have taken that horseshit about compulsive behaviour. Well, he thought, I didn't take it. But I'd have shown him the bloody door.

He couldn't be sure which way Julia Musgrave would jump. Her calm personality was a tremendous asset in a school like this. She was approachable and open to suggestions; which meant inconveniently that people like Dickinson got a hearing. Under pressure from the shrinks, the Japanese Embassy and the borough council, she was going to find it difficult, if not impossible, to hold on to Naomi. She was massively outgunned. One failed policeman convinced that everyone else was mistaken wasn't exactly the US Cavalry riding to the rescue.

His thoughts were interrupted by the jingle of tambourines being carried along the corridor, and the music teacher tottered in with the instruments stacked in her arms and the guitar slung across her back, and still wearing her fedora. She dumped everything onto a chair and went to the kettle. 'Want a coffee?'

'I wouldn't say no.'

'Thanks for bringing Naomi in. I didn't know where she was.'

He nodded. 'Does she take to the music?'

'Not that I've noticed. Would you prefer tea?'

'Whatever you're having.'

They waited for the kettle. The girl, an Australian from her accent, said, 'Your name is Diamond, right?'

'Yep.'

'Hold on, then. I've got something to show you. I won't be long.' She left him to make the coffee.

Presently she was back, with a large sheet of paper. 'Did you know you have a secret admirer?' She held the paper up.

He stared, disbelieving. 'Naomi did this?'

'Who else?' she said. 'And in my lesson. The little hussy won't bash a tambourine for me while you're on her mind.'

The mark on the paper was bold and unmistakable:

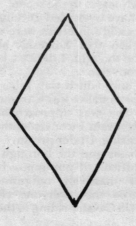

Chapter Eleven

A NARROW BLUE RECTANGLE WAS visible between the World Trade Center and the New York Telephone Company. It was the Hudson River. Viewed from Manny Flexner's office on the twenty-first floor of the Manflex Building on West Broadway, it glittered brilliantly in the morning sun. Manny's office had windows from floor to ceiling, divided at the centre, which was about head height. The upper sections slid open, a feature Manny had insisted on. He liked his air-conditioning natural when he could get it. Today was one of those blissful days when the wind was minimal and the temperature ideal.

While his eyes were on the river he was speaking on the phone to his son David in Milan, and the things he was hearing pleased him immensely. Why couldn't every Monday morning be like this?

'The meeting went more smoothly than I had a right to expect,' David was saying. 'Okay, we had a few tough questions about the decision to close the plant, but most of them understood the problems and appreciated the trouble we were taking to relocate them. It was all incredibly civilized.'

'Thanks to the hard work you put in last week,' Manny said with approval. 'You did your homework. People appreciate that. How many want to transfer to Rome?'

'Fifteen to twenty. Another twenty or so want more time to reach a decision.'

'How many of those are researchers?'

'Eight, at the latest count.'

'Not bad. You want to keep the ratio of research high. The norm in the industry is one-third research, two-thirds development. I always tried to better that. How did the buy-out offer do?'

'The union is asking for more, but that's a union's job. My feeling is that they're willing to settle.'

Manny let out a long, contented breath. 'Dave, you did a fine job. Is there any more news how the fire started?'

'No, the police haven't been back. I sent them a list of everyone at the meeting. I figure that won't please them much because we've accounted for every man jack on the books. The cops I saw here were pushing the theory that it was an inside job.'

'They still haven't identified the bodies in the Alfa Romeo?'

'Not so far as I know.'

'Are the insurers any wiser?'

'I doubt it. Everyone is resigned to long delays. Pop, if it's still okay with you, I thought I might take a couple of days off at the end of this week, go and see Venice, like you suggested. Rico can hold the fort.'

'Venice?' Manny brooded for a moment, then came to a decision. 'Sure, son, you've earned it. I'm proud of what you're doing. But don't wait. Go now. Today. And, Dave, don't tell Rico where you're staying. Make it a real vacation. You understand?'

'Pop, I'm in no hurry. I have a couple of appointments in the morning.'

Manny said earnestly. 'Cancel them. Do this for me. I know what I'm saying. Get the hell out of there if you want to see Venice. And, Dave . . .'

'Yes?'

'I love you, son.'

'Love you, Pop,' David answered in a bemused tone.

'Take care.'

'Sure.'

Manny cradled the phone. On his desk were a number of letters he'd written by hand. He picked out the one addressed to his son and wrote on the envelope *Hope Venice was magic.* Then he got up and poured himself a large brandy at the drinks cabinet and swallowed it rapidly.

He removed his reading glasses and replaced them in the case on the desk. Then he took out his pocketbook containing credit cards and some paper money and positioned it beside the spectacle-case.

On the other side of the office was an oval mahogany table with four matching chairs. Manny collected one of the chairs, carried it to the window and used it to climb onto his teak filing cabinet. His movements were ordered, automatic, and, for a man with a malignant illness, remarkably spry. He could easily step up to one of the open windows from there, and that was what he did. He got both feet on the metal frame and balanced there momentarily supported by his hands. The space was tall, so there was no need to stoop.

Manny didn't look down. His gaze was on the glittering section of river way ahead. The Hudson. And beyond, New Jersey. To Manny, in his fatalistic state of mind, the river might as well have been the Jordan, and beyond that was the promised land – a comforting thought. He was still looking ahead when he jumped. He kept watching the far shore while he started to drop, kept watching for as long as he was able.

Chapter Twelve

BEFORE EVERYONE EXCEPT MRS STRAW arrived at the school next morning, Diamond was in the staffroom making an island of the desks and other furniture. He'd called early at a do-it-yourself shop in Hammersmith and purchased two three-litre cans of vinyl matt emulsion in a shade described as apricot. On the chart it had looked the sort of colour that would blend with the furnishings – or so he'd easily convinced himself on seeing that it was offered at a special never-to-be-repeated discount. With the money he'd saved he'd gone straight into a toyshop across the street and bought a toy car with a friction motor. Later, he would give it to Clive; he had a place in his heart for the school vandal in spite of the extra work he had created.

So he was in his overalls applying the roller to the wall behind the door by eight-fifty, when the first of the teaching staff put in an appearance.

'What's all this?' Sally Truman, who took the youngest children, asked.

'A cover-up.'

'Oh, it's you.'

He dipped the roller into the paint tray and applied another band of apricot. Now that people had started arriving he wasn't going to down tools, just when he was entitled to some credit for this public-spirited effort. 'And how are you this morning?' he asked Sally.

'Tired, until I looked in here. The colour's woken me up.'

'Do you like it?'

She evaded the question. 'I expect it fades as it dries. They generally do. What is it?'

'Apricot.'

'Looks more like tomato to me. Now would you mind if I lift the dust-sheet and find my desk?'

He was gratified by a spate of congratulations in the next half-hour, even though the consensus of the teaching staff seemed to be that he should have paid a pound or two more and got magnolia or some other insipid shade. He listened with good humour and carried on obliterating Clive's eye-swivelling murals. By ten he was ready for a coffee break, and that required a rearrangement of the desks to get at the kettle. He'd covered two walls. Now that he stood back, the effect did appear more red than apricot.

He was earning plenty of good will for trying, however, and no one had complained about the disruption. They rummaged under the dust-sheets for chairs and sat as usual with their coffee-cups, catching up on developments since they had last shared a break. The news from yesterday of Naomi's drawing was the main topic this morning. In this small school every child was known to the teachers.

'It's got to be good news, Peter,' the deputy head, John Taffler said. 'And by God, you deserve some encouragement after all the time you've put in with that kid.'

Diamond was less sanguine. He'd had a night to think it over. 'I'd be more encouraged if it was something I'd taught her.'

Taffler wagged a finger at him. 'Don't be so ungrateful, man. It's recognition. It's your name. She's registered that you exist.'

'I wouldn't bet on it.'

'Oh, come on — why else would she draw a diamond? She knows your name.'

He looked around him at the faces of the staff. 'How would she know the symbol for it? I didn't tell her, and nor did anyone else, so far as I can make out.'

'Maybe she plays poker,' someone said, and got a few laughs.

Sally Truman said, 'It proves that she speaks English. Surely that's apparent now?'

Diamond pointed out gloomily that she didn't speak anything.

'Understands it, then,' Sally insisted. 'She heard your name and related it to the shape. She's trying to communicate.'

Someone else, one of the part-time teachers, then voiced the uncertainty that Peter Diamond himself was feeling. 'Let's not read too much into this. The kid could have drawn the shape in a random way. She may never repeat it.'

'She may not have the opportunity,' Taffler commented in the arch tone of someone with inside information. 'Not in this place, at any rate. Did you hear that Olly Dickinson, the shrink who was here yesterday, confirmed her as autistic? She's off to America as soon as they can organize it.'

Diamond had feared he would hear something like this before much longer, but it still raised his blood pressure by many points. He slammed down his mug, slopping coffee over the table. 'So it's the tidiest outcome for everyone,' he said bitterly. 'This school unloads a kid it can't do anything for, and so do the social services. The police stop making inquiries. Dickinson pockets a fat fee. The embassy stumps up and salves its collective conscience. Out in America they cash the cheque and add a new name to the roll. Bully for everyone – except one small girl who can't speak a word to prevent it.' He got up and marched out, straight to Julia Musgrave's office.

He swung the door open. 'When is she due to leave?' he demanded without preamble.

Julia looked up from some paperwork she had on her desk. Her eyes widened, no doubt at the sight of his overalls. She hadn't been near the staffroom yet. 'Peter, why don't you sit down a moment?'

'I'm too bloody angry, that's why. Just tell me how long I've got. That's all I want to know.'

'What do you mean – how long you've got?'

'Isn't it obvious? To find her people.'

The colour had drained from her face. She said, 'Peter, I'm not ungrateful for all the efforts you made with Naomi, only I have to remind you that you volunteered. It gave you no stake in her future.'

He didn't exactly shake his fist at her, but he clenched it and pounded the space in front of him as he declared, 'You talk about her future. I'm still trying to reconstruct her past. You and your cronies are about to blow it away.'

She looked as if he'd struck her. Pitching her voice lower in the effort to control it, she said, 'I resent that remark. I resent it deeply. If you want to know, I argued, I pleaded, for Naomi to remain here until we'd exhausted every possibility. I was in a minority of one.'

There was a moment of strained silence.

'I'm sorry.' Completely deflated, he took a couple of steps towards her, raising his hands in a futile gesture of disavowal. 'Christ, that's me mouthing off again without getting a grip of the facts. Julia, I'm more sorry than I can say.'

She shook her head in a way that seemed to mean words of any sort could only distress her more. She simply said, 'Probably Sunday.'

Sunday.

Four days.

By the time he returned to the staffroom everyone else had left. Instead of picking up the roller, he dragged the phone and the Yellow Pages from under the dust-sheet and started calling television companies, trying the shows he'd targeted for a slot about Naomi and asking each time for the senior person on duty. If he found himself palmed off with a research assistant, he had no conscience about using his former police rank and asking for someone more senior. In the robust style of his days in the murder squad, he badgered his way steadily through the BBC, Thames TV and Sky, all the breakfast shows, the mid-morning studio debates, the women's interest programmes and the talk shows, early evening and night. He missed nothing out in selling the idea of an unsolved mystery involving a small girl who'd triggered the alarms in Harrods and still hadn't been identified two months later. From the majority came dusty answers. A few referred him elsewhere and some took his number and promised to call back if their editorial team (or whatever) expressed any interest.

After that, there was nothing for it but to pick up the roller again. By lunchtime the job was finished and no one had phoned back. His shoulders ached and his throat was dry. Mrs Straw came in, obdurately ignored the immaculate, gleaming walls and pointed out some paint marks on the floor. He assured her that the paint was water-based and easily removable. Feeling as he did, he didn't actually undertake to clear the offending spots immediately, so Mrs S. made a production number out of fetching a bucket and squeegee and soaking the entire floor just as the staff were arriving for their lunch-break.

But there was something to lift his spirits, and it wasn't a compliment on his decorating. John Taffler grabbed him by the arm and said, 'Come and look at this, mate.'

Diamond followed him out to the garden, where the children had already started their playtime. Seated on a low wall beside the vegetable garden was Naomi. She had the drawing pad on her knees and she was using the marker, entirely absorbed.

With stealth, Diamond approached close enough to get a sight over her shoulder of what she was doing. She had drawn a series of fifteen or so diamond shapes, roughly similar in size, each one in isolation.

'How about that?' Taffler said. 'Random, my arse. She's turning them out in batches.'

Pleasing as it was to Diamond, the drawing left him mystified.

Taffler was crouching on Naomi's level and talking to her. 'Nice work, my darling. Beautiful! Diamonds.' He tapped several of the shapes consecutively. 'Diamond, diamond, diamond.' Then he pointed upwards. 'Mr Diamond. That's what you're telling us, sweetie, right?'

The child paused in her work and actually glanced up for a moment at Diamond. Inconveniently there was nothing in her look to support John Taffler's assumption, nothing remotely indicating that Diamond was on her mind. She frowned and turned away.

'Let's be thankful for what we've got,' Diamond said, determined to be positive. 'She's using the pen, and that's progress.'

'Well, yes.' Taffler stood upright again. 'At least she's coming out of that totally passive state. On the other hand,' he added as they started back towards the house, 'it's a little worrying that she isn't drawing anything else. It could get obsessional.'

Diamond was in no frame of mind to face that particular scare. Nor was he overjoyed to find Dr Ettlinger in the staffroom when he returned there. The psychiatrist was holding forth to an audience of one – Mrs Straw – about colour in the working environment. Apparently apricot, or orange, as Ettlinger termed it, was a highly unsuitable choice for a common room, liable to stimulate aggression. Predictably, too, from a psychiatrist, there were sexual implications. Red and orange were the colours of heat and passion. Listening to all this, Diamond could hardly wait for the orgies over coffee and cheese sandwiches. Not content with putting suspicions of carnality into Mrs Straw's head, Ettlinger went on to speculate that whoever had chosen such an unsuitable colour must be in urgent need of therapy. There was a deep-seated and dangerous aggression in such a personality.

To which Diamond, dressed in his paint-spattered overalls, responded, 'Rest assured, Doc, if I find him, I'll strangle him with my bare hands.'

Hearing this, Mrs Straw quit the room without her squeegee and bucket.

Ettlinger, the dour Dr Ettlinger, actually raised a smile. He could appreciate a psychological quip, even if it was directed his way. 'I didn't know you had suicidal tendencies,' he said ponderously to Diamond. 'Self-strangulation is difficult to achieve, I hear.'

Curiously enough, this bizarre conversation got both men off on a better footing. Diamond admitted that he was feeling angry — not suicidal — about the decision over Naomi. This was the first Ettlinger had heard of it. He shared in the indignation. After all, he regarded himself as the school's pet shrink.

Diamond suggested a coffee and switched on the kettle.

'I shouldn't say this about a professional colleague, but I will,' Ettlinger declared. 'Oliver Dickinson ought to be ashamed of himself. I defy any psychiatrist to diagnose autism in one session, particularly in the case of a child like Naomi, whose behaviour is predominantly passive.'

'He could be wrong?'

'I keep an open mind.'

'I remember,' said Diamond, sensing a way to prise more information from his new chum. 'But without committing yourself, is there any other explanation for the fact that she refuses to speak?'

Ettlinger's eyes twinkled in triplicate through his thick lenses. 'You want to muddy the waters a little?'

'I wouldn't say that, but I'm fishing.'

'Well, it's not impossible that this is a case of elective mutism.'

'Say that again.'

Ettlinger obliged. 'It's a psychological disorder that affects some children of three years and upwards. Something inhibits them from speaking. In certain cases this manifests itself at school and they talk normally at home. The most serious cases go totally silent, and keep it up for months and even years.'

'Can it be treated?'

'There is no cure, as such. They grow out of it, and some

of them are given help, but it's hard to say whether they would have recovered regardless. The best results are achieved one-to-one. Putting such children into a class with others is not always advisable, particularly if those others are disturbed in other ways. The child may imitate them, consciously or unconsciously.'

'And ape their behaviour?'

Ettlinger nodded.

'Such as biting?'

This drew a sly smile. 'Why not?'

Diamond was finding elective mutism increasingly plausible as a theory. 'Would this also explain the avoidance of eye-contact?'

'I wouldn't regard that as the sort of behaviour a child would notice in another,' Ettlinger said. 'However, if she is anxious to avoid speech, she will very likely shun situations requiring responses. So for that reason she may look away from people.'

'You say nobody knows the cause of this, em, what did you call it? . . . Elective, er . . .?'

'Mutism.' Ettlinger shrugged. 'One can't generalize. Sometimes school phobia is thought to trigger it. You move the child to a new school, or a new class, and the speech returns. But in most cases the onset comes earlier in the child's life and the problem isn't so clear, or so easily resolved. It may result from some emotional disturbance of which adults are unaware.'

Diamond made the coffee and handed over a steaming mug. 'In Naomi's case, she's been parted from her parents. Abandoned, possibly. Is that the kind of disturbance you mean?'

'Yes, an experience as shocking as that could amount to a trauma.'

'Trauma? That's a different ball-game.'

Ettlinger pulled a face at the analogy, making it plain that matiness had its limitations. 'I would define trauma as a deep emotional wound, an injury to the psyche.'

'Can it make a child mute?'

'Certainly.'

'And is it curable?'

'Let's say that the condition is usually of limited duration.'
'So she will recover her speech?'
'I wasn't discussing a particular case.'

Diamond conceded with a nod. 'That's another possible explanation, then. So far we have autism, elective mutism, and now, trauma.'

Ettlinger beamed. 'Have we muddied the water sufficiently?'

Diamond nodded. Confusion wasn't the object, of course; quite the contrary. He'd enlisted the support of an expert in questioning the assumption that Naomi was autistic. He hadn't enough clout to prevent her being put on that flight to Boston on Sunday, but he felt more clear in his own mind that he was right to protest.

Late that afternoon there was another boost. A call from the BBC. A generous-minded producer who had given him not a glimmer of hope that morning had since talked to someone's PA over lunch at the Television Centre, and she'd passed on the word about Naomi to her producer, who was now on the line. A new programme Diamond had never heard of called *What About the Kids?* had been running on BBC2 for two weeks, a Friday afternoon show featuring children and presented by children. It consisted mainly of two- or three-minute items such as song and dance, circus acts, animal training, a word game, demonstrations of toys, interviews with kids who'd been in the news and with adults like writers and artists who produced work for children.

The whole thing sounded like a dog's breakfast, but Diamond was careful not to say so. 'I bet the kids love it.'

'Surprisingly, the audience figures aren't all that encouraging,' the producer, who revelled in the name of Cedric Athelhampton, admitted, 'but we are back-to-back with Tin-Tin and Jackanory. The controllers are willing to live with moderate figures as long as we have some educational content, social issues and so forth. We're trying to include some items with more weight.'

Try me for size, Diamond frivolously thought. In fact, he felt lighter than air at this minute. 'You're looking for serious issues?'

'Exactly — only they have to be conveyed simply and

directly. And they must involve children, which is why I pricked up my ears when I heard about your Japanese girl. She *is* the child found in Harrods?'

'Yes.'

'And she still doesn't speak a word?'

'Not a syllable.'

'And nobody has identified her in all this time? I'll tell you how I see this, Mr Diamond. I've had a rather creative idea. We'll present it as a challenge. Do you follow me?'

With admirable self-restraint, Diamond indicated that he was keeping up.

Cedric Athelhampton's voice thickened and swelled in anticipation. 'This will really engage our audience. Kids adore playing detective. See if they recognize her from school or the park or the street where they play. Tell me, Mr Diamond, what exactly is your connection with this girl?'

He was primed for this one. 'I just took an interest in her case. Speaking of detectives, I'm ex-CID myself.'

'How divine.'

It was the first time he'd heard it so described.

The only hitch in all this euphoria was that Cedric was thinking in terms of the programme a week on Friday.

'Sorry. No chance,' said Diamond. 'Can't you slot her in this week?'

'I wish I could, ducky, but we're in pink script for Friday.'

'Does that make a difference?' he enquired, trying manfully not to let the 'ducky' unsettle him.

'It's a live show, Mr Diamond. We can't take more risks than we have to.'

'A live show for children? Is that usual?'

'Nothing about our show is usual. That's why it's so riveting. Can you come in on Friday week?'

'No. She'll be in America by then.'

'America! Whatever for?'

Without hesitation, he said, 'Prime-time television. She's going to be a sensation over there, they tell me.' He could be creative too, when pushed.

Chapter Thirteen

DAVID FLEXNER TURNED OVER THE envelope for the umpteenth time and looked at the four hastily scribbled words *Hope Venice was magic*. Schmaltz, pure schmaltz, he told himself, as an all too genuine tear misted his vision. Pop, you always knew how to pluck the heart-strings; and you always succeeded.

No question, Venice had been magic. He'd acted on Manny's advice and driven there the same night. Dropped everything, or almost everything. Bullish from handling his first executive assignment so effectively, he'd invited the winsome Pia to accompany him. To his delight, she'd laughed, squeezed his hand and accepted. They'd stayed three days and two unforgettable nights in a palace – the Hotel Cipriani on the tip of Guidecca Island, facing the Lido. Venice had been magic and so had Pia.

All of which made the aftermath – the return to Milan – even more distressing. Rico's, 'Where were you? We had no way of contacting you,' may not have been meant as a recrimination, but sounded like it. On being informed what Manny had done, David had felt overwhelmed by guilt. Only afterwards, during the flight to New York, did he mentally run through the sequence of events and accept that his father had wished it this way, wished him to get away – actually to enjoy himself – before he learned the terrible news.

Manny had fallen twenty-one floors and died on impact with the parking lot. Cancer would have taken him in a matter of months. A double shock for David.

On arrival at JFK, he was met by Michael Leapman, who embraced him supportively and handed him the letter from his father. He didn't immediately open it. The message on the back was as much as he could take at this time. At David's own suggestion, they drove straight to the morgue and went through the necessary ordeal of identification. Amazingly Manny's face was unmarked. There was damage to the base of the skull, the mortician explained, but he had hit the ground feet first. For the viewing of the corpse, everything was covered except the face. Prepared for injuries so extreme that he would have difficulty in recognizing his father, David was surprised and deeply moved to see the features he'd known and loved. He stooped to kiss Manny's forehead and whisper a farewell, and, as he did so, a curious thing happened. David's hair, fastened as usual in a ponytail, slipped off his shoulder and flopped over the pale face. Quickly he drew it aside and Manny's left eye opened. The dragging movement of the hair must have been responsible, but the effect was startling. It was almost as if his father winked at him. Straight away he stroked his hand over the face and closed the eyelid. The incident was over so rapidly that the others may not even have noticed. Certainly nothing was said.

Out in the daylight, Michael Leapman suggested a drink before returning to the office. They picked an Irish bar on the next block. 'You may wish to catch up on your letter,' Leapman suggested when they were seated. There was something else besides sympathy in his manner, and it was not unlike respect. In their previous encounters in the boardroom, more often than not he'd disregarded David – but then so had most of the other directors.

'Later.'

'Don't get me wrong. I don't want to be a drag, only I think you should look at it now, before we check in at the office. If it's anything like the letter I had, there are things to be done real soon.'

Leapman was right, David discovered. It was that sort of letter – Manny still calling the tune. Just one sentence to indicate that this was a suicide note: *'Sorry it had to happen like this, Davey, but you know me – couldn't ever wait for a darned thing.'* Then straight to business: *'I want you to take* over as Chairman. *My entire estate, including my holdings of shares, will come to you. I told Michael Leapman my wishes and he's promised his support. He'll propose you for Chairman at an Emergency Meeting I've asked him to convene. The Board will back you. It's essential there's no delay, no perceived reluctance from you, or the stock will drop and the predators will swallow us. Handle it as positively as you just handled the problem in Milan and we'll get through without damage, hell, no, we'll prosper. Take my word for it, Davey, when you're in charge, you'll be on a permanent high. Just remember you're the boss. You take the initiative, right? You need technical advice, take it, only don't let anyone railroad you. I don't mind admitting Manflex is short on new products that will pay off in the next decade. You have some major decisions to take. In this industry you can't play safe for ever. I could go on, but I figure I've said enough. You're going to make it, I know you are, kid.'* He'd signed it: *'Your loving Pop.'*

David sat rigidly in his chair and read the letter a second time. You can take so many shocks and then you enter a catatonic state. He felt close to that. *Chairman of Manflex —* it was bizarre. He'd never seriously contemplated such an outcome. He'd always assumed that the family would retain a major stake in the business after Manny went, but that others would undertake the management. He'd be content to keep his nominal seat on the Board without ever burdening himself with policy decisions. He was into creative things, not pesky pills.

He leaned against the banquette and looked towards the ceiling.

'He surprised you?' Leapman queried.

'That's an understatement.'

'I urged him to speak to you, tell you his plans. He wouldn't have it. Said something about having management thrust upon you. Thought you'd function best if it came without warning.'

David's eyes switched to Leapman. 'Do you mean he told you he was planning to kill himself?'

'No. Well, not in a way that I understood.' Leapman nervously fingered his tie.

'He told you about the cancer?'

'Yes.'

'And what exactly did he say he would do about it?'

Leapman examined his beer intently, as if the answer to David's question might rise to the surface.

'Go on,' David insisted. 'I want to know.'

'He, em – this is embarrassing – he said he was going to . . . step down.'

David's lips softened slowly into a grin and the grin turned to a laugh, the first breach in the gloom since he'd heard that Manny was dead. 'And he stepped down twenty-one floors. That's typical of Pop. A bad-taste joke about his own suicide. Come on, Michael, I don't mind if you laugh. Pop certainly wouldn't. You bet he enjoyed saying it.'

Leapman mustered a smile from somewhere. He'd never been in tune with Manny's humour.

David found it comical, the more so when he imagined his father's secret enjoyment in seeding the idea to his solemn sidekick. 'So did he also tell you he wanted me to step up, so to speak?'

Leapman nodded.

'Did you think he was out of his mind? Be honest.'

'It was unexpected. But you can count on my total support,' Leapman added quickly.

'I'm going to need it.' A declaration of intent from David. Suddenly, intuitively, but irreversibly, he'd made the greatest decision in his life. He would give the job his best shot, in spite of his contempt for the business world. The mission to Milan had boosted his estimate of his own ability as an executive. Manny had been wise, as well as witty. He was right about the high to be had from being in control. 'The shareholders have to be reassured,' he said as if the matter had been utmost in his mind for weeks. 'What's been happening to our stock price? I saw in the plane it fell sharply when the news broke.'

'Down another six points this morning. Someone is going to stage a raid unless we buck the trend.'

'A takeover, you mean?'

'That's the danger. The bastards know that there's value there. It's all about loss of confidence. We go into decline and they wait for the moment to strike.'

'And then they break us up.'

'It could happen very soon.'

'Unless we act.'

'Right.' Leapman ran his right forefinger slowly around the rim of his glass. 'To restore confidence you need something positive to tell the market. Thanks to your father, we have the reputation of being rock-solid, or did, until the last couple of weeks. We have a good base of OTC products—'

'OTC?'

Over the counter. Consumer brands. And Kaprofix is still one of the top prescription drugs for angina.'

'But could be overtaken soon?'

'Already has been. Adalat-Procardia has raced ahead of us.'

'Whose is that?'

'It's jointly produced by Bayer and Pfizer. And Marion-M Dow are making inroads with their drug.'

'We must have plenty of things under development.'

Leapman shook his head. 'Not for the angina market. And the patents of Kaprofix start expiring in 1993.'

'That means our competitors can market me-too imitations?'

'Right.'

There was a bleak period of silence.

David resumed, 'It's becoming screamingly obvious that I need to bone up on our research and development programme. You're closer to it than I am, Michael. Is there anything at a promising stage? My father implied in his letter that decisions had to be taken soon.'

'That's a tough one,' Leapman hedged. 'Sure, I can run through the possibilities with you, only I'd rather do it in the office with some figures in front of me.'

'Good enough. Let's go.'

Leapman hesitated. 'Something I wanted to mention. There's a guy you really should meet. Professor Alaric Churchward, from Corydon University.'

'Corydon? Where in hell is that?'

'Indianapolis. They specialize in the biological sciences. I think they were established during the Kennedy

Administration, or soon after, about the time when the potential of genetics began to be appreciated.'

'After the DNA code was broken?'

He nodded. 'Churchward joined them from Yale about 1981, I believe. If you had to pick out a future Nobel Laureate, he'd be the obvious choice.'

'And you think he would be useful to us?'

'He already is. We have strong links with Corydon, thanks to your father. We're funding a good proportion of the research that goes on there.'

'In genetic engineering, you mean?' David's voice was pitched on a note of unease.

'You don't have to sound so dubious,' Leapman gently chided him. 'Genetically-engineered drugs are the future of our industry. The great advances in medical health from now on are going to be made by geneticists. They already provided us with safer and better insulin for diabetics. In the next twenty years, they're going to produce vaccines for every disease you care to name.' He paused and took more beer. 'But as it happens, the latest breakthrough owes nothing at all to biotechnology.'

'A breakthrough? You really mean that?'

Leapman actually summoned up a smile. 'From old-fashioned chemical compounds, David.'

'A drug?'

He nodded.

'What for – which disease?'

'The most prevalent killer of all.'

'Cancer?'

'Old age, David. Old age.'

Chapter Fourteen

MANNY FLEXNER'S FUNERAL SERVICE TOOK place in the ante-chapel of the Temple Emanu-El on Fifth Avenue, the world's largest synagogue. The attendance of over two hundred and fifty was a measure of his popularity; Jews, gentiles, a broad cross-section of New York society. 'He was a much-loved man,' the rabbi said in his address, admittedly something of a cliché in funeral orations, but in this case it was true on several counts, most obviously the high count of attractive women in the congregation.

Later the same afternoon, while most of the family were still crowded into the house on the Upper East Side eating sandwiches and trading stories about Manny's escapades in love and business, an Emergency Board Meeting was held at the Manflex headquarters. David Flexner was proposed as the new Chairman and elected unopposed. Michael Leapman, his proposer, made it clear that this had been Manny's wish. The seven executive and two non-executive members applauded politely and a bottle of champagne was opened. The price of Manflex stock, which had been falling all week, picked up a few points by the close of trading.

'Better news, then,' David remarked, when Leapman told him.

'Sorry, but it isn't. The price rose on a rumour that someone is buying shares in significant numbers. The market senses a takeover bid.'

'So soon?'

'Sharks are fast movers. We've taken a hard knock and they scent blood.'

Vehemently, by his easy-going standard, David said,

'They can go to hell, Michael. No asset-stripper is going to tear Manflex apart. It was my father's life. Thousands of other lives are staked in it. I have a responsibility to the work-force.'

Leapman rested a hand on his shoulder. 'Don't let it get to you, David. This is the way the market works, unfortunately.'

'It's all about confidence, right?' said David. 'We have to demonstrate that Manflex has a future under my management.'

'Sure – and if we play it right—'

'I know what you're going to say, but it seems incredible to me that the survival of a great pharmaceuticals group like ours can hang on one blockbuster. Damn it, we sell hundreds of products.'

'So do our competitors. But where would Glaxo be without Zantac, or SmithKline Beecham without Tagamet? In reality what you need is a steady flow of new products, but that requires an incredible outlay on research. Have you any idea how many drugs are patented and tested for every one that is successful? Five thousand, David. Five thousand to one. Those are the odds in this business. We're not equipped to compete on that scale, not any more.'

'Okay, I get the point. I must meet with Professor Churchward just as soon as possible. Does that mean a trip to Indianapolis?'

Leapman nodded. 'How soon do you want to go?'

'The next available flight, I guess. Really I should be back at the house with the family right now. They'll have to make allowances.'

'Can't you tell them it's important business?'

'You know what they'll say? "Isn't he just like his father?" '

They took the plane that evening and spent the night at the Hilton-at-the-Circle in Indianapolis. After breakfast, they took a taxi out to Corydon University, some fifteen minutes' drive west along Washington Street and beyond the airport. Leapman filled in some background on the man they were about to meet. 'He didn't discover PDM3, but he was the first to see its potential. He's been working on a treatment for Alzheimer's disease for at least ten years, originally for his PhD, I believe. About five years ago he started testing a compound that seemed to have some potential in combating the memory loss associated with Alzheimer's. We called it Prodermolate, or PDM3. The first results were promising, no more, but lately – and I mean just in the past few weeks – he's come up with some results that can only be described as sensational, David. They have implications not just for Alzheimer's, but for the mental capacities of the population at large.'

'You said my father knew about this project?' David enquired.

'Sure, Manny knew. He met Prof Churchward several times.'

'So what was his assessment?'

'Of Churchward?'

'Of PDM3.'

'He gave it his backing.'

'You mean he was willing to stake the future of Manflex on it?'

Leapman shook his head. 'He didn't have the information we have.'

'But it's only just over a week since he died. Has it all taken off since then?'

Leapman put his hand to his face and as if heralding a sensitive matter. 'Well, David, Manny was a terrific guy and we all loved him—'

'But?'

'But towards the end he had his mind on other things. I don't blame him for that. When he told me about his terminal illness, I saw problems for the business, so I did what anyone in my position would do – discreetly took the pulse of the company. I asked for an update on all the research that we were undertaking, right across the world. That was how I learned that Churchward was almost ready to publish these fantastic results with PDM3.'

'You didn't discuss it with Pop?'

'I left it too late.'

Corydon University campus was compact and unfussy. Not an ivy leaf in sight. Solid sixties pre-structured building with some computer-age additions. Security cameras at the entrance. A black-uniformed receptionist flanked by video screens and with a console in front of him. He keyed in their names and they watched them appear on one of the monitors. Then they had to go through the ritual of being photographed for identity tags. Finally, Professor Churchward's secretary arrived — a demure young woman with a tag that read *Bridget Walkswell* fixed on her shirtfront. She looked the sort who would suffer acute embarrassment if anyone made a joke of her name. With a walk so innocent of any suggestion of a wiggle that she must have worked on it in front of a mirror, she escorted them to an elevator.

They stepped out into a low-ceilinged laboratory bristling with equipment, huge transparent cylinders on stands and metal structures festooned with white tubing and electric flex. Buff-coloured notices were prominent everywhere warning of biohazards such as mouth-pipetting. The steady hum of computers from the far end drew their attention to a series of keyboards and screens ranged along a bench. Something very like a submarine periscope was mounted there. It was being used by a slight, dark-haired man in a white coat.

Bridget Walkswell announced them.

'One moment,' the professor said without moving from the eyepiece. He touched an adjustment control. Beside him on a video display there was a small movement in a pattern looking like a Chinese ideogram which David recognized as a configuration of DNA, the genetic blueprint. The professor continued with what he was doing for another half-minute or so. When he eventually drew back, he still didn't give his visitors a glance. His chair was on casters and he glided to his right and tapped something into the nearest computer.

Without exactly apologizing for her boss, Ms Walkswell spread her hands in what amounted to a gesture of helplessness and then brought out two stools from under the bench. David and Leapman sat and waited.

Finally Professor Churchward swivelled around and said, 'So are we in business, gentlemen?' – at the same time snapping his fingers and gesturing towards the door. Ms Walkswell left the room.

Obviously the great man had more interesting things to do with his time than talk to a couple of business execs from New York. However, he offered them coffee, gesturing to a beaker of water simmering over a Bunsen burner. Beside it were some chipped mugs and unwashed spoons. Speaking almost in unison, they said they'd only just finished breakfast.

Churchward looked like a marathon runner, without an ounce of spare flesh, but his metabolism didn't require athletics to keep him in shape. He was one of the type who burn up energy without getting out of a chair. His intense blue eyes, lodged in a small, bony face, flicked over David's casual attire, missing nothing. There was no clue as to what he thought. He wore a plain brown tie and his own hair was as short as a marine's.

'David took over as Chairman of Manflex yesterday,' Michael Leapman explained.

Churchward nodded as if he already knew. No words of regret about Manny's passing. 'And you want an update from me on Prodermolate. You know the background?'

'Let's assume I know nothing,' said David, who knew not very much.

'As you wish. The compound that we call PDM3 was discovered as long ago as 1975 by a team at Cornell. They were funded by Beaver River Chemicals, which is now a Manflex subsidiary, as I guess you know. The formula was registered along with a million others, but it wasn't considered to be of any commercial use until about five years back, when a decision was taken in this department to initiate research into protective agents. You know what I mean?'

David frowned. The question was addressed to him and he felt that he ought to make a stab. 'Contraceptives?'

The professor closed his eyes and took a deep, restorative breath before opening them again. 'Protective agents are drugs that appear to protect certain of the nerve cells in the brain from dying. Nobody understands why. Your father, who kept up with developments, knew that some of his rivals in the industry were doing work in this field. The richest prize in the industry is a drug to treat Alzheimer's disease.'

'That much I do know,' said David.

Churchward nodded. 'Companies like Janssen and Miles had already started preclinical trials with drugs they had patented, so your father asked the people here to see if they had anything of potential use in the treatment of Alzheimer's.'

'And someone remembered PDM3?'

'Not at all.' Professor Churchward had no inhibitions about putting David down. 'Things don't happen like that. It was one of numerous compounds that were dusted off and tried. Targeted research is more rare than you would think in the discovery of medicines. We still rely heavily on blanket testing for biological activity. The first results were interesting, but not spectacular. PDM3 didn't promise anything remarkable in preclinical. Do you have any idea what I'm talking about? Do you know about the testing procedure?' he asked with intimidation.

This time David restricted himself to raising his eyebrows equivocally.

'I'm referring to the series of tests every drug is put through before it gets approval.'

'Ah – I'm with you,' David responded. 'In the preclinical stage, you're restricted to experiments on animals.'

Grudgingly, Churchward conceded, 'Correct. If that's satisfactory you go on to Phase One, which is merely testing for safety in a small sample of humans. In Phase Two you test for effectiveness, still using small numbers of humans. We've done all that. PDM3 has gone through Phase Two and now we're ready to undertake the third phase, the extensive clinical trials. Assuming they go well – and I've no reason to think they won't – we take it in front of the FDA.' He added, as if to a child, 'The Food and Drug Administration.'

'And when they recommend approval, we're in business?'

'And how!' murmured Leapman.

'You really believe this drug is something special?' David asked.

'Something special?' The professor hesitated, as if weighing his response. 'What we have, Mr Flexner, is the equivalent, in pharmacological terms, of the splitting of the atom.'

Goosebumps formed on the backs of David's arms. In his experience, scientists weren't given to such extravagant claims.

Professor Churchward said, 'PDM3 is not a protective agent. It is a regenerative agent. It enables dying nerve cells to grow and regenerate. No other substance in the pharmacopoeia is capable of that.'

'Brain cells *regenerate*?'

'Yes. Do you see the possibilities? This goes way beyond the treatment of Alzheimer's disease. We have the means of sustaining our mental ability indefinitely. There's no reason why we shouldn't make the drug available to healthy people. Young people. Men and women of forty can expect their brains to function just as efficiently when they are eighty. The drug will eliminate the process of ageing.'

'You mean mental ageing?'

Churchward reddened. 'Be reasonable. I wasn't suggesting we can make old men young again. That's a job for plastic surgery.'

'So it doesn't increase the expectation of life?'

He spread his hands in exasperation. 'What do you want from me, Mr Flexner?'

David told him coolly, 'I'm trying to get a grasp of this discovery, Professor. If you're looking for congratulations, fine. I salute you. I also want to make sure I fully understand you.'

'David, the potential is fantastic,' Leapman waded in fast. 'People will be capable of a longer working life if they want it. They won't be such a drain on the social budget. They can look after themselves for longer. Men and women of genius will be enabled to go on enriching the world for the rest of their lives instead of fading into senility.'

'And we're ahead of the field on this?'

'There are no other runners,' said Leapman.

110

'Some research is being done with nerve growth factor from naturally occurring brain substances,' Churchward thought fit to add, 'but it's at an early stage, and of course it's organic in origin.'

Leapman said, 'They can't compete with a drug.'

'You're quite sure we have it patented?'

'You bet we do.'

'What about ADRs?' David wasn't entirely ignorant of the jargon. An ADR was an adverse drug reaction, a side-effect.

'As you doubtless know,' said Churchward with unconcealed irony, 'every drug has ADRs. It's a matter of weighing them against the benefits. PDM3 has some temporary contra-indications. It produces mild headaches in some subjects, nausea and dizziness, but we also noted those effects in people receiving a placebo drug.'

'To the same degree?'

'Not quite the same,' he admitted. 'However, a high proportion of the subjects manifested no ADRs at all.'

'What proportion?'

'Up to sixty-eight per cent.'

The figure was meant to impress David, and it did. 'What about long-term effects? I suppose it's too soon to judge.'

The professor said, 'There is no evidence of any long-term ADRs.'

'There wouldn't be, would there? Did you detect any ADRs in the animal tests?'

'In a few cases, slight elevations in liver enzymes.'

'Isn't that a problem?'

' "A problem" would be putting it far too strongly. The liver has an excellent facility for regeneration, so if the dosage is monitored correctly, there is no danger.'

'How do you tell, Professor?'

'By taking blood samples.'

'If we want to market the drug, we can't expect people to subject themselves to blood-tests,' said David, realizing as he spoke that the remark was naive.

Churchward clicked his tongue and said nothing.

Leapman cleared his throat and said, 'I think there's a slight confusion here.'

'I'm confident that we can resolve the matter in the trials,' said Churchward. 'It comes down to an acceptable dosage, if that is a term we all understand.'

Almost everything the professor said was laced with contempt, and David couldn't understand why. He felt inept. He was sure his father would have handled this interview with less confrontation — in fact, with a mix of humour and cheek — yet Manny would still have managed to elicit the crucial facts. 'Don't get me wrong,' he said. 'I'm just trying to cover every angle. I understand about adverse reactions. I take your point that every drug has them to a greater or lesser degree. If you want to stop a cancer, you don't care so much if your hair falls out, right? The difference is that we wouldn't be treating a *disease* with PDM3.'

'We'd treat Alzheimer's,' said Leapman.

'Yes, but the professor is talking about offering this drug to fit people.'

'Hold on,' said Churchward. 'The first thing is that PDM3 is remarkably effective in the treatment of Alzheimer's, which was the subject of my research. We can safely go to Phase Three now.'

'But you're also confident that it improves the function of the healthy brain.'

'Improves, no,' Churchward corrected him. 'It can extend the time-scale of its efficiency.'

'Fine — but if we sell it to healthy people we're not balancing those ADRs, the nausea and the giddiness and the increase in liver enzymes, against a dangerous disease. We're asking them to accept risks.'

'I don't accept that. Let's not talk about risks. We would eliminate risks. There might be some inconvenience or discomfort,' said Churchward. 'That's up to them. Plenty of popular foods and drinks produce more disagreeable symptoms than PDM3. Health products, too. You take a multivitamin and there's a chance it will give you constipation.'

'So PDM3 is as safe as a vitamin tablet?'

'In the proper dosage, yes.'

'It's what Manny was looking for all his life,' said Leapman, spacing his words and speaking on a rising, evangelical note. 'A surefire product that will take the mass market by storm.'

David thought of his father. He remembered that bizarre wink in the morgue. The incident couldn't have meant anything, but it would never be erased from his memory. 'So when do we go public on this?'

'I'd say tomorrow if we want to keep Manflex afloat,' said Leapman. Quick to note David's startled reaction, he added, 'At this stage, we just have to announce tomorrow that we'll be hosting a conference soon to present the first studies of a new drug for Alzheimer's. That's enough to restore some confidence.'

The decision couldn't be put off. Now David felt his sweat go cold against his T-shirt. He looked towards Churchward.

'That's fine by me, gentlemen,' the professor said, positively fraternal. 'I'm ready to publish.'

'We're not going into production yet,' Leapman told David in reassurance.

'Yes, but once we've made this announcement, there's no drawing back, or it'll play hell with our rating on the stock market.'

'Agreed,' Leapman said cheerfully.

David was still troubled. 'The next step is going to require funding. Millions, probably. Clinical trials on a wide scale don't come cheap. And if we get FDA approval, we'll require massive new investment to launch this drug.'

'So we raise capital.'

'In a world recession?'

'We've got to be bold, David, or, frankly, Manflex is finished.' Leapman moved closer and said confidentially, 'Actually, I have some suggestions about additional finance that I can put to you later.'

Chapter Fifteen

WITH HER DRAWING PAD TUCKED under her arm and the marker pen in her fist, Naomi stepped into the waiting taxi as confidently as royalty. Just in case the little girl was more uneasy than she appeared, Diamond tried to enliven the short journey by pointing out the London buses they passed. After ten or so, he gave up. Naomi didn't need distracting.

Julia Musgrave had wanted to buy her a special dress with a lace collar until Diamond had reminded her of the reason why the child was going in front of the television cameras. So she was in clothes similar to those she had been found in – a brown and white check dress from Marks and Spencer, and white tights and trainers.

For a moment when the taxi circled the fountain in front of the Television Centre at Shepherd's Bush, a small hand reached for Diamond's and gripped it tightly. Nerves? He wasn't convinced. Maybe she thinks I'm looking jittery, he told himself.

In the course of his police career, he had notched up plenty of television appearances, so by rights he shouldn't have had any anxieties. But he was nagged by doubts whether an appeal for information on *Crimewatch* was any preparation for *What About the Kids?*

He had been asked to report to the reception desk with Naomi by ten on Friday morning, and also to be patient, because Cedric was going to fit them in when an opportunity came; there was no way of predicting how soon it would be.

They were taken up to the hospitality suite. The purpose of such places is allegedly to put visitors at their

114

ease. Diamond's confidence plunged as he stepped inside. He was a misfit here. The hospitality amounted to a stack of canned cola and plates of doughnuts and Penguin biscuits. Toys of various kinds were scattered invitingly around the leather and steel furniture. Naomi, for her part, appeared as indifferent to the food and the toys as Diamond was. She squatted on the carpeted floor and was soon completely absorbed in her drawing.

There are certain pivotal moments in any fanatical enterprise when you are compelled to pause, look around you and take stock. It wasn't the toys or the doughnuts that pulled Diamond up short, nor the arrival of three small girls in pink satin frocks, nor the boy with a punk haircut who came in on a skateboard. The critical factor was Sally, a deceptively docile-looking chimpanzee accompanied by a grey-haired woman wearing gauntlet gloves. Hardly had Sally been carried in and deposited at the far end of the settee where Diamond was seated before she started jumping and shrieking. The creature wasn't in distress, the woman assured them, nor was she nervous about appearing on TV. Sally, it seemed, was a regular, the mainstay of the programme. No, Sally was screaming out of sheer high spirits, because she was happy.

Moreover, she wanted to share her happiness with Diamond. Dressed in a red leather harness, but given a fair amount of play on the rein held by her trainer, she was allowed to venture within a yard or so of Diamond (it was a fine judgment on the trainer's part) and flail her arms in his direction. Then she bared her teeth and screamed.

Because she was happy.

That morning over breakfast, he'd told Stephanie where he would be spending the day, remarking bleakly that a kids' TV programme was a far cry from police work. Steph had pointed out that he was a free agent now. If he wanted to go through hoops for young Naomi, fine, but he'd better not forget that it was a self-imposed quest. 'What you mean,' he'd summed it up for her, 'is stop griping.'

She hadn't disagreed.

So if Peter Diamond, notoriously short-fused, was willing to share a settee with a screaming ape, something fundamental must have happened in his life, and it had. The fate of one small, silent girl now governed him; and all she had done was place her hand in his a few times.

Not wanting to make waves, he endured a full fifteen seconds of Sally the chimp before moving to another chair. He even smiled good-naturedly at the trainer, acting on a shrewd suspicion that if it came to a show-down, he and Naomi would be out on the street, not Sally.

Not to be denied, the chimp continued to make screaming sorties in his direction.

'She likes you,' the woman declared in that evasion often used by owners of animals that terrorize other people. 'She's really taken a shine to you.'

Relief presently arrived in the person of a bright-eyed young woman who introduced herself as Justine and said she was Cedric's personal assistant. At her side was a black boy looking not much older than Naomi. 'This is Curtis who'll be interviewing you,' Justine said, and explained as Diamond's eyebrows shot up, 'The programme is entirely presented by kids.' And with that, Justine smiled and left.

Curtis winked. He was wearing a red baseball cap and a black T-shirt with the programme's title across the front in white lettering. He extended a small hand to Diamond. 'Pete – you don't mind if I call you Pete? – I'm really sorry I can't tell you when we'll do our spot,' he said, sounding like someone five times his age, 'but I thought you and Naomi might like to see inside the studio while we have the chance.'

'We'd appreciate that,' Pete confirmed. About the only other person in the world who used the short form of his name was Stephanie. On a snap assessment, Curtis was worth making an exception for. No one else in the hospitality suite had been winkled out by their interviewer to become familiar with the studio.

Naomi had to be helped to her feet, she was so engrossed in her drawing.

'Is that Japanese writing?' Curtis asked.

'It's a nice idea, but I don't believe so,' Diamond answered after a glance at the sheet, which was decorated once again with diamond shapes. 'You know, of course, that she doesn't speak?'

'You bet I do, Pete,' came the answer. Curtis led them at a springy step through a couple of swing doors into the studio, a cavernous place, in semi-darkness except for the set of a pirate ship, where the technicians were setting up. With a caution to watch out for cables, Curtis made a beeline for an unlighted stage dressed up as an airport departure lounge, but scaled to child-size. Through a window, a model Jumbo jet was visible on a realistic-looking runway.

'It's one of our permanent sets, no kidding. Isn't it the pits?' Curtis apologized. 'You're supposed to think this is where the action is. The jet-set, get it? It's where Cedric wants to shoot us.'

In view of the flight to Boston being planned for Naomi, the choice was not inappropriate and Diamond said as much to Curtis. 'The only problem is that I'm going to look like King Kong in a set that size,' he added.

'No sweat, Pete,' Curtis assured him. 'The cameraman can take care of that.' Whether such touching faith was justified was another question, but the boy couldn't have been more reassuring as he went on to outline the kind of interview he wanted to conduct. 'The way I see it, we need to get across the story of how Naomi was found. You were in Harrods that night, am I right?'

Diamond nodded.

'So we'll talk about how she caused a major alert, and then I'll ask you who she is and how she got there, and you'll say nobody knows, right? Then you'd better tell me she doesn't speak at all. Cedric says we should skip the reasons for that. Keep it simple.'

'Agreed,' said Diamond, warming to these people. He didn't want Naomi labelled as autistic, or in any way mentally impaired. Far better if her mutism was just presented as a fact.

'Okay, then,' said Curtis. 'The point I'll be making is that we need help with this mystery.' He paused, made quote signs with his fingers and spaced his words. 'Who . . . is . . . Naomi? Cut to a close-up of Naomi. We want people to look at her and say to themselves, "Jeez, where have I seen this chick before?" '

No question – the boy was a pro.

'And that's it?' said Diamond.

'Unless you have something else you want to throw in.'

'You've covered it.'

'Like to see the other sets?'

While this was going on, Naomi had remained at Diamond's side, her drawing pad held across her chest. Now that the conversation had entered a new, less earnest phase, she began shifting her feet as if she wanted to leave the studio.

Curtis shot her a glance and asked, 'Does she want the girls' room?'

'What?' Diamond was nonplussed.

'The girls' room. The loo. How do you know if she wants to go?'

This wasn't a contingency he'd foreseen. Being responsible for a small girl brought complications. 'You'd better show us where it is, Curtis.'

The toilets were next to the hospitality suite. As soon as Naomi sighted the doors she handed her drawing pad and marker to Diamond and ran ahead. Interestingly she understood the symbols, because she didn't falter over the choice.

Curtis looked up at the clock and promised to rejoin them after lunch, when they'd be wanted in make-up. He gave directions to the canteen. With a wink and a smile he left Diamond waiting uncertainly outside the toilets. There was no telling whether the little girl could manage unaided, and as luck would have it, no woman came by, or he'd have asked her to check.

Strewth, if the lads in the Avon and Somerset Police could see me now, Diamond mused.

Then she emerged composed and in good order. Together they went to explore the BBC canteen. The pace started to accelerate.

Lunch.

Make-up.

Back to the hospitality suite.

Curtis, by now dressed in a red shirt and black bow-tie, kept them up to date with the programme schedule. It

118

seemed they might be included between the trio in pink satin and the skateboarder. Meanwhile Naomi continued with her drawing.

'She may be trying to tell you something. Have you thought of that?' Curtis commented.

'With the drawing, you mean? Certainly I have,' Diamond said, 'only I haven't cracked it yet.'

Curtis took another look over Naomi's shoulder. 'Is it a logo? You know, like you see in ads?'

'The diamond shape? Off the cuff I can't think of any business that uses it.'

'Have you noticed she doesn't shade them in? When most kids draw a shape like that, they fill it in.'

This was an observation he hadn't considered. For the moment he couldn't see its relevance, but Curtis was ahead of him.

'Could be something you see through, like those funny windows in old houses.'

Leaded windows.

'That's a fascinating suggestion, Curtis.'

'No fee,' said Curtis. 'I'd better get back to the control room now. Stay cool.' He strolled out, clicking his fingers to some tune pounding in his head.

Diamond weighed Curtis's idea. If Naomi had lived in a house with lattice windows, this could be a genuine clue. He levered his weight out of the chair and ponderously lowered himself to kneel beside her.

She stopped drawing and eased back on her thighs.

He studied the marks she had made on the paper. Some of them, at any rate, were joined at the corners. Maybe it was inevitable when she was drawing so many. He held out his hand and said, 'May I use the marker?'

She handed it to him. Not only did she understand, but she trusted him with the precious marker. A good sign.

He turned to a fresh sheet and started drawing diamonds linked at the corners. It would have been simpler to have drawn two sets of intersecting diagonal lines, but he reckoned Naomi's conception began with the basic shape, so he worked from that, gradually building a grid.

She watched him at work, and he was encouraged, even though she remained passive. He completed the drawing by squaring it off with straight lines to represent a frame, and he had a passable lattice window. He handed it back to her. 'How about that?'

She gave his work serious attention, studying it as earnestly as if she were one of the Hanging Committee at the Royal Academy. She put out her hand and traced the grid with her fingertips. It seemed that something wasn't done to her satisfaction.

'You want curtains?' said Diamond. He reached for the drawing pad, but she refused to give it up. Instead, she held out her hand for the marker.

He passed it across.

Concentrating deeply, she leaned so far over the drawing pad that her hair flopped forward, exposing the narrow white nape of her neck. She was working on the area at the top of the sheet, above the window Diamond had drawn. He couldn't see it until she sat back.

This time she had baffled him completely by adding two rectangles and a small circle:

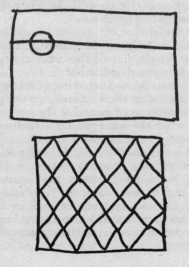

He was beginning to feel as if this were some kind of game for people with higher IQs than he possessed. He'd never mastered the Rubik Cube. He'd given up trying after one of Steph's brownies had demonstrated how to do the thing in a few rapid twists.

Curtis released him from further brain strain by coming back and saying they were wanted in the studio now. Naomi stood up immediately, not only appearing to understand, but seeming keen to get on with the real business of the day. The visit to the Television Centre had animated her; a pity Julia Musgrave hadn't been here to see it.

On the set, an adult-sized chair had been found for Diamond, the only drawback being that it was so low to the ground that he suspected six inches had been sawn off the legs. 'Just don't expect me to stand up while the cameras are rolling,' he warned Curtis, who was standing beside him for the interview.

Opposite them, Naomi perched serenely on a child-size upholstered bench. She appeared more interested in the model air-liner visible through the window than the cameras, and the floor manager had to snap his fingers to get her attention.

Then came the signal.

Smoothly, Curtis talked to the camera. Kids everywhere, he said, fancied themselves as detectives, and now they were getting the chance to solve a real-life mystery. In a few graphic sentences he gave the background, the terrorist alert in Harrods and the discovery of the small girl, his cue to introduce Diamond.

The interview went precisely as planned, with no trick questions and no stumbling answers. Afterwards, there was a chance to watch a recording, and Diamond was pleased to see how strongly the appeal to the viewers came over. Cedric Athelhampton emerged at last from the control room, a pencil-thin man dressed entirely in white, and shook Diamond's hand. 'Stunning, my love, simply stunning. You must have been hand-crafted for television, every chunky pound of you, did you know that? Such a substantial presence, a marvellous contrast with the little

121

girl. My only problem now is that I didn't warn the BBC about the calls. I'm perfectly certain the switchboard's jammed already. I'm going to get it in the neck, but it was bloody good television, and I'll say so in my defence.'

'What about these calls?' Diamond asked. suddenly perturbed.

'What do you mean?'

'Who's taking them?'

'They're being put through to my office, to my assistant, Justine, at present. Between you, me and the BBC, ninety-nine per cent will be duff. The proverbial pisspot full of crab-apples. Kids get carried away when someone with Curtis's charm and flair makes an appeal for information. Isn't he irresistible?'

Diamond was in no frame of mind for discussing anyone's charm and flair. He was furious with himself for failing to think ahead. He'd been far too preoccupied with the programme. 'Right now I'm interested in the calls, the one per cent. Is Justine capable of recognizing the real thing?'

Cedric smiled roguishly. 'The real thing? How would I know?' Reacting fast to Diamond's glare, he added, 'She's bright, as bright as a guardsman's buttons. Don't fret.' He squeezed Diamond's arm. 'We'll let you know if we strike lucky.'

But Diamond wasn't satisfied. He insisted on being taken to the office where Justine was answering the phone.

She had a notepad open and a pencil in her hand, and was talking into a headset. 'Thank you, dear. Now give the phone to Mummy.' She glanced up at Diamond. 'Sodding little brats.' She pressed another switch and said wearily, '*Where Are the Kids?* . . . Where exactly did you see her? . . . *The King and I?* Do you mean the film with Yul Brynner? . . . Thank you, I've made a note of it . . .'

Maybe it wasn't opportune to ask if any of the calls seemed promising.

Justine said, 'The parents give them these ideas. They must do. They're dafter than the kids.' She told Diamond, 'I know why you're here. I've been doing this for over an hour and they're still coming in non-stop. Do me a favour and get me a sarnie and an orange juice from the canteen, would you? By then I might have got myself sorted.'

He didn't argue; he was going to have to rely on Justine.

She'd removed the headset when he returned. She bit hungrily into the sandwich. 'Thanks. What do I owe you?'

'Just a summing-up,' he told her. 'Have we struck gold, or not?'

'You're the judge of that. What it boils down to is at least twelve callers who swear they know her, at school, or in a dancing class, or something. I've got their numbers so you can call them back. And there was one spooky call.'

'What do you mean – spooky?'

'I didn't like the sound of it one bit. A Japanese woman. Well, I think she was Japanese. She sounded Japanese to me.'

'Did she give her name?'

'No. That's the point. She refused. And she didn't say anything about knowing who Naomi is, like all the other callers did. All she would say was that she was under instructions to send you a message. A taxi would be sent for you at seven.'

'Sent here?'

'Yes. If you really want to help Naomi, you're to get into the taxi, both of you.'

'Naomi as well?'

'Yes.'

'That was all? She didn't say where the taxi would take us?'

Justine shook her head. 'Will you do it?'

'Did you get the impression she was serious?'

'Mr Diamond, she was so serious that if I were you I'd think twice about going.'

'I'm not looking for a bunch of laughs,' said Diamond. 'What time is it now?'

Chapter Sixteen

QUICK REACTIONS CAN BE VITAL to success; they can also get you into trouble. In the taxi, Diamond remembered he was no longer a senior policeman. He was doing the professional thing, following the only real lead to come out of the television programme. But as a detective acting on a tip-off he would have routinely radioed his movements to headquarters.

He asked the driver where they were going.

'My lips are sealed, mate.'

'Oh, come on!'

'The Albert Hall.'

'Get stuffed.'

He should have phoned the school, or at least got someone to pass a message to Julia Musgrave. For a middle-aged man to transport a small girl around London without informing her guardians wasn't just misguided, it deserved all the outrage it would trigger. The point wasn't that Julia would suspect him of abducting the child – she'd credited him with some responsibility up to now – but others would. Sexual abuse of children, an evil he was incapable of understanding, had come under the media spotlight in recent months and it wouldn't require much for a woman like Mrs Straw to brand him as a pervert. To be fair to Mrs Straw, any policeman would be duty-bound to treat such an allegation seriously. He resolved to get to a phone as soon as possible after they reached their destination.

And it was the Albert Hall.

The moment he and Naomi stepped out in Kensington Gore, opposite the north door, they were approached by a

Japanese woman. Diamond cupped a hand around Naomi's head and steered her protectively towards him. He was taking no chances.

The woman gave a deep, ceremonious bow. She looked about sixty, far too old to be Naomi's mother. There was a wart at the left edge of her upper lip. 'Mr Diamond?'

'Yes.'

'Please come with me.'

'In a moment, madam.' He settled the fare. As his right hand returned to his side he felt Naomi clutch the ends of his fingers tightly. Clearly she didn't regard the woman as family. They followed her towards the building and he noticed Naomi's head go back, to take in the scale of the building's red-brick exterior. A casserole-dish for the gods, he always thought when he saw the Albert Hall. You could imagine a Divine hand lifting the roof, inserting an enormous ladle and giving the contents a stir during the singing of 'Land of Hope and Glory' on the last night of the Proms.

The woman moved briskly up a short flight of steps and through the arched entrance as if the Albert Hall were her home. She was dressed in expensive western clothes, a fawn silk jacket and finely tailored dark brown trousers. Her gold-framed glasses had a long retaining-chain that danced on her shoulders.

By the time they entered the building, Naomi's grip was threatening to stop the circulation in Diamond's hand. The woman turned right, leading them along the main passage that surrounds the auditorium. Others were moving about in there, young people for the most part, with the age and appearance of students. Yet Diamond didn't have the impression that the Hall was being used for a concert, whether pop or classical. Precisely what was being staged down here this week he didn't know. Slack thinking, he chided himself. He ought to have asked someone at the Television Centre.

Their guide stopped by a door marked 'Private' and tapped with her knuckles.

Diamond was uneasy about taking Naomi into an enclosed area. 'Do you mind telling me what this is about?' he asked.

The woman turned to face him. 'I am sorry. It is not for me to say.'

'Who are you? I don't even know your name.'

'I am nothing. Disregard me.'

'You speak good English.'

'That is the only reason I am here.'

The door was opened by a burly young Japanese in a black tracksuit. The woman bowed. The young man dipped his head in a formal greeting directed more to Diamond than their guide and revealed that his hair was bunched and fastened in a topknot. Something was said in Japanese.

'Please enter,' the woman told them, standing aside to gesture them forward.

The sickly-sweet fumes of a floral perfume wafted over them. It was coming from the young man's hair, and the scent was camellia, Diamond registered, recalling a more subtle variety sometimes used by Steph. This was looking less and less like a homecoming for a lost child, but there didn't appear to be anything threatening about the invitation. He led Naomi through the door.

They were greeted by a spectacle that nothing had prepared them for: an enormous pair of buttocks, naked except for a strip of black silk squeezed into the cleft.

For reasons too complex to explore, the over-fleshed male bottom is not a feature much revered in modern Western society. It can be the object of mockery — literally, a butt — or, more positively, a source of extra poundage in the rugby scrum, or the tug-of-war team. This bottom manifestly aspired to higher planes of experience. It was monumental, as awesome in its way as the Albert Memorial across the road.

Motionless, pale gold in hue, smooth as traffic beacons, sturdy as two barrels stored side by side, it dominated the centre of the room and much of the sides as well. The rest of the owner's body was for the moment hidden, except for a partial view of stocky legs and bare feet. He was bending forward in a position that must have been painful to hold.

From Naomi's eye-level, the spectacle would have rivalled Mount Fujiyama.

Belatedly, Diamond recalled an item he had seen a

126

couple of days before on a television newscast. A Japanese Festival had opened and one of the main attractions was a tournament for Japanese wrestlers. The sport had a devoted following here. He mouthed the word, 'Sumo?'

The man who had just admitted them nodded.

Although Diamond hadn't watched much sumo wrestling on television, he felt some sympathy with a sport for which the training amounted to gorging oneself with food and the action rarely lasted longer than fifteen seconds.

The buttocks flexed, shuddered and shifted position with astonishing rapidity as their owner, regardless of his guests, went through a physical routine, raising his body level with his hips and lifting his right foot to shoulder height and then slapping it down heavily.

'The *shiko*,' murmured the woman from the doorway. 'To frighten evil spirits and the opponent.'

'Tell him the opponent isn't here,' Diamond muttered.

The *shiko* was repeated with the left leg. The great domes of flesh completed their movement, quivered, and were still. If anything, the reek of camellias had intensified. The wrestler, as well as his Jeeves, must have been pomaded with the stuff.

'I rather think someone has made a mistake inviting us here,' Diamond insisted.

Shocked that anyone should speak while the workout was in progress, the man in the tracksuit held up a restraining hand.

The wrestler treated them to the panorama of his backside again, bending so low that his head must have been between his knees. He was wearing the silk loincloth used in combat by the highest-ranking *sumotori*. The enforced intimacy with this mountainous rump was unsettling Diamond, and he didn't care to think what effect it could be having on the child. Actually, the room wasn't small. Indeed it must have been the star dressing-room. But when shared with a sumo wrestler and two heads coated in essence of camellia, it seemed minute. He turned to see if the woman was still present. She was standing just inside the door trying to be unobtrusive.

Diamond asked her, 'Are you sure this is right?'

127

She nodded and signalled to him to be silent by pressing her fingers against her lips.

The wrestler grunted, raised himself from the jack-knife position and suddenly turned about to face them. He was vast all over. His thighs looked as if they could have supported an overpass and in a sense they did, because his huge belly jutted so far over the belt of his loincloth that he appeared naked. A thick band of pectoral muscles lay over his torso, forming a deep, undulating crease. Above all that, almost extrinsic to the show, was his small, moon-shaped head. Its only real distinction was the hair tied at the back and folded forward in the traditional fan shape worn by the highest ranked *sumotori*. He exchanged the briefest of glances with the man in the tracksuit, who picked up a black jacket not unlike an undergraduate gown and wrapped it around the colossal shoulders.

Then the great man bowed in greeting and Diamond did the same. For once in his life, he was feeling physically diminished, skimpy, if not slender. A hand was extended for him to shake. Having seen the agility of Japanese wrestlers, he wouldn't have been surprised to have found himself on his back in the far corner. Instead he received nothing worse than a firm handshake. Something was said in Japanese, the voice high-pitched and husky.

The woman spoke up from behind Diamond. 'The *Ozeki* Yamagata wishes to introduce himself and welcome you to the Albert Hall, his temporary quarters.'

Diamond identified himself and Naomi. Chairs were produced for them. Yamagata squatted on a wooden bench and said something to his dresser, who spoke in turn to the woman interpreter.

She told Diamond, 'I have the honour to translate for Mr Yamagata. He instructs me to explain that *Ozeki* is the second highest rank in sumo. Mr Yamagata is a very important wrestler in Japan, and the most senior in this tournament. You are welcome to be his honoured guests in the arena tonight if you wish.'

'We are honoured indeed,' said Diamond, fitting smoothly into the formal style of address, 'but I think the child is too young.'

When this was translated for Mr Yamagata he appeared to take it well, nodding sagely.

Naomi still had a tight grip on Diamond's fingertips. With some justification, she regarded these proceedings with the deepest suspicion.

Yamagata spoke again and the interpreter explained that by chance the Very Important Wrestler had watched the transmission of *What About the Kids?* A portable set had been brought in for him to see a Channel 4 programme about sumo, but it had concentrated too much on a rival sumo stable and he had switched channels. 'Mr Yamagata was deeply moved by the unhappy situation of this Japanese child who appears on British television and says nothing. He asked me to make enquiries, so I phoned the BBC,' she explained.

Diamond's hopes of a breakthrough were dashed. 'You mean he didn't recognize Naomi?'

She shook her head.

'He doesn't know who she is?'

'It was only a TV show.'

'For crying out loud!' Diamond jerked up from the chair, accidentally hoisting Naomi to her feet as well, because she still had hold of his fingertips. 'You brought us here for nothing, because this ... this lump of lard happened to see the kid on the box? That's ludicrous. Who else have you dragged in – Arthur Daley?'

'Please! I cannot possibly say these things to Mr Yamagata.'

'Don't trouble. We're off. We've been conned by this heap of flab.' He turned to leave and found the way barred by the henchman in the tracksuit, hunched forward combatively, looking as if he wasn't messing. Naomi gave a whimper, dropped her precious drawing pad, and flung both arms around Diamond's waist, or as far around as she was able.

Not the ideal conditions for a first encounter with a sumo wrestler.

'Do you mind?' Diamond articulated in a straining-to-be-civil, British fashion. 'We would like to leave now.'

A volley of Japanese came from Yamagata, and the

interpreter pushed herself between Diamond and the henchman. 'Mr Diamond, I implore you! Mr Yamagata has not finished speaking. You cannot leave yet.'

'There's nothing else to say,' Diamond told her. 'The only reason we came was to find out who Naomi is. He doesn't know. He hasn't the faintest idea.'

'He wishes to help.'

'By questioning her in Japanese? The Embassy people tried. She doesn't respond. Now will you do me a favour and ask this buffoon to let us pass?'

'You should not turn your back on Mr Yamagata.'

She spoke this dictum like a universal truth. Probably it was well known and wisely heeded among the wrestling fraternity. Diamond heeded it and looked over his shoulder.

Thankfully, Yamagata hadn't moved from the bench. He was beckoning to Diamond to return to the chair.

Maybe, after all, Diamond rationalized, the guy has something constructive to suggest. I won't gain anything from an angry exit. I shouldn't let the frustration get to me. If I'd been questioning a witness in the nick, any old witness, I'd have heard him out in hope of eliciting something useful, wouldn't I?

'Okay,' he said, resting his hand on Naomi's shoulder. 'Two minutes.'

They sat down again.

'Mr Yamagata would like to hear from your own lips the story of this little girl.'

'I thought *he* had something to tell me.'

'Please, Mr Diamond.'

'As you wish.' Striving to be tolerant, he picked his way through the few known facts, starting with the bomb scare in Harrods and ending with Naomi's drawings, which she was willing to hand over for Yamagata's inspection.

The wrestler methodically turned the pages of the drawing pad, studying the diamond shapes and coming finally to the lattice window.

'That's my own work,' Diamond said, thinking how ridiculous he sounded, like some amateur artist looking for compliments. 'This drawing above is Naomi's. I wondered at one stage if she was writing in Japanese characters, but I was told not.'

When this was explained to Yamagata, he shook his head. He seemed as mystified about the significance of the drawings as everyone else. He closed the pad and handed it back to Naomi, graciously, with both hands, as if it were some precious item in the sumo ritual. He said something in Japanese to her, but she made no response. He then turned to Diamond and actually managed some halting words of English.

'Yamagata love little girl.'

Diamond had dreaded something like this. 'No. That's out. Definitely not possible,' he said, reinforcing it with a sweeping motion with his hand.

Yamagata frowned.

'I didn't bring her here to give her away,' Diamond tried to explain. 'She doesn't belong to me, anyway. I'm taking her back to the school tonight, and that's how it is.' He turned to the interpreter. 'For God's sake tell him what I'm trying to say.'

There was a consultation in Japanese. The woman then told Diamond with another bow, 'Pardon me for mentioning this, but I think you misunderstood Mr Yamagata. He was beginning to tell you that he had a young daughter about Naomi's age. He loved her deeply, but she died of meningitis last year.'

Yamagata's eyes moistened noticeably while this was explained.

'I'm sorry to hear that,' Diamond said in sincerity. 'A child's death is the worst kind of grief to bear. But please get him to understand that Naomi belongs to someone else.'

'He understands that.'

Yamagata spoke again in Japanese, flattening his palm to his chest to reinforce his message.

'He says he wants to help this little girl.'

'Naomi? He wants to help Naomi?'

Yamagata was nodding.

'That's kind,' said Diamond. 'I appreciate the offer, but what could you do? Do you understand me? What could you do to help?'

131

She put this into Japanese and got a quick answer. 'He says you tell him.'

This exercised Diamond for some time. He didn't like to appear ungrateful. Finally, he answered, 'I suppose you could do what I've been trying to do – drum up some publicity.'

When this was conveyed, Yamagata curled his lip in a clear signal of distaste. He spoke again. The interpreter told Diamond, 'Mr Yamagata has heard your story and he trusts you. You have been a police detective, so you are well qualified to find out the truth about the child. Mr Yamagata is a famous wrestler, not a detective. He is a rich man. He will pay all expenses. When you travel, fly to other places, stay in hotels, he will pay.'

A sponsor.

'I wasn't planning on flying anywhere.'

'Mr Yamagata thinks it will be necessary.'

Diamond shook his head. 'I doubt it.'

Another consultation, then she said, 'Mr Yamagata wishes to examine the drawing book again.'

'Again?' It was back on Naomi's lap. She allowed Diamond to take it from her and hand it across.

The wrestler turned the pages until he came to the drawing of the lattice window that Diamond himself had started. He traced a finger around the shapes Naomi had drawn and said, 'Aeroplane.' To reinforce the message he rested the drawing pad on his thighs and spread his arms wide.

'What?' By no stretch of imagination could the drawing represent an aircraft of any description.

Yamagata called his interpreter closer and spoke earnestly to her. She turned to Diamond. 'He says you should look closely at this drawing.'

On cue, Yamagata turned the drawing book in his hands and held it for Diamond to inspect.

'He believes this may be the child's view of inside an airliner.'

'Well, I wouldn't describe myself as a jet-setter, but I've flown a few times and not one of the planes had lattice windows.'

'Please study the drawings with Mr Yamagata.'
Yamagata held it higher.

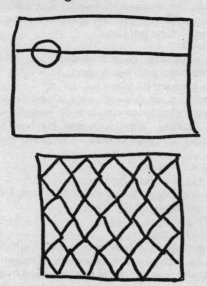

As Yamagata spoke and traced the shapes with his fingers, the woman interpreted. 'This grid-shape that you have assumed to represent a window may be something else.'

'I drew it myself.'

'You drew it from the patterns the child was making. Mr Yamagata believes it may represent the document storage pocket that is fixed to the back of each seat.'

Diamond knew what was meant. 'That string thing that everything is stuffed into – the safety instructions and the airline magazine and so on? That's a thought. She *would* be on a level with it if she sat in a plane. And this other shape could be the flap that you rest your tray on. I believe he's right.' He snapped his fingers. 'That's brilliant. Bloody brilliant. She's letting us know that she was in an aircraft.'

'Or an Intercity train.'

An uneasy pause ensued.

'Did he say that?'

'I did,' said the woman. 'I live in England. Many train seats have these flaps. The aeroplanes I have travelled in generally have fabric pockets.'

She was right.

'Hang on a minute,' Diamond said. 'May I have the pad back?' He gestured with his fingers.

Yamagata handed it to him.

He turned to a fresh page, took a pen from his pocket and made two rapid drawings, very basic in shape, of an aircraft and a train. 'Now, let's see.' He held them up for Naomi's inspection and covered the train with his hand. 'This one?'

She made no reaction.

'Or this?' He revealed the train.

After a worrying delay, the child put out her hand and touched the drawing of the train.

'This one? This one, Naomi?'

She tapped it again.

'So you're right. He was only partly right. He worked out what the drawing represented,' Diamond told the woman, 'but she was telling us she travelled by train.'

'Japan Airlines,' said Yamagata, nodding.

'British Rail,' Diamond said, turning to speak to the woman. 'Fancy you working it out.'

She told him, 'The credit for interpreting the drawings belongs to Mr Yamagata.'

'You got it between you, then. Bloody brilliant!'

'Oriental people write their language in ideograms. We have a sharp eye for symbols.'

Yamagata spoke again in Japanese and his interpreter said firmly, 'Mr Yamagata must prepare for the *basho*. We should not delay him. He said he will pay whatever you need to find Naomi's parents.'

Diamond's eyes widened in surprise. 'He'll pay?'

'That is so.'

'Let me get this right. He's offering to hire me?'

'Yes.'

'Does he really mean whatever I need?'

More consultation ensued. Then: 'Mr Yamagata possesses the Gold Card of American Express.'

'I'm impressed, but—'

'He will give you his Gold Card number. If you need to make expenditure, you quote the number. I will write this down for you.'

'He's giving me *carte blanche* to spend his money?'

'American Express,' said Yamagata himself, but with some difficulty over the letter 'R'.

'Mr Yamagata has satisfied himself that you are honourable.'

Encouraging as it was to have found unlimited sponsorship and been judged honourable, Diamond still had mixed feelings about the encounter. His expectation that these people had recognized Naomi had been dashed. He was pleased to have her drawing explained, but disappointed that it indicated nothing more than a journey on BR's Intercity.

After another bout of bowing and handshaking, he withdrew with Naomi to the blessedly unscented air outside.

The interpreter followed them out and handed him a card with Yamagata's Tokyo address. Below it she had written his credit card number. She said solemnly, 'And my phone number is on the back.'

The impulse to smile, or wink, or say something suggestive was hard to resist. But there are people you don't risk upsetting, and this oriental dowager was one. Actually the mention of the phone jerked Peter Diamond back to a matter of more urgency. He still hadn't called the school. He thanked her, pocketed the card and went to look for a callbox.

To his immense relief, Julia Musgrave answered. She agreed that it had been right to follow up the summons from the sumo wrestler. She'd watched *What About the Kids?* Everyone in the school had watched it and there had been high excitement among the children when Clive had recognized Naomi. Julia was sorry that nothing of real substance had resulted from the programme, apart from Mr Yamagata's offer, because — she reminded Diamond,

135

as if it wasn't paramount in his mind – Naomi's time in England was almost up. In less than forty-eight hours, she would be on that flight to Boston.

Miss Musgrave had gone home, Diamond learned when the school's front door was opened.

It was a good thing he'd phoned first. The worst Mrs Straw could find to complain of was that the child looked worn to a frazzle, poor mite. 'Look at her. She can hardly stand up, she's so done for.'

Naomi slipped her hand free from Diamond's and ran inside and up the stairs in quick, light steps, still holding her drawing pad.

He raised his trilby to Mrs Straw and went off to catch the tube.

Chapter Seventeen

STEPHANIE'S ADVICE ACROSS THE BREAKFAST table was eminently sensible, if totally unacceptable.

'Face up to it, Pete – you've run out of time. You can't solve that little girl's problem.'

'Which problem is that?'

She sighed. 'Oh, don't get pernickety, love. It's too early in the day.'

To demonstrate good-will, he offered to put a slice of bread in the toaster for her. 'I was only asking you to explain what you're on about. Which of her problems am I incapable of solving?'

'The speech.'

'You mean the absence of it.'

She sighed, rested her chin on the bridge she had made of her hands and gave him a look that said he was being unreasonably reasonable.

He told her, 'I never expected to restore her speech. All I've been trying to do is find her people. I'm a policeman, not a speech therapist.'

'You're neither,' she reminded him mildly.

'An ex-policeman, then.'

'But you weren't dealing with abandoned kids.'

'I've been through the training. I know the procedures. Look, Steph, you know me well enough. I'm not giving up now.'

She got up from the table and carried her plate to the sink. 'What can you do? It's Saturday morning. You told me they're flying her out to Boston tomorrow.'

'Correct.'

'Can't you see it may be the best possible thing, Pete?

137

The school is run by the Japanese. They have a wonderful reputation.'

He had nothing against the school. 'You want to know what I can do?' he said. 'I can get her to draw things. She is definitely trying to communicate through the drawing. I'm getting her confidence now. She holds my hand.'

Stephanie looked down at the water she was running over the dishes. Unseen by Diamond, she was smiling. By the simple act of holding his hand, one small, silent girl had succeeded in taming the bear.

'Would you like to come with me?' he offered.

'To the school?'

'We could take her out together.'

She thought for a moment, pleased that he'd suggested it, and then shook her head. 'She doesn't know me. She's not going to open up if there's a stranger tagging along. She's seen too many well-meaning women already, social workers and embassy people and special teachers trying to coax something out of her – worthy, I'm sure, but not what the kid wants. Heaven knows how or why, but you seem to have reached an understanding with her. You go alone, love, only don't pin your hopes on it.'

Knowing the school routine on Saturdays, he timed his arrival for just before ten, after breakfast was finished, the rooms cleared and the kids dressed and playing. It was one of those brilliant, cloudless London mornings that make urban pollution seem like a myth. He could hear the children outside in the garden at the rear, so he walked around the side of the house. Clive spotted him immediately and came running, holding the toy car Diamond had given him and making a convincing engine sound. Diamond stopped and spread his hands in welcome, but the boy veered off to the left, as if he had just remembered that he was autistic and didn't, after all, relate to adults.

Mrs Straw was on duty, seated on the bench under the sycamore, sedulously knitting something in a revolting shade of green.

He greeted her civilly and asked if Miss Musgrave was

about. When speaking to Mrs Straw, everyone on the staff referred to everyone else as Miss, Mrs or Mr.

'She's busy.'

'In her study?'

'Busy, I said.'

'Yes, but where can I find her?'

'She doesn't want disturbing.'

'I understand that. I'm asking where she is.'

'On the phone.'

Some of Mrs Straw's statements, if taken literally, had a surreal quality. Diamond had a mental picture of Julia doing a balancing act on top of the phone. 'I didn't actually ask you what she was doing.'

Silence.

'The one in her office?' he asked. There were three phones that he knew about.

Still no word.

'I'll go in and see for myself, then. Where's young Naomi this morning?'

If anything, Mrs Straw pressed her lips more tightly shut. This morning she was even more unobliging than usual. She continued to knit with tight, tense movements.

'Aren't you in charge?' Diamond asked, nettled by the dumb show. 'Shouldn't she be out here with the others?'

'She's gone.'

He tensed. 'What do you mean – "gone"?'

'It's plain English, isn't it?'

'Gone away?'

She gave a nod.

'Left altogether, do you mean?'

'Collected this morning.'

Mrs Straw hadn't even looked up from her knitting. She gave the information casually, as if it were common knowledge, and now she had started the next row.

Diamond was so astounded that he could only say an inane, 'What?'

'Are you deaf?'

He turned away and went to look for Julia Musgrave.

Just as Mrs Straw had said, Julia was on the phone. Seeing him in the doorway of her office, she said into the phone, 'It's all right. He's just walked in. I can tell him myself.' She put down the phone and said, 'I was talking to your wife.'

'My *wife*?'

'Trying to contact you. I didn't know you were coming in. I have some news that might upset you.'

'Mrs Straw just told me about Naomi.'

Her face tightened. 'That woman! She handed the child over without informing me or the social services or anyone else.'

'Weren't you here?'

'It all happened before I arrived. About eight this morning, when the children were having breakfast. The only staff here were Mrs Straw and the Malaysian girl who cooks. I gather that this Japanese woman knocked at the door and announced that she was the mother and had come to collect her child. As proof of identity, she produced a passport and a photo of Naomi and Naomi definitely recognized her, according to Mrs Straw.'

He was trying to assimilate the information. 'A passport and a photo, or a passport containing a photo?'

Julia shook her head. 'The photo was separate. The passport belonged to the woman, but the child was mentioned in it.'

'Naomi?'

'Some other name. Naomi was the name we gave her, if you remember.'

'What was this woman like?'

She shook her head. 'You know what it's like trying to drag information out of Mrs Straw. I was so incensed when she told me that she'd handed Naomi over without reference to anyone that I lost my chance of a normal conversation with her.'

'We'd better have her in here immediately,' said Diamond. 'She's got to give a proper account of what happened.'

'All right. You'll stay?'

'You bet I will. I'll fetch her now.'

In the garden he got a glare fit to petrify, but Mrs Straw folded her knitting and went with him.

140

They sat stiffly among the children's toys and pictures in Julia's office, Diamond on the wooden trunk, Mrs Straw on a chair just inside the door, as if poised for a quick exit.

Julia explained that she wanted to go over the details of what had happened that morning.

Pointedly ignoring what was said to her, and thrusting out her chin defiantly, Mrs Straw demanded, 'What's he doing here?'

Diamond drew breath to lambast her, but Julia got in first, and her rebuke was the more effective for being spoken in a soft, measured voice. 'Mr Diamond, as you very well know, takes a special interest in Naomi. He has worked for the police.'

'It's nothing to do with the police.'

'I didn't say it was, but I have to be sure about this woman who claims to be Naomi's mother. She could be an impostor.'

'Impossible,' said Mrs Straw.

'Not at all. It's quite possible that some childless woman could have seen Naomi on television and decided that she could pose as the mother.'

Mrs Straw was unimpressed. 'The woman had the photo of Naomi.'

Diamond intervened. 'Before we go into that, can we have it from the beginning, when the woman arrived?'

Without a glance in his direction, Mrs Straw said, 'I already told Miss Musgrave.'

'You gave me the essential facts,' said Julia. 'Now we need to know more.'

Mrs Straw sat back, exhaled noisily and folded her arms. 'There isn't any more.'

'Then tell me again, so that Mr Diamond can hear exactly what you recall.'

She rolled her eyes upward in protest. 'It's simple enough. I answered the door when the children were having breakfast.'

'What time?' Diamond asked.

'Round about eight. I don't have a watch. It was this Japanese woman. She asked if the little girl who was on the television yesterday was here. She said, "I am the

141

mother." '

'What was she like? Can you describe her?'

'She was Japanese.'

This, apparently, said it all, so far as Mrs Straw was concerned.

'And . . . ?' Diamond prompted her.

'They all look the same to me.'

'What age would she have been?'

'I can't say. You can't tell.'

'Young enough to be the mother of Naomi?'

'I suppose so.'

'What was she wearing?'

'I'd have to think about that.'

'Please do. Now.'

After a pause, she said, 'A grey jacket of some kind and trousers to match.'

'Shoes?'

'Black, I think.'

'With heels?'

'I didn't notice.'

'Would you describe her as smartly dressed?'

'The clothes were Rohan, if that's what you mean.'

He hadn't meant it. He didn't know anything about Rohan clothes, or how you recognized them, but from Mrs Straw's tone, he took it that she was sure. 'How did she wear her hair?'

'Short.'

'Very short, do you mean? Cut close to the head?'

'No. It was permed.'

'In curls?'

'Waves.'

Little by little, he was getting a mental picture, though not one that would distinguish the woman from a million other Japanese.

'What height would she have been?'

'Average.'

'Average for a Japanese?'

She responded once more with the unsatisfactory, 'I suppose so.'

After some more probing as to skin quality and

142

colouring, and make-up (the woman had been well-groomed, it appeared), Diamond gave a nod to Julia, who said, 'Shall we continue, then? You invited the woman in.'

'Only after she showed me Naomi's photo and the passport.'

'Her own passport?'

'Her picture was in it.'

'A Japanese passport?'

'Any fool could see she wasn't from Timbuctoo,' Mrs Straw said with contempt.

Diamond just about contained himself. 'She might have held an American passport, or Australian.'

'How would I know?'

'Couldn't you see the writing on the passport?'

'I can't read Japanese.'

'So you think it was Japanese script. We're getting somewhere. We're not trying to catch you out, Mrs Straw. We just want all the information you can give us.'

'It was in some foreign language. That's all I'm prepared to say.'

'And she also showed you this photo of Naomi?'

'Yes.'

'You're certain it was Naomi?'

'I said so.'

'You just implied that all Japanese people look alike to you.'

'If they're strangers. I've seen Naomi plenty of times.'

The point was fair.

'So was it a recent photo of Naomi?'

'Must have been.'

Julia asked. 'Did she have a name for Naomi?'

'Can't remember.'

'Come on,' Diamond urged her. 'Surely she gave a name?'

'I said I can't remember. It was double-Dutch to me. Anyway,' said Mrs Straw, willing to move on with her account to avoid further discussion of the child's name, 'I told her Miss Musgrave wasn't here and she said she wanted to see her little girl. She kept on saying it. She wouldn't be put off. So I let her come through to the dining-room.'

143

No one could doubt that any person who had talked her way past Mrs Straw was uncommonly persistent.

'The children were on their own,' she explained, to justify her capitulation. 'I was forced to leave them when I went to the door. I couldn't stand arguing on the doorstep.'

'Please go on.'

'There's nothing else. She came in and went straight to Naomi and anyone could see she was the mother.'

'How?' asked Diamond.

'You wouldn't understand,' Mrs Straw told him loftily. 'It takes a woman to understand.' She looked towards Julia for support.

Julia declined to conspire in this evasion. 'We want to know precisely what happened. Did Naomi get up and run to her?'

'Yes, of course.'

Diamond put up his hand too late to intervene, realizing that he couldn't caution Julia for putting words into Mrs Straw's mouth, as he might if some raw police constable were asking leading questions. The damage was done now. Mrs Straw was launched and away.

'They cuddled and kissed and wept a few tears and talked to each other in Japanese.'

'Talked? Naomi *talked*?'

'The mother I mean. Then she said she was going to take Naomi home, so I said I didn't think she should until she'd seen Miss Musgrave. I tried my level best to keep her there, but you've got to remember I was on my own here apart from the girl in the kitchen. The other children had to be looked after.'

'Why wouldn't she stay?' Diamond asked. 'What was the hurry?'

'I can't say. You can't tell with foreigners.'

'What happened then?'

'I asked the cook to keep an eye on the children while we went upstairs and collected the clothes Naomi came in. I let them take the things she was wearing. I knew Miss Musgrave wouldn't mind.'

'Then what?'

144

'They left.'

'Without leaving a name or address?'

'I forgot to ask.'

'Brilliant.'

'She was in a hurry to go,' said Mrs Straw in her defence.

'And you couldn't wait to show her the door.'

'That isn't fair. And it isn't true, either.' Reacting to a convenient scream from the garden, Mrs Straw said, 'Lord knows what the children are getting up to. I'd better go.'

Diamond said firmly that he hadn't finished. He wanted to see the room where Naomi slept.

'Suit yourself. There's nothing to see,' Mrs Straw declared.

'Take us there now, if you please.'

She took a sharp, indignant breath and turned in protest to Julia Musgrave, who told her firmly to do as Mr Diamond instructed.

As if every step were on red-hot coals she led them upstairs and opened a door to a room containing three small beds. The quilts were thrown back.

'Which is Naomi's?'

Mrs Straw pointed to the one nearest the door. A light green pair of child's pyjamas lay over the pillow. Diamond picked them up.

'School property,' Mrs Straw informed him.

He tossed them back and opened the locker beside the bed. Nothing was inside. But before rising, he happened to notice the hard, straight edge of something squeezed between the bedstead and the mattress. He slipped his hand inside.

A remark of Julia Musgrave's came back to him: *They can hide a favourite toy and weeks, months later, go straight to it.* What he had found was Naomi's drawing pad. He withdrew it and flicked through the pages to be quite certain.

'She left this.'

'Must have forgotten it,' Mrs Straw said tersely.

'That isn't likely. She carried it everywhere, as you very well know.' He felt under the mattress again and this time found the marker pen. 'She kept the things here because they were so precious to her. She's unlikely to have left without them. Not freely.'

Ridges had formed at the edge of Mrs Straw's mouth.

'You were here,' Diamond pointed out. 'Did she have the opportunity of collecting her things?'

She gave no answer.

'Just now you gave the impression that this was a joyful reunion with mother,' Diamond commented. 'Hugs and kisses and a few tears into the bargain. Were they tears of joy, Mrs Straw, or distress? You see, this discovery has rocked my confidence. I'm beginning to wonder if the child was taken from here against her will. If that is the case, you'd better say so, fast.'

She shook her head vigorously, either in defiance or to contest his interpretation.

Confronted with the familiar challenge of the unco-operative witness, a trained interrogator like Diamond might have coaxed out the truth, but while Naomi was under threat, he wasn't wasting time on refinements.

'You lied.'

Mrs Straw arched her mouth and glared.

He shoved the drawing pad towards her, forcing her to sway back. 'She wouldn't have gone without this.'

'Get away from me,' she muttered.

He felt Julia Musgrave's hand on his arm, wanting to restrain him, without result. 'Admit it. That woman took Naomi off by force.' He portrayed the scene vividly. 'She dragged the kid out of here screaming and kicking.'

'No.'

He gave her a moment for a more considered answer.

She added, 'That isn't true – about the screaming. You can ask the cook.'

'I intend to.'

'She only struggled a bit.'

'We're coming to it,' said Diamond.

'There wasn't no screaming.'

'Crying?'

'No.'

'And there wasn't any kissing and cuddling, was there, Mrs Straw? You lied about that.'

'No.'

'But you just said the child struggled. Come on, what are we to believe — that after this touching reunion her so-called mother had to wrestle with her to get her out of the place?'

She emitted a sound between a gasp and a sob and clamped her teeth over her lower lip. The dragon who deterred visitors was a cornered creature now.

Julia, probably succumbing to the tension, said, 'No one is blaming you, Mrs Straw' — which wasn't strictly true, and Diamond didn't let it pass. He was angry. And, more vitally, he was conscious of the minutes passing.

'Blame is exactly what this is about,' he said without deflecting his eyes from Mrs Straw. 'You thought you could avoid more blame by telling this crap about kissing and cuddling. You don't want us to know what really took place this morning. And while you feed us horseshit, this woman is heading for God knows where with a child who was in your charge. You're in deep trouble, Mrs Straw. By Christ, you'd better speak up.'

The force of his speech had a dramatic result. Mrs Straw turned ashen. The rigid mouth softened and quivered. Her hand fumbled in a pocket of the apron she was wearing and extracted a large red handkerchief. She pressed it to her nose and, instead of blowing it, emitted a long, low moan of distress. Her eyes reddened and dampened. Huge sobs convulsed her. The outburst was the more disturbing because she had always seemed so implacable.

'Now, now,' said Julia in sympathy.

Unmoved, Diamond remarked, 'We don't have time for this, Mrs Straw.'

Dabbing her tears, she launched into a confession punctuated by frequent sobs. 'I was too frightened to tell you exactly what happened. Naomi didn't want to leave. She put up a fight. What I said was true — about the picture and everything — and I'm positive they knew each other, only when it was obvious that the woman wanted to take Naomi with her, she went berserk — Naomi, I mean. She tried to run away and the woman grabbed hold of her arm and wouldn't let go. What could I do? I'm only supposed to be the help here. She kept on and on saying she was the mother and the passport was proof of it. In the end I went upstairs for Naomi's things. What I told you about the two of them coming up here wasn't true. Naomi was in no state to do anything, so I collected her things myself. I didn't think to look for the drawing book. I put the spare clothes in a carrier and handed them over. Naomi had to be pushed and dragged all the way to the taxi.'

'There was a taxi?'

'Yes, it must have been waiting. I noticed it when I first opened the door. And when they left, Naomi was struggling and kicking by the taxi door and only went in after her leg was slapped.'

'Oh, no!' said Julia, who wouldn't allow anyone to strike a child in her school.

'What sort of taxi?' asked Diamond, trying to exclude everything but the essential information, though, he, too, was disturbed at the treatment of Naomi.

'The usual. I won't lose my job, will I, Miss Musgrave?'

'Black?'

'What?'

'The taxi, Mrs Straw. Was it black?'

'Oh. Yes.'

'I suppose it's too much to hope that you took the number?'

She shook her head.

'Anything about it — adverts on the doors. Try and remember.'

'I can't. Anyway, I couldn't see it properly because of the hedge.'

'What time did they leave? How long were they here?'

'I don't know — about twenty minutes, I suppose. It might have been less. It seemed like twenty minutes.'

'Before eight-thirty, then?'

'I suppose so.'

He told Julia, 'I'm calling the police. We're going to need them.'

Mrs Straw covered her eyes and moaned.

Chapter Eighteen

THE PERSON WHO TOOK THE call at Kensington Police Station expressed doubt whether it would be possible to trace an unnamed Japanese woman and child who had stepped into a taxi in Earls Court at eight-thirty.

Diamond hadn't reprimanded a policeman for months, but he still had the knack. 'Who the hell do you think you are – God Almighty?' he boomed down the line. 'This is a bloody emergency. It isn't your job to look down from the clouds and say what's possible and what isn't. Action the call. I was in the police, son. I know what I'm talking about. The morning rush-hour is the busiest time of day for taxis.'

'That's just the point,' said the hapless officer.

'What are you, a civilian? Put me through to someone in uniform, will you? Who's the station sergeant?'

'I am.'

'God help us. Listen, I'm not telling you your job, sergeant, but there are ways of tracing taxis. Most of them work in fleets and radio their positions to the girl on the intercom, right? At the busiest times there's a large demand for cabs. If one was standing outside a school for twenty minutes, someone is going to remember – because it was unavailable for other work – follow me?'

'Yes, but—'

'And this cab driver, whoever he may be, is going to remember sitting there. He's also going to remember picking up a Japanese woman and a kid who was most unwilling to be with her. Now, you can't trace every taxi in London, agreed, but you can call the offices telling them to check with their controllers, or whatever they call themselves.'

'Have you any idea what you're asking, Mr—'

'Diamond. Ex-Superintendent Diamond. Yes, I know exactly what I'm asking, and it's the obvious course of action apart from questioning the neighbours round here, which goes without saying. If you want help—'

'That won't be needed.'

'Good. I'm glad you can handle that,' Diamond said and added before the sergeant had time to come in again, 'In that case I'll come straight down to the station. I can be more useful there.'

This had the desired effect, a definite infusion of urgency. 'Will you listen to me, sir? I want you to stay where you are. I'll be sending someone to take a statement from you.'

'Sod that. I've given you the facts. Do I have to repeat that this child was taken from the school against her will? Abducted, sergeant. We've got to know where she was taken, and we've got to know fast.'

He ended the call.

Julia Musgrave had overheard all this. She was pale, clearly disturbed by Diamond's bulldozing, without knowing that it was the sure way to get things done in the police. 'You said this is an emergency.'

His response was guarded. 'I know that sergeant's type. If you told him a bomb had been planted in Buckingham Palace, he'd want it in writing first.'

'Is Naomi in danger?'

'We've got to assume she is. Whoever this woman is – and she may be the mother, for all I know – she behaved suspiciously.'

'Maybe,' she commented. 'But you can't expect a mother deprived of her child to act rationally. She turned up here at breakfast time. Is that really to be interpreted as suspicious? If my child were missing, I wouldn't think twice about knocking on someone's door any time of the day or night.'

'In that case why didn't she come here yesterday, directly after the television programme?'

'We don't know where she was when she saw it. If she was in Manchester, for example, she'd have had to travel

150

to London, wouldn't she?'

'She could have phoned.'

'Perhaps she tried. You told me yourself that the BBC switchboard was jammed.'

He wasn't going to get far with this line of reasoning and he hadn't started it anyway, so he mentioned another obvious cause for mistrusting the Japanese woman. 'I can't believe a genuine mother just reunited with her child would hit her.'

'Stress.'

He gave up. He knew really that his motives in treating the matter as an emergency were more instinctive than rational. Naomi had eventually come to trust him – at least to the extent of holding his hand. He wouldn't have admitted to Julia Musgrave or anyone else – bar Stephanie – that the child had captivated him. He'd felt the small hand in his own and now it was a self-imposed duty to find out whether she was safe. But he didn't want anyone running away with the idea that he – the veteran of a dozen murder inquiries – was a soft touch, literally a soft touch. He didn't particularly want to admit it to himself.

There was more to it, he insisted. He was deeply suspicious about the mother. How could she have allowed herself to be parted from her child for so long? Why hadn't she alerted the police, or at least her own embassy, when Naomi first went missing? Foreigners could be forgiven some confusion in a strange country, but anyone, of any nationality, ought to have reacted promptly to a crisis as basic as that.

So he wasn't giving up without satisfying himself that the 'mother' *was* the mother, and was capable of looking after her child.

Before carrying out his promise (or threat) to call at the police station, he decided to give the area car ten minutes to drive up. Someone may have seen the woman forcing Naomi into the taxi and it was worth making sure that the right questions were asked. Thus far, he wasn't over-impressed by the calibre of the Kensington plod.

Two PCs – male and female – arrived with a couple of minutes to spare, looking like extras in a TV soap opera.

Why was it that no one in police uniform looked genuine any more? To do them justice, they went about their duties efficiently and agreed to divide forces, one knocking on doors while the other questioned Mrs Straw.

Diamond waited long enough to learn that not one of the neighbours had witnessed Naomi being bundled into the taxi. One man raised hopes by saying he had spotted the cab standing outside, and then could only add that the vehicle had been black and the driver white.

Down at the nick in Earls Court Road, someone must have issued a warning of imminent invasion. Two sergeants and a plainclothes CID officer – an inspector, as it turned out – were at the desk to repel Diamond. They didn't succeed, of course. He'd long ago checked the identity of the Deputy Assistant Commissioner for Six Area West and nothing opens a door better than naming the man in charge.

This being Saturday morning, the Big White Chief wasn't about, so Diamond had to settle for his surrogate, Chief Superintendent Sullins, another name usefully committed to memory from the police directory in Kensington Reference Library. For his part, Sullins, a foxy little character in white shirt and red braces, trying strenuously to look the part of the Kensington supremo, claimed to have heard of Diamond, though they had never met until this handshake on the stairs.

'Everything under control' was Sullins' text for the day, at least for Peter Diamond's consumption. He was giving this matter of the missing child high priority. The police already knew all about Naomi ('I wish I did,' Diamond commented in passing) from the night of the alarm in Harrods. They'd gone to extraordinary lengths to try and establish who she was. And now everything possible was being done to trace the taxi. Cab firms all over London were being contacted. So Diamond was free to leave in the sure confidence that nothing he could do would speed the process.

'Thank you, but I'd prefer to stay,' he said amiably.

'I'm afraid that won't be possible,' Sullins told him.

'Why?'

'We don't allow members of the public—'

'Ex-CID,' Diamond interjected.

'I appreciate the offer, Mr Diamond, but we have our procedures.'

He countered with: 'You mean you need to get the Chief's consent? Understandable.' He smiled disarmingly. 'I'll fix it. What does he do Saturday mornings – play golf or go shopping with his good lady? I'm damned sure he carries a beeper, wherever he is. And if he has to trot back to his car for the phone, I dare say he won't mind. Do you want me to mention you asked me to get clearance, or should I leave your name out of it, Mr Sullins?'

No ambitious policeman was proof against that kind of blackmail. 'Ex-CID, you said,' Sullins remarked as if he had only just registered the information. 'I suppose it's possible you may be of use. It's highly irregular.'

Diamond nodded. 'Cheers. I'll keep myself inconspicuous.' Which was by some way the most unlikely assertion anyone had made that morning.

In the communications room, a WPC was keying something into the computer. Diamond squeezed around her to reach for the log of calls that the switchboard operator had beside her. 'Got anything back from the taxi firms – about the Japanese kid?'

'Zero so far,' she told him.

'How many are there?'

'Cab firms? Have you looked at the Yellow Pages?'

He picked a directory off her desk. What he saw depressed him. 'How many have you done?'

'About twelve.'

'Keep going.'

She gave him a withering stare. 'Who *are* you?'

'It is a young kid,' he said.

'Japanese, aged about five,' she chanted without looking at a note, 'red woollen dress, black tights, white trainers, accompanied by a Japanese woman about thirty, of smart appearance, with short, dark, wavy hair, grey jacket and matching trousers believed to be made by Rohan.'

He took the opportunity to ask how anyone would

recognize Rohan garments and was told that the name was displayed on them.

So Mrs Straw was not, after all, a connoisseur of fashion, but her information was probably reliable.

'They're not cheap,' the girl added, 'but they're smart. Kind of sporty. Rohans are really something else in trousers – all those pockets.'

He thanked her. 'Now can I help in any way, by calling over the numbers, perhaps?'

'Is that meant to be a hint, or something? I was going as fast as I could before you interrupted.'

'What if one of them calls back?'

'Harry over there will take it. He's had nothing up to now.'

Harry over there was wearing earphones. He looked up from a copy of *Viz* and raised his thumb in greeting.

'I'll let you get on, then,' Diamond told them tamely.

'Ta.'

He moved away. He fancied a cigarette now, and he hadn't smoked in years. Didn't even approve of it.

Feeling alien and ineffectual, a sensation he'd never have dreamed was possible in a police station, he went to look for the canteen. Five cigarettes and two black coffees later, he went back upstairs, only to be greeted with Harry's palms spread wide in a negative gesture.

In an hour he returned and the operator said that she'd contacted every taxi firm except three that had probably gone out of business. Most of them had said they'd need to check with their controllers or their drivers, some of whom had changed shift since eight in the morning. The standard arrangement was that they'd ring back if anyone could remember picking up the Japanese woman and child in Earls Court.

Harry was filling in a football pools coupon.

'Nothing yet?'

'Zilch.'

Diamond went in search of Superintendent Sullins. He found him in an office upstairs dictating a letter. 'About to leave, Mr Diamond?'

'We seem to have drawn a blank with the taxis.'

'*Nil desperandum*. One of the firms could ring back any time.'

'I know, but it's almost six hours since they were last seen.'

'Let's not be melodramatic,' Sullins unwisely commented. 'We're not dealing with a mine disaster.'

'*Melodramatic*? This is a missing child.'

'Possibly.'

'Have you alerted the airports and the main line stations?'

'Alerted them to what? A mother slapping her child's leg? Let's keep this in proportion. And now you're going to tell me that we don't know if she's the mother.'

'We don't.'

'But she produced a photograph, Mr Diamond.'

An eruption was imminent. Only a buzz on the intercom prevented it.

Sullins touched a switch. 'Yes?'

The voice was female. 'Sir, we're taking a call from a taxi firm in Hammersmith called Instant Cabs.'

'Put it on,' Sullins ordered.

A man's voice was saying, ' . . . went off duty at twelve, and we've only just been able to trace him. He's your driver, all right. He picked up a Japanese woman at seven-fifty this morning in Brook Green. She had a suitcase, dark blue. He drove her to Kempsford Gardens School in Earls Court – would that be right? – and waited until eight twenty-five, or soon after, when she came out with a child, a small girl. Japanese, like the woman. She seemed to be playing up, he said. He drove them to the airport.'

'Heathrow?'

'Yes.'

'Which terminal?'

'Three. The inter-continental.'

Diamond didn't wait to hear any more. He was out and down the stairs and telling Harry to get Immigration on the line.

Chapter Nineteen

WEDGED INTO SEAT 11B IN Concorde, Diamond was about as comfortable as a stout person may expect to be on an aircraft noted for its slim contour. 11B was immediately behind the serving-bay, providing the dual advantage of increased leg-room and a tray arrangement that allowed him to stand his champagne glass on a level surface rather than having it on a slope created by his stomach.

Rapid decisions were responsible for his being on the flight. Around 5.30 p.m., he had learned from Immigration at Heathrow that someone remembered a Japanese woman and child passing through the departure gate about one p.m. More importantly, the woman had been wearing what was described as grey sportsgear and the child a red corduroy dress, black tights and trainers. Soon after this, British Airways check-in staff had confirmed that a Mrs Nakajima, accompanied by her daughter Aya, had boarded flight BA177 at 1415, due at John F. Kennedy Airport, New York, at 1705, local time.

New York. This wasn't a game for faint hearts, but Diamond was totally committed. By using his former police rank, he succeeded in extracting a promise from the Immigration Service at JFK that Mrs Nakajima and daughter would be detained for up to an hour. From British Airways he had already learned that by taking the last Concorde flight of the day at 1900, he could be in New York fifty minutes after BA177 arrived – the sort of schedule that would have him looking at his watch all the way across. He'd booked a passage immediately, quoting Yamagata's Gold Card number. The thought crossed his mind that he ought to have called the Albert Hall to get his sponsor's approval, but he decided against it. 'Mr Yamagata is a rich man. He will pay,' the interpreter had promised when they had met, and presumably Mr Yamagata, a man of honour, wouldn't quibble over a mere five thousand and thirty pounds. Diamond preferred not to enquire at this stage.

Remembering just in time that he was a considerate husband, he did phone Stephanie to let her know that he was leaving the country. She wasn't quite as devastated as he'd expected. 'See if you can get me a pair of genuine New York sneakers while you're over there. White, of course. Remember I take a seven, but that's eight and a half in their size.' How did she know these things? he wondered.

He checked his watch again, thinking ahead. The US Immigration officials would be the first test. They were trained to spot con-men. He'd need to be sharp to convince them that he was on an official investigation. Then there was the Nakajima woman, who had thoroughly outfoxed the formidable Mrs Straw. She was a real challenge. Even if she folded under questioning and admitted to abducting the child, there was still the matter of what action could be taken, and where. Extradition law had never been his forte.

A stewardess came along the aisle and handed him a note that must have been transmitted to the cockpit.

To: Supt. Diamond
From: US Immigration
Time: 1721 NYT
Will meet you on arrival. Ms Nakajima and child detained.

A tingling sensation, a mixture of relief, anticipation and champagne, spread through Diamond's veins.

'Good news, sir?' the stewardess enquired.

He gave a dignified smile. 'Just confirming an appointment.' In truth, it deserved a fanfare. For one indulgent moment, he likened himself to Chief Inspector Dew, the man who had crossed the Atlantic in 1910 to arrest Dr Crippen and his mistress. A telegraph message, a dash across the ocean, and Crippen had been copped.

157

There the comparison ended. Crippen had been a murderer. Mrs Nakajima was guilty, at most, of abduction.

Concorde had already started its descent. The fasten seatbelts order came over the public address.

They touched down five minutes before schedule at 1750.

When the doors were opened, a woman immigration officer was waiting. Diamond introduced himself.

'May I see your ID?' she asked, taking stock of him. He didn't fit the stereotype of a British detective, judging by the way she eyed his waistline.

'Will my passport do?' Helpfully, it had been issued four years ago and still listed his profession as police officer.

'Would you come with me, sir?'

The 'sir' was encouraging. Stiff from the journey and slightly disorientated, but eager to see Naomi, he was taken through a roped barrier and along a corridor lined with filing cabinets. Another door, another corridor, and into an office looking like a scene out of a television police series with its sense of stage-managed activity as people walked through, stopped, exchanged words, presumably to develop different plotlines in the story, and moved on. A black officer in tinted glasses carved a way around a couple of desks and said, 'You've got to be the guy from Scotland Yard.'

'Peter Diamond,' he said, offering his hand without going into the matter of where he was from. 'You still have these people detained, I hope?'

'Sure have.' The man didn't need to give his name. He had a tag hanging from his shirt that identified him as Arthur Wharton.

'Are they giving any trouble?'

'No, sir.'

'What have you told them?'

'The usual. A small technical problem over their passport. They're yours.' Arthur Wharton nodded to the woman who'd brought Diamond this far and she beelined determinedly between two people crossing the office from different directions and into another corridor. Diamond realized that he was meant to go with her. Striving to go

158

the same way, he found that he wasn't so adept at dodging people.

He caught up with her by an open doorway. A uniformed member of the airport police was sitting outside, drinking coffee from a paper cup.

Diamond looked into the room.

He stared.

A woman and child were in there, certainly, but the child wasn't Naomi.

She was at least two years younger. Seated on a steel-framed chair, swinging her legs, this little girl still had a baby face, tiny features and chubby cheeks. She wasn't even dressed like Naomi. She had a blue dress, white socks and black shoes made of some shiny material like patent leather. She was Japanese, admittedly, but there the resemblance ended.

The Japanese woman who looked up anxiously at Diamond didn't match the description he'd been given either. She was in a red skirt and jacket and she was wearing rimless glasses.

At a loss, he turned to his escort, but she'd already gone. He spoke to the man at the door. 'Those aren't the people. There's some mistake.'

The cop shrugged.

He found his way back to the hub of the Immigration Department, and vented his frustration on Officer Wharton. 'You detained the wrong people. I've never seen that kid before and they're wearing different clothes, for Christ's sake.'

'Hold on, Mac,' Wharton told him, pointing a finger. 'Don't give lip to me. We held the people you wanted. You gave us no description, just a name. That's Mrs Nakajima in there, no mistake. You want to see the passport?' He handed one across.

Diamond opened it. No question: these people were called Nakajima. 'But they don't match the description,' he said.

'You mean this passport belongs to some other woman?'

'No. What I mean is that the people who were seen at Heathrow were dressed differently from Mrs Nakajima and child.' Even as he spoke the words, the mistake he'd made dawned on him. 'Oh, no!'

Wharton eyed him dispassionately.

'I assumed because Mrs Nakajima and her daughter were Japanese and travelling alone that they had to be the woman and child seen going through the departure gate at Heathrow. After BA came up with these people, I just didn't check the other airlines. They must have taken some other flight. They could have gone anywhere – any damned place in the world.' Mad with himself for being so obtuse, he ended by thumping his fist down so hard on Officer Wharton's desk that paperclips jumped.

Three thousand five hundred miles on Concorde chasing the wrong people. What a pea-brain! 'Listen,' he said to Wharton, 'it may be too late, but I want to contact Terminal Three at Heathrow. I want to fax every airline to check their passenger lists for a Japanese woman travelling alone with a child some time after one p.m. today. Could you arrange that for me?' Sensing that the request was too stark, he added, 'Arthur?'

'You want me to authorize these faxes?' Wharton's expression didn't look promising.

'You have the facilities here,' Diamond told him frankly.

'But you want me to handle this?'

'Exactly. If my name is given, there's so much to explain. If the request comes from US Immigration, they'll act on it promptly. No explanation needed. Speed is the key here.'

'Checking passenger-lists? You've got to be joking, man.'

'They're computerized,' Diamond pointed out. He'd not often thought of modern technology as an ally, but he had no scruples in this emergency. 'It's just a matter of tapping a few keys.'

Wharton rubbed the side of his face.

'Listen,' Diamond steamed on, 'while you're doing this for me, I'll go back to Mrs Nakajima and make your apologies. Fair enough?'

It wasn't fair, and he knew it. Wharton knew it, too, but the urgency in the way it was put to him was compelling. 'You'd better write down the message you want me to send,' he said with a sigh.

The crucial reply from London came in forty minutes later. By that stage of the exercise, Officer Wharton had been thoroughly briefed about the quest to find Naomi and now he identified himself totally with the challenge. 'Hey, man, this is it.' He held up the fax he had just taken from the machine. 'You want some good news? She's here after all!'

Diamond was galvanized. 'Here? In New York, you mean?'

'Right on. They flew in this afternoon on a Pan Am flight. A Japanese woman and a kid.'

'Brilliant! When did they land?'

'Seventeen-twenty. About an hour ago.'

'An *hour*?' Diamond's elation withered and died. 'By now they must have cleared customs and left the airport.'

But Wharton gave a reassuring grin. 'Not this airport. Takes a while to get through Immigration in JFK. The Pan Am flight?' He looked at his watch. 'I figure they *could* be as far as the customs hall by now, but I wouldn't bet on it.'

Diamond was on his feet. 'Which way?'

'Hold on, Peter,' Wharton told him. 'You're in serious danger of doing yourself an injury. We can check from here.' He pointed upwards to a set of eight television monitors mounted on the ceiling. 'Video-surveillance. See if you can spot your people. I'm going to see if I can raise the crew of that flight.'

Cameras were in positions where they could pan slowly over the entire queue snaking around the system of barriers towards the kiosks where their passports were examined and stamped. Diamond studied each screen keenly, looking for a child. Some were tantalizingly half obscured by adults.

Wharton was busy on the phone. 'I've spoken to the chief steward on the Pan Am flight,' he presently informed Diamond. 'There's no question they were on board. He remembers Naomi in the red corduroy, and the woman in the grey Rohan jacket.'

'That's wonderful, but where are they now, I'd like to

know,' said Diamond. 'I can't see them in the queue.'

'You won't. Seems the Pan Am flight has cleared Immigration. Take a look at the baggage claim hall – the monitors to your right. They should be in there somewhere. I'm trying to establish which of our officers dealt with them.'

He would rather have been in the baggage hall himself instead of staring at the grey screens. The figures grouped by the baggage carousel looked about as remote and unfocused as the pictures of the first moon landing. True, he could just about make out enough to distinguish one individual from another.

'If you think you spot them, we have a zoom facility,' Wharton explained, taking the phone away from his ear for a moment. 'We can take a closer look.'

'Thanks.' But he hadn't spotted them, and the possible explanations were depressingly simple to supply. They may have collected their luggage and gone. Or the woman may have owned a US passport, in which case they would have passed through at least half an hour ago. Or they'd carried everything as hand luggage.

Then Wharton started talking earnestly on the phone. He told Diamond, 'Okay, they just passed through Immigration. The woman's name is Tanaka – get that? – Mrs Minori Tanaka, Japanese passport-holder. The kid is travelling on her passport, name of Emi.'

'Amy?'

Wharton spelt it. 'Mrs Tanaka put down the Sheraton, Park Avenue as her address. We can check with the hotel whether they have a reservation.'

Diamond's eyes hadn't left the monitors and a moment later he was rewarded by the image of two grainy figures of a woman and small girl approaching the carousel with a trolley. The child appeared to have Naomi's fringe and black hair.

He pointed. 'That one. Second from the end. The child.'

Wharton reached for a remote control and pressed a button to operate the zoom. The child's face increased in size until it filled the screen, placid in expression, gazing nowhere in particular, as if preoccupied in thought.

Naomi, without question.

'Let me see the woman with her,' Diamond requested.

'In close-up?'

The screen blurred momentarily, then he had his first sight of Minori Tanaka, a keen-eyed, intelligent face with prominent cheekbones and a small nose. The mouth, defined with an intense lipstick, was wider than usual in a Japanese, giving a suggestion of waywardness, or sexiness, according to interpretation. She was probably in her thirties.

'Attractive,' was Arthur Wharton's opinion.

Unexpectedly, the face slid out of shot.

'Can you pull back?' Diamond asked, and as the camera was being adjusted to give the longer view, even before it was complete, he saw that the woman was stooping over the carousel. 'Christ, she's collecting her suitcase! She'll be gone.'

Watching the screen, they had been lulled into a near-disastrous passivity. In seconds, Mrs Tanaka could wheel her trolley through customs to the cab-rank and be driven away with Naomi.

'How do we get to them?' Diamond demanded.

'You need a stamp on your passport first,' Wharton told him.

'Oh, for crying out loud! That child has been abducted.'

'Passport.'

He handed it across. Wharton opened it, selected a rubber stamp from the drawer of his desk, adjusted the date and made the imprint in the passport. 'Now that you're legal we can go find them, Peter.'

Diamond was speechless. Speechless, then breathless, as Wharton led him at a jog along a moving walkway and down two sets of stairs. Through a door and they emerged into the main concourse of the air terminal, opposite the arrivals gate. It was busy with friends and relatives crowding the barrier for a first glimpse as the passengers wheeled their trolleys through.

They were in time to see Mrs Tanaka emerge, pushing one large blue suitcase on a trolley. At her side – and there could be no doubt any more – was Naomi.

The little girl appeared uninterested in the new scene unfolding in front of her, the mass of faces turned their way. She walked mechanically at Mrs Tanaka's side, one hand on the trolley. They passed the point where the drivers stood with notices displaying people's names.

'You gonna stop them?' asked Wharton, giving him a shove. 'You'd better go now, man.'

Diamond started forward, and it was brought home to him forcibly – for the second time – that he wasn't in shape for dodging and weaving. A man in a wheelchair skidded to a stop and yelled at him to watch where he was going. He didn't have time to point out that he was doing exactly that – it was the stretch between that he'd ignored.

Just as he found a clear way through, he hesitated.

Someone had moved in to speak to Mrs Tanaka, a white man, tall, with cropped, dark hair and a distinctive nose that made Diamond think of Charlton Heston, though the resemblance ended there. He was in a black leather jacket and white jeans. He spoke to Mrs Tanaka and she nodded and frowned, apparently startled by the approach.

Naomi was looking past the man, straight at Diamond. But it was the stone-faced autistic stare that he knew so well. Nothing to suggest she recognized him, no reaction of surprise, or pleasure, or dislike, come to that. She simply let her eyes focus on him for a moment and then she was distracted by the electronic chime that signalled an announcement on the public address. She turned her face upwards towards the source of the sound.

A decision born of professional experience trailing suspects had made Diamond stop that split-second before going up to them. The man might be some predator muscling in to 'help' with the luggage for an exorbitant fee – easy bucks when the victims were women with children in tow. Yet his presence could be more significant. So the right move was to go straight past them, veering off to the left, and stand close to the queue at an information desk and keep tabs on what happened next.

Mrs Tanaka's body-language suggested she was agreeing to whatever the man was proposing, yet not without some reluctance. After some head-shaking and spreading of the arms, she twice took a step away from him. Finally she allowed him to take over the trolley and wheel it towards the nearest exit, so quickly that Naomi — still with her hand on the side — had to trot to keep up.

Diamond followed closely, secure in the knowledge that neither of the adults knew him and Naomi was unlikely to react. Allowing them to get this far without being challenged was something of a risk, yet he reckoned their movements were going to be limited by the trolley, whatever they did next.

They were heading towards the taxi-rank. If necessary, Diamond decided, he would let them get into a cab and drive off, and he'd follow in the next vehicle. If the man in the leather jacket travelled with Mrs Tanaka, one question would be answered: he'd be involved in this business.

Outside was the line of yellow cabs, superintended by a man with a whistle in his mouth. But Leather-jacket wheeled the trolley straight past and across the road. The air-shuttle buses, then? Apparently not. They were going into the short-stay parking lot, which was a possibility Diamond hadn't considered, and he clapped his hand to his face in self-rebuke. He wasn't thinking sharply at all since arriving here; he put it down to the flying.

He had to cross the road quickly, zigzagging through traffic, following them into the ground floor of the parking lot, where his problems increased. Leather-jacket and Mrs Tanaka weren't more than twenty-five yards ahead with Naomi when they turned right and entered the elevator. The doors had closed before he got to them.

What now?

There were stairs close by. He had no idea whether to go down to the basement or up to the decks above. There was no indicator to tell him which floor the elevator had reached.

He'd have to plump for one and hope they were still in sight when he got there. One direction was as likely as any other, so he went down, taking the stairs two at a time and bursting through the swing doors at the bottom.

No one was in sight among the ranks of cars.

Behind him, the elevator doors opened. Nobody was

inside. He was certain now that he should have tried one of the upper levels. He got in and pressed the second-floor button, cursing the delay before the doors slid across.

He'd be fortunate if he hadn't lost them completely. The cage moved upwards, the doors opened and he stepped out and started running. No point in stalking the quarry now. If they stepped into a car and drove away, he hadn't the slightest chance of pursuing them. There were no taxis up here. But he *had* spotted them. They were three or four aisles to his right, about eighty yards ahead. So he ran, shouting to them.

'I say! Mrs Tanaka!'

She turned to look.

Leather-jacket also turned. He was in the act of unlocking a car door.

Diamond was still thirty yards from them.

Mrs Tanaka said something Diamond couldn't pick up and opened a door herself and bundled Naomi into the car.

'I'd like a word,' called Diamond.

But he didn't get a word. Instead, he got the trolley slammed into him as he advanced. Leather-jacket used it like a battering-ram, driving it at him viciously. It had the weight of the suitcase behind it and the full force of a large, young man.

Diamond's ankles could have suffered ugly damage if he hadn't reacted a split-second before the impact and jumped six inches off the ground — about as high as a man of his size could hope to achieve. He pitched forward, making the suitcase take the main impact. His head crunched against the metal basket mounted at the top of the trolley. But for the cushioning caused by the suitcase, he might have ended with his head in the basket like a victim of the guillotine.

As it was, he rolled aside, tipping the trolley over and denting the wing of a car with his left shoulder. He was in no condition to spring up and fight.

Leather-jacket wasn't staying. He grabbed the suitcase (now split across the centre) from under the trolley, swung it into the back of the car, slammed the door, and got into the front with Mrs Tanaka.

A faceful of exhaust-fumes didn't help Diamond's condition one bit. The car – a large, white Buick with red strips along the side – roared. The tyres shrieked and it powered away.

Chapter Twenty

EXTENSIVE BRUISING, DEFINITELY. SOME TORN skin on the shoulder and left arm, which was smarting. A rapidly developing headache. Really, though, there was no serious injury, except to his confidence. He'd blundered. Blown it. Gone down the tubes, as they would say in this city of fertile phrases. After flying thousands of bloody miles and actually catching up with Naomi, he'd allowed her to be snatched away again. She was being driven God knew where.

Hopeless.

He hauled himself painfully upright, more stricken with self-reproach than pain. Damn it, he'd ignored even the most basic procedures. Hadn't even got the car's number.

He could imagine the reception he'd get from the New York cops if he asked them to trace a white Buick with red trimmings and no number.

What now, then?

Was this really the end of the chase?

He glanced around, at the trolley, still lying on its side in the space the car had occupied. He supposed he ought to look over the side of the car lot in the hope of seeing the Buick making its getaway, but he was damned sure his eyesight wasn't good enough to read a licence plate from up here – even if he had the good fortune to spot the car.

And then it occurred to him that a vehicle making a getaway from here still had to conform to the procedures. The designers of car lots made sure everyone was obliged to check out in an orderly way. There would be a barrier downstairs and a place where you paid. Maybe, in a busy car lot like this, where you *lined up* to pay. Even if this place had automatic gates, you could only get out as fast as the machinery and the cars in front allowed you. Actually, he was quite sure Leather-jacket hadn't stopped at a pre-payment facility.

So they couldn't race out without paying. A car, however fast, took a little time to get out to the street.

He hobbled across to the lift at the best pace he could manage. The only point of exit from the car lot was on the basement level, and this was the quickest way down. By good fortune — and he was overdue for some — the lift door had remained open, so he stepped in and pressed the control. Each delay was mental agony — the pause before the door operated, the slow progress down — saying a silent prayer that the cage wouldn't stop at the floors between — and the hesitation before it opened. Then he was out and looking for the exit signs, trying to see the shortest way across the floor, because he didn't need to go by the same roundabout route as the cars.

He decided on a line to his left, through the ranks of cars, which meant some tight squeezes and several wing mirrors being knocked out of alignment, but it proved the quickest route.

Ahead five or six cars were curving out of sight up a ramp. He ran past four and was in time to see the barrier descend and the Buick — or at least a red and white car — on its way out.

He wasted no more time. The car now at the head of the queue was a pink Chevrolet. He dragged open the passenger door. The woman driver was in the act of paying her charge. She swung around. 'What is this?'

'Police.' With no credentials to show except a passport, he tugged it from his pocket and held it up like a warrant. 'Do you mind? Would you kindly follow the car in front?'

'Would you say that again?' She was young, in her twenties probably, with dark hair in a mass of loose curls that stirred as she spoke.

'I'm asking you to follow the Buick.'

'Are you from England?' she asked.

He groaned inwardly. 'This is an emergency.'

'You'd better jump in, then. I can take you into

169

Manhattan, if that's what you want.'

He didn't prolong the conversation.

She moved off at a promising rate and soon got them out of the airport complex and on to the Van Wyck Expressway to Manhattan. There was no sign of the Buick.

'Can we go faster?'

'You said you're police?'

'I did.'

'You don't happen to have one of those portable sirens with you?'

He supposed she was being sarcastic.

'No.'

'Do I have police permission to break the limit?'

'It's a kid at risk, a small girl,' Diamond stressed.

She moved into the fast lane.

Two miles along, Diamond asked her to ease off a little. He could see the white Buick.

It was in a centre lane doing about seventy-five. He could see the outline of Mrs Tanaka's head above the front passenger seat.

'Not too close.'

'So you don't want me to force them off the road?'

'Not at this juncture. I'd prefer to stay inconspicuous.'

'I just love the way you say things.' She steered smoothly into a space three cars back from the Buick and they cruised in convoy. 'This kid – is she from England too?'

'Er, yes. What's your name?' he said to change the subject. Telling her the little he knew about Naomi would just confuse her. *He* was confused.

'Ken.'

'You said Ken?'

'Mm.'

'That's a girl's name here?'

'Short for Kennedy. I was born the week the President was killed. I get tired of explaining.'

'It's nice to have an unusual name. Mine is common enough. Peter.'

'Peter the Great.'

'Unfair.'

'What's wrong with that?' Ken asked.

He slapped the curve of his belly and she grinned. 'I didn't mean it that way.'

The line of cars was still cruising steadily in the same formation. The New York skyline was in view now. 'We're on Long Island here, am I right?' Diamond asked.

'This is the Long Island Expressway we just moved onto,' she confirmed. 'We're heading for Queens and the toll tunnel under the East River.'

'Is this the route you would have taken anyway?'

She shook her head. 'I live in the Bronx. It doesn't matter.' After a pause she added, 'You appeal to my curiosity. You're not really a policeman at all. I may look dumb, but I can tell the difference between a police ID and a passport. On the other hand, you don't have the look of a hitch-hiker. Or a rapist. Is it, like, a fight with your wife over custody of the child?'

He told her that Naomi wasn't his own child. He was almost persuaded, after all, to explain how the little Japanese girl had taken over his life. Then they entered the toll tunnel and he concentrated instead on the uncertainty of what would happen at the other end. 'Where exactly does this come out?' he asked, as if he had a map of Manhattan imprinted on his brain.

'East 34th,' Ken told him. 'It won't be so simple trailing them from now on.'

'Could you try and get closer, then?'

After they were out of the tunnel, she succeeded in passing one of the cars ahead and another turned off at the first traffic lights, leaving them with just a blue Volvo between their car and the Buick. But the tension grew as they crossed the city, negotiating lights, willing the Volvo not to hesitate. They passed the Empire State and Macy's before turning right, onto 8th Avenue, heading north.

The Buick picked up some speed.

'Can you pass the car in front?' Diamond asked.

When she moved into the next lane the driver of the Volvo took it as a challenge and blocked their way through. At the next lights he braked hard, forcing them to stop, while the Buick cruised on.

Diamond swore and turned to see if there was room to

move out, but it was impossible.

'They won't get far,' Ken said in reassurance. 'The lights will hold them up.'

He wasn't so confident. He'd already watched them go through on the red at the next intersection. 'We've got to pass this clever dick.'

She did, on the next block, in front of the Port Authority Bus Terminal, to a crescendo of car-horns. They had lost position badly. A glimpse of white some way ahead might just have been the Buick. They had to assume it was. Diamond strained forward with his face to the windshield. 'Keep going straight ahead. If they turn I'll tell you.'

She overtook cars at each opportunity and sometimes when the opportunity scarcely existed. He couldn't fault her commitment to the chase. Occasionally he caught sight of the white car through the traffic about a block ahead and he just hoped to God it was still the Buick they were following. Central Park came up on their right.

'We keep going far enough, we'll get to the Bronx and I'll be home,' Ken told him.

But they didn't get that far. They had almost reached the northern limit of the Park when the white car ahead moved into the left lane and turned.

'Can you move over?'

'Sure.'

'That must be 109th.'

She handled the Chevrolet with confidence, accelerating into a space and taking the turn at a speed that made the wheels screech. But there was no white car ahead of them on West 109th Street.

'He could have doubled back down Manhattan Avenue,' Ken suggested.

'Try it, then.'

She turned left again. Mistakenly, for two blocks ahead there were only yellow taxis and grey saloons.

'Sorry. I'm really sorry,' she said, and her voice was desolate. 'Want me to turn?'

'Where do you think they were heading before we lost them?'

'Hard to say. We're not far from Columbia.'

172

'You mean the University?'

'Yes.'

'Can you work your way back in that direction? If we're lucky the car may be parked on the street somewhere.'

They turned right, onto Amsterdam Avenue. No sign of a white car. A vast church loomed up on their right. 'It's really popular with the students,' Ken remarked.

'The Cathedral of St John the Divine?' Diamond read from the board in a disbelieving voice.

'I mean the Hungarian Pastry Shop on this side.'

'Ah.' Neither of them felt like smiling. The confusion was indicative of their helplessness. Nothing is so hard to accept as the knowledge that you have failed. They were floundering, trying to buoy each other up with words, but the words gave no real support.

'The Columbia campus comes up on this side in a block or two,' she informed him.

'We ought to be checking these. Can you turn up the next one?'

It was 113th Street, and they drove as far as Broadway, then made two lefts onto 112th. Three white cars were parked there, not one a Buick. Almost ten minutes had passed since they had lost sight of the car; and ten grew to twenty while they continued to tour the streets without result.

'I can transfer to a taxi,' Diamond offered.

'I won't allow it,' Ken said. 'I'm as keen to find the damned car as you are.'

'It could have left the area by now.'

'We owe it to that little girl to keep looking.'

He didn't need telling.

It took them just under an hour to find the Buick. It was parked near the Broadway end of 114th Street. They would have found it sooner if they hadn't chosen to start at 113th and work back as far as 108th, but the enormous relief at picking up the trail wiped out any regrets.

'What now?' Ken asked.

'I'm more grateful than I can say.'

She frowned, not understanding his English avoidance of the direct statement.

'I can manage,' he said.

'Hey, you don't think I'm quitting now? I want to see the kid for myself.' Her eyes dispelled any doubt that she meant what she said.

'In that case, I'll tell you what we do next. We go doorstepping.'

This section of the street was lined with apartment blocks and small hotels. They tried the hotels first. 'I'm hoping to find a couple with a small girl who may have registered here an hour ago,' was the disarming way he phrased his enquiry. 'The lady is Japanese and so is the child.' He was trying to project himself as the caring English gent, as if friends of his had left behind some lost property that he was anxious to reclaim for them.

After trying three hotels and getting suspicious looks and shakes of the head, but no verbal response, he changed his approach at the Firbank, a shabby brownstone with a sign in the window saying *Vacancies*. The window needed cleaning.

The door stood open and a man in a black singlet and jeans was behind a hinged table that passed for a reception desk.

'Is Mrs Tanaka staying here?'

'Who the fuck are you?'

It was, by certain lights, an improvement on silence. Diamond said that he'd been sent by Immigration. 'And who the fuck are you?' he added.

'George De Wint.'

'Manager?'

'I have no illegals in my hotel,' De Wint said defensively. For a beefy, tattooed man with a Cagney profile, he suddenly sounded pathetic.

'But you have Mrs Tanaka, in this afternoon from England?'

'From England?'

'Japanese, with a male partner, and a small girl.'

'So what exactly is the problem?'

'Is she here, or not?'

'Sure, she's here. You want me to phone the room?'

Mentally, Diamond turned a black flip of triumph. 'Could I see the register?'

George De Wint leaned to his left, placed a hand on a dog-eared exercise book, and slid it along the counter.

Diamond opened it at the latest entry, which was *M. Tanaka*. 'There's only the one name here.'

'So what? Kids don't have to register.'

'How about the man?'

'The guy isn't staying here. He carried the suitcase.'

'Has he left yet?'

'Not to my knowledge. What exactly is this about, mister? I don't want trouble.'

'Which room?'

'Twelve.'

'Upstairs?'

'Third floor. She wanted a twin with bathroom, so I gave her my biggest.'

'Show us up.'

The Firbank reeked of some cheap scented spray. It didn't run to a lift and the stairs creaked like rowlocks, so there was no point in trying to approach the room by stealth.

A '*Do not disturb*' notice was hanging from the handle of room twelve. Diamond knocked.

No one responded.

'Seems they went straight to bed,' De Wint suggested.

'With a child in the room?' said Ken in disbelief.

'To sleep. They could be jetlagged if they came from England.'

Diamond called out, 'Anyone there?'

Still silence.

He rattled the handle. The manager unhooked a bunch of keys from his belt.

When the door was unlocked, there was still no word from inside. And the room was not in darkness.

Diamond stepped in.

A moderate-sized, cheaply furnished room. Twin beds, one with the bedding pulled back. On the other, an open suitcase.

'They went out, then,' De Wint commented. 'People are so dumb, leaving notices on the door like that. When are my staff supposed to make up the rooms?'

'You said they were up here.'

'So I made a mistake. Mister, this is a hotel, not the city jail.'

Diamond crossed to the bathroom door, tapped once and opened it. The light was on. A saturated towel lay on the floor. There was water in the bath to the level of the overflow. He stepped closer.

'Someone is in after all,' he said.

The manager went closer. His reaction was less restrained. 'Jesus – why in my hotel, of all places?'

Lying along the base of the bath under several inches of water was a body, face down and dressed in a white blouse, grey trousers and shoes. The hair was short and dark.

Diamond warned Ken not to look.

Discovering a death is disturbing in any circumstances. What made this the more shocking was that the wrists were fastened behind the woman's back, bound with cord. Around the ankles a belt had been wound several times and fastened.

Diamond took off his jacket and handed it to De Wint, who was still carrying on about his misfortune. He rolled up his shirt-sleeves and stooped over the bath in an attempt to turn the body face upwards. The New York Police Department wouldn't be too thrilled at having the corpse disturbed; however, he needed to confirm the victim's identity at once. Taking a grip of the clothes, he tugged, but his figure wasn't shaped for turning over bodies in baths and he had to ask for the manager's assistance. 'Come on, man. I'm not talking to myself.'

De Wint was backing out of the bathroom. 'I can't touch it. No way.'

Fortunately, Ken was less inhibited. She came forward and said, 'Let me help. I'm not bothered.'

Splashing themselves liberally in the process, they managed the manoeuvre at the second attempt.

Without any doubt the body was that of the Japanese woman they'd followed from John F. Kennedy Airport, the woman who had brought Naomi from England.

He turned to De Wint, water dripping from his arms. 'Is she the woman who occupied this room? Come forward, man. Now, do you recognize the lady, or don't you?'

'Oh my God, yes. She's the one.'

Now the head could be lowered under the water again.

The question no one had spoken because it was so horrible to contemplate had to be faced, and quickly: where was Naomi?

Diamond felt some unsteadiness in his legs. He was literally shaking at the knees, and it wasn't brought on by what he had just discovered. He feared for what he might discover next. Without a word, he straightened, turned and moved back to the bedroom, leaving the manager bowed over the toilet bowl in the act of retching.

There weren't many places where a child's body could have been concealed. He could tell without pulling back the bedding that nothing was trapped beneath it. And the space under the divan beds was far too narrow. He opened the wardrobe. It contained only a woman's jacket, grey, with the name Rohan embroidered on the front in yellow.

There remained the window to check. In truth, he didn't expect to find Naomi dead inside the room. Some combination of intuition and experience told him she wasn't here. He felt less secure about looking out of the window.

It faced the rear of a building in the next street, and overlooked a narrow yard bounded by grime-stained brick.

He had to brace himself to look down.

Plastic bins. Some tired-looking geraniums in pots. A few dead leaves and scraps of paper shifting fitfully with the breeze. Nothing resembling a small body. A pigeon eyed him from a window ledge opposite.

He leaned out further. 'This fire escape on the left,' he called to De Wint. 'How do you reach it from inside?'

'The door at the end of the corridor.'

'And if I had to go down it, how would I get to the street?'

'There's a passage to 113th. You can't see from up here.'

'That's the way he left with the child, I reckon.' He withdrew from the window.

Time was precious. Faced with the dilemma of

immediate pursuit, or trying to make sense of what was happening by going through the woman's things, he chose the latter and started a rapid search of the bedroom. No doubt he'd be hammered for disturbing the scene of a murder. Sod that: Naomi's safety came before anything else, and if there were clues here, they had to be found fast.

He went through the suitcase first, a blue fabric case with no manufacturer's name and no labels on the exterior.

The dresses and underwear folded neatly in layers were of fine quality. There were also some clothes for the child, bearing the Marks and Spencer label. He ran his hand several times through the contents of the case in the hope of locating documents or an address book. There was nothing more helpful than an A–Z Street Atlas of London and a copy of *The Times*, three days old. A toilet-bag contained wash-things, lipstick and other make-up and some Aspro Clear in tinfoil. A brush and comb. A portable hair-dryer. It was all very predictable.

He flicked over the pages of the A–Z and found a cross pencilled in against the location of the school. That, finally, made a categorical connection with Naomi.

With a face not markedly different from the pale green of the bathroom he was emerging from, the manager reappeared in time for more questions from Diamond.

'This man who was with them, did he say anything when they registered?'

'Do you figure he could have done this thing?'

'Would you answer me? Did you hear him speak? Was he British?'

'No, the woman was doing all the talking, trying to shut the kid up.'

'The child was upset?'

'She was giving them hell.'

From across the room Ken's tough front suddenly gave way to the realization of what that small girl must have been through. 'Oh, my God.'

Diamond, rigidly holding his imagination at bay, said to De Wint, 'Let's concentrate on the man for a minute. How was he behaving when they arrived?'

'He was smiling plenty.'

'While the child was giving them hell?'

'Yes, as if it embarrassed him.'

'Did he seem possessive towards the child?'

De Wint shook his head. 'He just grinned and left the woman to it. Don't know if this is any help, but there was a gold tooth somewhere. I noticed it when he smiled.'

'*Somewhere,*' Diamond repeated without gratitude. 'The front? The sides? Upper jaw or lower? Come on.'

'Upper. This side.'

'The left.'

The mention of the tooth must have brought the rest of the face into focus in the manager's recall. 'His eyes were brown and he had a nose you wouldn't forget easy, kind of narrow and elegant, like some movie actor.'

'Charlton Heston?'

De Wint looked impressed. He didn't know Diamond had been charged down with a trolley by the man with a Charlton Heston nose.

Resuming the search, he found a handbag upended and left between the beds. The ejected contents – comb, another lipstick, pens, compact, some keys, two matches and a roll of peppermints – lay scattered over the carpet. A purse was left containing six hundred dollars and a handful of British coins. This was not a murder for money.

He picked up the handbag. Every section had been unzipped and emptied.

So what was missing?

The passport.

The photo of Naomi that the woman had shown to Mrs Straw.

Presumably a chequebook and credit cards.

The Pan Am flight tickets and boarding pass. She may have discarded these at JFK, but it was unlikely. People tended to dispose of them later.

In short, any documentary evidence that might have been used to identify the woman and child had gone.

He moved the beds and looked under them. Lifted the

pillows and bedding. Went through the pockets of the jacket in the wardrobe.

Nothing.

Leather-jacket had taken what he wanted as efficiently as he had killed. With a terrified child looking on, he must have behaved with exceptional single-mindedness. Or callousness.

Diamond drew a hand across his bald crown, trying to decide if there was anything more to keep him here. The impulse to go in pursuit of the killer was almost irresistible. The man had Naomi. He might be taking her to some place to kill her too.

Yet where? It had to be faced that the trail was cold. Leather-jacket could have gone in any direction, anywhere in New York. Finding them wasn't a one-man assignment. It required the resources of the police.

He picked up the phone, got an outside line and dialled 911.

A patrol would be on its way directly, they promised. He was to stay where he was and touch nothing.

A bit bloody late for that, he thought.

He was racked with the helplessness of the situation. What a cock-up. Those cops were going to throw the book at him for handling the body and the dead woman's possessions, and so they should.

He'd defied the rules for Naomi's sake, and achieved precisely nothing.

He was so wound up that when Ken spoke from across the room there was a delay before her words got through. If the police were about to take over, she was telling him, she figured she didn't really want to stay, particularly as she couldn't do anything else to help.

He thanked her with as much warmth as he could muster, saying that she had come to his aid in a crisis and put up with him heroically. She said something about wishing the kid would be rescued real soon, and then she shook his hand and left.

This was no time for self-pity, but he was sorry she was leaving.

Alone in the room — De Wint having taken the

180

opportunity to escort Ken downstairs – he found the wait unendurable. With nothing else to occupy him in the bedroom, he entered the bathroom again.

The corpse of Mrs Tanaka lay face upwards, submerged, the eyes closed, the mouth gaping. There was no point in turning her face down again, even if he could have managed it. He'd tell the patrolmen exactly what he had done since entering the room.

As he looked down at the body he recalled the rigidity of the thigh when he had gripped the clothes to turn her. He'd handled the dead as a matter of necessity in his work on murder squads; for some reason the rigor mortis – experienced through the sensation of touch – always affected him more profoundly than the sight of the corpse. The loss of flexibility in the muscles, transforming the body into something like a plaster cast, was such a contrast with living flesh.

Then he thought, hold on, this is wrong. She was killed less than an hour ago. I know that. I saw her at the airport. I followed her here in the car. Rigor mortis takes effect after *hours*, not this short time.

He bent over the bath and put a hand on the upper arm. The flesh was soft to the touch. He placed his hand on the thigh again, where he had gripped it before. It still felt rigid.

A memory was triggered, and he had the explanation. He recalled something the switchboard operator at Earls Court Police Station had said. 'Rohans are really something else – all those pockets.'

The stiffness wasn't the result of rigor mortis at all. On each side of the trousers there were two front pockets fitted over each other, the inner one fastened with a zip. He pulled the tab. The cause of the rigor mortis effect was inside that inner pocket.

He drew it out: a substantial leather wallet. He opened it and found a Japanese passport, issued in December 1988. The water had seeped through, damaging the edges of the pages, but the entries inside were unimpaired. Everything was written in English as well as Japanese. The passport-holder was Mrs Minori Tanaka, aged thirty-six.

The photo was clearly of the dead woman.

She had a Yokohama address. He took out a pen and pad and noted it.

There was an entry for her child Emi, date of birth 2 February 1984, sex female.

He sighed and shook his head. Emi . . . Naomi. Poor little kid.

Voices sounded downstairs and the tone was familiar to anyone who has worked in the police. They hadn't come to read the gas meter. There were solid footsteps on the stairs, and De Wint's voice came in at intervals, pitched high as he played the respectable hotelier who has never had trouble before.

Quickly Diamond examined the rest of the wallet. Those missing boarding-passes were there, and the flight-tickets. Also, tucked inside, a small batch of photographs. He glanced through them, picked one out and then stared at it in some surprise before slipping it into his pocket. On this occasion, he decided, he wouldn't declare everything to the police.

Chapter Twenty-One

THE TWO PATROLMEN FIRST UP the stairs had one thing, and one only, lodged in their brains: if this was murder, the scene had to be sealed until the Crime Scene Unit arrived. Having viewed the body, they didn't go so far as to take off their shoes and tiptoe from the room, but they were pretty fastidious about avoiding contact with anything except the carpet. Such discipline ought to have sounded a warning bell for Diamond, but his mind was on other things. He followed them out and told them that something else had to be done, and urgently. He gave them descriptions of Naomi and the man in the leather jacket, and the white Buick, including its licence number. The patrolmen seemed to take umbrage at this big, bluff Englishman issuing orders, so he changed to a more respectful approach. Patiently, more patiently than anyone who knew him would have credited, he repeated everything until one of them took the decision to transmit the message to Central that a murder suspect was at large with a seven-year-old Japanese girl believed to be mentally handicapped. He could do no more. The machine took over.

The scene of the killing became a honeypot for homicide detectives, the forensic team in white overalls, police photographers, the coroner's assistant and the medical examiner. Procedural activity compartmentalized the horror of violent death and made it manageable.

For the next three hours Peter Diamond was put through the grinder by detectives.

Violent deaths are commonplace in New York, but the case of Minori Tanaka had unusual features. More than one of the interrogators commented that it was a cruel killing. Even murders have their scale of acceptability and a bullet through the head rates several points above a drowning. The tying of the victim's hands was picked out as a particularly nasty feature. One officer commented that drowning may have been used because it was a relatively silent way to kill. It was true that the manager, De Wint, hadn't heard anything to alert him. If Diamond hadn't arrived and demanded to be let into the room, the body would have remained undiscovered until next day.

The workover he was given was outrageous, in his opinion, considering who he was, and he told them so. Homicide were unrepentant. As an ex-detective he'd conducted himself, in the words of one lieutenant, like Winnie the Pooh in a James Bond movie. While he didn't accept the comparison, he pretended to see it their way after a couple of hours of being shouted at.

He was driven to the 26th Precinct stationhouse to assemble a photofit of Leather-jacket; a task he'd often demanded of witnesses himself, without appreciating how difficult it was to arrive at a likeness. Afterwards, they got him to look through photos of known criminals. A fruitless exercise that had to be gone through.

By eleven that evening there was still no news of the Buick except that it was identified as a stolen car, taken from a street in Queens early that morning. If a car isn't stopped within the first two hours of a call going out, he was told, the chances of arresting anyone are slim. They abandon the car and take another if they're professional crooks, and who in New York would admit to being an amateur? He asked if the patrols were being reminded of the details. The transmitter was red-hot, he was told. When a kid is at risk, really at risk like this Japanese girl, the alert has top priority.

'So is there anything else I can do?'

He got the answer he expected.

'You're asking me to leave, then?'

'You got it. What's your address?'

'What?'

'Where are you staying, man?'

He hadn't even considered until this moment. 'I, em, haven't checked in yet.'

'Mister, it's a little late in the day.'

He settled for a room in the Firbank. Downstairs, without bath, at sixty dollars. Probably a sensible choice. While his sumo sponsor might conceivably have stumped up for a five-star hotel downtown, this was where the action was. And a five-star hotel downtown might have looked askance at a guest without any baggage at all.

The *action*? Why do I kid myself, he thought. I'm sidelined here. A killer is holding a handicapped child somewhere in this city. Even the police are getting no information.

Patience, self-discipline, confidence that something will turn up – these are the props a senior detective learns to support himself with when everything has been done and nothing seems to be happening. He'd been through it many times. The pressure was extreme, but you had to be strong.

In the privacy of the first-floor bathroom, he took from his pocket the photograph he'd found in Minori Tanaka's wallet, having suppressed his curiosity for hours. A curious picture to carry in a wallet. Not the kind of snap people hand out to friends when families are mentioned. It was a shot of a gravestone.

Most of the inscription was in Japanese, with the exception of some numerals showing the dates of birth and death of the deceased. He had to squint to read them: 2.2.1984–12.12.1988

He dipped into his pocket for the notes he'd made of the passport details and found that his memory wasn't at fault. The child named in the passport, Emi Tanaka, had been born on 2 February 1984, which was identical to the date of birth on the gravestone.

A coincidence?

No.

A twin?

Unlikely.

Most probably Emi Tanaka was dead.

If so, she had been dead four years. Yet Mrs Tanaka

had brought Naomi through immigration at Heathrow and JFK by using this passport, suggesting that *she* was the child born on 2 February 1984. The age was about right. No other identification is required when children travel on their parents' passports. No photo. No birth certificate. Not even descriptive details.

He returned to his room and lay on the bed pondering the reason why a woman should take a child – an autistic child – all the way from Japan to England, pretending it was hers. The obvious assumption was that she had kidnapped Naomi. Maybe she was one of those unfortunate mothers who snatch somebody else's child because their own has died. He'd investigated a similar case in England, although both children had been much younger, just a few months old in fact. The distress had affected everyone, not least himself. He'd been relieved that the woman was treated with leniency by the court. Anyone who has suffered the loss of a young child, or the grief of a miscarriage, can understand the motive for such actions, criminal as they may be.

With the facts so far, he started putting together a scenario. Somewhere in Japan in 1988, Mrs Tanaka's child Emi had died, aged four years and ten months. The grief-stricken mother had been unable to come to terms with her loss. She had to endure the sight of her dead child's friends growing up and enjoying the world, as Emi should have done. Either by chance or intention she observed the children in a school for the handicapped. Naomi was one of them, and Mrs Tanaka noticed her particularly because she was about the age Emi would have been. She coveted her. Not understanding Naomi's autism, she persuaded herself that this beautiful and apparently normal child was merely unwanted and unhappy, and that she could be a good mother to her and give her the love she craved.

So she contrived some way of snatching her from the school.

Then she'd flown to England, using her own dead child's entry on the passport to get Naomi past the immigration checks.

186

In London (the scenario went on), in fact, on a shopping trip to Harrods, Naomi had succeeded in escaping from this woman who had kidnapped her. She had hidden in the furniture department, and there she had been found after the store closed.

Distraught, Mrs Tánaka had not known how to get the child back. Afraid of contacting the police or the Japanese Embassy, she had waited for news of where Naomi was being looked after. Eventually, perhaps by recognizing her on television, she had tracked her to the school. By calling there early in the morning, she had avoided meeting the teaching staff. Her strength of will had outmatched Mrs Straw's. Reunited with Naomi, she had made her escape to New York.

There the theory foundered. The events in America were inexplicable. Leather-jacket's involvement didn't fit any facts at all. Apparently he'd been waiting to meet Mrs Tanaka and the child – with murder in mind. If not, then he was a killer who picked up women randomly at airports and murdered them – but would a random killer approach a woman with a young child? Surely he'd have the sense to foresee the problems that would bring. Anyway, the nature of the killing didn't square with a casual pick-up. The usual motives of sex and theft just didn't apply.

Well into the night Diamond grappled with the inconsistencies, trying to develop the scenario and finding it impossible. Somewhere earlier in the chain of events there must have been an American connection he'd missed, he decided, but that was the limit of his speculation. At some stage he left the room and went upstairs to check whether anything new had emerged. He found a solitary cop slumped in a chair outside the murder room. No one was inside. Homicide had left, and the inquiry was now being conducted from Headquarters, wherever that was.

He returned to his room, stripped and got into bed. Back in England, it would be morning already. He didn't feel like sleep, but he was dog-tired.

Chapter Twenty-Two

THE CRIME SCENE UNIT WERE running the inquiry their own way, and the detective skills of Peter Diamond were not included in the plans. He was finding that being a bystander was more stressful than heading the murder squad.

Early in the morning, realizing he hadn't eaten anything since the flight from London, he went looking for a coffee shop and found Hungry Mac's on Broadway and 114th. Number Seven on the menu, with just about everything in the kitchen included, carried the promise of what he regarded as a basic breakfast, and he ordered a double portion. He was on one of the stools at the counter – an uncomfortable perch for a big man – in order to get a view of the TV set. The Firbank wasn't the sort of hotel that provided television in the rooms, so he hadn't yet seen if there was any news coverage of the murder and Naomi's abduction. To add to his frustration, some kind of idiot game show was on the screen at present and two of the customers were watching as if it were the high point of their week.

He should have realized he'd get the information he wanted from the man who took his order.

'You think you can put away two breakfasts?'

'I'm certain I can.'

'You visiting?'

'Er, yes.'

'From England?'

'Yes.'

'Where you staying?'

He hesitated. He hadn't personally experienced

rapid-fire interrogation by a New York waiter, though he'd seen others getting the treatment. 'The Firbank.'

'Where they found the dead woman?'

'Yes.' He tried to make light of it. 'Hot and cold in all rooms. Towels and corpse provided by the management.'

'You get some crazies these days,' the man remarked to the shop in general, and it wasn't entirely clear whether he meant Diamond. 'This guy slept in the Firbank last night.' Evidently he did mean Diamond.

The place was pretty full, but no one else seemed interested where Diamond had slept.

When the plateful of bacon, sausages, hash browns and four eggs, easy and over, was served with toast and coffee, there was an extra tidbit in the form of some hard information from the waiter. 'I hear they found the car the killer used.'

Diamond had the knife and fork poised over the plate. 'Where?'

'Some cop spotted it in Chinatown.'

'No one in it, I suppose?'

'No chance.'

He bolted his double breakfast at a rate that would be a talking point in Hungry Mac's for weeks to come and legged it rapidly down to the 26th Precinct stationhouse. There, his air of authority carried him through as far as Sergeant Stein of the Detective Bureau, a gangling, grizzled man in a faded pink shirt and black jeans, who — this morning — was the senior detective on the case.

'You're the British cop,' Stein said in a tone that suggested he'd been warned to look out for Diamond.

'I hear you found the car.'

'A patrolman did.'

'Chinatown. Is that somewhere near the Bowery?'

'You could say that.'

'Where exactly is it, then?'

'Chinatown?'

'The Buick.'

'They moved it,' said Sergeant Stein, and added, after a considerable pause, 'for forensic examination.'

'So what time was it found?'

'A statement will be issued later.'

'Come on,' said Diamond in a flush of annoyance. 'I'm not here out of morbid curiosity.'

'What *are* you here for?' Stein asked.

'For a missing child out there with a murderer. Isn't that a good enough reason for the New York Police Department?'

Stein was unrepentant. 'Mister, I should be asking you the questions.'

'Like what?'

'Like what is your special interest in this kid?'

Diamond tensed. 'What exactly are you driving at, Sergeant?'

'We take a good look at middle-aged guys who follow little girls.'

The sergeant came within an ace of being thumped, and he knew it, because Diamond advanced on him until they were almost nose to nose like boxers staring each other out. 'That is not only insulting, it's also provocation,' he said on a note from deep in his gut. 'If you want to hang onto your shield, don't ever give horseshit like that to a senior policeman.' The minor detail that he was no longer a senior policeman didn't arise. He'd reacted as if he was. In the heat of the moment, he'd have needed to think hard to remind himself that he was not. And Sergeant Stein wasn't to know.

Stein backed down, actually raising his right palm like an Indian making peace. 'Just overlook what I said, would you? It was a heavy night.'

'Tonight could be heavier,' Diamond told him. 'Well? What time did they find the car?'

'Around two a.m. on Mulberry Street.'

'Anyone see anything?'

'No witnesses yet.'

'Where was the car taken to be examined?'

'Forensic have a workshop on Amsterdam.'

'Is that a walking proposition?'

'You want to visit? You can ride with a patrol. Just wait here, Mr Diamond.' Nodding a number of times to demonstrate his new-found co-operativeness, Stein departed thankfully from Diamond's presence.

The ride to Amsterdam Avenue in the company of a

laconic, gum-chewing officer allowed Diamond to weigh Stein's remark. Child-abuse had always been around, yet lately its notoriety had increased sharply. Whether the practice was on the increase was another question. As with rape and other sexual offences, the statistics needed to be put in the context of the greater opportunities for reporting and detecting the crimes. Whatever the truth, the public perception was that any man not actually a parent or a teacher had better not be seen alone with a young kid. He understood the need for vigilance, but he still regretted the fact that a few sexual deviants and sensation-seeking newspapers could make trust between man and child seem so unlikely as to be impossible any more.

Without a kid of his own, he couldn't truly view the question as a parent would, but were childless people who liked children fated to be treated as potential perverts?

The place where vehicles were taken for the forensic tests was hardly the squeaky-clean workshop-cum-laboratory Diamond had expected to walk into. It was a converted garage with a couple of ramps and inspection pits manned by young men in greasy overalls. The Buick was parked on the forecourt and was getting no attention at all.

He soon found an easy-going and friendly 'evidence technician' who appeared not to have been warned to watch out for a trouble-making British cop, and was quite willing to talk. 'The Buick? It'll take us at least a week. From what I can tell so far, half of New York seem to have driven that car and used it for sex and smoking. My guess is that it was owned by a syndicate of students.'

'You've done some preliminary work, then?'

'Had a look inside, removed most of the litter for examination.'

'What does it amount to?'

'The litter? Cigarette packets and butts, sweet papers, sandwich wrappers, Kleenex, condom packets, gasoline receipts, Alka Seltzers, chewing gum, ballpoints, parking tickets, panty-liners, takeaway containers — want me to go on?'

191

'Quite a heap, I should think,' Diamond commented. 'Or have you bagged it up already?'

'Give me a break, man. Four cars were brought in last night.'

'May I take a look at this collection? I am assigned to the case.'

'You're welcome.'

He was led to the back of the garage, through an office into a large room where the items he'd just heard listed were displayed on a long trestle table. The impression he'd first gained, of good-natured inefficiency, was given a sharp corrective. Every piece was already labelled and assigned a number, with the position where it was found in the car duly noted.

The Buick's interior hadn't been cleared of rubbish since February at least, judging by the date on a gasoline receipt. Someone had collected a stack and clipped them together. It would be the devil's own job to try and identify something discarded by Mrs Tanaka's killer.

'You checked the boot, I suppose?'

'Which boot was that?' his informant asked.

He could do without differences in the language adding to his problem. 'The storage place at the rear of the car.'

'The trunk. Yeah. We checked.'

'Just that I didn't see any mention of the boot on these labels. Now I understand why.'

'Right.'

He bent over to look at the ballpoint pens. 'I suppose you can tell if these were used recently. It's okay, I'm not going to touch.'

'How would we know that?'

'If a ballpoint hasn't been used for some time, it gets dry. When you write with it, you have to run the point over a surface for a moment to get some ink.'

His friend the evidence technician received this statement of the obvious more solemnly than it deserved. 'That may be true, but I know of no test that would tell you how long it is since a pen was used. It would depend on certain variables, such as the temperature where it was stored. Jesus, man, we can't even tell with accuracy how

192

long a body has been left someplace, so I don't see us succeeding with ballpoints.'

'No, but if the pen delivers the ink straight away, the chances are it was used not long ago.' He was sounding like Sherlock Holmes, except that this wasn't impressing anyone, least of all himself. Better say no more about ballpoints. 'May I examine the receipts?'

'Sure. Just hold them by the clip and use this probe to separate them.'

'I can't imagine the killer stopped at a gas station anyway,' Diamond commented, picking up the sheaf of receipts. 'It's unlikely any of these would carry his prints.'

'We can check the date, no problem,' said the technician.

'I'm not looking for a date,' Diamond told him. He was acting mainly on impulse now, as he turned the receipts over and used the wooden probe to flick through the blank squares of paper. The pens had suggested a possibility, a long shot.

'You think there might be something written on the backs of those receipts?' the technician asked.

'Have you checked already?'

'Haven't had time. Why would anyone do that?'

'The little girl – the one who was kidnapped – was a dab hand at drawing.'

'And you figure that could give you a clue?'

'It might,' said Diamond. 'Unfortunately,' he added, replacing the receipts on the table, 'none of these are marked.'

He picked up the parking slips and inspected them in the same way. Naomi had not used them for drawing either. He clicked his tongue in exasperation.

'Seen enough?'

'Am I holding you up?'

'It's okay.'

'Then I'd like to sift through the rest of this stuff. If you want to get back to your work, I can promise I won't leave my prints on anything.'

'That's okay by me.'

It was nice to be trusted.

The chance of finding anything significant was remote,

but even sorting through a collection of rubbish was better than doing nothing at all. Using two probes like chopsticks, he examined the items systematically, looking for signs of recent use. There was a roll of peppermints, and it occurred to him that Naomi might have been offered one to pacify her, but the mint that was visible was so dusty that it must have been unwrapped months ago.

With his thoughts still on the possibility that Naomi might have been offered something edible to stop her from protesting, he turned to the takeaway containers – a stack of six of different shapes from various fast food places. Odours of sweet and sour – sweet *what* and sour *what* he preferred to pass over – lingered around them. Nor did he care to imagine what the interior of the Buick must have smelt like on a warm day when the windows had been closed for some time.

There were two containers apparently of fairly recent origin, so he extracted them from the stack. These weren't polystyrene like the others, but were boxes made from thin white card. Judged by the grease-stained, sugary interiors, they had probably contained doughnuts.

He turned one over to look at the underside. It would have made a good surface for drawing. However, it was blank. Why was he so reluctant to drop this supposition that Naomi had left a drawing – a drawing, moreover, that provided information? He had a sense of being driven by some force akin to telepathy, as if the child were willing him to find what she had left. This wasn't entirely illogical, for occasionally in his life he'd experienced premonitions that had been fulfilled, such as the certainty that he would meet a particular old friend in a strange town.

So when he picked up the second box and saw pen-marks on the underside of the lid, his pulse may have quickened, but he did not punch the air with his fist or shout, 'Eureka!'

He explained with great patience to Sergeant Stein at the stationhouse how Naomi liked to make drawings, probably to compensate for the non-communication enforced by her muteness.

'And you think this is her work?' said Stein.

'Not this precisely. It's a copy I made of the drawing on the food-container. I left the box down at the workshop with all the other things found in the car. The ink matched one of the ballpoints found on the floor beside the front passenger seat. There's no way of proving Naomi did the drawing, but I could tell from the state of the box that it hadn't been lying in the car for long. I think the killer may have stopped at some point to feed her, or she may simply have found the box in the car and used it for the sketch.'

'You call that a sketch?' said Stein. 'Don't get me wrong, but it looks more like a doodle to me. What is it?'

'I'm not certain myself yet,' Diamond admitted. 'The original is about twice the size, or a little more,' he added, placing his notebook open on the desk.

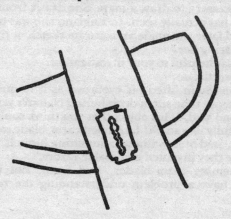

Stein said after a pause, 'You really think this represents something?'

'If Naomi did it, yes. She has an individual way of looking at things, but her drawing is pretty accurate.'

'Is it a map?'

'I suppose it could be.'

'If it's going to be any help to us, it *has* to be,' said Stein. 'I mean, what have we got here? Is this some kind of overpass? Because they're not common in New York City.'

195

Diamond stared at the drawing. He saw what Stein had obviously seized on — the broad causeway stretching south-east to north-west, apparently crossing minor routes. 'If so, what's the rectangular object there?'

'Automobile, I guess.'

'A bird's eye view, you mean?'

'Could be.'

'Then what is this elongated shape along the centre?'

Stein considered for a moment. 'You say this kid has an original way of seeing things. Maybe we're looking at the underside of the Buick. This could be the exhaust.'

'The *underside*?' Diamond doubted whether a child of that age had such technical know-how, and said so. He also doubted whether Naomi was capable of the conceptual ability necessary to draw a map. 'She draws from memory what she has actually seen. In England she was taken on a train, and later she made an accurate sketch of the back of the seat facing her.'

'Was that helpful to your investigation?'

'Not directly, no.'

Sergeant Stein lifted his eyebrows as if to question the value of more time spent deciphering Naomi's work.

Diamond said, 'This object that you think could be a car looks awfully like an old-fashioned razor-blade to me.'

'Uhuh,' said Stein without committing himself.

'Before they invented disposable razors.'

'I remember razor-blades,' said Stein, 'but if that's a blade, I have a problem understanding the rest of the drawing.'

'Me too.'

'I'll just attend to a couple of other things that came up.'

Abandoned to ponder the mystery alone, Diamond tried turning his notebook to see if the picture made more sense orientated differently. There was no certainty that what he'd taken to be the top was actually so; you can turn a food container any way you like and draw on it. No new possibilities leapt out. The rectangular shape still looked like a razor-blade from every angle. Now that he'd lodged that idea in his brain, he couldn't visualize anything else.

Towards noon, Lieutenant Eastland, the officer in

charge of the case – the man who had compared him to Winnie the Pooh – came in and said there was some progress in identifying the dead woman. The Japanese police had checked the Yokohama address in the passport. Mrs Tanaka was divorced and lived alone. Until the previous November she had been employed as a secretary at Yokohama University.

'A secretary? That begs a few questions,' Diamond commented. 'It could mean she was a high-powered administrator or simply a typist.'

'My information is that she worked in the faculty of science as one of a team of people operating word-processors,' Eastland told him. 'As for the kid—'

Diamond interrupted. 'Lieutenant, there's something I should tell you about the kid.' This would be embarrassing, but it had to be admitted. 'I'm pretty sure Naomi wasn't Mrs Tanaka's child. She had a daughter of her own who died. I, em, found this picture of the grave. This was the child listed in the passport.' He produced the photo from his pocket and prepared to be sliced into small pieces. The withholding of evidence wasn't the way to win friends and influence people.

The inevitable question came: 'Where did you get this?'

He answered, explained and apologized.

'Why are you showing it to me now?' Eastland asked without otherwise reacting. He was a tight-lipped, gaunt-looking cop in his forties, with a measured style of speech.

'Because it may have a bearing on the case.'

'You knew that last night.'

'I only examined it after you'd finished with me.'

'Couldn't take more of the same, huh?'

'That wasn't the reason.'

'So what was?'

'Priorities. I wanted to keep it simple. The first thing was to get the machinery in place to find Naomi, never mind who she is.'

'Did you remove anything else from the wallet?'

'No.'

'Can I rely on that?'

'Absolutely.'

'You know what you are?'

'I know what you think I am.'

'So long as we both understand,' said Eastland flatly. 'Now would you be so gracious as to share with me the drawing you were discussing with Sergeant Stein?'

The sarcasm couldn't have been more blatant, but at least there was some recognition of Diamond's efforts at consultation.

He opened his notebook again. Not wishing to pre-empt any ideas the lieutenant might have, he said nothing about the razor-blade.

'You believe the kid drew this?'

Diamond explained that he had made a copy.

Eastland frowned at the drawing for some time. Finally, all he could find to say was, 'What's your opinion?'

'I think the small object is a razor-blade.'

'Could be. In that case, what is it standing on – a shelf? Are we in a bathroom here? This semi-circular section – does this represent a hand-basin?'

'I hadn't thought of that.'

'The bathroom attached to the murder room has a similar basin, only the shelf is at quite a different angle. No bathroom shelf I ever saw is suspended across the width of the basin. Mind you, kids draw things from strange angles.'

'She'd have needed to be taller than you or me to look down on the shelf in that bathroom,' Diamond commented.

'I'm saying kids get things out of line.'

'She's an accurate artist.'

'And you think this is significant?'

'With not much else to go on . . . ' said Diamond, his voice trailing away as a new possibility dawned.

'Even if it is a drawing of the bathroom,' said Eastland. 'Even if there was a razor-blade in there – and I don't have any recollection of one – where does it lead us?'

Suddenly the marks made sense to Diamond. Everything clicked into mental focus. 'It's a tattoo.'

'A *what*?'

'The razor-blade is a tattoo. Take another look. This thing you thought was the shelf is obviously someone's arm against a steering wheel. She draws what she sees in front of her. I think that's the suspect's arm. It's the view Naomi must have had if she was strapped into the front seat beside him.'

Eastland stared at it for some time. 'You could be right.'

Chapter Twenty-Three

ONE OF THE OLDER COPS passing through the office had a memory of the razor-blade tattoo. It had been the emblem of a teenage street gang of the late 1970s that had created a certain amount of mayhem in a rundown area of Brooklyn, inspired by the punk-rock movement. The membership had reached about forty at the peak around 1978. By the eighties new gangs had taken over.

'Presumably you keep records of tattoo-marks of known criminals?' Diamond asked.

'They'll be on computer, sure.'

They ran a check. Eleven males were listed as having a razor-blade tattoo on one arm or the other. Not all had been members of the Brooklyn gang. Several, it seemed, simply liked the razor-blade design; one extreme case had a chain of them running from the back of one hand, up his arm and over his shoulders down to the opposite hand.

The computer-operator accessed the details of each. Three of the Brooklyn gang had descriptions promisingly close to Diamond's memory of Leather-jacket. He asked for mugshots. This entailed a visit to Records, in another building on the same block. The files were spread on a table for inspection by the time he got there. His pulse quickened.

Naomi's picture had paid off.

One of them was Leather-jacket. No question. The mean, narrow face, the eyes and, in the profile shot, the Charlton Heston nose.

'That's him.'

'Lundin? He isn't nice.'

The name was Fredrik Anders Lundin. Aged thirty-two.

A history of juvenile crime followed by two sentences for armed robbery. Sandwiched between them was one for murder, but he had been released on appeal. There was information that since coming out after serving three years of the second rap for armed robbery, Lundin was offering his services as a contract killer. He was currently under police surveillance (the file claimed), presumably in prospect of putting him away for a long term, rather than some token sentence for the charge of intent.

'It says you have tabs on him.'

Lieutenant Eastland said in his slow-speaking way, 'You're one hundred per cent certain this is the guy?'

'Absolutely.'

'You saw him meet with Mrs Tanaka and the kid in the airport car lot?'

'Lieutenant, I was as close to him as I am to you right now.'

'Okay, we'll pull him in.'

'How?'

Eastland gave a shrug that said English detectives were dense. 'That's what patrols are for.'

'Look, this isn't a simple arrest,' Diamond pointed out. 'This man is a killer. He's abducted a child. Her safety is paramount. You send two patrolmen in and people could start shooting.'

'What's your advice, then – a stake-out?'

'He's already under surveillance, according to this.'

'Don't believe everything you read in records,' Eastland cautioned. 'Surveillance could mean we have a guy who watches him play pool a couple of nights a week.'

Diamond couldn't be certain how much of this laid-back attitude was the New York detective's insulation against the dangers out there on the streets. He was in earnest, and he meant to leave nothing to chance. 'Lieutenant, you asked for my advice. I'm suggesting some subtlety is necessary. I don't think you should attempt to arrest him in the room where he's holding Naomi. That's putting her in real danger.'

'Mr Diamond, I'm deeply obliged to you,' said Eastland, affecting an English accent with about as much success as

Dick Van Dyke in *Mary Poppins*. 'Let's take a jolly old spin out to Queens where the gentleman resides and be subtle. I assume you want to be on the team.'

Diamond wasn't amused by the sarcasm, but he accepted an offer from Sergeant Stein to ride in his car. When they emerged from the Mid-Town Tunnel, the afternoon was drawing on. Some of the streetlights were switched on.

'Do you carry a piece?' Stein asked at some point on the journey.

'No.'

'Is that right – that English cops go unarmed?'

'Generally, yes.'

'Didn't you ever need one?'

'Not up to now.' He could have added that he was notoriously cack-handed, that in his possession a gun would go off when it was least expected, like now, from the jolting he was getting. The seat had no springs at all that he could discern.

Stein commented, 'Me – I'd have been dead five times over without my automatic.'

The area they were driving into was neither the best of Queens, nor the worst. The turn-of-the-century tenements had probably been smart addresses when they were built. The fire escapes that fronted them were still festooned with evidence of the warm afternoon that had just come to an end: canvas chairs, pot-plants, bedding, beer cans, takeaway boxes.

A patrolman flagged them down on a street corner. 'You can't drive past here. The suspect has a view of the street.'

'Which side is his apartment?' Stein asked.

'The right.'

'Anyone sighted him yet?'

'No. But there's a light.'

'So we could get lucky.'

They got out and joined Lieutenant Eastland and two more detectives, who had pulled up behind. A third car of uniformed officers had arrived from another direction. Eastland used his mobile radio to make contact with people already in position closer to the apartment. Then he issued orders. He wasn't messing now, and Diamond formed a better opinion.

'We're getting good co-operation from the people in the adjoining apartments,' he told Diamond presently.

'Have they seen the child?'

'Sorry, but no.'

'Or heard her voice?'

'Nobody mentioned it yet.'

'Maybe the walls are too solid.'

'Could be.'

'So what's the plan?'

'We can afford to wait a while,' said Eastland. 'With luck, he may come out for food in the next hour, and then we grab him. You want to go closer?'

'Why not?'

Stein was told to accompany him. Like two local residents walking invisible dogs, they strolled along the sidewalk until they were level with number 224, where the lighted second-floor windows gave promise of Fredrik Lundin being at home. Any chance of a sighting was forestalled by venetian blinds. Even so, it wasn't wise to linger. A finger's-width gap between the slats could give a clear view of the street.

They walked almost to the end of the block before stopping. Stein offered his pack of cigarettes.

Tempted, Diamond remembered that he was supposed to be a non-smoker now.

Stein's personal radio crackled. Eastland's voice asked, 'See anything?'

Stein reported back, 'Light at the window. Blinds. First floor in darkness, apparently unoccupied. Front door looks easy. Want us to go in?'

'Not yet.'

'The problem with this,' Stein confided to Diamond when he'd switched off, 'is that if Lundin gets suspicious, we could have a siege on our hands.'

It was a risk Diamond was willing to take, in spite of the fact that darkness was setting in rapidly.

'Sieges can be heavy on man-power,' Stein explained. 'We don't let them happen.'

Three cigarettes later, the radio broke the silence. 'Okay, we can't wait all night for this jerk,' Eastland announced. 'You and Diamond can enter by the front and occupy the first-floor apartment. Be ready to go upstairs as soon as the suspect is flushed and separated from the kid. Check?'

'Check, Lieutenant,' said Stein.

Diamond had an impulse to wrench the radio from him and urge Eastland not to provoke a shoot-out, but cold reason told him it wouldn't alter anything. This was Eastland's operation, and with half his men looking on he wasn't going to take instructions from a limey detective. It was some reassurance that he'd expressed some intention of separating Lundin from Naomi.

He and Stein returned up the street towards 224. It was much darker by now and the front wasn't well-lit. They could barely see their way up the stoop to the door. Stein put a hand in his jacket, evidently feeling for the grip of the gun he wouldn't be without. He nodded to Diamond to try the door. It opened easily.

No sound came from upstairs. They were in a wide hallway with stairs facing them. Halfway along, on the right, was the door of the apartment where they were supposed to take up position. Diamond gripped the handle. Was it too much to hope that this door, also, would be unlocked? It was securely fastened. Probably a well-aimed kick would resolve the matter, but only at the risk of disturbing the entire house.

Fortunately Sergeant Stein had come prepared, with the strip of plastic known to housebreakers and policemen as the indispensable aid to easing latches aside. He used it confidently, the door opened inwards and they stepped inside. Warm air wafted over them, reeking of cheap perfume and body odour. Just like a knocking-shop, Diamond found himself thinking – a thought that lingered and lodged more firmly when he heard a female voice murmur sleepily but without alarm, 'Hi, who is this? What time is it?'

A sofa creaked and something stirred. The woman who had been lying there said, 'Is there one of you, or two?' She got up and moved unsteadily towards a table-lamp. 'I'm not taking two – not together. Sorry, guys. One of you has to wait.'

Her hand was on the lamp.

'Leave it,' said Stein in a stage whisper.

She started to say, 'What the fuck—' before Diamond moved fast towards her and clapped a hand over her mouth. She struggled, and he had to grab her round the back. She was wearing some kind of silk wrap that made her slippery to hold, because she was obviously naked under it. His terse, 'It's all right, we're police officers,' was not a message calculated to reassure a lady of her calling, but it was the first thing to come to mind.

Stein told her more bluntly, 'You make one sound and you're busted. We've come for the guy upstairs. Know him?'

Diamond relaxed his hold on her.

She said, too loudly for comfort. 'You mean Fredrik?'

They both made shushing sounds.

With less voice, she said, 'What's he done now?'

'Is there a kid with him?' Stein asked.

'A kid?'

'A girl.'

She hesitated. 'You mean, like, under-age?'

'A *small* kid, child, this high, Japanese.'

She seemed genuinely shocked. 'Fredrik? He never puts kids to work. I'm damned sure he never uses baby-pros. I wouldn't work for a guy who uses kids.'

Diamond remained quite still and said nothing, but a pulse was hammering in his head and his mouth had suddenly gone dry. Until this moment, child prostitution hadn't crossed his mind as a possible motive for Naomi's abduction. Now it had to be faced as a sickening possibility. Clearly Lundin had an income from pimping. Pray God the woman was right and he drew the line at selling children for sex.

'You heard any sounds from up there?' Stein asked her.

She shook her head.

'Nothing at all?'

'You can't hear anyone talk.'

'But you can hear them move about.'

'Well, yeah. I hear that sometimes.'

'Last evening?'

'I guess so.'

'More than one?'

'I can't tell.'

'Have you talked to Lundin since yesterday?'

'No.'

'You think he's home right now?'

'How would I know? I was asleep until you arrived. Did someone give you a key?'

'Why don't you go back to sleep?' suggested Stein without much generosity in his tone.

He radioed Eastland and updated him.

'Okay,' came their instruction, 'stay where you are. Send the pavement princess out to us. She can help us.'

'Did you hear that?' Stein asked the call-girl just as she was reclining on the sofa. 'Get dressed. Fast.'

'And, Stein . . . ' the voice on the radio went on.

'Lieutenant?'

'When he comes out, leave him to us. You go right in and find the kid.'

Complaining bitterly, first that she wanted no part in the police operation and then that she couldn't see to get dressed, the woman stumbled about the apartment picking up clothes. Diamond scarcely noticed; he was still reeling from the suggestion he'd just heard. A minute ago, he'd been ready to urge the police to go easy on Lundin so that he'd be fit to give information; now, if this grotesque scenario was true, they'd have to restrain *him* from laying into the bastard.

'Jesus, what are you trying to find?' Stein demanded of the woman. He was standing at the open door.

'My face.'

'Your what?'

'The bag with my lipstick and things. It's here somewhere.'

'I don't believe this! Get your ass out of here.'

She went.

Eastland would use her as a lure. There was a better

chance of Lundin opening his door to the woman who worked for him than to the New York Police.

Above their heads the floorboards creaked. Someone was definitely up there. Stein immediately radioed his lieutenant. Up to now, this operation couldn't be faulted. No doubt there were men at front and back, waiting for the swoop.

Diamond waited too, striving to apply concentration to the job he and Stein were about to do. He had to believe they would find Naomi unharmed in the apartment upstairs. He kept thinking how small her hand had felt in his. Usually he remembered the eyes of people. He could picture her eyes, but because of the nature of her disability, they weren't so eloquent. It was still the memory of a touch that moved him.

He and Stein took up position with the door fractionally ajar for a view of the hall. They knew this would take time to set up, and they waited at least twenty minutes before anything else happened.

Then there was the sound of the front door opening and footsteps across the tiled hallway. The call-girl passed her own door and started climbing the stairs, her leather-soled boots, tokens of her trade, clattering on the wooden treads.

Stein drew his gun.

Two shadowy figures crossed the hallway a short way behind the woman. They made no sound.

She turned on the landing and started to ascend the second flight. Her escorts followed.

Down in the hallway, more cops crept across the narrow bar of vision between the door-jamb and the edge of the door.

The woman was out of sight now, but the sound of Lundin's doorbell being pressed was loud and clear and so was her voice saying, 'Fredrik, it's only me, Dixie.'

Diamond heard footsteps cross the room above them, but he didn't hear Lundin's front door being opened. Presumably he was looking out through the peephole.

The bell sounded a second time.

By now the two gunmen would be flat to the wall on

207

either side of the door.

'Fredrik, are you there?'

Something was being unfastened.

The woman's voice said, 'Hi, Fredrik, could you possibly step downstairs a minute?'

'What the fuck do you want?' Lundin's voice demanded.

'I have a small problem with a client. Please.'

'What kind of problem?'

'Em . . . he won't leave.'

'What do you mean?'

Come on, come on, Diamond mentally urged him. *Just step outside, will you.*

'Like I said. He's being difficult.'

'He won't leave the apartment? He had a trick and he won't leave?'

'I can't force him.'

'Who is he?'

'Some guy. I don't know him. I can't work if he won't leave.'

'Okay, okay, you go back. I'll see to it.'

The door closed.

Diamond clapped his hand to his head in frustration.

Dixie the call-girl came downstairs markedly faster than she'd gone up. She pushed her way in past Diamond and Stein. 'That's all I'm doing for you guys,' she told them. 'You'd better not mess up now, or I'll be dead meat.'

'Zip it up,' said Stein. There isn't much credit in helping the police.

The wait began again, and it seemed longer, even though it was under five minutes.

Then footsteps crossed the floor upstairs and Lundin could be heard unfastening the latch on his door. This time he definitely stepped out onto the landing, because there was a shout of, 'Freeze – police!'

Rashly, Lundin chose not to obey the order. He could be heard making a dash for the stairs. He must have got down two or three when a shot was fired, followed by two more almost immediately. A shriek of pain gave way to the sound of a body hitting the stairs and thumping down several steps.

'They got him,' said Sergeant Stein. He stared through the gap while shouts were being exchanged by the police in the hall, checking that it was safe to close in on the wounded man. 'Let's go.'

When they opened the door, a man in a white T-shirt and black jeans was lying near the bottom of the stairs and one of the cops was standing over him. Stein ran straight past, up the two flights, with Diamond close behind.

The door to Lundin's apartment stood open. The light from inside was dazzling after the long wait in darkness. The place was lavishly furnished in brown leather furniture, cream-coloured units and a Chinese carpet. There were huge indoor plants and pieces of bronze abstract sculpture.

But there was no little girl.

Diamond checked the other rooms – bedroom, kitchen and bathroom. He tugged back the bedding, flung open cupboards, and – with grim apprehension – looked into the bath.

She was not there.

He went back into the living-room, looking around for some place he may have missed.

'Mr Diamond.' Stein had followed him into the bathroom and was still there.

Diamond found him kneeling by the toilet pedestal.

'Would this be the kid?'

A question that struck horror into Diamond.

'I always look in the john,' the sergeant explained. 'They panic and try and flush things away.' He was holding up some small torn pieces of a photo.

Diamond arranged them on the floor. There were seven altogether, and they made an incomplete, but recognizable picture.

'Yes,' he said. 'That's her.'

Chapter Twenty-Four

DIAMOND WAS BEING DIFFICULT AGAIN.

'Apart from anything else, I just don't think you're built for this,' Lieutenant Eastland told him. 'Stein can drive you to the hospital in comfort.'

'I'm going in the ambulance,' Diamond insisted. He had his foot on the step and it was just a matter of climbing inside. He would have appreciated a helping hand, because it was a high step for a heavy man.

'The paramedic has to travel in the back and so does one of our officers.'

'Let the officer ride in the front,' said Diamond. 'I'll keep an eye on the prisoner for you. Look, the man isn't going to run away with two bullets in his leg.'

'You can question him at the hospital.'

'I want the answers now, Lieutenant. You've wasted too much time already.'

This touched Eastland on a raw nerve. '*We* wasted time? You wanted to run this thing like a Thanksgiving party, not me. The subtle approach. You were bothered about the kid, remember?'

'Correct. And I'm still bothered about her.' With that, Diamond leaned into the ambulance and grabbed the end of the stretcher to hoist himself aboard, with near-disastrous consequences, because the stretcher was mounted on a trolley and started rolling towards him. He had just about enough momentum of his own to climb in and stop the thing from upending himself and the hapless Lundin in the street. Then he sank onto the spare seat beside the paramedic. For a man of his bulk, occupation was more persuasive than argument. 'See you later, Lieutenant.'

Eastland glared and delivered his parting shot. 'If you're typical of England, I'm not surprised it pisses with rain every day. It should crap as well.' He nodded to the driver to close the doors.

'How long will this take us?' Diamond asked the young man beside him as suavely as if nothing had been said.

'You mean to the hospital? Six – seven minutes.'

'Right.' He leaned forward to get a better view of the prisoner's face at the far end of the stretcher.

'Careful of his leg,' cautioned the paramedic.

'Careful of my leg,' said Lundin with even more concern. He'd been given a pain-killing injection, but a stray hand hovering over the wounded limb must have been painful in prospect.

'Never mind his leg,' said Diamond. 'Show me his arm. The right.'

The paramedic pulled aside the sheet from Lundin's torso. On the right arm was a razor-blade tattoo.

Lundin spoke up, 'You think I'm a needle freak, you're wrong.'

'You're not too far gone to talk, then,' said Diamond. 'I want to know about the child. Where is she?'

'I want a lawyer.'

That old gambit, thought Diamond. 'You know something, Lundin?' he remarked. 'Nobody likes weirdos like you who play around with little girls. Accidents keep happening to them in jail.'

'Little girls? What are you talking about?'

'Don't give me that. I saw you pick her up at JFK. With her mother.'

'So that's who you are,' said Lundin as realization dawned.

Diamond was rather put out that he hadn't been recognized right off. Once seen, he was seldom forgotten. To be fair, Lundin had a difficult view from his stretcher. Anyway, they seemed to have got over the potential difficulty of requiring a lawyer in attendance. 'Right. So we know each other. I'm the fellow you knocked over and you're the child-molester.'

'That's a lie.'

'You definitely knocked me over with a trolley.'

'The other part – I'm no pervert.'

'You're acting for someone else who is – is that what you're telling me?'

'I'm telling you nothing.'

'That's even more despicable, supplying children to people like that.'

'You're talking horseshit.'

'Don't tempt me, Lundin.'

'What? Get away from my leg!'

'Where is the child? What did you do with her?'

'I don't have to talk to you. Who are you?' Lundin asked.

'A man with a weight problem,' said Diamond, folding his arms ostentatiously and inching closer to the wounded leg. 'Sometimes I need to prop myself up.'

'Bastard! Get away from me, will you?'

'Better not call me names, then. Where is she?'

'The kid?'

'Yes.'

'She's okay. It's nothing like you say.'

'Her mother isn't okay. Did you kill the child later?'

'No, I tell you. No!'

'She's alive?'

'Yes.'

'So where can I find her?'

Silence.

'Where can I find her, Lundin?'

'No, get off! I handed her over. The deal was that I would hand her over.'

'Who to?'

'I can't say – I don't know.'

'Do you care about the child?' Diamond asked.

'What do you mean?'

'Yes, I know it doesn't make sense to a hired killer to care about a child, but let me put it to you this way. You're going to stand trial for Mrs Tanaka's death. If the child is also killed, you're an accessory to a second murder.'

'She's okay.'

'You keep saying that, but how do you know? This person she's now with may already have killed her.'

'I don't think so.'

'They hired you to kill the mother. Why should they draw the line at the child?'

He hesitated and asked yet again, 'Mister, who are you?'

'My name is Diamond.'

'You a cop?'

'I am not.' Sometimes candour is rewarded with the truth. It was worth trying. 'I'm a private citizen. I came over from England because of the child. Naomi was taken illegally from a children's home, and I care very much what is happening to her.'

'You're not a cop?'

'That's what I said.'

'Are you taping this conversation?'

'No.'

After a pause, Lundin plucked up enough confidence to say, 'There was a contract on the woman, not the kid.'

'You were hired to kill the woman?'

This was a matter Diamond should have sidestepped, he realized the moment he'd spoken. It added nothing to his knowledge and it pulled Lundin up with a jolt. 'Forget it — I don't need to talk to you.'

'Who hired you?'

Silence.

Diamond adroitly switched to another question. 'You said you handed over the child. When was this?'

Grudgingly, Lundin muttered. 'Last evening.'

'By arrangement?'

Lundin started to say, 'I don't have to answer these damnfool—' and then interrupted himself when he noticed Diamond unfolding his arms. 'They told me to bring the kid to the Trump Tower and leave her at the top of the escalator on the second floor at nine p.m.'

'Hand her over to someone?'

'No, just leave her.'

'And you did?'

'I figured somebody was going to be waiting for her.'

'Did you see anyone?'

213

'Mister, in this game, you don't *want* to see anyone.'

'How did you get the instructions, then?'

'The phone.'

'Man or woman?'

'Man, I guess.'

All of this was leading nowhere. Fredrik Lundin didn't know where Naomi was, or who was holding her. He would be charged with Mrs Tanaka's murder, but the people who hired him had made damned sure he was incapable of putting the police onto them. The trail had gone cold.

'Let's go back to the first instructions you had. Who made the contact?'

'I don't know. I was phoned.'

And so it went on. Lundin had met nobody. A voice had told him what to do, where to pick up the money that was his down-payment for the elimination of Mrs Tanaka. He made it sound as commonplace as selling a house, with ninety per cent payable on completion, except that 'completion' had a more sinister interpretation.

Diamond didn't need the six or seven minutes the journey took. In four minutes flat he'd learned all he was likely to learn from Fredrik Lundin. The police would take up the questioning at the hospital and no doubt they'd extract enough information to put him behind bars for a long term, but they would find out nothing Diamond wanted to know, nothing of immediate use in tracing Naomi.

They got to the hospital and Lundin was wheeled away to have his wounds seen to. Diamond shared his disappointment with Lieutenant Eastland.

Eastland was still sore from the earlier exchange. 'What did you expect?' he commented when he'd heard how little had emerged about Lundin's paymasters. 'The guy is a functionary. Why keep a dog and bark yourself?'

'I hope you're not giving up on the child.'

'Did I say that? Did you hear me say that?'

'No, but—'

'Okay. What are your plans, Diamond?'

'Mine? I, em, I haven't decided.'

'Are you still staying at that two-bit hotel, the Firbank?'

Diamond had to think for a moment. 'I suppose I am.'

'You can ride back with me. I'm leaving soon. Stein will take over here.'

He saw, of course, that this wasn't an olive branch. Eastland wanted him away from the hospital while the questioning took place, and for once it seemed sensible to comply.

'Okay, I got a little above myself,' Diamond admitted when they were together in the back of the police car. 'I need your help more than you need mine.' It was the nearest he would come to an apology.

'I thought you would strangle the guy.'

'Lundin, do you mean? No, I was wrong about him. I really believed this was part of a vice racket. Now, I think the child was kidnapped for some other reason. Lundin happens to be a pimp, but that's not what he was involved in here.'

'He runs three or four girls in the street where he lives. He's small beer,' said Eastland. 'So what's behind this? What's the motive? Why would anyone pay to have a woman murdered and a kid handed over to them? What are we dealing with here – a custody dispute?'

'The tug of love?' said Diamond. 'Not the way I see it. Nobody has shown much affection for Naomi. She was abandoned in London until Mrs Tanaka came along – and she didn't treat the child with noticeable kindness.'

'She wasn't the mother.'

'Right. Where are the parents? They've been conspicuously silent. If they *were* in dispute for custody of the child, they'd have declared themselves by now. The people in these cases need publicity.'

'Do you have a theory, then?'

Diamond stifled a yawn. 'Lieutenant, I'm jetlagged. It's all I can do to stay awake. I'll say this much: whatever we're dealing with, it's high risk and there's big money behind it. But why a small, handicapped girl should be mixed up in it is a mystery to me.'

'For a ransom?'

'The parents would have to be very rich.'

'Japanese industrialists?'

'Surely they'd have reported by now that their daughter is missing. You've been in touch with the Japanese police. Did they say anything about a tycoon whose child has been taken away?'

'No,' said Eastland. 'But you and I know that kidnappings don't get reported every time. The parents could be dealing with the kidnappers directly.'

'How does Mrs Tanaka fit into this theory?' Diamond asked in a tone that betrayed how unimpressed he was. 'Why was she killed?'

'She was caught in the middle somehow. Maybe she doublecrossed the people who hired her.'

'Do you really believe this?' Diamond asked.

'Can you think of anything better?'

He didn't answer, and for a time all that was heard was the car's suspension being tested by the uneven Manhattan street surfaces.

Finally, Eastland said, 'If we could positively identify the kid, we'd stand a better chance.'

'We've been trying to do that ever since she was found,' said Diamond.

They pulled up outside the hotel and he got out and thanked Eastland for the ride, adding that he might drop by in the morning.

He was deeply dispirited, and the prospect of another night in the Firbank did nothing to lift him. It occurred to him when he caught sight of the payphone in the front hall that he hadn't spoken to Stephanie since leaving London. She wasn't the sort to panic, but she must have wondered why he hadn't been in touch before now. He felt in his pocket for some change, badly wanting to hear Steph's voice, even if she gave him some aggro.

Then he made a mental estimate of the time in London. About four in the morning.

Nothing was working for him.

Chapter Twenty-Five

IN THE MORNING WHEN HE tried phoning Stephanie, his timing was still wrong. After listening to the dialling tone until his ear ached, he worked out that it was noon in England and she would be at the Save the Children shop. He went out to breakfast convinced already that this would be another frustrating day.

But when he returned to the Firbank and tried again, she answered, and still the timing was wrong. Even five thousand miles and a time-zone away the disapproval in her tone was unmistakable. He was in the doghouse. He didn't make much impression explaining that he'd tried phoning earlier. The legendary Diamond charm was put to the test, and he had to dredge deep. 'The reason I'm calling you now — apart from wanting to hear your voice, my love — is to check something you mentioned just before I left, about shoe-sizes. Am I right? Is an English seven equal to an eight-and-a-half over here?'

There was time out for thought during which he could sense the reproach evaporating. Then they had a normal conversation. He didn't mention that Mrs Tanaka had been murdered, but he told her Naomi was still missing, and she sounded genuinely concerned.

He admitted, 'I may be forced to abandon this.'

'You wouldn't give up,' she said, shocked. 'Peter, you couldn't leave the poor little soul a prisoner in New York. Besides, what would you tell that wrestler — the man who paid your fare?'

'I haven't even thought about that.'

'Listen, if it's me you're bothered about, I'll be perfectly all right for a few more days. Don't worry. Just do what you can for that child. There must be some way of tracing her.'

'I hope you're right.' And he added, meaning it, 'Love you.'

'Love you, too.'

'Thanks, Steph. You're very understanding.'

There was a distinct pause before she said, 'Sometimes I understand more than you give me credit for, pussycat.'

Outside, it had started to rain, so he borrowed an umbrella from the hotel before stepping out to the stationhouse, where pandemonium reigned. He learned rapidly that Naomi's abduction was yesterday's news. Overnight, there had been a triple killing in a shooting gallery in West Harlem. It took him rather longer to work out that a shooting gallery was the slang for an abandoned house frequented by drug-addicts and pushers. Some of them were having their prints taken while he waited to talk to anyone he knew.

Sergeant Stein came in and nodded. He would have walked straight through to another office if Diamond hadn't called across to him.

'Did you get any more out of Lundin?'

'Not much. He was sleepy.'

'Any clues about what happened to the child?'

'Zilch. Now, if you don't mind, I have the arrest report to type.'

'Nothing else has come through about her?'

Stein shook his head. 'Why don't you go sightseeing, look at the Empire State or something?'

'Is Lieutenant Eastland about?'

'This afternoon. Maybe.'

Biting back a sarcastic remark, Diamond walked out and hailed a cab, not to go sightseeing, but to drive out to Lundin's apartment at Queens. An idea had surfaced; when he was feeling fractious, his brain sometimes went into overdrive.

The van in the street indicated that a forensic team were at work in the house. Meeting one of them on the stairs, he explained who he was, which was received with a narrowing of the eyes, and then mentioned Eastland's name, which made more of an impression. 'When we were here yesterday, we found some torn pieces of a photogaph of the missing child.'

'In the toilet. Yeah, we have them. We found a couple of extra pieces trapped on the inside.'

'Could I examine them?'

'You'd better talk to my boss.'

The fragments of photograph were in a polythene bag in the van, and there was some reluctance to let Diamond see them until he explained his thinking to the senior man, giving it the sales pitch he'd noticed was obligatory when you wanted results in New York. 'The style of picture, from what I remember of it, full face with a pale blue background, strikes me as typical of a school photo. These commercial photographers are smart. They persuade a school to let them take shots of all the kids, one by one. The style is pretty much the same the world over. You see beaming kids in their school uniforms on businessmen's desks, the mantelpiece in the White House, everywhere. Are you a family man?'

'Yeah, we've got a grandchild.'

'So the photographer has to print dozens, maybe hundreds of photos to order, right? And he has to have some way of identifying them. He can't get each kid to hold up a board with his name on it like a mugshot. So what does he do? He pencils some kind of serial number on the reverse. If we're lucky, one of those torn scraps may have the number that identifies the child.'

The senior man was sufficiently interested to send someone down to the van.

Diamond, pink with the effort, said casually, 'We may be unlucky, of course.'

Presently the pieces of the photo were tipped onto a table. No number was visible at once, but they started turning pieces over.

'How about that?'

It was not unlike a conjuring trick, except that this was no illusion. Just as Diamond had predicted, the number 212 was pencilled on a corner-piece. His luck seemed to have changed at last.

'That was just a hunch?'

'Yes.'

'Cool,' the senior man conceded.

'Thanks.'

'Now you have a number.'

'Yes.'

'So next you have to find the photographer, out of all the school photographers in all the world.'

'Right,' said Diamond without stopping to explain that there was a way of narrowing down the hunt. He was going to have inquiries made in Japan, and in particular, in Yokohama, where Mrs Tanaka had lived and worked. Of course there were plenty of schools in Yokohama, but fewer junior schools and even fewer children given the number 212.

Buoyant with his discovery, he returned to the stationhouse and told Sergeant Stein. In a matter of minutes they typed and faxed a memorandum to police headquarters in Yokohama. Unfortunately, it was already past midnight in Japan. Policemen might be on duty; school photograhers probably not.

London, he knew, was awake. He asked Stein if he could make an international call connected with the case.

'You want to make a local call,' said Stein with a stage wink. 'No problem. We can make local calls whenever we want.' Evidently the NYPD, like the rest of the city, paid lip-service to economy measures.

Diamond tapped out the international code for Great Britain, took a card from his pocket and referred to the number hand-written on the reverse, realizing that he still didn't know the woman's name.

'Yes?' It was a man's voice.

'Could I speak to the lady who works as a Japanese interpreter?'

'One moment.'

She came on the line, still guarding her identity. 'Yes?'

'This is Peter Diamond, from New York.'

'I remember.'

'The sumo wrestler, Mr Yamagata, kindly agreed to underwrite my expenses.'

'That is so.'

'I thought I should let him know what is happening. I'm working with the New York Police. The little girl is still, unfortunately—'

She interrupted. 'Mr Diamond, before you say any more, I should tell you that I am no longer employed by Mr Yamagata. The London *Basho* finished on Sunday. The entire party of wrestlers and officials has returned to Japan.'

'Oh.'

'If you remember, I handed you a card with his Tokyo address.'

'Yes, I have it right here in front of me.'

'Then I suggest you make contact with him in Tokyo later tonight.'

'With Yamagata himself?'

'He lives in the *heya*, the stable of wrestlers. They have someone who will interpret.'

'You think he'll stand by his promise? I'm running up some hefty expenses.'

'Of that there is no doubt.'

Without enquiring whether she was referring to the promise or the expenses, he thanked her and hung up.

The rest of the morning and the afternoon were notable only for the fact that he moved out of the Firbank to a better class of hotel, on Broadway, a place with phones in the rooms and a bar downstairs. It was still only a short walk from the stationhouse, where he returned at regular intervals, only to be told each time that no reports had come in of the missing child. Plenty of progress was being made on the shooting gallery murders.

'Has Lundin been put through the grinder to find out who hired him?' he asked Stein.

'Lundin knows nothing. The only thing he cared about was the money, and we think he was paid most of that in advance.'

'How much?'

'Probably twenty grand.'

About five, a fax arrived from Yokohama stating formally that inquiries would be pursued as requested.

Further information would be dispatched if and when it became available.

'If and when. Doesn't sound too positive,' Stein commented.

'It sounds to me like computer-speak,' said Diamond, 'but I'm willing to wait around until late.'

'You can go back to your hotel. We'll call you straight away if anything comes through.'

Diamond cast a glance around the office, still teeming with drug-addicts, detectives and patrolmen, and had more than a flicker of doubt. 'Thanks, but I'll stick around.'

Soon after nine p.m., he tried making a call to Yamagata in Tokyo. Over there it was eleven a.m. next day. Someone explained in English that the *sekitori* were at lunch, and could not be disturbed. He should call back in two hours. He was sympathetic. For these big fellows, lunch, he imagined, was more than a coffee and a quick sandwich.

He got through later, and talked to the same person, whose English was impeccable. Apparently Yamagata was somewhere close to the phone this time, because the interpreting was fast and to the point. Diamond reported on what had happened in the hunt for Naomi, ending by admitting that he was making some hefty use of the Gold Card number. This was not a problem, he was told. Yamagata wished to do everything in his power to assist the investigation. In fact, he would immediately contact the Yokohama Police Department to see what progress there was in checking with the school photographers.

The result was impressive. Just under twenty minutes later, a fax came through from Yokohama. All school photographers had been told to check their records. Another fax would be transmitted as soon as more information was supplied.

'I like that better than "if and when",' Diamond remarked to no one in particular. Sergeant Stein had long since gone off duty.

Just before two a.m., the first positive news came humming through the fax machine:

Police Headquarters, Yokohama
To: Detective Superintendent Diamond, NYPD

Reference your fax, PD/2, inquiries among Yokohama photographers reveal that thirty-five children, nineteen male, sixteen female, at nine different junior schools, were issued with school photographs, serial number 212, during the last two years. Kindly advise if further information is required.

'You bet it is,' he said, reaching for a pen.

26th Precinct, NYPD
To: Police Headquarters, Yokohama

Immensely grateful for your attention to my inquiry. It is vital to discover whether any of the female children is at present missing and has been absent from school for the past six weeks. Please include special schools for the mentally handicapped. Your urgent attention to this matter will be deeply appreciated.

A woman detective who had recently come on duty told him he was looking pooped, and he couldn't deny it. She offered to check the incoming faxes regularly while he caught up with some sleep on one of the cots used by officers forced to take off-duty spells in the stationhouse.

Police Headquarters, Yokohama
To: Detective Superintendent Diamond, NYPD

Further enquiries reveal that among the female children listed as 212 in photographers' records, none is reported as missing from school. Two were absent for periods of two weeks and ten days respectively with minor illnesses, but are now back at school. One left the city three months ago to live in

Nagoya. All others accounted for.

He looked at his watch. 5.20 a.m. He ached in every muscle. 'Thanks.'

She said, 'You want coffee?'

'I must reply to this first.'

26th Precinct, NYPD
To: Police Headquarters, Yokohama

Many thanks. Kindly send details as soon as possible of the girl who moved to Nagoya. Could you double-check whether the family live there?

Maybe it was the time of day, but he was inclined to believe that the night had been wasted — a night he could have passed in a comfortable hotel instead of an iron and canvas cot. He decided to go for an early breakfast.

Police Headquarters, Yokohama
To: Detective Superintendent Diamond, NYPD

A search made of Nagoya school computer records has been unsuccessful in the case of the child you asked us to trace. We therefore transmit information from previous school records:

Noriko Masuda, aged 9, born 20 December 1983. Last known address: care of Dr Yuko Masuda, MSc, PhD, (mother), 4-7-9, Umeda-cho, Naka-ku, J227 Yokohama. Father, Jiro Masuda, occupational therapist, died in automobile accident, January 1985. Mother engaged in postgraduate research in Yokohama University Department of Biochemistry until 1985. Child attended Noge Special School, Yokohama, September 1987, until March of this year. Diagnosed autistic, 1987. School progress: slow, hampered by muteness. Above average skill in drawing. Temperament: good. Conduct: good. IQ rating (non verbal): 129.

He read it a second time, dazzled by this treasure hoard of information after the weeks of guesswork and despair. To have so much confirmed was beyond expectation, beyond anything he had dared to hope when the faxes had started coming. There were more than enough indications that the child was Naomi. Or, rather, that the child he knew as Naomi was actually Noriko. For her to be anyone else would be stretching coincidence to a ridiculous degree.

Noriko.

A simple name for a Westerner to get his tongue around. Personally, however, he was going to find it impossible not to continue to think of her as Naomi, so he'd have to stay with it. He justified the decision by telling himself it would avoid confusion in dealing with the police in New York. They weren't very adaptable.

The autism, then, was confirmed. As a corrective to the elation he was experiencing, he tightened inwardly upon seeing the word. Against all the evidence, he'd cherished the hope that something could be done to unlock the little girl's mind.

By fleshing out the report with a few reasonable assumptions, he pictured Yuko Masuda, the mother, a bright young woman who had given up her studies to marry, devastated by the death of her young husband, struggling to raise this difficult child who refused to respond in the way other women's children did. A problem she probably didn't understand until Naomi was three or four.

Was the poor mother under so much strain, Diamond pondered, that Mrs Tanaka, who worked in the university, had offered to take the child on a visit to Europe and America? A temporary reprieve for Dr Masuda from the stress of raising an autistic child?

How could such an act of kindness have led to murder and kidnap?

He shook his head, sighed and scribbled a note of thanks to Yokohama and, as a personal touch, added the one word of Japanese he knew: *Sayonara*. Then tore it up. Damn it, he wasn't functioning properly yet. This wasn't the time to sign off with Japan. It might be late over there, but the case had just opened up.

26th Precinct, NYPD
To: Police Headquarters, Yokohama

Your co-operation is appreciated. The details tally with the missing child. Request that you trace the mother, Dr Masuda, as a matter of urgency. We need to know the circumstances in which the child travelled to London prior to September this year. She was believed to be in the company of Mrs Minori Tanaka, 36, former secretary in Yokohama University. Request fullest possible information about these two women.

When he'd fed this into the machine, he left the stationhouse and walked to his new hotel to get a shower and a shave. He'd managed three hours' sleep at most, but this morning he felt like a billion *yen*.

Chapter Twenty-Six

THE FIRST PERSON HE SPOKE to in Columbia University Library said with a sense of discovery, 'You must be from England!'

He said tamely, 'How right you are!' Each time this happened – and here in New York it was commonplace – he felt that simply admitting his Englishness didn't come up to expectations. Something extra seemed to be expected of him: a burst of *God Save the Queen*, or a hitch of the trousers to reveal Union Jack socks. He couldn't manage either.

He introduced himself, claiming that he was a detective attached to the New York Police Department, a slight distortion of the facts, but he'd never had a conscience about embroidering the truth in the cause of justice.

The senior librarian he was addressing, a strange, thin man with the peculiar fixed smile seen usually on the faces of politicians and the earliest Greek statues, said that he just adored the British police, and was he at the library on official business, or personal?

Diamond explained that he hoped to consult an international databank of postgraduate research projects, if the library possessed one.

He already knew it did.

En route to the computer suite, the librarian confided that his knowledge of Scotland Yard owed much to the British film industry. 'Did you know that the late Lord Olivier once played a lowly English bobby in a movie?'

Diamond undermined this promising conversation by saying, '*The Magic Box*.' It happened that he'd seen the film quite recently on TV one afternoon when it was too wet to go walking in Holland Park.

'Oh, you saw it. The story of the man who invented cinematography.'

'Friese-Greene.'

'You're so right!' the librarian said admiringly.

'But Friese-Green wasn't the inventor of cinematography.'

'Wasn't he?' The smile began to look strained.

'My understanding is that several people in different countries, including yours, made the significant discoveries. Friese-Greene was a minor figure.'

'You're sure of this?'

'Check the facts, if you like. We're in the right place.'

'No need, Mr Diamond, I'll take your word for it, of course.'

'The film was a flag-waving exercise,' Diamond went on without much tact. 'Britain needed cheering up at the time. As a nation we're unequalled at making heroes out of nobodies.'

After a pause, the librarian said staunchly, 'This doesn't affect what I was about to say about the movie. The acting was superb. Do you recall the scene?' Without pausing for a response, he added, 'Just a cameo performance by Laurence Olivier as the bobby invited in to look at the images being projected, but one of his greatest, in my opinion. If he'd done nothing else, you'd have known from that scene that the man was a genius. Hardly a word spoken.'

Diamond nodded. 'Pity it wasn't true.'

'Ah, but remember the *Ode on a Grecian Urn*: "beauty is truth, truth beauty. That is all ye know on earth, and all ye need to know".'

'Not in my job,' said Diamond. He'd never believed in mixing poetry and police work.

They entered the computer suite, a place, he reflected, that a more cultured policeman might have observed had a hum like a hedge of lavender on an August morning. Ranks of display units stretched far back. The librarian showed Diamond to a vacant position and demonstrated how to access information. 'It was a directory of scientific 'research you required?'

'The International Directory of Research Projects in Biochemistry. I'd like to know what a certain Japanese graduate was working on a few years ago.'

'We should be able to locate it.' He tapped something into the controls. 'Maybe I should leave you to find your own way to the information. It's straightforward now. You just follow the instructions when they come up in highlighted text.'

'I'd rather you stayed,' Diamond admitted without shame. 'My brain goes dead when I sit in front of one of these things.'

'That's reassuring to hear. From some of the things you've been saying, I thought you were information-oriented, and nothing else. Do we have the researcher's name?'

'Yuko Masuda.'

The librarian keyed in an instruction. 'I hope you weren't serious — about not being able to appreciate the film because it wasn't strictly true.'

'Don't let it depress you,' Diamond told him. 'It's the way I was trained.'

'Too much left hemisphere.'

'Too much what?'

'Of the brain. The left side of the brain marshals facts. I've always thought the police would do well to recognize that they have a right hemisphere as well, with a capacity for intuition.'

'How, exactly?'

'Not "exactly" at all, Mr Diamond. I'm suggesting you clear your mind of all those facts you collect and allow it to be receptive to psychic forces.'

'You mean tea-leaves and Tarot Cards?'

'No, no, I'm being serious. I think you detectives might benefit by tapping into your sixth sense occasionally.'

'Don't give me that. That's how the wrong people get stitched up,' said Diamond. 'A detective who thinks he knows the truth in advance of the evidence is a dangerous man. I've met a few in my time.'

'Isn't this a hunch — looking up a research student?'

'No, this is desperation. I know damn all about this woman. I've got to start somewhere.'

'And I think we've found her,' said the librarian, who had been scrolling the text as they talked.

Diamond stared at the screen and saw, midway down:

Masuda, Yuko. PhD. Yokohama Univ. 'An insult to the brain: coma and its characteristics.' 1979–81. S. Manflex. 'Narcosis and coma states.' (American Journal of Biochemistry, May 1981.) 'The treatment of alcoholic coma.' Paper presented to Japanese Pharmacological Conference, Tokyo, 1983. Drug and alcohol-induced comas, 1983. S. Manflex.

'Talk about an insult to the brain,' he said. 'My brain-cells turn their back and walk away when I'm faced with stuff like this. S. Manflex. Narcosis. Can you understand any of it?'

'That phrase "an insult to the brain" is faintly familiar,' the librarian said. 'Where have I heard it? Give me a moment.' Given a moment, he said suddenly, 'I've got it. That wonderful poet from your country, Dylan Thomas.'

'Not my country,' Diamond interjected. 'From Wales.'

'Isn't that the same thing? Anyway, they wrote "an insult to the brain" on Dylan Thomas's death certificate. Seemed appropriate – a kind of irony, considering he imbibed so much alcohol. I thought the doctor must have had poetic leanings himself. I didn't know it was a medical term.'

'I was talking about these other words,' Diamond said, becoming impatient with the frequent digressions.

'Hold on.' The librarian tapped some keys on the console and an insert appeared above the text explaining the abbreviations. 'S stands for sponsor, right? The research was sponsored by Manflex. I figure that must be the pharmaceuticals giant. You've heard of Manflex?'

'Vaguely.'

'If you buy something for a headache in this country, it's a fair bet it's made by Manflex.'

'And what's the other thing?'

'I have no idea. Science isn't my area at all.'

230

'Nor mine. Tell me about Manflex. Is it a Japanese company, by any chance?'

'You mean Japanese-owned? I doubt it.'

'It sponsors Japanese research.'

'That doesn't make it a Japanese company.'

He accepted the correction. He'd been thinking aloud, trying to make connections that didn't exist, but should.

'You could be right,' the librarian conceded. 'They have their base in America, certainly, but, who knows who owns it? The Japanese have taken over large slices of Manhattan. Even the Rockefeller Plaza. Would you like the address?'

This time it wasn't displayed on a screen. Diamond was handed the Manhattan telephone directory. In a few minutes he was phoning the Manflex Corporation on West Broadway, or trying to, because the number was busy. After ten minutes of dialling and swearing, he got through to a telephonist who, if anything, was in a more irritated state then he: 'Who is this?'

'Am I through to the Manflex Corporation?'

'Uhuh.'

'My name is Diamond and I'd like to speak to the managing director.'

'Sorry. No chance. Are you press?'

'No I am not.'

'Mr Flexner is unavailable.'

'When do you expect him to be available?'

'No comment.'

'Listen, I don't know who you think I am. I'd simply like to speak to somebody in authority. Is there anyone else?'

'You people are so persistent,' the voice said accusingly. 'A statement will be issued in due course.'

'About what? I just want to make an inquiry—'

'I'm sorry,' she said. 'I'm just too busy to prolong this.'

And she cut the call.

He could tell that the rudeness wasn't personal. She was clearly under intense pressure.

'Can anyone tell me why a pharmaceuticals firm called Manflex should be under siege by the press?' he appealed to the librarians at the desk nearby.

There was some shrugging and head-shaking before one of them piped up, 'I heard something about Manflex. Their price is rocketing on the stock exchange, that's what's happening. They slumped badly and now they bounced back, only more so.'

If Manflex was currently reversing a fall on the New York stock market, people were making money. And if Manflex had been the sponsor of Naomi's mother's postgraduate research, then perhaps there was some reason why Naomi had been kidnapped just as the company's stock was soaring.

He tried phoning again, but the line was busy.

There was plenty to occupy him in the library. He located some reference books on medical science that were written in English he could follow, so he made a determined effort to interpret the gobbledygook he'd copied from the computer. Yuko Masuda's research papers were all concerned with the treatment of comas induced by alcohol and drugs. All comas were attributed to some kind of insult to the brain, as it was so evocatively expressed. Dr Masuda specialized in comas induced by poisoning of the brain, rather than by injury, pressure, infection or lack of sugar.

The half-hour's concentrated study may not have turned Peter Diamond into a neurological specialist, but he reckoned he was better equipped to talk to the people at Manflex.

He pressed out the number again. No one was answering.

Instead, he left the library and went to look for a taxi.

The Manflex Building was one of the older landmarks on West Broadway, tall by most standards, yet dwarfed by the twin towers of the World Trade Center close by. When Diamond got close, he saw that the two sets of revolving doors to the entrance hall appeared to be locked. Armed security guards were preventing anyone from using the doors at the side. Two young women with the look of secretaries quite junior in the firm came out and were routinely approached by press people with microphones.

They said with equal casualness that they were making no comment. It had the look of a ritual that had been going on for some while.

He ambled across to one of the reporters, a woman in an oversize suede coat and white boots. 'Excuse me, could you tell me what's going on here? Is someone famous in there?' He added in excuse for ignorance, 'I'm from England.'

She gave him a sympathetic look. 'This is the Manflex Building.'

'Should I have heard of it?'

'Pharmaceuticals.'

'Ah? Is that of interest to the press?'

Now she looked at him as if he were Rip Van Winkle. 'Manflex's rating on the stock market has been rocketing on rumours of a new wonder drug. They're due to make an announcement Tuesday and there's any amount of speculation.'

'Manflex – is that an all-American firm?'

She was obviously starting to think that she was stuck with a headcase. 'Haven't you heard of Manny Flexner? He was a legend in the pharmaceuticals business. Very dynamic. His son just became chairman.'

'David. What's he like?'

'Nobody knows yet. He only took over a few weeks back. He's keeping his head down right now.'

'If this rumour is true, he's off to a good start.'

'He needs it. There was a big loss of confidence after Manny jumped.'

'Jumped?'

'Out of his office on the twenty-first floor.'

Diamond stared upwards.

'He fell the other side,' the reporter informed him. 'A small executive parking lot.'

Diamond thanked her and took a walk along Broadway, past City Hall, working out what to do next. He'd heard enough about the seesawing fortunes of Manflex to justify more inquiries, but he doubted whether he'd be able to convince Lieutenant Eastland that something should be done. For the present he preferred to pursue this tenuous line of inquiry independently. However, he wasn't going to be able to bluff his way past the security guards. Some different strategy was wanted.

He found a stationery store and went in to buy a notepad and envelope. Then he wrote a letter to David Flexner, the Chairman of Manflex, introducing himself as a detective from England conducting an inquiry involving murder and the abduction of a child. As a matter of extreme urgency, he went on, he needed an interview with the Manflex management to discuss the mother of the child, Dr Yuko Masuda, who had carried out research sponsored by Manflex at Yokohoma University in the early 1980s. He gave the address and phone number of his hotel and added the words 'Detective Superintendent' below his signature. He addressed the envelope to Flexner, marking it 'Personal – Extremely Urgent'. Then he returned to the Manflex Building and handed the letter to one of the security guards, stressing that it was vital that it was delivered to the Chairman immediately. And once again his old police identity card came in useful; security staff are invariably ex-policemen themselves.

Before returning to the hotel he called at a bank and used his credit card to get more cash to patronize a deli he'd just passed. Later, he thought, he'd be able to tell Steph that for lunch he'd restricted himself to a sandwich. She'd never seen the size of an American sandwich garnished with dill pickles.

It wasn't surprising that he took a post-prandial nap in his room.

The phone woke him.

'Hello.'

'Superintendent, er, Diamond?'

He sat up in bed. The digital clock beside it said 3.36. 'Yes.'

'David Flexner. You wanted to speak to me about this Japanese lady.'

'Correct.'

'There isn't much I can tell you at this point in time, and you'll understand that things are pretty busy here.'

'I appreciate that, but the child's life—'

'Sure.' There was a pause. 'I can meet you, but it would

234

be easier some place else, not in this building. Let me think a moment. You know the Staten Island Ferry?'

'I can find it.'

'Battery Park. Anyone in New York will tell you. I'll see you in the ticket office around seven-fifteen. That's the earliest I can do. How will I know you?'

'I wear a fawn-coloured raincoat.'

'Like Columbo?'

'Like five Columbos. I'm well-fed. I'm also bald, but you won't be able to tell, because I wear a brown trilby.'

'A what?'

'I believe it's called a derby here.'

'Fine. Look out for a stringbean with long, blond hair and a red windbreaker. We shouldn't have much trouble, Super.'

He got up and took a shower. Super. No one had ever called him that before. Flexner had sounded like a sixteen-year-old. If he had anything to be ashamed of, it hadn't come through in the voice. When this comes to nothing, Diamond thought, where do I go next? No messages had been left by the police, so they hadn't made any progress. These intervals of inactivity were the devil to endure. In his days on the force, he'd have spent this time chivvying the murder squad, or – as they would put it – making their lives a misery. Here, in this godforsaken hotel room, he had only himself to goad.

He went out and took a walk in Central Park that didn't deserve to be called a walk when compared with the gait of the exercise-minded fanatics who continuously strode past. When he rested on a bench he was immediately accosted by someone who wanted to compose a poem in his honour for five bucks. He said grouchily that he'd already heard enough poetry for one day and the poet spat on his shoe.

He tried some creative work of his own, devising scenarios in which Naomi's mother had given up her research as a result of getting disillusioned with the drugs industry; or that she had become a whistle-blower on malpractices in Manflex; or even a victim of some drugs experiment that had failed. He still couldn't work out why she had been parted from her child if she was still alive.

About six, no further on in his conclusions, he took the subway south and found his way to Battery Park. The Statue of Liberty was already a blue silhouette fading in the evening light. A ferry boat came in and he watched the procedure as the iron trellis snapped back and the passengers disembarked. With a strong breeze blowing, he was glad of his raincoat – which he'd never thought of as anything like Lieutenant Columbo's. It was a trenchcoat really, well-lined and with flaps that could button across the chest. With the hat, it was definitely more Bogart than Peter Falk.

He watched the ferry fill up and depart and then strolled across to the ticket office. Just after seven, too soon to be looking out for Flexner. The benches were fast filling up with passengers for the next ferry. Guessing that he might face a wait of twenty minutes or more, he claimed a seat.

Ten minutes passed. A mother brought her fractious toddler to the place beside Diamond and waged a noisy battle of wills over some chocolate that was certain, the mother said, to make the child very sick indeed after all he'd eaten. When junior had screamed enough to get his way, Diamond decided maybe the mother had not been bluffing. To safeguard the trenchcoat – which in his size wouldn't be easy to replace – he got up and moved away.

Nobody matching young Flexner's description was in sight.

'Are you Mr Peter Diamond, by any chance?'

He turned. Someone he must have seen and mentally dismissed had stepped over to talk to him, a pretty, dark-haired young woman in a cherry-coloured bomber jacket and jeans.

'That's my name.'

'Mr Flexner sends his apologies. He had a problem escaping from the press, so the meeting-place had to be changed. I'm Joan. I'm going to drive you there.'

'Drive me where, exactly?'

'I'm sorry but I can't tell you yet. There's a phone in the car. He's going to let us know.'

'You want me to come with you now?' What was being

236

suggested sounded reasonable enough. He checked his watch and saw that it was already past the time Flexner had suggested that they meet.

'It must be such a burden for him, all this pressure from the media,' she remarked, leading Diamond across the park towards a place where several cars were parked.

'I appreciate that,' he said. 'Are you his PA or something?'

She smiled. 'Or something – I've no idea what you could possibly mean by that.'

'So you're on the payroll?'

'I drive a car. That's all.'

It was a smart car, a long, black limousine, the sort that would cause heads to turn in England but make no impression in New York. From some distance away, Joan used a remote control to disengage the security system. The indicator lights flashed briefly and the locks clicked. Just as automatically, Diamond went towards the left side.

She said quickly, 'I'm driving.'

He came to his senses. 'My mistake.'

Inside, she picked up the phone and pressed out a number. 'This won't take a minute,' she told him.

He sat back casually, trying to listen without appearing interested, but the voice on the end of the line was inaudible.

She said into the mouthpiece, 'We got here . . . Sure, he was . . . Yes, Mr Flexner, I know it. You want to speak to him? . . . Fine, we won't be long.' She replaced it between them and started up. 'Talk about cloak and dagger. You won't believe where we're going.'

Deviously, he suggested, 'The Trump Tower?'

It made no visible impression. 'No.'

'Where, then?'

'It's on the West Side.'

'You're being mysterious yourself. Is it anywhere I'm likely to know?'

'I shouldn't think so, but it's one of the "in" places.'

He had a depressing image of a trendy nightclub, the sort of venue a wealthy young hotshot like David Flexner might frequent. 'Am I dressed all right?'

'Just fine.'

237

She would keep this going indefinitely, and he didn't know New York well enough to pin her down. He didn't like secrecy when he was the one being kept in ignorance. They were heading north, along the Hudson River waterfront. Occasionally they had glimpses of the lights of New Jersey. A diversion sent them away from the river, and they picked up their northward route on 10th Avenue. The Lincoln Tunnel was signposted, but they passed the approach roads and soon after slowed. Joan the driver was obviously counting streets, so Diamond helped.

'Forty-seventh.'

'Thanks.'

'Which one are we looking for?'

'Forty-ninth will do.'

They turned left and tracked the street to its limit, under the girders of the highway. Soon they were back in a dockland area. Presently she turned onto a tarmac stretch between warehouses. Red hazard lights marked the tops of some cranes.

'He's *here*?' said Diamond in disbelief.

'I told you it was cloak and dagger,' she said. She flashed the headlights a couple of times.

A figure came from the shadows of one of the warehouses. 'Doesn't look like David Flexner,' Diamond commented as if he knew him well.

'This is one of his team,' she said, touching the control to let the window down on Diamond's side.

'I hope you'll be waiting,' Diamond remarked to Joan as he prepared to get out. 'I wouldn't want to walk back to my hotel from here.'

'I'm in no hurry,' she said.

The man stooped to look in. 'Mr Diamond?' The face was unshaven and smelt of liquor. As the face of an executive's personal aide, it wasn't convincing.

Diamond turned to look at the woman who called herself Joan. Even at this stage she returned a level look without a trace of perfidy. If this was a set-up — and he now believed that it was — she had played her part immaculately. She'd disarmed him with her poise.

238

The man outside reached for the door-handle. Diamond snapped down the lock.

Joan said, 'Why did you do that?' And before she'd got out the words she had released the lock from the central control at her side.

The man outside swung open the door. He was built like the stevedore he probably was.

Joan shrilled, 'Take him!'

Diamond jerked away from the door and made a grab for the steering wheel, whereupon Joan stabbed the sharp end of the keys into the back of his hand. The searing pain weakened his grip. She opened her door and leapt out on her side, yelling something across the quayside.

At the same time the thug leaned inside the car and put an arm-lock around Diamond's throat. It was painful and disabling, but it wasn't enough to eject him. He braced his legs to press his back against the seat and groped for the man's face, which was close to his own. He found a handful of hair, but he knew better than to work on that. You go for the eyes and ears.

He slid his hand across the surface of the face, got bitten badly in the fleshy area under his thumb, but succeeded in thrusting the same thumb hard into a fold of soft, moist flesh that could only be the man's eye-socket.

There was a scream and the arm-lock loosened.

But there were voices. Someone was shouting, 'Get out of my way!'

Something swung in a huge arc towards Diamond's skull. He couldn't duck. He put up an arm a fraction too late. The impact was terrific. His face hit the dashboard and smashed through glass. A second blow crunched into his shoulder. He was lucky to be registering anything.

'You got him,' someone was saying.

What now? he thought. Do I come quietly, or play dead?

Someone had two hands under his armpits and dragged him off the car seat. He went limp before hitting the ground.

'Bastard.'

Words, he guessed, wouldn't be enough for the man whose eye he had damaged. Two kicks in his kidneys

239

followed. He couldn't stop himself crying out in pain. For this, he got another mighty crack on the head.

He was losing consciousness.

'Grab a leg, will ya?'

He didn't expect to survive. Joan had said this was the 'in place' and now he knew what she meant. They were going to dump him in the Hudson River.

Chapter Twenty-Seven

HE HAD SWALLOWED A BELLYFUL of foul-tasting liquid. His eyes were smarting and his nose was blocked. Repeatedly he spluttered and vomited and felt no better for it. Once or twice he opened his eyes and saw nothing. He was aware only of an occasional nudge against his right arm and shoulder. And that he was cold, indescribably cold. Parts of his body must have ached, but the cold subdued every other sensation.

He was face-up, most of him submerged.

He remembered nothing. For all he knew, he could be lying in a primeval swamp.

Waiting to die.

A stronger jolt forced his arm across his chest, turning him almost on his side. More of the liquid washed over his face, filling his mouth and nostrils again.

If this was drowning, he wouldn't recommend it as a way to go.

He turned his head and emptied his mouth.

Coughed.

Gasped for air.

Whimpered.

Your strength is going, Diamond. If you don't do something to help yourself, this is where you go under for ever.

He flung out his right arm. His hand slapped against a surface slimy to the touch, but solid. He'd hardly begun to examine it when he felt the structure being moved out of reach. He groped for whatever it was and missed, realizing as this occurred that the surface hadn't moved, but he had. As he was towed back to the right, he tried again, made contact and felt for the texture under the slime. Maddeningly, the action of the water rocked him away again.

His brain was beginning to function now. He realized that what he had taken to be nudging was the action of a current pressing him against some kind of obstruction. He pressed his hand hopefully towards it, grasped an object strange to the touch that he let go when he recognized its shape and texture as that of a large, dead bird. Then felt his knuckles come into contact with something smoother, some kind of container, a beer-can, perhaps. Mentally he was back in the twentieth century. He was part of the floating rubbish that collects along the banks and shores of waterways.

But there was some reason why the rubbish was trapped here. The current should have carried it downstream. Presumably he was caught against some obstruction.

As his thinking process sharpened, so did the cold — penetrating, demanding to be recognized, persuading him that it was futile to struggle. Feebly, he reached out again.

His fingers found something that didn't move, about the shape and thickness of a prison bar, only this was horizontal. He held on.

It was securely anchored. Without releasing his grip, he explored the shape, discovering a ninety-degree angle, a shorter length and then, coated with waterweed, the masonry from which it projected. He had found an iron rung attached to a stone structure.

He flexed his arm to draw closer. Then reached over and upwards with his left hand to see if a similar rung was located above the one he was holding.

The hand scrabbled against weed and stone.

Yes. His fingers curled around a second rung.

There was a ladder set into the wall.

But had he the strength to drag himself out of the water? Such an exercise would require an exceptional effort any time, and he was weak.

Try, or die, he told himself. One rung at a time.

He released his hold on the first and reached up with his right hand. Gripped and pulled. Found himself too feeble.

Got both hands on the rung and slackened his body. His shoulders were out of the water, and now one of them was giving him pain he hadn't felt before. From the chest down he was submerged, and he just hung there, cursing his size, unable to achieve any more.

Then he was aware that his thighs were in contact with something. There was distinct pressure above his knees.

He'd found a lower rung. The ladder extended below the water-line. Not so far down as his feet, unfortunately, but if he could raise his legs high enough to get a foothold on this rung, he'd have a chance of making progress.

He raised his knees to the required level but found that, being pudgy, his knees wouldn't give him any purchase. The only way was to hoist himself up a couple of rungs by using his arms alone.

He breathed deeply and reached up. Got his fingers around the next rung and immediately felt such a searing pain in the shoulder that he let go. Now he knew he was injured. The right arm was virtually useless.

With the imminent prospect of sinking back into the filthy water, he braced himself for one more effort to go higher, reaching up with the left hand while holding on agonizingly with the right.

He made fingertip contact, got a grip and hauled himself higher one-handed, immediately releasing the right arm from its painful duty. The sense of achievement set the adrenalin flowing. Without pause, he forced the right hand into use again and held on, while jack-knifing his body in an attempt to get a foothold on the lowest rung.

He managed it.

Now it was a matter of leverage rather than brute strength and stoicism. With both feet securely positioned, he heaved himself upwards, raising his torso clear of the water. Clawing at the higher rungs, he began a steady ascent up the side of what he now perceived was a stone pier.

And as he climbed, his brain began to deal with his bizarre situation. Dimly at first, but with increasing clarity, he recalled where he was and why. He understood the reason for the pain that afflicted him, not just in the shoulder, but – as his circulation was restored – in his head and lower back. It had been a savage beating, and his attackers had assumed he would drown. Maybe the extra poundage that he was finding such a handicap while climbing the rungs had saved him. The body blows – apart from those to his skull – had been cushioned. In the water, his in-built insulation had kept him alive for longer.

But he still felt grim.

Not to say unsafe. He hesitated on the higher rungs, wondering whether anyone would spot him and throw him back again. A mere push in the chest would be enough. He wouldn't survive another ducking.

The darkness was an ally. He put his head above the wall, satisfied himself that no one was near and then climbed up the remaining rungs and flopped like a beached whale.

With no choice but to lie still, he waited for his pulse and breathing to reduce to rates he could cope with. He was getting messages from parts of his body that had suffered injuries he hadn't registered. Now his face was smarting. He put his hand to his left eye and felt a large swelling. There was a cut across the centre of his nose.

He couldn't tell how long he'd been in the water. There had certainly been an interval while he was unconscious. Presumably the shock of immersion had revived him.

In the open, darkness is never total. He rolled over and peered across the expanse of open ground between the pier and the warehouse from which his attackers must have come. The limousine had gone, maybe – he told himself optimistically – with the men as passengers. The instinct of killers is to leave the scene.

What now?

Clearly, he needed to get to the police. It was vital that they were informed what had happened, for the Manflex connection was no longer tenuous. Those people were revealed as willing to kill, and he wanted them interrogated as soon as possible. He wanted to hear David Flexner's explanation.

He just hoped he was capable of staying on his feet long enough.

Staying? He realized that he had yet to *get* on his feet, and now he was about to try. The effort required was immense. He achieved the standing position by a process of crouching for a while, then stooping, propped with hands on knees, and finally trying unsuccessfully to straighten and groaning at the effort. Movement was going to be a painful, shuffling process that made him think how useful a zimmer-frame would have been. Even the light shore breeze threatened to bowl him over.

Obviously he needed to find a way back to the streets, but getting there would be like finishing a marathon. To be positive, he still had both shoes on. All he seemed to have lost was his hat.

In the next twenty minues he made it across the waterfront, over a no-man's land cluttered with rubbish, and down a slope to where one of the West Side streets terminated. The nearest block of tenement buildings didn't really have the look of a haven for a half-drowned, badly-beaten Brit, but he staggered to the first door he could find, and looked for a doorbell — a facility the household lacked. He rapped the woodwork with his knuckles. Nobody came. He could hear nothing from inside.

He tried two more houses before anyone appeared, and this was a small, black boy who stared. Anyone would have stared.

'Hi,' said Diamond with an effort of the imagination.

The stare persisted.

'Are your parents about?'

A blink, and then a resumption of the stare.

'Your Mum and Dad? Sonny, I need help.'

The boy frowned and said, 'Where you from?'

He didn't want to go through that again, not in the state he was in, but the kid had broken his silence, so: 'From England.'

'England?' The kid raised a hand as if to strike him.

Just in time, Diamond saw what was intended and let his own right hand come in a sweeping movement to slap against the boy's in salute.

A short time after, wrapped in a blanket, he was seated

in a wicker armchair in the living-room of the basement apartment, surrounded by a large Afro-Caribbean family. They brought him coffee laced with rum and they put a Band-aid on his nose.

Twenty minutes or so of this treatment revived him remarkably. He was ready to move on. They wanted to know where he was going and he named the police at the 26th Precinct.

When the amusement had subsided, the boy's father offered to drive him there.

Thus it was that towards ten p.m., Sergeant Stein of the 26th, passing the 'front counter', was confronted by the disturbing spectacle of a grinning man, notorious across New York for the terms he'd served for armed robbery, carrying a heap of wet clothes, accompanied by Superintendent Diamond dressed in a blanket, a plaster on his nose, his left eye black and closed.

The explanation had to be given twice over, because Lieutenant Eastland, who was off duty, was called in to take decisions. He didn't go so far as to smile at Diamond's state, but he wasn't sympathetic. 'So what we have,' he summed up, 'is a link with Manflex through the child's mother. You set out to investigate, and you were beaten up and tipped in the river. Who by?'

'Come on,' said Diamond angrily. 'There were no lights out there except the car headlights. The girl who called herself Joan I'd know. But the point is that David Flexner himself must have given these people their instructions. Something I said must have really upset him.'

'You surprise me,' said Eastland.

'What *did* you say?' asked Stein.

'Just that I wanted information about the research Dr Masuda was doing some years ago in Yokohama on a grant from Manflex.'

'I wouldn't have said this was grounds for murder,' commented Eastland. 'Are we sure of this connection?'

'What do you mean?'

'I mean can we be certain that these people who jumped you were sent by Flexner?'

'It's inescapable. The girl told me she was working for

246

him. She knew about the meeting. She knew where to find me, and when.'

'Okay, we'll pull him in and see what this is about.'

'One more thing,' said Diamond.

'You want to see a doctor?'

'I want to get my clothes to a laundry.'

'Okay. How you feeling now?'

'Impatient . . . to see Flexner.'

'You should rest.'

'Go to hell.'

In fact, he did get almost an hour on the cot he'd slept on the previous night. They had to wake him when Flexner was brought in, and then he felt worse than ever for the short sleep. Every part of him ached.

It was agreed that he should observe the first interview on closed-circuit TV. Lieutenant Eastland pointed out that Flexner had no reason to believe that Diamond had survived the attack. A first principle of interrogation was to give nothing away.

The young, long-haired man on the screen certainly looked uneasy, revealing in body language how agitated he was at being brought in for questioning. He flicked the tip of his tongue repeatedly around the edges of his mouth and worked his hands around his face like some actor over-playing Hamlet.

Eastland's voice started up, giving the routine information about the taping of interviews. 'You give your permission?'

Flexner nodded.

'Would you mind giving a verbal response?'

'I don't mind.'

'You agree to us taping the interview?'

'I agree.'

'Okay.'

While Eastland went through the preliminaries of establishing Flexner's identity and address, Diamond watched the young man keenly. For a business tycoon, he was pretty unconventional in style, dressed in T-shirt, jeans and windcheater with the mane of blond hair extending to his shoulders. It was pretty well the description he'd given of himself over the phone.

'You know a guy called Diamond – a British cop?' Eastland asked. He wasn't in shot. The camera was continuously on Flexner.

'I know the name, that's all. He called me this afternoon.'

'He called you? Is that an accurate answer, Mr Flexner?'

Flexner raked a hand nervously through his hair. 'What I mean is, he wrote me a note. I called him at his hotel.'

'Let's have the truth, huh?'

'I'm sorry. Was that important?'

'Everything's important. Do you still have the note?'

'Not here.'

'Can you tell me the contents, accurately?'

Flexner closed his eyes as he spoke, as if trying to visualize the note. 'He wrote that he was an English detective inquiring into a murder and an abduction, the abduction of a child. He wanted to meet me for information about the kid's mother who carried out research sponsored by my firm in Yokohama, Japan, in the 1980s. Her name was Dr Yuko Masuda. He signed himself Peter Diamond, Detective Superintendent.'

'And he gave a number for you to call?'

'The Brightside Hotel on West 106th. I took it seriously. I looked up the records on this woman. Then I called Mr Diamond and fixed a meeting at Battery Park, in the ticket office for the ferry.'

'Strange place for a meeting.'

Flexner gave a shrug. 'My circumstances are pretty unusual right now, for reasons unconnected with this. It was simplest to meet him someplace outside the office.'

'Battery Park? Why not his hotel?'

'Battery Park is a short taxi-ride from my office. It's also a place a stranger to New York could find easily.'

'So did you go there?'

'Sure, but I was delayed. He wasn't there.' Flexner leaned forward in his chair as if a sudden thought had come to him. 'What happened to this guy? Is he okay?'

'You tell me what happened to you,' said Eastland.

'I turned up at Battery Park—'

'No,' said Eastland, who was letting nothing by. 'You tell me what delayed you.'

'A smoke alarm.'

'What?'

'A smoke alarm went off in a storeroom on the twentieth floor.'

'What time?'

'Around six forty-five, just when I was ready to leave. Someone had dumped a cigarette in a trash-bin. It ignited some tissues.'

'In a storeroom?'

'That's where it was found. The result is I didn't get down to Battery Park until twenty-five after seven, and the guy wasn't around. I looked around, I asked—'

'Okay,' said Eastland. 'So let's have this very clear. Did you at any point instruct anyone else to meet Detective Diamond?'

'No. I just told you. I went myself.'

'Who else knew you made this appointment? Your secretary?'

Flexner shook his head. 'I handled it myself.'

'Is your phone system secure?'

'So far as I know.'

'You said that you consulted the records on this woman. Did somebody fetch them for you?'

'No, we have them on computer. We keep records of all our sponsorships and research programmes. I accessed them on the modem I have in my office.'

'Anyone see you?'

'I was alone in there. Look, would you mind telling me what happened?'

'Detective Diamond was met by a woman who said she was sent by you. You know about this?'

Flexner swayed back in his chair, frowning. 'Sent by me? No, I don't. I didn't speak to anyone.'

'Take your time, Mr Flexner. Think back. You're quite certain you mentioned this meeting to nobody?'

'Positive.'

'Maybe someone overheard you speaking on the phone. Is that possible?'

'I was alone in my office. The door was closed.'

'Yet this woman – who called herself Joan, by the way – found Detective Diamond in the ticket office, told him you were unable to get there and drove him in a black limousine to the waterfront area in the West Forties, where some goons were waiting to work him over good and sink him in the Hudson.'

'I can't believe this.' To his credit, Flexner was looking as if he meant what he said. He'd gone extremely pale.

'You'd better,' Eastland told him. 'And you'd better start thinking who this woman is, and why it was necessary to do that to a guy you arranged to meet. You don't have to answer right off.'

'He's dead?' Flexner asked.

'Go over it in your mind, Mr Flexner. There may be something you forgot. I'll be back.'

Flexner was left staring. There was only the sound of the interview room door being closed.

Eastland came into the room where Stein and Diamond had been following the interview. 'Well?'

'I'd like to question him,' Diamond said. 'I still want the information he was going to give me.'

'You think he's speaking the truth?'

'He made a pretty good impression.'

'Yeah?' said Eastland with heavy irony. 'Maybe none of this happened. That's a phantom black eye you have.'

'I still want to question him.'

'Not yet.'

'This is urgent.'

'We can break this guy, no problem,' Eastland bragged. 'He claims he told nobody he was meeting you. That's got to be horseshit.'

Diamond contained himself, but with difficulty. There was a real danger that Naomi's plight would be overlooked in the eagerness to break David Flexner. Breaking him, as Eastland candidly put it, was not the way to get the crucial information. 'Listen, I think we should test the truth of what he's saying this way. He arranged to meet me. That's not in dispute. So he must have had something to pass on about Naomi's mother.'

'It was a blind, just to set you up.'

'Let's find out. Let's ask him what he can tell us. If he *is* telling the truth, it may lead us to Naomi.'

The lieutenant obviously wasn't impressed. He spread his hands as if his point had just been proved. 'Peter, my friend, you were asking about research the woman was doing seven, eight years back. That's not going to tell us who's holding the kid tonight.'

'It scared someone into wanting me killed. It can't be all that remote,' said Diamond. 'Let him talk while he still has an interest in co-operating. If you go in there and scare the shit out of him, we may get nothing.'

'Keep him sweet, you mean?'

'Play along with him. It won't take long, for God's sake.'

Eastland weighed the suggestion. 'You could be right.'

'I'll do it,' Diamond offered.

'You? No way. He thinks you're stashed away in the morgue, and we don't want to disillusion him. Okay, Diamond, we'll play it your way for a while. Just tell me what you would have asked him.'

Diamond outlined the strategy. Without going all the way to convincing Eastland, it seemed to mollify him somewhat.

In a few minutes, the questioning started up again. Eastland went straight to the point. 'Tell me about Yuko Masuda.'

'There isn't much. I haven't met her,' David Flexner replied. 'She's just one of thousands who have carried out postgraduate research funded by Manflex or one of its associate companies.'

'She's unimportant?'

'I didn't say that. According to our records, we've been sponsoring her researches for ten years or more. She's written some papers on the treatment of drug and alcoholic comas using sympathomimetic drugs.'

'Using *what*?'

'They imitate the effects of the sympathetic nerves. Adrenalin and ephedrine are examples.'

'I've heard of adrenalin.'

A sigh from Flexner betrayed some impatience.

251

'Alcoholic comas, you said?' Eastland continued. 'You mean these drugs pull the patients out? Restore them to their senses?'

'Inspector, all my information comes from a file entry on a computer. I am neither a biochemist nor a doctor.'

'Okay, okay. And what else does your computer tell you?'

'The usual stuff. Her age, address, qualifications. She isn't one of our employees, you understand, just a postgraduate research student.'

'Does the file show that she is married?'

'Yes. Masuda is her married name.'

'And is her child mentioned?'

'It wouldn't be. That's irrelevant to us.'

'She's based in Japan?'

'Yokohama.'

'And she's been doing research continuously since when?'

'1979.'

'Long time.'

'Research sometimes does take a long time.'

'Do you get updates on her work?'

'Not personally. The company keeps tabs on all our research programmes.'

'Did you know that she's been missing from her home for a couple of months?'

'No, I didn't know that. It wouldn't necessarily come to our attention for some time unless someone reported it.'

There was a pause in the questioning, as if Eastland was reluctant to move on, but couldn't think what else to ask. Finally he said, 'Is there anything else on this woman's record that you planned to tell Detective Diamond?'

'No,' answered Flexner. 'Naturally, I wanted to be as helpful as I could, but that's all I could have told him. You've heard it all.'

'Forgive me, but it doesn't sound like the secret of the Sphinx,' Eastland commented. 'Why did you need to meet with Diamond like a couple of CIA agents? Why not simply call him on the phone and tell him what you had?'

Flexner shrugged again. 'I guess I wanted to be sure

who I was dealing with. We don't give out information about people as a rule.'

'You didn't trust him?'

'I thought it right to meet him and make sure. I couldn't invite him to the office. He'd have had to run the gauntlet of the press. They're camped outside my building.'

'I've seen them. You're getting plenty of attention,' said Eastland. 'This is the wonder drug you're about to launch?'

Flexner shifted position in his chair. 'Look, this has no bearing on the matter of the Japanese woman.'

'How do you know?'

'It's unrelated.'

'We'll judge that for ourselves, Mr Flexner.'

'I'd rather not discuss the drug. If any of what I said leaked out prematurely, it could get us suspended on the stock market.'

'Everything you tell me stays within these walls,' Eastland assured him while the unseen watchers in the room across the corridor continued impassively to follow the interview.

David Flexner passed his hand agitatedly across his mouth. 'You're putting me in a difficult position.'

'The hot seat.'

'Excuse me?'

'I'm putting you in the hot seat.'

'Oh.' An unhappy smile flickered across the young man's lips. 'You appreciate that I only took over as Chairman quite recently, when my father died,' he explained. 'Frankly, the business hasn't gone too brilliantly for some while. We slipped badly in the pharmaceuticals league table. Our competitors like Merck and Lilly have developed new drugs and gotten away from us. And quite recently our stock market rating took a dive because of a fire at one of our major plants in Italy. The place was gutted.'

'And that hit confidence here?'

'Manflex Italia is our main European subsidiary. The investigation is still going on. We could be dealing with a case of arson.'

'But you hope to restore confidence with this new drug, is that it?' said Eastland.

David Flexner gave a nod. 'One mass-selling product can make one hell of a difference. Without saying more than I have to, I can tell you that Prodermolate—'

'Prodermolate?'

'PDM3. It's one of thousands of compounds that we patented over the years. The great majority never come to anything. Well, it happens that this drug – which was developed getting on for twenty years ago – is more effective than anyone suspected.'

'For what?'

'Forgive me, but I can't tell you that, Lieutenant. We're due to make an announcement in a couple of days and the future of Manflex rests on it. And thousands of jobs. We're under tremendous pressure to leak the information before Tuesday. I can't tell anyone, not even you, not even in this place.'

'You can't withhold information,' said Eastland in a voice more offended than threatening. 'I need to know.'

'I'm sorry, but—'

'You think I'm going to rush out tomorrow and buy shares in Manflex?'

'Well, no.'

'I have better things to do than gamble on the stock exchange, Mr Flexner. If I wanted to be a rich man, I wouldn't be in this job.'

'But I'm under an obligation.'

Eastland lifted his voice a fraction. '*You're* under an obligation? What about me? I have to find a child, a handicapped child, as a matter of fact, who is in real danger of losing her life. This isn't hide and seek, it's child murder unless I find her.'

'Murder?'

After a sufficient pause, Eastland added, 'We've had one killing already.'

The quickness of Flexner's reaction, a spasm of shock that produced a rictus-like baring of the mouth, showed that he was primed for the bad news. Clearly he took the statement to mean that Diamond was the victim. This was the fear most on his mind. In a tone that showed he was about to capitulate, he said, 'I wish you'd told me right out.'

'You haven't been entirely open with me. Tell me about this drug,' said Eastland with the timing of a skilled interrogator.

Flexner had whitened noticeably. 'You give me your word it goes no further?'

'Secrets are my business.'

'Okay. I, em, I'm not the best-informed person to talk about the potential of the drug, but I gather it was patented back in 1975 at Cornell. The original research was carried out on a grant from Beaver River Chemicals, who became a subsidiary of ours when my father took them over about 1976. Nobody found much use for the stuff. That's the way things are. You discover thousands of compounds and register them without knowing if they're any use. Not many are chosen for development, which is extremely costly. It can run into millions. Professor Churchward has discovered that PDM3 is effective in regenerating the nerve-cells of the brain.'

'Is that special?'

He looked pained that such a question had to be asked. 'I said regenerating. It's unknown to science. It's a tremendous breakthrough. It means that we can arrest the process of mental ageing.'

'Alzheimer's?' said Eastland.

'Yes, but more than that, vastly more. PDM3 fosters the production of new cells. We can foresee its being used to sustain the brain at peak efficiency into advanced old age.'

'For anyone?'

'Exactly.'

'So it's a surefire money-spinner,' Eastland said in a swift descent to market economics. 'On Tuesday, you're launching this drug?'

Flexner raised his hands like a man looking into a gun barrel. 'No, no. That's still at least a year off. We're staging a conference to report on the work so far and announce that we're going into the third stage of testing, which is extensive pre-clinical trials.'

'But the mere fact that you are starting the trials will lead to massive investment in Manflex.'

'That is likely.'

'You mentioned a professor just now.'

'Churchward. He's at Corydon University, Indianapolis. I flew out there to see him last week. He's leading the teams at work on PDM3.'

'Did you form a good estimate?'

'What do you mean?'

'Did you like the guy?'

'I didn't have to.'

'Trust him, then?'

'My judgment is that he's a good scientist, or I wouldn't be putting our resources into the drug.'

'So you see a bright future, Mr Flexner.'

'For mankind, with an advance like this? Certainly.'

'For Manflex Pharmaceuticals.'

He looked faintly embarrassed. 'I expect so.'

'You can do without a murder inquiry on your doorstep right now.'

'Too damned true.'

'And you say you mentioned Detective Diamond to nobody?'

'Not a living soul.' Impulsively, Flexner said, 'Could we keep it out of the papers until after Tuesday?'

Eastland behaved as if the question hadn't been put. 'When you called him on the phone, did you dial the number yourself?'

'Yes.'

'You didn't ask the switchboard to get the number for you?'

'No.'

'Can they listen in to outside calls?'

'I'm pretty sure they can't.'

'Let's take another view of this,' suggested Eastland. 'Who else beside yourself knows what you intend to announce on Tuesday?'

'About PDM3?' He cast his eyes upwards, as if the names were written on the ceiling. 'My deputy, Michael Leapman, and Professor Churchward, of course. They'll both be at the conference.'

'The professor is in New York?'

'He flew in tonight. He's staying at the Waldorf Astoria.'

'No one else knows about PDM3?'

'I can't think of anyone. There are people working on various phases of the project, but only Michael and Professor Churchward know the whole picture.'

'Your wife?'

'I'm unmarried.'

'Girlfriend?'

Flexner shook his head.

'So who are the opposition?' Eastland asked. 'Who has an interest in screwing up your big announcement?'

'Competitors, you mean?'

'If you like. *Someone* took the child. Who do you suspect, Mr Flexner?'

'I've no idea. I'd rule out our competitors. They wouldn't get involved in anything criminal. Can't you find out from the mother if anyone has approached her?'

'I told you the mother is missing.'

Flexner let out a long breath. 'I can't explain any of this.'

'It's pretty obvious that someone in Manflex reacted quickly when Diamond got in touch with you. My guess is that your office is bugged. Have you thought about that?'

His eyes widened.

Eastland added, 'I can think of no other way they could have set this thing up, hired the team to take care of him and also set off the smoke alarm in your building. It was an inside job, Mr Flexner. No question.'

The young man shook his head, more as a way of coming to terms with the unthinkable than as a denial.

Eastland said, 'Where do I find Michael Leapman?'

'Michael? He has no reason to—'

'Was he in the building this afternoon?'

'Yes, but—'

'His address, please.'

'I don't know. He lives in New Jersey.'

'You have a phone number?'

'Somewhere.' He felt into the back pocket of his jeans. 'But Michael is the last man on earth to want to screw up our plans. PDM3 is his baby.'

257

Chapter Twenty-Eight

IT COULDN'T HAVE HAPPENED IN England. Deep in New York's Chinatown at close to midnight a patrolman had acquired from a clothing emporium for outsize men called Chunky Chang a pair of white cotton trousers with a fifty-inch waist, an XL T-shirt, a loose-knit pink sweater, socks and white sneakers. Diamond was clothed again, if not remotely to his taste. And now he was being driven with Lieutenant Eastland and Sergeant Stein via the Holland Tunnel to New Jersey.

'So what have we got on this guy?' Eastland asked.

Stein had been assigned the problematic task of obtaining a profile of Michael Leapman by radio contact while they were driving to interview him. 'No record of arrests,' he said. 'Vice Chairman of Manflex for the past five years. Unmarried. Thirty-seven, originally out of Detroit. He worked there for a pharmaceuticals firm called Fredriksson and Lill. Worked his way up to executive director and then the firm got taken over by Manflex. You want to know the letters he can put after his name?'

'We get the picture,' said Eastland. 'Old man Flexner must have rated him to make him Vice Chairman.'

'David Flexner has a good opinion of Leapman, too,' Diamond chipped in, wanting to justify his presence in the party. 'And if we believe young Flexner – as I'm inclined to, having watched him under questioning – Leapman has a personal stake in the success of PDM3. He promoted it strongly inside the company. He arranged for Flexner to meet the professor in Indianapolis.'

The car moved on a couple of blocks before anyone

followed up the remark, and then it was Stein who spoke. 'So why would a good company man like Leapman risk everything on the eve of their big announcement by putting out a contract on a British detective?'

'You mean what made me a threat?' said Diamond.

'No, I mean what made the little girl a threat? You're just a pawn in the game.'

Such offensive remarks were best treated with indifference, in Diamond's experience. 'I think it has to be connected with this drug, doesn't it?' he said without betraying the slightest resentment. 'PDM3 could be the jackpot of all time, as David Flexner made clear. Leapman is pushing like mad to get it licensed. We don't know yet how big his personal involvement is, but it's possible that he's seen this as a once-in-a-lifetime opportunity and invested his own capital in the company. He must have been shattered when the Chairmanship of Manflex was bequeathed to David Flexner. As I see it, he uses his inside knowledge to get a big payday as compensation.'

'Are you saying this could be a scam, this whole thing about the drug?' asked Stein.

'No, I think it would be difficult to fool so many people. There are all kinds of safeguards in the drugs industry. They must have had some very promising results from the pre-clinical trials. They couldn't fake them. But the timing is amazing, isn't it? They're ready to go public on the miraculous properties of this drug now, just when Manflex is nose-diving. The stuff has been around for twenty years.'

'He explained that,' Eastland pointed out. 'They didn't know it was useful until the professor started work on it.'

'But he's been working on it for some years.'

'You think they sat on it until now?'

'I'm just trying to account for Leapman's behaviour – if he really is the villain. Of course it may be that Manny Flexner knew about PDM3 and wasn't so convinced as his Vice Chairman. Manny may have put the brake on it.'

'If there is anything suspect about the drug, it won't stay secret for long,' said Eastland. 'Like you said, every drugs company in the world will want to know the formula and scrutinize the results, not to mention the analysts who advise the stock market.'

Diamond wouldn't be shaken from his conviction that the decision within Manflex to press ahead with PDM3 had triggered the crimes they were investigating. 'Yes, the results so far must be watertight, or they wouldn't risk publishing them. Let's accept that everything we've heard about the drug is true, and that it's the most exciting discovery since penicillin. Then isn't it certain – as sure as God made little green apples – that the criminal fraternity will have got to hear of the payday in prospect?'

'The mob?'

'The barons who run crime in this city of yours, from whatever community. They could be calling the shots.'

'Maybe,' said Eastland. 'Maybe.' After a moment he admitted, 'It's plausible.'

Sergeant Stein said wistfully, 'It's a terrific pay-off.'

Eastland then followed up his double 'maybe' by commenting insensitively, 'This is all very neat except that we're investigating a missing kid, not a killing on the stock exchange. The only link we have is that the kid's mother happens to be sponsored by Manflex.'

Of all people, Diamond didn't need reminding about Naomi, but he wasn't going to be shaken from the point he'd made. 'Come on, there's ample evidence that professional crooks are involved. Mrs Tanaka's was a contract killing. And the people who attacked me weren't amateurs.'

'So why was Mrs Tanaka killed?' asked Sergeant Stein.

'My guess is that she was given a job to do and she failed. They considered her untrustworthy.'

'She was expendable.'

'Just a pawn, like me.'

'How about the kid?' said Stein. 'Is she expendable, too?'

'No,' said Diamond, quick to dismiss the unthinkable. 'If they'd wanted to harm Naomi, they'd have done it long ago.'

'I may be dumb,' said Eastland, 'but nobody has explained to me yet how one small, mentally handicapped girl is so important in this case.'

Diamond had no answer. He'd long since reached the conclusion that Lieutenant Eastland was anything but dumb.

Leapman's house was one of six in a cul-de-sac north of Hoboken, spacious two-storey wooden buildings with attached garages owned (Diamond guessed) by the kind of people who couldn't yet afford a prime position overlooking Manhattan, but had their hopes. They had plaster geese on their porches and flagpoles in their lawns.

No lights showed at the windows of the end house, but that wasn't remarkable considering that it was already 1.15 a.m. Two households were watching TV and the others were dark.

The police car glided to a stop in the street outside the Leapman address. Diamond reached for his door-handle and gasped with pain. His right arm still hurt.

'I don't think so,' Eastland told him. 'You've seen enough action for one night. We have our procedures. Ready to go, Stein?'

Submissive for a change, Diamond remained in the car and watched them approach the house, guns drawn, moving with stealth. At the front door, Stein stood well to one side when he pressed the bell, probably mindful of cops who had been shot through doors.

The chimes were audible from the street.

No lights went on.

Eastland moved around the side of the house, leaving Stein, who sounded the chimes several times more without response.

When a light did appear, it was only Eastland's flashlight bobbing around the other side, past the garage entrance. He pointed it through a front room window and beckoned to Stein to join him. They stood together staring inside for what became to Peter Diamond an unbearable interval.

Diamond told the driver, 'Blow this for a lark. They've spotted something. I'm going over.'

The action of removing himself from the car gave him another uncomfortable reminder of the strains he'd put on his physique that night. No catlike movement across the drive for him. He hobbled.

Lieutenant Eastland turned and came towards him.

'What have you found?' Diamond asked, but Eastland walked right past him and used the radio in the car.

'What is it?' He was addressing Stein now, but the question was superfluous.

Michael Leapman's front room looked as if it had stood in the path of stampeding buffaloes. The moving flashlight picked out a unit lying tilted across a sofa, with books and ornaments strewn across the floor. The television set was face-up, smashed. A chair lay across a table.

'Is he in there?'

'We can't see,' said Stein, still with his gun drawn. 'We don't know.'

'Shouldn't we go in?'

'The lieutenant wants a back-up.'

'I can provide that. Have you checked all the doors? The windows?'

'Don't get me wrong, but he wouldn't want back-up from you.'

'Why not?'

'Do you have a piece?'

'A piece of what?'

Stein gave a shrug that said he wouldn't want back-up, either, from a man without a piece and without knowledge of what a piece was.

'Any signs of a break-in?' Diamond asked.

'No.'

Eastland came back and reported that the Emergency Service Unit was on its way. 'The perps could still be inside. I'm taking no chances.'

Diamond awaited his opportunity to sidle closer to Sergeant Stein, from whom he learned that a perp was a perpetrator. The common language had its pitfalls.

A van was with them in six minutes, followed soon after by two cars. Armed men were sent around the side of the house. Lights were set up. There were dog-handlers and men in white overalls who spoke briefly with Eastland and then forced open the front door and went in.

Diamond stayed close to Eastland and followed the

262

search of the interior as it came over the personal radios. The house was unoccupied, they learned, but there were more signs of violence, including blood spots on the wall in one corner of the living-room. There were bloody fingerprints on the phone, which was pulled from its socket and lying upside down on the floor. A bloodstained baseball bat was found beside it.

'Looks like someone used the phone after the victim was struck,' the voice reported.

'Or tried to,' said Eastland. 'Have you checked all the rooms now?'

'Yeah. No disturbance anywhere except the living-room. This don't look like robbery to me, Lieutenant. The drawers and cupboards are closed.'

Then a crackle of static was followed by the voice of the other searcher. 'I wouldn't bet on that. His car isn't in the garage.'

'They took the car,' said Eastland. He turned to Stein and asked him to get a computer check on Leapman's licence plate number.

Diamond groaned in frustration. 'Can we take a look for ourselves now?'

'Not yet. Crime Scene has to go through.'

'How long before they get here? Look, I'm not asking to tramp through the room where the assault took place. I'd like to see the rest of the house.'

'What exactly is your problem?' asked Eastland. 'Not satisfied with the search?'

'I'd like to take a look for myself, that's all.'

'There's no evidence that the perps went anywhere except the living-room.'

'In that case, there's no risk of disturbing anything.'

But they wouldn't permit Diamond to step inside until an hour and twenty minutes later, after the crime scene people had been through. The possibility that Eastland was exacting some kind of revenge for the liberties Diamond had taken at the murder scene in the Firbank Hotel did occur to him at the depth of his frustration while he was waiting, but probably he was wrong. They had their procedures and they observed them rigidly. Nevertheless he was hunched and resentful as he limped about the drive.

He was unsure what he might find, if anything. He just felt driven by some inner force. Maybe, he reflected, he'd taken to heart that advice from the librarian, to unlock his sixth sense, or right hemisphere, or whatever the man had been rabbiting on about. It wasn't easy to recall at two on a chilly morning.

Eventually, the Crime Scene Unit passed on the word that, apart from the living-room, the house was open to inspection. Leaving his new sneakers on the doorstep, he stepped inside with Eastland.

'You're looking for evidence that the kid was here, aren't you?' the lieutenant said.

'I'm keeping an open mind.'

'Yeah?'

The lights were on all over the house. It was very much the bachelor businessman establishment, with the feel of a furniture showroom rather than a home. Leapman seemed to be a man of tidy habits who favoured light oak and muted colours. The pieces of furniture had their functions, and there was little in the way of ornament, and certainly no clutter.

'Want to start upstairs?' Eastland suggested.

'The bedrooms.'

It wasn't entirely Diamond's sixth sense that was motivating him. If Naomi had been kept here for any appreciable time, it was likely that she would have been confined in a room out of sight of the neighbours.

At the top of the stairs, they glanced into a couple of rooms, getting their bearings. A guest bedroom attracted Diamond's attention. It was small and it faced the back of the house. However, there was nothing to suggest anyone had occupied it. The duvet was positioned four-square on the divan, the pillow plumped and tidy. Eastland went systematically through the chest of drawers and found only some spare bedding in the bottom drawer.

'Satisfied?' he enquired of Diamond.

'Almost.' Intuition was prompting him strongly now, spurred on by something Julia Musgrave had said. He told

264

Eastland, 'Autistic kids quite like to hide things, toys and so on, objects that they value. If I'm right, it's just possible that she used a hiding-place she once favoured before, in another place.' He crouched by the bed. 'It was this side last time.' He slipped his hand between the mattress and the spring box of the divan with a sense of anticipation little less than Lord Caernarvon's at the opening of Tutenkhamen's tomb. His fingertips had touched something solid. He took it out in triumph: a ballpoint pen. 'I would say that it's ninety-nine per cent certain that Naomi was here.'

'You knew it would be in there?' said Eastland.

Elated, Diamond risked more strain on his battered body by pulling up the mattress. There may be something to intuition, but good luck is a deception. There was no drawing pad lying under the mattress. Not even a sheet of paper.

Cause for celebration: Naomi was alive – or had been at the time she hid the pen here. Cause for concern: the trail had gone cold again; there was no telling who was holding her now. The forensic tests might provide clues, but the men in white coats always take days to report their findings.

'Did Sergeant Stein get anything on the stolen car?' he asked Eastland.

'Leapman's car? It was a dark blue Chevy Citation. We have the licence plate number from Central. Every radio car in New York has it.'

There was nothing to detain them any longer. Knowing that he would keel over if he didn't get some sleep soon, Diamond asked for a lift to his hotel.

Chapter Twenty-Nine

ONE CAN ONLY GUESS AT Lieutenant Eastland's thoughts next morning when he arrived at the stationhouse to find his office occupied by Peter Diamond wearing just an unbuttoned shirt and red jockey shorts. The fat Englishman was standing with the phone anchored between his shoulder and his fleshy jowl. The desk was heaped with clothes, some discarded, some obviously back from the cleaner. Judging by the clutter of phonebooks, notepads, pens and screwed-up Kleenex, he had been installed there for some time. 'Beef, for a start,' he was saying. 'Have you got beef? . . . Right. What else? Liver, I should think. Lamb, yes . . . Well, as much as you can manage at short notice . . . Excellent. How soon? . . . Oh, give me strength! I'm talking about lunchtime today. . . . Yes, *today* . . . Right, I know you will. I'll call you back around noon. . . . One o'clock, then. No later.' He put down the phone. 'Morning, Lieutenant. Did you oversleep?'

Eastland regarded him with glazed, red-lidded eyes.

Diamond told him, 'My clothes came back.'

'So I see.'

'There's just time to get down to the Sheraton Center.'

Eastland said, 'This used to be my office.'

Diamond announced in the same up-lads-and-at-'em tone, 'The conference opens at eleven.'

'Conference?'

'Manflex. Remember? This is the big one, when they unveil the wonder drug. David Flexner will be there and so will Professor Churchward. We've got to be there.'

'Who do you mean — *we*?'

'You and I. Sergeant Stein as well if you want.'

Eastland ran his fingertips down the side of his face as if to discover whether he'd shaved yet. 'The Sheraton Center, you said?'

'Seventh Avenue and Fifty-third.'

'I know where the Sheraton is,' Eastland said in a growl.

'Snap it up, then.'

'Diamond, you have all the finesse of a sawed-off shotgun.'

To be charitable to Eastland, he hadn't seen Diamond so animated before. The Englishman was unstoppable. Within three minutes they were in a sector car heading downtown.

'I've been turning things over in my mind,' Diamond said, as if to explain the transformation. 'Last night, the scene at Leapman's house seemed all wrong.'

'Wrong?'

'What we found.'

'The ballpoint?'

Diamond stared in surprise at the lieutenant. 'No. The ballpoint wasn't wrong. That was a genuine find. Just about everything else was wrong.'

'For instance?'

'The damage to the front room. It looked impressive at first, as if there'd been a fight, but what did it amount to in breakages? One smashed TV screen. The shelf unit had tipped across the sofa and some books and things were on the floor, a chair was overturned and lying across a table and that was it.'

'The phone was pulled from its socket,' Eastland added.

'True – but it wasn't damaged. To me, the scene looked as if it had been staged by a rather fastidious owner who didn't want to damage his living-room more than was necessary.'

'You think that was staged?'

'I think it's more than likely.'

'Aren't you forgetting the bloodstains?'

'No, I haven't forgotten them. First, consider the state of the bedroom where the child was held. Immaculate – apart from the ballpoint. There was no other evidence that

267

Naomi had ever been there. Not so much as a hair on the pillow. Wouldn't you expect some sign that she'd been removed from there in a hurry?'

'Maybe she was already downstairs when the fight started,' said Eastland.

'Dressed in her coat and shoes and everything? They're not in the house.'

'Whoever took the kid must have taken her things.'

'Picked them up with his bloodstained hands and helped her into her coat? Does it sound likely?'

'Do you have a better explanation?' asked Eastland.

'Then there's the matter of the car,' Diamond continued as if the question hadn't been put. 'How did the assailant – what do you call him, the perp? – how did he travel to the house. On foot? If he came in a car, where is it, because he couldn't have driven *two* vehicles away from the house after the attack.'

'Two perps,' said Eastland doggedly. 'One drove their car, one drove Leapman's.'

'Taking Leapman with him?'

'Yeah.'

'All right – then why was it necessary to take Leapman as well as the child?'

'Maybe they killed him. There's enough blood, for sure. They got rid of the body.'

'To hinder your investigation, do you mean?'

'Sure,' said Eastland. 'They carried him to the integral garage, loaded him in the car and then opened the garage door and drove out with the body in the back. That way they avoided carrying him out into the street in the view of the neighbours.'

'And that's how you see it?'

'Do you have a better explanation?' Eastland asked for the second time.

'Let me take you back a bit,' said Diamond. 'Leapman definitely took the child to his house at some stage. We found the ballpoint where I said it would be. We agree on that, right?'

'Uhuh.'

'Look at this from Leapman's point of view. Yesterday

268

when David Flexner arranged to meet me at the ferry, Leapman was listening. Either the office or the phone was bugged. He has links with organized crime and he alerted his criminal friends and asked them to meet me and dispose of me, while he created a smoke alarm diversion at Manflex Headquarters to delay David Flexner. Is that a reasonable inference from the facts as we know them?'

'It's conceivable.'

'Conceivable? I was dumped in the river. You won't question that?'

'No, I don't question that.'

'Leapman must have believed I was dead, but he still had a problem, because you – the cops – brought David Flexner in for questioning the same night. He couldn't understand how you made the connection, but he knew how dangerous it was. It was getting too close to home. And home was where he was holding Naomi.'

Eastland was waking up. 'He didn't want the cops calling. This is not a good time in his life to get arrested.'

'Right. If he's going to cash in on PDM3, it's essential that the conference goes ahead. Are you with me so far?'

Eastland only gave a shrug and said, 'Let's say I've been listening.'

'Now, Leapman isn't the spokesman for PDM3. He's just the Vice Chairman. It isn't absolutely necessary that he puts in an appearance at the conference. David Flexner and the professor can handle it. The only thing liable to ruin the day – and the big hike in his shares – is if he – Leapman – has a visit from the cops and is found to have the child in his possession. That would be a disaster.'

'So?'

'So he arranges to disappear. He will take the child with him, leaving no evidence that she was ever in the house. First he dresses the child and puts her in the car. Then he tidies her room so well that you wouldn't know she was ever there.'

'Unless you were smart enough to look under the mattress,' said Eastland in a bland tone that didn't amount to mockery, but wasn't respectful either.

Diamond's eyes narrowed, and one of them hurt. The

black eye was still swollen. He sensed that he was being sent up, but he refused to be deflected. 'Then he fakes the attack. Tips over several items of furniture and smashes the TV screen.'

'How about the blood? You telling me it was ketchup?'

'No.'

'Self-inflicted?'

'I don't know.'

'That makes a change.'

There followed an interval when neither man spoke. Diamond needed to draw breath and Eastland was gathering himself to demolish the theory. 'It's one hell of a scenario to build on one ballpoint,' he said finally. 'In a nutshell, you believe Leapman arranged the scene himself, leaving us to deduce that he was beaten up and probably murdered?'

'Yes. I think you'll find that the only prints are his own. Probably he wore gloves to handle the baseball bat and the phone.'

Eastland supplied unexpected support here. 'It's true that whoever handled those objects wore gloves. That much we have established. And you think Leapman is alive and well? He drove off with the kid sometime before we arrived?'

'That's it.'

'Where to?'

'I've no idea, but at least we know who to look for. We can put out a description.'

'We circulated details last night,' Eastland said with a yawn.

'No response?'

'None.'

Diamond didn't have to be told about the problems tracing cars in New York.

'What's your reaction, then?'

'To what?' said Eastland.

'To what I've just been telling you.'

'I don't buy it.'

And that was that.

They arrived at the Sheraton Center and shared an

elevator to the third floor with a throng of people wearing name-tags marked with the Manflex logo. The conference was to be in the Georgian suite. Young women in red blazers and white skirts were handing out information packs. Diamond took one and saw with grim satisfaction that an amendment sheet was included: *Mr Michael Leapman, Vice Chairman, will not, after all, be chairing the session with Professor Churchward. His place will be taken by the Chairman, Mr David Flexner.*

Seated inconspicuously towards the back, Diamond and Eastland watched David Flexner enter, accompanied by the professor, a slim, brown-suited man with cropped hair who took a chair beside the podium. Flexner was the first to speak. He addressed his large audience confidently, unaffected, it seemed, by the alarms of the previous twenty-four hours. After welcoming everyone, he briefly outlined the history of Manflex under his father's management, listing the principal drugs for which the firm was known. This was a stage of the proceedings when a few latecomers were still finding seats and many of the audience were looking around them to see which faces they recognized.

To a scattering of polite applause, the man in the brown suit was introduced as Professor Alaric Churchward. Gaunt and pale, but well in control, Churchward surveyed the audience with pinpoint blue eyes for a few seconds before opening with an attention-grabbing statement. Some four million Americans, he said, could no longer remember the names of their friends and families. They couldn't put names to everyday objects, such as chairs and tables. They were sufferers from Alzheimer's disease and they included people who had held highly responsible and demanding jobs. The roll of victims of Alzheimer's was as impressive as it was distressing, including the actress Rita Hayworth, film director Otto Preminger, mystery writer Ross Macdonald and artist Norman Rockwell. The cause was unknown; it was likely that a number of different areas of the brain contributed to the symptoms. Research scientists the world over had been working intensively for the last fifteen years to find a successful treatment.

271

He summarized the main targets of the research in a way that signalled something new and revolutionary, describing how the bulk of the work had concentrated on finding ways of increasing supplies of the brain chemical acetylcholine, which has a vital and mysterious process in the functioning of the memory. The brain's supply of this chemical was known to diminish rapidly with the onset of Alzheimer's.

Churchward went on to say that his own approach (and now more pens came out in the audience and tape-recorders were switched on) was different because it was directed towards the nerve cells themselves. For twelve years, teams of scientists under his direction based in America, Europe and Asia had made animal studies to test the effectiveness of certain compounds as protective agents that could delay, or even prevent, nerve cell death. In the last eight years their work had been concentrated on a compound known as Prodermolate, or PDM3, that had proved to be something more than a protective agent.

Alaric Churchward was quite a showman. Having got to his product, he kept everyone in suspense by introducing film footage of some Alzheimer's patients he had tested five years previously, prior to the administration of PDM3.

The bemused people who were shown on the screen being asked which month it was and when they were born and who was the current President of the United States were not exclusively the elderly that Peter Diamond associated with the illness. There was a woman of forty-seven and a man of fifty-two, although the others were over sixty-five. The spectacle of people of intelligent appearance puzzling over quite basic facts was profoundly disturbing, particularly a couple of men who demanded angrily to be told who they were and where they came from.

'I guess this is the "before",' Eastland commented to Diamond.

'Is it? I don't think I . . . Oh — I see what you mean.' In his concentration on the film, he must himself have sounded mentally lacking. These pathetic people moved him more than he had expected. Progressive loss of memory was a deep-seated fear of his own, and he had no difficulty in identifying with their distress.

After the lights were turned up, the professor talked at length about PDM3, a technical briefing couched in scientific terminology that Diamond found increasingly difficult to follow. His attention drifted back to the poignant images of the Alzheimer's patients.

Then the room was darkened for another sequence of film, the 'after' interviews. Introducing them, Churchward explained that some of the volunteers (as he insisted on calling them, rather than patients, or subjects) had been administered with PDM3, and some, as a control, with a placebo.

The film was eloquent. The effects on those who had been given the drug were striking. Not only did they answer the questions they had found so baffling before, but they went on to give unsolicited accounts of the improvements in their lives. They could dress themselves, go for walks, use shops, write letters. In the standard word-test, they had averaged a seven-point improvement. The results contrasted cruelly with the steady deterioration of the group who had taken the placebo. For Diamond, cynical as he felt about the sales pitch, it was difficult to remain detached, difficult not to wish that every one of those sad, benighted people had been given the drug.

In a neat *coup de théâtre* when the lights went on, Churchward was seen to have been joined by a man and a woman, whom he introduced as people just seen in the film, volunteers whose lives had been transformed by PDM3. Each answered two or three questions lucidly and testified to the improvement in their memory and concentration. They left the platform to spontaneous applause.

David Flexner stepped up to play his part as Chairman. He invited questions.

A bearded man near the front made the point that certain drugs patented by other pharmaceutical companies had appeared to produce remarkable improvements in Alzheimer's patients, but the effects had proved only temporary. In two years, the deterioration had set in again. Was there any real possibility, he asked, that PDM3 could sustain the improvement?

Churchward answered the question so smoothly that it might have been seeded before the conference, and perhaps it had been. 'Of course I'm aware of the products you're referring to, sir, and I agree that they have disappointed as long-term remedies. There are six drugs to my knowledge that have been undergoing tests intended to give a boost to the cholenergic system that produces acetylcholine. It is beyond dispute that a certain amount of success has been achieved. Unfortunately, as you just implied, the duration is severely limited. The reason – and this is a personal opinion – would appear to be that the nerve cells that produce the acetylcholine continue to die. Our own approach, with PDM3, is quite different, for we are actually regenerating those cells. Our experiments in Indiana and at our other centres in Tokyo and London have been running for seven years, and no significant deterioration has been observed. Clearly the patients get older – let's not forget that we are dealing mainly with geriatrics – but our tests and interviews are consistently encouraging. There is, of course, documentary back-up that some of my colleagues will present this afternoon. Next question.'

A woman to the right of Diamond asked if any adverse drug reactions to PDM3 had been reported.

'Remarkably few,' Churchward told her. 'Every drug produces some unwanted reactions, but in this case they are negligible. The majority of volunteers reported no untoward effects.'

'Maybe they forgot,' Diamond muttered to Eastland in a facetious aside. He was becoming irritated by the smoothness of Churchward's presentation.

'Fewer than twenty per cent of our volunteers reported mild dizziness, but this is notoriously difficult to assess, and was of short duration,' Churchward added. 'Five per cent of those taking the placebo also reported dizziness. It isn't perceived as a serious problem.'

Diamond leaned closer to Eastland and told him in a low

voice that he was going out to make a phone call. It may have sounded remarkably like a smoker's excuse for a quick drag outside the room, but it was genuine. He was in the seat closest to the aisle, so he was able to move out without disturbing anyone.

When he returned ten minues later, the question and answer session was still in progress. Someone asked if PDM3 could be described as a 'smart drug'.

'That's not a term a serious biochemist would use, madam,' Churchward answered, 'but I know what you're referring to, and you have touched on a matter of real significance. It's estimated that up to 100,000 healthy Americans take drugs daily in the expectation of increasing their mental capacity. Call them cognitive enhancers or smart drugs, the point is that their effects are as yet unproven. I read somewhere that as many as 160 cognitive enhancers are under development, many of them being vasodilators. Do you know what I mean by that? A vasodilator has the effect of widening the blood vessels, thus increasing the supply of blood to the brain. However, if your blood supply is normal, there's no evidence that vasodilators will make you any smarter. I have yet to be convinced that any of the so-called smart drugs are effective. And yet . . .'

The professor paused, smiled slightly, and then leaned forward like a preacher, with one finger raised to focus the attention of his listeners. He need not have troubled, for they were totally attentive. '. . . PDM3 raises exciting possibilities. This afternoon, I shall give you details of a limited experiment that we undertook with a group of student volunteers. It's well known that certain highly intelligent people have poor memories. We administered PDM3 to twenty undergraduates from the University of Corydon in Indianapolis. Three of them were consistently below average scorers on memory tests and there is no question that the drug produced a marked improvement in their mental performance. We're not talking about forgetful elderly people here. This is something else. And now . . .' Churchward folded his arms and kept everyone in suspense for a moment. '. . . I want to take it a stage further. In Phase Three of our tests, I propose to examine in a wide-scale test the ability of this remarkable drug to regenerate and prolong the mental capacities of normal people. If our preliminary findings are right, the implications – for individuals, for society as a whole, for the economy, for the welfare of our nation, the progress of mankind, are truly—'

'Mind-blowing?' the questioner suggested.

Churchward smiled. 'I'm tempted to say that anyone taking PDM3 runs no risk of having his mind blown. But, yes, we can scarcely imagine the potential of such a discovery.'

It seemed a good note on which to end, or so David Flexner thought, because he reached for the microphone. 'Unless there are any other questions, ladies and gentlemen—'

'Yes, I have one more, if you don't mind.' Suddenly Peter Diamond was on his feet. He hadn't planned to intervene so publicly as this and he hadn't discussed it with Lieutenant Eastland (who muttered, 'Jesus!'). Only in the last few minutes had he come to a decision to fire a broadside across the bows of the two well-defended men at the front. A scare at this stage, when they thought they were fully in control, might panic them into revealing something really culpable – if they were implicated. 'This session was to have been chaired by Mr Michael Leapman. What is the significance of his absence?'

Flexner's right hand went straight to his long hair and raked through it. 'Mr Leapman is, em . . . Excuse me, sir, this is an organizational matter. I don't see that it has any relevance to what we have heard.'

'Ah, but it has,' Diamond insisted. 'It's well known that Mr Leapman is strongly identified with this drug. He promoted it actively within your company. He, more than any other individual, is responsible for this conference, for the decision to go into Phase Three of the testing. Yet he isn't here this morning. What are we to make of this, Mr Flexner? Does it mean that Michael Leapman has gone cold on the project?'

Flexner was staring. 'Sir, would you mind telling me

who you represent?'

'My name is Diamond.'

This simple statement made a satisfying impact. Men don't return from the dead all that often, and David Flexner had not been informed that Diamond had survived his dip in the Hudson River. His hair didn't stand on end, but in every other respect he gave a fair impression of a man seeing a ghost.

To give him time to find his voice again, Diamond went on to say, 'I'd better identify myself properly. I'm a detective working with Lieutenant Eastland of the New York Police Department, with whom you are acquainted. He's sitting beside me, in case you can't see from there. But my question was about Mr Leapman. As you no doubt know, he has gone missing. I think your audience are entitled to know the circumstances.'

Flexner looked more bloodless than the spectre in front of him. 'It has no relevance,' he managed to say.

Churchward got up and spoke to Flexner and his remark was close enough to the mike to be heard all over the room. 'Let's wrap this up fast.'

No one else had any desire to leave. Diamond said, 'You may prefer to wrap it up fast, gentlemen, but the rest of us won't be impressed if you do. Mr Michael Leapman has disappeared from his house in suspicious circumstances. A certain amount of damage has been done inside his house in New Jersey. There are signs of a scuffle. Overturned furniture. Bloodstains. His car is missing. I believe you were informed of this when you tried to call him this morning.'

Flexner appeared to give a nod.

Seeing that his Chairman was bereft of words, Professor Churchward reached for the microphone and said, 'This is a scientific conference, not a police investigation. We're sorry to hear about the attack on Michael, but with all due respect it has no bearing on what we are discussing today.'

Diamond said at once, 'I believe you're mistaken there. You've assumed that Mr Leapman was the victim of an attack.'

'But you just described it,' said Churchward.

'No, Professor, I described the scene at the house. The evidence is that the attack was faked.'

There were gasps. Everyone had turned to hear what Diamond was saying.

'I was doubtful of the set-up anyway, so I asked the forensic lab to check the blood-spots found at the scene. I phoned to get the results a few minutes ago.' Savouring the moment, he found a wicked way of prolonging it. 'As there are so many scientists present, you may care to know that they test whether it's human by diluting it and bringing it into contact with animal serum. There should be a precipitin reaction between the human protein and the animal serum. A white line forms. No white line was found in this case. The forensic people have a good stock of anti-sera from a variety of animals.' He paused. He was as capable as Churchward of working an audience. 'The blood-spots in Michael Leapman's living-room were bovine in origin, probably from calf liver, which is as bloody as most things one keeps in a freezer.' Again he waited, allowing the facts to sink in. 'So I'm bound to ask whether either of you gentlemen has any idea why Mr Leapman should have gone missing in these suspicious circumstances at this crucial time.'

Churchward was careful to switch off the mike before conferring with Flexner, who had a glass of water to his lips.

Diamond remained standing.

Without getting up, Lieutenant Eastland muttered reproachfully, 'You could have told me first.'

'There wasn't time.'

'Was this what you were setting up this morning when I came in?'

'With the lab, yes. I called them back just now. The beef test was the first they tried.'

'I thought you were ordering a sandwich.'

David Flexner switched on again and did his best to sound composed: 'We are not aware of any reason for the incident that has just been described. Michael Leapman has served as our Vice Chairman with honour and distinction for many years. We regret what has just been

278

reported, but we can't see that it has any connection with our business here today. The programme will resume after lunch. That is all I have to say at this time.'

The press closed in on Diamond.

'Satisfied?' Eastland asked, when Diamond had finally shaken off the last of them.

'I'm not here for satisfaction. I'm here to find out how much Flexner and the professor know about Leapman's activities.'

'So what did you learn?'

'Flexner, at least, was genuinely fazed. I'm less certain about the professor.'

Eastland appeared to concur. 'He's a different type. More mature as a personality. His mind was on damage limitation.'

'That was my impression, too. A cool customer. I suspend judgment on Professor Churchward.'

'His sort wouldn't be fazed if King Kong stepped into the conference.'

'But that doesn't make him a guilty man.'

'Want another look at him? He's taking the afternoon session.'

Diamond said he had other plans. While the big-shots were away, he was going to visit the Manflex Building. He meant to find out for himself whether Flexner had concealed anything of importance the evening before when he was being questioned about Yuko Masuda's file entry.

'You won't get in there without a warrant,' Eastland told him. 'They have security like a state pen.'

'Want a bet?'

'Sure.'

'I bet you the price of a meal, then,' Diamond suggested.

'One of *your* meals? Get away.'

Both men grinned. They worked better now they had the measure of each other.

Later, fortified by a sandwich (or two) he bought himself, Diamond stepped from a limousine and strutted confidently towards the front entrance of the Manflex

Corporation. The security guard – happily one he hadn't met on the previous visit – asked for his pass.

Diamond admitted that he didn't possess a pass. He had something better.

'What's that?'

'A British passport.'

'Mister, are you trying to be funny?'

'No, I'm giving you the chance to verify my name. I'm Peter Diamond.'

'Am I supposed to have heard of you?' said the guard, a mite more cautiously.

'I'm glad you asked the question. You'd better give some thought to the answer.' Diamond peered at the man's identity disc. 'Officer William Pinkowitz.'

Anyone who has played the power game knows that you put a man on the defensive by using his name. 'Are you something in Safe Haven Security?'

Diamond repeated in a scandalized tone, 'Something in it?'

'Do you work for us?'

'I wouldn't put it that way, but you're getting there.' All this was an exercise in psyching out that he had used in various guises many times before.

'But you're not American.'

'Didn't I just make that clear?' He left the wretched man dangling a moment longer before saying, 'Safe Haven is just a subsidiary of Diamond Sharp International.'

'Diamond Sharp . . .'

'International. Do you want to check with your superior?'

There was a certain amount of hesitation before Officer William Pinkowitz apparently decided that to cast any more doubt on the word of Peter Diamond was a risk he'd rather not take. 'I'll just take a look at that passport, sir.'

'Certainly.'

After an interval came the inevitable, awed, 'You're a Detective Superintendent?'

'You're doing a good job, Pinkowitz. Keep it up.' He walked into the building. Behind him, he heard Pinkowitz's heels click in salute.

He got out of the elevator at the twenty-first floor, from which, he'd been told, Manny Flexner had jumped to his death. A woman was coming along the corridor and wasn't the sort to walk shyly past. Thirtyish, with dark hair, brilliant make-up and, of all things, a kiss-curl in the centre of her forehead, she couldn't wait to find out what he was doing there with his black eye and battered face. She called out when she was still fully fifteen yards away, 'Can I help you?'

'Personnel records?' he said.

'They're all on computer now.'

'Where could I, em. . .?'

'Are you Australian?'

'English.'

'Oh, you can't be!' she checked the position of her curl. 'I have some very dear friends in England. Which part of England?'

'London.'

'Really? My friends are in Welwyn Garden City. Is that near London?'

'Tolerably near.'

'Tolerably near — I love it! But what's happened to you? I hope you haven't had a bad experience in our country.'

'No, just a fall. I'm fine.'

'I wouldn't have said so! Are you here on a vacation?'

'Research,' he said, divining a way to get back on course. He wasn't sure how long he could rely on Officer Pinkowitz to keep his privileged knowledge to himself. 'Family history. Mr, er, Leapman suggested I consult the records for information about a distant member of the family.'

'Michael Leapman? He isn't here today. Isn't that just too bad?'

'It doesn't trouble me in the least. But if I could be shown how to use a computer . . .'

'I don't know if there's a spare desk. Hold on — I'll think of something.'

'Mr Leapman's desk?'

'Why, yes — of course!'

Neat and simple, satisfyingly simple. At least, he told himself, I'm functioning again.

She showed him into Leapman's office, a place with signs of long occupation. A comfortable reclining chair, worn at the arms. A desk with cup-stains apparently impervious to cleaning. Some far-from-new executive toys, including a Newton's cradle that Diamond couldn't resist disturbing. A poster of Stockholm, curling at the corners. Even the computer keyboard at a separate desk had the glaze chipped off some of the main keys.

He sat in front of it, and his latest help-mate pressed a switch. While the machine was booting up, she had a spasm of uncertainty. 'Are you quite sure Michael said you could inspect the personnel files? Only a few of us have the password to get into them.'

'That's all right,' he assured her. 'I'm not out to discover how much you people earn or what age you are. I just want to look up a research scientist, someone who is sponsored by Manflex.'

'That's no problem,' she said, with obvious relief. 'It's much easier to access researchers than permanent staff. What name are you hoping to find?'

'Masuda. Dr Yuko Masuda.'

'That doesn't sound English.'

'It isn't. I have a cousin who went to Japan.'

'Let's try, then. Masuda. Would you spell that?'

When the name appeared on the screen, Diamond's hopes of new information were dashed. It was a thin account of twelve years of research.

Name: MASUDA, Dr Yuko (female) *Date of Birth*:——
Address: Care of Dept of Biochemistry, Univ. of Yokohama, Japan.
Qualifications: MSc, PhD
Dates of Sponsorship: From: September 1979.
                       To: Continues.
Subject of Research: Drug and alcohol-induced comas.
Drugs Under Research: Sympathomimetic.
Publications: 'An insult to the brain: coma and its characteristics.' Postgraduate thesis, 1981.
             'Narcosis and coma states.' American Journal of Biochemistry, May 1981.

'The treatment of alcoholic coma.' Paper presented to Japanese Pharmacological Conference, Tokyo, 1983.

'It isn't much,' he complained. 'Hasn't she published anything since 1983? I thought research scientists were constantly publishing.'

The woman gave a shrug. 'Maybe the file hasn't been updated.'

At least the file confirmed that David Flexner had been entirely frank about Yuko Masuda. This was all familiar stuff from the interview at the stationhouse.

'Is there any way of telling when this file was put together?'

'Oh, sure. There's a check-list of all the dates when entries or deletions were made.' She pressed two keys and a window was displayed on the right of the screen. 'Just two entries. As you see, the file was created on 10 September 1987, and the latest entry was only three months back.'

He hesitated. Something was wrong. 'But the last entry on file refers to a conference in 1983. Which piece of this data is new? What did anyone find to enter three months ago when all I can see here relates to work published up to 1983?'

'I'm sorry, I can't answer that. I have no idea.'

'The computer can't tell us?'

'No.'

He sighed. Three months ago would have been shortly before Naomi was brought to London. Possibly there was a connection. Apparently there was no way of finding out.

He had another thought. 'Can *anyone* make additions to these files?'

'If they can get into them, sure, but only a few of us have the password.'

'That would include the Chairman. . .?'

'The Vice Chairman, Personnel Director, Research Director, Senior Systems Analyst and some secretaries, including me.'

'Whose secretary are you?'

'Mr Hart's. He's Personnel.'

'And you are. . .?'

'Molly Docherty. I thought you were never going to ask.'

'I'm Peter Diamond. And who is the Research Director?'

'Mr Greenberg. Would you like to meet him?'

'How long has he been in the job?'

'About two years.'

'Then I don't think I want to meet him.' Diamond tapped the screen with his finger. 'Tell me, Molly, where was this information stored prior to September 1987?'

'It was all on a card index. Mr Flexner — Mr Manny Flexner, I mean — was a sweet man, but he was a little slow in catching up with the computer age. He didn't trust modern technology.'

Nor I, thought Diamond. 'And all the information on the card index was transferred to the computer?'

'Oh, yes. Everything. And triple-checked. I was one of the operators.'

Before asking the next question, he sent up a silent prayer. He was agnostic in his thinking, but if help was to be had from any source he needed it now. 'Do those filing cards still exist?'

There was an agonizing pause for thought before Molly Docherty said, 'I believe they were put into store somewhere.'

'Where?'

'Now you're really asking. The basement, I guess.'

'Would you mind escorting me?'

She laughed, he supposed at the way he'd expressed himself. 'I'll have to clear it with my boss.'

'You don't have to mention me.'

On the way down in the elevator, she said, 'You must be very devoted to your family.'

'Why?' He was thrown briefly, and then remembered his trumped-up reason for inspecting the files. 'It isn't just a matter of making a family tree. I want to get the background on these people.' Even to himself, he sounded pretty unconvincing.

The basement was a cold, echoing place stacked with outmoded office furniture: wooden desks with the veneers exposed, grey metal cupboards of the kind so popular in the sixties and a great variety of chairs with their covers ripped and frayed. The discarded personnel files were easy to locate, stored in five metal boxes – locked, but Molly had thoughtfully collected a set of keys from upstairs.

'These go back thirty years at least,' she told him. 'There must be a thousand in each box.'

'Let's open one.'

She stooped and found the appropriate box. As she tried the keys, she remarked, 'This is like treasure-hunting. I do hope it's worth your trouble.'

She flicked through the cards rapidly with a long, lacquered fingernail, picked one out and handed it to Diamond. 'Voilà!'

He didn't need long. 'This doesn't match the computer entry.'

'It wouldn't,' she said. 'We're constantly updating.'

'Deleting information?'

'No, adding it.'

'What do you make of this, then?' He handed back the card.

Name: MASUDA, Dr Yuko
Address: c/o Dept of Biochemistry, Yokohama University
Qualifications: MSc, PhD.
Dates of Sponsorship: From: September 1979
                             To: July 1985
Subject of Research: Comas, drug-induced and alcoholic
Drugs Under Research: Jantac
Publications: 'An insult to the brain: coma and its characteristics.' Postgraduate thesis, 1981.
           'Narcosis and coma states.' American Journal of Biochemistry, May 1981.
           'The treatment of alcoholic coma.' Paper presented to Japanese Pharmacological Conference, Tokyo, 1983.

'What's the problem?'

Clearly the details weren't written so indelibly in Molly Docherty's memory. Diamond explained. 'It says here that the sponsorship terminated in July 1985. On your computer, that isn't mentioned. It states that the sponsorship continues. That's a big difference, surely?'

'I guess she resumed the research at a later date.'

'Wouldn't that be recorded upstairs?'

'The point is that she's back with us now. I guess whoever updated the entry did the simple thing, deleted the date she stopped and substituted "continues".'

He wasn't satisfied with that. 'It gives the impression she was continuously doing research. There must have been a gap.'

'For a short period.'

'Of about two years? The computer was installed in 1987, you said. And everything was triple-checked from these cards?'

As if resenting the implication that someone had erred, she said, 'I'll just see if there's an entry on another card. Maybe the data from two cards was collated.'

But there was no second card for Yuko Masuda.

'This drug — Jantac — isn't listed on the computer, either,' Diamond pointed out. 'There's something quite different and unpronounceable. Sympatho— something or other. What exactly is Jantac?'

'Sorry,' she said, 'but there are thousands of drugs. I can't tell you.'

'Is it a Manflex product?'

'It isn't familiar to me, but we can check the list upstairs.'

'And could we also make a photocopy of this card?'

She looked doubtful. 'Is this really for family history?'

'Only remotely, I'm afraid. I'm a policeman on the trail of a little girl who is missing from home. Dr Masuda is her mother.'

'And what did you find out about this drug?'

Eastland looked more at ease sitting at his own desk in the stationhouse.

'Jantac? Not much,' Diamond admitted. 'It was on the Manflex list of experimental drugs.'

'*Was?*'

'It isn't any longer. They pulled it in 1985.'

'The year your Japanese lady's research stopped.'

'Exactly.'

'Do we know why it was withdrawn?'

'No, but I intend to find out.'

'You think it could be important?'

'Someone wiped it from the computer record. I'm satisfied that it must have been transferred accurately from the cards. Molly – the woman who helped me – insisted that everything on those cards went on to the computer and was triple-checked. But listen to this – the computer entry was altered for the first and only time three months ago.'

'About the time you found Naomi in London?'

'Yes.'

Eastland leaned back in his chair. 'Where will you get this information – about Jantac?'

'Yokohama University, I reckon. That's where the work was done. I'll fax them.'

'Before you do that, there's something I should tell you. We found Leapman's car.'

'Where?'

'JFK.'

'The airport.'

'It was in the parking lot. Been there some time.'

'How do you know?'

'He flew out last night. Japan Airlines, direct to Tokyo. I've spent the afternoon checking passenger schedules.'

'Tokyo. Have you told them?'

'Too late. He's already landed and cleared. With Naomi.'

Chapter Thirty

A JAPAN AIRLINES BOEING 747 taxied down the runway at the International Airport at Narita, thirty-five miles east of Tokyo. From his window over the wing Peter Diamond could see watchtowers, water cannon and riot policemen in full battledress. He'd read somewhere about the mass riots here in the mid-eighties and the long-running dispute with the local farmers over landing rights. Even so, this degree of security was daunting. It led him to wonder how stringent the immigration arrangements would be. Narita was not the most auspicious airport at which to arrive if your luggage consisted of a carrier bag containing only a pink sweater, cotton trousers, disposable razor, face-cloth, toothpaste and toothbrush. His apprehension was borne out when he produced his passport and it was taken away. He was asked to step into an interview room, where he waited under video surveillance for twenty minutes while, presumably, they checked their lists of undesirable aliens.

Finally he had an opportunity to tell an immigration officer (who spoke faultless English) that he was a detective engaged in an investigation.

The young man eyed him dubiously. 'Scotland Yard Special Branch?'

'No.' He had the strong impression that anything he said was liable to be checked, so he kept to the truth. 'I've been working with the New York Police. Twenty-sixty Precinct.'

'You are with the NYPD?'

'In co-operation with them. I am a senior officer. My passport, if you examine it—'

'I already have. Is Detective Superintendent your

present rank, Mr Diamond?'

He noted a distinct emphasis on the 'Mr'. 'Former, actually. I have retired from the regular police.'

'Retired? So you are a private agent?'

'Er, yes, in a sense.'

'And are the Japanese police aware of your present mission?'

'No – em, not yet. There wasn't time. They know about the case, but they didn't know I was flying here. Look, this is an emergency. I'm pursuing a suspect who has abducted a child. When I heard he had flown to Tokyo I took the next available flight.'

'The suspect is. . .?'

'An American by the name of Michael Leapman.'

'And the child?'

'The child is Japanese.'

'Japanese? You say the Japanese police have not been informed yet?'

This was sounding more reprehensible by the minute. He could see himself spending the rest of the day repeating his story to policemen – and not necessarily policemen with as good a command of English as this beacon of the immigration service. 'It's an extremely urgent matter. Obviously, I'll notify the police, but even as we're speaking, the trail is going cold, if you understand.'

'I understand, Mr Diamond. But I am not certain if you understand the difficulties you would face tracking a suspect in Tokyo. You don't speak Japanese?'

'No.'

'You don't know anybody in Tokyo?'

'Oh, I know someone.'

'Who is that?'

'A sumo wrestler by the name of Yamagata.'

'Yamagata?' The name had a remarkable effect on the immigration officer. He gripped the edge of the table, blinked several times and swayed back. 'You know the *Ozeki* Yamagata?'

'Yes.'

'You're quite sure of this?'

'I wouldn't have mentioned him if I wasn't.'

'You have actually met him?' It was if they were speaking of the God-Emperor.

This, Diamond thought, is an opportunity. Without trying too obviously to impress, he underlined his links with Yamagata. 'We met when he was in London. He's paying my fare. He hired me, in fact. He's taking a personal interest in the case.'

'You should have mentioned this.'

'I just have.'

'Yamagata-Zeki?' He repeated the name as if having difficulty in believing what Diamond was saying.

'He lives in Tokyo. I'm sure he'll vouch for me. Would you like to check with him?'

'I would.' The man's face lit up. 'I would indeed. Thank you.' This, it emerged, was an inspired suggestion, the bestowal of an honour. The immigration officer reached for a phone book. His face was flushed. The pages shook as he turned them.

He stood up to make the call, rigidly, like a soldier. Without understanding a word, Diamond watched fascinated as the stern face of the immigration department become coy, then ingratiating and finally elated.

After the conversation ended, the young man continued to hold the phone, gazing at it as if it were a thing of beauty.

'You got through all right?'

'Yes.' The voice was dreamy. 'I have just been speaking to Yamagata-Zeki.' He put down the phone and flopped into his chair.

'Is that all right, then?'

'I can't thank you enough.'

'May I have my passport?'

It was handed across. 'Now I must call a taxi for you. Yamagata-Zeki looks forward to greeting you in the *heya* where he lives.'

'There isn't time,' Diamond said flatly.

'You can't refuse.'

This was infuriating. How could he make a social call when he was chasing Leapman? But while thinking actively how to get out of the arrangement, he began to see that a detour to Yamagata's *heya* might actually be necessary. As the immigration officer had pointed out, a complete stranger to Tokyo faced problems. He couldn't begin to go in pursuit without some practical help from the locals, and that would be difficult if most of them spoke no English.

Not long after, still fretting over lost time, he was in a taxi being driven to the *heya*, which the immigration officer had informed him was one of thirty or more 'stables' for sumo wrestlers in Tokyo, most, like this one, in the district of Ryoguku, east of the Sumida River. His new friend for life ('forever in your debt, Superintendent') had assured him that no fare would be required. Diamond wasn't sure whether it would be settled by the Immigration Department or Mr Yamagata. He couldn't believe that the taxi-driver would make the trip for no other reward than the honour. Yet undoubtedly the support of a famous sumo patron was going to be useful.

He wasn't really taking in his first sights of the real Japan. Instead he was trying once again to understand Leapman's motive in coming here. The necessity of escaping from New York was clear, but to escape to an alien country whose language the man didn't, presumably, speak was extraordinary unless he had something else planned. Something Leapman believed was vital to his survival.

On the plane, Diamond had been handed a *New York Times*. The conference at the Sheraton was reported in the business section under the heading MANFLEX DIRECTOR MYSTERY. Leapman's untimely disappearance was given a couple of paragraphs rich with innuendo, yet it appeared that the market had still been impressed by the claims Flexner and Churchward had made for PDM3. Manflex stock had soared by more than five dollars, offering large profits to insiders whose stake had been purchased cheaply. In all probability, Leapman was still set to make a fortune if he could keep clear of the law. He could take his profits simply by calling his stockbroker — from Tokyo, or anywhere else.

But why Japan?

Was it possible that the man had some humanity after all and had come here to return Naomi to her mother? Clearly, he didn't want to remain in charge of a small child. He knew she was being sought. To hold her for long was dangerous as well as impractical. He was a swindler, hand in glove with professional criminals, but maybe he drew the line at murdering a child because she was in the way. Could it be as simple as that?

Not likely.

The smoke-stacks of industrial Tokyo gradually gave way to city streets crowded with purposeful people in sharp dark suits. The taxi-driver said something in Japanese with a man-to-man chuckle recognizable in any tongue and pointed to a lighted sign in English saying *Soapland*.

'Massage parlour?' hazarded Diamond.

'You want?'

'No, no. Sumo.'

He was doing his best to get his bearings from the odd assortment of English words on signboards. They passed through an area thick with cinemas, theatres, and restaurants, and eventually came to the Kuramae subway station. Almost beside it was a sign for the Kuramae-Kokugikan Sumo Hall, of which all that was visible was a long stretch of white wall and a vast, pyramid-shaped roof.

'Is this it?'

It was not. They crossed a bridge over the Sumida River into a district signposted as Ryoguku. The *heya*, a building of much older design than the Sumo Hall, proved to be only a three-minute drive away.

The driver kindly left his cab and showed Diamond the door to use. He offered a five-dollar tip – not possessing any *yen* – but it was refused. This was certainly another civilization.

A bunch of teenage girls, evidently groupies – or whatever they called them in the sumo jargon – stood near the entrance and regarded him speculatively, but with reserve. He was big enough to join the ranks, but other factors ruled him out. The place he entered had a table just inside the door manned by a young fellow in a striped kimono with the oiled black topknot.

Diamond bowed self-consciously and said, 'Visiting Mr Yamagata.'

'You are?'

'Peter Diamond.'

'You wait, please.' He picked up a phone.

There was nowhere to sit, so he interested himself in a poster for a forthcoming *basho*, trying to decide whether the exorbitant rear of the figure in the foreground belonged to his patron.

The place was extremely clean, with strips of wood horizontally around the walls, not unlike the reception area of an upmarket health club. He looked down and noticed a rip in his bulging carrier bag; he wasn't adding much to the ambience.

Another hefty young lad in a kimono appeared from a door and approached Diamond. They exchanged the obligatory bow and he said in good English, 'Welcome to our stable, Mr Diamond. I am Nodo. I have the honour to escort you to Yamagata-Zeki.'

Nodo's thong-sandals scraped the wooden floor as he led Diamond through a place where wrestling practice was in progress in a rope-edged ring with a clay floor on which sand had been shovelled. Observed by a dozen wrestlers, two masses of living flesh shaped up to each other, encouraged by a silver-haired trainer with a bamboo stick that he wasn't hesitating to use on the exposed rumps. Nobody turned to look at the Occidental dressed in a suit who was being escorted past.

'These are lesser ranks,' Nodo explained with lordly confidence that none of the lesser ranks spoke English.

At the far end, on a shelf above a radiator, was a kind of altar-piece with candlesticks. Nodo clapped and bowed his head briefly as they passed it. Before opening the door, he confided, 'Shinto shrine. We call it *kamidana*.'

'Ah,' responded Diamond, doing his best to sound enlightened.

'Now you will meet the Yamagata-Zeki. He is printing the *tegata*. You will see.'

They entered another large room where Diamond immediately recognized his famous patron. If it were possible, Mr Yamagata looked mightier than he had in London, barrel-chested, with his broad face resting in folds of flesh indistinguishable as chin or neck. He was seated cross-legged between two acolytes. In front of him was a stack of large blank cards and he was making palm-prints by pressing his hand repeatedly onto a red ink-pad and then banging it down onto the stack, from which each print was adroitly removed by the man to his left. The great wrestler made eye-contact briefly and dipped his head in a perfunctory bow which Diamond returned. Some Japanese was spoken.

Nodo explained that Yamagata-Zeki had many fans and sponsors, who liked to receive *tegata*, or hand-prints, as personal souvenirs. They sent the cards to the *heya* with a small cash donation, and the *rikishi* obliged by printing up to a thousand in batches. With Diamond's indulgence, the printing would continue while they talked.

Nodo added, 'He invites you to be seated.'

Chairs aren't provided in sumo stables; they wouldn't last long if they were. Diamond wasn't equal to the cross-legged position, but he showed willing by lowering himself to the floor and sitting in front of Yamagata with his knees bent. Up to this minute he'd felt like a detached observer, but the feeling wasn't going to survive the pressure of the floorboards against his backside. He was now emphatically part of the scene.

The rhythmic thump of the palm-printing distracted him at first, but with perseverance and the help of Nodo he succeeded in bringing Yamagata up to date on the hunt for Naomi. He was thorough, treating it as the sort of briefing he would have given to the murder squad in the old days.

Another burst of Japanese was uttered without interruption to the printing.

Nodo translated, 'He says you should go to Yokohama as soon as possible. This is where the answers to these mysteries will be found.'

'I agree,' said Diamond, privately thinking that he hadn't needed to come here to be told that. 'How do I get there?'

'Better by train than taxi at this time of day.'

'The Bullet?' he asked, airing his fragmentary knowledge of Japanese life.

'No. The Yokosuka line is faster. I am to call a taxi to take you to the Central Station. Do you need money?'

He was answering when one of the apprentice wrestlers came in with a portable phone and handed it to Yamagata. Without hesitating, the wrestler grasped it with his inky right hand. Apparently a call was on the line. He listened, grunted some response, and handed a red-smeared instrument back to the unfortunate who had brought it in. Then he spoke to his helpers. It seemed that the printing session was over, because the blank cards were hastily taken aside. With a rocking motion, Yamagata prepared to get up. He pressed his clean hand against the floor, leaned on it and rose. Then he spoke to Nodo.

When translated, the news was ominous. 'That was a call from Immigration at Narita Airport. The officer who saw you has been checking to see if anyone has a recollection of the small girl and the American passing through yesterday. It seems they were noticed, and they were not alone. Two other Americans travelled with them, male, in their twenties, six foot plus, names Lanzi and Frizzoni.'

'I get the picture,' said Diamond gravely. 'He's got minders.'

'They were under surveillance by Customs and their luggage was inspected, but they were clean.'

'They can get guns here. They'll have contacts. I thought at one stage he was acting independently, but I was naive. The stakes are too big. This is bad.'

'Yamagata-Zeki agrees with you. He is going with you to Yokohama.'

This was hard to credit. 'He's planning to come with me?'

'He says you can't handle this alone.'

Diamond gave a low whistle as he tried to imagine it. 'I'm grateful, but doesn't he think he's rather conspicuous? I mean well-known,' he corrected himself.

'I don't think it would be wise to question his decision,' said Nodo.

'Are you coming too?'

'Oh, no.'

'Why not? We need a translator.'

'It isn't necessary. You are in Japan.'

Events moved on with the positiveness of a *basho*. In a matter of minutes, Yamagata, dressed only in a bright-patterned kimono and flip-flop sandals, was squeezing into the back of a taxi. There was no question of Diamond's sharing the seat, so he travelled with the driver. At intervals along the route to the station, whenever the taxi was forced to slow for lights, people reacted with double-takes to the sight of the passenger in the back. Whatever the benefits of having a famous sumo in support, secrecy could be forgotten.

The problem was worse at the station. A crowd gathered almost immediately and stayed with them all the way from the ticket booths to the train. Yamagata accepted the attention as his lot in life. He wore a frown that seemed calculated to keep people from actually asking for autographs or striking up a conversation. They chatted excitedly among themselves, but they didn't trouble him, apart from staring and generally obstructing the view. When he moved, no one was unwise enough to stand in the way for long.

The up-side of travel with a sumo hero was that seats were instantly offered on a crowded train, a double for each of them. Once settled, Yamagata closed his eyes as if to shut out the attention. Someone spoke something in Japanese to Diamond, so he followed Yamagata's example. There was no risk of falling asleep because the announcements over the public address system came every few moments with a staccato ferocity that would have woken the dead.

In thirty minutes they reached Yokohama station and changed trains. Yamagata led the way, still oblivious of all the attention he was getting. It was fast becoming apparent to Diamond that he would never have fathomed the intricacies of the railway system without help.

Two stations along, they got out again and went for a taxi. Other people were waiting for cabs, but the front of the queue melted away when Yamagata arrived with his entourage of the starstruck and the starers.

They climbed into the first one on the rank and Yamagata gave the driver his instruction.

Next stop, the University, unless I've been totally misled, thought Diamond.

Chapter Thirty-One

YOKOHAMA UNIVERSITY WAS LITTLE DIFFERENT from Tokyo Central Station in the way people reacted to having a sumo celebrity among them. The administrative staff flocked into the reception hall to stare at the illustrious guest, who conducted himself in the same imperious manner, staring into the mid-distance as if to show disdain for an opponent. At the desk, however, he became animated and explained the purpose of the visit in fast, forceful Japanese. Confused and overcome, the young woman on duty didn't appear to take in what he was saying, so he repeated it. There was an embarrassing hiatus until one of the staff, a demure, blushing girl with wide, intelligent eyes and a tiny mouth exquisitely defined in brilliant lipstick, took Diamond aside and asked if he was American.

'English. Is there a problem?'

'We are not accustomed to visits from *sumotori*.'

'I can understand.'

'Of course we are honoured. We wish we could have made preparations, arranged a proper tour.'

'We don't want a tour, thanks. We just want to speak to someone in the Biochemistry Department — a research scientist. It's very urgent.'

'He said something about a missing child.'

'That's right. We want to speak to the mother, Dr Yuko Masuda. Could you find out whether she's on the campus today?'

'I'll ask them.'

She came back without an answer, but with an instruction: 'Please, they say you should proceed to the

298

science building and go to the Department of Bio-chemistry.'

'What's your name?'

She looked slightly dismayed to have been asked. 'Miss Yamamoto.'

Diamond tried repeating it exactly as she had spoken. He wasn't being familiar just because she was pretty. 'Can you come with us and translate for me?' She lowered her head decorously. 'That would be an honour, sir.'

'Excellent. And one more thing.'

'Yes?'

'It would not be wise to let Dr Masuda know who her visitors are. We don't want to alarm her.'

'I shall tell them.'

They were escorted through a labyrinth of cloisters to the science blocks, modern pre-cast structures several stories high. The news had travelled. Faces were at most of the windows and there was a gathering of interested students at the entrance, some taking photographs and some ready with pens and paper, but no one went so far as to ask for an autograph. Yamagata's look wasn't inviting.

Biochemistry was on the second floor. Diamond had doubts about sharing the elevator with so much poundage, but their guide didn't hesitate and the machinery survived the test.

As the doors parted, a silver-haired man in a white lab-coat stepped forward and greeted them in the traditional Japanese manner.

'This is Dr Hitomi, principal lecturer in postgraduate studies,' the indispensable Miss Yamamoto explained.

They were taken to the departmental office and offered seats. Yamagata looked dubiously at the plastic chair that was expected to support him and shook his head, so Diamond tactfully remained standing also. Anyway, he expected to meet Dr Masuda shortly, which would mean hoisting himself upright again.

A crushing disappointment followed. It emerged that Naomi's mother was not based at this campus after all. She had last worked here some seven years ago, researching into a drug for the treatment of comas.

'Jantac?' said Diamond when this had been translated.

Dr Hitomi nodded.

'But we heard that she is still carrying out research here, with a grant from Manflex Pharmaceuticals,' Diamond said.

This created some uncertainty.

'He repeats that Dr Masuda is not working here,' Miss Yamamoto told him. 'Her research here terminated in 1985.'

'Terminated? Definitely terminated?'

'Definitely.'

Dr Hitomi spoke some more.

'He says he knew Dr Masuda personally. She was a good scientist. Her work came to an end when Manflex took a decision to stop further experimentation with Jantac.'

'Why? Why was it stopped?'

When this was put to Dr Hitomi, he shrugged before giving his answer.

'He says Dr Masuda had worked with Jantac for more than two years and was getting good results in reversing coma symptoms, but about this time she detected side-effects from the drug.'

'Side-effects?' Diamond's antennae were out.

Dr Hitomi had taken a Japanese/English dictionary from the shelf behind him. He pointed out a word.

'Cirrhosis?' said Diamond. 'Liver disease?' His brain darted through the implications.

After another explanation, Miss Yamamoto translated, 'The side-effect of this drug was difficult to detect, because the coma patients were alcoholic and alcoholism is a major cause of what is that word?'

'Cirrhosis.'

'He says alcoholism causes cirrhosis anyway. However, Dr Masuda discovered that Jantac also caused an increase in liver enzymes, producing cirrhosis. A small side-effect is acceptable, but this was too much. When she reported her findings to Manflex, they terminated the programme.'

Dr Hitomi added something.

'He says Mr Manny Flexner, is that correct?'

'Manny Flexner, yes.'

'Manny Flexner himself took the decision to stop working with Jantac. Mr Flexner always put the safety of patients first.'

Diamond gave a nod while he wrestled with the implications. What he had just heard conflicted with the computer records he'd seen at Manflex headquarters in New York, yet confirmed and expanded on the information he'd seen on the record card in the basement. Jantac had proved to be a dangerous drug and as a result Yuko Masuda's research had been axed.

'Would you ask Dr Hitomi if the department has copies of any correspondence dealing with this matter?'

This, it seemed, was doubtful. Dr Hitomi picked up a phone.

It emerged that the correspondence had been returned to Manflex some months ago at their request.

Suspicious.

'This year?'

'Yes.'

Someone in New York had gone to unusual lengths in covering tracks. Diamond sighed and folded his arms. It was a strange situation, being surrounded by a group of people so willing to help and watching him intently, but without understanding the problem. It was down to him, and he was far from certain what to suggest next.

'Does the University possess copies of the papers Dr Masuda published?'

Almost certainly they did, in the library.

'In English as well as Japanese?'

It was likely.

The entire circus struck tents and removed to the library, where the by now predictable excitement and confusion prevented anything useful happening for several minutes. At length, Diamond was presented with a copy in English of Yuko Masuda's research paper on the treatment of alcoholic coma presented to the Japanese Pharmacological Conference in Tokyo in 1983. He sat down to see what he could discover in it, while everyone waited.

Inwardly he groaned. The text was way beyond his

comprehension. He stared at the first page for some time before turning to see how many pages like this there were. Thirteen.

Then his attention focused on a paragraph towards the end of the last page:

'The research continues. Present studies are concentrated on a compound patented by Manflex Pharmaceuticals and given the proprietary name Jantac, and early results are encouraging.'

He looked for the footnote and found that it gave a chemical formula.

Ideas rarely come as inspirations. More usually they develop in levels of the brain just above the subconscious, over hours, days or years, and most of them never come to anything. He had kept a vague idea on hold ever since he had stood in the basement of the Manflex building with Molly Docherty and looked at Yuko Masuda's record card.

'May I use a phone? I want to call New York.'

They took him into the chief librarian's office. Fortunately he could remember the number he wanted.

'Police,' said a weary American voice.

'Is that the 26th Precinct? Lieutenant Eastland, please.'

'Who is this?'

'Peter Diamond. Superintendent Diamond, speaking from Yokohama.'

'Lieutenant Eastland isn't here just now, sir.'

'In that case, would you give me his home number. It's extremely urgent.'

'We can't disturb him right now, sir. Do you know what time it is here?'

Diamond erupted. He didn't care what the sodding time was in New York. A child's life was at stake and he needed to speak to Eastland right now.

She took the number and promised that she would ensure that the lieutenant called right back within the next few minutes.

The promise was kept.

The familiar voice, husky with sleep, protested angrily, 'Diamond? For Chrissake—'

'Listen. That conference at the Sheraton. Are you with me?'

'Yeah,' said Eastland, already capitulating. He *must* have been tired.

'Do you still have the literature?'

'Literature?'

'The press pack. The stuff about PDM3.'

'I don't know. I could have slung it out. It may be downstairs. Do you want me to look?'

'Oh, come on. Would I be phoning you?'

'Hold the line. I'll be right back.'

Through the door he could just see Yamagata doing an exercise that involved propping his left leg on a bookshelf. It looked liable to cause a disaster.

'Peter, you there?'

'Of course. Have you got it?'

'Yeah.'

'Good. Now, turn to the first page of that blue leaflet, the one that introduces PDM3. Somewhere, there's a chemical formula. Know what I mean?'

'Hold on. . . . Okay. You want me to read it out?'

'No, let me try. Listen carefully. Check every figure, would you? C_{18}.'

'Correct.'

'H_{13}.'

'Check.'

Diamond's pulse beat more strongly. He was reading out the formula for Jantac. 'NO_3.'

'Yeah.'

It *had* to be the same now. His voice breaking up with tension, he completed the formula. It was precisely the same. Jantac, the drug dumped by Manny Flexner in 1985, had been resurrected as Prodermolate – the miraculous PDM3.

'Is that all you wanted?' said Eastland in a less than cordial tone.

'That's all I wanted – unless you can give me the form on a couple of hatchet men called Lanzi and Frizzoni.'

'Never heard of them. Can I go back to bed now?'

Diamond thanked him and put down the phone. He gestured to Yamagata to come into the office and the big fellow thoughtfully grasped Miss Yamamoto's wrist and brought her in as well. Blushing as only a Japanese girl can, but not displeased — for his grip was gentle — she remained standing beside him when he released her.

It was vital that Yamagata understood the significance of this discovery. Others, including Dr Hitomi and a couple of librarians, had followed him in, but Diamond couched his explanation in terms meant for the wrestler. 'Do you see what I'm driving at?' he said when he'd given the gist of the phone call. 'Jantac was discredited here. It's dangerous, and shouldn't have been used again. We now know that another team of researchers, headed by Professor Churchward, worked independently with the same compound and came up with sensational results in the treatment of Alzheimer's disease. I'm not going to speculate whether Churchward knew that he was working with a dangerous drug, but someone at Manflex headquarters certainly knew, which is why all mention of Jantac was erased from Yuko Masuda's computer record.' He waited for this to be translated, and he had to repeat it more slowly. In his eagerness he'd strung too many sentences together. Also he suspected that Miss Yamamoto was distracted by Yamagata.

Yamagata said recognizably, 'Leapman.'

'Yes, it had to be Leapman. All his actions confirm that he's responsible. And something else was altered on the computer. Dr Masuda's project was stopped in 1985, but the computer record was falsified to make it appear that her research continues. Some other group of drugs is mentioned, but that's just a smoke-screen. On second thoughts,' he said quickly, 'don't try translating that last bit.'

After Miss Yamamoto had filled in, Diamond resumed, 'It isn't just a matter of falsifying the records. Leapman is in deep with organized criminals, who are set to make big profits out of PDM3. Manflex was on the slide at the beginning of this year.' He mimed the downward slope of a sales graph. 'Before Manny Flexner committed suicide, there was a big fire at one of their plants in Europe. Milan. Manflex dropped even lower on the stock markets. There's a police investigation still going on into a possible arson attack. To me, that suggests this plot was being hatched many months ago.'

He paused for the translation. Yamagata nodded gravely. He seemed to be following what was said.

'If they're capable of doing that, they're capable of murdering Yuko Masuda, who could have exposed them. I can't say for certain yet, but I very much fear that she is dead. I believe her little daughter – the child I know as Naomi – was given to Mrs Tanaka, a woman desperate to adopt. Maybe they drew the line at killing a child. Mrs Tanaka was ordered to get the child out of Japan, to Europe. She was horrified to discover that Naomi was autistic. She couldn't cope and she abandoned her. I'm sorry, I'm not giving you a chance,' he admitted to Miss Yamamoto.

'It's all right,' she said launching into a translation directly, looking up earnestly at the wrestler.

'As you know,' Diamond picked up his thread again, 'in England we did all we could to publicize Naomi's plight. After I went on television, Mrs Tanaka panicked and snatched Naomi back. She was in trouble now. She couldn't possibly stay in Britain, so she phoned her contact for orders. They told her to fly to New York, and she obeyed, a fatal move, if only she'd realized. Obviously the people behind this scam had decided Mrs Tanaka was unreliable and dispensable, and they hired a man to meet her and murder her.'

He stopped. He'd told most of it now. It all hung together so well. And yet . . .

Yamagata listened to the Japanese version and then spoke a few words that, translated into English, pinpointed the problem. 'If Dr Masuda is dead, why has Leapman come to Japan with Naomi and two American strongmen?'

Diamond was about to admit he was stunned for an explanation when someone interrupted in Japanese. It was Dr Hitomi, speaking in the modulated tone he had used before.

Modulated it may have been, yet it brought a swift, excited response from Yamagata.

The translation followed for Diamond's benefit. 'Dr Hitomi says he thinks you are mistaken in saying Dr Masuda is dead. He saw her here on the campus only last week.'

He made an effort to stay calm. 'Is he certain? When the police checked her last address, she was missing.'

Now one of the librarians chimed in, using imperfect, but perfectly comprehensible English. 'Is true. She alive. She sometimes use library. If you like I show you her name on computer.'

'No need,' said Diamond. 'I believe you, both of you.' He loosened his lips and blew out, making them vibrate. It eased his tension, somehow. 'And now we know the answer to Mr Yamagata's question. Leapman and his friends are in Japan to do the job properly this time and silence Dr Masuda for good.'

'With a child?' Miss Yamamoto said spontaneously.

'They'll use the child as bait. The point is, have they found her mother already?'

When this had been turned into Japanese, Yamagata spoke.

'He says the real point is, where to look for Dr Masuda.'

He was right. They did the obvious thing first, and checked the library records for an address. It proved to be the same place that Diamond had been informed by the Yokohama police was now let to someone else. A phone call confirmed this.

'So where in the whole of Japan do we turn now?' he said aloud, but speaking more to himself than anyone present, so that he was caught by surprise when Miss Yamamoto translated.

This time, no one had an answer.

And this was the nadir, the most depressing moment of the entire quest. To have come this far and be thwarted was hard enough, but to know for sure that every minute of inaction made it more likely that Naomi and her mother would die – that was intolerable.

He asked them to call the police. He was told that they had been notified hours before, apparently by the zealous young man in Immigration.

'Then we'll call and ask if they have any information yet.'

A call was made and the police had nothing to impart. Not even a sighting of the Americans.

Someone suggested coffee. Diamond wasn't interested.

'What else do they have on that library computer?' he asked Miss Yamamoto.

Only the titles of the books borrowed.

'What are they?' he asked, more to give an illusion of activity than anything else.

Yuko Masuda had one book out. On comas.

He wondered.

'Is there a hospital in this city, or in Tokyo, that specializes in treating alcoholics?'

Three.

'Would you phone each of them and ask whether Dr Masuda carries out research there?'

The second hospital they called said Dr Masuda was a regular visitor.

Chapter Thirty-Two

DIAMOND HAD BEEN TOLD THAT the hospital was south of the city, in the foreigners' quarter, Yamate-Machi, known as the Bluff. For about a mile the taxi-driver took a route along the north bank of the River Nakamura. He drove fast, with the horn blaring most of the time, on orders from Yamagata, who kept urging him to overtake more vehicles; you didn't need Japanese to understand. And there was no complaining from the driver. He was obviously a sumo worshipper having the trip of a lifetime. If he lived to tell the tale, he'd be the envy of every taxi-driver in Yokohama.

In the front passenger-seat, Diamond ground his teeth and braced himself for a collision. This kind of travelling, he reflected grimly, shouldn't be inflicted on the middle-aged. It was a bit much when the quickest you normally experienced was a bus up Kensington High Street. But he still hoped to God that he would get to Yuko Masuda before Leapman and his two gorillas.

They screeched right, the mudflaps rasping on the road, forced lower by the weight on the rear seat. They crossed a bridge, zigzagged along a busy stretch beside Ishikawacho Railway Station, and then onto the access road for a stretch of expressway. God help us, Diamond said to himself, he can really put his foot down now. But the taxi was close to its optimum speed anyway. They fast-laned under a tunnel and all the way to the next exit which took them into the Yamate-Machi area. Not a moment too soon, the hospital came up on the left, dominated by four high-rise blocks, a huge, modern site with its own system of roadways.

Yamagata had his door open well before they braked outside the main reception hall. Gesturing to Diamond to remain in the cab, he moved inside at impressive speed for a big man. It would have been interesting to see the reactions inside. When a *sumotori* charged in and demanded to know the way to the coma unit, you'd assume that he'd been rough with someone.

Yamagata emerged, running, shouting directions, and clambered in, causing the whole vehicle to rock, and they powered off again. The speed was even more reckless in hospital grounds with limit signs at every turn, but the driver wasn't slowing for ambulances, food trolleys or zimmer-frames; he could steer, couldn't he?

They rounded the out-patient block, swerving to avoid an unconscious patient being wheeled between two buildings, and raced through a narrow space between parked cars. Ahead was the building they wanted, if Yamagata's frenetic instructions meant anything. It was a one-storey, flat-roofed wooden structure that looked like an afterthought. The taxi screeched to a halt and the passengers leapt out and shoved open the door.

They were in a short corridor with doors along one side. A woman was walking towards them.

At this critical stage of the operation, with timing that can only be described as inopportune, Diamond had a deeply disturbing thought. He hadn't the faintest idea what Yuko Masuda looked like. If this woman were she, he wouldn't know. Nor, come to that, had he ever laid eyes on Michael Leapman.

He was looking for total strangers.

He told Yamagata, 'We need help,' and the big man seemed to understand because he spoke to the woman. When the name Masuda was mentioned, she didn't react as if it were her own. She came back with a question of her own that Yamagata answered. Then she pointed to a door just behind them.

Diamond opened it and walked into a ward about forty metres long, with five bays separated by glass-walled partitions. In the nearest they could see a patient surrounded by the apparatus necessary to monitor and sustain life in the unconscious state. Most of one wall was covered with photos and cards and there was a mobile of cardboard goldfish suspended above the bed. A nurse wearing a face-mask was attending to the drip-feed. She turned, her eyes widening in amazement.

Yamagata spoke.

The nurse pointed to the bay at the far end, nearest the window, and Diamond's heart-beat stepped up.

A small Japanese woman in a white coat was in conversation with two Caucasian men. They didn't have the look of hospital staff. One was tall and blond, wearing a dark, expensive-looking suit, white shirt and club tie and the other had reddish-brown hair with a flat-topped cut that might have been made with one sweep of a scythe. This second man was marginally shorter, but very large in the chest and shoulders, and was dressed more casually, in a suede jacket and black denims. Presumably he was one of the heavies seen arriving at the airport. If so, it was a fair bet that the blond man was Michael Leapman. Intent in their discussion, they hadn't yet noticed that anyone had come in.

Diamond approached to within a few yards without catching their attention.

'Mr Leapman?'

Both men wheeled around.

'Hold it! Who are you?' the blond man asked in an American accent.

'Someone you people thought you'd disposed of,' Diamond answered.

'You're that English cop.'

Confirmation, if it was required, that this had to be Michael Leapman. 'Drop it.'

The heavy had just whipped out a knife.

'You're joking.'

Diamond wanted no violence. But if necessary, he backed Yamagata — even against a hitman armed with a dagger. He beckoned to the woman with his right hand, inviting her to step away from the two Americans. 'Dr Masuda.'

Her face crinkled as if in pain and she pinched her lips

together, but she made no move other than to shake her head and draw her arms across her chest.

Leapman said with confidence, 'We're walking right out of here with Dr Masuda and you can do shit-all about it. Let's move, Dino.'

Dr Masuda seemed petrified. She could have stepped away from them. It wasn't as if the knife was at her throat. She turned her head and glanced behind her.

There was a slight movement to Diamond's left and he saw that Yamagata had hunched into the position the *sumotori* adopt immediately before the charge. Then Dr Masuda cried something in Japanese.

Leapman said, 'Hey, tell blubbergut to take it easy, will you? This little lady has made up her mind.'

Whatever it was that Dr Masuda had just said, it appeared to confirm Leapman's last statement, because Yamagata suddenly straightened and gripped Diamond's arm to restrain him.

A sumo champion backing down? It was difficult to credit.

Leapman gave the grin of a man who had won without so much as a scuffle. 'I won't say it's been good to meet you, gentlemen. Have a nice day, just the same.' He gestured to Dr Masuda to walk ahead and she obeyed. 'See what I mean?' He started to follow. The minder went, too, walking backwards to cover their exit, the knife held threateningly.

Yamagata's grip on Diamond's arm tightened. He would not allow Diamond to go in pursuit.

When they were out of arm's range, the reason why Masuda had gone so compliantly was made clear. Yamagata steered Diamond to the windows and pointed to where a figure was standing beside a red saloon car. Two figures, in fact. On first sight they had merged as one, for a man was holding a small Japanese child directly in front of him. She looked pale and passive, her hands limp at her sides, in spite of the cord around her throat.

It was Naomi.

Having anguished over her fate for so many days, having put so much into the search, this was a nightmare.

311

To do nothing now – while she was there in view, under threat of murder – would be unforgivable.

Leapman had reached the door. He told Diamond, 'She's coming with us because she wants her kid back. She hasn't seen her in months.'

'You'll kill them both.'

'Maybe, but she doesn't know that. She can't understand one word we say. And just in case you were thinking of following, I'm asking Dino to guard the door while we get clear.'

Dr Masuda had already gone through and Leapman followed. The henchman waited just inside, guarding the only exit with the knife held ready.

Although his heart was sick, Diamond knew in his head that Yamagata was right. To have made a move now would certainly have put Naomi at risk. It wouldn't require much for the thug out there to strangle her. Very likely he'd been hired to kill mother and child anyway. One unexpected move might precipitate the deed. But it must have required astonishing self-restraint on Yamagata's part to hold back when all his training, all his pride, was based on the the concept of the fight.

Even at this stage, he continued to hold Diamond's right arm in the iron grip.

'They're getting away, for God's sake!' The scene unfolding on the other side of the glass appeared as remote as television. In fact, the windows were about the size of portable TVs, much too narrow to have climbed through.

'Will you let go of me?' Diamond demanded.

Now he could see Yuko Masuda running towards her child, her hands oustretched.

The henchman released Naomi, probably on orders from Leapman, who was following closely. The child stood still, unaffected, and then was gathered into her mother's embrace.

'It's too bloody late now!'

Leapman had the car door open and bundled mother and child into the back seat and got in beside them. The other man got into the driver's seat.

Only at this point did Yamagata release Diamond, by now rigid with anger and frustration. 'Too bloody late!' he shouted.

Yamagata plainly didn't agree. Timing is fundamental to sumo wrestling and for him the fight wasn't over yet. The huge man moved at astonishing speed before Diamond had even got the last words out. He went straight to the bed in the end bay. It was a good thing it was unoccupied, because Yamagata tucked his hands underneath, tipped it over, grabbed the underside and lifted the entire thing as if it were polystyrene. In the same forward movement he charged at the window frame and crushed the bed against it with tremendous force. Such was the impact that the entire casement and a section of wall collapsed at the first contact, leaving a gap framed by splintered wood and plaster. The rage, the humiliation of the last few minutes was being expelled in one eruption of action.

Yamagata almost fell across the bed when it landed upside down in a flower-border outside, but he just succeeded in stayng upright and clambering over it. His kimono was half off one shoulder, so he ripped it from his body without shifting his gaze from the focus of his anger.

The car was moving off, but it would have to pass Yamagata on the narrow road.

He stooped, legs astride, rubbing his hands, preparing to meet the car as if it were a rival in the wrestling ring. He actually indulged in some intimidatory action. He placed his left hand across his heart, stretched out his right, raised his right leg high in the *shiko* movement and slammed it down on the road.

There wasn't time to complete the ritual. The car was coming at him. Hunkering low again, he waited for the crunch. There was no question of giving way to two tons of automobile. Much more than his self-esteem was at stake.

With exquisite timing, he launched himself straight at the car at the moment it would have smashed into his legs. His huge body was visible rising over the bonnet in a movement that looked like a dive at the windscreen. The effect was made more spectacular by the car's acceleration, because all he needed to do was dip his torso and jump as the bonnet moved underneath him. His head shattered the windscreen and hit the driver with tremendous impact. The car veered off the road and smashed against a speed limit sign.

Peter Diamond was standing in a dust-cloud of plaster, mesmerized by what he had just witnessed. Whether Yamagata had survived, he couldn't tell. The wrestler's head and torso were entirely inside the car and the rest of him lay on the bonnet, ominously still.

Diamond shook himself out of the trancelike state and was preparing to clamber over the rubble to give help when there was a warning shout from behind, more of a scream than anything intelligible. Just in time he glanced behind and saw Leapman's other henchman charging towards him with the knife raised to strike.

Diamond was no sumo wrestler. Nor was he particularly fit. His right arm still ached from the beating he'd had in New York. But he still had quick reactions and his police training had given him some elementary judo. Until now he'd never been required to use the shoulder throw in a real fight. It was quite a contortion to twist sufficiently to grab the man's right sleeve and left lapel without being stabbed, but he succeeded. He bent his knees to get under his attacker's centre of gravity, and gave a terrific tug. The man somersaulted over his back and thumped the ground heavily. Not bad for an amateur. Diamond grabbed the knife, but there was no need because the man was out cold.

The shout must have come from the nurse they'd seen attending to one of the coma patients. Now she was running straight past Diamond to the car. He followed.

One of the rear doors opened and Leapman climbed out, scattering fragments of broken windscreen from his clothes. Seeing the knife in Diamond's hand, he raised his arms. He was not the sort to fight for himself. Diamond ordered him to lie face down on the verge.

Naomi got out next, making a whimpering sound, in some distress, but not visibly injured. Her mother followed and held her.

Yamagata's body was lacerated extensively, but to

314

Diamond's immense relief, he began to move. He must have been stunned for a while, and no wonder. Slowly but without assistance he withdrew his bleeding torso from the front of the car. Astride the heavily dented bonnet he sat tidying his hair.

The nurse had been examining the man in the driver's seat, feeling for a pulse. Presently she stood back and shook her head. From the look of him, his neck must have been broken. He'd taken the full impact of Yamagata's head.

Hospital staff rapidly appeared from all sides, some just to watch or take pictures – for a Japanese is never far from his camera – and others ready to help.

Diamond stooped and picked up one of Yamagata's flip-flop sandals, or *bedi*, lost or discarded in the action. He looked for the other and found it. A doctor who spoke English made himself known to Diamond and arranged for the security staff to take charge of Leapman and the surviving henchman, who was regaining consciousness. The police were called.

The sightseers surrounded Yamagata until a nurse persuaded him to remove himself from the car bonnet and go for treatment. He was extensively marked, but the cuts were superficial. In a few days there would be no scars. Diamond eased a path through the admirers and handed the flip-flops to their owner. He would have liked to apologize for the way he'd ranted and tried to break free. Instead, he bowed. They both bowed. Then Yamagata made a generous gesture. First, he pointed to the henchman being helped to his feet by a security man and then he tapped Diamond's chest with his forefinger, nodding at the same time as if to express approval. He bowed again and with a sense of ceremony returned the flip-flops to Diamond. Words weren't required. There was actually a scattering of applause. Diamond was glad he didn't have to speak because he couldn't have trusted his voice at that moment.

Yamagata looked around. Something still troubled him. He spotted Dr Masuda standing a short way off, holding Naomi by the hand. He strode across to them, exchanged a bow and a few words and then stooped and lifted the little girl into his arms.

She looked comfortable. Even contented.

The cameras clicked.

Chapter Thirty-Three

'LOOK AT THESE! JESUS, WHAT do they think I'm going to do?' The handcuffs on Michael Leapman really weren't necessary, but as the Yokohama police had insisted on this formality when they allowed Diamond to interview him, it was respected. They sat facing each other in leather armchairs in an office belonging to the senior detective, who observed from behind his desk with an interpreter beside him.

Diamond waited indifferently. He was confident that the protest would pass. If he'd ever seen a man who was ready to talk, it was Leapman, desperately wanting to justify his actions to somebody.

And the switch to sweet reasonableness was not long in coming. 'You know, in a way I'm relieved. I wasn't in control of my life any more. Mind if I tell it my way?'

A nod from Diamond and he was away.

'I can scarcely believe what an idiot I've been. Less than a year ago, I had things pretty well sorted. I was Vice Chairman, on a good salary in a prosperous company, although I have to say I could see the clouds gathering. Manny – the Chairman – wouldn't admit that we were slipping back in the pharmaceuticals league. He was a great personality, a real nice guy, a terrific manager in his time, but frankly he wasn't in tune with modern business. It's a shark pool now and Manny shouldn't have been there any more. I know the drugs industry. I was ambitious for his job and I expected to get it soon.'

'Through a boardroom coup?'

'Right. I had a surefire plan to reverse the slide, but I knew he wouldn't back it. Unknown to Manny, I'd already given the green light to certain research projects that he wasn't even aware of. Nothing unethical, just things that I considered Manflex should support to stay competitive. I diverted some funds quite legitimately from other projects we were phasing out and when the accounting got a little complex I actually injected some cash from my own pocket. It was an investment, the way I saw it. There was this project in Indianapolis with terrific potential.'

'Churchward's?'

Leapman nodded. 'Every drugs company in the business was looking for a breakthrough with Alzheimer's. Alaric Churchward was getting some sensational test results with PDM3. I was damned sure we had an all-time winner, and I was aiming to torpedo Manny with it. I knew he wouldn't back it without all kinds of guarantees we weren't ready to supply. The Board were unhappy with Manny and I expected to make my bid for Chairman any time. When I became boss I could give the drug my backing and turn Manflex into a top company again.'

'You had support on the Board?'

'For sure. But they didn't know about PDM3 yet. That was the ace up my sleeve. I told nobody.'

'You told the mafia.'

'I needed money to fund the project. More money than I possessed.'

'But from the mafia?'

Leapman's cuffed hands moved apart in a parody of a man gesturing that he'd acted in good faith. 'At the beginning I didn't know they were the mob. They crept up on me. I wanted large injections of cash without questions being asked and I approached one guy I knew from way back, who promised to talk to a venture capital person, and so on. One day a wad of money arrived. I didn't know it was mafia money until they followed up. Then I found myself talking to Massimo Gatti, who everyone knows is a mafioso.'

'Yet you didn't back out at that stage?'

He glared at Diamond. 'You should try backing out on a man like Gatti.'

'So you were in his pocket.'

'They saw ways of making big bucks on the stock market. It was crazy. They set fire to one of the Manflex plants in Italy. Reduced it to ashes. You know why? To depress the market price so they could buy in on favourable terms. I wasn't a party to that, believe me. I only heard about it later. That was when I realized I was way out of my depth.'

'Did you know at the time that PDM3 was dangerous?'

'At the time I borrowed the money? Christ, no. What kind of monster do you think I am?'

'You trusted Professor Churchward?'

'Sure. He's a great scientist. Believe me, he wasn't part of this mess. Okay, he knew there were some ADRs – adverse drug reactions – but he believed they could be kept to a minimum with the right dosage.'

'When did you find out the truth?'

'About Jantac? Six or seven months back. By that time, there was no going back.'

'How did it come to light?'

'Alaric called me one afternoon with some technical query. He said he was aware that a number of preliminary studies had been started with the compound and not proceeded with. That's quite usual. Testing new drugs for biological activity can be a long and frustrating process and on top of that you're sure to have plenty of failures trying to discover if they have any medical potential. He wanted to know if there was anything still on file. I promised to run a computer check. I keyed in the chemical formula—'

'And found the file on Jantac?'

Leapman remembered and winced. 'It was a real kick in the guts. The crucial decisions were taken back in 1985, a couple of years before I joined the company. Dr Masuda had done two years of testing here in Japan in her research into alcoholic comas, using the same compound as PDM3 under the proprietary name of Jantac. I learned that Manny had personally axed the research after Dr Masuda detected liver damage that was caused by Jantac. The name Jantac was deleted from our list of drugs under research. I was deeply shocked when I learned this. By this

319

time I'd staked my career and my personal savings in the same lousy drug.'

'Didn't you inform Churchward?'

'No.' Leapman shook his head, and it was an expression of regret. 'I faxed him some of the other studies I found, but I kept quiet about this Jantac bombshell. I hoped it might not be the serious problem it first appeared to be. Sometimes Manny Flexner was too cautious for his own good. He took no risks whatsoever with drugs. Every drug has ADRs, and I argued to myself that alcoholism causes liver damage anyway, so maybe those Japanese results wouldn't show up to the same degree in patients who drank in moderation. Alaric Churchward's brilliant work on Alzheimer's didn't have to be jettisoned just because Manny was so ultra-careful.'

'All right, you rationalized,' said Diamond, becoming impatient. 'What did you do about it? Altered the records, for a start.'

'That was no problem. I could do that sitting in my office and I did.'

Diamond refrained from pointing out that he should also have gone down to the basement where the old file cards were kept.

'Computer records are simple to wipe,' Leapman was saying. 'But this had a human dimension.'

Diamond gave a nod. 'And you can't wipe humans so easily.'

Leapman glared in defiance. 'I am not a killer. Sure, I could foresee problems with Dr Masuda. She was a real risk if she got to hear about PDM3. It was quite possible that she had a grudge against Manflex for what happened. I made some enquiries and learned that after her research was axed she stopped work altogether. She hadn't gone back since. So I flew to Yokohama to see her.'

'Independently – without telling the mafia?'

'Yes. My idea was to buy her good will. I'd get her back to work on coma research, using some safe drugs we'd developed recently. Then I would change her file to make it appear that we'd continued to sponsor her without a break. But there was a complication.'

'Naomi?'

'Excuse me?'

'The child. Naomi is what I call her.'

'Ah. I understand. Yes, discovering that the little girl existed was a real shock, and even more so when I found that she was autistic. She needed round-the-clock attention. The only way I could get Dr Masuda back to work was by finding a surrogate mother. Well, I discussed it with Dr Masuda. After seven years of caring for a kid who doesn't respond one bit, she was ready for a break if we could find someone. I agreed to meet the cost. She already knew a woman in the University who'd had a kid who died. She'd wanted to adopt, but she was a single parent and the adoption agencies wouldn't play ball.'

'Mrs Tanaka?'

'Right. There was no question of letting her adopt, but we were willing to let her care for the kid. In fact, she could take her on a vacation. It worked out quite neatly in theory. Mrs Tanaka knew the kid a bit. I put up the money for a trip to England, to get – what name did you give her?'

'Naomi.'

'. . . to get Naomi right away at the time I was planning to unseat Manny Flexner. PDM3 was going to be the resignation issue and it had to be watertight.'

'But why. Why go to so much trouble over a little girl?'

'Because she was the living proof that Dr Masuda quit researching in 1985. I could buy Dr Masuda's silence, but I couldn't explain away the child if someone did some digging.'

'Who did you fear? Manny?'

Leapman shook his head. 'He was unlikely to make the connection with Jantac, even though he dumped it himself. He wasn't really a scientist. No, the people I feared were outside the company. The medical press, the stock market analysts, our rivals in the drugs industry. They're damned quick in dredging up anything adverse they can find on a new drug. Nothing was published on Jantac, but somebody somewhere could have heard a whisper.'

'So you sent Mrs Tanaka to London with Naomi.'

'It seemed like a neat solution, but she fucked up everything. Everything. Maybe those adoption agencies knew something, because Mrs Tanaka couldn't cope. An autistic child was all too much, and one day she panicked and abandoned her in Harrods. The next thing it was all over the British press and on TV. It was a news story. There was even an item in the *New York Times*. Far from hushing up the child"s existence, we'd got it all over the media. Our billion-dollar project was about to blow up in our faces, all because of one small girl.'

'But nobody knew the child's identity,' Diamond reminded him.

Leapman erupted. 'For God's sake! Every tabloid in England and Japan wanted to know who the dumb kid in Harrods was. It was a great human interest story. Our papers carried it. The only question was which smart-ass pressman would be the first to trace her mother.'

'Through Mrs Tanaka? You're telling me that's why Mrs Tanaka had to be murdered?'

'Listen, I was facing annihilation myself. Soon as one of those guys got to Mrs Tanaka she would blow the whole project. She'd tell them about the arrangement with Dr Masuda. The connection with Manflex would be out in the open. All those wiseguys looking for some flaw in PDM3 would be alerted. I had to act fast, and I couldn't do it alone.'

'So you explained the problem to your mafia friends and they put out a contract on Mrs Tanaka.'

'Not my friends. And I was never a party to murder.'

'But you kept them informed. She must have got in touch with you before she flew to New York with Naomi.'

'Listen, you've got to understand that these people were breathing down my neck. When Manny committed suicide and nominated David to succeed him, my plans went —'

'Out of the window?' said Diamond with the suggestion of a smile, but he could hardly have expected a laugh from Leapman at this point in his story and he didn't get one.

'I was horrified when I heard what they did to Mrs Tanaka. Appalled. And, you know, first of all, I thought the kid must be dead as well.'

'I never heard of the mafia killing a child.'

'Well, no.'

'But they didn't object to throwing me in the Hudson and leaving me for dead,' Diamond added.

'You were too close to the truth. When you fixed that meeting with David Flexner, they had to act.'

'Yes, how was that done? Am I right in thinking Flexner's room was bugged and you tipped off your mafia friends?'

'Listen, by that time, I was being threatened too. Those people don't forgive anything.'

'But that's how it was done?'

'Essentially, yes.' He hesitated. 'Should I apologize?'

Diamond shrugged. He could be magnanimous now. 'And what exactly was the purpose of coming here to Yokohama?'

'Quite simply, to liquidate Dr Masuda. I want to make it clear that I came under coercion. I was under constant threat of being murdered myself. Those two who travelled with me were mafia hitmen. I was to lead them to her and Naomi would be used as bait. They planned to drive into the country, kill Mrs Masuda and abandon Naomi.'

'Do you really think they would have let you live?'

Leapman pondered this for a moment. 'Maybe not. Like I said, I'm glad it's over. I don't mind giving evidence when all this comes to court. I've been a damned fool, Mr Diamond, but I was never a willing party to the violence.'

Diamond felt a twinge in his back as he got up to leave. He wasn't quite the fighting machine he'd appeared to be earlier. 'You say that, Mr Leapman, but you were blithely prepared to sentence untold numbers of Alzheimer's patients to serious liver damage and maybe death so that you could be rich and successful. In my book, that's on a par with murder.'

'Are you leaving?' Leapman asked, sidestepping the accusation.

'As soon as I can get a flight.'

'What will happen to me?'

'You'd better ask a lawyer. I dare say they'll extradite you in time to give evidence against Massimo Gatti and his hitmen.'

Leapman twitched.

'You'll be safe behind bars for a while,' Diamond reassured him. 'After that, there's always plastic surgery.'

On the way out, he was stopped by one of the clerical staff and invited into another office, where, unknown to him, Yuko Masuda and Naomi had been waiting. The interpreter followed him in.

Dr Masuda was standing hand in hand with Naomi. She bowed and delivered a little speech.

'She says that she has learned of all the trouble you took to help her daughter and the danger you faced. She says that you saved both their lives.'

'Mr Yamagata did that,' Diamond said.

'She insists that she owes her life to you. She would like to repay you in some way.'

'That isn't necessary.'

'Excuse me if I take the liberty of speaking myself,' the interpreter said. 'It is our way in Japan. If you can think of some small service she can perform, it will ease the burden of debt that she has to carry now. A token of gratitude. Small thing, but very important.'

He glanced towards Dr Masuda. 'In that case, what I would really like is to hold her daughter's hand for a moment.'

'I think that would satisfy decorum.'

After it was explained, Dr Masuda nodded.

Naomi was standing beside her, gazing at the wall.

Diamond took a step closer and offered his hand.

Dr Masuda said something in Japanese.

Naomi placed her hand in his. She didn't look up, or do anything else, but that was enough. It satisfied decorum for a Japanese lady and it brought a lump to the throat of an unsentimental Englishman.

The ceiling still wanted decorating in the basement flat in Addison Road.

'I'll get some more paint tomorrow,' he promised.

'A bit of a comedown after all your globetrotting,' Stephanie said.

'Not at all. Domestic life has its attractions.'

She smiled faintly. 'That doesn't sound like the man of action I read about in the paper this morning.'

'Man of action? With my figure?' He dismissed the idea with a laugh.

'You don't fancy yourself as a sumo wrestler, then?'

'No chance.'

'The paper says you tossed an armed man over your back. It says you're Britain's sumo champion.'

'Get away!'

'Really. Do you want to see.'

'No, it's rubbish, and we both know it. I'm just glad to be home with you.'

Her smile became more definite. 'Did you, by any chance, remember the sneakers?'

Big he may have been, but he felt himself shrinking. 'There just wasn't an opportunity. Sorry, my love.'

She said, 'I wouldn't have mentioned it, but you did phone me from New York to check the size.'

He got up abruptly to delve into the hold-all he'd brought back from Japan. He took out a shoe-box. 'But I got these for you yesterday afternoon in a Yokohama shoeshop. They don't look quite so comfortable as American sneakers, but I was told they're better for the feet. They call them *geta*.'

With anticipation she lifted the lid. Then she gave Diamond a frown. She lifted out a small pair of the traditional wood and leather flip-flops.

'No sneakers?'

He shook his head. He'd been tempted to call them Japanese sneakers, but there were limits.

She took off her shoes and tried on the *geta*.

'Do they fit?'

She tottered over and aimed a mock punch at him. 'You're the bloody limit. I suppose I can wear them around the house.'

'Good,' he said, removing Yamagata's *geta* from the bag. 'I was given this pair myself and I'd quite like to wear them sometimes.'